WIDOWMAKERS

WIDOWMAKERS

The Widowmaker
The Widowmaker Reborn
The Widowmaker Unleashed

MIKE RESNICK

SCIENCE
FICTION

THE WIDOWMAKER Copyright © 1996 by Mike Resnick. All Rights Reserved.

   Printing History: Bantam Spectra paperback August 1996

THE WIDOWMAKER REBORN Copyright © 1997 by Mike Resnick. All Rights Reserved.

   Printing History: Bantam Spectra paperback August 1997

THE WIDOWMAKER UNLEASHED Copyright © 1998 by Mike Resnick. All Rights Reserved.

   Printing History: Bantam Spectra paperback September 1998

First SFBC Science Fiction Printing: November 1998

Published by arrangement with:
Bantam Spectra
A division of
Bantam Doubleday Dell Publishing Group, Inc.
1540 Broadway
New York, NY 10036

ISBN # 1-56865-950-4

Visit The Science Fiction Book Club online at
http://www.sfbc.com
Visit Bantam Spectra's website at *http://www.bdd.com/forum/bddforum.cgi/scifi/*
Visit Mike Resnick's website at *http://www.fortunecity.com/tattooine/farmer/2/*

Join the Mike Resnick e-mail discussion group! For information, e-mail *resnick@groups.com*

PRINTED IN THE UNITED STATES OF AMERICA

Contents

The Widowmaker

To Carol,
as always,

———————

And to Anne Groell
and Jennifer Hershey,
for encouragement and patience

Prologue

A mile beneath the glittering surface of Deluros VIII, the capital of mankind's sprawling Oligarchy, two men rode a slidewalk down a long, dimly lit corridor, their voices echoing in the vast emptiness. One wore gray, one white. They passed a door, then four more.

"I wonder what he'll be like?" mused the man in gray.

The man in white shrugged. "Old and sick."

"I know," agreed the man in gray. "But I've seen so many holos of him when he was . . . well, you know."

"When he was the most famous killer in the galaxy?" asked his companion sardonically.

"He did most of his killing on the side of the law."

"So the legend goes."

"You sound like you think otherwise," said the man in gray.

"No. But I know how legends get made."

The slidewalk brought them to a security checkpoint, then stopped until their ID badges and retinas had been scanned. It began moving again, only to stop once more at a second checkpoint fifty yards farther on.

"Is this really necessary?" asked the man in gray.

"The richest men and women in the Oligarchy lie helpless down here," came the answer. "They are totally defenseless—and believe me, *nobody* gets that rich without making enemies."

"I know," said the man in gray. He gestured ahead to two more checkpoints. "I was just wondering if we're going to have to pass through one of these stations every forty or fifty yards."

"Absolutely."

"I was afraid of that."

"Add it to your bill," said the man in white.

After another two hundred yards the corridor branched off, and they chose the slidewalk that veered to the right. The doors came more frequently now, as did the checkpoints, but finally they came to a halt in front of a door that appeared no different from any of the others.

"We're here," said the man in white, allowing the scanner above the door to verify his retina and palm print.

"I feel nervous," said the man in gray, as the door slid into the wall long enough for them to pass through.

"It's a simple enough procedure."

"But he doesn't know who we are."

"So?"

"What if he's happy the way he is? What if we annoy him? What if he kills people for bothering him?"

"If he was in any condition to kill people, he wouldn't be here," said the man in white. "Lights!"

The room was instantly bathed in a dim blue glow.

"Can't you make it any brighter than this?" asked the man in gray.

"He hasn't opened his eyes in more than a century," replied his companion. "The room will wait until it knows his pupils are adjusting before it gets any brighter." He walked past a number of drawers built into the wall, checking their numbers, then came to a stop. "Drawer 10547."

A drawer slowly emerged from the wall, stretching to its full eight-foot length. The two men could barely make out the shape of a human body beneath the translucent covering.

"Jefferson Nighthawk," mused the man in gray. "*The* Jefferson Nighthawk." He paused. "It's not what I expected."

"Oh?"

"I thought there'd be all kinds of wires and tubes attached to him."

"Barbaric," snorted the man in white. "There are three monitoring devices implanted in his body. That's all he needs."

"How does he breathe?"

"He's breathing right now."

The man in gray stared, trying to detect the tiniest sign of movement. "I don't see anything."

"He's doing it so slowly that only the computer can tell. DeepSleep slows the metabolism down to a crawl; it doesn't *stop* it, or we'd be down here with thirty thousand corpses."

"So what do you do now?"

"I'm doing it," said the man in white. He walked over to the drawer

where the body lay, laid his hand over a scanner until it identified his fingerprints, then tapped in a code on a keyboard that suddenly extended from
the scanner.

"How long will this take?"

"For you or me, probably a minute. For the people we've got down
here, maybe four or five minutes."

"Why so long?"

"If they weren't dying, they wouldn't be here in the first place. In their
weakened conditions, they take longer to respond to external stimuli." The
man in white looked up from the body. "More than one has died from the
shock of being awakened."

"Will he?"

"Not likely. His heart reads pretty close to normal, considering."

"Good."

"But if I were you, I'd brace myself for when he finally wakes up."

"Why? You've already told me he won't die, and that he's too sick to
pose a threat even if he wanted to. So what's the problem?"

"Have you ever seen a man in the advanced stages of eplasia?"

"No," admitted the man in gray.

"They're not pretty. And that's an understatement."

They both fell silent as the body in front of them gradually began
acquiring color. After two more minutes the translucent top slid into the
wall, revealing an emaciated man whose flesh was hideously disfigured by
the ravages of a virulent skin disease. Patches of shining white cheekbone
protruded through the flesh of the face, knuckles pierced the skin of the
hands, and even where the skin remained intact it looked like there was
some malignancy crawling across it and discoloring it.

The man in gray turned away in disgust, then forced himself to look
back. He half expected the air to smell of rotting flesh, but it remained pure
and filtered.

Finally the eyelids flickered, once, twice, and then, slowly, they opened,
revealing light blue, almost colorless eyes. The diseased man remained motionless for a full minute, then frowned.

"Where did Acosta go?" he croaked at last.

"Who is Acosta?" asked the man in gray.

"My doctor. He was here just a minute ago."

"Ah," said the man in white, smiling. "Dr. Acosta has been dead for
more than eighty years. You yourself have been here for one hundred and
seven years, Mr. Nighthawk."

Nighthawk looked confused. "One hundred and . . . ?"

"And seven years. I am Dr. Gilbert Egan."

"What year is it?"

"5101 G.E.," said Egan. "May I help you sit up?"

"Yes."

Egan lifted the frail, skeletal figure until it was sitting erect. The moment he stopped supporting it, it collapsed onto its side.

"We'll try again when you're feeling a little stronger," said Egan, adjusting Nighthawk so that no ravaged limbs flopped over the side. "You've been asleep a long time. How do you feel?"

"I'm starving," said Nighthawk.

"Of course you are," said Egan with a smile. "You've gone more than a century without a meal. Even with your metabolism slowed down a hundredfold, your stomach has probably been empty for a decade or more." Egan attached a tube to Nighthawk's left arm. "Unfortunately, you're in no condition to eat, but this will supply your body with the nourishment it needs."

"I might as well get used to eating," rasped Nighthawk, "now that I'm cured." He paused. "A hundred and seven years. It sure as hell took you long enough."

Egan looked at the frail, diseased man with some compassion. "I am afraid that a cure for eplasia has not yet been developed."

Nighthawk turned and stared at the doctor. It was the kind of stare that made Egan happy his patient was not armed and healthy.

"I left explicit instructions that I wasn't to be awakened until I was cured."

"Conditions have changed, Mr. Nighthawk," said the man in gray, stepping forward.

"Who the hell are *you*?" demanded Nighthawk.

"My name is Marcus Dinnisen. I am your solicitor."

Nighthawk frowned. "My lawyer?"

Dinnisen nodded. "I am a senior partner in the firm of Hubbs, Wilkinson, Raith and Jiminez."

"Raith," said Nighthawk, nodding vaguely. "He's my lawyer."

"Morris Raith joined the firm of Hubbs and Wilkinson three years before his death, in the year 5012. His great-grandson worked for us until his retirement last year."

"All right," said Nighthawk. "You're my lawyer. Why did you feel I had to be awakened?"

"This is somewhat awkward to explain, Mr. Nighthawk," began Dinnisen uneasily.

"Spit it out."

"At the time you elected to undergo DeepSleep, you turned your entire portfolio over to my firm."

"It wasn't a portfolio," said Nighthawk. "It was six and a half million credits."

"Exactly so," said Dinnisen. "We were instructed to invest it and to keep up the payments for this facility in perpetuity, or until a cure for your disease was developed."

"So it took you one hundred and seven years to lose all my money?"

"Absolutely not!" said Dinnisen heatedly. "Your money remains intact, and has been earning an average of 9.32% per annum for more than a century. I can supply you with all the figures if you wish to review them."

Nighthawk blinked, a puzzled expression on his grotesque face. "Then if I'm not broke and I'm not cured, what the hell is going on?"

"Your account has been earning slightly more than six hundred thousand credits a year," explained Dinnisen. "Unfortunately, due to an inflationary spiral in the Deluros economy, this facility now charges a million credits a year. This makes for a shortfall of almost four hundred thousand credits per annum. We cannot make the payments with your dividends, and if we dip into capital, you will be destitute in a decade. Nor is there any guarantee that a cure for eplasia will be found by then."

"So you're telling me that I'm being thrown out of here?" asked Nighthawk.

"No."

"Well, then?"

"I require a decision from you," responded Dinnisen, staring at the hideous countenance in fascination. "If anyone else could make it, I would never have awakened you until . . ."

"Until I was broke," Nighthawk concluded wryly. "All right, go on."

"We—that is to say, your solicitors—have received a most unusual communication, one that may solve your financial problems and allow you to remain here until the cure for your disease has finally been found."

"I'm listening."

"Have you ever heard of Solio II?"

"It's a planet on the Inner Frontier. Why?"

"The governor of Solio II was assassinated six days ago."

"What's that got to do with me?"

"Simply this," said Dinnisen. "Knowledge that the notorious Widowmaker was still alive has somehow reached the Frontier, and the planetary government of Solio II has offered you a bounty of seven million credits to hunt down the killer—half now, half when you succeed."

"Is this some kind of joke?" demanded Nighthawk. "I can't even sit up!"

Dinnisen turned to Egan. "Doctor, would you explain, please?"

Egan nodded. "While we have not yet effected a cure for your disease, Mr. Nighthawk, we *have* made progress on other fronts, especially in the field of bioengineering. When the offer was tendered to Mr. Dinnisen, he came up with a proposal that is acceptable to the government of Solio II if it is acceptable to you."

"Bioengineering?" repeated Nighthawk. "You're going to clone me?"

"With your permission."

"When I went into DeepSleep, I was told that I had no more than a month to live," said Nighthawk. "How do you expect me to wait until the clone has grown to manhood? Or, if you're going to put me away and awaken me in another twenty or thirty years, what makes you think Solio will be willing to wait?"

"You don't understand, Mr. Nighthawk," said Egan. "We no longer have to raise a clone from infancy to maturity. During the past quarter century, we have devised a method whereby we can create a clone of you at any age: sixty minutes or sixty years. We propose to create a twenty-three-year-old Jefferson Nighthawk, a young version of yourself at the peak of your physical abilities."

"Will he have the disease?"

"If we took the cells from you today, the answer would be yes. But there is a museum on Binder X that has on display a knife with which you were stabbed when you were a young man. Do you recall the incident?"

"I've been stabbed more than once," replied Nighthawk.

"Well, yes, I suppose you have," continued Egan uneasily. "At any rate, we have been in contact with them, and they say that they can supply some of your blood cells from the blade. In all likelihood they'll be contaminated, but we have ways of purifying them."

"You still haven't answered my question: if you make my clone from these blood cells, will he have the disease?"

"Almost certainly not, since *you* didn't have it at that age. However, he will be susceptible to eplasia, and will very likely contract it as he grows older—just as you did."

Nighthawk frowned. "This disease rots my flesh off my bones. I look like a child's nightmare. I wouldn't wish it on my worst enemy; how can I give it to someone who's even closer to me than a son?"

"He's just a shadow, a copy of the original," said Dinnisen. "His sole purpose, the only reason he will be brought into existence, is so that *you* can remain alive until a cure is found."

"Consider it this way," added Egan. "If you give your permission to create a clone, you may both survive long enough for us to develop a cure. If not, one of you will surely die and the other will never be born."

"It's an easy choice when you put it that way," admitted Nighthawk. He sighed deeply. "God, I'm tired. You'd think I'd have a little more energy after a hundred-year nap."

"I anticipated that," said Dinnisen, producing a pocket computer. "I've got a copy of the Solio II agreement here, as well as permission for us to create the clone. Your thumbprint is all that we need to make them legal and binding." He paused and smiled. "Then we'll put you back into Deep-Sleep."

"How soon will the clone be ready?" asked Nighthawk, struggling helplessly to lift his hand. Finally Egan helped him place his shriveled thumb on the surface of the lawyer's computer.

"If we accelerate the process, perhaps a month."

"That fast?"

"I told you: we've made enormous progress in the field of bioengineering."

Nighthawk nodded, then looked up at the medic. "I need some food."

"No, you don't," said Egan. "Now that you've satisfied the legalities, there's no need for you to remain awake."

"And find me a bed," continued Nighthawk.

"I don't think you are listening to me . . ." began Egan.

"In a month you're going to have a perfect, twenty-three-year-old, disease-free replica of me, right?" asked Nighthawk.

"Yes."

"Are *you* going to teach him how to kill?"

"No," said Egan, surprised.

"How about you?" said Nighthawk, turning to Dinnisen.

"Of course not," replied Dinnisen.

"Then it's up to me."

"I'm afraid not," said Egan. "You probably can't live for a month, and I can't put you back into DeepSleep until the clone is ready and then awaken you—the process of starting and stopping your metabolism would be harder on you than just keeping you awake."

"You can't send him out there without any training!" snapped Nighthawk.

"We have no choice," said Egan. "You are in no condition to train him."

"He won't last a week," mumbled Nighthawk, his eyelids drooping, his speech slurring. "You've killed us both."

Suddenly he lost consciousness, and Egan straightened the bedding beneath him.

"Well, that's your client," he said. "What do you think of him?"

"I don't think I'd have liked meeting him when he was young and healthy."

"That's too bad," said Egan, touching a button that caused the translucent cover to lock into place. "Because that's precisely what you're going to do in about a month."

"I'll be meeting the duplicate, not the original," replied Dinnisen. "He won't be carrying any of Nighthawk's grudges, just his skills."

"His *potential* skills," noted Egan. "Nighthawk was right about that."

"They'll be enough," said Dinnisen. "Why do you think Solio wanted *him*, when there are so many other killers and bounty hunters to be had?" He looked down at the diseased body. "When Jefferson Nighthawk was twenty-three years old, he had already killed more than *thirty* men. Gun, knife, freehand, there wasn't a man alive who could touch him. The instincts will be there, all right."

"Instincts aren't skills," said Egan. "What if you're wrong?"

"We've fulfilled our end of the contract. We'd rather have all seven million, but half is better than nothing."

Egan studied Nighthawk's face for a long moment. "Have you considered what might happen if you're right?"

"I beg your pardon?"

"What if the clone's every bit as efficient a killer as the original was?"

Dinnisen looked puzzled. "That's what we're hoping for."

"How will you control him then?"

"The original Widowmaker repressed all his emotions. This one won't have any reason to—and loyalty has an emotional basis."

"Have you considered the fact that you'll only have a few weeks to give him a moral and ethical code of behavior at the same time you're teaching him a hundred ways to kill?"

"*I'm* not teaching him anything," answered Dinnisen defensively. "I'm a solicitor. I'll be hiring specialists—not just specialists in killing, but in behavior as well. How difficult can it be?"

"I'll bet Pandora said those very words just before she opened the box," replied Egan as the drawer containing Jefferson Nighthawk slid silently back into place.

Chapter 1

The jungle planet of Karamojo was the jewel of the Quinellus Cluster. A fierce, primitive world, it was a hunter's paradise, overflowing with enormous horned grass eaters and deadly carnivores.

The Oligarchy, having seen what happened to such overexploited worlds as Peponi and Karimon, had declared Karamojo off-limits for colonization. Instead, it became an exclusive planet for sportsmen, and hunting licenses were strictly limited. It took an awful lot of money, or clout, or both, just to land on Karamojo, and even more to be allowed to hunt there.

Aficionados said that the fishing was better on Hemingway, out in the Spiral Arm, but everyone agreed there was no better hunting to be found anywhere. It made the men who visited the planet willing to put up with its hardships: swarms of deadly insects, an atmosphere so thin that a hunter's blood had to be medically oxygenated every fifth day, a temperature that rarely dipped below 30 degrees Celsius even at night, and a landscape that made adrenaline pills all but mandatory.

Only nineteen hunters in the planet's history had been granted permanent licenses. One was the fabled Fuentes, considered by most experts to be the best hunter who had ever lived. Another was Nicobar Lane, whose trophies filled museums across the galaxy.

And yet another was Jefferson Nighthawk, known as the Widowmaker.

It had taken almost a day for Nighthawk and his companion, a small, balding man named Ito Kinoshita, to clear Customs. His fingerprints checked out. So did his retinagram and his voiceprint. Preliminary DNA tests seemed also to confirm his identity—but he was more than a hundred and fifty years old, and the man who bore his name was clearly under twenty-five, and hence a clone.

Finally the authorities decided that a clone had the right to use the original's license, and he and Kinoshita disappeared into the endless alien bush for four days. When they emerged, it was with the carcasses of two enormous Demoncats, the seven-hundred-pound carnivores that preyed on the huge herds.

Kinoshita drove their safari vehicle toward Pondoro Outpost, a luxurious fortress in the middle of the bush where tired, wealthy hunters could relax in comfort. The outpost contained a restaurant, a tavern, an infirmary, a weapons and ammunition shop, a map shop, a taxidermist, and one hundred chalets, which could hold up to four hundred men. There were only three such outposts on the planet—Pondoro, Corbett, and Selous—and at no time were more than fifteen hundred humans hunting or relaxing on a planet that possessed almost twice Earth's surface area.

Upon reaching the outpost, they unloaded their Demoncats at the taxidermy shop, retired to their chalet to bathe, shave, and change into fresh clothes, and then met at the restaurant for dinner. The menu consisted of imported game meats, as there was something about the indigenous Karamojo animals that humans couldn't metabolize.

Then they headed over to Six-Finger Blue's, the tavern run by a huge human mutant whose skin was tinted a striking shade of blue. His left hand ended in a shapeless mass of bone, while his right possessed six long, multi-jointed, snakelike fingers. He had been a fixture on Karamojo for the better part of thirty years; if he had ever left the planet during that time, no one could remember it.

Blue himself was no hunter, but he believed in creating an ambience that would appeal to his clients, and so the heads of Demoncats, Fire Lizards, Battletanks, Silverskins, and half a dozen other local species were stuffed and mounted on the walls, making the tavern look far more like a rustic hunting lodge than a bar from the 52nd Century of the Galactic Era.

Blue kept a colorful blue-red-and-gold Screech-owl in a large cage over the bar. Customers were encouraged to feed it, and a small supply of live lizards was always handy. Just beyond the cage was a computer readout, constantly being updated, of the current exchange rates in credits, Maria Theresa dollars, Far London pounds, and half a dozen other currencies.

One wall was lined with a discreet set of holographic screens, as remote cameras stationed all over the area flashed scenes of animals and where they could be found. A few short-timers, men and women in for one-day safaris, watched the screens intently. Whenever the animal they were looking for came up, they went out after it. There was no such thing as a white hunter or a guide, not in an age when the safari vehicle could read spoor and track game on its own.

Upon reaching the table, Kinoshita moved the chairs, then sat down and gestured for his young companion to do the same.

"You're through rearranging the table?" asked Nighthawk, staring at him curiously.

"Never sit with your back to a door or a window."

"I don't have any enemies yet," replied Nighthawk.

"You don't have any friends either, and where you're going, that's more important."

Nighthawk shrugged and took a seat.

An alien servant, humanoid in form and speaking Terran with a harsh accent, approached them and asked for their drink orders.

"A pair of Dust Whores," said Kinoshita.

The alien nodded and walked away.

"Dust Whores?" repeated Nighthawk.

"You'll like them," Kinoshita assured him.

Nighthawk shrugged and looked around the room. "Interesting place. Feels exactly like a hunting lodge should."

Kinoshita nodded in agreement. "There's a place just like this on Last Chance."

Nighthawk shook his head. "No, it's on Binder X."

Kinoshita smiled. "You're right, of course. My mistake."

Well, your memory—or whoever's memory you've got—is functioning perfectly, you poor bastard.

The alien waiter returned with the drinks. Nighthawk stared at his dubiously.

"They're good," Kinoshita assured him.

"They're green," he replied.

"Trust me, Jeff," said Kinoshita. "You'll love it."

Nighthawk reached out for a glass, brought it slowly to his lips, and took a sip.

"Cinnamon," he said at last. "And Borillian rum. And something else I can't quite put my finger on."

"It's a fruit they grow on New Kenya. It's not quite an orange or a tangerine, but it's in the citrus family—as much as an alien fruit *can* be, anyway. They wait until it ferments, then process and bottle it."

"Good," said Nighthawk, taking another sip. "I like it."

Of course you like it. The real Widowmaker was practically addicted to these things.

Nighthawk downed his drink, then looked across the table at his companion.

"Are we going out again tomorrow?" he asked.

"No, I don't think so. We wanted to see how good you were with your weapons after a month of training. We saw."

"Too bad," said Nighthawk. "It was fun."

"You think being charged by a Demoncat is fun?"

"Well, it's certainly not dangerous," came the answer. "Not when I've got a rifle in my hands."

"The taxidermist would probably agree with you," remarked Kinoshita.

"I beg your pardon?"

"When I brought the carcasses in, he said that you didn't just shoot them in the *eye* to avoid damaging the heads, you shot them in the *pupil*."

"Like you told me when we started, it's just like pointing your finger."

"I lied," said Kinoshita. "But you seem to have turned it into the truth."

A disarmingly boyish smile crossed Nighthawk's face. "I did, didn't I?"

Kinoshita nodded. "You did."

"Damn!" said the young man happily. "That calls for another drink!" He signaled to the alien waiter. "Two more Dust Whores." Then he turned back to Kinoshita. "So what do we do next?"

"Nothing," said Kinoshita. "Today is your graduation."

"Wasn't much of an exam," said Nighthawk.

It hasn't started yet. Aloud, he said, "You'd be surprised how many men have been killed by Demoncats. You had less than half a second to aim and fire, you know."

"*You* were the one who wanted to go into heavy cover after them," noted Nighthawk.

"I wanted to test your reactions under the harshest field conditions," said Kinoshita.

"Do you do this a lot?"

"Go into thick bush after Demoncats? No, thank God!"

"I meant train men to fight."

"You're the first."

"What *do* you do, then?"

"A little of this, a little of that," replied Kinoshita noncommittally.

"Have you ever been a lawman or a bounty hunter?" persisted Nighthawk.

"Both."

"And a soldier?"

"A long time ago."

"What about an outlaw?" asked Nighthawk.

"I give up," said Kinoshita. "What *about* an outlaw?"

"Have you ever been one?"

"Depends on who you ask," said Kinoshita. "No court ever convicted me of anything."

"How did you wind up working for Marcus Dinnisen?"

"He's got a lot of money to spend. I need a lot of money. It's only natural that we got together."

"When is your job over?"

Kinoshita stared at the head of a Fire Lizard, which stared blindly back at him. "Soon."

The young man frowned unhappily. "How soon?"

Kinoshita sighed. "Oh, I might come out to the Frontier with you for a week or two, until you're settled, but after that I'd just be in the way. It's not very likely that the man you're after will simply announce himself. You've got a lot of work to do, and the sooner you start, the better." Kinoshita sipped his own drink. "The Frontier's as empty as the Oligarchy is crowded. It's almost impossible to sneak up on anyone out there. They see you coming from too far away."

"They won't see me at all," said Nighthawk. "I'll be in a ship until I land."

"I was speaking metaphorically." Nighthawk looked unconvinced. "Look," continued Kinoshita, "I was right about the drinks. Trust me, I'm right about this too. I'd be a hindrance."

"If I'm the guy who has to do the dirty work, I should be able to make some of the decisions."

"Once you're out there on your own, you'll be making *all* the decisions," Kinoshita assured him.

"Then I should decide whether I go alone or not."

"I don't want to argue with you," said Kinoshita. "We had a nice, satisfying hunt and a nice, satisfying meal. We'll talk about it later." *If I can figure out a graceful way to explain to you that you're expendable but I'm not.*

Nighthawk shrugged and nodded his agreement. "All right. Later."

The young man was considering ordering yet another round of drinks when suddenly Six-Finger Blue walked over to the table.

"Hello, Ito!" he said in his deep bass voice. "I *thought* I spotted you when you came in. Where the hell have you been keeping yourself?"

"Oh, here and there," said Kinoshita.

"Last I heard, you were shooting bad guys out on the Rim."

"Gave it up," answered Kinoshita. "Decided I liked the thought of living to an old age."

"Yeah, making it past forty has got a lot to recommend it," agreed Six-Finger Blue. He turned and stared at Nighthawk. "Who's your friend? His face is familiar, but I can't quite place it."

"His name's Jeff," said Kinoshita.

Nighthawk extended his hand, and Blue wrapped his six fingers around it. "Howdy, Jeff. You been out here to the Frontier before?"

"No," answered Nighthawk.

"Well, if you're half the man your pal is, you'll make out just fine," said Six-Finger Blue. He stared again. "Damn! I could swear I've seen your face somewhere!"

He wandered off to greet other patrons, and Kinoshita turned to Nighthawk. "An old holograph, probably," he suggested as a possible explanation. "I could almost guess when and where, because by the time you were twenty-three you were wearing a huge handlebar mustache. It didn't look like much, but it added ten years to your appearance."

"It wasn't a holo of *me*," answered Nighthawk. "You're confusing me with *him*."

"You *are* him, in a way," said Kinoshita. "Now that I've worked with you, in a *lot* of ways."

Nighthawk shook his head. "He's an old man, dying of some horrible disease. I'm a young man with my whole life ahead of me. Once I take care of this business on Solio II, I've got a lot of places to see and things to do."

"What kind of things?" asked Kinoshita.

Nighthawk tapped his head with a forefinger. "As real as these things seem to me, I know they can't be my memories. I'm going to replace them with *real* ones. There's a whole galaxy out there to see and experience."

"It sounds like you've been giving it some serious thought."

"Well, I've been working all my life—all forty-eight days of it." Nighthawk smiled awkwardly at his rudimentary attempt at humor. "I'm looking forward to my first vacation." He paused thoughtfully. "Though for the time being, I'll settle for just one night of sleep when I'm not plugged in to an Educator Disk."

"It was necessary," replied Kinoshita. "You've been force-fed the equivalent of twenty years of living in little more than a month. We couldn't send you out there with no knowledge and no social skills. Hell, you wouldn't even be able to speak yet if it hadn't been for the Disks."

"I know, and I'm grateful," said Nighthawk. "But I still have *my* life to live, once I'm through saving *his* life." He looked around the room, over the mounted heads on the wall, then back to Kinoshita. "I want to see him before I leave."

Kinoshita shook his head. "He might not survive being awakened again—at least, not until we have a cure for him."

"I don't have to talk to him," persisted Nighthawk. "I just want to *see* him."

"They say he looks pretty awful."

"I don't care. He's the only family I've got."

"They won't allow it, Jeff. Why not plan on seeing him after you've done your job and science has found a way to cure him?"

"Science hasn't made any progress in a century. Why should I expect them to find a cure now?"

"I'm told they're getting close. Just be patient."

Nighthawk shook his head. "I don't have a father or a mother. All I've got is him."

"But there's more to it than that, isn't there?" said Kinoshita.

"Why should you think so?"

"Because I've already told you what an unpleasant experience it will be to see him. Now, what's the real reason?"

"I want to see what's in store for me if they *don't* come up with that cure."

"You've got enough things to think about, Jeff. You don't need to carry around an image of what this disease can do to you."

"*Will* do."

"*Can* do. You might not contract it."

"Come off it, Ito. I'm not his son; I'm his *clone*. If he got it, *I'll* get it."

"They could have a vaccine in two years, or ten, or twenty. You're physically twenty-three years old. He didn't contract it until he was in his late forties."

"That's not so far off," said Nighthawk.

"It's far enough."

"You won't let me see him?"

"It's not up to me," said Kinoshita.

Nighthawk sighed. "All right." He paused. "I'll have another Dust Whore. They kind of grow on you."

You gave in too easily, Jeff. The real Nighthawk would have demanded what he wanted, and then if I hadn't helped him, he'd have taken it himself. If he wanted to see a frozen body, God help anyone who stood in his way. That's what made him the Widowmaker. We had to tone you down, make you controllable, but now I wonder if you're tough enough to do what must be done.

Two more drinks arrived, and Kinoshita looked around the tavern. His gaze fell on two burly men standing at one end of the bar.

They're here, just as we'd been tipped they would be. He glanced sur-
reptitiously at Nighthawk. *It's time for your final exam, Jeff. I hope you're
up to it.*

"You see those two guys at the bar?" asked the small man.

Nighthawk nodded. "You know them?"

"In a manner of speaking," answered Kinoshita. "I know *of* them." He
paused and studied the two men. "The one with the beard is Undertaker
McNair, an assassin from out on the Rim. The other one's his bodyguard."

"What does an assassin need with a bodyguard?"

"Everyone needs someone to watch his back—especially a man with
his reputation and enemies."

Nighthawk frowned. "If you know who he is, so must Customs. Why
would they allow a hired killer to hunt here?"

"Because he can afford it."

"That's the only reason?"

"This is an exclusive place. People are expected to pay for that."

"How much has this cost *us* so far?"

"Don't worry about it," said Kinoshita. "You're about to earn more
than enough to cover the cost."

"You're being optimistic. It could be months before I finish my work
on Solio II."

"No. You're going to earn it right now."

Nighthawk looked puzzled.

"There's paper on Undertaker McNair—half a million credits, dead or
alive." Kinoshita paused. "Dead is easier."

"I don't even know him," said Nighthawk uncomfortably.

"You won't know the man you're after on Solio, either."

"That's different. Besides, I'm not armed."

"I've taught you forty-three ways to kill with your hands and feet,"
said Kinoshita. "This is as good a time as any to see how much you've
learned."

"But he's not bothering anyone," said Nighthawk. "I can't just walk
up to him and kill him."

"I agree. Kill the bodyguard first."

Nighthawk looked at the two men, then back at his tutor. "Don't make
me do this, Ito."

"I can't make you do anything," said Kinoshita.

"What'll happen if I say no?"

The small man shrugged. "We'll pack our bags and go back to
Deluros."

"And then?"

Kinoshita paused a moment and stared into Nighthawk's eyes. "And then they'll destroy you quickly and painlessly, and we'll make the next clone a little more aggressive."

"You'd let them do that to me?" demanded Nighthawk.

"I couldn't stop them," said Kinoshita. "They're playing for huge stakes, and their first duty is to the old man who pays their bills."

Nighthawk looked at the two men, then back to Kinoshita. "What do I say to them?"

"Anything you want, or nothing at all."

"What if they're armed?"

"They're not supposed to be, not in here."

"But *if* they are?"

"Then you'll have to think fast, won't you?" said Kinoshita.

"That's *it*?" said Nighthawk. "That's all the advice you're going to give me?"

"I won't be around to give you advice when you go up against the man you were created to kill. You might as well get used to it."

Nighthawk stared at Kinoshita silently.

All of a sudden you'd rather kill me than them. What the hell did I say that got you so pissed off? Suddenly a sense of outrage possessed him, outrage that his sole purpose for existing was to kill. Yet he couldn't change it, so he tried to focus it on his targets.

"Wait here," said Nighthawk.

The young man got to his feet and walked over to the bar, where Undertaker McNair and his bodyguard were standing. He strolled casually past them, then suddenly whirled and brought his hand down heavily on the back of the bodyguard's neck. There was a loud cracking sound, and the man dropped like a stone.

McNair was startled, but his instincts were good, which is all that saved him from Nighthawk's first blow: a haymaker that was aimed at his head but struck his shoulder as he turned and tried to protect himself.

"What the hell is going on?" muttered McNair, backing away and striking a defensive posture.

Nighthawk said nothing, but launched a spinning kick that would have beheaded McNair if it had landed. McNair blocked it, reached inside his tunic, and suddenly was holding a long, wicked-looking knife in his hand.

"Who *are* you?" demanded McNair, feinting twice with the knife, then thrusting toward Nighthawk's neck. Nighthawk blocked the thrust, grabbed the assassin's wrist, ducked and twisted—and McNair flew through the air and landed next to his bodyguard with a resounding *thud*!

The young man, not even breathing hard from his exertions, kicked the knife out of McNair's hand and across the room, then gestured for him to get to his feet.

"What do you want?" rasped McNair. "Is it money? We can deal!"

Nighthawk feinted for McNair's groin, then took the heel of his hand and landed a powerful blow to McNair's nose, driving into his brain and killing him instantly.

Nighthawk heard a humming noise behind him, and turned to find himself facing a fully charged laser pistol.

"Hold it right there, son," said Blue, holding the pistol in his good hand.

"There was paper on them," said Kinoshita, who hadn't left his table.

"Not my concern," said Blue. "You don't kill people in my establishment."

Nighthawk shot a quick glance at Kinoshita. It seemed to ask: *Do I kill him too?*

Kinoshita shook his head, and the young man relaxed.

"We'll be happy to leave as soon as you put your pistol away."

"I haven't said that I'm going to put it away," replied Blue.

"And we'll make restitution," continued Kinoshita.

"Yeah?" The interest was in Blue's voice; his face was without emotion, his unblinking eyes trained on Nighthawk.

"There's six hundred thousand credits due on those two," said Kinoshita. "Half a million on McNair, the rest on his friend. We can't have racked up *that* big a bill in just three days. I'll instruct the authorities to turn the reward over to you. Pay our tab with it, and keep the rest."

"And the Demoncats?"

"What about them?"

"Always a market for good trophies."

"They're yours."

Blue stared at Nighthawk for another moment, then put his pistol back behind the bar. "You got yourself a deal," he announced. "Have one more Dust Whore—on the house."

"That's very generous of you, Blue," said Kinoshita, gesturing Nighthawk to leave the bar and rejoin him at the table. "We accept."

Nighthawk plunked a coin down on the bar. "I can afford to pay for *my* drink," he said with a hint of childish pride.

"You did well, Jeff," said Kinoshita. "Those were tough, hard men you killed. You pulled it off with a minimum of effort, and with no damage to yourself."

"So what?"

Kinoshita smiled. "*That* was your graduation ceremony. We will each drink a Dust Whore. Then we'll go back to the chalet, and in the morning you'll take off for Solio II." The small man paused. "When we entered this establishment, you were a clone, all potential, all promise." He raised his glass in a salute. "Now you are as good as any man, and better than most."

"I always was."

"I know, but—"

"You don't know anything," said Nighthawk angrily. "You think I was created in a laboratory just to kill someone on Solio II."

"You were, Jeff," said Kinoshita. "We've never hid that from you."

"*I'll* decide what I was created for," said Nighthawk in low tones. "I'm a man, just like you." He stared unblinking into Kinoshita's eyes. It was not a pleasant stare. *"Don't you ever forget it."*

Well, now I know what got you so riled.

"You saw what I did to those two," continued Nighthawk, gesturing toward the corpses and downing his drink with a single swallow. "I could get to where I *like* killing things."

He got to his feet and stalked out of Six-Finger Blue's, heading toward his chalet.

Kinoshita watched him go.

Yeah, no question about it; you're the Widowmaker, all right. You just needed to get your blood up. Kinoshita smiled a strangely satisfied smile. *I guess maybe we made you tough enough after all.*

Chapter 2

Solio II wasn't much of a world, not for a young man who had been born two months earlier on Deluros VIII and whose head was full of memories of glittering worlds he had never been to. There were less than a million inhabitants: about eight hundred thousand were human, the rest aliens of various species.

The planet's primary business was trade. It served as one of the handful of transitional worlds, officially part of the Frontier but in reality acting as an economic conduit between the mining and farming worlds of the Inner Frontier and the conspicuous consumers of the Oligarchy. It was said that Solio II was the Breadbasket to a Thousand Worlds, though it was a supplier rather than a breadbasket, and it traded with closer to three hundred worlds than a thousand, which was still not exactly a trifling number.

The Solio system had been ruled by dictators for the past half century. The most recent, Winslow Trelaine, had been in office for almost eight years before his assassination. He was the fourth governor in the past half century to die violently; governors of Solio II had a habit of not surviving long enough to retire.

Colonel James Hernandez, the government's chief of security, had made the initial contact with Nighthawk's legal representatives, and it was to his office that the young man reported when he finally touched down on Solio II.

Hernandez was a tall, lean man with thick black hair, an aquiline nose, a narrow jaw, and dark brown eyes. His chest was covered by row upon row of medals, despite the fact that the Solio system had never gone to war with anyone. A stack of orders was piled neatly on one corner of his desk, awaiting his signature—although his computer, which hovered above the left side of the desk, was quite capable of duplicating his signature thousands of times per minute.

The rest of the office was spotless, as if he'd just completed inspection. Every cabinet top was pristine, every painting was hung at the perfect angle to the floor, the various holoscreens were arranged by size. Nighthawk imagined that a speck of dust would be treated as an enemy invasion.

Hernandez got to his feet, his eyes appraising the young man who had entered his office. "Welcome to Solio, Mr. Nighthawk. May I offer you something to drink?"

"Later, perhaps."

"A cigar? Imported all the way from Aldebaran XII."

Nighthawk shook his head. "No, thanks."

"I must tell you I can hardly believe I'm here speaking with the Widowmaker himself!" said Hernandez enthusiastically. "You were one of my heroes when I was a boy. I think I read everything ever written about you. In fact," he added with a smile, "you might say that *you* are the reason I became what I am."

"I'm sure the Widowmaker would be flattered to know that," said Nighthawk in carefully measured tones as he sat down opposite Hernandez on a straight-backed chrome chair. "But I am not him."

Hernandez frowned. "I beg your pardon?"

"The Widowmaker is currently on Deluros VIII, awaiting a cure for the disease that afflicts him. My name is Jefferson Nighthawk, and I'm just someone who's here to do a job."

"Nonsense," said Hernandez, genuinely amused. "Do you think we haven't heard of your exploits on Karamojo? You killed Undertaker McNair with your bare hands." He paused, staring at Nighthawk. "You're the Widowmaker, all right."

Nighthawk shrugged. "Call me what you want. It's just a name." He leaned forward intently. "But remember that you're dealing with me, not him."

"Certainly," said Hernandez, studying him carefully for a moment. Finally he turned and lit a thin cigar. "Mr. Nighthawk, do you mind if I ask you a couple of questions that are not related to your mission here?"

"What kind of questions?"

"You're the first clone I've ever met," continued Hernandez, taking a puff of his cigar, "and I'm naturally curious about you. For example, I know that you didn't exist two months ago. How did you learn to speak the language so rapidly?"

"You make me sound like a freak," said Nighthawk, openly annoyed. "I'm a flesh-and-blood man, just like you."

"No offense intended," said Hernandez smoothly. "It's just that I will almost certainly never have the opportunity to speak to another clone. It is said that there are less than five hundred of you in the galaxy. Your creation is outlawed on almost every world in the Oligarchy. We had to cash a lot of political IOUs to get you made." He paused. "So it's only natural that I take advantage of the opportunity while you're here."

Nighthawk stared coldly at him for a long moment, then forced himself to relax. "I was given intensive sleep therapy," he replied at last.

"I know we've made great strides in sleep therapy," said Hernandez. "But I can't imagine anyone could master colloquial Terran that quickly. Did they perhaps start teaching it before you were . . . ah . . . fully formed?"

"I don't know," said Nighthawk.

"Fascinating! Did they use the same means to teach you to use the physical attributes you so obviously possess?" A tiny bit of ash fell on the desk; Hernandez meticulously ran a miniaturized vac over it.

"I suppose so. I also worked out with Ito Kinoshita."

"Kinoshita," repeated Hernandez. "I've heard of him. A formidable man."

"A friend," said Nighthawk.

"Far preferable to having him for an enemy," agreed Hernandez.

"Now let me ask you a question."

"Certainly," replied Hernandez. He noticed that his cigar had gone out and lit it again.

"Why me?" demanded Nighthawk. "You could have hired Kinoshita, or someone like him. Why did you spend all those IOUs and all that money for *me*?"

"I think the answer's obvious," said Hernandez. "You are the greatest manhunter in the history of the Inner Frontier. Greater than Peacemaker MacDougal, greater than Sebastian Cain, greater than any of the legendary lawmen and bounty hunters." He paused. "Winslow Trelaine was a good leader and a dear friend; he deserves to be avenged by the best."

"I've done my homework, Colonel Hernandez," said Nighthawk. "Winslow Trelaine was a dictator who grew fat at the public trough."

Hernandez chuckled. "You sound as if you were contradicting me."

"Wasn't I?"

"Not at all," said Hernandez. "Do you think only democratically elected leaders can attain greatness? Let me suggest that how one reaches power has nothing to do with how one exercises it."

"I think it does."

"And well you should," replied Hernandez. "You speak with the innocence and idealism of youth, and I can appreciate that."

"I'm not that young."

An amused smile crossed Hernandez's face. "We'll discuss it again when you're a year old."

"Are you *trying* to insult me?" asked Nighthawk, an ominous note in his voice.

"Not at all," Hernandez assured him. "*I'm* the reason you exist. Of all the men that I could have had, I chose to create you. Why would I insult you?"

"*You* didn't create me."

"Oh, I didn't take the skin scrapings and fill the test tubes and prepare the nutrient solutions or whatever it is they do, but you exist for one reason and one reason only: because *I* threatened some politicians, bribed others, and paid an inordinate amount of money to your legal representatives for the sole purpose of creating a young, healthy Jefferson Nighthawk to hunt down the assassin of Winslow Trelaine." Hernandez stared at him. "Don't tell me they also gave you the Book of Genesis during your sleep therapy."

Nighthawk stared at him but said nothing.

Finally Hernandez shook his head. "We've obviously gotten off on the wrong foot. Perhaps we should talk about what you plan to do now that you're here."

Nighthawk waited for the tension to flow out of his body. "I'll have that drink now," he said at last.

Hernandez crossed the office to an ornate cabinet and pulled out an oddly shaped bottle and two large crystal glasses. "Cygnian cognac," he announced. "The best there is."

"I've never had any."

"Well, you're starting at the top," said Hernandez. "From this day forward, every cognac you drink will be a disappointment, for the memory of this will never leave you."

Nighthawk took a sip, resisted the urge to ask for a Dust Whore, and forced a smile to his face. "Very good," he said.

Hernandez took a small sip from his own glass. "Wait for the aftertaste," he said.

Nighthawk waited what seemed an appropriate amount of time, then nodded his head in agreement.

"And now," continued Hernandez, "I think it's time to get down to business."

"That's what I'm here for."

"As you know, Winslow Trelaine was assassinated nine weeks ago."

Hernandez grimaced. "He was killed with a solid beam of light from the muzzle of a laser rifle, fired at a distance of approximately two hundred meters."

"Where did it happen?" asked Nighthawk.

"Ironically, as he was getting out of the car to attend the opera."

"Ironically?" repeated Nighthawk.

"Winslow *hated* the opera," said Hernandez with a smile. "He was there to make peace between two feuding factions among his supporters."

"Could one of them have done it?"

"Not a chance," replied Hernandez with absolute certainty. "We had all of them under surveillance."

"Could one of them have commissioned it?" persisted Nighthawk.

"One of them *did*," answered Hernandez. "They knew he'd be attending the opera that night, though his loathing for it was well documented. They even knew which government vehicle he'd be arriving in." He paused. "That information could only have come from an insider."

"Was this the first attempt on his life?"

"The third."

"Tell me about the first two," said Nighthawk.

Hernandez sighed. "I would love to tell you that my quick-witted security staff anticipated and thwarted them, but the fact of the matter is that both attempts were thoroughly botched or else they might well have succeeded."

"I assume you captured the perpetrators?"

"The *would-be* perpetrators," Hernandez corrected him. "Yes, we caught them both."

"And I assume they had no connection to the assassin who succeeded?"

"Not as far as we can tell," agreed Hernandez. "Both were members of the lunatic fringe. Well, *different* lunatic fringes. One wanted to help the sales of his book, which was a dismal critical and commercial failure. The other thought Trelaine and his entire administration were puppets of some alien race and were preparing to enslave the planet for his dark masters."

"Is either one alive?" asked Nighthawk.

Hernandez shook his head. "Both were executed. Besides, as I said, they acted alone—and they were crazy. *This* was a meticulously planned political assassination."

"And there are no leads at all?"

"None."

"Well," said Nighthawk thoughtfully, "there's no sense questioning Trelaine's cabinet or his personal friends, at least not yet. They'll all deny everything, whether they're telling the truth or not, and I don't suppose I have the authority to . . . ah . . . *extract* the information I need?"

"No, I'm afraid not."

"Pity." Nighthawk followed Hernandez's gaze, saw that it had come to rest on his almost-untouched glass of cognac, and forced himself to take another sip. "Well, Trelaine was obviously killed by a hired gun. Who's the likeliest?"

The smile returned to Hernandez's face.

"Did I say something funny?" asked Nighthawk.

"Not at all. I am just pleased to see that you are reasoning like the Widowmaker."

Nighthawk sighed and placed the glass down on the edge of the desk. "All right. Who am I looking for?"

"I will give you his name in a moment," said Hernandez. "But first, I want it made clear that I am not accusing him of murder. I am not saying that he pulled the trigger." He paused. "But out here killers and bandits tend to be territorial. If this man didn't take the commission himself, he undoubtedly approved whoever *did* take it."

"Fine," said Nighthawk. "Who is he?"

"Have you ever heard of the Marquis of Queensbury?"

Nighthawk shook his head. "No."

"He is the most lethal man within hundreds—perhaps thousands—of light-years," said Hernandez, not without a tiny note of admiration. "Present company excepted, I hope. Anyway, armed or unarmed, you couldn't ask for a more formidable opponent. Further, having built a criminal empire, he has demonstrated remarkable skill at running it."

"Have you any idea where he might be?" asked Nighthawk.

"I know precisely where he is."

Nighthawk frowned. "Then why haven't you—?"

"It's not that simple," interrupted Hernandez. "Not only do most of the Frontier worlds make their laws in a haphazard fashion, when they have any laws at all—but almost all of them lack extradition treaties with each other. That's why bounty hunters flourish out here."

"So he's on a world that won't extradite him?"

"He's on a world that hasn't seen a lawman or a law since the first Man set foot on it eight centuries ago."

"If they don't have any laws, it should be easy enough to just go there and hunt him down," suggested Nighthawk.

"Ah, the exuberance and confidence of youth!" replied Hernandez with a smile. "How I wish I still shared it with you!"

"Okay," said Nighthawk. "What am I missing *this* time?"

"Seven light-years from here—three star systems away—are the nearest habitable planets. And I use the word 'habitable' *very* generously. They are sister planets, mining worlds named Yukon and Tundra. Each is an almost unbroken sheet of ice. The average daytime temperature lingers around minus-twenty degrees Celsius—and each possesses literally hundreds of outlaws who are totally loyal to the Marquis."

"Which one is he on?"

Hernandez shrugged. "I've no idea. He divides his time between them."

"They sound . . . unappealing," remarked Nighthawk.

"They're unappealing on good days," said Hernandez. "On bad days they're a lot worse—but they're his headquarters."

"Why not just drop a bomb?"

"Because you would be killing thousands of innocent men and women," answered Hernandez.

Nighthawk shrugged. "Oh, well—it was an idea."

"Not a practical one."

"I assume there's no way to sneak up on him?" continued Nighthawk. "I mean, if he controls the planets, he knows who comes and goes."

"I'll give you credentials as a miner," said Hernandez. "That should get you through the door, anyway."

"An interesting situation," commented Nighthawk dryly.

"It is an outrageous situation," said Hernandez. "That is why we have come up with an outrageous solution and are paying an outrageous price." He lit another cigar. "Remember this: The Marquis is as dangerous as you are. If I were you, I'd shoot him on sight."

"I don't know what he looks like."

Hernandez reached into his desk drawer and withdrew a small, multicolored cube. He studied it for a moment, then tossed it to Nighthawk.

"Run that through your ship's computer. It's got all the data we possess on the Marquis, including a current holograph."

"Thanks," said Nighthawk, putting the cube into a pocket. He stared across the desk at Hernandez. "If I shoot him on sight, how will he be able to identify his employer for us?"

"If you can get it out of him, so much the better," said Hernandez. "But frankly, my office is under enormous pressure to produce the killer. My own preference, of course, is for finding the man who hired him, and we'll continue to work on it, but there are certain political realities that I must face if I wish to keep my job."

"Give 'em someone to hang or they'll hang you instead?" suggested Nighthawk with a smile.

"Something like that."

"Is there anything else I should know?" asked Nighthawk.

"Probably," said Hernandez. "If I think of it, and it's not on the cube, I'll transmit it to your ship."

Nighthawk got to his feet, and Hernandez rose as well. "I'll spend tonight in orbit about Solio, just in case you remember anything else you want to tell me." He paused. "I assume the coordinates and star maps are on the cube?"

Hernandez nodded.

"Thank you for your time," said Nighthawk. "I'll report to you whenever it's practical."

"Good luck," said Hernandez as Nighthawk left his office.

The officer sat down and took a final sip of his drink. "Did you hear that?" he said at last.

A small, olive-skinned man wearing a major's uniform entered the office through a hidden door. "Every word of it," he said.

"Have somebody follow him," said Hernandez. "If he goes anywhere except straight to his ship, I want to know about it."

"Do you really think he can take the Marquis, sir?" asked the major.

"I hope so. He's the best there's ever been—or at least, he *was*." Hernandez paused, lost in thought for a moment. "Yes, I think he's got a chance."

"Can he also come out of there alive?"

"Well, that's a different proposition. He might be good enough to get in there and kill the Marquis, but there's no way that he's going to be able to fight his way back out. And that, of course, will save us the completion fee for the job." He contemplated his cigar thoughtfully for a long moment. "Poor, ignorant clone. The real Widowmaker would doubtless have spotted my purpose halfway through our interview; this one is too young and too innocent to even know what he's dying for."

Chapter 3

Tundra was everything Hernandez had said, and more. Almost as large as Earth, it was completely shrouded in snow and ice. Mountains, valleys, plateaus, buttes, all shone such a brilliant white in the midday sun that a man without polarized lenses would go snow-blind in a matter of minutes.

The planet had once provided the Oligarchy with a bounty of gold and diamonds and fissionable materials. For almost two centuries it had been ripped open and plundered until, at long last, its vast riches were only a memory. Ghost towns littered the face of the planet. Smelting and refining plants stood empty, encrusted in ice or buried under hundred-foot snow-drifts. Here and there small communities of Men still existed, extracting the last bits of treasure from centuries-old mines, but most of the miners had long since moved on to younger, riper worlds.

There were still goods to be assayed and shipped, miners to be fed and medicated and entertained, remnants of businesses to be tended. Most of the people remaining on Tundra gathered in Klondike, a once-prosperous city.

Nighthawk set his ship down at the Klondike spaceport, checked the outside temperature, found that it was 46 degrees below zero Celsius, and decided to travel the half mile to the city in his spacesuit rather than in the protective outer garments that Hernandez had supplied.

As he passed among the spaceships that stood like frozen needles in the sun, he noted that two of them were transport vessels from Solio II, delivering foodstuffs and liquor to the isolated dome-dwellers. Almost all of the others, some four hundred in number, were private ships and bore insignia from all across the Inner Frontier.

He had cleared the spaceport and was riding a rented powersled toward the city when he saw a sudden movement off to his left. He stopped, turned, and tried to pinpoint it against the glare of the snow. Then he saw it again—a brief, feeble, jerking motion. Curious, he altered course and a moment later came to a small, underweight man twitching in the snow, his thick coat, fur gloves, and fur boots obviously not adequate against the cold.

Nighthawk crouched down and helped the man to a sitting position. His eyes focused briefly and he said something, but Nighthawk, wearing his space helmet, could not hear, nor did he have any intention of removing the faceplate in this temperature.

By gestures he tried to ask if the man could stand. The man shook his head, and Nighthawk set him onto his feet, pointed toward the city, and prepared to load him onto the powersled. The man resisted weakly, then passed out, and a moment later the sled was taking them both toward Klondike.

When he reached the city, Nighthawk tried to figure out what to do with his burden. The deserted streets and sidewalks were being plowed continuously by robotic machines, but he couldn't spot any people. There were some imposing buildings—an opera house, a theater, a museum—but all were deserted and coated with ice, as if they belonged to some more prosperous era in the planet's history.

Nighthawk slowly surveyed the city, left to right. Offices, stores, bars, a sports arena, a small colosseum—all frozen, all deserted. Finally he felt a hand poke him weakly. It was the small man he had rescued, and he pointed to a building off to the right.

Nighthawk immediately directed the sled toward it, and as he got closer he saw the glow of artificial light coming from a small window. When he reached the front door it dilated long enough for him to enter with the small man slung over his shoulder, then quickly contracted back into place.

He passed through an airlock and found himself in a small tavern. Two orange-skinned aliens in the corner glanced briefly at him, then went back to conversing in low hisses. A man standing at the bar stared at him in open curiosity, but made no motion to join or help him. The bartender—tall, broad-shouldered, potbellied, and golden-eyed—nodded to him, smiled briefly, and then went back to whatever he had been doing.

Nighthawk carried the small man to a table, lowered him gently into a chair, then quickly clambered out of his spacesuit and walked over to the bar.

"Dust Whore for me, something hot for my friend," he said. "Bring them over when they're ready."

He returned and sat down next to his new companion, who seemed to be recovering his senses. Now, in the light, Nighthawk could see that the man's skin was leathery, giving the impression of row upon row of hard scales.

"How do you feel?" asked Nighthawk.

"Awful." Pause. "Where are we?"

"We're in Klondike."

The man moaned. "Now I feel even worse. I was trying to tell you to take me to your ship."

"I have business here," responded Nighthawk.

"Well, I have business anywhere else," said his companion, coughing feebly. "I was trying to get *away* from Klondike when you interfered."

"You'd have been dead in another ten minutes," replied Nighthawk.

"I might have made it to my ship."

"Not even if you had wings."

"Well, at least it would have been painless," muttered the little man. "Freezing to death's not a bad way to go."

"Compared to what?" asked Nighthawk.

"Compared to what's gonna happen to me if I don't get off this iceball of a world right away."

"You're in no condition to go anywhere."

The small man sighed. "You've got a point," he admitted. "By the way"—he extended his hand weakly—"I haven't thanked you for saving my life." Nighthawk stared at the scaled fingers without moving. "It's okay, friend. They wouldn't have let me on the planet if I had anything contagious." Nighthawk considered the statement, then reached out and shook his hand. "The name's Malloy—Lizard Malloy."

"Jefferson Nighthawk."

"I've heard that name—or something like it," said Malloy. "A long time ago. So it couldn't have been you, could it?"

"No," said Nighthawk. "And I've never met anyone called Lizard Malloy before."

"Used to be simple John Jacob Malloy," answered the little man. "Asteroid miner. Made a goldstrike over in the Prego system, just before the star went nova. They warned us it was going to blow, but I thought I had another day's time to get my stuff out. Turned out I was wrong. Sun exploded into a zillion glowing dustballs. Stuff went right through my spacesuit. When I got out of it, I found my skin looked like *this*." He held out his arm for inspection. "You should have seen what I did to Geiger counters for the next three years! Drove my doctors crazy. And of course, I had to dump my gold for a tenth of its value; it's got to sit in a vault somewhere for a couple of centuries before anyone can touch it."

"But you're not hot anymore?"

"Nope. I can walk through a spaceport today and not set off a single machine. One day I woke up and all the radiation was gone. Drove my doctors crazy a second time!" Malloy chuckled in amusement. "Whenever I need to raise a grubstake, I go back to the hospital and let them try to figure out what happened."

"I assume they haven't come up with an answer yet?"

Malloy shook his head. "Nope. I'm one of nature's mysteries." He paused. "You'll find a lot of us on the Frontier, one way or another." He gestured to the approaching bartender. "Even Gold Eyes here is one of us. Only he was born that way."

The bartender set their drinks on the table and grinned down at Malloy. "Word is out that he's looking for you," he said.

"Now tell me something I *don't* know."

The bartender chuckled and walked back to the bar.

Malloy rose to his feet. "I gotta get out of here." But he was overcome by dizziness, tried to steady himself, and collapsed back onto his chair.

"The only place you should be going is a hospital," said Nighthawk.

The small man shook his head vigorously. "I'll be okay in another minute."

"Sure you will," said Nighthawk sardonically.

"They don't call me Lizard just for the scales," countered Malloy. "The damned nova gave me a lizard's metabolism, too. I get too cold, I go comatose. You warm me up, I'm fine." Suddenly he grinned—a reptilian grin. "Put me in a sauna, I have so much energy I can't sit still." He paused. "Anyway, I'll be fine soon, and then I'm gone before *he* knows I was here."

"Who are you talking about?"

"Who else? The Marquis."

"The Marquis of Queensbury?" asked Nighthawk.

Malloy grimaced. "You know any other Marquises?"

"What does he have against you?"

"Well, that's kind of a long and involved story," said Malloy. "I'm sure it wouldn't interest someone like you."

"Everything about the Marquis interests me," said Nighthawk.

Malloy stared at him long and hard. "Look, Jefferson Nighthawk," he said, "you saved my life, so let me return the favor. You're a nice young man. If you want to live to be a nice old man, go home."

"Explain yourself."

"There are only two reasons for a man on Tundra to be interested in the Marquis. You either want to join him or kill him—and somehow you don't strike me as the joining type." He paused. "You're just a kid. He's the Marquis. You haven't got a chance."

Nighthawk downed his Dust Whore. "I haven't got a choice."

"He'll kill you."

"I doubt it," said Nighthawk seriously. "I'm pretty good."

"Every graveyard on the Frontier is filled with kids who were pretty good," said Malloy. "Go home."

"I can't. But there's something I *can* do. From this moment on, you're under my protection."

"What are you talking about?" demanded Malloy.

"Just what I said," replied Nighthawk. "Anyone wants you, they have to go through me to get you."

"Fuck it!" said Malloy, jumping to his feet. "I've got better things to do than play bait for the Marquis. He'll kill us both." He turned toward the door. "I'm out of here!"

Nighthawk shoved the small man back onto his chair, and an instant later Malloy was staring down the barrel of a wicked-looking gun.

"You don't have any choice in the matter," said Nighthawk, his conversational tone belying the meaning of his words. "I saved you. Your life is mine. I'll spend it any way I choose."

Malloy looked long and hard into Nighthawk's eyes before moving, or even breathing deeply.

"You'd really do it, wouldn't you?" he said at last. "You'd really kill me!"

"I'd prefer not to."

"Yeah, but you'd do it."

"Without hesitation," said Nighthawk, holstering his gun and sitting back down.

Malloy was silent for a moment. "I could make a break for it," he said at last. "The door's not that far away."

"You could," agreed Nighthawk.

"Just how good a shot are you?"

"Pretty good."

"Pretty good," repeated Malloy sardonically. "I'll bet you could hit a speck of dirt at four hundred feet."

"Maybe even five hundred," said Nighthawk easily. "Now, have a drink and relax. I'm buying."

Malloy frowned. "I don't understand you at all. First you save me, then you threaten to kill me, and now you're buying my drinks."

"It's easy enough. As long as you are under my protection, I pay your way."

"And how long is *that*?" asked Malloy suspiciously.

"You'll know when it's over." Nighthawk signaled the bartender to bring two more drinks.

"No more for me," said Malloy. "I want to be sober enough to duck if I have to."

"Just relax. Nothing's going to happen to you."

"What makes you any better than every other kid who's gone after the Marquis? They were all good, and now they're all dead. Are your hands any faster? Are your eyes any better? Why should you succeed when so many have failed?"

"Because I'm the best there is."

"You're just a kid, maybe twenty-two, twenty-three years old," said Malloy derisively. "Who'd you ever kill? What makes you the best?"

"Take my word for it," said Nighthawk.

"If we were just two guys talking in a bar on some other world I would—but we're on *this* world and you're using me as bait, so no, I don't take your word for anything. Who have you killed?"

"Cherokee Mason," said Nighthawk. "Zanzibar Brooks. Billy the Knife."

"Wait a minute!" said Malloy. "What kind of idiot do you take me for? Those guys are all out of the history books!"

Nighthawk shrugged. "So am I."

Malloy stared at him and frowned. "Jefferson Nighthawk, Jefferson Nighthawk," he repeated. "It's familiar, but I don't place it. And you're not out of any book more than a year or two old."

"Maybe you know me by another name," said Nighthawk.

"Maybe I do," replied Malloy dubiously. "What is it?"

"The Widowmaker."

"Bullshit! He died a century ago."

"No he didn't."

"Well, if he's alive, he's a hell of a lot older than *you*."

"He's in DeepSleep in a cryonics chamber on Deluros VIII," said Nighthawk.

"What are you trying to tell me?" demanded Malloy.

"I'm his clone."

"I don't believe it!"

The two orange-skinned aliens looked up briefly at Malloy's exclamation, then went back to conversing in their low, hissing voices.

Nighthawk shrugged again. "Believe what you want."

Malloy stared at him, puzzled. "Why would they clone him? You even *think* of cloning a human, you're looking at thirty to life on a prison planet." Suddenly his eyes narrowed. "Are you telling me they cloned you just to kill the Marquis?"

"That's right."

"What happens to you after you're done? Do they send you back to the factory?"

"I don't think they've thought that far ahead," said Nighthawk. He paused. "But *I* have."

"And you're really the Widowmaker?"

"Yes."

Suddenly Malloy grinned. "I'll have that drink now." He turned to the bartender. "Hey, Gold Eyes. Another round here!" As the bartender prepared the drinks, he turned back to Nighthawk, speaking in low tones. "You know, there may be a way for everyone to profit from this."

"How?"

"Watch."

The bartender approached them and delivered their drinks.

"Hey, Gold Eyes, what's the odds on the kid here living till tomorrow?"

The bartender shrugged. "Beats me."

"What are the odds if he goes up against the Marquis tonight?"

Gold Eyes stopped and scrutinized Nighthawk for a long moment. "Three hundred to one, against."

"I'll take twenty credits' worth of that," said Malloy.

"Where's your money?"

"Hey, Jefferson," said the small man, "loan me twenty credits, will you?"

"I buy your drinks," said Nighthawk. "I don't pay for your bets."

Gold Eyes kept staring at Nighthawk. "Are you here to kill the Marquis?"

"I never said that," replied Nighthawk.

"Then you're not?"

"I didn't say *that*, either."

"Want a piece of advice?" said Gold Eyes.

"How much are you asking for it?"

"It's gratis."

"Then keep it," said Nighthawk. "It's probably worth about what you're charging for it."

Gold Eyes chuckled. "I like you, kid. Take my advice and get the hell out while the getting's good. He already knows you're here."

"Where is he?"

"Who knows?" said Gold Eyes. "But this is his world. Nothing goes on here that he doesn't know about." He picked up the empties and headed back to the bar.

"What happened to your money?" asked Nighthawk, turning to Malloy. "When you said the Marquis was after you, I figured you'd swindled him somehow."

"I did," said Malloy unhappily.

"How?"

"I had the most perfect set of cards you ever saw," said Malloy. "They were beautiful. I mean, *nobody* could spot them. Even if you knew they were marked, you couldn't read them until I showed you how." He paused. "I took the Marquis for two hundred and seventy-five thousand credits last night."

"And he spotted them?"

"No. I told you no one could spot them. Hell, if he had, I'd have been dead before morning."

"What happened, then?"

"Since I was planning to leave, I sold the deck to one of the locals for a couple of thousand credits." Malloy smiled ruefully. "Wouldn't you know we'd have the first blizzard in a month? No ships could take off, so I came back here for a little warmth and companionship—and found out that the son of a bitch I'd sold the deck to had cashed in by fingering me to the Marquis! I hid out until morning, and then tried to make it to the spaceport."

"So?"

"So what?"

"So where's the money?"

"Taped behind one of the chemical toilets in the men's room in his casino," answered Malloy.

"All right," said Nighthawk, slapping some money on the table. "Let's go get it."

"I beg your pardon?"

"Your money," said Nighthawk. "I assume you want it?"

Malloy blinked furiously, like a lizard suddenly exposed to the sun. "You don't propose to just walk into the Marquis' casino, take the money, and walk right back out with it?" he demanded.

"Oh, we might stop for a drink or two, just to make sure we're spotted."

Malloy studied him for a long moment. "You're *sure* you're the Widowmaker?"

Nighthawk didn't answer but started putting on his spacesuit, and Malloy finally climbed into his coat and boots.

"How far?" asked Nighthawk.

"Halfway down the next block," answered Malloy.

"Can you make it?"

"I have two hundred and seventy-five thousand credits waiting for me there," said Malloy. "What do *you* think?"

The door dilated as they passed through to the frigid street.

"God, I *hate* this iceball!" said Malloy, already starting to shiver. But Nighthawk, as before, refused to remove his faceplate, and so could not hear his companion. They walked rapidly to the casino and wasted no time entering it. Nighthawk left his spacesuit and helmet in an Anti-Thief Field just inside the airlock, and Malloy—who couldn't afford the protective device—simply hung his coat on a wall.

If Gold Eyes' tavern had been empty, the Marquis' casino was overcrowded. The walls changed color to match the mood of the live music, and the place was brilliantly illuminated although no light source was visible. Built to comfortably accommodate perhaps one hundred and fifty men, it currently held upward of two hundred, plus another forty aliens. Floating three feet above the floor were tables for roulette, baccarat, ten variations of craps (with six-sided, eight-sided, and twelve-sided dice), and even two tables of *jabob*, an alien game that had become incredibly popular all across the Inner Frontier. A sleek chrome bar, stocked with intoxicants from a hundred worlds, lined one wall, and hovering a few feet above it was a tiny stage that featured a sultry half-clad girl whose undulations passed for dancing. Holographs of beautiful females—both human and alien, mostly nude—lined the walls, glowing gently as they spun slowly in the air.

"He does pretty well for himself," remarked Nighthawk.

"Ninety percent of these guys work for him," answered Malloy, his features becoming more animated as he became warmer. "They're just playing with money he gives 'em." He looked around nervously. "I don't want to ask any embarrassing questions or anything—but have you thought of how you're gonna get out of here if you *do* kill him? There's a couple hundred guns in here. Even the Widowmaker wasn't *that* good."

Nighthawk made no answer, but scanned the crowd, checked all the exits, and measured the distances involved while his brain computed the odds.

"You know, if *I* could figure out what you're here for, it ain't gonna be too long before someone else does, too," whispered Malloy. "Let's get the hell out of here. I can get my money some other time."

He started walking toward the door, but Nighthawk reached out and grabbed his arm. "We're staying."

Malloy seemed about to jerk his arm free, then thought better of it.

"Well?" he insisted as they turned back in to the casino. "Are you taking them *all* on?"

"Not unless I have to," said Nighthawk.

"Then what *are* you gonna do?"

"I'm working on it."

"What if one of *them* works faster?"

"He'll wish he hadn't."

"Look," said Malloy in low tones, "maybe you Frontier legends don't feel any fear, but us real people, we get scared shitless at the thought of facing a couple of gunmen, let alone a couple of hundred. Tell me something comforting about why I shouldn't worry."

"Shut up and think about your money."

"Right now all I can think is that it'll pay for one hell of a fancy funeral," complained Malloy. "I mean, you *seem* sane, but you don't look even a little bit afraid, and that makes you either stupid or crazy." He paused. "*Are* you crazy? Did you maybe just imagine all this about the Widowmaker and everything?"

Nighthawk turned away from Malloy, an expression of distaste on his face. As he did so, his gaze fell upon a new dancer atop the floating platform. Her appearance was striking: her hair was auburn, her eyes almost colorless, her figure lean and lithe. But it was her skin that captured Nighthawk's attention: it was light blue.

The music began again, an alien melody with an insistent rhythm, and the blue-skinned girl started dancing atop the platform. Tiny chimes attached to her fingers and ankles augmented the primal rhythm as she spun and whirled in the confined quarters with an almost inhuman grace.

"Who is she?" asked Nighthawk.

"Her?" replied Malloy. "I don't know her real name. They call her the Pearl of Maracaibo. Comes from somewhere in the Quinellus Cluster."

"A mutant?"

Malloy grinned a reptilian grin. "Unless you know anyone else with blue skin."

Nighthawk continued staring at her. "Just that mutant bartender." Pause. "She's very beautiful, isn't she?"

"A lot of people think so. The smart ones keep it to themselves."

"Oh?"

"She belongs to the Marquis."

"You mean she works for him?" said Nighthawk.

"I meant what I said."

"Didn't they fight eight or nine wars to abolish slave labor?"

"For all the good it did."

Nighthawk smiled. "I stand corrected." He paused. "Interesting man, the Marquis."

"Does that matter?"

"Maybe so, maybe not," said Nighthawk without taking his eyes off the Pearl of Maracaibo. "You never know."

Chapter 4

The music stopped and the blue-skinned girl vanished behind the floating platform.

"Go tell her that I'd like to buy her a drink," said Nighthawk.

"I don't know where she is," said Malloy with obvious relief.

"Then tell the bartender to send her one with my compliments."

"Doesn't it bother you that you're completely surrounded by all these cold-blooded killers whose only loyalty is to the Marquis?"

"The only thing that bothers me is that you're talking to me instead of walking over to the bartender."

Malloy got up and stared long and hard at Nighthawk. "You ain't *him*," he said at last.

"I beg your pardon?"

"I know *he* lived to see forty. No way you're going to." And turning on his heel, Malloy approached the bar. He forced his way between two shaggy Lodinites, signaled to the bartender, said something to him, pointed to Nighthawk, then returned to the table.

"You know any prayers?" asked Malloy, taking his seat.

"Nope. Why?"

"Probably just as well. I don't think you're gonna have time for one."

"What's it like to spend your whole life being afraid?" asked Nighthawk, genuinely interested.

"Healthy," said Malloy. "And if you're *not* afraid, you've got a gene missing or a screw loose or something. These guys don't know you're a legend come back to life. They think you're just a kid—and any moment now, when the bartender shoots his mouth off, they'll think you're a kid who listens to his gonads instead of his better judgment."

"I can't help what they think."

"Yes, you *can* help it," said Malloy bitterly. "Or at least you could have until you sent me over to buy a drink for some goddamned mutant who probably can't metabolize it anyway."

"You worry too much. It's going to make you old before your time."

"Yeah? Well, you're going to make me dead before my time!"

"I saved you, remember?"

"To use as bait!"

"Only if I have to." Nighthawk looked over Malloy's shoulder. "And it's starting to look like I won't."

Malloy spun around on his chair and saw two men and a hulking, gray-skinned alien from Pellenorath VI approaching the table.

"I don't have a weapon!" whispered Malloy urgently.

"You won't need one."

"You don't know who they are! The one on the left is Bloody Ben Masters. He's killed maybe twenty men all by himself—and I've seen the Pellenor rip men to pieces!"

"Shut up and keep out of the line of fire," said Nighthawk calmly. He looked up as the three killers reached his table. "Is there something I can do for you, friends?"

"Yeah," said Masters. "You can be very careful who you buy drinks for when you're in Klondike."

"You mean my friend Lizard?" he asked innocently, gesturing toward the leather-skinned Malloy. "He looked thirsty."

"You know exactly who I mean," said Masters.

"Ah! You're speaking about the lovely young dancing lady."

"You got it."

"But she looked thirsty, too. Besides, it hardly seems fair that the Marquis of Queensbury should have a whole world and her, too."

"You are pushing your luck," said the Pellenor in heavily accented Terran.

"Just consider this a friendly warning," continued Masters.

"Well, I thank you for your concern," said Nighthawk. "And I'll certainly be careful about who I buy drinks for."

"Good."

"Oh, I'll still buy them for the young lady," said Nighthawk, getting to his feet as the three were turning to leave. "But I'll make sure I never offer any to scum like you or your ugly gray pet here."

Bloody Ben Masters had his pistol out before he had fully turned back to the table, but Nighthawk was even faster. There was a brief hum of power, and Masters and the other human collapsed to the floor, their flesh charred and smoking from Nighthawk's laser gun.

The bulky Pellenor emitted a roar and lunged for Nighthawk, but the young man was too quick, sidestepping him and bringing the barrel of his gun down with killing force on the back of the alien's head. The skin broke open, shooting out jets of purple blood, and the alien collapsed to the floor.

"You all saw it," said Nighthawk without raising his voice.

"A clear-cut case of self-defense," added Malloy, amazed to find himself still alive. "Bloody Ben went for his gun first. I'll testify to it!"

Nobody said a word for almost a full minute, while Nighthawk kept his laser pistol in his hand, hanging down past his hip but ready to use again if he had to. Finally someone spoke up: "So whose deal is it?" and a few seconds later everyone went back about their business.

"Have you got any law officers here?" asked Nighthawk, holstering his weapon and sitting back down.

"Not much point to it," answered Malloy. "We ain't got no laws on Tundra, except those the Marquis makes up."

"So who's going to take care of the bodies?" continued Nighthawk, staring at the three corpses that lay where they had fallen.

"There are some maintenance mechs somewhere," said Malloy. "When they see the mess, they'll come on over and cart the bodies away."

"And they're just going to lie here until then?" asked Nighthawk, surprised.

"I suppose so."

Nighthawk looked around the casino. No one paid any attention to the bodies; they could have been invisible. "It's like it never happened. I thought maybe you were kidding when you said they didn't have any laws here."

Two small robots suddenly approached with an airsled. They placed both human corpses on it, then piled the alien atop the humans. There was a whirring of overtaxed motors, and the sled gently sank to the floor. The robots studied the situation for a moment, then rolled the alien off the sled and left with the two men.

"You're awfully good," said Malloy admiringly. "I half think you might have a chance against the Marquis after all. In a fair fight."

"Thanks."

"Doesn't make much difference, though," added Malloy. "The Marquis doesn't believe in fighting fair."

"I assume he's on his way here?"

"If he's on Tundra."

"And if he's not?"

"Don't worry—*someone* will be laying for you," answered Malloy.

"You killed three of his people. He can't let you get away with that. It's bad for business."

Nighthawk studied the room again, wondering where the next attack might come from. Finally he turned to Malloy.

"I want you to go up to the bartender again," he said.

"You're not buying her another drink?" said the little man incredulously.

Nighthawk shook his head. "I want you to go and tell the bartender that if the next person to come after me isn't the Marquis, I'm going to consider it a direct attack by *him* and this place will need a new bartender two seconds later."

"Are you sure?" asked Malloy. "I mean, hell, *he* can't help who tries to kill you."

"Who do you think passed the word to those three?" responded Nighthawk irritably. "I'm through with underlings. If the Marquis is around, he'll know how to contact him."

The two robots came back with an empty airsled to collect the Pellenor. Malloy watched them load the body and leave, then looked up. Suddenly his leathery face registered total fear.

"Uh, that ain't gonna be necessary," he said, his voice shaking.

Nighthawk turned in the direction Malloy was looking. A tall man was staring at him. He had wild red hair, bright blue eyes, and as square a jaw as Nighthawk had ever seen. He was tall—close to six feet eight or nine inches—his shoulders were broad, his waist solid without being fat, and he possessed an animal grace that was rarely seen in men a foot shorter. There was a deep scar on his left cheek, from just below the corner of his eye down to his jaw, but rather than looking bizarre or ugly it only seemed to add to his charisma.

And charisma he had: he seemed to fill the room just by being in it. Everything about him was just a bit bigger than life. He wore no visible weapons. He carried a bottle of alien liquor in one hand and an empty glass in the other.

Nobody had to tell Nighthawk that this was the Marquis of Queensbury. The crowd parted as if by prior signal as the huge redheaded man approached his table.

"You're dead," he said to Malloy, then ignored him as if he were some insignificant insect and turned his attention to Nighthawk. "Your name's Jefferson Nighthawk."

Nighthawk simply stared at him.

"You killed three of my men."

Nighthawk made no reply.

"You don't talk much, do you?" asked the Marquis of Queensbury.

"I haven't heard any questions," replied Nighthawk.

The Marquis nodded his approval. "A good answer." He sat down at the table, commandeered an empty glass, and poured himself a drink from the bottle he was carrying. "You want a question? I'll ask one." The blue eyes bored into Nighthawk's own. "Who gave you permission to kill three of my men in my casino?"

"They went for their weapons first," answered Nighthawk.

"Makes no difference," said the Marquis. "They belonged to me, and you killed them." He paused ominously. "How are you going to make that up to me?"

"Well, I suppose I could go out and recruit three more fools," said Nighthawk.

"Are you calling my men fools?"

"Yes."

The Marquis stared at him for a long moment, then laughed aloud. "I *like* you, Jefferson Nighthawk!" He shook his head with mock sadness. "It grieves me to have to make an example of you."

"Then don't," said Nighthawk.

"It can't be helped," said the Marquis. "How long could I stay in business if I let everyone make advances to my woman and kill my men?"

"Longer than you can stay alive if you don't walk away," said Nighthawk. He placed the muzzle of his laser pistol against the Marquis' belly beneath the table, where no one else could see it.

The Marquis looked nonplussed. "You're going to kill *me* in front of two hundred witnesses?"

"I'd rather not."

The Marquis chuckled. "I'll just bet you'd rather not."

"On the other hand, I don't plan to let you kill me in front of two hundred witnesses, either," said Nighthawk.

"Put the pistol away," said the Marquis. "I'm not armed."

"I'm told you're a man of your word," said Nighthawk. "Promise not to kill me and I'll let you walk away."

"I can't promise that," said the Marquis. "Who knows what the future holds?" He paused. "But I'll promise not to kill you today. Good enough?"

Nighthawk nodded.

The Marquis got up, turned his back, and began walking away—but just as Nighthawk thought the situation had been diffused, or at least postponed, he felt his arms being grabbed and twisted behind his back. He was yanked painfully to his feet and held motionless by half a dozen men.

"It's nice to have friends," said the Marquis as he turned back to Nighthawk. "Of course, you wouldn't know about that, would you?"

Nighthawk grimaced, and for a moment his gaze fell on Malloy, who hadn't moved since the Marquis had entered the room.

"*Him*?" said the Marquis with a contemptuous laugh. "That's not a friend, that's a parasite."

"Let me go, and you'll be surprised how few friends I need," Nighthawk countered.

"Ah, the bravado of youth!" said the Marquis, amused. "Half adrenaline, half testosterone, and totally foolish."

He nodded to two of his men, who quickly removed Nighthawk's visible weapons, frisked him for hidden ones, and came away with two knives and a small sonic pistol.

"You have an impressive number of toys," observed the Marquis. "Now that we've removed them, perhaps you'll tell me why you were looking for me."

Nighthawk glanced around, found himself surrounded by a hostile crowd of men and aliens, and then looked back at the Marquis.

Think fast. What would he have done?

"I have a business proposition for you," he said at last.

"Well, it's fortunate I came by when I did, isn't it?" said the Marquis. "Before you had totally decimated my customers, that is."

"I thought it might get your attention," admitted Nighthawk.

"Oh, it did that, young Jefferson," said the Marquis. "You offer whiskey to my woman, and instead of announcing your presence like a normal visitor, you kill three of my men. It certainly does attract my attention." He paused and stared at Nighthawk. "Just what is it that you want?"

"Hire me."

"I beg your pardon?"

"I'm better than any twenty men you've got," said Nighthawk. "And I'll only charge what you pay ten of 'em."

The Marquis stared at him with an amused expression. "I can't decide whether you're very young or very foolish."

"I'm very good."

"Do you know how many very good men I've killed?"

"I haven't the slightest idea."

"Sixty-four."

"And how many of them were being held motionless before you?" asked Nighthawk.

Another grin, half amused, half satisfied, appeared on the Marquis' face. "Let him go."

Suddenly Nighthawk's arms were hanging loose at his sides.

"All right," said the Marquis, folding his hands into a massive pair of fists, "let's see what you can do. And in the meantime, I'm going to show you what happens to brash young men who kill *my* men on *my* world."

His hand shot out. Nighthawk saw it coming, but even his youthful reflexes weren't good enough, and an instant later he felt the cartilage in his nose give way.

"You okay?" asked the Marquis with false solicitation. "You look terrible."

"I'll live," answered Nighthawk, spinning and delivering a kick that would have knocked the Marquis halfway across the room if it had landed, but the Marquis sidestepped it.

' Oh, one more thing," said the Marquis, feinting with a left, then barely missing with a thunderous right.

"What's that?" asked Nighthawk, connecting two quick jabs to the Marquis' chin, then attempting a chop to the bridge of the nose, only to have it blocked.

The Marquis picked up a glass filled with Cygnian cognac and hurled the contents into Nighthawk's eyes. "We fight by the Marquis of Queensbury rules."

"What the hell are they?" said Nighthawk, backing away quickly and blinking his eyes furiously.

The Marquis grinned. "I thought you'd never ask," he said, lifting a chair over his head and hurling it at him. "They're whatever I say they are."

He followed up with a flying kick, but Nighthawk ducked, reaching an arm beneath the Marquis' legs, and lifted upward. His equilibrium upset, the Marquis landed on his back with a loud thud.

Nighthawk kicked him twice, and was about to deliver a third when the Marquis recovered, grabbed his foot, and twisted. Nighthawk went sprawling, but was up in an instant.

"You know, you're not half bad," said the Marquis as he slipped a punch, stepped in close, and delivered a flurry to Nighthawk's belly.

Nighthawk doubled over to protect himself. Then, as the Marquis moved even closer, he brought his head up quickly, splitting the Marquis' chin open.

"*Goddamn!*" bellowed the Marquis as blood gushed down over his shirt. "That *hurt!*"

"It was supposed to," rasped Nighthawk, following up with a left that closed the Marquis' right eye.

The Marquis fell to the floor, but even as he did so, he whipped out his legs and tripped Nighthawk.

"You're good, I'll give you that," panted the Marquis as he regained his feet.

"You're not so bad yourself," mumbled Nighthawk through his split lips.

"Tell you what," said the Marquis. "Let me buy you a drink and then we'll have Round Two."

"Sounds good to me," said Nighthawk, following him to the bar. The bartender slid two large beer mugs over to them.

"You're not going to be too proud to let me pay, are you?" demanded the Marquis.

"I like it when other people pay," said Nighthawk.

"Good," said the Marquis. "We're going to get along fine."

"We've made a pretty good start, haven't we?"

The Marquis threw back his head and guffawed. "You've got a fine sense of humor, Jefferson Nighthawk!" Suddenly he hurled the beer mug at Nighthawk's head. It split his forehead open and careened off.

Nighthawk almost dropped to his knees, but managed to hang on to the bar with one hand. He saw a kick coming, and just managed to grab a floating barstool to protect himself. The Marquis bellowed in rage as the stool upset his balance; the huge man's head bounced off the bar, and his knees were suddenly wobbly.

Nighthawk wiped away the blood that was pouring down into his eyes and cautiously closed in for the kill. He landed a left, two rights, and a chop to the shoulder that deadened the Marquis' arm. He was so intent on putting the Marquis away that he didn't see the huge thumb coming for his ear until it was too late. A million bells chimed inside his head, and suddenly he had difficulty keeping his balance.

He sensed that the Marquis was coming toward him, but all he could do was spin crazily to his left, extend his arms, and hope for the best. He felt the edge of his hand chop across the Marquis' neck, and then he was grabbing the bar again, trying desperately to stay on his feet.

He waited for the Marquis' final charge, wondered what form it would take, wondered if he would even be able to see it coming . . . but for a moment nothing happened.

Then the Marquis laughed again. "By God, Jefferson Nighthawk, I do believe you're as tough as you think you are!"

Suddenly Nighthawk felt a powerful arm supporting him.

"We'll have another drink, and then we'll go to my office and talk business." The Marquis paused and looked out at the crowd. "From this minute forward, this man works for me and speaks for me. An insult to him is an insult to me, and if anyone cheats him in any way, they've cheated me. Is that clear?"

The crowd reaction—total silence, and a number of bitter glances—told him that it may not have been popular, but it *was* clear.

"What about my friend?" asked Nighthawk, indicating Lizard Malloy.

"I'm feeling generous today," answered the Marquis. He turned to Malloy. "Listen to me, you little swindler: You return my money before you leave the casino, and maybe I'll let you live. You take one step outside before I get what's mine, you're dead meat. Do you understand?"

"What's this 'maybe' shit?" demanded Malloy. "If I give you your money, I get to walk."

The Marquis turned to a burly bearded man. "Kill him."

"Wait a minute!" shrilled Malloy. "Wait a minute. It's a deal!"

The man aimed his weapon at Malloy and looked at the Marquis.

"You're sure it's a deal?" asked the Marquis. "I mean, I do admire bravery in a man."

"It's a deal," repeated Malloy, deflated.

The Marquis nodded, and the gunman put his weapon away.

"And now, my friend," said the Marquis, turning to Nighthawk, "let's go enjoy the comfort and privacy of my office."

"If your furniture's any good, maybe we'd better stop bleeding first," suggested Nighthawk.

"Good idea," said the Marquis. He pulled a banknote out of his pocket and slapped it on the bar. "Fifty credits says I stop before you do."

Nighthawk matched the bet. "You're on."

The Marquis grinned again. "Jefferson, my boy, I have a feeling that this is the beginning of a beautiful working relationship."

Chapter 5

The Marquis of Queensbury's office reflected its owner's tastes. The furniture was rugged, built for large, muscular men. The bar was well stocked. There was a glass-enclosed room filled with boxes of cigars from all over the galaxy. Music—*human* music—was piped in. A reinforced window offered a view of Klondike. Paintings and holographs of human and alien nudes, far more provocative than those in the bar, hung on the walls or floated just in front of them. A trio of display cases held jeweled alien artifacts.

As they sat down, the huge man looked intently at Nighthawk for a long moment, trying to see past the blood and the swellings.

"You're a clone, aren't you?" he asked at last.

"Yes."

"I *thought* so!"

"It was the name, right?"

The Marquis shook his head. "No. Out here people change names like they change clothes. There are probably a dozen Jefferson Nighthawks on the Frontier."

"Then . . . ?"

"There are other ways of telling. For one thing, I've seen holos of the Widowmaker." He paused. "I've never seen a clone before. I find *that* more interesting than whose clone you happen to be."

"Oh?"

"Yes. For example, how old are you?"

"Twenty-three."

"Not physically, but actually?"

Nighthawk sighed. "Three months."

The Marquis grinned. "I *thought* so!" He continued to stare at Nighthawk. "What's it like to have no past, no memories?"

"I have them," answered Nighthawk. "They're just not my own."

"Whose are they?"

Nighthawk shrugged. "I've no idea."

"Who trained you? The original?"

"No, he's dying from some disease he picked up more than a century ago. He was in his forties when he contracted it, and he was sixty-two when it finally disabled him."

"Frozen?"

Nighthawk nodded. "On Deluros VIII."

"Let me see if I can put it together," said the Marquis. "Someone had a job for the Widowmaker. Somehow they knew he was alive, but when they tried to find him, they discovered that he was frozen. Probably they knew it up front, since he'd be well over a century old. But old or not, he was supposed to be the best, and they wanted him anyway—so they bribed every well-placed official they needed in exchange for a clone."

"That's about it."

"Oh, no, there's more," continued the Marquis. "Why are you here, at this place, at this time? Well, it could be that you're after one of my men—but the message you sent was for me, not for them. So why are you after me? What crime have I committed that's so important they cloned the Widowmaker?"

"You're doing pretty well so far. What's the answer?"

"Easy. You're obviously here to hunt down Winslow Trelaine's killer."

"That's right."

"Well, I didn't kill him," said the Marquis. "Hell, I *liked* him. He left me alone, I left him alone. We had an understanding."

"An understanding?"

"He and Hernandez let me plunder the planet six ways to Sunday in exchange for a few favors."

"But you know who *did* kill him—and who paid for it?"

"It's possible," said the Marquis easily. "I know a lot of things."

"So why not tell me?"

The Marquis chuckled. "If I told you other people's secrets, you'd never trust me with your own."

"I don't plan to anyway." Nighthawk paused. "So what happens now?"

"What happens?" repeated the Marquis, leaning back on his chair, which floated gently just above the floor. "Back in the casino you offered to come to work for me, remember? We're negotiating your contract right now. I don't give a damn what brought you here. I need a good lieutenant; there's none better than the Widowmaker."

"I'm not the Widowmaker. I'm *me*."

"Same thing."

"It's not," protested Nighthawk. "He's not even a man anymore. His skin is covered with a hideous disease, and he's more than a hundred years old. He's a *thing* that used to be Jefferson Nighthawk."

"And you're a laboratory creation, three months out of the test tube," said the Marquis. "So what? I prefer to think of you both as men."

Nighthawk grimaced. Thoughts about his own relationship to humanity made him uncomfortable.

The Marquis lit up a thin cigar imported from distant Antares III. An ashtray sensed the smoke and floated over to hover just beside his hand.

"Care for one?" he asked, offering a cigar to Nighthawk.

"I don't know. I can't remember."

"Try one. It's the only way to find out."

Nighthawk agreed, accepted a cigar, and lit up. He decided he would have to try a few more before he knew if he liked them.

"Anyway," continued the Marquis, "what the hell do you owe those people back on Deluros? If they didn't want something, you wouldn't be here. You're not legal anyway; it's a felony to clone a human, so they broke a bunch of laws just to make you. You catch their man for them, they'll probably hire you out again or turn you into a vat of protoplasm; either way you haven't got much of a future to look forward to."

"What kind of future are *you* offering me?" asked Nighthawk.

"The very best," answered the Marquis with a smile. "Skip being a man altogether. Go right from test tube to kingship! I control eleven worlds already; by the time I'm through, I'll have an empire of twenty-five worlds, maybe thirty. You'll be my majordomo. You want a couple of worlds of your own, just prove your worth to me and they're yours."

"I thought the Oligarchy didn't look too kindly on upstart emperors," remarked Nighthawk wryly. "Even when the total populations of their empires don't equal the population of Solio II."

"We're doing them a favor," answered the Marquis firmly. "No matter how vast the military becomes, the galaxy's always going to be too big for us to gobble up whole. So out here on the Frontier, enterprising men assimilate it piecemeal. In the long run, what difference does it make to history whether the Oligarchs control these planets or *I* do? They're controlled by the race of Man, and that's what really matters."

"That's as eloquent a justification for pillage, plunder, and wholesale slaughter as I've heard," said Nighthawk.

"*I* thought so," agreed the Marquis, still smiling. "You don't like that explanation? Then try this one: You'll have more power than you ever dreamed of."

"I don't know," said Nighthawk. "I have pretty big dreams. I might even want something *you* have."

The smile vanished and the Marquis stared coldly at him. "You try to take anything that's mine and you're the sixty-fifth footnote to my biography, just a slab of dead meat waiting to be carted away." He paused. "On the other hand, do what I tell you to do, and do it well, and you'll find that everything's negotiable."

"Including the Pearl of Maracaibo?"

"*Almost* everything," amended the Marquis. "She's private property, Widowmaker. Don't even think of it."

"I told you: I'm *not* the Widowmaker. And she's free to make her own choice."

"Nonsense. No one's ever free. You belong to your masters on Deluros—and when you leave them, you'll belong to me."

"And who do you belong to?" asked Nighthawk.

"I owe bits and pieces of me all across the Frontier."

"I thought you were in the business of killing and robbing people, not owing them."

"Would you rather I killed and robbed you?" asked the Marquis with an amused laugh. "I can, you know."

"Maybe."

"I thought I just proved it out in the casino."

"You're as good as you're going to get," responded Nighthawk seriously. "I'm still learning."

"A telling point. Let's hope we never have to find out how much you've learned."

Nighthawk got to his feet.

"You leaving?" asked the Marquis.

"Just looking around at the spoils of conquest," replied the younger man, studying the alien artifacts in the display cases.

"I haven't got an eye for art," said the Marquis. "I just pick up what appeals to me. The rest gets sold to collectors on the black market."

"How did you get started?" asked Nighthawk. "Were you a thief? Or a killer?"

"Me?" said the Marquis. "I was a detective."

"You're kidding!"

"Not at all. About fifteen years ago I tracked down a suspect out here on the Frontier. Jewel thief. He was sitting on a pair of diamonds as big as your eyes. I tried to take him alive, but he put up a fight and I had to kill him. Well, the more I got to thinking about taking those diamonds back and turning them over to my superiors—who I knew were corrupt enough to pocket the diamonds and kill my report—the more it seemed like an exercise in futility."

"And they were worth a fortune."

"And they were worth a fortune," agreed the Marquis. "So they vanished, and I vanished with 'em. I took a new name, got into some trouble, shot my way out of it, and then I became the Marquis of Queensbury."

"What's a Marquis?" asked Nighthawk.

"Damned if I know, but some guy called the Marquis of Queensbury created the rules for karate, or maybe it was judo. Anyway, on my world I create the rules, so it seemed an appropriate name." He paused. "After a couple of years I realized that a competent motivated man could become a hell of a lot more than a successful thief out here. He could, in fact, become an emperor. I started with Tundra and Yukon—it's not hard to take over a couple of worlds that haven't got two thousand inhabitants total—and then I just started expanding."

"What does owning a world entail?"

"Well, for starters, I'm the tax collector."

"Protection money?"

"That's such a vulgar term," said the Marquis with an expression of distaste. "I prefer to call it a Security Assessment."

"Have you ever had to supply security?"

"Not yet, knock wood," answered the Marquis. "But I've got enough manpower to hold off almost anyone except the Navy."

"If those three I killed were an example of it, I'd say you're in big trouble if someone tries to move in."

"Apples and oranges. They were just three men, and you're the Widowmaker. That's different than sending three hundred hardened killers against an expeditionary force controlled by another . . ."

"Warlord?" suggested Nighthawk.

"I was going to say *entrepreneur*," replied the Marquis.

"Yeah, well, I still wouldn't count too heavily on them."

"I don't," replied the Marquis. "I'm counting on *you*."

"My first obligation is to find Trelaine's assassin."

"I'm counting on *that*, too." The Marquis flashed him a grin. "You know he couldn't have killed Trelaine without my approval. You know you can't beat his name out of me, and that if you luck out and kill me, you still won't get it. So the logical course of action is for you to do such a brilliant job that you win my trust and place me under obligation to you—right?"

"Perhaps," agreed Nighthawk. "On the other hand, I may disappoint you and find the assassin without your help."

"I've been disappointed before. I'll survive." *You may not*, was the strong implication, *but I will*.

"Still, until I do find him, I might as well work for you. I'll need a job once my current one is over."

"Even the Widowmaker must genuflect to logic," said the Marquis with a satisfied smile.

"From time to time," agreed Nighthawk. "Where do I start? What do I do?"

"First, you take a few days to recover. I'm just egocentric enough to think I did you some damage. Use the time to learn your way around Klondike, meet some of the men and women who work for me. I keep a suite on the sixth floor of the hotel down the block; it's yours for the time being."

"Where will *you* stay?"

"On the tenth floor," replied the Marquis with a grin. "I like penthouses." He paused. "Anyway, I'll send a medic by to stitch you up and straighten your nose. If there's anything you want, just order it through room service. If you go anywhere in town for food, drink, clothes, anything at all, just tell 'em who you are until they get to the point where they recognize you. I'll pass the word before you leave that you're working for me."

"Does everyone who works for you get this kind of service? I'm surprised the merchants haven't left for better pickings."

"I'm a businessman, not a philanthropist," laughed the Marquis. "How can I tax them if they don't make any money? No, only you and Melisande have carte blanche."

"Melisande?"

"That's the girl you're never going to touch."

"The Pearl of Maracaibo?"

"Her professional name. Like the Marquis of Queensbury, or the Widowmaker."

"Okay, she's Melisande and I'm Jefferson Nighthawk. Who are you, really?"

"My name wouldn't mean a thing to you."

"I'd like to know it anyway."

"I'm sure you would," said the Marquis. "But I've no intention of telling it to you. It's much better if everyone thinks I'm dead."

"As you wish," said Nighthawk with a shrug. "But it hardly seems fair."

"Of course it's not fair," said the Marquis. "I'm the boss and you're not. What's fair got to do with anything?"

"Not much, I guess."

"You have an interesting expression on your face."

"I do?"

The Marquis nodded. "It says, 'Someday when he least expects it, I'm going to remind the Marquis of what he just said—probably after I take his woman away and shoot his legs out from under him.' " He paused. "Forget it. It's not going to happen."

"It's your fantasy, not mine," said Nighthawk.

"What's yours—and how many women does it involve?"

"None."

"No women at all? What kind of fantasy is that?"

"I'll tell you someday when I know you better," said Nighthawk. "I might even enlist your help."

"How comforting."

"It is?"

"Certainly," said the Marquis with a smile. "It means that it doesn't involve killing me."

"To borrow an old expression," said Nighthawk, "I've got bigger fish to fry."

And perhaps a very old one to kill, before his attorneys and medics decide to kill me.

"Really?" said the Marquis, interested. "So you think the assassin is a bigger fish than I am?"

"You want the truth?"

"Definitely."

"I think you *are* the assassin."

"I told you I wasn't," replied the Marquis.

"I know. But I don't believe you."

"And what do you plan to do about it?"

"I plan to hunt for evidence. As slowly as I can. And hope that you're right."

"I don't think I understand," said the Marquis, frowning. "I thought you explained to me that your first obligation was to bring in the assassin."

"My first obligation is to hunt for him. I'll be just as happy if I don't find him."

"Ah, I was right!" said the Marquis with a smile, finally comprehending. "You fulfill your mission and it's back into the vat with you."

"Not if I can help it."

"Just stay out here and they'll never find you."

"There's one man back there who can find me wherever I go," responded Nighthawk.

"Nonsense! You're the Widowmaker."

"So is *he*—and if they cure him, he'll be after me the next morning."

"What makes you think so?"

"It's what I'd do—and I'm him."

"It's foolish," protested the Marquis. "Why should the Widowmaker want to kill his clone—especially if no one is paying him to do so?"

"You can't have two Jefferson Nighthawks walking around at the same time. I've got something that he spent his whole life acquiring: his identity. He'll want it back."

"I don't know how you can be so sure."

"Because I want to kill him for the same reason," answered Nighthawk. "As long as he lives, I'm just a shadow. I'm not even legally alive. Every credit I make is his, everything I do, both good and bad, accrues to him." He paused, trying to order his thoughts. "Jefferson Nighthawk's just a name. I can answer to it as well as any other. But Widowmaker's a *definition*. I won't be the Widowmaker until *he's* dead."

"But he doesn't have that problem," noted the Marquis. "He *is* the real"—Nighthawk winced—"forgive me, the original, Widowmaker. His money, his identity, they're his own."

"But who will they hire when they want the Widowmaker—an old man they can't even stand to look at, or me? He can't let me live any more than I can let *him* live. God didn't mean for there to be two of us alive at the same time."

The Marquis stared at the young man for a long minute. "I wouldn't have your dreams for anything," he said at last.

"My dreams are very pleasant," said Nighthawk wryly. "It's just my life I have problems with."

"Well, we'll simplify and improve it, starting tomorrow."

"I hope so," said Nighthawk, getting up to leave. He heard a door dilate behind him and saw the Pearl of Maracaibo's image in a mirror as she emerged from another room, one with a large unmade bed in it.

But somehow I doubt it, he added mentally as he left the office and went back to join Malloy in the casino.

And for just a moment it seemed that a very old, very diseased man was walking beside him with an unseemly vigor.

You think it's going to be this easy? asked the old man. *You think you're going to kill the bad guys and get the girl and spend your life hunting villains on the Inner Frontier?*

I hadn't thought that far ahead, admitted Nighthawk. But it's a pleasant future.

It's a pipe dream. Do you really think I'll let you live once I'm out of that frozen tomb? God made one Widowmaker, not two.

How will you stop me? You're an old man, and I'm in my prime.

But I'm the real Widowmaker. You're just a shadow that will vanish in the light of my day. Think about it: The better you are, the sooner I can dispose of you.

Then the image vanished . . . but the words stayed with Nighthawk long after he reached the casino.

Chapter 6

The Marquis proved to be a man of his word. Whatever Nighthawk asked for he received, and payment was never requested.

Nighthawk spent a couple of days exploring the city of Klondike. He visited each of its four restaurants, all of its many bars and casinos and brothels. The drug dens he avoided; his borrowed memories were increasingly vague as they were replaced with his own experiences, but those that remained told him that nothing good or useful ever came of drugs or their users.

Most of his time, though, was spent in the Marquis' casino, where he was on call for anything the Marquis might want. Lizard Malloy stuck close to him, as if he were the little man's only protection in this hostile environment, and in exchange for offering that protection Nighthawk picked his mind, learning the names and dubious accomplishments of most of the men and women who worked for the Marquis.

There was another reason for spending time in the casino, and Malloy was quick to spot it.

"Don't even think about her," he said as Nighthawk watched the Pearl of Maracaibo undulating atop her floating platform.

"Last time I thought about her, it got me a job with the Marquis," replied Nighthawk.

"All the more reason not to push your luck twice," said Malloy.

"I wonder what she sees in him?"

"You mean, besides the fact that he's ten feet tall and owns forty or fifty worlds?" asked Malloy.

"He's not that tall, and he only owns eleven worlds."

"Well, that makes all the difference in the universe," said Malloy sardonically.

"Where does she come from?"

"I don't know."

"Find out for me, by tomorrow," said Nighthawk, smiling up at the Pearl of Maracaibo as she finished her dance.

"You got yourself a serious death wish, you know that?" said Malloy.

"Just do it."

Malloy shrugged and fell silent. A moment later one of the Marquis' men approached Nighthawk and took him to the office.

"What's up?" asked Nighthawk as he sat down opposite the Marquis.

"We've got a little problem over on Yukon that I want you to clean up."

"Oh?"

The Marquis nodded. "Seems someone has set up shop there without my permission. I sent an emissary to explain that this was a breach of etiquette, and she killed him on the spot. We can't allow her to get away with that. Too many other people might start flexing their muscles."

" 'She'?" repeated Nighthawk.

"Name's Spanish Lace."

"Sounds intriguing."

"There's nothing intriguing about her. She's operating on my territory without a permit. That's against the law."

"*Your* law?"

"You know of any other?" said the Marquis.

"Not on Yukon and Tundra," admitted Nighthawk.

"Well, then, that's your job."

"I'm not quite clear," said Nighthawk. "Do you want me to sell her a permit to operate, or run her off?"

"I want you to kill her," said the Marquis. "And then I want you to take what's left of her and nail her to a cross or hang her from a tree—anything out in the open—as a warning to anyone else who might be having similar ideas."

"There are only a few thousand people on Yukon," noted Nighthawk. "How many are likely to see her stretched out on a cross or spinning slowly in the wind?"

"It's cold there. She'll keep."

"Why not just charge her a couple of million credits and send her packing?" suggested Nighthawk.

"I'm going to answer you this time," said the Marquis, "because you've just started working for me and you don't know that I have a reason for everything I do. You haven't learned that you *never* question one of my orders; that's the same as arguing with me, and I won't tolerate that in an employee." He paused. "If you ever question another order, you'd better have a nice cemetery plot picked out. I don't care how good you are, I'll kill you on the spot—and if *I* can't, I've got two hundred men who'll see to it that you don't live long enough to leave Klondike."

Nighthawk simply stared at him without saying a word.

"All right," continued the Marquis. "If you fine her and chase her off Yukon, you'll have made a powerful enemy who'll think that I have wrongly humiliated her and appropriated her money, though of course I have every right to whatever money is brought to one of my worlds. If, on the other hand, you kill her, we'll have at least as much of her money, probably even more, and we *won't* have a bitter and successful woman out there"—his vague wave encompassed half the galaxy—"plotting ways to get her money back and punish me for appropriating it."

"So you don't really care whether anyone sees the body?"

"Certainly I do, but that isn't my primary purpose for killing her." The Marquis paused. "Any more questions?"

"What's her line, and how many men has she got?"

"Spanish Lace? It all depends on which world you ask that question. She doesn't believe in specialization. She's a bank robber, an arsonist, an extortionist, an assassin. She usually works alone, but she may have brought a little protection along."

"She's an assassin, you say?"

"Don't look so interested. She had nothing to do with Trelaine."

"How do you know?"

"Nothing goes on in this sector that I *don't* know."

"All right," said Nighthawk. "When do you want me to leave?"

"Immediately. Why else would I be telling you all this?"

"Where will I find her?"

"I've already had the landing coordinates fed into your ship's computer. Take that little snake-skinned bastard Malloy along with you. He's been to Yukon before; maybe he can be of some use to you." The Marquis chuckled. "At least he won't block your vision or get in your line of fire. I don't think I've ever seen a bigger coward."

"That's probably why he'll outlive us both," replied Nighthawk.

"It's possible—but you have to consider the quality of that life."

"*He* considers the quality of his death," said Nighthawk with a smile. "Hasn't found one that lives up to his high standards yet."

"Somebody should explain to him that very few of us fuck ourselves to death," said the Marquis.

"I'll try to remember that."

"Especially when you're around Melisande," added the Marquis meaningfully.

"I'm not going to get myself killed over a blue-skinned mutant," said Nighthawk.

"Nothing personal," replied the Marquis. "I like you, I really do. But you were put together in a lab three months ago. How the hell do *I* know what you will or won't get killed over?"

"I'm as much a man as you are!" snapped Nighthawk heatedly.

"If you weren't, I wouldn't worry about your doing something stupid because of Melisande."

The answer seemed to mollify Nighthawk, and he relaxed visibly.

"Well, now that you've made up your mind not to kill me, get the hell out of here and go kill the person you're being paid to kill," said the Marquis.

Nighthawk nodded and got to his feet.

"Cigar?"

"I still haven't decided if I like them," answered Nighthawk.

"By the same token, you really can't know if you like blue-skinned ladies, can you?" asked the Marquis meaningfully.

"Don't start on me again!" snapped Nighthawk. "There's more to me than just a killing machine!"

"And you'll kill me to prove it?"

Nighthawk glared at him for a moment, then turned and left the office.

He hunted up Malloy, got into a spacesuit, and found one for his companion. Then they made their way across the ice fields to the spaceport. Within an hour they were ensconced in the pilot's cabin of Nighthawk's ship, leaving Tundra behind them and heading for Yukon.

"I *hate* traveling within a solar system!" complained Malloy, looking at a viewscreen. "It takes longer to go from one world to another than from one *star* to another."

"Can't do light speeds within a system," answered Nighthawk. "You know that."

"Yeah, but I don't have to like it."

"Find some way to occupy yourself. Like telling me about Melisande, for instance."

"I found out what you wanted to know," said Malloy. "She comes from Greenveldt."

"That's a Frontier world?"

"Right."

"Are all the colonists on Greenveldt blue-skinned?" asked Nighthawk.

Malloy shook his head. "She didn't evolve, she mutated."

"Explain."

"She's a sport—there's just one of her."

"I like that," said Nighthawk.

"You do? Why?"

"Let's just say I have a certain fondness for people who are one of a kind."

"Then you ought to love Spanish Lace," said Malloy. "There ain't never been anyone like her."

Nighthawk checked his navigational computer and found that he had almost forty minutes before the ship entered Yukon's orbit. "We've got time," he said. "Fill me in."

"Didn't the Marquis tell you?"

"Just that she's moved in on his territory and he wants her off."

"He didn't tell you that she's killed the last three men who had your job?"

"No."

"Or that she's not quite human?"

"Explain," said Nighthawk.

"She *looks* pretty much like a normal human woman," said Malloy. "But I've heard stories about her. She's got powers that no human ever had."

"For instance?"

"I don't know."

"So it could just be bullshit."

"If it was, would the Marquis' last three hired guns be dead?"

"Go on," said Nighthawk. "I need details."

"Nobody knows any. She's robbed some banks back in the Oligarchy, I know that. And they say she killed Jumbo Willoughby with her bare hands. Oh, and there was that affair on Terrazane—"

"What affair?"

"Somebody blew up the whole parliament. Killed about three hundred men and women. Nobody ever proved anything, but they say it was *her* doing, that if she didn't set off the bomb herself she at least arranged for it to go off."

"She sounds interesting."

"What she is is *deadly*," said Malloy devoutly. "Don't worry—you won't have to meet her."

"No way. I'll be at your side."

Nighthawk stared at him. "You don't have to."

"I don't care. I'm coming with you."

"I'd have thought you'd be happier keeping out of the line of fire."

"I'm supposed to wait in the ship or some bar wondering who's going to come to meet me, you or the worst killer on the planet?" demanded Malloy. "No, thanks! First time a door or a hatch opened, I'd be wound so tight I'd probably explode."

"To hell with your reasons," said Nighthawk. "I thank you for your loyalty." He paused. "It's strange, but you're just about the only friend I've got."

"I'm not your friend," said Malloy. Nighthawk started to protest, but Malloy raised his hand for silence. "But let's pretend that I am for a minute, so I can give you a piece of friendly advice." Nighthawk stared silently at him, and he continued. "I know you've never had a mother or a family, and you've probably never even had a woman, let alone lived with one. I know you're probably looking for people to talk to and drink with at the same time you're hunting for victims. Well, let me tell you something, something the first Jefferson Nighthawk must have known to have lived so long: Out here on the Frontier, you must never mistake self-interest for friendship. They're a harder breed out here than back in the Oligarchy. They came out here for a reason, and they *stay* out here for a reason, and friendship isn't it. So be as cordial as you like, Widowmaker, and most people will be cordial right back at you because of who you are and what you can do if you get mad at 'em—but *never* think that a cordial overture out here will lead to friendship. If it leads to another day's survival, that's enough."

Nighthawk considered what Malloy said for a long moment, then shook his head. "I don't buy that. You're too cynical by half."

"You were created solely to kill people, and *I'm* cynical?" said Malloy sarcastically.

"Killing is what I *do*," said Nighthawk. "It's not what I *am*."

"Not yet," agreed Malloy. "But you'll grow into it. Or die."

They fell silent for a few minutes, and then Malloy spoke again.

"What's he paying you to go up against her?"

"Nothing."

"You're facing Spanish Lace for *free*?" demanded Malloy.

"Not exactly," answered Nighthawk. "He's paying me a ton of money to do a job. This is part of the job description. Probably today I'm being underpaid; yesterday and tomorrow I'll be overpaid. It all evens out in the end."

"That depends on when the end comes," noted Malloy.

"If you can tell me what to prepare for, maybe it won't come too soon," suggested Nighthawk.

"I don't know her powers. I just know that a couple of times they had her dead to rights, but she's still alive and everyone who's ever tried to kill her is dead."

"Maybe she's just good with her weapons," offered Nighthawk.

Malloy shook his head again. "She's faced odds even *you* wouldn't face, Widowmaker."

"But she comes of human stock. Just how many strange talents can she have?"

"Enough," said Malloy unhappily, as the ship entered Yukon's frigid atmosphere.

Chapter 7

The ship touched down in the city-state of New Siberia, which differed from its namesake only in that it was bigger, colder, and a few hundred thousand light-years away. Nighthawk and Malloy were about to exit the ship and take the heated tram to the spaceport tower when a voice rang out through the ship.

"Passports, please."

"When we get to Customs," answered Nighthawk, staring at the young woman's face that had suddenly appeared on all the viewscreens.

"This *is* Customs, sir," she replied. "So few people come and go here that we found it more convenient to clear you before you leave your ship rather than set up a permanent booth in the tower."

The two men held up their titanium passport cards for scanning.

"Welcome to Yukon, Mr. Nighthawk. Welcome back to Yukon, Mr. Malloy. What is the purpose of your visit?"

"Tourism," said Nighthawk.

"We don't have a tourist industry, Mr. Nighthawk."

"That's hardly my fault," he said. "I plan to see such natural wonders as your lovely planet affords."

"I think you are here to gamble, Mr. Nighthawk," continued the woman, oblivious to his answer.

"You make it sound like it's against the law."

"Absolutely not. In fact, it is encouraged. I see that you have recently opened an account on Tundra. We can bill your account for a gambling license if you will give us permission."

"And you don't have tourist licenses, is that it?" asked Nighthawk with a smile.

"Verbal permission will be sufficient," she continued. "A holocopy of this conversation will be kept on file."

"You have my permission."

"I am sure you will enjoy your stay here, Mr. Nighthawk, and I wish you good luck at the gaming tables." Pause. "Your purpose for visiting Yukon, Mr. Malloy?"

"I'm with him."

"I cannot find any account bearing your name and voiceprint in either the Inner Frontier or the Oligarchy, Mr. Malloy," she said. "How will you pay for your gambling license?"

"Bill me," interjected Nighthawk.

"If you wish," she said. "However, the laws of Yukon require me to tell you that the purchaser of a license is responsible for all debts incurred on that license."

"I see," said Nighthawk. He paused for a moment. "Mr. Malloy will purchase his own license with cash when he finally reaches one of your casinos. Is that acceptable?"

"Quite," said the woman. "I should further point out that until he places a certain minimal amount on deposit here, any purchase he makes is payable in cash. In advance."

"He understands."

"I must hear *him* say it."

"I understand, I understand," muttered Malloy.

"Fine. You are each cleared to remain on Yukon for seven days. If you wish to go beyond the borders of New Siberia, you will have to ask and receive permission from whichever country you plan to visit. If you wish to extend your vacations, please check in here again more than one Galactic Standard day before your current visa expires. Are there any further questions?"

"Yes. Where can I find a map of New Siberia?"

"Please wait. . . . A map has just been transferred to your ship's navigational computer."

"And how does one get around on New Siberia?"

"There are powersleds for rent at the tower," was the answer. "They are heated, and come with radar, a radio, and a three-day supply of food for a crew of six men."

"Do I *need* a crew of six?"

"No. That is the maximum number a sled can transport at one time."

"Thank you," said Nighthawk. "You've been most helpful."

The screen deactivated.

"Bring up the map and find Spanish Lace," Nighthawk ordered the computer. "We might as well see exactly where the hell we're going."

The computer threw the map on a viewscreen, then cross-indexed it against the planetary census, and suddenly a tiny spot, some forty miles distant, began blinking brightly.

"Nearest city?" demanded Nighthawk.

There was a blinking right next to the spaceport.

"Nearest neighbor?"

Another spot, some fifteen miles away, began blinking.

"Off."

The screen went dark, and Malloy turned to Nighthawk. "She doesn't seem to like crowds."

"An understatement."

"So what do we do now?"

"We rent a powersled and pay her a visit."

"She's got to have defenses," said Malloy. "She'll know you're coming."

"Probably."

"Why not contact her from here? You could talk."

"I'm not being paid to talk."

"You're not being paid to get killed, either," said Malloy.

"I don't plan to die."

"Neither did the three guys who went before you."

"If you're frightened—" began Nighthawk.

"Of course I'm frightened!" snapped Malloy. "Only a crazy man wouldn't be frightened!"

"Then stay here."

"What if she kills you?"

"You've got more chance to get away if you're here than if you're standing next to me."

"Too cowardly," said Malloy.

"But you *are* a coward," replied Nighthawk with a chuckle.

"But I'm not blatant about it."

"In other words you want to stay here, but you want a good reason to—one that will keep your self-respect intact."

"Basically," admitted Malloy.

"All right. You don't know what powers she possesses, right?"

"Right."

"Does anyone?"

"Not to my knowledge."

"Then stay here and keep in radio and visual contact with me, and if she uses those powers to kill me, you can report what she's got to the Marquis. You might even get yourself a nice reward for that kind of information."

"You really think so?"

Nighthawk smiled. "Not a chance. But you *will* be bringing him information he needs."

"Well, that's all fine and well for *you*," said Malloy. "After all, you work for him. But I don't."

"Then don't go back to Tundra. Get as far away as you can and send him a subspace message offering to sell what you know."

"Now, *that* makes sense!" said Malloy.

"And it's more in keeping with your character," added Nighthawk sardonically.

"We can't all be heroes and killers," said Malloy defensively. "Some of us are just normal men." He looked at his scaled hands and arms and smiled ruefully. "Well, maybe not exactly *normal*," he amended.

Nighthawk donned a spacesuit, then began going through the ship's minimal stores.

"What are you looking for?" asked Malloy. "You're already packing three different kinds of weapon."

"Four," corrected Nighthawk. "I'm looking for an eye."

"You leave your eyes lying around in cabinets?" asked Malloy, confused.

"A three-hundred-and-sixty-degree camera," explained Nighthawk. Suddenly he reached out and picked up a small, circular object, less than an inch in diameter. "Got it."

"That must be spy gear," said Malloy. "I never saw anything like it before."

"I'll put it down on a chair or table," said Nighthawk, ignoring his remark. "It'll transmit a visual of the entire room it's in—walls, floor, ceiling, everything. The computer will receive the signal, sort out all the angles and images, and display something that makes sense to you."

"What if she's got a killer pet that eats it?"

"Then you'll see what the inside of its digestive system looks like, and you'll have to sell your information to a exoveterinarian instead of the Marquis." He paused. "I'll keep my communicator activated. If she hasn't got some way to nullify the signal, it should transmit everything we say."

"Are you sure you'd rather go alone?"

"As a matter of fact, I'd much rather have company," said Nighthawk, repressing a smile. "Give her two targets instead of just one."

"Damn it!" exploded Malloy. "You were supposed to say that you wanted to face her alone!"

"I do, really. I just wanted to see your reaction."

"Cold-blooded killers aren't supposed to have a sense of humor," muttered the little man.

"Then I must be a hot-blooded killer."

"Let's just hope you're a long-lived one."

"One of me is."

Nighthawk left the ship, found a waiting tram, and got off at the tower, where he rented a heated powersled. It was a type with which he was unfamiliar, so he had the saleswoman program it for him.

"You're *sure* these are the coordinates you want?" she asked.

"Why not?"

"I'll need a larger deposit," she said apologetically. "Lots of people go out to the Ice Palace. Almost none of them come back."

"What happens to them?"

"Beats me," she said. "I don't know. I don't *want* to know. I just want a bigger deposit."

Nighthawk pressed his thumb against a contract rider that she produced.

"You got any advice for someone going to the Ice Palace?" he asked while waiting for the thumbprint to be cleared and approved.

"Don't believe your eyes."

"I don't think I understand," said Nighthawk, as the computer approved his print.

"She *looks* human, but she's not."

"What is she?"

"If you survive and return the sled, maybe you can tell me," said the woman.

Chapter 8

Nighthawk could see the Ice Palace from five miles away. It appeared, truly, to be a structure of snow and ice, blindingly white in the midday sun. There were huge turrets, crenellated walls, towers and ramps and balustrades, and literally millions of icicles hanging down from every section and structure. All that was missing was a moat, and he was sure it was only because it was too cold for water.

He approached to within a mile, then slowed the powersled to half speed, alert for any possible danger. Small white animals scurried to and fro, some even racing alongside the sled for a moment, but they veered off as he neared the main gate.

Finally he came to a halt in front of the Ice Palace and stepped off his sled. He looked around for guards and was mildly surprised not to find any. He walked up to the gate and tried it. It was locked, and he turned his laser pistol on it, melting both the locking mechanism and the latch itself.

He stepped cautiously inside. The walls and floor still seemed to be made of ice, but his spacesuit told him that the temperature was 23 degrees Celsius. He cautiously removed his helmet, then quickly slipped out of his suit. He touched some icicles that hung down from the ceiling; they were quartz, and quite warm to the touch. Spheres of light—not quite solid, with no discernible power source—floated near the ceiling, illuminating the room.

He walked through a number of chambers, accompanied by about half the spheres, which seemed to sense his presence and anticipate his needs, racing to provide light whenever he turned his head to look in a new direction. The walls and floors glittered like polished diamonds. Some of the chambers were furnished with pieces that matched the magical decor of the palace; others were empty. Nowhere was there any sign of life. No humans, no aliens, no pets, no guard animals, nothing.

Finally he came to an exceptionally large room, perhaps sixty feet on a side. Lilting alien music came from a tiny speaker that hovered near the ceiling at the exact center of the room, and a number of the light spheres floated about it in a stately dance that had no pattern but displayed a form and grace that seemed to match the music perfectly. Lining the walls were exquisite statues of ice, or perhaps quartz that resembled ice; Nighthawk couldn't tell which.

As he crossed the room, a door slid into place behind him. He whirled, gun in hand, as he heard the sound, then quickly moved toward the next doorway. A glittering white door slid shut before he was halfway there.

A low chuckle told him that he wasn't alone, and he turned to find himself facing a small, lithe woman with wild dark hair and matching eyes. She was dressed in a formfitting black outfit made of a delicate lace.

"How did you get in here?" demanded Nighthawk.

"This is my home," she replied. "I come and go as I please."

"You're Spanish Lace?"

"And you are Jefferson Nighthawk."

"Who told you so?"

"I have my sources," she replied. She stared at him. "Of all the lackeys the Marquis of Queensbury has sent, you are the youngest. You must be very skilled at your trade."

"I'm not a lackey."

"But you *are* a killer?"

"I'm many things," he said. "That's one of the less important ones."

She uttered a mocking laugh. He stared at her for a moment, then began examining the room, walking through it, studying the artifacts, while she stood perfectly still, watching him intently. Finally he stopped and turned back to her.

"What's so special about you?" he asked. "Why does he want you dead?"

"He wants me dead because he fears me," said Spanish Lace.

"He doesn't strike me as a man who is afraid of anything," replied Nighthawk.

"If he doesn't fear me, why did he send you to do his dirty work?"

"Because I'm not afraid of you either—and he's got all the money," answered Nighthawk with a smile.

"Have you thought of how you are going to get back?"

"Same way I got here."

"I don't think so," she replied. "Why not go and check for yourself?"

"After you."

She shrugged and retraced his route through the palace. Doors dilated or slid back as she approached, and in less than a minute she came to the main gate. As it slid into the wall, she stepped aside and Nighthawk saw what remained of his powersled, a crushed, twisted mass of metal.

"What the hell happened to it?" muttered Nighthawk, more to himself than to Spanish Lace.

"Poor Jefferson Nighthawk," she said. "How are you to leave here now?"

Suddenly Nighthawk was aware of the freezing cold, of the wind whipping across his face and body. He turned to Spanish Lace, who stood next to him, totally oblivious to the wind and cold. His first instinct was to stay out there and outlast her, to prove that he could stand anything she could stand, but he quickly realized that it was precisely that kind of machismo which could get him killed, for she seemed truly impervious to the elements.

He turned and walked back into the Ice Palace. Spanish Lace fell into step behind him.

"You asked a question a few moments ago," she said when they had reached the chamber they had left.

"I did?"

"I think your precise words were: 'What the hell happened to it?' " She smiled. "*I* happened to it."

"You were with me."

"I know."

"You did it before you came into this room?"

"I did it *while* I was in this room," she replied.

"How?"

"I promise you will discover that before this day is over, Jefferson Nighthawk." She sat down in a chair that looked like sculpted ice. "Have you decided how you will kill me yet? Will it be death by heat or death by sound? Will I die before a weapon, or beneath your fists? Will my end be swift or slow?"

"I haven't said I would kill you at all," replied Nighthawk. "I only said that I was *sent* to kill you."

"Ah," she said, smiling again. "You await a counteroffer."

"Not necessarily."

She looked puzzled. "Then what?"

"Let's just talk for a while."

"Why?"

"Have you got anything better to do?" asked Nighthawk.

She stared at him for a long moment. "What kind of killer *are* you?"

"A reluctant one. Why does he want you dead?"

"I am a rival, and he is very territorial. What better reason is there?"

"Offhand, I can think of hundreds," said Nighthawk. "Why is life held so cheaply on the Frontier?"

"Probably because it *is* the Frontier. Life is never very expensive on the farthest borders of civilization."

"You people have pasts and futures. Don't you want to hang on to them?"

"*You* have a past and a future too," she pointed out. "Why should anyone else's attitude puzzle you?"

He shook his head. "I have no past, and my future is, at best, uncertain."

"How can you have no past?" she demanded.

He merely stared at her.

Suddenly her dark eyes widened. "Of course! You're a clone!"

He nodded an affirmative.

"Remarkable! I've never seen one before." She got to her feet and approached him. "And that explains why you are so young." She reached out a hand. "May I touch you?"

He shrugged and made no reply as she ran her fingers over his face and neck.

"Remarkable!" she said again. "You feel human."

"I *am* human."

"I mean that there is nothing artificial about you."

"That goes with being human."

She stared at him, obviously fascinated. "And who were you, Jefferson Nighthawk? A mass murderer? A decorated soldier? A celebrated lawman?"

"I am . . . I *was* . . . the Widowmaker."

"Ah. A bounty hunter!"

"And a lawman."

"Perhaps, but that is not why we all remember you." She returned to her chair. "So I am to be killed by the Widowmaker."

"I told you, I just want to talk."

She closed her eyes and nodded her head. "Of course you do. Poor little clone, with all the Widowmaker's skills and none of his experiences. He *chose* to become a killer, was probably driven to it, doubtless reveled in it. But you were *created* to become one, ordered to be one. No one ever asked you if you wanted to kill, did they? No one ever thought you might have other goals and desires."

Nighthawk exhaled deeply. "You understand."

"Certainly I do. Even among the outcasts and misfits who inhabit the Frontier, you are different, as I am. You were given certain physical attributes that you did not ask for, as was I. You find yourself an outsider in a galaxy of outsiders, as do I. How could I *not* understand?"

"What do you mean?" asked Nighthawk. "You look normal to me."

"Never trust the eye, which sees only the facade and never the truth," she replied. "You appear perfectly normal to me, too—and yet you are the Widowmaker, and how many men did he kill? Two hundred? Three hundred?"

"A lot."

"But less than me," she said proudly.

He frowned. "You've killed three hundred men?"

"More. And before this day is over, I will add to that total."

"We have nothing to fight about," said Nighthawk. "As you pointed out, we're two of a kind."

"What I didn't point out is that I'm as territorial as the Marquis, and you have invaded my home."

"I'll tell him I couldn't find you."

"Poor clone," she said with mock sympathy. "*You* may need a friend and confidant, but *I* do not. My life was not forced upon me; I have *chosen* to be an outlaw and a killer. You will not leave here alive."

"This is stupid," he protested. "I'm offering you your life! I could kill you in two seconds if I wanted to."

"Try," she said, amused.

"Don't push me!"

"*Push* you?" she repeated with a laugh. "I *challenge* you, Widowmaker!"

"I don't want to kill you."

"But *I* want to kill *you*."

"You're not carrying any weapons. This is murder."

"Do you really think the Marquis would want me dead if I were harmless?" responded Spanish Lace. "I don't *carry* my weapons like you lesser beings. I *am* a weapon."

Nighthawk faced her and reached for his laser pistol, but it leaped out of his holster before he could touch it and hovered, tantalizingly, about four feet away from him.

"What the hell?" he exclaimed.

"What is the loss of one weapon to a man like you?" she said, still amused. "Try another."

He reached for his sonic pistol. He closed his fingers on the handle and pulled. Nothing happened. He tightened his grip and yanked. And found that he couldn't budge it so much as a millimeter.

"*Now* do you know what happened to your powersled?" she asked.

"You're telekinetic?"

She nodded. "I have always had the ability to move material objects with the power of my mind alone. In fact, I think I was seven or eight years old before I realized that no one else could do it." She held out her hands to grab his weapons as each in turn left him and flew across the room into her grasp. "How do you feel *now* about killing a poor, helpless woman?"

"A lot better," he said, reaching into a boot, removing a knife, and hurling it at her all in one fluid motion. It flew straight and true toward her heart, and then froze in space about six inches from its target.

"Fool!" she said, allowing a contemptuous sneer to replace the look of amusement on her angular face. "Don't you realize that you are completely helpless?" Nighthawk heard a sound above him and dove to one side just before a section of the ceiling crashed down where he had been standing. "Can you fight the Ice Palace itself?"

He began approaching her cautiously. Just as he was tensing his muscles for the final charge, a small chair flew into his back, sending him sprawling on the glittering floor.

He was on his feet in an instant, and managed to duck another chair that came at him out of nowhere.

"Very good, Widowmaker," she said. "You inherited good instincts—if 'inherit' is the proper word, and I suspect it isn't. I shall almost be sorry to dispose of you."

He stared at her, reluctant to approach, unwilling to retreat.

"Now, how shall I kill you?" she continued. "It might be amusing to use your own weapons."

Suddenly his three pistols—laser, sonic, and projectile—formed a line just to her left, five feet above the ground, and spun until they were aimed directly at him.

He dove behind the couch to get out of the line of fire. An instant later the couch moved rapidly to his left, and he scrambled on hands and knees to remain behind it as her laughter reverberated through the large chamber. He saw a doorway some fifteen feet away and dove for it. Weaponfire followed him, but he made it intact and raced through another doorway.

He moved quickly from room to room, aware of the danger behind him, unwilling to plunge blindly into potentially greater dangers ahead of him. Once he was too slow, and a beam of solid light singed his ear.

And then he came to a room from which there was no exit. It contained a huge circular bed that spun slowly a few inches above the floor, a pair of glittering silver chests, a large mirror, and a holograph of Spanish Lace herself. A small circular computer hovered near the bed. Dominating the room were some fifty clocks of all types and makes, from an ancient grandfather clock to a complex mechanism giving digital readouts in thirty-six different languages to a rotating holographic representation of Yukon divided into time zones. Nighthawk pulled his tiny circular camera out and tossed it onto the bed; if he was going to die, Malloy might as well see how it happened so the next man the Marquis sent would be better prepared.

"Ah, here you are!" said a voice from the doorway. He spun around and found himself facing Spanish Lace, with his weapons still floating in the air just next to her. "You led me quite a chase, Jefferson Nighthawk, but now it's over."

Nighthawk's gaze darted around the room, trying to find something, anything, he could use to his advantage.

He *survived a hundred or more battles. Some of them had to be against aliens or mutants with even greater powers than she possesses. Think! What would* he *have done?*

"These are my prizes," she said, gesturing to the clocks. "My booty. All else I sell or trade, but the clocks I keep, to tick off the minutes and hours of my life until I am no longer in bondage to this unwanted body." Her face suddenly became a mask of fury. "And you dare to stand among them and insult me?"

A shot rang out and a bullet ripped into the wall behind him, spraying his face with dust. He dove behind the nearest chest for cover. Two small alien statues stood atop it. He grabbed one of them, hurled it at her, picked up the second as the first bounced off an invisible barrier a foot from her head, and hurled it more carefully. She grinned as it whizzed harmlessly by her, but it hit what Nighthawk was aiming at, shattering the sonic pistol and careening off the projectile gun.

"You think I need weapons?" she said harshly, as a portion of the ceiling came loose and fell on top of him. He was up again in an instant, positioning himself directly in front of the mirror. When he sensed that the laser pistol was about to fire, he fell to the floor, and the beam bounced off the mirror. The angle brought it within inches of Spanish Lace. She ducked instinctively, then grabbed the laser pistol and hurled it through the doorway into a corridor.

You ducked! You weren't expecting the beam to bounce back at you, and you had to duck. That means it takes you a fraction of a second to erect those invisible walls and shields. Now, if I can just find a way to use that . . .

"On your feet, Jefferson Nighthawk."

He saw no reason to keep hiding, so he stood up and faced her. "What now?"

"Now we end it," she said.

And suddenly the furniture, the walls, the ceiling, *everything* began closing in on him. Vases flew at his head, lamps at his chest, the floor began swaying beneath his feet. He struggled futilely to keep his balance, fell heavily to the floor, got up again, and backed away from her until he was pressed up against the ancient grandfather clock, clinging to it desperately.

Another section of the ceiling came away, burying him. He moaned once, then lay absolutely motionless in the rubble.

Spanish Lace approached him cautiously, poking his spine to see if there was a reaction. There wasn't. She knelt down next to him, still half expecting him to jump at her, but he was motionless.

"All right, clone," she murmured, turning him onto his back and feeling for his identity disk. "Let's see if you're who you said you were."

She deftly removed the disk, and as she was studying it his hand suddenly rose and came down on the back of her neck—burying the grandfather clock's minute hand into the base of her brain. She fell across him without a sound, dead.

Nighthawk shoved her body off his and stood up. He reached out a foot and turned her over. Her face was serene in death, as if an overwhelming burden had somehow been lifted.

You were as much of a freak as me. You could have been my friend. Why did you make me kill you?

He shook his head, as if to physically rid it of that train of thought. It didn't help.

The Widowmaker must have had brothers. Maybe cousins. Maybe even a son or two no one knows about. There could be twenty or thirty men carrying his blood. None of them are doomed to spend their lives killing everyone they meet. Why me?

But of course, they were carrying *some* of the Widowmaker's blood. He was carrying *all* of it, because he *was* the Widowmaker. Not a brother. Not a son. Not Version 2.0. But the Widowmaker. And what the Widowmaker did was kill people. Even people who might have been his friends.

Suddenly he found that he was shivering, and he realized that what had kept the interior of the Ice Palace warm was not a furnace or any heating plant but Spanish Lace, who had used a tiny portion of her abilities to keep the molecules of air in constant motion, spinning them fast enough to make the temperature habitable.

He began searching the room. The chests contained only clothes, but behind the mirror he found a small safe embedded in a quartz wall. He couldn't open it, so he cut it out with his laser pistol, tucked it under his arm, and was about to return to his ship when something caught his eye.

He walked over to it, and found it was a small holograph of a group of girls, perhaps ten or eleven years of age, their arms interlinked, all smiling at the camera. He studied it for a long moment, trying to pick out the girl who would someday become Spanish Lace, and found that he couldn't.

Interesting. One of you might have grown up to be an artist. One an accountant. One a mother of six. One a bitter, barren old woman. One a spaceship mechanic. One a professor of ancient languages. And one a notorious thief and assassin.

And suddenly he understood why she should keep that, of all holographs, of all mementos.

It was the last time you could be mistaken for normal, the last time you fit *anywhere.*

He stared at the holograph again, at all the smiling girlish faces.

I envy you. At least you had ten years.

He located his laser pistol on the way out, then hunted up her powersled and was about to take it back to his ship when he decided that she deserved to be buried. He walked back into the Ice Palace, attached his laser pistol to his power pack, rigged the charge to overload, and left both the gun and the pack right next to her corpse. Then he returned to the powersled and began racing over the frozen plains. When he was five miles away he stopped and looked back, shading his eyes against the sun and its blinding reflections. He could just barely see the Ice Palace. He waited five seconds, ten, fifteen—and suddenly he could hear the explosion. Another moment and the towers and turrets began collapsing inward upon themselves. He thought it would be appropriate to whisper a prayer, and was surprised to discover that he didn't know any.

He rejoined Lizard Malloy at the ship. The leather-skinned little man had witnessed the entire fight on his receiving device and wanted nothing more than to talk about it, while Nighthawk wanted only to put it out of his mind.

"What's the matter with you?" complained Malloy as their ship took off for Tundra. "You kill the most dangerous woman on the Inner Frontier, and suddenly you're acting like you just lost a friend."

"Maybe I did."

"Are you crazy?" said Malloy. "She did her damnedest to kill you."

"We had a lot in common, she and I," answered Nighthawk thoughtfully.

"You think so, do you?"

Nighthawk nodded his head. "She was just a friend I hadn't made yet."

"You're crazy, you know that?" said Malloy.

Nighthawk shrugged. "You're entitled to your opinion."

Malloy pulled a small cube out of his pocket. "If I show this to the Marquis, if he sees you offering that bitch her life, you're history. He'll throw you out on your ass so fast you won't know what happened."

"I can live with that."

Malloy tossed the cube into the ship's atomizer. "*I* probably can't," he said wryly. "You're still the only thing standing between me and a very slow, very painful, death."

"Then you're still under obligation to me."

"I suppose, if you put it that way," acknowledged Malloy uncomfortably.

"I do."

"I have a funny feeling you're bringing that up for a purpose."

"When we land, I want you to take a message to the Pearl of Maracaibo for me."

"I thought the Marquis told you she was off-limits," said Malloy.

"He did."

Malloy stared at him. "You're crazy, you know that?"

"I've decided that life is too short to worry about what you or the Marquis or anyone else wants," said Nighthawk. "I'm going to start thinking about *me* while there's still time, because every other person I've met, without exception, has either tried to use me or kill me."

"Not me!" said Malloy devoutly.

"You, too—or don't you want me to protect you from the Marquis?"

"That's a trade," said Malloy. "I do favors for you, you do them for me."

"Right," answered Nighthawk. "And it's about time you started fulfilling your end of the bargain."

"What the hell happened to you in the Ice Palace?" demanded Malloy. "You're different somehow."

"I realized that life is short, and that everybody goes through it alone," said Nighthawk. "Today is the first day of the rest of my life, and from now on I'm living it for *me*."

"All that from killing one woman?"

"All that, and more," said Nighthawk, wondering idly why he didn't *feel* more free for having declared his freedom.

Chapter 9

"Well, Widowmaker, you're as good as you're supposed to be," said the Marquis of Queensbury as he looked across his desk at Nighthawk.

"I'm not the Widowmaker. And you didn't warn me what I was going to be up against."

"You're who I say you are," replied the Marquis. "And as for the rest of it, I want my second-in-command to be resourceful. View it as a test."

"I thought my test was fighting you in the casino."

"It was."

"Well, then?" said Nighthawk.

The Marquis looked amused. "Did you think life involves only one test?"

"You're supposed to be a good businessman," said Nighthawk, trying to hide his anger. "It was bad business to send me up against someone with Spanish Lace's powers without letting me know what she could do. Why risk getting me killed by not telling me everything I needed to know before I went up against her?"

"It'd be worse business to keep you in your current high position if you couldn't improvise well enough to kill her," answered the Marquis. "Just out of curiosity, how did you finally do it?"

"By deceit and trickery. If she could be killed in any other way, it still hasn't occurred to me."

"You're young yet."

"How would *you* have killed her?" asked Nighthawk.

"Me?" The Marquis laughed aloud. "I'd have someone else do it for me. That's what being the boss is all about."

"I suppose so," acknowledged Nighthawk. "The thing is, talk like that makes me want to be a boss too."

"That's good. I admire ambition in a man." The Marquis' smile vanished as quickly as it had appeared. "But you would do well to remember that this organization only has room for one boss—and I'm him."

Nighthawk stared at him, but made no reply.

"You know," continued the Marquis, "in most employees that kind of sullen look would constitute insubordination. In your case, I think I'll write it off to the arrogance of youth. *This* time. But don't press your luck. You'll need it all just to kill our enemies."

"*Your* enemies."

"You work for me. That makes them your enemies too."

"If you say so."

The Marquis stared at him through narrowed eyes. "You know, I can't decide if you're *trying* to annoy me, or if you're so socially maladroit that you can't help it. I have to keep reminding myself that you're only a couple of months out of the lab."

"And now *you're* trying to annoy *me*," responded Nighthawk.

The Marquis shook his head. "Not at all. I'm just stating facts."

"Let's say, then, that you choose very unpleasant facts to state."

"You've got a lot to learn," answered the Marquis. "Facts are true or false. Pleasant or unpleasant is just the spin you put on them."

"That sounds reasonable, but it's bullshit and you know it."

"You're in a lousy mood. They tell me this happens in three-month-olds, so I'll forgive it this time, but if I were you I wouldn't make a regular habit of it—at least, not when you talk to me. Are we clear?"

Silence.

"Are we clear?" repeated the Marquis.

Nighthawk nodded. "We're clear."

"I think I know what's got you depressed," said the Marquis. "I'll tell you what: Let me catch up on business here and maybe I'll go to Deluros in a week or two and kill the real Nighthawk for you."

"I *am* the real Nighthawk."

"Let's not get into semantics. Once I kill him, you'll be the *only* Nighthawk."

"That's no good."

"Why not?"

"Because *I* have to kill him."

"You know, you could become a real pain in the ass without half working at it," said the Marquis irritably. "Get the hell out of here before we really *do* come to blows."

Nighthawk left the office without another word and, still annoyed with the Marquis, returned to the casino. The place was more crowded than usual. Most of the gaming tables were operating at capacity, and whores of both sexes were cadging drinks and trying to make their business arrangements for the night. The *jabob* table was surrounded by humans who found the alien game fascinating, while the craps table was populated by Lodinites, Canphorites, and a six-limbed golden-shelled Lambidarian.

Malloy was busy playing poker with a couple of flashily dressed miners and a green-hued creature of a species Nighthawk hadn't seen before. He watched as the little man bet up a flush and lost to a full house. Finally he wandered over to the bar, ordered a Dust Whore, and idly watched the various dancers until the Pearl of Maracaibo appeared on the floating platform.

He was sipping his drink and staring at her intently when she suddenly winked at him, then laughed at his reaction. He waited until her dance was through, then made his way to her dressing room, a glass in each hand. The red eye of the security system scanned him and reported his presence to the room's occupant.

"Come in," she said, and the door dilated long enough for him to step into the room.

She sat on an elegant gilt chair, naked from the waist up. A small mirror hovered in the air perhaps thirty inches from her face. She had been staring into it, meticulously removing her stage makeup, but she turned to face Nighthawk as soon as he entered.

"How nice to see you again," she said. "The Marquis tells me you're a hero."

"The Marquis exaggerates," said Nighthawk.

"A *modest* hero," she said. "Now that *is* a rarity around here."

"I brought you a drink," he said, placing it down next to her.

"I didn't ask for one."

"Try it," he said. "You'll like it."

"In a moment, perhaps." She paused and stared at him. "Do you know what the Marquis would do to you if he knew you were here?"

"I know what he'd *try* to do," answered Nighthawk, his anger returning at the mention of the Marquis.

"And you have no fear of him?"

"None." He paused. "Besides, you invited me here."

"I did?"

"You winked at me," he said. "I consider that an invitation. And you haven't told me to leave."

"Leave, then."

"Not just yet."

She smiled but chose to make no reply, and an uncomfortable silence ensued. She stared at her mirror and he looked at her. "You're a very good dancer," he said at last.

Still no reply.

"I noticed that the first time I saw you."

Silence.

"You don't have to be afraid to talk to me," he said. "I'll settle for just being friends."

She uttered a disbelieving laugh. "Just friends?"

"Yes."

"Why?"

"Because I'm lonely."

"There are many women here. Why me?"

He stared at her for a moment before answering. "Because we're both freaks," he said. "I'm sure the Marquis has told you what I am, and with that blue skin you're some kind of sport or mutant. We're each the only one of our kind here. I thought you might be lonely too."

"You were mistaken."

"I'm not so sure of that. Except when you're with the Marquis, you keep entirely to yourself."

"Did it ever occur to you that I might enjoy my own company?"

"No, it never did."

"Why? Just because you don't enjoy yours?"

He stared into her clear, almost colorless eyes for a long moment. "We're getting off on the wrong foot here," he said at last.

"Yes, I know," she said in amused tones. "You just want to be my friend."

"That's right."

"Funny," she said, making no attempt to shield her naked breasts from his gaze. "I thought you wanted to look at my body."

"That too."

"Does your notion of friendship include sharing my bed?"

"If you ask me to."

"And if I don't?"

"Sooner or later you will," he replied. "In the meantime, two lost souls can take some comfort in each other's company."

" 'You do not look at me like a lost soul," she said, arching her back and stretching sensuously, "but rather like a lustful man."

"You're a very beautiful woman. How would you prefer that I look at you?"

"Perhaps, given your situation, you shouldn't look at me at all."

"The Marquis just told me that he wants his employees to display initiative," said Nighthawk with a smile. "Besides, if no one looked at you, you'd be out of a job."

"Very clever," she said. "Now, if you're all through looking, I think you'd better leave."

"I'm still looking," he replied. "Why not have the drink?"

"I could call the Marquis."

"Yes, but you won't," said Nighthawk confidently.

"Why not?"

"Because you don't want me to kill him."

She laughed "*You*? Kill *him*?"

"That's right," he answered seriously.

"So instead of merely a lustful underling, I find myself confronted by a lustful egomaniac," she said. "I suppose I shall have to accept your drink or you will kill *me*, too."

"Now you're making fun of me."

She shrugged and turned back to her mirror.

"I've had very little experience with women," said Nighthawk awkwardly. "Believe me, the very last thing I want to do is seem comical to you."

"Not comical. Just suicidal," she replied. "And the Marquis tells me that you have had very little experience with *anything*." She stared at him with open curiosity. "Is it true that you are only three months old?"

"In a manner of speaking."

"What is it like, to remember no childhood?"

"I have vague memories of a childhood," he replied. "It's not my own, though, and the memories fade daily."

"How wonderful not to remember one's childhood," she said. "I wish I could not remember mine."

"You didn't enjoy it?"

"Would you enjoy being—how did you call it—a sport?" she asked. "Children can be very intolerant." She paused, frowning at the memories. "That is why I came to the Inner Frontier. Here they care no more that I have blue skin than that you are three months old. They care only about what we can do—who we *are* rather than who we *aren't*."

"Interestingly put," said Nighthawk. "But I thought the Oligarchy was based on that same principle."

"They may give lip service to it, but it is valid only out here."

"Perhaps when I'm a year old I'll be less trusting," he said in self-deprecating tones.

She laughed. "You can be very amusing."

A satisfied smile spread across his face.

"You look happy," she said.

"It's nice to be appreciated for something other than my ability to kill people."

"Who was the original Jefferson Nighthawk?" she asked.

"He was the best bounty hunter who ever lived," answered Nighthawk. "He spent most of his life on the Frontier. They called him the Widowmaker."

"The Widowmaker? I've heard of him."

"I think just about everyone has."

"How did he die?"

"He didn't."

She frowned. "But I thought he lived more than a century ago."

"He did. He came down with a disease, and went into the deep freeze before it could kill him."

"It must be very strange for you to know he still exists."

"It makes me feel like a ghost."

"A ghost?"

"Insubstantial," said Nighthawk. "Like he's the real thing, and I'm just an ephemeral shadow, here to do his bidding and then vanish."

"I would hate that feeling!" she said passionately.

"I'm not especially pleased with it myself," he replied. "But it's probably no worse than dancing half-naked so all the men in the audience can lust for your body."

"Nonsense," she said heatedly. "For men to admire my body is perfectly natural. What you have described is sick!" She reached out, grabbed the drink he had brought her, and downed it in a single swallow.

"Tell me—how did you come to be known as the Pearl of Maracaibo?"

"I think we are through talking."

"We are kindred souls," said Nighthawk. "We have many things in common, many things to share. I told you how I came to be the Widowmaker; now you tell me how you came by *your* name."

"I have agreed to no trades or bargains," she said. "If you have a kindred soul here, it is more likely Lizard Malloy than me. Each of you wants things you cannot have. In his case, it is money."

"And in my case?"

"Don't play the buffoon," she said. "You are here right now because of what you want." She stood up and removed the single garment that had been wrapped around her waist. "Take a good look, Jefferson Nighthawk, for this is as close as you're going to get to it."

"I don't give up easily," he said, staring at her nude body.

"Even if I felt attracted to you, I have a strong sense of self-preservation," she said. "I belong to the Marquis as surely as you do. He would kill one or both of us."

"I'll protect you," said Nighthawk.

"Don't be a fool. This is *his* world."

"Just promise to give it some thought."

"All right, I promise," she said. "Now go. I have to get ready to dance again."

"Your last dance of the night is coming up, right?" asked Nighthawk.

"Yes."

"I want to see you after it's over."

"You are a fool."

"I know. But you didn't answer me. Can I stop by here afterward?"

"You are a notorious killer. How can I stop you?"

Nighthawk grinned, then got up and left her in order to secure a spot at the bar where he could watch her dance again.

Chapter 10

Nighthawk lay on his back, head propped on a pillow. The bed floated a few inches above the floor, and constantly changed shape to mold itself to the forms of its occupants.

"That was great!" he said. Suddenly he grinned. "I'm glad I didn't have to wait twenty-three years for it."

"From now on, whenever you go to bed with a woman, you'll have me to compare her to," said Melisande, the Pearl of Maracaibo.

"What makes you think I want anyone else?"

"You're a man. If you don't now, you soon will."

"No," he said. "You're the woman for me."

She turned on her side and looked into his eyes. "But you're not the man for me."

He frowned. "I don't understand."

"I belong to the Marquis. You know that."

"But I thought . . ."

"You thought that just because I went to bed with you once, I was prepared to leave him forever?" she asked with a smile. "You really *are* very young, you know."

"Then why *did* you go to bed with me?"

"Because you looked at me like a hungry puppy dog," she said. "And because I was curious to see what it felt like to have sex with a clone."

"And?"

She shrugged. "You've got a lot to learn."

"You can teach me."

"Teaching awkward young men is not part of my job," she said with a chuckle.

"I'm sorry the experience was so unpleasant," said Nighthawk bitterly.

"I didn't say it was unpleasant," she replied.

"Not in so many words."

"It was all right."

"But nothing more."

"That's right."

"Nowhere near as good as with the Marquis."

"Don't feel badly," she replied. "Most men do a lot worse their first time."

"I don't find that especially comforting."

"Would you rather I lied to you?"

"Much," said Nighthawk.

"But then you'd insist on doing it again."

"Why not?"

She shook her head. "Once was curiosity. Twice would be infidelity."

"You've got a funny notion of morality," said Nighthawk.

"I've developed mine over a period of thirty Standard years," she replied. "How long have you been honing *yours*?"

He made no reply, but swung his feet over the edge of the bed, stood up, and walked to the window that overlooked the frozen streets of Klondike.

"Notorious killers aren't supposed to sulk like spoiled children," she said.

"Look," he snapped, turning to her, "this is the first time I've been with a woman, and also the first time I've been rejected by one. Now, maybe the Widowmaker would know how to handle it, but I'm having a little trouble."

"You *are* the Widowmaker."

"I'm Jefferson Nighthawk."

"Is there a difference?"

"More than you can imagine."

"Well, whoever you are, do you know how silly you look, standing there without any clothes on?"

He walked over to the bed, ripped the covers off, and threw them on the floor.

"Now we're even."

"Do you feel better?" she said.

"Not much."

She stood up, examined her image in the mirror with a critical eye, brushed a few strands of hair into place with her fingers, and started searching for her clothes.

"What are you doing?" he demanded.

"I'm getting dressed and leaving," she replied. "You stopped being fun a long time ago. Now you're not even interesting."

"You're going to the Marquis."

"That's right."

He walked over and grabbed her arm. "And what if I decide not to let you?"

She winced and pulled her arm loose. "That *hurt*! Keep your god-damned hands to yourself!"

"I didn't squeeze that hard," he said. "What's the matter?"

"Nothing," she said, turning away and picking up some clothing from the floor.

"Let me see your arm," he demanded, grabbing her by the shoulders and turning her around.

"Leave me alone!"

He took her arm in his hand and studied it carefully. "That's a hell of a bruise. I can't imagine how I missed it when you were dancing."

"I cover it with makeup."

"How did you get it?"

"None of your business," she said, trying to pull her arm free.

"The Marquis gave it to you, didn't he?"

"I fell and bumped it."

"Not there you didn't, unless you fell with your arms splayed out. The Marquis did it."

"What if he did?" she said defiantly. "It has nothing to do with you."

"How often does he beat you?" demanded Nighthawk.

"I deserved it."

"For what?"

"For something a lot more serious than sleeping with a three-month-old," she said.

"He won't beat you for sleeping with me?"

"Who's going to tell him? You?"

"What kind of man beats a helpless woman?"

"What kind of man *kills* a woman?" she shot back. "Isn't that what you just came back from doing?"

"I'm not going to let him hit you ever again," said Nighthawk.

"I have no further interest in you," she said. "I want you to display none in me."

"I can't."

"Why not?"

He stared at her for a long moment. "I might be in love with you."

" 'Might'?" she repeated.

"I don't know. I've never been in love before."

"You're not now. You had a good time in bed; let it go at that."

"I don't like to think of you going back to him."

"Fine. Think of something else."

She finished dressing and walked to the door. "I have every intention of forgetting tonight. I'd strongly advise you to do the same."

"Not a chance."

"That's *your* problem," she said, walking out as the door sensed her presence and dilated.

Nighthawk walked back to the window and stared out at the frozen landscape for a long moment. Then he slowly climbed into his clothes, no longer interested in sleeping. Finally he walked over to a mirror to comb his hair, but as he looked into the glass, it seemed to him that the reflection he saw was that of a horribly disfigured old man, his eyes sunken, his cheeks hollow, the bones of his face sticking out through his rotting flesh.

The Widowmaker.

"What would *you* have done?" demanded Nighthawk bitterly.

I'd never have gotten into such a situation. I never let my libido rule my mind.

"How can you say that? I've been to bed with a woman exactly once."

You haven't been able to think of anything else since you saw her.

"You wouldn't have, either."

Never tell me what I would or wouldn't have done. You are the student here, not me.

"All right, then. What would you do now?"

Forget her.

"I can't."

She's just a woman. You're just a man. The only difference is she's had enough experience to know she can forget you. Sleep with a few more women, and you'll find her face harder to remember each time.

"Is *that* what made you such a killer? The fact that no one ever meant anything to you?"

I never said that no one meant anything to me. I said that you can't let your gonads rule your mind.

"I'm tired of hearing that. Say something else."

Don't give me orders, son. I'm the Widowmaker. You're just my shadow, my surrogate.

"Then help me, damn it! I'm out here on the Frontier trying to help *you*!"

Why do you think you're seeing me? You'd better start taking the help you can get. Don't hold out for the advice you want.

"What are you talking about?"

You want me to tell you how to win the blue-skinned girl. I'm not going to. Forget her.

"Maybe *you* could. *I* can't."

Then be prepared to kill the Marquis.

"I'm ready to do it tonight."

I know. And once you do, who's going to finger President Trelaine's assassin? Or have you forgotten why you were given life in the first place?

"The Marquis has got to be worth over five million credits. Why don't I just kill him, confiscate what's his, and send it back to Deluros?"

Because all you really want to confiscate is the girl. And because the Widowmaker has a code of honor. If he said he'd accept an assignment, he always kept his word.

"But I'm not the Widowmaker."

You will be, one day.

"No! I'm Jefferson Nighthawk!"

So am I—and I was Jefferson Nighthawk first.

"I'm my own man! I'm not you, and I don't take orders from you!"

You are more me than you can imagine.

"No!" shouted Nighthawk furiously.

Oh, yes, flesh of my flesh and blood of my blood. You don't really think I'm here in the mirror, do you? This is just your mind's way of rationalizing my presence. I'm your conscience. More than that, I'm your essence. We are intertwined mentally, physically, in every possible way. You fall and I hurt, you laugh and I rejoice, you reach for your weapon and I aim the gun and pull the trigger. There's no getting away from yourself, son, and that's what I am: your true self. I'm the man you are striving to become. I'm the ideal you strive to achieve, and I'm always out of reach. No matter how hard you try, you'll always know in a secret chamber of your mind that I am the better man with a weapon or a woman.

"The hell you are!"

The hell I'm not. I'm thirty percent man and seventy percent disease, and I'm frozen away like a piece of leftover meat, but you're still afraid of me, still jealous. I haunt your dreams, young Jefferson; you don't haunt mine.

"I don't have to listen to this!" yelled Nighthawk. He pulled out his sonic pistol and pulled the trigger. The beam of sound shattered the mirror into a thousand pieces.

He calmed down as suddenly as he had become enraged, and realized that he still hadn't settled on a course of action. He walked into the bathroom and stood, contritely, before the mirror.

"I'm sorry," he said. "I lost my temper. Probably you went forty years without losing yours."

A handsome young man stared out at him.

"I said I'm sorry," he repeated. "And I still don't know what to do next."

It seemed to him that the face in the mirror turned rotten with disease just long enough to say, *Of course you do,* before reverting to the handsome young man whose uncertainty and indecision showed in his every expression and gesture.

Chapter 11

Nighthawk rode the ramp down to the subbasement level beneath the casino. He walked past the swimming pool and the sauna, and finally came to the shooting gallery where the Marquis of Queensbury was taking aim at a tiny target fifty meters away. The target spun, rose, and fell, remaining in constant motion—and unlike any other target Nighthawk had ever seen, this one fired back.

It was a holograph of a Navy officer, kneeling, with his pistol clasped in both hands. Tiny laser beams eminated for it—not enough to do serious damage, but more than ample to cause a painful jolt.

Nighthawk stopped and watched, silent and motionless, as the Marquis swayed back and forth, bobbing and weaving like a boxer as he evaded the laser beams and finally squeezed the trigger of his pistol. An instant later, the Electric Monitor signaled a bull's-eye.

"Nice shot," said Nighthawk, finally stepping forward.

"Thanks," said the Marquis. "You haven't been down here before, have you?"

Nighthawk shook his head. "It's impressive."

"It's more than impressive. It's essential."

Nighthawk stared at him curiously.

"There are a thousand men carrying weapons up on ground level. If I'm to be their undisputed leader, it's because they know they can't kill me and take over the operation. The reason they know it is because every month or so I'm called upon to prove it." He paused. "Most of them never pull a weapon out of a holster except to kill someone—or to try to. Their reflexes get rusty. The sights on their weapons fall out of synch. The power levels on their pistols get low. Me, I work with targets at least an hour a day, and my weapons are always in prime condition. It's the difference between the amateur and the professional."

"Very impressive," said Nighthawk.

"How are *your* weapons?" asked the Marquis.

Nighthawk, who was facing the Marquis, spun and drew his weapons and fired them, all on one fluid motion. The gun in his right hand put a bullet through the left eye of a holographic Navy man who was peeking up over a protective barrier, and an instant later the pistol in his left hand burned a hole in the Navy man's chest with a beam of light.

"They seem okay," he said, replacing each weapon in its holster.

"Even more impressive," said the Marquis. "Though somehow I knew that, of all the men on Klondike, you were the one most likely to keep his weaponry in perfect working order. And of course, the Widowmaker could probably hit his targets at fifty meters even if he were blindfolded."

"You didn't ask me down here to watch me shoot," said Nighthawk. "And I didn't come to watch *you* shoot. So what's up?"

"They didn't teach you any small talk back on Deluros, did they?" asked the Marquis with a smile.

"No."

"All right. I sent for you because we have some business to discuss."

Here it comes. He's going to mention the Pearl of Maracaibo, and demand that I never touch her again, and I'm going to have to kill him.

"Ever hear of Father Christmas?"

"You mean like in the kid's nursery story?" asked Nighthawk.

"You should be so lucky," replied the Marquis with a laugh. "No, this Father Christmas works the Frontier. Or, rather, he used to until he got ambitious. He just pulled off a job in the Oligarchy, and now he's headed back here with maybe a dozen police ships on his tail."

"Why is he called Father Christmas?" asked Nighthawk.

"Out here you choose your name," replied the Marquis. "Or sometimes it chooses you. At any rate, he only steals from churches."

"Is there a living in it?"

"Well, if he only went after priests and poor boxes, no. But there's a lot of gold and artwork in some of the churches. Not too many of them are out here on the Frontier, which is why he went into the Oligarchy looking for a big score."

"Sounds like he got it."

The Marquis nodded. "Yeah. I gather he stole about five hundred pounds of gold from a church on Darbar II, as well as a couple of religious paintings by Morita."

"Morita? I never heard of him."

"I suppose there was a limit to what they could teach you in two months," said the Marquis. "Morita was the finest artist of the late Democracy period. His paintings go for millions, and last time I looked, gold was going for seventeen hundred credits an ounce. Which means Father Christmas has what used to be called a king's ransom in his ship's cargo hold. His problem, as I mentioned, is that he's also got a bunch of police ships on his tail."

"What sort of lead does he have?"

"Oh, maybe seven hours, maybe eight."

"He'll lose them. Seven hours is forever at light speeds."

"He's riding a Model Three-forty-one Golden Streak."

Nighthawk looked blank.

"High speed, limited range," continued the Marquis. "He's good for maybe six more hours, but then he's going to have to stop to refuel."

"I assume all this has something to do with me?"

"Of course it does," said the Marquis. "My computer has projected the possible worlds where he can freshen his atomic pile. There are only four. Two of them are military outposts, and he's too smart to stop there. The third is at war with a neighboring system, and no matter what assurances they give him, there's a fair to middling chance that he'll get blown out of the sky by one side or the other."

"Let me guess. Tundra is the fourth."

"No—but I run the fourth world. It's a little planet called Aladdin. I want you there immediately."

"And once I'm there?"

"My guess is that's where Father Christmas will put down. I want you to meet with him."

"Okay, I meet with him. What do I say?"

"You transmit my personal greetings and felicitations to him, and tell him, gently but firmly, that the price of fuel and safe passage has gone up."

"How high?"

"*Very* high," said the Marquis. "I want fifty percent of his haul."

"And if he says no?"

"Do whatever you have to do," said the Marquis with a shrug. "Just make sure that when he leaves, half of what he stole remains behind."

"How many men has he got?"

"A Three-forty-one Streak can only hold a crew of four, so the most he'll have with him will be three."

Nighthawk nodded. "Is there anything else I should know about Father Christmas?"

"You already know it: He's carrying cargo we want."

"You know what I mean," continued Nighthawk. "Has he any special talents or powers?"

"Not unless you believe that he and Jesus are in cahoots," answered the Marquis. "There are some people who believe exactly that, you know."

"Any reason why?"

"He blundered into a trap where all his men were killed and he got out unscathed. And another time the police found his hideout, back on Roosevelt III, and blew it to smithereens. He was down the block at a bar at the time. Heard the noise, stole a ship, and never looked back."

"You want me to take anyone with me?"

"You're the Widowmaker," replied the Marquis. "If I thought you needed anyone before, your last assignment proved just what you can do on your own."

"What do you have all these gunmen for if you won't use them?" asked Nighthawk.

"Oh, I use them when I need them. But you don't really hope to convince me at this late date that you need any help against four men?"

"You're a real sweet guy to work for," said Nighthawk caustically.

"Melisande thinks so."

Nighthawk took one look at the Marquis' smirking grin and knew that she had told him about the night they'd spent together.

"Every once in a while she has to go slumming, just to remind herself why she hooked up with me in the first place," continued the Marquis. "I don't blame her, since it reminds her why she stays with me. The problem," he added, "is that sometimes the man involved doesn't understand what's going on. He gets it into his head that she actually cares for him, and then he makes a nuisance of himself, and then, unhappily, I have to dispose of him." He pulled his gun out of his holster, flipped it in the air, caught it in his other hand, and pulled the trigger. There was a deafening *BANG!* and the Electric Monitor scored another bull's-eye.

"You're very good," acknowledged Nighthawk.

"We both are," replied the Marquis. "I hope we never have cause to find out who's better."

"No reason why we should," said Nighthawk.

But in his mind's eye he could see the Marquis running his hands and mouth all over Melisande's nude body. He felt a wave of jealousy sweeping over him, and he knew that they had more than ample reason.

Chapter 12

Aladdin had once held the promise of great riches—hence its name. But, like Yukon and Tundra, its mines were exhausted in less than two decades, the miners went farther toward the Galactic Core, and not much remained except a handful of prospectors who kept hoping to find another mother lode and the usual gamblers and outcasts and adventurers who were endemic to the Inner Frontier.

As with many of the Frontier worlds that no longer held major populations—or, indeed, never had—Aladdin was dotted with a number of deserted Tradertowns: quickly erected structures that had catered to the needs of a transient population. There were some worlds with forty or fifty functioning Tradertowns, but Man was an efficient animal, and usually within two or three decades of his arrival most of the Tradertowns had become ghost towns as the plunder of the planet was completed and the plunderers moved on. Such a planet was Aladdin, with seventeen ghost towns and one working Tradertown.

It was the first planet within his admittedly limited experience that allowed Nighthawk to land his ship without first requesting permission. The spaceport had fallen into disrepair and the landing pads were cracked and broken; most of the ships landed on a flat, open savannah about a mile from the Tradertown.

Nighthawk made sure that the fueling station was inoperative. Then, satisfied that his prey would have to go into town to obtain fuel, he set his ship down on the plain, activated the alarm system, and began walking across the hot, arid plain toward the Tradertown. Suddenly he became aware of the fact that he was not alone. A spherical ball—bright, yellow and fluffy, totally round, with no visible sensory organs—was rolling alongside him, purring gently to itself.

Nighthawk stopped; the ball of fluff stopped too. He started walking again, altering his direction every few strides; it matched him move for move. He stopped again, and it rolled over to him and rubbed against his boot, purring more loudly. Nighthawk kept his fingers poised above his weapon, just in case it bit, but after rubbing against him for a few more seconds it backed away, as if waiting for him to start walking again. He stared at it for a long moment, then shrugged and continued on his way.

He soon reached the town, still accompanied by the *thing*. He couldn't spot any place that was likely to sell fuel, so he tried to imagine what Father Christmas would do when confronted with the same situation.

He'd seek out some locals, of course, men who could tell him where to obtain his fuel. He'd probably keep clear of the bar and the drug den; there was always a chance that one of the patrons might consider playing bounty hunter and try to kill him for the reward. The assay office was closed; so was the postal station. That left the whorehouse, the restaurant, and the hotel. He arbitrarily chose the hotel and walked down the street until he stood opposite it. He took one more look up and down the street, just to make sure that he hadn't missed an even more likely spot, then turned and entered the hotel.

It was nondescript, much like Aladdin itself. It had changed hands so many times, and so many owners had tried to shape it to their tastes, that it seemed a catchall of influences—nonrepresentational holographic art sharing wall space with alien carvings and the stuffed heads of Aladdin's now-extinct carnivores.

The furniture was the same: angular chrome chairs floated above the floor, sandwiched between oddly shaped chairs for strangely jointed aliens and leather lounge chairs that recalled the gentleman's clubs of Earth's 19th Century.

Nighthawk approached the front desk, still accompanied by the little yellow ball of fluff. An alien, mildly humanoid, with green skin, protruding golden fangs, a bulbous forehead, and huge, luminous purple eyes, stood behind the desk. As Nighthawk approached, it spoke into a translating device that it wore attached to the shoulder of its shining silver tunic.

"Good morning upon you, sir," said its inflectionless translated voice. "How may I help you?"

"I ran short on fuel," answered Nighthawk. "I was forced to divert and land here. Where can I purchase some?"

"What type of ship do you have?" asked the alien.

"A Three-forty-one Golden Streak."

"Ah! You need your nuclear pile enhanced."

"I know what I need. Where do I go for it?"

"It is not necessary to go anywhere. I will send an experienced mechanic to your ship."

"Has he got an office?"

"No, sir. No more than one ship per Standard week needs work done on its pile. I will contact him immediately."

"Not right now."

"But you just stated that you had almost no fuel."

Nighthawk leaned halfway across the counter and lowered his voice confidently. "I have a young lady aboard the ship. Her social position is such that she must not be seen or identified. She's waiting until dark, and will then join me in the suite I intend to rent here." He paused. "Do you understand what I am saying to you?"

"Absolutely, sir," the alien assured him. "You may count upon my discretion."

"Good. What's available?"

"We have an exquisite corner suite on the third floor."

"That'll be fine."

"Will you be taking your Holy Roller with you?"

"I beg your pardon?" said Nighthawk.

"Your Holy Roller," repeated the alien. "I must know if you intend for it to stay with you."

"I don't know what you're talking about."

The alien pointed to the yellow fluffball that was about eighteen inches from Nighthawk's boot. "That is your Holy Roller, sir."

"Interesting name," said Nighthawk. "However, it's not exactly *mine*. It followed me here."

"I can see that, sir, but it's yours nonetheless," said the alien clerk. "They spend years by themselves, manifesting their presence to no one. Then, for reasons no one can fathom, one of them will suddenly appear and befriend a human. Though I have heard of such instances, I have never actually seen it prior to today—but legend has it that once it happens, they never willingly leave the human's presence again."

Nighthawk looked down at the Holy Roller, which purred and rubbed up against his boot. He frowned.

"Let me get this straight: You're telling me that I'm stuck with it?"

"Yes, sir."

"For how long?"

"They are said to be truly faithful companions," answered the alien, leaning over the counter to stare at the Roller. "It is almost always a lifetime relationship."

Nighthawk stared at the yellow fluffball. "Whose lifetime—ours or theirs?"

"They are virtually immortal."

"I don't *need* a lifetime companion."

"I'm not at all sure that your needs are meaningful to it, sir."

"Wonderful," muttered Nighthawk. "Who named them Holy Rollers?"

"They have been called that since I immigrated to Aladdin," said the alien. "I have always assumed that the name was given to them by Men." The alien paused awkwardly. "I really must know, sir: Will it be staying with you?"

"What's it to you?"

"I must program your room's security system, sir. It is quite sensitive: if I don't inform it that you are accompanied by a Holy Roller, the alarm will go off incessantly."

"I see."

"Would you like to see your suite now?"

"Not just yet." He tossed a disk on the desk. "Bill it to that account."

"Of course, sir."

Nighthawk leaned down and picked up the Roller. It made no attempt to elude him, and in fact began purring louder than before as he stroked it absently with his hand.

You'd have blown it away, wouldn't you, Widowmaker?

"Well, it's nice to find *something* that likes me," he said softly. "Maybe I'll let it stick around for a while."

He placed it back on the floor and walked through the lobby into the small restaurant. He found a small table, sat down, pressed his thumb against the scanner until it identified him and verified his credit, and read through the menu, touching his thumb to those items he wanted. He ordered coffee and a roll for himself, and a small bowl of milk for the Roller. When the robot trolley arrived, he took his food from it and placed the bowl on the floor.

The Roller approached it, circled it warily, and finally backed away, rubbing against Nighthawk's boot and purring loudly. Nighthawk reached down and gently pushed it toward the bowl. It emitted a piercing high-pitched whistle, bounced over the bowl, made a semicircular return to Nighthawk, and was soon rubbing up against his boot again.

"All right, have it your way," said Nighthawk, picking up the bowl and placing it on the table.

Suddenly the Roller started bouncing, gently at first, then higher and higher until it reached table height. One more bounce, and it landed gently atop the table and rolled to a spot just opposite the milk. It had no visible sensory organs, but Nighthawk would have sworn it was staring suspiciously at the bowl.

He finished his coffee and offered to show the empty cup to the Roller, which raced to the far side of the restaurant, then shyly returned to the table and lay up against his boot. He ordered another coffee, remained where he was for perhaps ten minutes, then walked out into the lobby.

"You left before I could tell you the number of your suite," announced the alien clerk. "It is three-zero-two-B, and it has been adjusted to recognize your voiceprint, thumbprint, or retinagram."

"Thank you, but I think I'll stay down here."

"Why? Nothing ever happens down here. In your room there are video entertainments, a liquor cabinet, an Imaginarium, and . . ."

"It'll give me something to look forward to."

The alien simply stared at him, as if it realized it was never going to comprehend this species into whose company Fate had thrust it.

Nighthawk walked over to a comfortable-looking chair that floated a few inches above the floor and sat down. He crossed his legs, and the Roller hopped onto the toe of his boot and remained there.

"Slow spin," he commanded, and the chair began spinning very gently in a circle. It didn't move fast enough to make him dizzy, and it allowed him to see the entire lobby in a matter of seconds without having to move or draw attention to himself.

A pair of women entered the hotel a few minutes later and went straight through to the airlift. A miner emerged from the restaurant, wearing his spotless smock, ready to direct his robots in the day's search for Aladdin's remaining riches.

Then, perhaps two hours later, a short, burly man entered the hotel, sweating profusely. He looked around briefly, then walked directly to the desk.

"How may I help you, sir?" asked the alien.

"Got a hungry Three-forty-one Golden Streak," replied the man. "I need someone to tickle its pile."

"I assume you landed to the west of town, out on the savannah?"

"That's right."

"If you will give me your ship's registration number, I can have a skilled mechanic there in fifteen minutes."

"R-three-two-zero-one-TY-four-J" was the man's answer. He slapped a wad of credits on the desk. "And get him there in *ten* minutes."

"Yes, sir!" said the alien, pocketing the money. He cast a map of the

Tradertown on his computer's holoscreen, highlighted the most likely places the mechanic might be, and directed the computer to begin establishing vidphone connections to each location.

Nighthawk got out of his chair and approached the man. "Buy you a drink while you're waiting?"

"Sounds good to me," said the man. "Mighty neighborly of you."

Nighthawk turned to the clerk. "The bar's closed," he said.

"Oh, no, sir," replied the alien. "The bar is open. It just doesn't have any customers."

Nighthawk handed a few bills to the alien. "The bar is closed," he said again.

"Yes, sir. The bar is closed."

Nighthawk accompanied the man to the bar, which was situated across the lobby from the restaurant. Like the rest of the hotel, it showed the influence of too many owners. Holographs of human and alien athletes mingled with paintings of nudes, a huge tank of alien fish, and a pair of Imaginarium games.

"What'll it be?" asked Nighthawk.

"Hot, dry day out. Anything that'll kill my thirst."

"You ought to be a little more careful how you say that," answered Nighthawk. "Someone could make the case that a bullet'll kill your thirst about as well as anything."

"A point well taken," said the man. "I'll have a beer."

"Let's make it two," said Nighthawk, punching the order into the computer. "By the way," he added, extending his hand, "my name's Jefferson Nighthawk."

"A proud name, that," said the man, accepting his hand.

"You've heard it before?"

"I think everyone's heard it before. Are you a relation, or just a pretender to the throne?"

"A little of each. And you are . . . ?"

"You know damned well who I am, Jefferson Nighthawk," said Father Christmas. "You weren't sitting in that lobby, carrying a small arsenal, just for the hell of it, and I didn't stop on Aladdin just to satisfy my thirst. You were waiting for me. Eventually you'll get around to telling me why. In the meantime, I propose to enjoy my beer."

"This world is under the protection of the Marquis of Queensbury," said Nighthawk. "He has no desire to hinder you in your flight from the police."

"That's right thoughtful of him."

"He asks only that you acknowledge that Aladdin belongs to him . . ."

"Gladly done."

". . . and that you pay him a small tribute for allowing you to refuel here."

"*How* small a tribute?"

"Half," said Nighthawk.

Father Christmas threw back his head and laughed. "Do you know what I have in my hold?"

"Yes, I do."

"And the Marquis thinks I'm going to give him the equivalent of twenty million credits just for letting me replenish my atomic pile?"

"He *hopes* you will," said Nighthawk.

"Well, he can hope. I take it you're the alternative?"

"That's right."

The two beers arrived, and each man took one.

"Well, if you're half as good as your namesake, you're twice as good as me. I freely admit it. So why don't we put off the shooting and talk a little business first?"

"That's what I thought we were doing."

"No," answered Father Christmas. "We were talking threats and extortion and the Marquis. Let's just you and me talk some business. Okay by you?"

Nighthawk sipped his beer and considered the older man's offer. Finally he nodded his agreement. "It doesn't cost anything to listen."

"By the way, what's that . . . uh . . . *thing* on your knee?"

"You should approve," said Nighthawk. "It's called a Holy Roller."

"What does it do?"

"Not much that I've been able to tell."

"That makes it holy, all right."

"I take it you're not enamored of religion," said Nighthawk.

"Yeah, that's a pretty fair assessment of the situation."

"Have you always hated churches?"

"Fact of the matter is that I used to be a minister," said Father Christmas with a grin. "Spent sixteen years saving souls, worshiping God, and avoiding the temptations of the flesh. You'd have been proud of me; I was what every mother wants her boy to grow up to be."

"So what happened?"

"There was a young man in our church. Looked a lot like you, though he was no killer. Still, he got arrested for raping and killing a pair of sisters in the congregation. A lot of the evidence pointed to him, but he swore to me on his Bible that he was innocent, and I believed him. So I did a little digging, and I found out that a surgeon, one of our wealthiest and most respected members, had actually committed the crime. Problem is, I didn't have any proof that would hold up in a court of law."

Father Christmas paused long enough to drain his beer glass. "So I figured, well, maybe I couldn't prove he was guilty to a court's satisfaction, but if I turned over all the facts to a good lawyer, he could at least give a jury a reasonable doubt that the young man had killed the girls."

"Did it work?"

"Never got a chance to. Next day my superiors contacted me and told me to tend to the spiritual and leave the temporal to those whose domain it was. The bishop explained to me that if we dragged the surgeon's name through the muck, he'd stop making generous donations to the church. Others pointed out that the young man had been arrested for robbery a few years earlier, and his loss wouldn't mean much. Then, when they couldn't scare me off, the surgeon hired the most expensive lawyer on the planet, and within two days they'd filed fifteen motions against *me*. I couldn't talk about this, I couldn't do that, I couldn't appear here, I couldn't offer an opinion on such and so. They really tied me up, let me tell you."

"Sounds like it," Nighthawk agreed.

"I went to the head of my church, back on Earth itself, and explained the situation. He promised to help me, and I went home—but when my ship landed, I found that his notion of helping was to transfer me to the Rim. And through a friend I had in his office, I learned that the surgeon had made a handsome donation to the church less than an hour before my transfer orders were written."

"So what did you do?" asked Nighthawk.

"I bought a laser pistol and burnt a hole in the middle of the surgeon's chest. Then I killed my superior, broke into jail and let the young man loose, took every credit from every bank account the church possessed, plundered half a dozen churches on Earth, and declared war on all churches from that day forward. It's my experience that they're all a bunch of money-grubbing hypocrites who deserve any misfortune I visit upon them."

"Why the name?"

"Father Christmas?" He smiled. "I declared my war on December twenty-fifth on Earth's calendar."

"So what?"

"Once upon a time, before we went to the Galactic Standard calendar, that was the date on which they celebrated Christmas." He paused. "I've been Father Christmas for fourteen years now. Never killed anyone who wasn't associated with a church, never robbed anything that wasn't owned by a church. You've got no argument with me, Nighthawk."

"Nobody's arguing."

"You're trying to exact tribute," said Father Christmas. "That's got a religious feel to it."

"I have a feeling anything you don't like has a religious feel to it."

"You put your finger on it, all right," said Father Christmas with a smile. "The Marquis wants half of what I have in my hold, right?"

"Right."

"So how much of that will he give to you?"

Nighthawk shrugged. "I don't know. Probably nothing."

"Probably, my ass," retorted Father Christmas. "You *know* you'll never see a credit of it."

"Okay, I'll never see a credit of it."

"Let me leave in peace and I'll give you ten percent. You won't even have to report it to him. Just tell him I never set down on Aladdin."

"He'll know you did."

"Tell him any damned thing you please," said Father Christmas irritably. "Do you know how much ten percent of what I'm carrying comes to?"

"A lot."

"You bet your ass!" he said emphatically. "So do we have a deal?"

"He'd know."

"All right, then. Come to work for me, and it'll be a down payment."

"Robbing churches and killing ministers?"

"And priests," added Father Christmas. "I wouldn't want it said that I was bigoted."

"God's not my enemy."

"He's everyone's enemy!" snapped Father Christmas, his eyes glowing with a private passion. "It's just that most people live their lives without knowing it."

Nighthawk shook his head. "Your god is a biblical deity with a long flowing white beard. I've *met* mine. He wears a lab coat and has a neatly trimmed brown beard . . . and I don't have any desire to kill him. I'm after the devil."

"How will you spot your devil?" asked Father Christmas. "If he doesn't have horns and a tail, what does he look like?"

"Just like me," said Nighthawk. He paused thoughtfully. "Have you got any help on that ship of yours?"

"No."

"You sure?"

"I never plan to work alone," admitted Father Christmas, "but that's the way it usually ends up."

"They desert you?"

"Or I desert them. It depends on the circumstances."

"Then why should I even consider working for you?" asked Nighthawk.

"I'm offering to pay you so much I'd *have* to keep you around. Couldn't let that kind of money loose in the galaxy; some of it might end up in a church."

The Holy Roller somehow bounced and rolled up to Nighthawk's shoulder and perched there, purring gently. He reached up and rubbed it gently. "I'm not going to come to work for you," he said after a moment's consideration, "but I'll tell you what I *am* going to do: I'm giving you a pass."

"You mean I'm free to get my fuel and leave?"

"That's right."

"Why?"

"Maybe I like meeting a dedicated man, and I don't much care what he's dedicated to."

"Maybe, but I doubt it," said Father Christmas. "As you yourself pointed out, the Marquis will know we've met. If you let me leave with my cargo intact, he'll probably kill you."

"He'll try, anyway," agreed Nighthawk.

"You *want* him to?"

She'll never come away with me if I call him out and murder him. But if I kill him in self-defense . . .

"I have my reasons."

"Pity you won't come with me," said Father Christmas, extending his hand. "I could use a man like you."

As Nighthawk reached out and clasped the outlaw's hand in his own, the alien desk clerk approached them, a pistol in one hand and a miniaturized receiver in the other.

"I regret to inform you that the Marquis foresaw this possible turn of events and commissioned me to spy upon you and take the appropriate action if it became apparent that Mr. Nighthawk was going to ignore his duty."

Slowly, leisurely, it aimed the pistol between Nighthawk's eyes. It was only a fraction of a second from squeezing the trigger when the Holy Roller went berserk.

Chapter 13

At first Nighthawk thought it was simply a shrill whistle. But it continued, and got louder, and higher, and louder still, and suddenly he couldn't think clearly. He doubled over and clasped his hands to his ears. Father Christmas fell out of his chair and rolled on the floor, also holding his ears. The alien fired its pistol, but it was in such sense-destroying agony that the laser beams burned two holes in the ceiling before the gun fell to the floor. The alien began shrieking. Droplets of blood appeared in its ears and nostrils, and soon became gushing streams. Still the Holy Roller's whistle continued.

Nighthawk realized through a haze of pain that the Roller was actually able to direct the force of its whistling—that as painful as it was, he and Father Christmas were not bearing the brunt of it. Glasses near the alien began shattering, bottles burst; the alien kept screaming and bleeding, and finally collapsed in a heap on the floor. Instantly the Holy Roller went back to purring and rubbing up against Nighthawk.

"That's some pet you've got there," said Father Christmas groggily, rising to one knee and staring at the Roller. "It sure packs a wallop."

"It does, doesn't it?" said Nighthawk, still trying to focus his eyes.

He waited until all his senses were working properly again, then got up, walked over, and examined the alien. It was dead.

"That gonna get you in a mess of trouble with the authorities?" asked Father Christmas.

"It was probably the closest thing to an authority this world had," said Nighthawk, gesturing toward the dead alien.

Suddenly two servomechs entered the room.

"Clean up the broken glass," ordered Nighthawk. "Leave the body alone until I tell you what to do with it."

They immediately went to work straightening up the room, with special attention to the shards of glass.

"Well," said Father Christmas, "it's obvious that the Marquis doesn't put a lot of trust in you, and when his stooge doesn't report back, he's going to figure out that you killed it."

"I didn't; the Holy Roller did."

"Same difference. Who do you think he's going to blame—you or an alien animal that looks like a kid's doll and purrs all the time?" Father Christmas smiled. "If it was me, I'd pack my belongings right quick and start considering finding employment elsewhere. *I'll* still take you on, of course, but I have a feeling not too many other people in this section of the Frontier will once word gets out that the Marquis is looking for you."

"He won't have far to look," answered Nighthawk. "I'm going back to Tundra."

"Without any part of my cargo?"

"I told you—you're free to go."

"But the situation has changed," noted Father Christmas. "Now you've got a dead spy on your hands."

"I'll say you killed it."

"And you just stood by while I walked away?" asked Father Christmas.

The Holy Roller began bouncing again, while still purring, and finally bounced high enough to settle on Nighthawk's shoulder. He reached over and petted it without thinking, and the fluffball began purring so loudly that it sounded like an engine.

"You have a point," admitted Nighthawk. "I suppose I'll just have to tell him the truth."

"Thereby guaranteeing that he kills you."

"Guaranteeing that he'll *try*, anyway. It's a little sooner than I'd antici-pated, but it was bound to happen. It might as well be now." The servomechs had finished sucking up the glass shards and now approached him for more orders. "Take the body to its office, lock the doors, and wait there for further orders," said Nighthawk. The machines left the bar, returned a moment later with a cart, placed the alien onto it, and took it away.

"None of this is necessary," said Father Christmas. "Just come away with me and forget about the Marquis."

"It's not the Marquis I can't forget," replied Nighthawk wryly. "He's just an obstacle."

"So it's a woman!" said Father Christmas with a grin. "But then, it always is at your age."

"It's a woman," admitted Nighthawk.

"She belongs to him?"

"People shouldn't belong to anybody."

"Absolutely," agreed Father Christmas. "It's against all the laws of God and man." He looked sharply at Nighthawk. "And you'd like her to belong to you."

Nighthawk nodded. "In a manner of speaking."

"So you need an excuse to kill the Marquis."

"Right. But . . ."

"But?"

"But he's been decent to me. He made me his second-in-command, he's trusted me . . ."

"He didn't trust you to kill me, did he?" noted Father Christmas. "If he had, we wouldn't have a dead alien on our hands."

"That's true," said Nighthawk, frowning. "But he knows what I am, and it doesn't bother him. He treats me like anyone else."

"You look like anyone else to me," said Father Christmas. "What are you?"

"I'm a clone."

"Ah! You are the Widowmaker reborn, risen from the ashes."

"He's not dead."

"He must be. He'd be a hundred and fifty years old."

"He's been in the deep freeze for the past century."

"Let me think about this," said Father Christmas. "He's alive, but he's frozen. They spent a lot of money and took a lot of risks to make a clone. Why would he freeze himself? Probably a lot of reasons. Disease. An enemy he couldn't handle. He invested a bundle of money at a good return, and hopes to be worth billions when he wakes up." He paused, considering all the possibilities. "But if it wasn't an enemy, he could wake up now. He wouldn't need a clone. If it was money, he definitely wouldn't want the potential legal hassle of sharing it with a clone. But if it was a disease . . ." He frowned. "But why a clone?"

"Costs have gone up."

"Of course," said Father Christmas. "He's been paying for the deep freeze with interest from his investments. As expenses increased, they had to dip into capital, and suddenly they're facing a situation where he won't have enough money to *stay* frozen. So they created you. . . ." He frowned again. "But what are you doing, working for the Marquis? If it's money they need, you should be here on an assignment. Gun down some killer, collect the reward, and return to wherever they're keeping the original Widowmaker."

"I'm working on it. Kind of. Things have become very complicated."

"Will killing the Marquis make it easier for you? Is *he* the one you're after?"

"No. He knows who I'm after, but so far he hasn't been willing to tell me."

"I imagine he won't be very willing, and even less able, after you've killed him."

"I've thought about it," said Nighthawk. "I'll claim he was the man I was after, take the reward, and . . ." He paused, momentarily lost in thought.

"And send it back to the Widowmaker?" suggested Father Christmas.

"No. I'll take it back to Deluros myself."

"Deluros? That's halfway across the galaxy. Why not send it?"

"I've got to deliver it in person."

"Why?"

"Because I'm probably the only man alive who can kill him," answered Nighthawk.

"I thought you said he was sick."

"I don't know if I can handle him once he's healthy. He's a killer by choice; I'm one by necessity."

"Comes to the same thing in the end," said Father Christmas.

A middle-aged man, his luggage hanging from his shoulder by a strap, entered the lobby of the hotel. When no one came to greet him, he wandered over to the bar and froze when he saw the still-wet bloodstains on the floor. Nighthawk and Father Christmas stared coldly at him, and after a moment he retreated without a word, backing up until he careered off the front desk. Then he raced out the front door.

"Well, son," said Father Christmas, "I think we'd better take our leave of this place."

Nighthawk began walking toward the door. The Holy Roller chirped in surprise, then bounced down to the floor and positioned itself about eighteen inches away from Nighthawk's left boot.

"I have no reason to stay," Nighthawk said, walking around the bloodstains and out into the lobby. He turned to Father Christmas. "Where are you heading?"

Father Christmas shrugged. "I don't know. Might be interesting to see if there are any religious goods worth stealing from Tundra."

Nighthawk looked at him, surprised.

"I've taken a liking to you," continued Father Christmas. "And I never did have much use for the Marquis. We thieves are supposed to stick together, not extort each other when we stop for a little fuel."

"You have half a dozen police ships on your tail," noted Nighthawk. "They're only a few hours behind you."

"I'll transfer all my goods to *your* ship," said Father Christmas. "With our alien friend dead, I'm not likely to find someone to enrich my ship's pile in the next hour anyway. Let 'em do whatever they want to my ship."

"I don't want to be responsible for your loot," said Nighthawk.

"Nobody's asking you to," said Father Christmas. "In fact, I'd deeply resent it." He paused. "Time's running short. Can I use your ship or not?"

Nighthawk considered it for a moment, then nodded his head. "I'm taking the Roller, too."

"Can't say that I blame you. Damned thing's more effective than most weapons I could name."

"I wish I knew what it ate," said Nighthawk as he walked out the front door of the hotel. "I'd like to take some along."

"It doesn't seem to have a mouth," observed Father Christmas. "Why not assume that it ingests through osmosis? Give it nice things to rub against and it'll do just fine."

"What constitutes nice things?"

"You," suggested Father Christmas with a smile.

"I beg your pardon?"

"I've seen animals with no ingestion orifices on other worlds, a couple of 'em. They feed by osmosis. Figure this critter probably kills small animals by draining the life force from them. You're too big for it to hurt, so it feeds off your energy when it gets hungry, and keeps you alive for future meals by killing off your enemies."

"You might be right," said Nighthawk. He stared down at the Roller. "But I liked it better when I thought it was protecting me because it cared for me."

"Maybe it does. I'm just guessing."

"I wonder if it'll even go into my ship," said Nighthawk. "Maybe it'll decide it would rather stay here."

"Not a chance," said Father Christmas.

"Why not?"

"If we were back in my preacher days, I'd say that the Holy Roller—especially with a name like that—is a sign from God."

"A sign?"

"That you're protected. If God hadn't supplied you with an alien entity that can't think and can't talk but nonetheless decided to attach itself to you, you'd be dead back there in the hotel. It means God had other plans for you."

"Like killing the Marquis?"

"Who knows?"

Or spending my life with the Pearl of Maracaibo?

"You're the preacher," said Nighthawk. "How will I know when I've accomplished what God had in mind for me?"

"Easy," answered Father Christmas. "Once you've done what you're supposed to do, your little fluffball here will stop protecting you."

As if to emphasize that it wasn't ready to part company yet, the Roller began purring loudly and bounced up to Nighthawk's shoulder again.

Chapter 14

Lizard Malloy looked up from his game of solitaire and saw Nighthawk and Father Christmas approaching him.

"Welcome back," said the leather-skinned little man. "Who's your friend?"

"Call me Kris," said Father Christmas.

Malloy suddenly stared at the Holy Roller. "You know you're being followed by something round and yellow?"

"Yeah."

"I assume it's alive, but I can't see any eyes or ears or anything like that."

"It's alive," said Nighthawk. "Where's the Marquis?"

"It's pretty late," replied Malloy. "I think he and the Pearl have gone off to bed."

Nighthawk tensed, but made no reply.

"Well, I'd like a drink," said Father Christmas. "You mind if we join you?"

"Ask *him*," said Malloy, indicating Nighthawk. "He's the boss."

"Sit," said Nighthawk, pulling out a chair and seating himself. The Holy Roller chirped happily and bounced up to his shoulder, where it settled down to do some serious purring.

"What the hell *is* it?" asked Malloy.

"Just a pet."

"Looks harmless," offered Father Christmas, suppressing a smile.

"Absolutely," said Nighthawk.

Malloy looked at it suspiciously for a long moment, then shrugged.

"When can we figure on meeting the Marquis?" asked Father Christmas.

"You know him, Kris?" asked Malloy.

"I know *of* him," replied Father Christmas. "I'd like to meet him. And I have a feeling that it's reciprocal."

"Well, once his lady is bedded down for the night, he usually comes back here for a nightcap," offered Malloy. "Stick around awhile and you'll probably run into him, or vice versa."

"Sounds good to me," said Father Christmas.

"And he'll probably want a report from *you*," added Malloy to Nighthawk. "Did everything go smoothly?"

"In a manner of speaking."

"Did you get the money, or did you have to kill him?"

"I've got his entire haul in my cargo hold."

"Then you killed him?"

"No."

Malloy looked puzzled. "I thought this Father Christmas was a big-time Bad Guy. What kind of crook gives you everything he's got without a fight?"

"One who wants to live to see the next morning," suggested Nighthawk.

"I happen to know Father Christmas intimately," added Father Christmas, "and I guarantee that he would do almost anything to avoid a physical conflict with young Nighthawk here. Or with the Marquis, for that matter."

"Too bad," said Malloy. "The name was so interesting, I kind of hoped a really interesting crook went with it."

"Oh, he's fascinating beyond belief," said Father Christmas. "I never tire of talking about him."

"Well, you'll have to fill me in on him, Kris," said Malloy. "Only later."

"I'm happy to do it right now."

"I don't think so," said Malloy, looking across the huge casino toward the large man who was approaching him. "Here comes our lord and master. It'll have to wait."

"That's the Marquis?"

"Big, ain't he?"

The Marquis of Queensbury strode up to the table. "Welcome, Widowmaker," he said. "I hear you had a little problem."

"No problem at all," answered Nighthawk.

"You shot the wrong man, you asshole!" bellowed the Marquis.

"I didn't shoot anyone—and it wasn't a man, it was an alien."

"All I know is that I told it to keep an eye on you, and suddenly it's dead and Father Christmas's ship is empty and you're sitting here with a stranger and some kind of idiot animal and telling me that everything is okay. So you'll have to excuse me if I seem a little out of sorts, but *I* don't think everything is okay."

"I've got Father Christmas's entire haul in my ship," said Nighthawk.

"Oh?" said the Marquis, genuinely surprised. "You killed him?"

"As a matter of fact, I didn't."

"You mean he just *let* you empty his ship and move all his cargo to yours?" asked the Marquis sardonically.

"No," said Nighthawk.

"I knew it."

"He helped me," continued Nighthawk.

The Marquis looked from Nighthawk to Father Christmas. Finally he turned to face the latter. "Father Christmas, I presume."

"You certainly do. Imagine trying to extort fifty percent for the privilege of refueling."

"What are you doing here?" demanded the Marquis.

"I wanted to see what kind of thief robs his fellow thieves," answered Father Christmas.

"You're looking at him," said the Marquis with no display of embarrassment. "And I'm looking at a man who robs the deeply religious. Which of us do you suppose has more demerits in the Book of Fate?"

"It'd be a close call," said Father Christmas.

"You'd win in a walk," said the Marquis firmly.

"I would, if it was written by the same hypocrites who wrote the Bible and the church services," agreed Father Christmas. "Fortunately, they don't speak for God."

"And you do?"

"God doesn't need *my* help. I'm just a stopgap, until He Himself razes the temples to the ground."

"Temples? I thought you robbed churches."

"A poetic flourish," replied Father Christmas. "Actually, I rob any religious institution I come across."

"I know. And now you've presented me with a serious ethical problem," said the Marquis.

"I have?"

The Marquis nodded. "I've never stopped you from practicing your profession. You've robbed churches on *my* world, and I've never lifted a finger against you. But now you've taken advantage of my hospitality on Aladdin without paying for it, and one of my most trusted employees is dead. Hell, for all I know, you've corrupted the Widowmaker here." He uttered a mock-theatrical sigh. "What am I to do with you, Father Christmas?"

"Well, the way I see it, you have three choices," answered Father Christmas. "First, you can kill me. That would unquestionably make you feel better—but I suppose it's only fair to tell you that I rigged the cargo hold on Nighthawk's ship, and if you try to remove any of my treasure without knowing the proper codes, you'll blow up the ship and everything in it. Second, you can let me go, but I don't *want* to go, and I probably wouldn't avail myself of the opportunity."

The Marquis stared thoughtfully at him, more amused than outraged. "And third?"

"Third, you can use your brain and offer to become my partner. There are thousands of churches on the Frontier, millions back in the Oligarchy. We could die of old age before we've plundered two percent of them."

"Why should I want to rob churches?" asked the Marquis.

"Because you're a thoroughly corrupt man, and there's a fortune to be made," answered Father Christmas.

"I rule eleven worlds already, and I influence twenty more," said the Marquis. "That's thirty-one worlds under my control. Why should I need a partner?"

"Because you want what every corrupt man wants."

"And what is that?" asked the Marquis.

"More," said Father Christmas.

"True," admitted the Marquis. "But if robbing churches won't make me any less corrupt, then I'll *always* want more."

"You always will," agreed Father Christmas. "That's why men like us never retire."

"And you only rob churches, right?"

"Who else forgives you for your misdeeds and prays for your soul?"

"Do I detect a note of cynicism?" asked the Marquis with a grin.

"Absolutely not," said Father Christmas earnestly. "Back on Earth—and I have plundered some of its finest churches, including Notre Dame and the Vatican—there is an insect called the ant. It lives in colonies, and is very industrious. It builds small mounds and creates incredibly complex passageways and food chambers and nurseries just beneath the surface. It takes days, sometimes weeks, to create these anthills . . . and yet you can destroy them in seconds, with the toe of your boot. And do you know what the ants do then?"

"Attack you?"

"No," answered Father Christmas. "They go right back to work rebuilding the mound."

"And you're saying churches are like anthills?"

"Only in this respect: They don't seek revenge once you've plundered them. They rebuild with all the industry of ants. It is counter to their philosophy to blame the thief. They prefer to consider me an agent of God, Who for reasons unknown to them is punishing them. It would make much more sense to think of me as the devil incarnate, but they don't really want to believe in a devil. It's easier to blame God, and hence their own sinful lives, for what I do without conscience or ethical consideration. And when disaster—meaning myself—strikes, they go about their business like the ants, rebuilding so that I can plunder them again."

Suddenly a huge smile spread across the Marquis' face. "I like you!" he exclaimed.

"Why shouldn't you?" asked Father Christmas. "I'm very likable."

"I think we can reach an agreement," continued the Marquis.

"Give me safe passage and asylum and I'll give you twenty percent," said Father Christmas.

The Marquis shoved Malloy out of his chair and sat down on it. "Take a walk," he said. "We're about to talk business."

Malloy, obviously feeling insulted, got up from the floor and left.

The Marquis turned back to Father Christmas. "Twenty percent isn't even worth talking about," he said. "Now, here's *my* proposal, my friend. You tell me what worlds you plan to hit. I'll supply you with all the firepower you need, and I'll give you safe haven on any world within my sphere of influence, for, shall we say, half?"

"I thought half was your criminal extortion rate, not your very best offer to possible partners," said Father Christmas. "I'll agree to it for, shall we say, a quarter?"

The Marquis turned to Nighthawk. "You brought back a good man, Jefferson Nighthawk. I *really* like him." He stared at Father Christmas. "In fact, I like you so much I'll do it for a third."

"Like me a little less and take thirty percent," said Father Christmas with a grin.

"What the hell, why not?" said the Marquis, sticking out his huge hand and shaking Father Christmas's much smaller one. "You've got a deal."

"Well, it's nice to be in business with you," said Father Christmas. "I think this calls for a little celebration. I'll treat for a bottle of your finest Cygnian cognac."

"I'll go get some from the bar," said the Marquis, getting up.

The Marquis of Queensbury returned a moment later with the bottle and some oddly shaped glasses on a glowing tray. He opened the bottle with a flourish, and carelessly filled each of their glasses, splashing some of the expensive cognac onto the tray and table.

"To friendship, partnership, and success," he said in a loud voice.

"To friendship, partnership, and success," echoed Father Christmas.

"And to death," added Nighthawk.

"Death?" repeated the Marquis curiously.

"In our business, how else will you know you've succeeded?" asked Nighthawk.

"True," agreed the Marquis after a moment's thought. "To death."

"May it visit our enemies first, and ourselves not at all," intoned Father Christmas.

If I work it right, thought Nighthawk, *that toast may just come true.*

Chapter 15

Nighthawk sat at the bar, next to Lizard Malloy, staring at the Pearl of Maracaibo in rapt fascination. His drink was untouched, and his thin cigar had gone out. The Holy Roller sat motionless on the bar, an inch from his left hand.

Father Christmas walked into the casino, spotted him, and walked over. He looked up at the undulating, nearly nude blue-skinned girl with a bored expression, ordered a drink, and turned to Nighthawk.

"Close your mouth," he said. "You never know what might fly into it."

"Shut up," said Nighthawk, never taking his eyes off the dancing girl.

"Just trying to be helpful," said Father Christmas with a shrug. He nodded a greeting to Malloy, waited for his drink to arrive, took a sip, and reached out to pet the Roller. It allowed him to touch it, but displayed neither interest nor pleasure, refusing to purr or move closer.

Finally the performance was over and Melisande vanished backstage.

"Never interrupt me when I'm watching her," said Nighthawk, finally turning to Father Christmas.

"She won't vanish if you take the time to say hello to a friend," replied Father Christmas. He got to his feet. "Come on over to a booth. It's more comfortable, and I'm an old man with all kinds of aches and pains."

Nighthawk and Malloy picked up their drinks and followed him. The Roller chirped twice, then bounced to the floor and soon caught up with them. When they reached a booth and sat down, it came to rest on the toe of Nighthawk's boot.

"You spend a lot of time watching her," noted Father Christmas.

"What's it to you?"

"He's in love," said Malloy with a smirk.

"Have either of you got anything useful to say?" demanded Nighthawk irritably.

"As a matter of fact, I have," replied Father Christmas. "You know, you'd be immature even if you were as old as you look—and I happen to know you're a good deal younger than that."

"Get to the point."

"The point, my young friend, is that you're in the throes of first love. You're not going to want to hear this, but trust me: You'll get over it."

"I don't want to get over it."

Malloy grinned. "They never do."

"Now, I know you won't believe this," said Father Christmas, "but girls like her are a credit a crate. Any Tradertown has a hundred just like her."

"There's no one like her!" snapped Nighthawk.

"She's the two T's, kid—trouble and trash."

"Be careful what you say," replied Nighthawk ominously. "You may be a friend, but there's a limit to what I'll let even a friend say about her."

"Listen to him," urged Malloy, enjoying Nighthawk's discomfort. "You don't know it yet, but there are a lot of women who look even better."

"And a handful who are even less trustworthy," added Father Christmas.

"What do you mean—less trustworthy?"

"I've seen her type," said Father Christmas. "They're drawn to power the way you're drawn to a good-looking girl."

"So I'll prove I'm more powerful than *he* is."

"You don't understand. I said *power*, not physical prowess. If it's not the Marquis, it'll be some millionaire or politician or something. Never an outsider like you or me."

"You're wrong," said Nighthawk stubbornly. "I can *make* her care for me."

"How? By killing her protector?"

"Oh, she'd love that," said Malloy sardonically.

"If it's a protector she wants, *I* can protect her better than *he* can."

"From outlaws, yes. From economic recessions, I doubt it." Father Christmas paused. "Let her go, Jefferson. All she is, all she'll ever be, is bad news. Believe me; I'm not an involved party."

"You don't understand," said Nighthawk. "I love her."

"You've been alive four months, and you've found the only woman in the galaxy that you can love?" chuckled Malloy.

"Doesn't that seem just a little far-fetched, even to you?" added Father Christmas.

"She's what I want."

"I know. I'm just suggesting that *you* are not what *she* wants."

"What do either of you know about it?" demanded Nighthawk. "He's a repulsive little freak, and you're a wrinkled old man! When did you ever love anyone?"

"You think being old and gray-haired and wrinkled stops you from falling in love?" asked Father Christmas with a chuckle. "Just because you don't appeal to nubile twenty-year-old women anymore doesn't mean *they* don't appeal to *you*." He paused. "But if age has made you any wiser, you realize that there's a big difference between *wanting* them, which is accept-able, and *loving* them, which must be done with judgment and discretion. Especially when you have as many enemies as I do, or as you will if you live to be my age."

"Did you come all the way over here from the hotel just to give me a lecture on women?"

"No, though it's obvious you need one," said Father Christmas. He paused and stared at Malloy. "I think it's time we considered our next career move."

Nighthawk turned to Malloy. "Go to the bar. The drink's on me."

"Damn it!" snapped Malloy. "I'm sick of everyone always trying to get rid of me!"

"I've got business to discuss with Father Christmas," said Nighthawk.

"You think this place isn't wired for sight and sound?" demanded Mal-loy. "Or that it's not making a permanent record of everything you say so that the Marquis can watch and listen to it later?"

"Go away."

"Some fucking friend you are!" muttered Malloy.

Nighthawk stared at him coldly. "You are no longer under my protec-tion. We owe each other nothing from this moment on."

"Big deal! He gives me back my life. Hallelujah." Malloy glared at him. "I don't *want* the goddamned thing back! As long as it belonged to you, people left me alone and I got to stay alive. If word gets out that I'm not beholden to you anymore, my life expectancy is about three hours, tops."

"Just go away," said Nighthawk. "You make my head hurt with all your convoluted reasoning."

"But am I still under your protection?" persisted Malloy, holding his ground.

"Whatever makes you happy."

"*That* does."

"Fine," said Nighthawk. "Now beat it."

"But if I belong to you, you shouldn't have any secrets from me."

Nighthawk whipped out a pistol and pointed it at the tip of Malloy's leathery nose.

"See?" said Malloy accusingly. "See? I *knew* you replaced me with the Roller!"

"The Roller always keeps its mouth shut and doesn't give me unwanted advice," said Nighthawk. "That's more than I can say for a certain half-pint gambler."

"All right, I'm going, I'm going!" said Malloy bitterly. "But someday you'll wish you'd been nicer to me."

"I saved your life," responded Nighthawk. "How much nicer do I have to be?"

"You'll see," muttered Malloy, stalking off to the bar.

"He's right, you know," said Father Christmas.

"You told me to dump *her*," said Nighthawk irritably. "Now you're going to tell me to be nice to *him*?"

"No," answered Father Christmas. "I mean that he's almost certainly right about the place being wired."

"Do you want to go outside and talk?"

Father Christmas considered it for a moment, then shook his head. "No. I think anything we have to say can be said in front of the Marquis."

"Okay," said Nighthawk. "Shoot."

"We have to have a serious discussion about the future, Jefferson," said the older man.

"I thought we had one on the way back from Aladdin."

"That was then, this is now."

"What's changed?" asked Nighthawk.

"I've got a bad feeling," replied Father Christmas. "The Marquis was too willing to forgive you for not doing what he sent you to do."

"I brought you back," said Nighthawk. "That was even better."

"I know you have your whole life ahead of you, but trust me: Outlaws live for the moment. He might ultimately be willing to deal with me, but it doesn't make sense that he wouldn't try to grab the gold and the Moritas first. That's hardly the mark of a criminal kingpin. It makes sense for me to deal with him; it makes less for *him* to deal with *me*."

"But you had the hatch rigged."

"That's another thing," continued Father Christmas. "He can't stay in power long if he lets people challenge his authority like that. Hell, it practically invites his henchmen to protect what they've stolen by booby-trapping the loot and then renegotiating terms with him. *I* would never allow it; neither should *he*."

"But he did."

"That's what makes me very uneasy."

"What do you think his motive is?"

"I can't spot it. Except I know that it has nothing to do with me."

"Why not?" asked Nighthawk.

"Because my plans were fixed before I met him, and I haven't changed them one iota."

"If it has nothing to do with you, then who—*?*"

"You, of course," said Father Christmas. "You disobeyed his orders, and if you didn't kill his spy, you at least didn't go out of your way to save it. So I have to ask myself: Why are you still alive? He's not afraid of you; a man like the Marquis can snuff you out in an instant. He's not being altruistic, because altruism is totally alien to a man like that. He hasn't forgiven your infraction; he's chosen to ignore it. Why? Why is a four-month-old clone suddenly his second-in-command?"

Nighthawk considered what the older man had said. "I don't know," he admitted at last.

"Neither do I," said Father Christmas. "But there *must* be a reason." He paused. "Why are you here?"

"I told you."

"All right, it's part of a mission. Who sent you here?"

"Marcus Dinnisen—the Widowmaker's lawyer, back on Deluros VIII," answered Nighthawk.

"He sent you to Tundra?"

"No. He sent me to the Inner Frontier. A man named Hernandez, the chief of security on Solio II, sent me here."

"What's his connection to you?"

"He's the one who arranged for me to be created."

"Interesting."

"Is it?"

"And frustrating," said Father Christmas. "We don't know enough. Or if we do, I can't see it yet."

"You're the guy with the bad feeling," answered Nighthawk. "I still don't know what's got you so bothered."

"There's something going on here, something that reaches at least to Solio II, and maybe all the way back to Deluros," said Father Christmas. "I think we'd be well advised to get the hell out while the getting's good. There are too many things going on here that I don't like."

Nighthawk looked around, his gaze coming to rest on Malloy, who sat at the bar, and he remembered what the leathery little man had said. "Are you sure you want to be saying all this where the Marquis can probably overhear you?"

"What difference does it make?" shot back Father Christmas. "If you agree to come with me, we'll be out of here before he can stop us. If you stay here, he'll know that my best arguments couldn't make you leave him."

"What if *I* stay and *you* leave?" asked Nighthawk. "Won't that bother him?"

"Probably. That's why it won't happen."

"I don't follow you."

"Malloy is no fool," said Father Christmas. "The only thing keeping him alive is you. I plan to put myself under your protection as well."

"That's the silliest thing I ever heard," said Nighthawk. "Why would you do something like that?"

"It's a fair trade," said Father Christmas. "You're the one person on this world who can protect me and my treasure from the Marquis. And I'm the only person on this world who's been honest with you, who's tried to talk you out of doing stupid things, and who's stuck with you even when you did them. You are friendless and alone in the galaxy. I aim to be your friend, and I'll be everything a friend should be—but my price is high: my life. You're in charge of safeguarding it." He extended his hand. "Have we got a deal?"

"You ask a lot for your friendship," said Nighthawk, staring at his hand.

"If you get a better offer, take it."

Nighthawk stared for another moment, then reached out and took Father Christmas's hand.

"Good!" said the older man. "Now we stay together or leave together."

"I'm not going anywhere," said Nighthawk. "Not until *she* goes."

"Then maybe we'll take her."

"Kidnap her? The Marquis will have two hundred men after us before we're out of the system."

"You overestimate the depth of his feelings for anyone besides himself," replied Father Christmas. "He didn't get to be who he is by developing a deep and lasting commitment to every nightclub dancer who comes along." He paused thoughtfully. "Still, it would be such a public humiliation that he'd have to do something." He paused. "No, it'd probably be better to talk everyone into it."

"Everyone?"

"Even the Marquis."

"What kind of prize could get both him and her to come along?" asked Nighthawk.

"The biggest."

"Deluros VIII?"

Father Christmas nodded. "The capital world of the race of Man."

"But it's half a galaxy away."

"It's got a lot of churches—and it's got the Widowmaker."

"So how do we convince them to come along?"

"We find something he wants," said Father Christmas. "Something he can't say no to."

"Like what?"

"I've got an idea," said Father Christmas. "But I need to work on it for a while."

"He knows you're trying to come up with a reason," noted Nighthawk. "Or he soon will."

"If it's a good enough reason, he'll come anyway," answered Father Christmas.

"And if it's not?"

"Then," said the old man grimly, "you'd better be prepared to prove your friendship."

Chapter 16

Father Christmas entered the casino, spotted Nighthawk sitting alone at a table, walked over, and told him to don his spacesuit.

"What's the problem?"

"You look like you need some exercise," said the older man. "A walk'll do you good."

"I'm comfortable here."

"Do it anyway."

Nighthawk stared at him curiously for a moment, then shrugged, went to the airlock, and climbed into his suit. Then he and Father Christmas walked out into the frozen streets. A few robots were out clearing the snow from the streets. Here and there men would rush swiftly and silently from one building to another; other than that, the city might have been deserted.

What frequency? Nighthawk mouthed the words.

Father Christmas signaled "4748" with his fingers.

"All right," said Nighthawk, making the adjustment. "Can you hear me?"

"Yes. And nobody else can."

"Let me check that out," said Nighthawk. "I've got a pretty sophisticated radio unit. Talk, and don't say anything important."

"Lovely morning," said Father Christmas. "Reminds me of the winters back home when I was a boy."

"That's enough," said Nighthawk, scanning a panel on his radio pack. "No one's monitoring us."

"Actually," continued Father Christmas, "I grew up on a beautiful agricultural world, with waving rows of mutated wheat as far as the eye can see. I *hate* snow."

"If you brought me out there to talk about your childhood, I'm going back in," said Nighthawk.

"Actually, I brought you here to talk about Colonel James Hernandez."

"Hernandez?" repeated Nighthawk. "What's all the secrecy about? You didn't mind being overheard three days ago."

"That was then, this is now."

"Okay," said Nighthawk. "What's Hernandez got to do with anything?"

"More than you imagine," answered Father Christmas. "Why do you think he sent you here?"

"To find out who killed Governor Trelaine and to bring him to justice one way or another."

"Bullshit."

"Yeah? What makes you think so?"

"He knows who killed Trelaine," said Father Christmas as they walked slowly across the frozen surface of Klondike.

"All right," said Nighthawk. "Who killed Trelaine?"

"The Marquis, of course."

"You're guessing."

"I don't guess, kid. I'm telling you, the Marquis is the man you're here to kill."

Nighthawk stared at him. "Before we go any further, suppose you tell me how you figured all this out?"

"I did just what you'd have done if you had a little more experience," answered Father Christmas. "Two days ago I paid a substantial fee to tie my personal computer into the Master Computer on Deluros VIII."

"And?"

"And I asked it to find out everything it could about the Marquis of Queensbury. It took this long because I couldn't supply it with a holograph or a retina ID, and we were only dealing in possibilities until last night. Then I managed to swipe a beer glass that still had his fingerprints on it."

"So what did the Master Computer say?" asked Nighthawk.

"His given name is Alberto da Silva. He had a couple of other names before he became the Marquis."

"Okay, he's had other names. So what?"

"He's also had other jobs," said Father Christmas. "The last one was working as a independent subcontractor for Colonel James Hernandez."

"An independent subcontractor?"

"He killed Hernandez's enemies, and in exchange Hernandez looked the other way when he plundered Solio II."

Nighthawk frowned. "That doesn't make any sense," he said. "If Hernandez hired him to kill Trelaine, why does he want him dead now?"

"Now we come to theory instead of fact," said Father Christmas. "But bear with me. I think it makes sense."

"Go ahead," said Nighthawk.

Father Christmas looked intently into Nighthawk's eyes and began. "What if someone saw the Marquis pull the trigger? Whoever it was would be one of the leading citizens of Solio II—remember, though Trelaine was killed at the opera, he was there to make peace between opposing factions of his party—and of course this citizen immediately took steps to protect himself. He probably hired bodyguards, and instructed his computer to release the truth about the assassination to every news organization in the sector if anything happened to him."

"Okay," said Nighthawk. "I'll buy that. What else?"

"Now that our citizen feels safe, he approaches Hernandez and says, in essence, This was *your* guy who killed Trelaine. I think you're preparing to seize power on Solio II. Hernandez denies it, of course; what the hell else can he do?"

"So far so good," said Nighthawk. "Keep talking."

"Okay. The citizen says to Hernandez, *Prove* your innocence to me. Bring in the Marquis and I'll believe you were telling the truth; otherwise, you're on the hook as much as he is. And maybe he gives him a deadline: six Standard months, a year, whatever. Now, Hernandez can't just call the Marquis in and shoot him. The Marquis has got a reputation; if he brings him in too easily, he's still a suspect. So instead he hires a bounty hunter. And not just *any* bounty hunter, but the best who ever lived."

"There are a lot of good bounty hunters out here on the Frontier," said Nighthawk. "Why me?"

"Because he could count on you not to bring the Marquis in, but to *kill* him."

"But—"

"Think back to your meeting with Hernandez," said Father Christmas. "I'll bet he told you not to take any chances, to blow the Marquis away the first time you saw him."

"Something like that," admitted Nighthawk grudgingly.

"Don't you see?" said the older man. "He expressly asked for *you* because, unlike your namesake, you've had no experience. You don't understand nuances. Subtleties are lost on you. You could never have figured this scam out by yourself. The one thing you can do is kill, and that's exactly what Hernandez was counting on."

"But sooner or later I'd have figured it out," answered Nighthawk, "and then I'd be just as dangerous to Hernandez as the Marquis is."

"He probably figures the Marquis' men will kill you before you leave the planet, once you do what you were hired to do. And I'm sure he's turned his office into a death trap, just in case you manage to make it back there." Father Christmas paused for a long moment, then shrugged. "He doubtless intends for you to die here or on Solio. And if not . . ."

He let the sentence hang, unfinished, in the air.

"If not, he figures that they'll 'decommission' me back at Deluros?"

"You're the consummate killing machine, kid," said Father Christmas, "and once this job is done, you're beholden to no one. That makes you too dangerous to live."

Nighthawk stood, silent and motionless, for a long moment while he considered what the older man had said.

"Yeah, it makes sense," he replied in a cold, passionless voice.

"It's conjecture," said Father Christmas. "Maybe Deluros will strew your path with flowers and send you out on more assignments. Maybe the Marquis didn't pull the trigger. Maybe I'm wrong about everything"—he rubbed his stomach—"but down here in my gut, it *feels* right."

Nighthawk fought back his anger at the notion that he had been *used*. His face was totally expressionless, a mask that was the very last thing 300 young men had seen more than a century ago. "It *is* right," he said at last.

"So that leads to the question: What do we do next?"

"You're the deep thinker," answered Nighthawk. "What do you have in mind?"

"Same as before: We all go to Deluros VIII. I rob some churches, you kill the original Widowmaker, and the Marquis . . . well, I'm still working on that."

"I have an idea."

"Let's hear it," said the older man.

"What if there is one man in the Oligarchy's Intelligence arm who knows he was the assassin, one person Hernandez confided in. Wouldn't it make sense for the Marquis to want to dispose of anyone who could finger him?"

"He'd have to believe the man hadn't told anyone else yet," responded Father Christmas. "Even the Marquis wouldn't try to wipe out the entire Intelligence Department." He paused. "Still, why should he believe that?"

"Because a sweet-talking old bastard like you ought to be able to convince him of almost anything," said Nighthawk. He stared at the older man, trying to martial his arguments. "For example, I fought him to a draw the day I arrived; one of these days I'll be able to beat him, and he knows it. All you have to do is convince him that once I kill the Widowmaker, I'm a free agent and I don't give a damn what happens to him or Hernandez. At the same time, come up with a name from Deluros VIII—real or phony, it makes no difference—and convince him that if he kills that name, there's no longer any connection between him and Hernandez anywhere in the Oligarchy's files."

Father Christmas lowered his head in thought for a moment, then looked up.

"You know, that's not bad at all," he replied. "You're going to be damned frightening if they let you live another twenty years or so." He paused. "No wonder they still talk about the Widowmaker."

"I don't want to hear about him," said Nighthawk irritably. "He's just a frozen old man who's never going to wake up."

"He's you and you're him, whether you like it or not," said Father Christmas.

"I don't," said Nighthawk. "And if you say it again, you'll wish you hadn't."

"You got a lot of hang-ups for a four-month-old," muttered Father Christmas.

"Just remember what I said."

"I'll remember," said the older man. "But sometimes you make it very hard to be your friend."

"It's a lot harder to be my enemy."

"Let's hope so." Father Christmas turned back toward the casino. "Shall we go back, or have you got anything else to say that we don't want the Marquis to overhear?"

"No, I think that's pretty much everything." Suddenly Nighthawk stopped in his tracks. "Well, there *is* one more thing to consider."

"Yeah?"

Nighthawk nodded. "I see how we're going to get the Marquis' permission to leave, and how we're going to convince him to come with us. But . . ."

"But what?"

"After you rob your churches and I kill the Widowmaker, what do we *do* with him?"

"Well, that's pretty much up to you, isn't it?" said Father Christmas.

"Yeah," said Nighthawk thoughtfully. "Yeah, I suppose it is. And of course, if he doesn't come back, if he's killed while he's away on a job . . ."

"Don't even think about *her*," said Father Christmas. "You kill him, she'll be on her way so fast it'll make your head spin."

"I'll be in charge here. I'll have the power, *and* the ability to protect her. She'll stay."

"Not a chance."

"You'll see," said Nighthawk. "I'm young. If she sticks with me, I can get her anything she wants."

"Others can get it faster," replied Father Christmas. "Some of them already have it. She's the type who can sniff them out from two thousand light-years away."

"Have you even spoken to her?" demanded Nighthawk heatedly. "What makes you think you know anything about her?"

"Experience."

"You don't have any experience with her, because there's never *been* anyone like her."

"Blue skin doesn't make her any different."

"It's not the skin," said Nighthawk. His voice lowered. "She's perfect."

"Son, take it from a minister," said Father Christmas. "Even God isn't perfect."

"What do you know about God *or* women?" demanded Nighthawk. "All you do is rob God's churches, and you're so old and wrinkled no woman would look at you."

"Kid, if I wasn't sure you'd blow me away, I'd show you just how fast I could get that dancing girl to go to bed with me." He sighed. "Let's skip it. We're agreed on what we have to do, right?"

"Right."

"Then let's get the show on the road."

He turned and began walking back to the casino.

Chapter 17

"So where is he?" demanded Nighthawk, stalking angrily through the control cabin of his ship. Father Christmas sat in a passenger seat, while the Holy Roller perched atop the navigational computer, purring softly to itself.

"He'll be here," said Father Christmas reassuringly.

"Are you *sure* he bought your story?"

"I'm sure."

"Then why isn't he here?"

"He's the Marquis of Queensbury, and he rules eleven worlds," answered Father Christmas easily. "He's allowed to be twenty minutes late. He knows you won't leave without him."

Nighthawk came to a stop and looked at Father Christmas. "What if he doesn't show? We're already committed to leaving. We'll look damned silly changing our minds just because he didn't come along."

"I don't know why old people, who have so much less time remaining to them, develop patience, while young men like you, with a century ahead of them, go a little crazy when they have to wait for anything."

"He believes someone in Intelligence can finger him, right?" said Nighthawk, ignoring Father Christmas's statement.

"Yes, he believes it."

"If *I* thought someone could put me out of business, or bring the authorities down on me, I'd be early, not late."

"Maybe that's why *he* runs the show, instead of someone like you," suggested Father Christmas. "Do you mind if I change the subject?"

"Talk about anything you damned well please," said Nighthawk irritably, as he recommenced his pacing.

"Fine. I will. Because you're worrying about the wrong thing. The

Marquis will be here, never fear. What *you* should be thinking about is how you're going to kill the Widowmaker."

"Gun, knife, hands, what difference does it make?"

Father Christmas shook his head. "You don't follow me. If you can make it to the chamber where he's frozen, I'll grant you can kill him by any means you choose. But only the very, very wealthy can afford to be frozen. The Widowmaker was only a millionaire when he went in there, but he's lying side by side with billionaires, with people who created financial empires and have every intention of waking up and ruling them again at some time in the future. How do you plan to get past the kind of security they've paid for with those enormous annual fees?"

"I'll find a way."

"Have you considered that you might not even be able to get through Customs on Deluros VIII? All they really have to do is report the Widowmaker's passport missing. You'll give them an ID disk, it'll set off twenty alarms, they'll incarcerate you until someone who can identify Jefferson Nighthawk shows up—and you can bet your ass he'll show up with a gun."

"Why?" asked Nighthawk. "They don't know I'm coming to kill the Widowmaker."

"They don't have to know why you're coming," answered Father Christmas. "All they have to know is that they've created the deadliest killer in the galaxy and told him to go out to the Frontier. Suddenly he's disobeying their orders and coming to Deluros without giving them any prior notice. Losing control of their creation will scare 'em more than knowing you want to kill the Widowmaker."

"All right," said Nighthawk. "I'll start thinking about it." He paused. "*You're* wanted on dozens of planets. How do you get around it?"

Father Christmas smiled. "I never go back, so it's a moot point."

"But even when you go to a new planet, they must know who you are, and that you're wanted."

"I mostly stay on the Frontier, and most Frontier worlds don't have extradition treaties with the Oligarchy. Hell, most of 'em don't have any laws at all."

"Okay," said Nighthawk. "But now we're going to the capital world of the Oligarchy. So how will *you* get past Customs?"

"How many passports do you possess?" countered Father Christmas.

"One."

"Well, I've got fifteen," replied the older man with a triumphant smile, "each and every one able to pass a close inspection by a Customs computer. I use the one that fits the situation."

"Tools of the trade?" asked Nighthawk.

"Even the original Widowmaker must have had a handful of them," answered Father Christmas. "No sense announcing your presence when you're trying to sneak up on someone who doesn't know you're on his trail."

"I may need some myself," said Nighthawk thoughtfully. "Where do you get them?"

"There are forgers all over the galaxy," said Father Christmas. "After we're through with our business on Deluros, I'll introduce you to some of them."

"Some of whom?" said a familiar voice from the direction of the airlock, and they turned to see the Marquis of Queensbury, his arm around the Pearl of Maracaibo.

"What's *she* doing here?" asked Father Christmas.

"I never go anywhere without the necessities of life." He ran his fingers through her hair and down her neck to her breast, then leaned over and kissed her on the ear while she grinned at Nighthawk. "Hi, Jefferson," he said when he looked up again. "How's it going?"

Nighthawk realized that he'd been staring at the blue-skinned girl. He had no idea what his expression had become when the Marquis fondled and kissed her, but he realized there was enough tension in the air that the Roller had stopped purring. Suddenly he snapped to life.

"You're late," he said. "I wanted to leave half an hour ago."

"Your victim can wait," replied the Marquis easily. "He's past knowing what time it is."

"You should have said you'd be late," repeated Nighthawk. "It's only common courtesy."

"This is *my* world," answered the Marquis. "It obeys *my* laws." He looked into Nighthawk's eyes and smiled. "That means you were leaving half an hour too early."

Melisande laughed, her eyes never leaving Nighthawk's.

"All right," said Nighthawk. "Let's get going now, if it's all right with you."

"Just fine."

"It'll be a little cramped. I didn't know we were going to have another passenger."

"No problem," said the Marquis easily. "We only need three beds."

"I was referring to oxygen and meals."

"Then we'll put down on some world or other and get more when we need it."

"There's only room for three people on the bridge," said Nighthawk.

"That's not a problem," said the Marquis. "She and I will share the captain's cabin. You can bunk with the old man." Before Nighthawk could protest, he added, "Take her down there and show her around."

Nighthawk could smell her perfume as she passed him. There wasn't much room, and she had to turn sideways to enter the corridor that led to the sleeping cabins. She took a deep breath, and he couldn't help looking down her neckline. She grinned at him and undulated her way past him, then slowed her pace so he had trouble avoiding bumping up against her.

"You've gone too far," said Nighthawk a moment later, stopping by the door to his cabin. She turned back and managed to lean against his arm and shoulder while the door slid into the wall. "This is it," he said, taking a step into it while she followed.

"This is your cabin?"

"It *was* my cabin."

"It's more like a prison," she said, looking around. "Like the kind of place where you spend long, lonely nights." She turned to him. "Do you?"

"This is the closet," he continued, ordering a door to slide open.

"What's that?" she asked.

"What's what?"

"That," she repeated, pointing to the Holy Roller, which had followed them and now bounced up to Nighthawk's shoulder. "I've seen it near you when I was dancing. At first I thought it was some kind of toy, and then I realized it was actually alive. Is it a pet?"

"Kind of."

"It doesn't *do* much," she said. "Why do you keep it?"

"It loves me and it's loyal to me," answered Nighthawk. "That's more than I can say for any person I know."

"Let me see it," she said, approaching him and reaching out for the Roller.

The Roller tensed and stopped purring.

"That's not a very good idea," said Nighthawk, stroking the Roller as he felt it stiffening. It calmed instantly beneath his touch.

She pulled her hand back and glared at the Roller. "Who wants to touch such an ugly thing anyway?"

There was an awkward pause, and then Nighthawk spoke again. "Behind that door's the bathroom. It's got a dryshower and a chemical toilet."

"Maybe you'll come by later and scrub my back," she said, lowering herself to the bunk and stretching.

Nighthawk stalked out and returned to the control cabin.

"Welcome back," said the Marquis, who was now sitting in the captain's chair. "What kept you?"

"That's *my* chair," said Nighthawk.

"Not anymore."

"I own this ship."

"And I own *you*," said the Marquis. "Now sit down."

"I've got to lay in a course to Deluros," said Nighthawk.

"I've already done it. We'll be jumping to light speeds any second now." He turned to Father Christmas. "Well, old man, have you got your churches all picked out yet?"

"Sure do," said Father Christmas. "Just waiting to narrow 'em down to a reasonable number."

"I take it you've been studying them?"

"All my adult life," answered the older man. "There's a lot of gold in the churches of Olympus. I think I'll take some of it back with me."

"Olympus? What is that—a city?"

Father Christmas chuckled. "A continent."

"So who can know the geography of a thousand worlds?" said the Marquis with a shrug.

"Anyone who wants to get rich off 'em," replied Father Christmas, as the ship suddenly lurched and jumped to light speeds.

"Touché," laughed the Marquis. He turned to Nighthawk. "What about you, Jefferson Nighthawk?" he asked with a certain smug amusement. "Do you plan to get rich on Deluros?"

"No," answered Nighthawk. "I plan to get free on Deluros."

"Free of what?"

"Of a lot of things."

"For instance?"

"Ghosts, mostly."

"Of men you killed?"

Nighthawk shook his head. "Of the man I was . . . or the man I was supposed to be."

"Not much profit in that," remarked the Marquis with a faint air of disapproval.

"More than you can imagine," said Nighthawk firmly.

The Marquis shrugged. "Whatever makes you happy." He glanced down the corridor toward Melisande's cabin, and added, "Within reason."

Nighthawk tensed again, and the Holy Roller reacted instantly. It stopped humming and began a very low whining sound. Nighthawk picked it up, cradled it in his arms, and stroked it gently.

"You ought to get rid of that thing," said the Marquis.

"I like it."

"As far as I can tell, it serves no useful purpose—and it wastes space."

"Not as much as Melisande."

"*She* has advantages that outweigh her disadvantages," said the Marquis.

Nighthawk forced himself to relax, muscle by muscle, and tried not to think of the blue-skinned woman stretched out on his bunk. Finally the Holy Roller began purring again, and he realized that he had succeeded.

"You're going to have to learn to control that hot young blood," remarked the Marquis, who had been watching him closely. "And you're also going to have to learn who gives the orders around here."

"We're learning just as fast as we can," said Father Christmas, before Nighthawk could make a caustic reply.

"That's what I like to hear," replied the Marquis.

Melisande suddenly appeared in the corridor. "I'm hungry," she complained. "What have we got to eat?"

"Don't ask *me*," said Nighthawk coldly. "Ask the ship."

Nighthawk walked to the galley and ordered it to life. Suddenly it was awash with lights, and an illustrated menu appeared in midair, the three-dimensional images of the food rotating slowly before the ship's occupants.

"Is that really steak?" she asked.

"It's all soya product," answered Nighthawk. "But you won't be able to tell the difference."

"Sounds good to me," said the Marquis. "If it looks like steak and tastes like steak, who cares what it is?"

And if someone looks like the Widowmaker and thinks like him and kills like him, thought Nighthawk, *don't ever get him mad by taking over his ship and flaunting your woman in front of him.*

"What'll you have, my love?" asked the Marquis.

"Nothing," replied Melisande.

"You're sure?"

"I don't eat substitutes." She paused briefly. "Besides, what I want now isn't in the galley."

She sauntered down the corridor and gave the Marquis a sexy smile as she passed by the cabin door.

"You can wait for him in the control room," suggested Father Christmas as she reached the end of the corridor.

She walked slowly through the galley and came to a stop a few feet from Nighthawk.

"There are only three chairs," she noted.

"That's right," said Nighthawk.

She stared at his lap until he shifted uncomfortably on his chair, then turned around and returned to the galley, brushing against Nighthawk as she did so.

"By God, she looks good when she walks away!" said the Marquis enthusiastically. He got to his feet. "I think we'll retire to our room for a little while." He headed toward the captain's cabin.

Nighthawk watched them, his face expressionless, his body rigid. The Roller bounced back down to the floor and began whining softly. Suddenly he felt a heavy hand on his shoulder, and found that Father Christmas had walked over to him.

"Don't do anything foolish, son," said the older man.

"Am I supposed to let him fuck her on *my* bed and just sit by doing nothing?" demanded Nighthawk in strained tones.

"It's her choice."

"It's *not*! He'd kill her if she said no."

"I don't want to disillusion you," said Father Christmas, "but she probably hasn't said no since she was twelve."

"Shut up!" snapped Nighthawk, and the Roller, still whining ominously, jumped to his shoulder.

"I'm not the enemy," said Father Christmas, back-backing away and lowering his voice. "Try to remember that. I'm just trying to keep you alive."

"All right," said Nighthawk after a long moment. "We'll stick to the plan. He lives until you've robbed your church and I've killed the Widowmaker. But then . . ." He reached out and absently petted the Holy Roller, which twitched a couple of times then rubbed up against him.

"Just make sure you don't underestimate him," said Father Christmas.

"I can take him," said Nighthawk grimly.

"You sound awfully certain."

"I didn't ask to be the best killer in the galaxy," said Nighthawk. "But that's what they made me." Suddenly Melisande's moans of ecstasy could be heard through the closed door of the cabin. Nighthawk's face became even grimmer. "They had their reasons back on Deluros, and now I've got mine."

A mechanical voice spoke out. "Pursuer alert. Ten minutes three seconds stroke four off the port bow."

Nighthawk frowned and ordered his ship to change course. The voice was silent for a moment, then repeated its message with slightly different coordinates. "What is it?" asked Father Christmas.

"Someone's on our tail."

"Who?"

"He doesn't want to identify himself. But we've ID'd his registry number, and traced a signal he's sent elsewhere to learn his frequency. The computer will find out who he is before too long."

"Maybe we should tell the Marquis."

Another muffled moan came from Nighthawk's cabin.

"And then again, maybe not," amended Father Christmas.

Nighthawk sat absolutely motionless, forcing himself to stare at a computer screen. A moment later an amused expression flashed across his face. "The gang's all here," he announced.

"What do you mean? Who's in the other ship?"

"Lizard Malloy. He's probably been on our tail since we took off."

"So tell him to go away."

"Don't be silly. He's not going to go away just because I ask him to. He's there for a reason."

"*What* reason?" demanded Father Christmas.

One final sound of sexual frenzy rang through the ship, reaching a crescendo and culminating in a satisfied moan.

"I wish I knew," answered Nighthawk.

"Maybe if you'd spend less time concentrating on what's happening thirty feet away from here and start worrying about what's a parsec away, we might get something accomplished," said Father Christmas.

"I *am* concentrating on Malloy."

"Sure," said the older man, unimpressed.

"*And* the Marquis."

"Did the Marquis order him to track us?"

"How the hell should I know?"

"Why not ask him?" suggested Father Christmas. "It sounds like they'll be through in a minute or two. Just give him a chance to put his pants on."

"And if he doesn't know why Malloy's out there?"

"Then it might be interesting to know who *did* send Malloy after us."

Nighthawk tried to think about Malloy, or the Marquis, or the Widowmaker, but he kept coming back to the same thing again and again: *Goddamn it, she never sounded like that with me!*

He knew he wanted to kill someone, but at the moment he wasn't sure if it was the Marquis, or perhaps the Pearl of Maracaibo, or maybe even himself.

Chapter 18

Nighthawk was sitting in the galley, nursing a cup of coffee a few feet away from the command chair, as the ship sped through the void on autopilot. Father Christmas was asleep in his half of the crew's cabin, and the Marquis was snoring noisily across the corridor.

Finally Melisande emerged from the captain's cabin, wearing nothing but a towel she had wrapped around her.

"May I sit down?"

Nighthawk indicated the empty chair across from him.

"And could I have some coffee, please?"

"Don't ask me," he said. "Ask the galley."

She repeated her request as an order, and a moment later a cup of black coffee was deposited on the table in front of her.

"Thank you," she said.

"If you're waiting for it to say you're welcome, you're out of luck," said Nighthawk. "Only the control deck talks back to you."

"Why?"

"Because that's the way I like it."

"Don't be so defensive," she said with a smile. "I'm not criticizing you."

"I'm not defensive."

"You sound like you are."

"I'm not!"

"Okay, have it your way," she said with a shrug. The shrug caused the towel to come loose and slip to her waist. "Excuse me," she said with a catlike smile.

"Cover yourself up!" snapped Nighthawk.

"What's the problem?" she asked innocently, as she slowly adjusted the towel. "This isn't anything you haven't seen before—or have you forgotten already?"

"I haven't forgotten."

"Come over and help me do this," she said, wrapping herself again in the towel.

"Fix it yourself."

"All right—but I can't promise that it won't slip again."

Nighthawk grimaced, got to his feet, and walked over.

"Right here," she said, pointing to the spot where she wanted it joined.

She handed Nighthawk a gaudy, ornate clasp and he put the two ends together, trying to ignore the scent of her perfume.

"You're all right now," he announced, walking back to his chair.

"You're sure?" she asked, getting to her feet. "It's very short."

"So what?"

"So what if I have to raise my arms like this?" she said, starting to do so.

"Just sit down and it won't happen again."

"I can't sit for the whole voyage."

"Then get dressed."

"I don't want to wake the Marquis." She grinned. "I think I wore him out."

Nighthawk made no reply.

"This is very good coffee," she said at last.

"How do you know?" he answered. "You haven't tasted it yet."

"But it warms my hands." She reached out and laid her hand on top of his. "See? No one wants to be touched by a cold hand."

"It doesn't bother me."

"Well, maybe it wouldn't bother your hand, but there are other places I could touch you where you'd jump." She paused. "Or you would if my hands were cold. Next time they are, I'll prove it to you."

"Not necessary."

"I don't mind," she responded. "After all, we're all friends here, aren't we?"

"Maybe you should stick with the friend that brought you," suggested Nighthawk tightly.

"But he's sound asleep," she said. "If you listen, you can hear him snore."

"So what?"

"He needs his sleep . . . but I've already had mine. It's boring in there, just watching him." Suddenly she smiled. "Of course, he *is* naked."

"I'm sure you find that wildly exciting."

"Well, it all depends," she said. "I mean, it's no fun being excited all by yourself. I *could* find it exciting if *he* did. Would you like me to tell you how I would excite him?"

"No."

"Are you sure?" she said. "It might even excite you."

"Leave me alone!" he snapped, getting to his feet and walking to the command chair.

"I thought you liked me."

"I do," he said softly.

"I even thought you wanted me," she continued.

"How come you only come on to me when both cabins are in use?"

"You think we have to have a cabin?" she said. "All a cabin has is a bed." She stood up and removed her towel. "We've got everything we need right here." Mock hurt. "You're frowning. Don't you like what you see?"

"I like it."

She approached him slowly, making sure to avoid the Roller, which was perched on a panel a few feet away. "Yes, I can see that you like it," she said, staring at his groin.

He grabbed her arm, pulled her onto his lap, and kissed her hungrily.

"Careful," she said, shifting her position. "You're going to impale me."

"That's the general idea," he said.

"What if the Marquis wakes up and walks out into the corridor right this second?" she said.

"I'll have to kill him."

"But how can you if I'm in the way?"

"Stop talking so much."

"Maybe I should check and make sure he's still asleep."

"Forget it."

"No," she said, getting up. "I really should. I don't want to be caught in the crossfire."

Before he could stop her, she walked back to the galley and wrapped her towel around her, then disappeared into the captain's cabin. She emerged a few seconds later and mouthed the words *Sound asleep.*

Then, as she was approaching Nighthawk again, Father Christmas's sleepy voice rang out. "What the hell's going on out there?" A moment later he emerged from his cabin, stopped apruptly, and sized up the situation as he stared at Melisande.

"Dressed in a bit of a hurry, didn't you?" he said sardonically.

"I just came out for some coffee," she said.

"Galley, serve up two coffees," commanded the old man. Two cups filled with black coffee appeared a moment later. The Pearl of Maracaibo turned to Nighthawk and shrugged helplessly, almost falling out of her towel.

"So how long was I asleep?" asked Father Christmas.

"Maybe four or five hours," replied Nighthawk.

"Too bad I didn't sleep another hour," he said. "You might have made a little progress with the lady here."

"Not a chance," answered Melisande. "I'm totally loyal to the Marquis."

"And I'm the reincarnation of Ramses II," said Father Christmas.

She turned to Nighthawk. "Are you going to let him talk to me like that?"

"You're totally loyal to the Marquis," said Nighthawk. "Let *him* defend your honor."

"Some hero," she snorted contemptuously.

Suddenly the Marquis stuck his head out into the corridor and stared at the galley. "What's going on?"

"Nothing," she said. "We're just talking."

"You woke me up."

"We didn't mean to," she said. "Go back to sleep."

"Come on back to bed," he said. "I don't like to sleep alone."

"Whatever you say."

"*That's* what I say," answered the Marquis.

She stood up, clutching the towel to her, and turned to Nighthawk. "Perhaps we can continue our discussion later."

"Perhaps," he said noncommittally.

"Get your ass in here," said the Marquis, withdrawing to the interior of the cabin. She joined him a few seconds later.

"You're a little young to have a death wish," said Father Christmas as the door to the cabin slid shut. "I hope what I think was going on here wasn't going on."

"I don't want to talk about it."

"I'll just bet you don't," said the older man. "I wonder how many pets she tortured to death when she was a little kid."

"Shut up!"

"Have it your way," said Father Christmas. He took a sip of his coffee. "How long until we reach the Oligarchy?"

Nighthawk looked at a screen. "We entered it about five hours ago."

"And when do we hit the Deluros system?"

"At this speed, maybe another thirty hours."

"Thirty hours more," mused Father Christmas. "That's a long time for her not to precipitate a killing."

"I don't want to discuss her," said Nighthawk ominously.

"We still got our shadow?"

"Malloy? Yeah, he's back there a couple of million miles."

"Sounds like a lot until you realize it's, what, maybe ten seconds?"

"A little less."

"You want some sleep?" asked Father Christmas. "I can keep an eye on things."

Nighthawk shook his head.

"You've been awake a long time," continued Father Christmas. "I want all your reactions to be one hundred percent when we get there. Get some sleep."

"How can I sleep when I know she's in bed with him not twenty feet away?" demanded Nighthawk irritably.

"So *that's* what it is," said Father Christmas. "You think if you stay here in the control room maybe he won't fuck her any more?"

"They're not fucking—they're sleeping," said Nighthawk. "Or, at least, *he* is."

"And you don't like that any better, do you?"

"No, I don't," said Nighthawk.

"Well, then," said Father Christmas, "I have a suggestion."

"Oh?"

"You won't like it, but it makes the most sense."

"Let's hear it."

"This girl is messing up your mind, son," said Father Christmas. "She's tying you into knots. She's all you're thinking about, and that's deadly."

"You want me to kill the Marquis?"

"You can't kill the Marquis . . . yet," said the older man. "Don't forget your original assignment: You need him to finger the assassin for you."

"Then what do you want?"

"Kill *her*."

"Are you crazy?" snapped Nighthawk.

"Not even a little bit," said Father Christmas. "Every time the Marquis takes a nap or turns his back she's teasing the hell out of you. Don't bother to deny it; I've got eyes. You let her live, eventually she'll precipitate a fight between you and the Marquis before you're ready for it."

"But the whole purpose of this trip was to kill the Marquis so I could finally have her," said Nighthawk.

"She's not worth having, son," said the older man. "Let me plunder my churches while you're killing the Widowmaker, and then let's both blow this life and go retire somewhere where neither the Good Guys *or* the Bad Guys will ever find us."

"Sounds good to me."

"It's a deal, then?"

"As soon as I kill the Marquis," said Nighthawk. "We'll take Melisande with us."

The old man sighed once, deeply, but made no reply.

Chapter 19

They were thirty-eight hours out of Tundra, and life wasn't getting any easier for Nighthawk. When he wasn't busy fantasizing about Melisande, she was there in front of him, sending him secret smiles, finding reasons to accidentally brush against him, taunting him with the touch and smell of her.

Her behavior radically altered whenever the Marquis was around. She never willingly left his side at such times. No portion of her anatomy was forbidden to his hands, even in plain sight of Nighthawk and Father Christmas. But the Marquis had no interest in the workings or navigation of the ship, and he spent most of his time in his cabin. As quickly as he was out of sight she went back to teasing Nighthawk with the same single-mindedness with which she ignored him when the Marquis was around.

Nighthawk was experiencing one of his few brief moments of solitude, staring absently at one of the ship's viewscreens. He ordered it to go to high magnification, hoping to get a glimpse of Malloy's ship, but all he could see were stars and the endless blackness of space.

Finally he decided to radio Malloy yet again to find out why he was being followed—but he couldn't raise Malloy's ship. It was there, it was tracking him, but it wouldn't respond to his signal. He frowned. Neither Malloy nor his ship presented a physical threat, but he didn't like things he couldn't understand, and he didn't understand why the little grifter was following him into the Oligarchy.

"If he bothers you so much," said a voice behind him, "let's slow down, let him catch up with us, and blow him into a million pieces."

It was the Marquis, who had wandered over while Nighthawk was preoccupied with the radio.

"I didn't say he bothered me," replied Nighthawk defensively.

"You didn't have to."

"I just want to know why he's there."

"Someone sent him, obviously," responded the Marquis.

"Who—and why?"

The Marquis shrugged. "Beats the hell out of me." He paused, then smiled as a thought came to him. "If you don't want to blow him away, let him catch up with us and then threaten to lock him in a room with the Holy Roller. Five'll get you ten that he'll suddenly be overjoyed to talk to us."

"It's a pet, not a weapon," said Nighthawk, stroking the Roller as it bounced up from the floor to his shoulder.

"It's a little of each," said the Marquis. "You're not the first I've ever seen with a Holy Roller. I've known two other men that Rollers attached themselves to." He paused and looked at Nighthawk's Roller admiringly. "Get one of those things angry, it can wipe out a roomful of men in ten seconds flat. *I'd* call that a weapon."

"I'd call it a friend."

"That's because you don't think big enough," said the Marquis. "You don't understand what you could do with a thing like that."

"But you do?" said Nighthawk sardonically.

"Of course I do," answered the Marquis. "That's one of the differences between us."

"If you're that hot to get one, go to Aladdin."

"I've been to Aladdin. Never saw one."

"So go again."

"Waste of time," said the Marquis. "I've been there a dozen times." He paused. "I think I'd rather trade for yours."

"It's not for trade."

"You haven't heard my offer yet."

"You don't have anything I want," said Nighthawk.

"Oh, I think I do," said the Marquis with a grin. "Melisande!"

The blue-skinned girl emerged from the cabin and walked over to join the Marquis.

"Well?" said the Marquis.

"Her?"

"For the Roller."

"It's a deal," said Nighthawk.

"Don't I get some say in this?" demanded Melisande.

"I'm afraid not, my dear," said the Marquis.

"You can't trade me for some alien animal as if I was a piece of property!" she said.

"We are all property," answered the Marquis. "It is only the intelligent ones who know it." He paused. "I am sure Mr. Nighthawk will cherish you as I have, my love."

"And what if I don't want to be cherished by Mr. Nighthawk?" she said.

"That's hardly my concern." The Marquis paused. "I'm sure that he'll treat you with the same compassion that I have displayed up to now."

"Which is to say, none at all," she snapped.

"Please don't make this more difficult than it is," said the Marquis. "You have given me an inordinate amount of pleasure, and I regret losing you"—he smiled apologetically—"but the galaxy is full of women. There are very few Holy Rollers. For all practical purposes, there is really only one. Surely you would do the same thing in my position."

"I've never been in your position," she said bitterly.

"Well, there you have it." He reached out for the Roller, which suddenly became rigid and started humming softly.

"I don't think it likes the thought of you touching it," offered Nighthawk.

"Well, explain to it that we've got a deal."

"I don't know its language."

The Roller began whistling a little louder.

"Make it stop!" said the Marquis. "I've seen them do this before."

Nighthawk plucked the Roller from his shoulder and cradled it against his chest, stroking it gently.

"We made a trade," said the Marquis, backing away slowly. "It's up to you to deliver your end of it."

"Don't you think I *want* to?" shot back Nighthawk. "It doesn't like you, and there's nothing I can do about it. The alien back on Aladdin told me that it chooses one person and sticks with him for life."

"Too bad," said the Marquis. "You had your chance, and you blew it." He turned to the Pearl of Maracaibo. "It looks like we're reunited in eternal love, my sweet." She glared at him but didn't say anything. "Go back to the cabin," he continued. "I'll join you in a few moments."

She stood still and glared at him.

"Now," he said in a tone that brooked no disobedience.

She stalked off to the cabin without a backward glance.

"My offer stands for the duration of this trip," said the Marquis. "You teach the Roller to accept me, and she's yours." He paused and suddenly grinned. "Maybe I'll have to teach her to accept *you*."

Nighthawk made no reply.

"Well, she may be yours any day now," said the Marquis, starting to walk back toward his cabin. "I think I'd better enjoy her while I can."

He grinned again and disappeared into the cabin. The Holy Roller squeaked loudly, and Nighthawk realized that he was squeezing it painfully. He released it, and it rolled down his leg onto the floor.

"Mind if I join you?" asked Father Christmas, emerging from his cabin and walking down the corridor toward the galley and the control cabin.

"Why not?" said Nighthawk without enthusiasm. "You heard it all?"

"Yep. Hard to keep secrets on a ship. Especially one as small as this." He paused. "Sounded like a soap opera. Makes for an entertaining trip."

"So how do I make the Roller like him?"

"You don't," said the older man. "They choose one person, and when all is said and done they're a lot more loyal than any man or woman I've ever met."

"You're not much help, are you?" said Nighthawk bitterly.

"I would be, if you'd ever listen to me."

"You don't say anything I care to hear."

"Nobody ever really wants the truth," agreed Father Christmas.

"Let it be."

Father Christmas shrugged. "Whatever you say." He glanced at the viewscreen. "Malloy still tracking us?"

"Yeah. I tried to raise him, but he's not answering his calls today."

"Assuming the Marquis was telling the truth—always a dangerous assumption—I wonder who the hell Malloy *is* working for?"

"I don't know."

"Why don't you think about it for a minute?" said Father Christmas.

"I'm thinking," said Nighthawk. "Nothing's coming."

"You know, the guys who built you could have spent two less school days on killing people and two more on spotting subterfuges."

"What are you talking about?"

"Use your brain, son," said Father Christmas. "What is Malloy doing?"

"Tracking the ship."

"Why?"

"I don't know," said Nighthawk, feeling just like a frustrated schoolboy.

"What *do* you know?"

Nighthawk frowned. "What do you mean?"

"Let's assume for a moment that the Marquis is telling the truth, that he has nothing to do with Malloy or the ship. What does that tell you?"

Nighthawk looked blank.

"Look," said Father Christmas patiently, "if he's not here for the Marquis, and he's not here for you, and he's not here for me, who the hell else *is* there?"

Nighthawk's eyes widened. *"Melisande?"*

"Right."

"But why?"

"Beats me," admitted the older man. "But I'd say she's probably a little more than she seems to be."

Nighthawk said nothing, but sat motionless, petting the Holy Roller absently, lost in thought. Finally he looked up, cleared his throat, and spoke.

"Maybe his employer wants to know where the Marquis is and what he's doing."

"Would *you* send someone like Malloy up against the Marquis of Queensbury?" retorted Father Christmas. "If it was up to me, I'd hire someone who could handle himself when the going got rough—someone like you."

"Then why is he following us?"

"I've got a notion or two, but let's wait a little longer and see what happens."

"How much longer?"

Father Christmas shrugged. "We'll know before we get to Deluros." He pulled out a deck of alien cards. "Care for a quick game of *jabob*?"

Nighthawk shook his head. "They never taught me the rules."

"The rules are easy," said the older man with a smile. "The odds are impossible."

"Then why do so many humans play it?"

"Because the rules are simple," answered Father Christmas. "So they figure they ought to be able to beat it." He paused. "Most men don't suffer from an abundance of intelligence—or hadn't you noticed?"

"I've noticed," said Nighthawk.

The two of them sat silently for a few minutes, the older man shuffling and reshuffling his cards. Then the Marquis emerged from his cabin once again.

"Still here, I see," he said.

"See what I mean?" whispered Father Christmas. Then to the Marquis he said, "We're traveling at sixty-four times the speed of light in a three-man ship. Just where the hell did you think I'd be?"

The Marquis shrugged. "Sleeping. Eating. Pissing. How should I know?"

Father Christmas laughed aloud. "You'd better work on your muscles, son," he said to Nighthawk. "It's a cinch she's not hanging around with him because of his brainpower."

"Watch your mouth, old man," said the Marquis ominously. "I want part of your haul, but I don't *need* it. Never forget that."

"My sincere and most humble apologies," said Father Christmas, bowing low from his seated position and somehow losing his smile before he straightened up again.

The Marquis glared at him silently for a long moment, muttered "Old fool!," then ordered a drink from the galley.

"Well, Nighthawk," he said at last, "are you still looking forward to killing the Widowmaker?"

"That's why I'm here," answered Nighthawk.

"It must feel a little like killing your father."

"Not really."

"Ah, I forgot," said the Marquis. "You don't *have* a father, do you?"

"Well, if I do, he's been dead a couple of centuries," said Nighthawk.

"Then maybe it's really more like killing your brother," suggested the Marquis. "Perhaps you are Cain to the Widowmaker's Abel."

"If you say so."

"I don't say anything. I'm just trying to understand what it feels like, as one killer to another."

"I'll tell you after I've done it," said Nighthawk. He sighed deeply. "I rather suspect it'll feel like laying a bad memory to rest."

"I thought you'd never seen him," said the Marquis. "How can you remember him?"

"Maybe I expressed myself poorly," replied Nighthawk. "He's the ideal to which I have always been compared. His accomplishments created the hopes and expectations that I've been measured against." He paused thoughtfully. "Most young men simply have to forget the role models that have been chosen for them. Me, I get to eliminate mine permanently. I find that a very satisfying notion."

"If he's half of what they say he was, you might not be able to kill him."

"He's a diseased, disfigured old man who can't move or breathe without help," said Nighthawk. "Besides, I have no intention of waking him up. This is an exorcism, not a contest."

"An exorcism," repeated the Marquis with a smile. "I like that."

"I'll like it when I've finished it."

Melisande stepped through the cabin door then, sauntered into the galley, and paused to run her hands through the Marquis' tousled hair.

"I want a drink," she announced.

"Order it yourself."

"I don't like this galley," she complained. "It doesn't mix them right."

"What the hell do you want *me* to do about it?" asked the Marquis.

She nodded toward Nighthawk. "Make *him* mix me a drink."

"I don't mix drinks," said Nighthawk.

"Just a minute," said the Marquis, turning to face Nighthawk. "It's okay for *me* to tell her you don't make drinks. It's not okay for *you* to."

"Why not?" said Nighthawk. "Has she suddenly become my commanding officer?"

"No," replied the Marquis. "But *I* give the orders around here, so when I'm around you don't refuse any request until you find out what I want you to do about it."

"Some chain of command," said Father Christmas with a contemptuous snort.

"You stay out of this, old man," snapped the Marquis. He turned to Nighthawk again. "Fix her a drink."

"I don't do coolie labor," said Nighthawk. "Let her fix her own."

"I'm ordering you to."

"I kill very dangerous people for you," said Nighthawk. "That's my job, and I'm goddamned good at it. It's *not* my job to mix Melisande's drinks just so you can prove to her that you can give me orders. Everything that makes you look good in her eyes makes me look like shit. If you want a drink mixed, mix it yourself."

The Marquis got to his feet. His left arm moved out slowly, sweeping Melisande behind him.

"I'm ordering you one more time. Mix her drink."

"Go fuck yourself," said Nighthawk, still sitting comfortably on his chair.

"I'm not going to ask you again," said the Marquis ominously.

"You didn't *ask* a first time," said Nighthawk. "Besides, what are you going to do? Fire me and make me walk home?"

"That's not a bad idea."

"Of course it's not," said Nighthawk. "*You* didn't think of it."

"You guys don't want to fight in here," said Father Christmas suddenly. "A stray shot could go right through the bulkhead and kill us all."

"Then it's damned lucky for you that I never miss, isn't it?" said the Marquis.

Suddenly the Holy Roller, distressed by the tension in the room, became rigid and started humming.

"Turn that damned thing off or I'll kill it," warned the Marquis.

"I wouldn't even if I knew how," said Nighthawk, finally getting to his feet. "Which of us are you going to shoot first, and what do you think the other's going to be doing in the meantime?"

"I beat you before and I can beat you again!" snapped the Marquis.

He pulled out his laser pistol and fired it—and a beam of solid light almost split the Roller in half. It screeched once, burst into flames, and died. But as it did so, Nighthawk had his own gun in his hand and fired one shot. The bullet lodged between the Marquis' eyes, and he plunged, face forward, to the floor.

Father Christmas knelt down next to the Marquis and rolled him over, examining the wound.

"Goddamned lucky the bullet didn't ricochet off and go through the bulkhead," he said. "Either of you idiots could have killed us all with one bad shot."

"What did you want me to do—arm-wrestle him?" said Nighthawk.

"No," said Father Christmas with a deep sigh. "But you might have mixed the lady's drink. He had information you needed, remember?"

"Fuck it," said Nighthawk. "I needed that information so I could deliver an assassin and collect enough money to keep the Widowmaker alive until they came up with a cure for what ails him." He paused. "Well, what's about to ail him is *me*, and there's no cure for what I plan to do. That makes the Marquis' information kind of meaningless, doesn't it?"

"What about *her*?" asked the older man.

"She's mine now," said Nighthawk, turning to face Melisande. But what he found himself facing was the business end of one of the Marquis' sonic pistols.

"I'll decide who I belong to," she said coldly. "If you take one single step toward me, you'll be dead on the floor right next to him." She looked him square in the eye. "I mean it."

Nighthawk gently holstered his pistol and sat back down on his chair.

"I hate to say 'I told you so,' " said Father Christmas with an ironic smile, "but . . ."

Chapter 20

"Well," said Father Christmas, breaking a long, tense silence, "we've got some decisions to make."

"I've made mine," said Melisande.

"You don't have the slightest idea of what I'm talking about," said Father Christmas, making no attempt to keep the contempt out of his voice. "Now put that gun away. I guarantee that Nighthawk's not about to pounce on you while I'm here and there's still a dead body on the floor."

She stared at Nighthawk for a long moment, then placed the pistol down on the galley table.

"All right," continued Father Christmas. "First thing we have to do is . . ."

"First thing we have to do," interrupted Nighthawk, "is jettison what's left of the Roller."

"Forget it," said the older man. "We've more important things to consider."

"How can you stand the smell?"

Father Christmas inhaled deeply, made a face, and nodded his consent. Nighthawk picked up the little Roller's charred corpse, carried it past the galley while Melisande and Father Christmas tried not to retch, and jettisoned it into space. On the way back he activated a small servomech that cleaned up the spot where the Roller had bled, and then had it deodorized.

"Better," agreed Father Christmas when Nighthawk returned to his chair.

"All right," said Nighthawk. "Now, what decisions do you think we have to make?"

"Well, the first one's already out of our hands," said the older man. "All we have to do is acknowledge it."

"What are you talking about?"

"We're going to have to alter course," said Father Christmas. "We can't go to Deluros."

"Why?" demanded Nighthawk.

"Because Deluros has the best security in the galaxy." Father Christmas paused. "In fact, we'd better get the hell out of Oligarchic territory while we have the chance."

"Why should you give a damn about Deluros's security now?" said Nighthawk. "It didn't bother you when we were planning this job."

"We didn't have a dead body in the ship when we were planning this job," answered Father Christmas. "There's no way you can hide that from Deluros security."

"Then we'll just jettison it, the way I did with the Roller," said Nighthawk.

Father Christmas turned to Melisande. "Do you want to tell him, or should I?"

"Tell him what?" she asked, honestly confused.

"Jesus!" muttered Father Christmas. "I wonder if either of you have enough brains to write your name in the dirt with a stick!"

"Get to the point," said Nighthawk irritably.

The older man turned to face him. "You can't jettison the Marquis' body because a slimy little bastard called Lizard Malloy is still tracking us, and the second you dump it into space he's going to pick it up and either blackmail us if we to return to Yukon or Tundra, or turn us in for the reward if we stay in the Oligarchy."

"Malloy," repeated Nighthawk. "Shit! I'd forgotten all about him."

"Well, it's a goddamned good thing that *I* don't forget the scum that's following me across the galaxy."

"All right," said Nighthawk, trying to control his temper. "We can't go to Deluros until we get rid of the body, and we can't jettison the body while Malloy's tracking us. That seems to leave us two choices: We land on a planet long enough to dump the body, or we go back to the Frontier with it."

"You've only got one choice, son," said Father Christmas. "You've got to go to the Frontier and lose the body there."

"But there are hundreds of thousands of planets right here," protested Nighthawk.

"You might park the ship in an orbiting hangar, or dock it at a space station without getting searched," said the older man, "but I guarantee that you'll be thoroughly scanned if you try to put down on a planet, and there's no way to hide the body from the kind of scanning they'll do. And if you can't jettison it with Malloy around, I guarantee you can't jettison it at an orbiting hangar or a space station."

"But I've got business on Deluros!" insisted Nighthawk.

"That's the seat of human government," said Father Christmas. "They're more sensitive about security there than anywhere else in the Oligarchy. They'll scan you ten times between the moment you enter the system and the moment you park in orbit around Deluros VIII. And a couple of hundred police will be waiting for you to emerge from the ship once they've spotted the corpse." He paused. "Now, if you'd killed him with your hands, we could try to pretend that he tripped and fell against something hard, and if you'd killed him with your sonic pistol we might have been able to blame the Holy Roller, at least if you hadn't jettisoned it—but it's gonna be god-damned difficult to tell them that he shot himself right between the eyes while he was cleaning his pistol. Or *your* pistol, once they got done examining the bullet. You see what I mean?"

"I see what you mean," said Nighthawk. "But I still want to get to—"

"Forget it!" snapped the older man. "First things first. We've got to go back to the Frontier and lose the Marquis. Otherwise, you'll never get within five hundred miles of Deluros VIII's surface, and that's a fact."

Nighthawk fell silent, considering his options, rejecting each in turn. Finally he looked up and stared at the Pearl of Maracaibo.

"Just a minute," he said, his eyes narrowing.

"What is it?" asked Father Christmas.

"We had a problem a few hours ago. We discussed it, but never solved it—and then, because of the killings, we forgot all about it."

"I don't think I follow you."

"Neither does Malloy," said Nighthawk. "But *he* follows *her*. Maybe we should ask why."

"You're making foolish accusations," said Melisande angrily. "Malloy is *your* friend, not mine."

"What reason would he have for following me?" asked Nighthawk.

"How the hell should *I* know?" demanded Melisande.

"Nobody knows," said Father Christmas. "There isn't any reason." He paused. "Now, what reason does he have for following *you*?"

"I don't even know him!" she protested. "I've seen him in the casino. He spends most of his time with you."

"Just a minute," said Father Christmas. "Suppose you tell us who you worked for before you hooked up with the Marquis."

"I don't have to tell you shit!"

"That's what you think, lady," said Father Christmas.

"Leave her alone," said Nighthawk.

"Damn it, son," said Father Christmas, "I know you've got the hots for her, but we're in a helluva dangerous situation here. You've killed one of the most powerful men on the Frontier, we've got a potential enemy tracking us—and we might have another one right here in the ship. So stop thinking with your gonads and start using your brain. We are in serious trouble, and I can't get us out of it alone."

"We'll get out of this," said Nighthawk. "Just stop harassing her."

"Goddammit!"

"You heard me."

"All right," said the older man with a heavy sigh. "We can't stay in the Oligarchy. We can't jettison the body. I say that we don't return to the Inner Frontier. Too many people know we left with the Marquis; they'll figure out that you killed him. Lord knows *I* couldn't have done it."

"So what?" responded Nighthawk. "He was just a crook, a little more powerful than most. It's not like some government will post a reward for me."

"You don't understand," said Father Christmas. "There was a limit to what they could teach you in a couple of months."

"What don't I understand."

"The very people who are thrilled that he's dead, so they can divide the spoils and advance up the ladder, will be the ones who come after you. If you could kill the Marquis, you could kill any of them, and since they don't know for a fact that your current employer won't finger them next, you're a marked man." The older man paused and cleared his throat. "So I say we stay away from the Inner Frontier."

"Where do we go?"

"The Rim, the Outer Frontier, the Spiral Arm—at least that portion of the Arm that's not officially a part of the Oligarchy."

"That's awfully far away," said Nighthawk.

"Of course it is," replied Father Christmas. "That's the whole point of this."

"I don't want to go the Rim or the Outer Frontier," said Melisande. "I haven't killed anyone."

"Fine," said Father Christmas. "We'll drop you off at the next oxygen planet and you can make your way back home—or hitch a ride with Malloy."

"The hell we will!" snapped Nighthawk.

"Son, she doesn't want you," said the older man. "Now, that seems pretty devastating to you right now, but there are trillions of women in the galaxy. Believe me: You're young, you'll find another."

Nighthawk stared into Melisande's eyes. "You're the one I want."

"That's *your* problem," she said. "I have problems of my own. One of them is getting back to Tundra."

"I'm stronger than *he* was," continued Nighthawk. "I can take better care of you, protect you better."

"But I don't want you to."

"I'll go back to Tundra and take over," said Nighthawk. "I'll be as rich as he was. Richer. I'll be able to buy you anything you want."

"I want the Marquis," she said. "Buy me that."

"You didn't give a damn about the Marquis," said Nighthawk. "It was the money, the power he wielded."

"It was *him*."

"Bullshit."

"It was him, and the way he could please me," she said. "But that's something you couldn't possibly know about, could you?" she added with a cruel smile.

"I'm naive, but I'm not stupid," said Nighthawk. "You enjoyed it. I know you did."

"You can enjoy many meals in a restaurant," she replied. "But there might be only one that you would pay to have again."

"There's nothing he could do that I can't do," persisted Nighthawk. "I'll learn."

"Not with me, you won't."

"It'll work out. You'll see."

"Foolish, foolish clone," she said, making no attempt to hide her contempt. "Conceived in a test tube, nurtured in a chemical bath. An educated blob of protoplasm. A laboratory *thing* that walks and talks like a man." She paused. "I'll bet the original Widowmaker knew how to please a woman. Bring *him* around and maybe I'll stay."

His gun was out and aimed at her so quickly that she couldn't even reach for her own. She just sat there, stunned by the speed with which he had moved.

"Don't ever say that again!" he whispered so softly that she could barely make out the words.

Both Melisande and Father Christmas had seen Nighthawk under many conditions. They had seen him angry, and they had seen him bitter, and just a few minutes earlier they had seen him kill a man—but neither had ever been physically afraid of him until that instant.

Chapter 21

Nighthawk carried the Marquis' body belowdeck, deposited it in the cargo hold, and sealed it in a quick-hardening plastic since he didn't know how long it would remain aboard ship. Then he returned to the control room, set a course that would take them to the Rim while avoiding the Oligarchy, and finally stopped by the galley. He couldn't remember the constituent parts of a Dust Whore, so he settled for ordering a beer.

"It should take us ten, maybe eleven days to get to the Rim," he announced. "I've never been there, so I don't know which worlds have been opened up, which ones might be friendly to us. Hopefully my ship's computer is up to date."

"Well, *I* don't want to go to the Rim," said Melisande. "I haven't killed anyone, and no one wants to kill me. I want to go back to the Inner Frontier."

"I'm afraid that's out of the question, my dear," said Father Christmas.

"Am I your prisoner?" she demanded.

"Nobody's a prisoner," said Nighthawk. "You're a guest. Hopefully more than a guest."

"The hell I'm a guest," she said. "I'm here under protest. I want to go home."

"Where *is* home, now that the Marquis is dead?" asked Father Christmas.

"What makes you think it's anywhere but Tundra?" she demanded pugnaciously.

"Because nobody goes to Yukon and Tundra unless they have business there," answered Father Christmas. "What's *your* business? Surely you're not going back there just to dance with your clothes off?"

"My business is none of your concern!" she snapped.

"Then you *do* have business there?" he persisted.

"I've told you before to stop baiting her," interrupted Nighthawk.

The older man shrugged. "Okay. What would you rather talk about?"

Nighthawk glared at him and made no reply, and an uneasy silence descended on the ship for the next ten minutes. Then he ordered another beer.

"I'll have one too," said Father Christmas.

"How about you?" said Nighthawk to Melisande.

She shook her head.

"Something to eat, then?"

"No."

"You must want *some*thing," said Nighthawk.

"I want to go back."

"I can't take you back just yet," he said.

"Why not?"

"I'm not ready to be a target. Once word gets out that I killed the Marquis, dozens of men, maybe hundreds, will be after my scalp. None of them live on the Rim."

"The Rim has *its* share of bounty hunters, too," she pointed out.

"Yeah, but there won't be a price on my head," noted Nighthawk. "Have you ever seen a bounty hunter kill anyone for free?"

"Just one," she said. "You."

"I'm not exactly a bounty hunter," he corrected. "And I didn't kill the Marquis for free. I killed him for you."

"I didn't ask you to."

"Not in so many words."

"Not in any way whatsoever!" she snapped. "You've killed him, and now you're taking me half a galaxy away from where I want to be. And then you wonder why I don't like you."

He stared at her. "Would you like me better if I took you back?" he asked.

"No," she answered. She smiled a slow, seductive smile. "But I might hate you less."

Nighthawk was silent, as if thinking about his options.

"You can't do it, son," said Father Christmas softly. "Not if you want to live to an old age."

"I know," said Nighthawk at last. He turned to Melisande. "You're coming to the Rim with us. It won't be so bad. You'll see."

She stared at him coldly, then stood up and stalked off to her cabin.

"You want a suggestion?" said Father Christmas.

"Not particularly."

"I'm going to make it anyway. If you join her in the cabin, frisk her before you climb into bed with her."

"I'm not joining her."

"Good decision."

"I don't want to rape her," continued Nighthawk. "I love her. I want her to love me."

"You're a little new to the game to understand what love is," said the older man. "As for her, she doesn't love anyone but herself. Never has, never will."

"Shut up."

"You're the boss."

They were silent for a few minutes. Then Nighthawk got to his feet. "I need some sleep."

He went off to the crew's cabin and fell into a deep, dreamless sleep . . .

. . . that was broken by the high-pitched wailing of the ship's alarm sirens.

He shot up, banged his head against the bulkhead, sat down heavily on the bed, tried to clear his head while the sirens kept screaming, and finally lunged out into the corridor. Father Christmas was in the control room, looking for the mechanism that would deactivate the alarms.

"Off!" shouted Nighthawk. The sirens stopped immediately. "They're keyed to my voice," he explained to the older man.

"No wonder I couldn't find a way to turn them off."

"What happened?" demanded Nighthawk, glancing around. "All the systems seem to be working."

"The airlock's been opened and closed," said Father Christmas. "So has the aft hatch. I tried to stop her—but it seems that half the ship's protective devices are keyed to your voiceprint."

"Her?" repeated Nighthawk. He turned to a viewscreen. "Magnify." He couldn't see anything. "Extreme magnification."

And now, suddenly, he was able to make out two tiny figures: the spacesuited Melisande, and the plastic-coated corpse of the Marquis.

"What the hell's going on?" murmured Nighthawk. "This doesn't make any sense."

"Now it does," said Father Christmas, as Lizard Malloy's ship suddenly came into view. It stopped and hung motionless in space, waiting for Melisande to maneuver herself and the corpse into an open hatch. A moment later they both disappeared inside the ship. It turned its nose back toward

the Inner Frontier, then accelerated and vanished from the screen as it reached light speeds.

"As soon as the ship's computer can dope out its course, we'll go after it," announced Nighthawk, finally looking away from the screen.

"And do what?" asked Father Christmas. "This isn't a military ship. We don't carry any weaponry. You can't blow him apart. So what will you do? Follow him into the middle of the Marquis' territory?"

"What makes you think he's going there?"

"They've got the Marquis' body. Where do *you* think they're taking it?"

"To claim a reward."

"There isn't one," said Father Christmas. "There was never any paper on him, or someone would have killed him long before you did." He paused. "Face it, son—Malloy and your ladyfriend are partners, or at least they work for the same employer." He paused. "I told you before that Malloy had to be following us because of her. It was the only logical conclusion. If you decide to chase them, someone's going to get blown out of the sky, all right—but it won't be *him*."

"All right," said Nighthawk bitterly. "You have all the answers. Who do they work for?"

"I don't have 'em all, but I do have a logical mind," answered Father Christmas. "You start by asking who wants the Marquis dead, and everything else follows."

"There's no price on him," said Nighthawk, frowning. "You said so yourself."

"There's no price on your head either, but I think we can safely assume there are people who want *you* dead."

Nighthawk lowered his head in thought for a moment, then looked up. "I don't know."

"Well, I suppose not many four-month-olds could dope it out," said Father Christmas. "But you're going to have to grow up fast if you want to survive out here."

"Spare me the lecture and get to the point," said Nighthawk in annoyed tones.

"All right," replied Father Christmas. "Who sent you after the Marquis in the first place?"

"Colonel Hernandez, back on Solio II."

"Well?"

"Well *what*?" demanded Nighthawk. "He told me the Marquis would know who shot Trelaine."

"The Marquis knew, all right," said Father Christmas. "But then, so did Hernandez."

"What are you talking about?"

The old man lit a cigar and settled more comfortably into his chair. "Let me do a little serious hypothesizing here," he said at last.

"Go ahead."

"All right. Let's say my name is Hernandez. I've been in charge of security on Solio II for years, which means I command the best-trained forces of armed men on the planet. Now, we call the big boss our Governor, but he's just a more accomplished tyrant than the rest. You with me so far?"

"So far," said Nighthawk.

"Let's say I decide that *I* would make a better Governor than Trelaine. What would I do?"

"Kill him."

Father Christmas shook his head. "Too many potential witnesses, too much chance of being seen. But that doesn't mean I can't carry out my plan. All I have to do is contact a criminal who operates on my world—and would like to operate even more freely—and suggest that *he* do it. Maybe I pay him money, more likely I forgive all his past crimes and promise him a free hand in the future. Now, I don't care if the Marquis pulls the trigger or hires it out; all I care is that he sees to it that Trelaine gets killed. And so he does."

"But you're not Governor."

"I know," said Father Christmas with a smile. "I guessed wrong. Remember, Trelaine went to the opera to make peace between two warring factions. What if neither of them was strong enough to take over, but both of them were strong enough to stop *me* from taking control? In fact, suddenly I have to prove that I had nothing to do with the assassination." He paused and puffed on his cigar. "Well, I can't bring the Marquis in. He'll never go quietly to the gallows; if he stands trial, he's a cinch to implicate me. So I want him dead. Now, how do I get about it so no one will know?"

"You hire me."

"Right," said Father Christmas. "Not because you're the best killer in the galaxy, though that's a pretty good job qualification. I insist on a clone of the Widowmaker because I know he'll be all of two or three months old in real time when he gets out to the Frontier. I not only need someone who can kill the Marquis, but I need someone so naive, so innocent, that in all the time he's out here he never puts two and two together to figure out *why* I've finessed him into a situation where he almost *has* to kill the Marquis rather than bring him in."

"It's an interesting hypothesis," said Nighthawk uncomfortably. "But what does it have to do with Malloy or Melisande?"

"Melisande is Hernandez's spy," answered the older man. "She wasn't there to have you fall in love with her. She was there to sleep with the Marquis and let Hernandez know if he ever had an inclination to talk—or to blackmail Hernandez, which was much more likely."

"And Malloy?"

"I doubt that he was working for Hernandez at all. From what you told me, if you hadn't shown up exactly when you did, the Marquis would have killed him or he'd have frozen to death trying to get away. No, my guess is that once you became friendly with him, Melisande reported it and that was when Hernandez hired him." Father Christmas took another puff of his cigar and looked at Nighthawk. "Well, what do you think?"

Nighthawk considered the scenario for a long moment. Finally he looked at Father Christmas. "I think you're probably right," he admitted.

"Probably?"

Nighthawk angrily slammed a fist against the arm of his chair. "Okay, you're right. Period. Are you happy now?"

"Thank you," said Father Christmas. "I presume this means you're going to set a course to the Rim?"

"I haven't decided."

"But I told you what a double-crossing bitch your Pearl of Maracaibo is!"

"I know."

"Well, then?"

"You don't love someone because she's perfect."

"You're kidding!" exclaimed Father Christmas. "We're not talking about a woman who falls a few notches short of perfection. We're talking about someone who is, and always has been, in the employ of the enemy and wants you dead. What the hell is the matter with you?"

"You haven't been to bed with her," said Nighthawk. "You can't know what you're asking me to give up."

"A quick death!" answered Father Christmas. He stood up as if to pace off his frustration, then realized there was no room to do so and sat down tensely. "If you'd ever fucked anyone else, you'd know there's nothing unique about her. And remember: It was all an act, all in the line of duty. She'll never go to bed with you again, now that you know who and what she is."

"She doesn't know I'm aware that she works for Colonel Hernandez."

"She jumped ship with the Marquis' corpse," said the older man sardonically. "She's got to figure that even you can draw the logical conclusion about whose side she's on."

"I want her."

"I want to be King of Deluros VIII," retorted Father Christmas. "We're both doomed to be disappointed."

"Speak for yourself," said Nighthawk.

Chapter 22

Father Christmas sipped his beer and tried to control his temper. "Goddammit, son—will you please, just for once, use your brain?"

"What are you talking about?" demanded Nighthawk.

"I know it's difficult, but try to think things through. You want to follow the girl, right?"

"Right."

"And you know she's with Malloy, and they're almost certainly in the employ of this Colonel Hernandez."

"Have you got a point?"

"Just this," said Father Christmas. "Where do you suppose they're going right now?"

"Probably Solio II."

"And if you follow them, that's where you'll wind up, right?" continued the older man.

"So what?"

"So how much does Hernandez owe your creators?"

"I'm not sure," said Nighthawk. "Somewhere around five million credits."

"But you haven't told your people on Deluros that you've accomplished your task and killed the Marquis," Father Christmas pointed out. "So if you land on Solio, what is Hernandez's most reasonable course of action?"

Nighthawk was silent for a moment, considering the possibilities. Finally he grimaced. "He kills me, or has me killed, and saves the money."

"Exactly!" said Father Christmas. "You've already killed the man he wanted dead. Now all he has to do is kill you, dump your body on any Frontier world except Solio II, and then report to your people on Deluros that you told him you were following a very promising lead. The next thing he knew you'd been ambushed and killed." The older man finished his beer. "Just remember that Hernandez controls security for the whole planet," he continued. "He's probably got ten times as many guns working for him as the Marquis had, and they're better disciplined. If you go there, you won't have a chance."

"All right," said Nighthawk angrily. "You've made your point."

"So we go to the Rim, right?"

"Wrong," said Nighthawk.

"But I've explained that it's suicide to go to Solio," said Father Christmas.

"You've warned me what I'll be up against."

"Then what's the problem?"

"I want her."

"There's nothing wrong with *wanting* her," said the older man. "Just don't go after her."

"I love her. I'm not leaving her."

"You're a fool!"

"Nobody says you have to come along," said Nighthawk. "I can set you down on the first inhabited world we come to."

"How do I know it'll have a church?" replied Father Christmas. "You need a keeper, son. That's me."

"Then you're coming with me?"

"When we're ready."

"I'm ready now," said Nighthawk.

"The hell you are," said Father Christmas. "The second Hernandez speaks to the Pearl of Maracaibo—and he doesn't have to wait for her to land on Solio to do that—he's going to know you killed the Marquis and that you're probably coming after the girl. First thing he'll do is put a price on your head."

"But I killed the man he wanted dead."

"Yeah—but now that the Marquis is dead, and there's no proof linking him to Trelaine's assassination, the easiest way to save however many millions of credits he owes to your people on Deluros VIII is to kill you before you can explain *why* you think the Marquis was the hit man or was at least connected to the crime. He'll have posters transmitted to every Frontier world, and if his people don't kill you, the bounty hunters will. Hell, once he tells your people on Deluros that their illegal clone is off the reservation and killing people on his own, they'll probably double the reward."

"So what do you suggest?"

"A little subtlety, a little misdirection," answered the older man. "Remember I told you about phony passports and IDs? That's what we need now. He's looking for you to sneak onto his world, to land where no one's around to challenge you and then come after him under cover of night. I think you'll do better walking boldly in the front door. You don't identify yourself until you're behind ninety-nine percent of his defenses."

"How long will that take?" asked Nighthawk, seriously considering the suggestion.

"It all depends," said Father Christmas. "How far are we from Purplecloud, Terrazane, or Antares III?"

"I have no idea," replied Nighthawk.

"Neither do I. That's what we have a navigational computer for."

A moment later the ship informed them that the closest of the three worlds, Purplecloud, could be reached in seventeen hours.

"Lay in a course for Purplecloud," said the older man, ordering another beer.

"That's where one of your forgers lives?"

"One of my equipment managers," Father Christmas corrected him with a smile.

"Equipment?"

"You'll see," Father Christmas assured him.

Chapter 23

Purplecloud wasn't all that impressive a world, despite the fact that it lay firmly within the boundaries of the Oligarchy. It had been opened as an agricultural world early in Man's galactic expansion, supplying food to fifteen nearby mining worlds. But the soil wasn't very rich in nutrients, and other worlds with far better farmland were soon opened up.

So Purplecloud was deserted and forgotten for close to two millennia. Then gold was discovered in one of its mountain ranges. There wasn't all that much of it, and the veins were soon played out, but not before half a dozen Tradertowns were built. Two of them still existed, one serving the employees of the huge corporations that had taken over the abandoned farmland and were now growing hardy hybrid crops, the other acting as a refueling stop on the way to the Inner Frontier.

Nighthawk set his ship down near Tomahawk, the second of Purplecloud's Tradertowns. He and Father Christmas emerged, passed a row of advertising and Wanted holographs, and caught an airbus into town.

"I know this place," said Father Christmas, as they came to a small restaurant. "Great food."

"Good," said Nighthawk, following him inside. "I was getting sick of the ship's menu."

The older man found a table that suited him and sat down. "It was a fine menu. Problem was that everything was made with soya products. You can get real meat here—a kind of mutated buffalo they farm a few hundred miles to the west. You ought to see those suckers: blood red, and maybe six thousand pounds apiece. They make great eating."

"What are they called?" asked Nighthawk.

"Redbison," answered Father Christmas. "Get yourself a tenderloin. Fabulous piece of meat."

They ordered, and as they were waiting for their meals to arrive, Nighthawk turned to Father Christmas.

"Where's your contact?"

"Just up the street."

"You're sure he's still here?"

"I'm sure, and he's a she."

"How did you ever find her on a little backwater world like this?" asked Nighthawk.

"I ran into some associates with better-forged papers than my own and asked them where they got the work done."

"I wouldn't have thought they'd reveal a source like that."

"I had a partner at the time. Young feller, a lot like you." Father Christmas grinned. "The survivor was more than happy to share his information with me."

"Yeah, I can see where he might have been," said Nighthawk, as the food arrived at the table. He cut off a small piece of meat, chewed it thoughtfully, and nodded his approval.

"Anyway," continued Father Christmas, "I came here, introduced myself by returning the dead men's papers to her, and suggested that since I had cost her some clients, it seemed only fair that I take their place. We did a little negotiating, and that's all there was to it."

"If she's so good, why do you also have forgers on Terrazane and Antares III?"

"Great steak—as good as I remember it," said Father Christmas, cutting into his meal. Finally he got around to answering Nighthawk's question: "You never know when you'll blow a particular identity, or need a new one in a hurry—and you can't go racing halfway across the galaxy when you need new papers. There probably aren't more than a dozen topnotchers in the whole damned galaxy."

"You'd think there'd be more," commented Nighthawk.

"There were."

"What happened to them?"

"People like you happened to them," said Father Christmas. "This is, shall we say, a highly competitive business. A man of your talents could make a handsome living hiring out as an assassin to one forger after another. In fact, a lot of men of your particular talents have done just that."

"Well," said the older man when they were through with the meal, "was it as good as I said?"

"Better," answered Nighthawk, wiping his mouth on his sleeve. "I'm going to have to stop here whenever I come to this part of the Oligarchy."

"Tell you what," said Father Christmas. "Before we leave, we'll buy a couple of dozen frozen Redbison steaks and put 'em in the galley."

"Sounds good to me," agreed Nighthawk.

"Let me pay for this," said the older man, pressing his thumb against a sensor. "You don't have any accounts in the Oligarchy, and it'll take forever for a Frontier account to clear."

The computer took less than twenty seconds to verify his thumbprint and match it with his bank account on a nearby world.

"What now?" asked Nighthawk, as they stood up and walked to the door.

"Now I visit my supplier and haggle out a price for everything we need," said Father Christmas. "It's probably best if you don't come along. If she doesn't know you, she might not let either of us in."

"No problem," said Nighthawk. He looked around as they left the restaurant. "I'll be at that bar across the street."

"Fine," said Father Christmas. "I'll meet you in about twenty minutes."

Nighthawk nodded and walked slowly to the tavern. It was dimly lit inside, and housed an equal number of Men and aliens. He entered, looked around for an empty table, spotted one, and walked over to it.

He sat down, lit a small, thin cigar, and surveyed his surroundings. Though well within the Oligarchy, the place was primitive even by Frontier standards. The furniture was made of a native hardwood and didn't float, or adjust to fit his form, or indeed do anything but sit there. The lighting, though poor, was direct: the lights didn't move, raise, lower, or adjust their intensity to accommodate his pupils; all they did was cast a dim illumination throughout the place. The bar was also made of a poorly finished hardwood; it neither sparkled, glittered, nor shone. It also didn't house a complex computer. A small three-legged alien, a native of Moletoi II, walked from table to table, taking orders and dispensing drinks, while a human bartender, a bored expression plastered permanently on his face, mixed the drinks and manned the cash drawer.

The little Mole approached Nighthawk and spoke into its translating device.

"How may I help you, sir?"

"Bring me a Dust Whore."

"I would love to oblige you, sir," responded the Mole, "but this is a tavern, not a brothel. I regret that I cannot bring you any kind of prostitute."

"That's the name of a drink."

"Truly?"

"Truly."

"I have never heard of it."

"I'll bet we could fill a book with things you've never heard of," said Nighthawk. "Just tell the bartender what I want. He'll know."

"Have you a second choice, in case he too has never heard of a Dust Whore?"

"Just do what I told you to do."

The Mole bowed and waddled off to the bar, where the bartender nodded and began mixing up Nighthawk's Dust Whore. When he was through he handed it to the Mole, who dutifully carried it back to Nighthawk.

"He has heard of it, sir."

"Why am I not surprised?" said Nighthawk sardonically.

"I have no idea why you are not surprised," answered the Mole, "but if I were to hazard a guess, it would be that this drink is popular among Men."

Nighthawk stared at the Mole without responding, and finally it began to feel uncomfortable and waddled over to another table to serve some Lodinites.

Nighthawk sipped his drink, and had just decided that the bartender might have heard of a Dust Whore somewhere but had never actually made one before, when Father Christmas entered, spotted Nighthawk, and walked over to join him.

"She's still in business?" asked Nighthawk.

"I told you she was," said Father Christmas, sitting down wearily.

"Well?"

"She can supply everything we need."

"How soon?"

"Tomorrow, if we want it."

"We do."

"There's just one little problem," said Father Christmas. "Oh, nothing we can't take care of before the night's over, or certainly by tomorrow," he added hastily.

"What is it?"

"She's got a computer expert handling her financial transactions," said the older man, "and this young man says that the police have put a Watch-and-Track on all my Oligarchy bank accounts."

"What does that mean?"

"It means any time I transfer funds, an alarm will go off in some computer somewhere, and they'll follow the money to find out who I paid."

"Well, hell, they already know you're here on Purplecloud," said Nighthawk. "You charged dinner, remember?"

"I know."

"So what's the problem?"

"Well, if all they find is that I charged dinner and some uranium rods for the ship's pile, there's nothing to lead them to my friend, who definitely doesn't care to have the government looking into her business."

"All right," said Nighthawk. "You said we could get around the problem. How do we do it?"

"The answer should be obvious," said Father Christmas with a smile. "We go out and rob a couple of churches."

"I don't rob churches."

"You can make an exception this time," said Father Christmas. "We need some untraceable money. The gold from Darbar II is too easy to spot."

"We wouldn't need a thing if you hadn't let Melisande go," said Nighthawk.

"No use dwelling on the past, son."

"The past?" exploded Nighthawk. "That was yesterday, for Christ's sake!" He glared at the older man. "You couldn't have slept through all that clamor. If you couldn't stop her yourself, why didn't you wake me?"

"Good riddance to bad rubbish," said Father Christmas. "That girl was going to get you killed."

"That girl is the reason we're here, trying to get new identities."

"Well, we're not getting anything until we rob a church," said the older man sullenly.

"And what happens if I agree to rob it?" demanded Nighthawk. "Will your forger accept payment in candlesticks?"

"Certainly not. We'll have to go to a fence first."

"The woman I love is racing for Solio, and you want me to go out robbing churches and visiting fences?" said Nighthawk angrily.

"You know a faster way?" said Father Christmas pugnaciously.

"You bet your ass I do!" snapped Nighthawk.

He pulled his gun out of its holster, aimed it at a man who was huddled with three friends at the bar, and shot him in the back of the head. Before the body had hit the ground every patron had ducked for cover.

"Have you gone crazy?" yelled Father Christmas.

"There's a reward for that man, dead or alive," answered Nighthawk. "I saw his face on a poster at the spaceport."

He stood up and faced the dead man's three companions.

"There's paper on all of you," he announced. "But I'm not interested in you. Your friend will bring me all the money I need. If you want to live, drop your weapons and walk out of here."

"Who the hell *are* you?" demanded one of the men.

"I'm the man who's offering you your lives."

"Yeah? Well, here's what I think of your offer!"

The man reached for his pistol. Nighthawk put a bullet between his eyes, then crouched and whirled to face the other two. Both had gone for their weapons. Nighthawk took out the man who actually had his hand on his gun, then waited for the other to take one wild shot and blew him away.

"Stupid," muttered Nighthawk. "They should have listened to me!"

"You think *they're* stupid?" said Father Christmas disgustedly. "How about the man who killed them for nothing?"

"What do you mean, nothing?" demanded Nighthawk. "The four of them are worth close to fifty thousand credits."

"And the second you collect it, your people on Deluros will know where you are."

"Who gives a damn?" shot back Nighthawk. "We're not waiting around to meet them. The second I collect it, we visit your forger and then we're out of here."

Father Christmas looked at the four bodies on the floor. "You sure as hell didn't give that first one much of a chance," he said.

"He was a killer with a price on his head."

"He was a man."

"He was an obstacle," said Nighthawk. "He stood between me and Melisande. I plan to handle any other obstacle the very same way."

And as he looked into the young man's eyes, Father Christmas realized that he meant every word of it.

Chapter 24

They picked up the reward money the next morning—fifteen thousand credits for the first one Nighthawk killed, ten apiece for the other three. Father Christmas immediately converted the credits into Maria Theresa dollars and Far London pounds. He then explained to Nighthawk that once they got back to the Frontier, where people had very little faith in the Oligarchy's longevity and even less in its currency, the other currencies would be worth much more. Nighthawk, who had seen all kinds of currency on Tundra and the other Frontier worlds, had no objection.

Then, their financial transactions completed, they went down the main street until they came to the forger's place of business: an apartment above a weapons shop. There was no airlift, not even an elevator, simply a set of stairs leading up to the second floor. The door was plain, made of wood, with no name or number in evidence. Still, as they approached it, it scanned them briefly, then opened long enough to let them through to the foyer.

A small, wiry woman, her auburn hair turning gray and in need of brushing, stood in the living room of the apartment, staring at them.

"Did you bring the money?"

"Yeah, we've got it," said Father Christmas.

"You know better than to bring credits," she said, anticipating him. "We'll use the exchange rates on Sirius V as of nine o'clock this morning, Standard time." She paused and stared at him, as if expecting an objection.

"Fine by me."

She walked over to Nighthawk and studied his face. "So this is your young friend."

"Any problem?" asked Father Christmas.

"Not if you have the money."

"Here it is," he said, pulling a wad out of his pocket.

"Just lay it on the table," she said, walking over to a desk, unlocking one of the drawers, and reaching in. She took out a large envelope, which she brought over to the two men.

"Now this," she said, withdrawing a small cube and handing it to Father Christmas, "is your passport. You are Jacob Kleinschmidt, a platinum miner from Alpha Bednares IV."

Father Christmas studied the cube for a moment. "Shouldn't this be round and flat?"

"They've changed them in the Altair sector, and that's where you're coming from." She reached into the envelope and pulled out more items, none of them more than an inch square, most made of titanium. "Your birth certificate. Your employment record. Your most recent tax form. Your health certificate. Three blank visas, good for most of the worlds within the Oligarchy."

She turned to Nighthawk. "Have you ever been to the Deneb system?"

"No, ma'am. I come from—"

"I don't want to know where you come from," she interrupted. "And if you're using your real name, I don't want to know that either." She paused. "You know," she added, studying his face, "you don't have to be from Deneb after all. You're young enough to be on a field trip from Aristotle."

"Aristotle, ma'am?" he repeated.

"A university world. I understand that you wish to approach the chief of security of one of the Frontier worlds."

"Yeah. He's—"

"I don't want to know who or where he is. Just his job." She paused thoughtfully. "You can't study security—they don't give degrees in it—let's see, yes, I think we'll make you a student of ciphers. That at least is associated with security, and should validate any request you have to speak to your prey."

"Will you need a holograph of me, ma'am?" asked Nighthawk.

"I took it when you were waiting for the door to open," she replied. "Your passport is being processed right now."

"Fine."

"It'll just take a moment."

She left the room.

"Has she got a name?" asked Nighthawk. "I feel awkward calling her ma'am all the time."

"I'm sure she does," replied Father Christmas. "But she's never felt compelled to reveal it to me."

"It doesn't make sense," said Nighthawk. "If you're caught, and they want to know where you got your papers, you can give them her address as easily as her name."

"There are no addresses on this street, in case you haven't noticed. And this building is identical to the next three or four. With no name for the police to ask after, by the time they get to this apartment, she's seen them coming for at least half an hour and has managed to hide anything incriminating."

"For a whole hour, actually," said the woman, returning to the room. She walked over to Nighthawk and handed him his envelope. "Everything is here. You are Vincent Landis, a student from Aristotle, majoring in ciphers with a minor in communications. You are twenty-one years old, and you come from Silverblue, out on the Rim. Your parents are farmers."

"Got it," said Nighthawk. He turned to Father Christmas. "Are we done here?"

The older man laughed. "Not by a long shot." He turned to the woman. "Have you got what we discussed last night?"

"The pistol?" she said. "Yes. But as I told you, it will be expensive."

"Makes no difference," said Father Christmas. "He'll never get past Customs or any of the security checkpoints with what he's carrying now."

"What are you talking about?" demanded Nighthawk. "I'm happy with the weapons I have."

"I'm sure you are," answered Father Christmas. "But they've got to go."

Nighthawk was visibly upset. "But they're the ones I was trained with!" he protested.

"Son, you try to get anywhere near the colonel with them," said the older man, scrupulously avoiding mentioning Hernandez by name, "and you'll set off every alarm on the planet."

"What kind of gun have *you* got for me?" asked Nighthawk unhappily.

"May we see it, please?" asked Father Christmas.

The woman walked to the desk, unlocked another drawer, and handed him a small carrying case.

Father Christmas opened the box.

"Lovely," he said, looking at the small pistol. "Just lovely!"

"It looks like one of *my* guns," said Nighthawk. "What's so special about it?"

"It's made of molecularly altered ceramics," explained the woman. "Trust me: it can pass through any security device yet created."

"Looking like *that*?" said Nighthawk sarcastically.

"Of course not." She quickly, expertly broke the pistol down into four pieces. "This part, with the trigger, will pass for your belt buckle," she explained, demonstrating for him. "These two pieces will act as orthodic inserts in your boots. And I've tampered with the molecular structure of this final piece: just touch a match to it and it expands and loses its physical integrity. You can use it as a hatband or belt or anything else you can think of. Then, when you're ready to assemble the pistol, just touch it to a cold metal surface and it will instantly revert to this shape."

"I don't see any bullets," said Nighthawk.

She smiled. "That's the beauty of it. Even if they suspect what it is, even if they confiscate it, they'll never find the ammunition, and eventually they'll have to return it to you and let you go."

"So where is it?"

"In your pocket."

"My pocket?" he repeated.

"It shoots coins," she said. "I have this one configured to shoot gold Maria Theresa dollars."

"Well, I'll be damned!" said Nighthawk.

"Nice idea," said Father Christmas. "Could get expensive in wartime, though."

She ignored the older man's attempt at humor. "I think you'd better practice with it before you use it," she said. "It's not balanced like a normal handgun. At more than thirty yards, you'll have to adjust for a tendency to shoot low—about an inch per yard."

"I won't be that far away."

"All right. Our business is done." She escorted them to the door. "Your face is familiar," she said to Nighthawk as he stood in the doorway, "yet I'm sure we've never met before."

"You don't want me to tell you why," he said.

"No, I don't."

"I'll let you know when I've succeeded."

"I'd rather you didn't," she said. "It would only remind me of all my clients who didn't succeed."

"How do you know there are that many?" asked Nighthawk.

"An identity is an ephemeral thing," she replied. "The successful ones come back for more."

The door opened.

"Go," said the woman. "And good luck to you."

"What about me?" asked Father Christmas with a smile.

"You don't need any luck, old man," she said. "You'll never be half the man your young friend is, but you're a survivor. I *know* I'll see you again."

Then they were walking down the stairs and heading for the ship. Father Christmas was basking in the glow of being called a survivor, but Nighthawk was too busy planning his approach to Solio to wonder why he had not been considered one as well.

Chapter 25

They were two hours out of Purplecloud and headed for the Inner Frontier when his lawyer on Deluros VIII finally tracked him down.

"This is Marcus Dinnisen of Hubbs, Wilkinson, Raith and Jiminez, trying to contact Jefferson Nighthawk."

Nighthawk ignored the signal.

"Please come in."

"You're gonna have to talk to him sooner or later," said Father Christmas.

"Damn it, I know you're on that ship, Jefferson!" said Dinnisen angrily. "Please respond. I'm not going to break contact until you do."

"All right," said Nighthawk after another lengthy pause. "How did you find me and what do you want?"

"Finding you was easy," said Dinnisen. "You put in a claim for forty-five thousand credits."

"You learned about it awfully fast."

"We're a very powerful law firm," replied Dinnisen. "We have connections all over the Oligarchy."

"All right, so you know I did some bounty hunting," said Nighthawk. "So what?"

"So what?" repeated Dinnisen, surprised. "So what the hell are you doing on Purplecloud?"

"Killing bad guys, just like you and Kinoshita told me to do."

"Damn it, Jefferson—you were sent to Solio II to accomplish a specific mission. If it's not done, I want you to go back there immediately. If it *is* done, then we want you to come back to Deluros VIII."

"What you want doesn't matter to me," replied Nighthawk easily.

"What the hell are you talking about?" yelled Dinnisen.

"You heard me. I have business to take care of. Leave me alone."

"The only business you have is working for the team that created you!"

"You're welcome to think so," said Nighthawk.

"Look," said Dinnisen placatingly. "Let's stop before we say things we'll both regret. Why don't you come to Deluros and we'll talk it over?"

"Not a chance," said Nighthawk.

"I think it would be best, Jefferson," continued Dinnisen in persuasive tones.

"Yeah? Well, *I* think it would be suicidal."

"What are you talking about?"

"The second you get your hands on me, you'll toss me back into a vat of protoplasm."

"Don't be melodramatic, Jefferson," said Dinnisen, trying to control his temper. "We don't have vats of protoplasm, as you well know. We just want to talk."

"Anything you've got to say, you can say right now."

"We're not the enemy, Jefferson," continued Dinnisen. "We *created* you. You're like family to us."

"That's funny," said Nighthawk. "You don't feel like family to *me*."

"You're being difficult, Jefferson," said Dinnisen. "You've changed since I last saw you. What's happened, son?"

"I'm not your son, and the galaxy is what happened to me. I've been out here, and I'm not going back."

"No one wants you to stay on Deluros VIII," said Dinnisen. "I'll be perfectly frank with you: You represent an enormous investment in time, money, and technology. Since you're alive, it means you've been able to interact with the scum that live out there on the Frontier and survive. We'll have many lucrative assignments for you."

"Most of the scum I've interacted with would look down their noses at a lawyer," said Nighthawk. "Any lawyer. But especially you."

"Why are you being like this? We just want to examine you and make sure you're holding up all right. One day and out. Is that so much to ask?"

"I have work to do."

"Our work?"

"*My* work."

"You don't *have* any work!" exploded Dinnisen. "You're less than six months old, for God's sake!"

"Wrong," said Nighthawk coldly. "I'm the Widowmaker, and I was an old man when your great-grandfather was less than six months old."

He terminated the communication.

"Well?" he asked, turning to Father Christmas.

"Does it bother you when I call you son?" asked the older man.

"No. But it bothers me when *he* does." He paused and suddenly grinned. "Hell, it bothers me when he calls me Jefferson."

"Well, I hope you enjoyed your conversation with him, because it's going to cost you."

"Money?"

"Everything *but* money," responded Father Christmas. "Five'll get you ten he's already contacting Hernandez to warn him that you're off the reservation."

"Why?"

"Because he and his people have created the perfect killing machine, and suddenly you've got your own agenda. They don't know what it is, but they're going to warn the guy who commissioned you." Father Christmas smiled suddenly. "And you can bet your ass *he'll* know what your agenda is."

"I hope so," said Nighthawk. "He's responsible for it all: Trelaine, me, the Marquis, Melisande, Malloy, everything. I want to look into his eyes when I kill him."

"He's awfully well protected," noted Father Christmas. "It may be a very short look."

"That'll be enough," said Nighthawk.

Chapter 26

They sold their ship as soon as they reached the Inner Frontier, then took their new ship and their new identities straight to Solio II.

"You know," said Nighthawk, when they were still half an hour out from Solio, "I know why *I'm* going back, but I sure as hell can't figure out why *you're* going."

Father Christmas shrugged. "Why not? Solio's got churches, just like every other world."

"It's also got a top-notch security force. We may fool them for a while with all the stuff we picked up on Purplecloud, but eventually they'll dope it out. If not before I kill Hernandez, then after. Either way, anyone who was seen with me is going to be pretty high up on their Wanted list."

"You want me to leave?" asked Father Christmas.

"I didn't say that," replied Nighthawk. "I asked why you *hadn't* left."

The older man leaned back on his seat, stared at the ceiling for a moment, then exhaled heavily. "I think it's curiosity more than anything."

"To see if you were right about Hernandez hiring the Marquis?" asked Nighthawk, puzzled.

Father Christmas shook his head. "No, I'm pretty sure about that. And if it's not that, then it's something similar. These guys feed on lies and subterfuge the way we fed on Redbison two nights ago."

"Then what are you curious about?"

"You."

"Me?"

"Yeah," said Father Christmas. "I want to see if you're as good as I think you are."

"I assume that's a compliment?"

"All depends. I don't think you can steal the girl and get off the planet, but I'm curious to see how close you come."

"You left out killing Hernandez."

"That, too."

"Getting to him will be the toughest part of the job," said Nighthawk thoughtfully. "Once I've killed him, the rest should fall into place."

"Have you given any thought as to how you're going to get to him?" asked Father Christmas.

Nighthawk lit a small, thin cigar. "Not really. Create some story that'll get me in to see him, I suppose."

"You can't be the only man who's ever wanted to kill him," suggested Father Christmas. "There probably aren't too many stories he hasn't heard— or that his subordinates haven't encountered."

"Well, if push comes to shove, I'll just shoot my way in and shoot my way out," said Nighthawk with a shrug.

"Just like that?" asked the older man, snapping his fingers.

"Why not? I took the Marquis, didn't I?"

"And if you run into someone better?"

"Anyone who's better than the Marquis isn't working for peanuts on some security force," answered Nighthawk. "He's set up shop somewhere on the Frontier, and he probably controls a dozen or more worlds."

"Well, at least consider this: There's no silencer for the gun you're carrying. The first shot will draw everyone within five hundred yards."

"There's only going to be one shot," responded Nighthawk. "That's all I ever take."

"One, five, a dozen—it'll make noise."

"Hernandez carries a laser pistol. By the time my gun's made a bang, I'll have his weapon, and it's silent except for a little buzzing. If no one hears a second shot, they'll think the first one was something else."

"You hope."

"Actually, I don't much give a damn. If they worked for Hernandez or so much as touched my Melisande, I *want* to kill 'em."

"Well, I, for one, would feel a damned sight safer if you had some means of approaching him other than to tell one ridiculous story and then shoot your way in if the story doesn't work," said Father Christmas.

"Just say the word and I'll put down on a neighboring world and let you get off."

"I don't want to get off, son," said the older man. "I just want you to take it a little slower and more carefully so that you live through this episode."

Nighthawk looked at Solio II, a green and blue world spinning in the viewscreen. "She's there right now," he said. "The slower I go, the longer it'll be before we're together again."

"Son," said Father Christmas, "I hate to keep bringing this up, but she doesn't *want* to be together with you."

Nighthawk's expression hardened. "She will," he said adamantly.

Chapter 27

They touched down at Solio II's single spaceport, about ten miles outside the planet's major city, which was also called Solio. Unlike many Frontier worlds, Solio II was large enough and busy enough to have a Customs department, and their documentation was given its initial test as they were ushered into separate booths.

"Please insert your passport, sir," ordered the Customs computer.

Nighthawk did so.

"Thank you. Please sit down."

Nighthawk sat down opposite the holographic screen.

"Name?" asked the computer.

"Vince Landis."

"Your passport says Vincent Landis."

"Vince is a shortened version of Vincent."

"Checking . . . verified. Home planet?"

"Silverblue."

"Your passport says you live on Aristotle."

"I do live there now, but I am a student and that is a temporary residence. My permanent residence is with my parents on Silverblue."

"Considering . . . accepted. Age?"

"Twenty-one."

"Purpose of visit?"

"Research."

"What is your area of study?"

"As you see," answered Nighthawk, "I am majoring in ciphers. My doctoral thesis will concern the use of ciphers by security forces on the

Inner Frontier. I intend to visit a number of worlds on the Frontier, questioning the security forces about the use of ciphers in their daily work."

"Where will you stay while on Solio II?"

"I have no idea," said Nighthawk. "Can you recommend a good hotel?"

"I will append a list of all hotels and room rates to your visa," said the computer. "Have you any weapons to declare?"

"I'm just a student," said Nighthawk with a smile. "What would I do with a weapon?"

"You did not answer the question."

"No, I don't have any weapons."

"Have you any existing medical conditions?"

"None."

The machine returned his passport, along with a thirty-day visa and a list of hotels.

"You have cleared Customs, Vincent Landis," it announced. "Welcome to Solio II."

"Thank you."

Nighthawk got up and walked out of the booth, and found Father Christmas waiting for him.

"How'd it go?" asked the older man.

"No trouble. And you?"

"Nothing to it."

"Then let's get out of here," said Nighthawk, heading toward an exit. They followed the departing crowd to an airbus and rode into the city. When they reached a street that seemed to have lots of hotels, they got off.

"What now?" asked Father Christmas.

Nighthawk studied the area carefully. "I'm trying to remember where the Security Division is." Finally he shrugged. "It doesn't make any difference. We'll find it later. Let's go get a couple of rooms."

They registered at one of the hotels, and met a few hours later for dinner.

"Did you locate it?" asked Father Christmas.

"The Security Division?" said Nighthawk. "Yeah, it's about half a mile away."

"And teeming with armed men?"

"It is now," said Nighthawk. "We'll walk by and see how it looks after dark."

They ate dinner in the hotel's restaurant, and Father Christmas spent most of the meal complaining that the meat seemed insipid next to a cut of Redbison. They waited until dark, then walked outside and headed over toward the large building that housed Hernandez's office.

"I'm nervous," said Father Christmas.

"Why?" asked Nighthawk.

"I don't know. Maybe because it's been so easy to get this far. I keep thinking someone's watching us and is getting ready to pounce."

"Won't do 'em much good," said Nighthawk with a grim smile. "I must be walking around with thirty Maria Theresa dollars in my pockets."

"You mean you've already assembled the gun?" asked Father Christmas.

"I thought I'd attract less attention assembling it in my room than in front of the Security Division," said Nighthawk wryly.

Father Christmas kept looking nervously off to his right and left. Finally Nighthawk stopped and turned to him.

"Look, if you'd be happier robbing a church, I'll point a couple out to you and—"

"I don't want to rob a church."

"Well, you sure as hell need *something* to do with your hands," said Nighthawk. "You're even making *me* nervous."

"Sorry," said Father Christmas, thrusting his hands into his pockets.

"All right," said Nighthawk, giving his companion a reassuring pat on the shoulder. "Let's keep going."

They walked another two blocks, and finally found themselves staring at a large building.

"This is it?" asked the older man.

"This is it."

"Well, how do you approach it—from the front, the rear, or the side?"

"The front," answered Nighthawk. "Isn't that why I'm a student from Aristotle? Tomorrow I'll just walk up and make an appointment."

They were about to leave when a window on the third floor opened, and a sleek figure stepped out onto a balcony. It was Melisande, dressed all in gold.

"It's *her*!" whispered Nighthawk.

"I *knew* those IDs were too good to be true," muttered Father Christmas.

"What are you talking about?"

"They know we're here, son, or at least they expect us any moment," said the older man. "Look at her, dressed in gold and glitter and leaning out over the edge of the balcony. They're using her as bait."

"For me?"

"Who else?"

"And they think I'm going to burst into the building and shoot my way up to the third floor because she's standing there?" continued Nighthawk.

"Yeah," said Father Christmas. "Pretty damned foolish, aren't they?"

"Sure are."

"So what do we do now?" asked the older man. "Go back to the hotel?"

"You can go if you want."

"What about you?"

"Me?" repeated Nighthawk. "I'm going to burst into the building and shoot my way up to the third floor."

"I thought I just explained: That's exactly what they're expecting," said Father Christmas.

"They're expecting a man," replied Nighthawk, checking his ceramic pistol and thrusting it back into a pocket. "What they're getting is the Widowmaker."

He turned and began climbing the ornate stairs to the main entrance.

Chapter 28

Nighthawk entered the building, passing through the security scanner without setting off any alarms. Father Christmas, after a moment's hesitation, followed him at a safe distance.

A young man sat behind a desk in the main foyer. He looked up at Nighthawk with a bored expression on his sullen face.

"May I help you?"

"My name's Landis. Vince Landis. I'm a graduate student from Aristotle. I'd like to arrange an interview with Colonel James Hernandez."

"Are you seeking employment?"

"I told you—I want an interview."

"Concerning what subject?"

"I don't see that it's any of your business," said Nighthawk.

"Rudeness will not get you your appointment," said the young man punctiliously. "I must know the purpose of your request."

"I'm a student of ciphers and communications," said Nighthawk. "I want to speak to him about his use of them."

"I will transmit your request to him, Mr. Landis," said the man. "Have you an address where you can be reached?"

"I'll wait right here."

"It may take days or even weeks for an appointment," said the man. "And that's *if* he'll agree to see you at all."

"I haven't got days or weeks," replied Nighthawk. "I'm leaving Solio II in a couple of hours. It'll have to be right now."

"That's out of the question."

"Contact him and let *him* decide."

"Are you giving me orders?" demanded the young man, rising to his feet.

"I'm trying to save your life," said Nighthawk. "Now call him."

"I'll do no such thing!"

Nighthawk pulled out his pistol and fired at point-blank range. The man collapsed behind his desk, and Nighthawk, without another look at him, sought out the nearest airlift.

"Don't go that way," said a voice behind him, and he turned to find himself facing Father Christmas.

"Someone's got to be monitoring the lobby here," continued the older man. "They know you've killed that young feller. You get into an airlift now, you've obliged them by confining yourself, and they won't let you out until there are more guns facing you than even you can handle. If I were you, I'd find a stairway instead. Even if they come after you, you'll have a little more room to maneuver."

"Makes sense," said Nighthawk, heading for the ornate curving staircase that led to the upper levels of the building. "Keep clear once the shooting starts."

"I ain't no hero, son," Father Christmas assured him. "Once the guns come out, you're on your own."

"That suits me fine."

"Somehow I thought it would," said Father Christmas wryly.

Gun in hand, Nighthawk began climbing the stairs, alert for any sign of movement above or below him. He made it to the second floor without any opposition. Then, as he was about to climb to the third floor, a door opened behind him and two thin beams of light burned into the railing. He whirled and got off three quick shots, and two men, each holding a laser pistol, fell to the floor.

"Nice job," said Father Christmas's voice from well below him.

"Thanks," said Nighthawk.

"Be careful," urged Father Christmas. "They won't be that dumb again."

Nighthawk surveyed the staircase. Given the way it curved, the top of his head would be a target for anyone on the third floor before he could see to fire back.

"Right," he said.

He stepped back and considered his options, then turned and walked quickly to the office in which the two men had been hiding. There was a large window, and he opened it and leaned out. The sides of the building were as smooth as glass; climbing up on the outside would be impossible.

He stepped back into the hall and picked up the dead men's weapons. Now that his presence was known, the more firepower he had, the better.

He approached the stairs, then paused. There had to be another way to the third floor besides the stairs and the airlift. Perhaps a service lift. He was about to look for it when a door opened at the far end of the hall. A man stepped out, saw him, and started shouting. Nighthawk quickly silenced him with a burst of solid light from a laser pistol.

There was certainly a service elevator, but he didn't have time to hunt for it. Besides, if he started walking down the hallway, he'd have cut off his options since the airlift and the stairway would both be behind him and it wouldn't take much to isolate him.

So it was back to the stairs. He began climbing them in a semi-crouch, ceramic pistol in one hand, laser in the other, not so fast that he was an easy target, not so slow that Hernandez had time to send more men to meet him. When he was almost halfway up, just reaching the turn where his head would become visible, he measured the angles by eye and fired his laser once more, holding the pistol steady as the deadly beam burned through the floor above him. There were exclamations of surprise and a scream of pain, and he knew he'd gotten at least one of the men who were waiting for him. The problem was that he didn't know how many were left, or where they were positioned.

He heard a footstep below him and spun around, half expecting to see Father Christmas. But it was a uniformed guard, taking aim. He dropped down and got off a shot as he tumbled down a couple of stairs. When he regained his balance long enough to look, the guard was dead.

He fired upward, blindly, just to make whoever was on the third level keep their distance, but he knew he couldn't remain trapped on the stairs between floors for much longer. He'd just about made up his mind to go back to the second floor and look for some other means of reaching Hernandez's office when he heard Melisande's voice ring out from above.

"Jefferson!"

He paused just an instant. Then, pocketing his ceramic pistol, he took a laser in each hand, swept every part of the third floor he could see with deadly light, and raced up the stairs, which were already starting to smoke. Two men moved to stop him; both were dead by the time he reached the top step. Two more bodies lay where he had shot them through the floor.

He looked around for Melisande but couldn't see her. The corridor ran about sixty feet in each direction from the stairway, and he began walking down the hallway to his left, guns at the ready.

Suddenly a man burst out of a room behind him and hurled himself at Nighthawk's back. Nighthawk went sprawling, and both laser pistols flew from his hands. He tried to get up, only to have a large forearm come down heavily on the back of his neck. He rolled onto his side, and was able to see his attacker: a huge man some six and a half feet tall, topping three hundred pounds without any fat on him at all.

Nighthawk twisted and turned, trying to free himself, but the man wouldn't budge. Finally he snaked his hand down to his side, then moved it slowly, painfully, inch by inch, until he found what he was looking for—his attacker's testicles. He grabbed and squeezed, and the man let out a howl of pain and tried to roll away. Nighthawk held on, squeezing and twisting; the man shrieked and squirmed, and finally, with one enormous effort pulled free.

The man, red of face, breathing heavily, got to his feet and pulled a wicked-looking knife from his belt. Nighthawk looked for his pistols, but they were too far away. The man hunched over, holding the knife like someone who was experienced with the weapon, and edged forward.

Nighthawk, his back to the railing, realized the man would reach him momentarily. He got to one knee, checked for escape routes, found none. Then, suddenly, he grabbed one of the railing's smoldering supports, pulled it loose, and swung it toward the man's head, all in one motion. It split his opponent's head open with a sickening thud. The man fell forward, and Nighthawk bent down, letting the huge body somersault over him and past the railing. By the time it hit the floor two levels below, Nighthawk had picked up his laser pistols and was once again stalking down the corridor.

He heard a sudden sound behind him and saw Melisande, well past the landing, almost at the end of the opposite corridor, struggling to free herself from two uniformed men. They overpowered her and pulled her back into the room from which she had come.

He raced down the corridor, past the landing, toward the room she was in. A shot rang out, and he felt a bullet bury itself in his shoulder from behind. The force of the bullet spun him around, and he got a quick glimpse of a man ducking back into a room, almost at the spot he had reached before seeing Melisande. He fired his laser, but it was too late; the corridor was empty. As he turned back, ready to race to Melisande's room, a sonic pistol hummed, and suddenly he staggered as a field of solid sound overwhelmed him. He fell to one knee, his ears and nose bleeding, and fired back. The man with the sonic pistol fell into the hallway, dead—but even as he did so, another bullet dug deep into the back of Nighthawk's left thigh. He turned and fired at where he knew the shot had come from, and this time he burned off the sniper's hand. There was a scream, then silence.

And now, suddenly, every room seemed to hold a sniper. Dozens of doors up and down the corridors slid open and shut, just long enough for the occupant to take a shot at Nighthawk. A laser put a smoking hole in his left foot, and another burned off part of his ear. He fired back, and two more men were dead. A bullet smashed his right knee. He fell to the floor, but he melted the man who'd shot him. Another bullet hit him in the back, then two more, and as he tried to regain his feet he found that he couldn't get up—either because of the knee or the bullet in his lower spine, he didn't know which. He dragged himself to a doorway, trained a laser on it, and tried to burn a hole through to the interior where he would momentarily be out of the line of fire. But the door, made of a tightly bonded titanium alloy, only glowed red and didn't melt. A bullet burst through his hand, and he felt the bones splinter as the laser dropped to the floor.

He inadvertently grabbed his broken hand with his left hand, dropping his other laser in the process. A molecular imploder disabled both lasers, and suddenly he was lying on the floor of the corridor, bleeding from more than a dozen wounds, unable to move.

A door at the end of the corridor opened, and James Hernandez stepped out. He walked over to Nighthawk and stared down at him.

"You should have stayed away," he said.

"Couldn't," rasped Nighthawk, choking on his own blood.

"Why? You killed the Marquis, you saved your . . . ah . . . progenitor—or at least bought him a few more years. You must have known that I'd kill you if you came back here."

Nighthawk couldn't force any words out. He settled for nodding his head weakly.

"Then why?" asked Hernandez, genuinely puzzled. "There's no price on *my* head. Why did you come back?"

He tried to mouth the word "Melisande" and found that he couldn't. "For *her*," he grated.

"Ah." Hernandez smiled. "I didn't think anyone was that young or that foolish." He turned and spoke to someone who was out of Nighthawk's line of vision. "Come say good-bye to the bold young hero who was going to rescue you from my nefarious clutches."

And then, suddenly, she was standing next to Nighthawk.

"You're a fool," she said.

He convulsed with pain. "I know."

"And now you're going to die."

"Everyone dies," he replied, coughing blood.

"You could have just stayed in the Oligarchy," said Melisande angrily.

"Probably," he grated, as a wave of pain and dizziness overcame him.

"Then why didn't you?"

His lips moved, but no words come out.

"Well, this is all very touching," said Hernandez, "but I'm afraid the time has come to deliver the coup de grace. Have you any last statement to make?"

Again the lips moved silently.

"Kneel down and tell me what he's saying," ordered Hernandez.

"Why me?" demanded Melisande.

"You slept with him. Who better to hear his final words?"

She glared at Hernandez for a moment, then knelt down next to Nighthawk and leaned over until her ear was next to Nighthawk's lips.

Suddenly there was the sound of a gunshot, and the blue-skinned girl jerked spasmodically just once, then rolled over with a coin-sized hole in her chest.

"I saved you the trouble," whispered Nighthawk as Hernandez kicked the ceramic pistol out of his hand and aimed his gun at the young man's head.

Epilogue

They buried Nighthawk the next morning, in an unmarked grave beside the Pearl of Maracaibo.

Father Christmas walked across the large cemetery, looking neither right nor left, ignoring the dozens of armed, uniformed men who watched his every move. When he reached the grave he stopped, crossed his hands sedately in front of him, and lowered his head.

"I rather thought I'd see you at the ceremony," said Hernandez, joining him.

"I hate services."

"But you like churches."

"This was a little one," said Father Christmas. "Hardly anything worth stealing, except for the cross behind the altar."

"How did you know about that?" asked Hernandez. "No one saw you check it out."

The older man smiled. "If people could spot me when I'm casing a job, how long do you think I'd stay in business?"

"You have a point," conceded Hernandez. "But a moot one. I'm putting you out of business this morning."

"Be quiet and show some respect for the dead," said Father Christmas.

"When you're through praying for *him*, you might say a brief one for yourself," continued Hernandez. "You're going to be joining him, wherever he's at."

"Don't be foolish," said Father Christmas easily. "You don't really think I'd show up here without protection, do you?"

Hernandez looked around the cemetery. "I don't see any protection."

Father Christmas chuckled. "And you won't—unless I turn up dead."

"What do you think you've got?"

"This is hardly the place to discuss crass worldly matters," said Father Christmas.

"What *is* the proper place?"

"You got any drinkin' stuff in your office?"

"Yes," replied Hernandez.

"That'll do."

The two of them turned and walked across the cemetery together, then entered the impressive Security headquarters, and took an airlift to the third floor.

"It's a lot easier to get here today," noted Father Christmas. "How many of your people did he take out before you killed him?"

"Enough," said Hernandez grimly.

They stepped out of the airlift and onto the third level.

"You cleaned up the mess pretty quickly," said Father Christmas.

"It looks better than it is," replied Hernandez. "There was some structural damage to the staircase. Everyone above the second floor is required to take the airlift.

"Well, when all is said and done, lots of things look better than they are," said Father Christmas. "I hate to think of how many industries would go broke if that weren't so."

"Spare me your quaint homilies."

They reached the door to Hernandez's office, where the colonel waited for the standard retina and palmprint scan, after which the door slid into the wall.

"What's your preference?" asked Hernandez.

"Anything that's wet."

Hernandez poured them two drinks, handed one to Father Christmas who seated himself on a leather chair, then went behind his desk and sat down himself.

"All right, old man," he said, "what do you think you have on me?"

"You hired the Marquis of Queensbury to kill Governor Trelaine," replied Father Christmas. "And then you got them to create young Nighthawk to kill the Marquis so you could cover it up."

"Why would I do that?" asked the colonel, lighting up a thin Antarean cigar.

"Oh, lots of reasons," answered the older man, sipping his drink. "The way I see it, you wanted to be Governor. You hired the Marquis to kill Trelaine . . . but then he began blackmailing you. He probably got a little too greedy, and eventually it was a matter of kill him or be exposed."

"You couldn't be more mistaken."

Father Christmas shrugged. "The reason doesn't make much difference. What matters is that you hired the Marquis to pull the trigger, and he confessed to it before Nighthawk killed him."

"Rubbish. Why would he tell you?"

"Maybe he was trying to buy his life."

"Nonsense," said the colonel. He noticed that his cigar had gone out and relit it. "The Marquis was as brashly fearless as young Nighthawk."

"Maybe he was bragging," said Father Christmas. "Who cares what the reason was? I've got recordings of it stashed on three different worlds in the Oligarchy. If I don't report in to each of them every month, those recordings go—"

"To the Oligarchy?" interrupted Hernandez. "Somehow, I'm not trembling in my boots."

"To the press on Solio II, and to half a dozen select politicians just down the street."

Hernandez stared at him. "I think you're bluffing."

"Ah, but would you stake your life on it?" said Father Christmas. "All I want is to go out to the Rim and plunder God's churches at my leisure. If you let me go, you'll never hear from me again. If you kill me, you'll be joining me within, not to be too pessimistic about it, a year."

Hernandez downed his drink in a single swallow, then carefully placed the empty glass on a corner of his polished desk. "Do you want to know the truth of it?"

"I'd like to," said the older man, glancing out the window at the cemetery. "But I can live without it. It's up to you."

"Trelaine was a tyrant, but he was a *weak* tyrant. He allowed the Marquis to rob the Solio system because he didn't have the guts to stand up to him." He paused. "The Marquis had once worked for me on, shall we say, a freelance basis. We'd had a cordial relationship. I finally managed to convince him that if he killed Trelaine, I would put in a puppet who would allow him even greater freedom in plundering Solio II."

"Yourself?"

"If I could have rounded up the support, yes. If not, then a man who was amenable to my suggestions. The Marquis' muscle would help keep us in power, and we'd show our gratitude by looking the other way. At least, that was the plan I laid out to him." He paused. "Of course, the moment we took power we'd have driven the Marquis and his henchmen out of the system"

"The Marquis might have considered that a bit of a double cross," observed Father Christmas.

"By then it wouldn't have mattered," answered the colonel. "I'd have had the power to make it stick, and he could have been just as rich and happy preying on other worlds."

"So he killed Trelaine. . . ."

Hernandez nodded. "But he was smarter than I had anticipated. He had his own puppet, and he took me by surprise. The new Governor kowtowed to him even more than Trelaine did. *That's* why I contacted Deluros about the Widowmaker. I'm a *patriot*, damn it!"

"Patriot, murderer, we'll leave it to posterity to judge," said Father Christmas. There was a meaningful pause. "Or we can leave it to your peers. It's your choice."

Hernandez stared at him for a long moment. "All right," he said at last. "You've got a deal."

"Good," said the older man. "It's a pity you had to waste a promising young man."

"Nighthawk? There was no place for him in our plans," said Hernandez. "And this way we justify our decision not to pay millions more to his people back on Deluros. The official line is that he died before accomplishing his mission."

"It just means they're going to make another one, you know," said Father Christmas. "Who knows? Maybe next time they'll do it right."

"What was wrong with this one?" asked Hernandez curiously. "He was good enough to kill the Marquis, and wipe out half of my staff."

"Oh, he had all the physical skills," said Father Christmas. "They made sure of that. Trained him to kill from the instant he was born, if 'born' is the right word." He finished his drink. "But when all is said and done, they couldn't give him the heart of the Widowmaker. He was too soft."

"Soft?" repeated Hernandez, surprised. "Look at the people he killed!"

"Makes no difference," said the older man. "He had a fatal flaw, one that's maybe even worse than a bad aim or a shaky hand: the poor son of a bitch *cared*. The one thing you can never do in his business is get emotionally involved." He paused. "The Widowmaker *chose* to become a killer. Jefferson Nighthawk's tragedy is that he was never allowed to choose *not* to become one."

"I think perhaps he was toughening up there toward the end," offered Hernandez.

"Oh?"

The colonel nodded. "His last words. He knew that I'd have killed her if he hadn't. She'd outlived her usefulness, and she knew too much."

"Well," said Father Christmas, "I think I'll have one more drink, and then I'll take my leave of you."

Hernandez got up and poured them each a refill.

The older man held up his glass. "To lost innocence."

"Whose?" asked Hernandez.

"Everybody's," answered Father Christmas.

The Widowmaker
Reborn

To Carol,
as always

———————

And to Richard Potter
and Andrew Rona,
two of Hollywood's Good Guys

Prologue

In a small, dimly lit room a mile beneath the glittering surface of Deluros VIII, the capital of mankind's sprawling Oligarchy, Jefferson Nighthawk opened his eyes.

"Good evening, Mr. Nighthawk," said a slender man wearing a white tunic. "How do you feel?"

Nighthawk gradually became aware that he was lying on a long, narrow table, staring at the ceiling. He tentatively lifted an arm, made a fist, and then began slowly opening and closing his fingers.

"Pretty good," he said, surprised.

He brought his hand up to his face and stared at it as if it were some alien object he had never seen before.

"It looks normal," he said at last.

"It is."

"Then I'm cured?"

"Well, yes and no," replied the man in the white tunic. "It's a complex situation."

Nighthawk eased his legs over the edge of the table and slowly, carefully, sat up.

"Yeah, I feel all right," he said. "I guess the clone did his job."

"You're getting ahead of yourself, Mr. Nighthawk," said another voice, and Nighthawk turned to see a stocky, bearded, middle-aged man dressed in gray staring at him.

"Who are you?" demanded Nighthawk.

"Marcus Dinnisen, a senior partner in the firm of Hubbs, Wilkinson, Raith and Jiminez." He smiled. "I'm your attorney."

"That's right," said Nighthawk, nodding his head slowly. "You told me the last time you woke me up that Raith was dead."

"He died more than three-quarters of a century ago," said Dinnisen. "His great-grandson worked for the firm until a few years ago."

"Okay," said Nighthawk. "You're my lawyer." He turned to the man in the white tunic. "I assume you're my doctor?"

"In a manner of speaking" was the reply. "My name is Egan. Gilbert Egan."

"I think I've met you before."

"Just over two years ago," said Egan.

"So what year is it now—5103?"

"5103 G.E.," Egan confirmed.

"Then this means you've come up with a cure for eplasia sometime during the past two years," said Nighthawk.

"No, Mr. Nighthawk, I'm afraid we haven't."

Nighthawk frowned, confused. He carefully touched his face with his fingertips. "But I'm cured," he insisted. "There's not a mark on me!"

"You're not cured," said Egan gently. "In fact, you're in the very earliest stage of the disease. It won't manifest itself for another year."

"What are you talking about?" demanded Nighthawk. "Look at me. The disease is gone!"

"Maybe *you'd* better look at you," said Egan, handing him a mirror.

Nighthawk carefully scrutinized his handsome, unblemished face, looking more and more puzzled.

"What the hell is going on?" he said. "I look thirty-five!"

"Our best estimate is thirty-eight," answered Egan.

"But that's crazy! I was sixty-one years old when I checked in here more than a century ago."

"Calm down, Mr. Nighthawk."

"*You* calm down!" said Nighthawk, and something about his manner made both men draw back. "*I* want to know what's happening, and I want to know now!"

"Certainly, Mr. Nighthawk," said Egan, stepping forward again. "You've been injected with tranquilizers to ease the shock. I hate to think of what might happen if . . ."

A hand shot out, grabbed Egan by the collar, and pulled him close.

"I'm not feeling very tranquil, Mr. Egan," said Nighthawk coldly. "Now talk."

"*Doctor* Egan," said Egan, pulling loose from Nighthawk's grasp and brushing the rumples from his tunic. He stared at Nighthawk uneasily. "You know, I've spent the past two days wondering just how to tell you—and I still don't know where to begin."

Nighthawk looked annoyed. "Try the beginning."

"All right," said Egan. "It's a matter of record that Jefferson Nighthawk, also known as the Widowmaker, a well-known lawman and bounty hunter on the Inner Frontier, contracted eplasia and voluntarily submitted himself to freezing in the year 4994 of the Galactic Era. His instructions were that he was not to be awakened until science had developed a cure for his disease."

"I'm right here," said Nighthawk. "You can stop referring to me in the third person."

"Please let me continue in my own way," said Egan. "We had every intention of honoring Jefferson Nighthawk's wishes, but a financial crisis arose two years ago. Due to an inflationary spiral in the economy of Deluros VIII, the interest on Nighthawk's principle was no longer sufficient to cover the very high cost of this facility. We were faced with the possibility of awakening a diseased, aging man and turning him out, when an offer made to Mr. Dinnisen's office provided us with an unique alternative: a world on the Inner Frontier required a man of the Widowmaker's talents, and they were willing to pay seven million credits for those talents. We could not use the real Nighthawk, of course; he was almost dead when he first came here, and he couldn't survive, unfrozen, for another month with the disease. But we could and did create a clone that cost about half of the amount offered, which allowed us to add more than three million credits to Nighthawk's principle."

"I know," said Nighthawk. "You woke me to sign a release allowing you to clone me."

"That's correct," continued Egan. "We cloned you and sent the clone out to the Frontier."

"I know," said Nighthawk. "What happened?"

"He did what he was paid to do," said Dinnisen, "but he was seriously flawed."

"He had the disease?"

Egan shook his head. "No. He was a perfect replica of the twenty-three-year-old Jefferson Nighthawk, with all of Nighthawk's physical abilities. But because of the urgency of the situation, we sent him out only two months after he was created. He was a remarkable killing machine, but that was the only thing he knew how to do, and emotionally he was only two months old. He proved totally unable to cope with his abilities. In the end, he was killed trying to help a woman possessed of what I shall term questionable character and loyalties."

"Get to the point," said Nighthawk.

"The point is that the government has not managed to control inflation. Furthermore, for reasons with which I strongly disagree, Colonel James Hernandez, the man who commissioned the clone, refused to make his final payment. Most of the money we received was spent creating the clone; the profits we anticipated did not materialize." He paused. "Science is very close to developing a cure for eplasia, but it's still two or three years in the future, and once again the interest on the Nighthawk account is insufficient to pay for this facility."

"If you're trying to tell me I'm a clone, you've picked a lousy audience for a very bad joke," said Nighthawk. "I can remember everything I've done, every man I've killed, every woman I've had."

"I know," said Egan. "Because the initial clone did accomplish its mission before its untimely death, Mr. Dinnisen's office has had more offers. He has winnowed them down and come up with the most lucrative. But based on our first experience, we felt that we couldn't send another physically perfect but emotionally immature specimen out to do the job. So we hired some of the top men and women in the field of genetics and have finally managed to create a clone—yourself—that possesses all, or almost all, of the memories of the host."

"I don't believe it," said Nighthawk.

"I didn't really expect you to," said Egan. He studied Nighthawk carefully. "Do you feel strong enough to stand?"

Nighthawk eased himself down to the floor. A sudden weakness swept over him, and he clutched for the table.

"What's the matter with me?"

"Nothing," said Egan. "You're just using muscles you've never used before. You may also experience some dizziness." He waited until Nighthawk was able to stand without using the table for support. "Can you walk now?"

"I think so."

"Then come this way, please," said Egan as Nighthawk and Dinnisen fell into step behind him. As they left the room they came to a slidewalk, which they rode down a long, dimly lit corridor.

After passing a number of doors, the slidewalk brought them to a security checkpoint, then stopped until Egan's ID badge and retina had been scanned. It began moving again, only to stop once more at a second checkpoint fifty yards farther on.

After another two hundred yards the corridor branched off, and Egan chose the slidewalk that veered to the right. The doors came more frequently now, as did the checkpoints, but finally they came to a halt in front of a door that appeared no different from any of the others.

"This is it," announced Egan, allowing the scanner above the door to verify his retina and palm print.

The door slid open, revealing a circular chamber with a number of large drawers built into the wall.

"Drawer 10547," ordered Egan, and a drawer slowly emerged from the wall, stretching to its full eight-foot length. A human body was discernible beneath the transluscent covering.

"The true Jefferson Nighthawk," said Egan, touching a control that turned the covering totally transparent.

Nighthawk peered into the drawer, and saw an emaciated man whose flesh was hideously disfigured by the ravages of a virulent skin disease. Patches of shining white cheekbone protruded through the flesh of the face, knuckles pierced the skin of the hands, and even where the skin remained intact it looked like there was some hideous malignancy crawling across it and discoloring it.

"That's the way I remember it, all right," he said, turning away.

"I realize what a shock this must be," said Egan sympathetically.

Nighthawk tapped his head. "But these are *my* memories. I *know* they are. They're *real!*"

"They're real, but they're not yours," interjected Dinnisen. "I know it's difficult to accept, but today is your birthday, in the truest sense of the word." He paused a moment while Nighthawk wrestled with the concept, then continued: "Physically you're thirty-eight years old, and free of the disease that brought you here."

"*Almost* free," corrected Egan. "It's there, but dormant."

"I didn't contract it until I was in my late fifties," said Nighthawk. "Why do I have it now, twenty years earlier?"

Egan shrugged. "You have a genetic weakness that invites the disease. Because we were able to get blood and tissue taken before the original Nighthawk developed eplasia, the first clone possessed nothing more than a tendency to the disease. We used that same sample with you, but you are almost twice that clone's physical age, and it has begun developing within you. Very likely it is due to the laboratory process that aged you so rapidly." He paused. "I should add that now that you are alive, you will henceforth age at a normal rate."

"The last clone never developed the disease?"

"No, but he died very young," answered Egan. "He would surely have contracted it if he'd lived long enough. Given your particular genetic makeup and immune system, it seems inevitable."

"All right," said Nighthawk. "Next question: why am I in my late thirties? I—*he*—is sixty-one."

"We were able to make you any age we wanted," replied Egan. "We decided to create you at the peak of your powers."

"I was quicker and stronger at twenty-three."

"Too many hormones," said Dinnisen. "They proved your undoing last time. We want the Widowmaker, not the Testosterone Kid."

"Okay," said Nighthawk. "Let's cut to the bottom line. What happens to *me* after I make enough money to keep *him* alive?"

"You assume a new identity—it's essential to maintain the original Nighthawk's legal claim to investments and personal property—and live a long and prosperous life. No one will mistake you for him, since he hasn't been seen in more than a century."

"What about my eplasia?"

"If science can cure his, it can cure yours," said Egan.

"And you should certainly possess enough skills to earn whatever it takes to effect a cure," added Dinnisen.

"How much will it cost?"

"For the next few years, maybe half a million credits. Within a decade, perhaps a hundred thousand. In a quarter of a century, we'll be immunizing fetuses for about ten credits apiece."

Nighthawk was silent for a long moment. Finally he turned to Dinnisen, who felt uncomfortable under the gaze of his almost colorless eyes.

"You know what I think?" said Nighthawk.

"What?"

"I think you're full of shit."

"I beg your pardon?"

"I may be a century out of date, but it's a big galaxy out there. There are still thousands of killers and bounty hunters on the Inner Frontier, and even more on the Rim and in the Spiral Arm."

"I don't follow you, Mr. Nighthawk."

"If whoever is paying for my services went to the time and expense to clone the Widowmaker when he had thousands of others to choose from, I would imagine the odds are so stacked against me that the smart money says I won't last a week."

"He wanted the best," replied Dinnisen, looking distinctly uncomfortable. "That's you."

Nighthawk fell silent again for a long moment. Then he looked up at Egan.

"Give me something sharp," he said.

"Sharp?" repeated Egan, puzzled.

"A knife, a scalpel, something like that."

Egan examined his pockets with no success.

"Never mind," said Nighthawk. He walked to the edge of the still-open drawer, pressed his thumb against it, and pulled it across the edge, leaving a deep gouge in the skin.

"Scanner?" he demanded.

Egan merely pointed at the glowing red mechanical eye.

Nighthawk walked over, wiped the blood from his thumb, and held it up to the scanner.

"Have I got an official name or number around here?" he asked.

"Just Jefferson Nighthawk Clone Number Two," answered Egan. "Serial number 90307."

"Good. Tell the machine that this is the thumbprint of Jefferson Nighthawk Clone Number Two, serial number 90307. The scar will differentiate it from any other Nighthawk clone you may be tempted to create in the future."

"It's listening. It knows," said Egan.

"Fine. Now I want you to go tell whoever is paying for me that our price just went up half a million credits. When he agrees—and he will, or he would have settled for a man with lesser credentials—tell him we want it in advance. Then put it in an account that can only be opened by my voiceprint and thumbprint."

"We've already agreed on a substantial price," said Dinnisen. "Holding him up for more at the last minute isn't ethical."

"You worry about ethics," said Nighthawk. "I'm worrying about getting enough money to cure my eplasia while it's still in the early stages—and I'll want cosmetic surgery so I don't resemble *him* too much."

"He'll be the one having the cosmetic surgery," said Egan. "Look at him. We can't let him go out in public looking like *that.*"

There was a tense silence.

Dinnisen finally nodded his agreement. "I'll do what I can, Mr. Nighthawk."

"I'm sure you will," replied Nighthawk. "Or I *won't* do what I can."

"Is that some kind of threat?" asked Dinnisen.

"Not at all. Just a statement of fact."

Another silence.

"I hope you won't be offended by my observation," said Dinnisen, "but your predecessor was much easier to deal with."

"Of course he was," replied Nighthawk. "He was a newborn baby in the body of a man. *I'm* the Widowmaker."

"I know you are. That's precisely why you have to fulfill this contract. Our client put up millions of credits just to create you."

"Then he can put up another half million to keep me alive after I finish this job."

"And if he won't?"

Nighthawk smiled. It was a smile that sent a chill down Dinnisen's spine. "If he had someone who could make me do something I don't want to do, he wouldn't need me in the first place."

"A point well taken," said Dinnisen, nervously returning his smile.

"I'm glad we all understand each other," said Nighthawk. "As soon as the money's been deposited, you can sit down with me and tell me just how many hundreds of men I have to kill for it."

"Possibly no one," said Dinnisen.

"That's the upside," said Nighthawk. "What's the downside?"

"I think you've had enough surprises for one day," said Dinnisen. "Especially considering that it's the first day of your life." He rose and walked to the door of the chamber. "We'll talk again tomorrow."

"Shall we go too?" asked Egan as Dinnisen left the chamber.

"In a minute," said Nighthawk, walking over to look at the original Widowmaker. "Jesus! I—he—looks awful."

"Eplasia is an awful disease."

Nighthawk stared down at the disfigured, skeletal body. "You've waited a long time," he said softly. "I know what it means to you. I won't let you down."

He stood in silence for a moment, then turned to Egan. "Okay, let's go see the world."

Chapter 1

Jefferson Nighthawk stood two hundred yards from the burning targets, a laser pistol in his hand, and grimaced.

"Six shots, five hits, elapsed time 4.13 seconds," announced Ito Kinoshita, the small, wiry man who was standing near him. "Very good."

Nighthawk shook his head. "It stinks. Set 'em up again."

"You're sure you don't want to rest? We've been at this for over an hour now."

"Not until I get it right." He looked around at the rolling green countryside. "It's not as if we're bothering anyone. I'd be surprised if there's a neighbor within five miles."

"You hit one hundred percent with your Screecher and your bullet gun," said Kinoshita. "And you've got the laser up from fifty percent to five out of six, and doubled your speed. I'd call it a good morning's work."

"The laser's the one I'll use the most often," answered Nighthawk, frowning at the targets. "Makes the least noise, lightest in weight. And that's not five out of six targets I just burned. It's five out of six armed men; the sixth one just killed me."

"You're a perfectionist."

"In my business you don't live much past twenty if you're not."

"How often did you practice when you were . . . ?" Kinoshita paused, trying to find the right word.

"Alive?" asked Nighthawk wryly.

"Actively engaged in business, let us say."

"Not regularly. But I was used to my body and my weapons. They haven't made any major changes to these pistols"—he indicated the various weapons that were laid out on a table beside him—"but they're a little lighter in weight. It makes a difference. As for my body," he continued, "it's in perfect shape, and *that* requires adjustments."

"That's a problem?"

"Absolutely."

"Why?"

"I broke my hand when I was twenty-eight," explained Nighthawk. "I didn't realize it until now, but it made a difference in the way I held a gun. Not much of one, but enough to throw my aim off. Also, I'd taken a few burns and bullets in my younger days; that made me hold my body differently. A tiny difference, to be sure . . . but the difference between a kill and a miss can be pretty small, too."

Kinoshita gave a brief order to his control board, and six more targets flashed into existence.

Nighthawk stared at them for a moment, then aimed and fired the laser pistol again. There was a soft humming noise, and an instant later all six targets were ablaze.

"Time?" he asked.

Kinoshita checked the automatic timer. "3.86 seconds."

Nighthawk laid the laser pistol down next to the other weapons. "Better. Not great, but better." He turned to Kinoshita. "Let's get something to drink. This afternoon we'll try again, and tomorrow we'll work on fast draws. Blowing away six targets in three seconds won't do you much good if it takes you a couple of seconds to get your gun out of its holster."

They stepped onto the carefully manicured sliding trail that took them past the large angular main house at the center of the compound. Dozens of impressive-looking machines were caring for the grounds, sweeping up fallen leaves and atomizing them, mowing the vast lawn to a height of exactly two inches, dispensing insecticides. A robot maid exited one bungalow and made its way to the next.

"How many people can this place accommodate?" asked Nighthawk.

Kinoshita shrugged. "Twelve bungalows plus the main house. Maybe forty people. Any given day there are usually three or four members of the firm and their mistresses of all genders, and I've seen up to three hundred at their parties." He paused. "Of course, it's empty now except for you and me and the chef. I don't think they want anyone trying to buy you away."

"Is this where you trained the last clone?"

"No. Dinnisen's firm only bought this place about a year ago." They reached the door to Nighthawk's bungalow, which slid back after identifying them. Kinoshita immediately walked into the kitchen. "What would you like?"

"Water or coffee," answered Nighthawk.

"We have beer and whiskey."

"I don't drink alcohol when I'm working. Besides," he added, "I don't know how my body will react to it, and I'd rather not experiment until all my reflexes are up to par."

"It's your own body. How can you not know?"

"It's never had any liquor before. The last time I was this age, I'd probably consumed a swimming pool's worth. I have a feeling that makes a difference to a body's tolerance."

Kinoshita nodded in agreement. "I'm beginning to see why you lived so long," he said. "You're a very cautious man. You think of everything."

"There's more to being a bounty hunter or a lawman than being good with a gun," answered Nighthawk as Kinoshita ordered the kitchen computer to prepare two tall glasses of ice water. "Especially out on the Frontier. Which reminds me: when will Dinnisen be here?"

"Any time now. Late morning, he said."

"Good."

"Is there a problem?" asked Kinoshita, carrying Nighthawk's drink to him.

"Could be."

"What is it?"

"I don't buy his whole bullshit story," replied Nighthawk. "I've got a lot of questions for him." He downed half his glass of water in a single swallow, then stared at Kinoshita. "Unless *you'd* like to answer them?"

"Not me" was the reply. "I'm just your trainer. Which," he added, "is ridiculous. You're already twice as good as I am, and you know your body far better than I do."

"Did you train the last clone?"

"Yeah . . . but he was a baby with your body. I had to teach him how to shoot a gun, how to break a skull, everything." Kinoshita looked at Nighthawk with open admiration. "There's nothing I can teach you, Widowmaker."

"Sure there is," said Nighthawk. "There's a computer in the next room. They've changed a lot in the past century. I don't even know how to turn it on."

"What do you need from the computer?"

"The Widowmaker file. I'm sure it's protected, but you work for the organization. You ought to know how to access it."

Kinoshita frowned. "Why?"

"This organization sent a clone out two years ago, and as near as I can tell, he did what they asked him to do, and no one in Dinnisen's firm lifted a finger to save him. That's not going to happen to me. If I find they can't be trusted—and I suspect they can't—then I don't plan to ever put myself in a position where I need their help. I want to learn everything I can about the last clone: what he did, where and how he did it, who killed him, and why."

"I doubt I can access all that," answered Kinoshita. "But I'll be happy to bring up my own file. The problem is that it stops the day he left for the Frontier."

"I suppose it's better than nothing," said Nighthawk. "Will you get in trouble for letting me read it?"

"I don't think there's anything all that sensitive in it," said Kinoshita, walking to the next room. "Besides, if push comes to shove, I'd much rather be in trouble with Dinnisen than with you."

Kinoshita opened the file, then left him alone until Dinnisen showed up.

Nighthawk looked up from the computer as Dinnisen entered the bungalow. He deactivated the machine, then walked across the glowing carpet, which was woven from exotic alien filaments. When he reached a formfitting chair that floated a few inches above the floor, he sat down.

Dinnisen and Kinoshita soon joined him in the small, cozy room. Dinnisen sat down opposite Nighthawk, while Kinoshita remained standing.

"Well, how are you coming along?" asked the lawyer.

"A couple of more weeks and I'll be ready."

"That long?"

"Just making sure I can properly protect your investment," said Nighthawk.

"*My* investment?" asked Dinnisen, puzzled.

"Me."

"I thought I explained that time was of the essence."

"Surviving is of the essence," said Nighthawk. "Time is secondary."

Dinnisen turned to Kinoshita. "Does he really need two more weeks?"

"It's not his decision," interrupted Nighthawk.

"Your predecessor was a much more pleasant person," said Dinnisen, making no attempt to hide his annoyance.

"That's probably why he's dead."

"I don't like your attitude, Mr. Nighthawk."

"I couldn't care less, Mr. Dinnisen. I'm not going out until I'm ready."

"I'm told that you put all three of your sparring partners in the hospital yesterday. How much readier do you have to be? Couldn't you at least have pulled your punches?"

"He *did* pull his punches," interjected Kinoshita. "That's why they're still alive."

Dinnisen stared at Nighthawk for a long moment, then shrugged. "All right," he said at last. "Two weeks." He took a deep breath, released it slowly, and made another attempt to be charming. "How do you like the facilities?"

"They're fine," said Nighthawk. "And Selamundi seems a nice enough world."

"And it's only two systems removed from Deluros, which is quite convenient," noted Dinnisen. He leaned forward. "Do you need anything? Different weapons? Protective clothing? Anything at all?"

"Yes, I need something."

"Just name it."

"Answers."

"I beg your pardon?"

"This cock-and-bull hunt you're sending me out on," said Nighthawk. "It reeks."

"I assure you—"

"Spare me your assurances," said Nighthawk. "I want the truth."

"I told you what you need to know."

"You haven't begun to tell me what I need to know, and I'm not putting my life on the line until you do."

"I'll go over it again," said Dinnisen irritably. He pulled out a tiny, pen-sized holo projector and cast an image of a slender young blonde woman in the middle of the room. "Cassandra Hill, the daughter of Cassius Hill, governor of Pericles V, has been kidnapped by a revolutionary named Ibn ben Khalid." The holograph of a ruggedly handsome man in his early thirties replaced the woman's image. "I have supplied you with dozens of holographs of each of them, and told you that he is presumed to be on the Inner Frontier. You have been given a considerable amount of money to draw from for whatever you need. You'll have your own ship. Ito will accompany you until you're comfortable with the changes that a new century has brought about. What more could you possibly want?"

"Plenty," said Nighthawk. "For starters, why me?"

"You're the best," said Dinnisen. "Or, once upon a time, you *were.*"

"Not good enough," said Nighthawk. "The governor of Pericles V has the entire resources of his planet at his disposal. He can send out the Navy, and post a reward that will attract hundreds of bounty hunters. After all, he'll only have to pay one of them." He paused. "But someone has already paid to create me—and they've paid more than the girl is worth. I want to know why."

"Rescuing Cassandra Hill is only part of your mission," said Dinnisen, looking just a bit uncomfortable. He paused almost imperceptibly. "The other part is killing Ibn ben Khalid."

"*He's* what's worth all those millions, not *her*," said Nighthawk. Then, sardonically, "My sympathies to the grieving father."

"He *is* a grieving father," said Dinnisen.

"Sure he is," said Nighthawk. "But if the only way to kill him is to kill her too?"

Dinnisen sighed. "Then you kill them both."

"Yeah, he sure loves his daughter, this politician," said Nighthawk. "How comforting to know that nothing's changed in a century." He paused. "Hell, if I were her, I'd choose Ibn ben Khalid over Cassius Hill every time. Maybe she wasn't kidnapped at all."

"Look," said Dinnisen, "he would much prefer that you rescue his daughter and bring her back to him in one piece. That is the ideal scenario."

"You've been a lawyer too long. You couldn't utter a simple factual sentence if your life depended on it." Nighthawk lit a smokeless cigar. "All right, we'll overlook all the nuances of the father's motives. My job is to rescue her and kill him, and that's what I'll try to do." He paused. "Now, he's enough of a revolutionary that his death is the most important part of this assignment. How big is his army?"

"I don't know," said Dinnisen. "Big."

"So big that Cassius Hill doesn't really expect anyone to try to earn the reward?"

"If someone can find the girl, by herself, of course they'll claim it."

"But they won't go up against Ibn ben Khalid." It was a statement, not a question.

"I doubt it. He's got informants all over the Frontier. It would be almost impossible for anyone to infiltrate his organization." Dinnisen stared at Nighthawk. "Anyone but you. That's one of the reasons Hill made us the offer. Not only are you the best at what you do—but you haven't been around for a century. His agents won't know who you are, won't spot you as a bounty hunter or an employee of Cassius Hill."

"You undercharged," said Nighthawk.

"What?"

"If Hill's afraid to go up against Ibn ben Khalid's men with his own planetary forces, you're not charging him enough."

"It's not a matter of fear. It's a matter of legality and cost. Pericles V has no authority on the Inner Frontier, and even if it did, equipping such a mission could cost billions."

"All the more reason to demand triple what he offered. If the alternative was putting billions into a military operation, with no guarantee of seeing his daughter alive again, he'd have paid."

"You're not going to hold him up for more money *again*?"

"No, I'm getting what I want," said Nighthawk. "But for a smart lawyer, you're a lousy bargainer, Mr. Dinnisen. It makes me wonder why."

"I assure you—"

"So you've said. Now let's get back to the business at hand. Has there been a second ransom demand?"

"No. Nothing since the tragedy on Roosevelt III."

"Let me make sure I've got this straight. Ibn ben Khalid contacted Hill through intermediaries, explained that he'd kidnapped his daughter, and demanded two million credits for her return. Hill sent his bag man to Roosevelt III with the money, as instructed. Once the man landed, he was killed and the money was stolen. Right?"

Dinnisen nodded. "Right."

"Is there any proof that Ibn ben Khalid was responsible for it?"

"Who else could it be?"

"Anyone who wanted two million credits in cash."

"It was *him*, take my word for it."

"I don't take your word for anything," replied Nighthawk. "In fact, until you tell me how Hill knew that Ibn ben Khalid had his daughter, I don't even take your word that he kidnapped her. He could just be an opportunist who heard she was missing and tried to pry a couple of million credits from a grieving father while she's shacked up somewhere with a lover. It wouldn't be the first time a smart man has pulled a bluff like that."

Dinnisen reached into a pocket, pulled out a small computer cube, and tossed it to Nighthawk.

"Here's a holo duplication of the first ransom demand. I just got it this morning."

"Okay, I see Ibn ben Khalid," said Nighthawk, looking at the cube. "Are you sure the girl's not an actress or a double?"

"The voiceprint checks out. It's her."

"I'll look at it later," said Nighthawk, placing the cube on a table.

"If we get anything further, I'll of course see that you get a copy."

"Fine. And I want everything you have on Hill."

"You have it."

"The father, not the daughter."

"Cassius Hill?" said Dinnisen, surprised. "Why?"

"He's involved. Why not?"

Dinnisen shrugged. "Whatever you say. I'll have it sent here this afternoon." He paused. "Do you have any more questions?"

"When I do, you'll be the first to know."

The lawyer turned to Kinoshita. "How's his progress?"

"He's the fastest and most accurate shot I've ever seen with every weapon he's tried," replied Kinoshita. "I should add that he's very disappointed in his performance. He's the Widowmaker, all right."

"That just means he's an exceptionally able killer."

"And you're an exceptionally able lawyer," said Nighthawk. "Ironic, isn't it?"

"What?"

"You get guilty people off the hook," said Nighthawk. "And eventually I get paid to hunt down your triumphs."

"You haven't liked me from the first moment you opened your eyes," said Dinnisen. "Why? What could I possibly have done to you in your four days of life?"

"To me? Nothing."

"Well, then?" demanded the lawyer.

"You sent my predecessor out without preparing him for what he would face."

"Nonsense. He knew what he had to do."

"Oh, he knew who to kill. But he didn't know how to live, and you didn't give him enough time to learn. That may work here in the heart of the Oligarchy, where you have laws, and lawyers, and more social safety nets than you can count—but out on the Frontier, that's a death sentence. And I think you knew it. I think you were fully prepared to kill him if he made it back alive."

"Kill him? Hell, we'd have rented him out again. He was a valuable commodity!"

"Well, I'm a human being and not a commodity," said Nighthawk. "Do you think you're going to rent me out after this assignment?"

"The firm of Hubbs, Wilkinson, Raith and Jiminez would be happy to enter into any such arrangement as your representative," said Dinnisen. "But I suspect you're too independent. I truly don't foresee us having a working relationship with you."

"You bet your ass."

"Have you any further questions before I leave?" asked Dinnisen.

"Just one," said Nighthawk. "You mentioned that I would have my own ship."

"That's right," replied the lawyer. "Mr. Kinoshita will handle it until you're able to fly it alone."

"Where is it?"

"It's due to be delivered either this evening or tomorrow morning."

"Good. Once we take off, I'll let you know where we're going."

"Your destination will be Innisfree II," said Dinnisen.

"Eventually," said Nighthawk. Both men looked at him questioningly. "I have some unfinished business to take care of first. It won't take long."

"Unfinished? After one hundred and nine years?"

Nighthawk dumped the nub of his smokeless cigar, lit another, and ignored the question.

Chapter 2

"You're sure you want to come with me?" asked Nighthawk, surveying the spaceport as their ship touched down.

"I feel like I've got a vested interest in you," answered Ito Kinoshita.

"I hardly know you."

"Then let me amend my statement," said Kinoshita with a smile. "I feel like I've got a vested interest in the clan of Jefferson Nighthawks." He paused. "I'm your biggest fan, as well as being your instructor in a previous incarnation."

"Then you know why I'm on this world?"

"It doesn't take a genius to guess."

"All right. Let's go."

They left the ship and took a shuttle vehicle to the spaceport's main terminal. When they arrived, Nighthawk approached an empty Customs booth, while Kinoshita sought out another.

"Name?" asked the computer's electronic voice as it scanned Nighthawk's retina, dentation, and skeletal structure.

"Jefferson Nighthawk."

"Passport?"

Nighthawk handed over the titanium disk.

"Purpose of visit?"

"Tourism."

"There was another Jefferson Nighthawk with an identical retinagram and—except for a scar on your thumb—similar fingerprints, who visited the Solio system two years ago, but he was sixteen years younger."

"That's no concern of mine," replied Nighthawk.

"My programming tells me that two men possessing the same names and retinagrams approaches the statistically impossible," responded the machine.

"Is the other Jefferson Nighthawk still here?"

"He died on Solio II."

"Then it couldn't have been me, could it?"

"I never stated that it was," answered the computer. "Still, the similarities are remarkable."

"What now?" asked Nighthawk.

"I am authorized to make value judgments after accessing my sixth-level programming. I am doing so now."

Nighthawk stood patiently as the computer buzzed and beeped while making its decision.

"How long will you be here, Mr. Nighthawk?" asked the machine after a moment's pause.

"Perhaps a day, possibly two."

"That is a very short visit for a tourist," noted the machine.

"Are short visits forbidden?"

"No, they are not," said the computer. It paused. "Your credentials are in order. Please note that we accept only Oligarchy credits. If you have any Far London pounds, Maria Theresa dollars, or New Stalin rubles, you may exchange them at the spaceport bank. All other currencies, including Kenyatta IV shillings from our neighboring system, should be left in your ship, as they are illegal currencies in this system, and our banks post no exchange rates for them."

"Understood."

"The penalty for selling or purchasing illicit drugs in any quantity, however minimal, is death. No legal appeal will be allowed."

"Understood."

"The atmosphere is seventeen percent oxygen, eighty-one percent nitrogen, two percent trace elements, and the gravity is 1.06 times Earth Standard. If you have any medical condition that will be affected by continued exposure to our air or gravity, please state so now and the proper life-support system will be supplied."

"None."

"Then you may be admitted. Welcome to Solio II."

The door at the far end of the booth dilated, and Nighthawk stepped through it. Kinoshita was waiting for him.

"What took you so long?"

"I'm not the first Jefferson Nighthawk with these retinas or fingerprints to land here," replied Nighthawk.

"Do you think you set off any alarms?" asked Kinoshita. "Will Customs send word ahead that you're here?"

"Why?" said Nighthawk. "I must be the last guy in the whole damned universe anyone expects to encounter. After all, Jefferson Nighthawk died here a couple of years ago; I can't imagine that the Customs computer has been programmed to keep an eye out for me."

"So where to now?"

"Now, since I don't feel like walking into the government building that houses Security headquarters and facing hundreds of guns, I find out where Hernandez lives, where he eats, where I can find him alone or nearly so." He paused. "I assume that megalopolis five miles east of here is the capital city, since this is the only spaceport on the planet. We'll go there, I'll spread a little money around, and before too long someone will tell me what I want to know."

"As simple as that?"

"The direct approach is usually the best."

Nighthawk and Kinoshita began walking through the spaceport. When they came to an exit, they caught a shuttle bound for the nearby city, and a moment later they were skimming a few inches above the ground as the shuttle raced across the flat, barren, brown landscape.

They got off in the middle of the city, a forest of angular steel-and-glass buildings with the streets crisscrossing in regular patterns. As he had predicted, it took Nighthawk less than an hour to get the information he sought. He soon stood before a small, elegant restaurant that was located just off one of the main thoroughfares.

"Are you really going in there?" asked Kinoshita.

"Why not?" responded Nighthawk. "It's lunch-time. Either he's here now, or he soon will be." He paused. "Do you know what he looks like?"

Kinoshita shook his head. "I never dealt with him. I've never even seen a holograph."

"It doesn't matter," said Nighthawk. "This place caters to businessmen and bureaucrats. If he's in uniform, I'll spot him."

"And if he doesn't eat here every day?"

"Then I'll pay him a visit at his home tonight," said Nighthawk. "But I'd much rather meet him here."

"There are more witnesses here," said Kinoshita.

"True. But the security's poorer."

"Are you sure?"

Nighthawk walked to the door. "Pretty sure," he said. "Still, there's only one way to find out."

"There are close to fifty men and women in here," whispered Kinoshita as Nighthawk paused in the doorway. "Some of them have got to be armed."

Nighthawk shrugged. "There's nothing I can do about it," he said, scanning the restaurant. Finally he stared intently at a uniformed man who was sitting with two other officers at a table in the farthest corner. "*That* has to be him."

"You've never seen him before," said Kinoshita. "How can you know?"

"He's the highest-ranking officer in the place," said Nighthawk. "Get a table halfway between him and the door and keep an eye on my back."

"I don't understand."

"This is the most powerful man on Solio II," explained Nighthawk. "Believe me, he'll have more than two bodyguards. Kill anyone who reaches for a gun."

"But—" said Kinoshita, but Nighthawk was already walking calmly through the room. Finally he stopped at the officer's table. "Do you mind if I join you?" he asked, sitting down before receiving a reply.

"Do I know you?" asked the officer, staring intently at him.

"That all depends," replied Nighthawk. "Are you James Hernandez?"

The man nodded. "You have the advantage of me, sir."

"Still a colonel, I see. You haven't advanced very far in the last two years."

Hernandez continued to stare at Nighthawk. "We met two years ago?"

"In a manner of speaking." Nighthawk leaned forward. "Look at me closely, Colonel Hernandez."

"Nighthawk!" exclaimed Hernandez after another moment had passed. Suddenly he turned to his two companions. "Leave us alone for a few minutes."

"But sir—" protested one.

"It's all right," Hernandez assured him.

The two officers got up reluctantly and moved to a nearby table.

Hernandez turned to Nighthawk and lit a Cygnian cigar. "You're much older," he noted. "I approve." He paused. "I suppose your friends on Deluros sent you here about the money?"

Nighthawk shook his head. "I'm on my own."

"Really?" said Hernandez. "Good. I can use a man like you, Jefferson Nighthawk."

"The way you used the last one?"

"He was a child masquerading as the Widowmaker," said Hernandez contemptuously. "You're the real thing—or at least you appear to be." He smiled. "We can do business together."

"Slaughter whole planetary populations?" asked Nighthawk, returning the smile.

"We'll start with three or four people who have been causing me problems lately and work our way up from there."

"Only three or four?"

"Do I look *that* beleaguered?"

"I'd rather expected you to be a general by now. There have to be more than three or four men standing between you and what you want."

"I found a properly malleable puppet to be governor," replied Hernandez. "Let him get the headlines and attract the assassins. I am content to rule the planet in obscurity." He grinned. "That's why I'm not a governor *or* a general."

"Very intelligent."

"So," said Hernandez, "can we do business?"

"Actually, I'm here on business," said Nighthawk.

Hernandez frowned. "I told you: if your people have sent you here about the final payment . . ."

"They haven't."

"Then why are you here?"

"Think hard, Colonel Hernandez. What is the very last thing you did to my predecessor?"

"I killed him," responded Hernandez. "But surely you know he was trying to kill *me* at the time." He paused, then added incredulously: "You're not going to tell me that you feel any loyalty to a clone you never met, a clone that was killed two years before you were created?"

Nighthawk stared coldly into Hernandez's eyes. "You didn't kill my father, or my brother, or my son," he said at last. "You killed someone even closer. You killed me. A younger, more innocent version, but me nonetheless." He continued staring at the colonel. "You never intended that I would survive my mission. You used me and set me up and when the opportunity presented itself, you killed me."

"Not *you*!" insisted Hernandez. "I killed a version of you that you never even knew!"

"It was a Jefferson Nighthawk—and I take it personally when Jefferson Nighthawks are killed."

"Fine. I won't kill you or that hideous monstrosity they cloned you from."

"You don't understand," said Nighthawk. "I'm not here to extract promises; I'm here to extract *payment*. And there is only one way you can pay for killing Jefferson Nighthawk."

Hernandez glanced quickly around the room. "You'll never make it out of here alive."

"You're not going to live long enough to know whether I do or not."

"Look, we can reach an accommodation," said Hernandez smoothly, his dark eyes seeking out the bodyguards who were spaced around the various tables. "Your principals think I owe them a few million credits. Come back to my office with me and we can work something out."

"I told you: I'm here for myself."

"Then I'll deal with *you*."

"I don't want your money," said Nighthawk firmly.

"Then why all the talk? Why didn't you just walk in and shoot me?"

"I wanted you to know *why*. In your last second of life, I wanted you to know that your death was neither a mistake nor an accident. It was because you used and betrayed and finally murdered Jefferson Nighthawk." He paused, then added with a sense of finality, "And now you know it."

Nighthawk got to his feet, pulled out a laser pistol in a single fluid motion, and as the weapon hummed softly with power, he burned a sizzling, bubbling hole between Hernandez's eyes. The officer slumped over, dead, as a woman shrieked. In the same motion he turned and killed the two officers at the next table.

Then, as Kinoshita watched, transfixed, Nighthawk, the one calm island in a sea of confusion, picked three more men from the crowd and burned them away. He surveyed the room, couldn't spot anyone else with the urge to be a hero, and walked through the restaurant, taking the stunned Kinoshita by the arm and heading for the door. As they stepped outside, he turned and melted the lock with his laser pistol, effectively sealing the staff and customers inside.

"You're everything they said you were!" remarked Kinoshita as they crossed the street and rounded a corner. He stopped and stared admiringly at Nighthawk. "I never saw anything like that!"

"Keep walking. There'll be a back entrance—and it'll only be a matter of minutes before someone remembers."

"So what do we do now?"

"We go back to the spaceport," answered Nighthawk, spotting a shuttle at rest and increasing his pace to reach it. "By the way," he added sardonically, "thanks for protecting my back."

"I never saw any guns," said Kinoshita defensively.

"You wait until their guns are out and you're dead. A man with that much clout figures to hire only the best."

"So he had some guardian angels spread around the restaurant in civilian clothes. How did you know which ones they were?"

"I didn't."

"But—"

"Anyone who ducked or sat still was a civilian. Anyone who reached inside his tunic or jacket was an enemy."

"And if they were just reaching for their wallets?" asked Kinoshita as they reached the shuttle.

"Then I'd say they timed it very poorly," replied Nighthawk as the shuttle doors opened.

"Are you saying that—?" began Kinoshita.

"Shut up," said Nighthawk. Kinoshita looked at him questioningly. "This isn't the time or the place for this discussion."

Kinoshita fell silent, but his active imagination played out thirty or forty scenarios, each grimmer than the last. To his amazement, they reached the spaceport without incident and were soon racing out of the Solio system at light speed.

The instructor poured himself a drink, stared at his calm, relaxed companion for a long moment, and began to understand, for perhaps the first time, exactly who and what he was traveling with. It had just been a morning's work for Nighthawk, nothing to get excited about, nothing to celebrate, nothing to turn into song or fable.

Just *business*.

Suddenly Kinoshita was very glad that he was not one of the Widowmaker's enemies.

Chapter 3

Nighthawk sat at the control panel, sipping a mutated fruit drink and staring at the viewscreen. Finally he looked across at Kinoshita.

"What planet do you want me to put you off on?" he asked.

"Do you think you're able to run the ship yourself?" responded Kinoshita.

Nighthawk smiled. "The panel looks different, and the galley cooks better meals, but if they've made a meaningful improvement in the past century, I sure as hell haven't been able to find it. You still say 'Take me to Binder X,' and then you relax for two days while the ship does what you ordered."

"Oh, they've made a few changes. Nowadays if it spots an ion storm or a meteor swarm coming up on its flight path, it won't bother you for instructions. It'll avoid them on its own and then recalibrate its course."

"Big deal," said Nighthawk. "As far as I'm concerned, an ion storm is one of the few things that keeps you from being bored in deep space."

"They also fly a little faster."

"You could cross the whole damned galaxy in less than a month back in *my* time, and if you didn't want to look out the portholes or play games with the computer, you could go into DeepSleep, so what the hell difference does it make that it can do it in twenty-seven days instead of twenty-nine?"

"Not much," admitted Kinoshita. "But when an object approaches maximum performance, any improvements will seem small."

"Fine," said Nighthawk. "You still haven't answered my question: where do you want me to put you down?"

"Nowhere."

Nighthawk stared at him.

"I'd like to come along," continued Kinoshita.

"As a watchdog for Marcus Dinnisen?"

Kinoshita shook his head. "I've been in the Oligarchy too long. It's time I got back out to the Frontier."

"You're crazy," said Nighthawk. "If the odds weren't hundreds to one against pulling this job off, you don't think they'd have cloned me, do you?"

"I have confidence in you."

"Bully for you." Nighthawk paused. "I don't take partners. Anything I earn is already earmarked for me or for my dying double."

"I have enough money," said Kinoshita.

"No one has enough money."

"Look, I'll explain it as simply as I can. I used to be a lawman and a bounty hunter. A damned good one, if I say so myself. I took enormous pride in my accomplishments." He paused, awkwardly trying to stake out a position halfway between admiration and hero worship. "You're the best I've ever seen, maybe the best there ever was. I want to watch you work."

"I'll have enough trouble protecting *me*. I won't be able to worry about you."

"I can take care of myself," said Kinoshita. "And I can be useful to you."

"Like you were at the restaurant?" asked Nighthawk with a sardonic smile.

"I'd never seen you in action before. I wanted to see just how good you really are, so I decided not to help unless you needed me." He paused. "It takes a hell of a lot to impress me, but I'm impressed. You're even better than the history books make you out to be." He looked into Nighthawk's eyes. "Next time I'll back you up. It won't happen again, I promise."

Nighthawk stared at Kinoshita until he shifted nervously in his seat. At last he said, "It damned well better not."

"Then am I coming along?" asked Kinoshita.

"For the time being."

"Thanks. I owe you."

"Fine," said Nighthawk. "Start paying."

"I beg your pardon?"

Nighthawk tapped his head with a forefinger. "I've got a lifetime of memories in here, but they're a century out of date." He paused. "For example, I *think* the biggest whorehouse on the Inner Frontier is Madame Zygia's on Tecumseh IV, but for all I know it's been out of business for ninety years."

"I see what you mean," said Kinoshita.

"So does Madame Zygia's still exist?"

"Madame Zygia's?"

"That's what we're talking about."

"I don't know," said Kinoshita. "I never heard of it."

"Find out," said Nighthawk. "And if it's not there anymore, find out where the biggest whorehouse is."

"I've heard that there's a huge one on Barrios II."

"Multispecies?"

Kinoshita shrugged. "I really couldn't say."

"Find out," repeated Nighthawk.

"All right," said Kinoshita. Then: "Why this sudden interest in whorehouses?"

"It's not sudden, and we're going to one."

"Now?"

"Now."

"Why don't we just stop at the next oxygen world? I don't suppose there's a world anywhere on the Inner Frontier that doesn't have a whorehouse."

Nighthawk shook his head. "I'm not looking for your everyday whorehouse."

"I'll find a luxurious one," Kinoshita assured him.

"That's not what I asked for. I need the biggest, not the best."

"Just what are you looking for?"

"I already told you," said Nighthawk, leaning back comfortably in his chair, putting one foot up on the panel, and closing his eyes. "Now let's see if you can find it."

"Is this some kind of test?"

"Just do it."

Kinoshita sighed and had the ship's computer start poring through its more esoteric data banks until he found out that Madame Zygia's was nothing more than a memory, and that the biggest brothel on the Inner Frontier was indeed the Gomorrah Palace on Barrios II. He directed the ship to set a course for the Barrios system, then went off to the galley to get some lunch, all the while wondering why, if the Widowmaker was addicted to interspecies sex, his multitude of biographies never made mention of the fact.

Chapter 4

The Barrios system was perfectly placed, on the main route between Terrazane, the huge world at the outskirts of the Oligarchy, and the Inner Frontier's vast Quinellus Cluster.

There were fourteen planets in all. Eight were gas giants. Four more were mining worlds that had long since been abandoned. The thirteenth boasted an ammonia atmosphere. But Barrios II was a bustling center of activity. It had started out as nothing but a refueling station. Then plutonium had been discovered, and it became the proudest of the system's mining worlds. When the plutonium ran out, it metamorphosed into an agricultural world, becoming the breadbasket for half a dozen nearby systems. Finally, thanks to its favorable location and its constantly increasing population, it became a major financial world, dealing in thousands of rare commodities from the Inner Frontier, and handling literally hundreds of different currencies.

One of Barrios II's landmarks was the Gomorrah Palace, easily the biggest brothel on the Frontier, and quite possibly the oldest as well. This was not a swank, elegant temple of luxury like the fabled Velvet Comet, which drew its clientele from the wealthiest men and women in the galaxy. Instead, it was an efficiently run operation, specializing in service rather than expensive fantasy. From its meager beginnings almost a century ago, it had undergone a series of facelifts and five additions, and now took up an entire city block. Some of the locals objected to it, as had their parents and grandparents, but since the Gomorrah Palace brought in more hard currency than any business on the planet except for the branch of the Bank of Deluros VIII, no one in authority ever seriously considered shutting it down as long as it paid its taxes.

Nighthawk looked at the front entrance to the Palace as he and Kinoshita approached it on foot.

"Not as impressive as one might expect, is it?" he remarked dryly.

"I told you it wasn't," replied Kinoshita defensively. "We could have stopped at Pollux IV."

"I was observing, not complaining. This is the place I want."

"I can't imagine why."

"Because the biggest whorehouse will have the biggest selection."

"Just as the best whorehouse will have the best selection," grumbled Kinoshita. "And the best whorehouse is about forty-five hundred light-years behind us."

"This'll do just fine."

"Whatever perverse needs you have, you could have taken care of them in much more luxurious surroundings on Pollux IV."

"I doubt it," said Nighthawk.

"Well, it may suit *your* tastes, but it sure as hell doesn't do much for *me*."

"Just as well. We won't be here long enough for you to avail yourself of their services anyway."

Kinoshita stared at him curiously.

"Just stay in the bar and have a drink or two. I expect to be through before you're done."

"Maybe you're right, after all."

"About what?" asked Nighthawk.

"If you're that fast an operator, a whorehouse like the one on Pollux IV would be wasted on you."

Nighthawk allowed himself an amused smile as they reached the front door, which melted before them and reconstituted itself after they had passed through to the large lounge. There were prints and holos—no originals—on the walls, and a long, gleaming bar along one wall. A few men were discreetly sitting inside "lineup booths," selecting their companions for the evening.

A once-beautiful and still strikingly handsome middle-aged woman, obviously the madam—or one of them, at least—walked up to Nighthawk and Kinoshita after they'd each ordered a drink.

"Welcome to the Gomorrah Palace," she said. "I don't recognize either of you."

"It's our first visit," said Kinoshita.

"Did you have anything special in mind?" she asked.

"Not really."

"How about any*one* special?" she continued with a knowing grin.

"It's possible," replied Nighthawk. "What have you got?"

"We have too many girls to do a live lineup," answered the madam. "But we can show you holographs of each of them."

"Fine," said Nighthawk. "Let's see them."

"Most men prefer the privacy of a booth when making their selection."

"My friend's just here to drink, and I'm not shy."

The madam shrugged. "Whatever you say."

She touched a small control on her bracelet, and suddenly a holograph of a gorgeous redheaded woman, no more that a foot high, floated a few inches above the bar. Nighthawk made no comment or gesture, and after a moment the holograph was replaced by another.

By the time the fortieth holo had appeared without eliciting any reaction from Nighthawk, both Kinoshita and the madam were wondering just what he was looking for. He found it in the forty-first holo.

"Stop."

Kinoshita stared at the holo in disbelief. "You're kidding!" he exclaimed at last.

"Why should you think so?"

"She's got to weigh three hundred pounds. And look at her features: she's not even human."

Nighthawk turned to the madam. "She's the one I want."

"I'm afraid that's not possible. She's in hospital."

"Have you got any other—?"

"—Balatai women?" She completed his sentence. "Just one other. They're quite rare, you know."

"So I've been told."

"And consequently they cost extra."

"How much?"

The madam stared at him, as if sizing him up. "Twelve hundred credits?" It was as much a question as an answer.

Nighthawk stared at her without speaking, and she became visibly uneasy.

"This your first time here, right?" she asked at last.

"Yes."

"Hell, make it an even thousand. I wouldn't want you to be unhappy with us." She paused. "We'll also take payment in Far London pounds, Maria Theresa dollars, or New Bombay rupees. There's a five percent conversion charge. If you have any other currency, you'll have to exchange it at a bank."

"A thousand credits is acceptable."

She turned to Kinoshita. "And how about you? Are you sure we can't find someone to interest you?"

"I'm sure you can," said Kinoshita bitterly. "But I'll just stay here at the bar and wait for my friend."

The madam shrugged. "Whatever makes you happy."

"Being happy's got nothing to do with it," muttered Kinoshita.

"Lead the way," said Nighthawk. "And put my friend's bar bill on my tab."

"Happy to," she replied, as Nighthawk followed her down a long, dimly lit corridor. A doorway dilated and they entered another building, then took an airlift to the third level.

"Here we are," said the madam, coming to a stop in front of an unmarked door. "You'll pay me now. Any tip you arrange will be paid directly to the lady of your choice."

She pulled out a pocket computer, which registered Nighthawk's retina and thumbprint, paused for about ten seconds, and flashed a credit approval code.

"Enjoy," said the madam, turning and walking back to the airlift.

Nighthawk looked for a handle or a knob, couldn't find one, and finally said, "Open." The door slid back into a wall as he stepped through, then closed behind him.

Lying on a bed in a corner of the room, wearing something black, lacy, and skimpy, was a female. At first glance she appeared to be a normal human woman, but there were enough differences so that even the casual observer would quickly realize that while she had come from human stock, her branch of the Tree of Man had been evolving and changing for more than a few generations.

Her ears were round and lobeless. Her fingers were all of the same length. She had only four toes on each foot. Her pupils were not round but vertical slits. Her knees and elbows seemed somehow exaggerated, almost swollen.

Nighthawk stood where he was, carefully observing her. At first the woman struck a provocative pose, then another. Finally she stared at him, studying him as carefully as he was studying her.

"All right," she said after a minute had passed. "What's going on here?"

"I just bought you for the night."

"Why?" she said. "You don't want me."

"I want you very much," said Nighthawk.

"You know you can't lie to me. I'm a Balatai woman."

"I know."

"Well, then?" she said. "Why did you pay for my time if you don't want to have sex with me?"

"Because I have a business proposition for you, and I didn't know how else to contact you."

"I don't know what you're talking about," she said. "You've already made a business proposition, and the house has accepted it. Otherwise you wouldn't be here."

"That was business with *them*. Now I want to talk business with *you*."

She frowned. "What the hell are you talking about? You have no more desire for me than I have for you."

"Less, probably," said Nighthawk. "Now, are you going to listen to me or not?"

"You've paid for my time," she answered with a shrug. "If talking is your notion of a good time, go ahead. And watch your temper; you're starting to get angry."

"Irritated," he corrected her.

"Irritated, angry, what's the difference? They both wind up with me getting beat up."

"I'll never lay a finger on you," said Nighthawk. "Consider it carefully. You should be able to tell if I'm lying."

She stared at him curiously for a long moment. "Okay, you're not lying," she said at last. "Go ahead. You do the talking, I'll do the listening."

"My name is Jefferson Nighthawk. Does that mean anything to you?"

"No. Should it?"

"Not necessarily. In some places I'm also known as the Widowmaker."

"I remember reading stories about the Widowmaker when I was a little girl."

"That was me."

"It couldn't be," she said, sitting on the edge of the bed and staring at him with a mixture of curiosity and disbelief. "He died a century ago."

"Check me out. Am I lying?"

She frowned. "No." A thoughtful pause. "But that doesn't mean you're not crazy. A crazy man might believe that he's the Widowmaker, and I couldn't tell he was lying because he'd truly believe it."

"Fair enough," said Nighthawk. "When I start acting crazy, activate that alarm by your headboard and call for the bouncers. But in the meantime, why not assume I'm sane and hear me out? After all, I've paid for your time."

She continued staring at him, more curious than frightened. "All right, Jefferson Nighthawk, let's hear what you've got to say."

"To begin with, I'm a clone of the original Widowmaker."

"I thought clones were illegal."

"Most of them are."

"Including you?"

"Probably," said Nighthawk.

"Okay, you're a clone," she said, walking to the bar and pouring herself a drink. "So what?"

"I'm a clone with a difference. I was given the original's memories."

She looked him up and down, as if appraising him. "Can they do that?"

"They can." A pause. "They did. I've got 'em."

"So who's after you?"

Nighthawk smiled. "*I'm* after someone."

"Me?" She put the drink down, suddenly tense. "What did I ever do to you?"

He shook his head. "No, not you. I've been commissioned to rescue a woman who's been kidnapped, and to terminate her kidnapper."

"Terminate?" she repeated. "You mean kill him?"

"Right."

"I still don't understand: what does all this have to do with me?"

"The kidnapper is a revolutionary," said Nighthawk. "He's got an entire army protecting him and the girl. That means I can't approach him directly. I'm going to have to infiltrate his forces to get to him." He paused. "I had to infiltrate a gang of smugglers in 4986 . . . ."

"You?"

"No, I mean the original me," said Nighthawk irritably. "Sometimes I get confused separating us." He grimaced. "He's the one who did it, but I'm the one who remembers it."

"What about it?"

"I used a Balatai woman," he said. "I think it's time to use another."

For the first time the woman's face came alive with interest. "You used one of us?"

"Yes," answered Nighthawk. "I think I would probably have been killed if I hadn't."

"What was her name?"

"I couldn't pronounce her real name. She had a human name she used, but it wouldn't mean anything to you."

"How interesting," mused the woman. "Someone actually had the good sense to use one of us for something meaningful, instead of games in a whorehouse." She paused and scrutinized him intently. "But why did you seek me out here? Why not go to my home world?"

"I don't know where it is."

"She never told you?"

Nighthawk shook his head. "It was a well-kept secret a century ago. If it's been made public since then, I wouldn't know about it."

"It hasn't," she answered. "We have enough problems without being exploited."

"Seems to me you're being exploited right here."

She shook her head. "I have my reasons for working here."

"What are they?"

"Personal."

Nighthawk sat down on the room's only chair. "I just paid a thousand credits for your time. How much of that do you get?"

"Three hundred, plus whatever tip we agree to."

"Come with me and I'll pay you two thousand a day for as long as the job takes."

She smiled at him. "You'll pay more than that, Widowmaker. Someone went to a lot of expense to create you. They can spend a little more and protect their investment."

"Twenty-five hundred," said Nighthawk.

"Five thousand."

"Don't get too greedy," he said. "That's a raise of almost seventeen hundred percent."

"Maybe I'm only worth three hundred credits a night here, but I'm worth a hell of a lot more than that to you. After all, who else but a Balatai can tell you if your cover has been penetrated, if your identity is known, if your enemy is aware of your presence?" She paused. "Of course, if you think you can get some other Balatai cheaper . . ."

"Maybe I can, maybe I can't," said Nighthawk. "But I don't have the time to find another one."

"There's another consideration," she said. "I have a contract with the Gomorrah Palace."

"Don't worry about it."

"Why not?"

"For the same reason the bouncer who's monitoring this conversation won't try to stop you from leaving." He paused. "Would *you* go up against the Widowmaker because some prostitute decided to break her contract?"

"No, I don't think I would." She paused and then smiled. "Have we got a deal, then?"

He shrugged and nodded. "What the hell, it's not *my* money I'm spending."

"You shouldn't have said that, Mr. Nighthawk," said the woman. "That'll cost you another thousand a day."

"Forget it. You named a price, I agreed to it. I don't renegotiate."

"If you don't, I'll stay here."

"Then stay," he said, walking to the door.

"You're bluffing."

He turned and faced her. "Am I?"

She stared at him for a moment. "No," she said slowly. "No, you're not."

"Well?" he said. "Am I leaving alone or with you?"

"Give me a moment to get dressed." She got to her feet and walked to a closet, then turned to him. "Mr. Nighthawk, you've bought yourself an empath."

Chapter 5

"Why not a telepath?" asked Kinoshita after they had taken off and were heading deeper into the Inner Frontier.

"Find me one and I'll hire him," responded Nighthawk, relaxing in the pilot's chair.

"They say the Domarians are telepaths."

"They're aliens."

"They have less reason to fear or distrust you than most humans."

"Swans swim with swans, ducks swim with ducks," answered Nighthawk.

"What the hell does *that* mean?"

"It means I'll attract enough attention with a Balatai."

Kinoshita turned to the Balatai woman, who was sitting near the navigation tank, watching holographs of the ship making its way among the stars of the Inner Frontier. "I meant no offense," he said. "But my fortune is intertwined with his, so I want him to have the best chance."

"I know," she replied. "You don't believe it, Mr. Kinoshita, but reading your emotions isn't very different from reading your thoughts."

"It isn't?"

"Nine times out of ten."

"And the tenth time?" asked Kinoshita.

She smiled. "That's why he's the Widowmaker. Because the tenth time can get messy."

Kinoshita stared at her for a long moment and finally nodded his approval. "You'll do," he said decisively. "What's your name?"

"What name do you like?" she responded.

"I didn't realize it was up to us."

"Choose one."

"Melisande," said Nighthawk.

"Fine," she said. "Then I'm Melisande." She paused. "Who was she?"

"Nobody very important," said Nighthawk.

"Your emotions say you're lying," said Melisande. She turned to Kinoshita. "Perhaps *you'll* tell me."

"She was the woman who betrayed his predecessor," said Kinoshita. She turned to Nighthawk. "Do you expect me to betray you?"

"No."

"Then why—?"

"It's a pretty name. I thought you might redeem it."

"In that case, I'm honored."

Kinoshita studied Nighthawk carefully, and finally spoke. "First Hernandez and now Melisande. I think you'd be better off if you forgot about the previous Nighthawk's life and concentrated on your own."

"I'm an orderly man with an orderly mind," answered Nighthawk. "I'm just taking care of the things that affect *all* Jefferson Nighthawks."

"I'd concentrate on Ibn ben Khalid if I were you."

"If you were me you'd be six inches taller and a hell of a lot faster with a gun—and you'd be an orderly man."

"It seems to me that an orderly man wouldn't proceed without a plan. How do you intend to make contact?"

"The simplest and most efficient way possible."

"Jeff—your predecessor—shot up a bunch of the Marquis of Queensbury's men and offered himself as their replacement," noted Kinoshita. "I seem to remember from the reports that he also fought the Marquis to a standstill."

"My predecessor was two months old," said Nighthawk. "He can be forgiven for his methods."

"So what do *you* plan to do?"

"I plan to use the tools at my disposal."

Kinoshita frowned. "Your weapons?"

"God gave you a brain," said Nighthawk irritably. "You offend Him when you refuse to use it."

"Why don't you just tell me what tools you're going to use and stop insulting me?"

Nighthawk stared calmly at him. "I'm going to use you and Melisande, of course."

"How?"

"She'll enter a bar or a restaurant and sit down alone. A few minutes later you and I will come in and sit elsewhere. After we've had a drink or two, we'll start discussing Ibn ben Khalid, and we'll make sure we're over-heard. I'll praise him to the skies, you'll argue that he's the worst kind of slime—and Melisande will read the emotional reactions. When she finds one that's strong enough, we'll assume he's working for Ibn ben Khalid and I'll follow up on it."

"If he doesn't kill me first," added Kinoshita ruefully.

Nighthawk shrugged. "You want to come along. That's the chance you take when you play for high stakes."

"I'm *not* playing for them," Kinoshita reminded him.

"Of course you are," said Nighthawk. He leaned forward on his seat and stared intently at the smaller man. "Do you really think I haven't figured out that you're here to keep an eye on me for Dinnisen, and that you're to report to him the second it looks like I might wander off the reservation?"

"There no sense denying it," said Kinoshita. "Sure I'm being paid to keep tabs on you—but I just look on it as found money. I can't stop you from doing anything you want to do. Hell, I wouldn't if I could. Like I told you, I'm a fan."

"I know that," said Nighthawk. "But you'd better understand that there'll come a day when you'll have to choose between me and your em-ployer."

"Easy choice. Dinnisen can't kill me; you can." Suddenly Kinoshita grinned. "You see? I *do* have an orderly mind."

"In the meantime," continued Nighthawk, ignoring his companion's attempt at humor, "I'll dictate your reports back to Deluros VIII."

Suddenly Melisande spoke up. "You're *good,* Widowmaker!" she said admiringly. "You don't need me. Hell, you don't need anyone!"

"I'm flattered that you think so, but I know what I need. My job is to kill Ibn ben Khalid. Let's suppose, just for the sake of argument, that he has a million followers; that's just a tiny drop in the bucket when you con-sider that there are almost two trillion Men abroad in the galaxy. But it means the odds are a million to one against me. If you can lower the odds, then I'll use you."

Melisande broke in. "So where are we going?"

"I'm not sure yet. Deeper into the Frontier."

"Any world in particular?"

Nighthawk shook his head. "I don't suppose it makes much differ-ence—except that I don't want to set down on any world where my prede-cessor landed."

"Why not?"

"Just in case he wasn't as efficient as I am."

"I don't follow you."

"He may have left some enemies alive. I won't know who they are, but some of them might recognize me. That's a suicidal situation, and if the Widowmaker was suicidal, he would have taken his life when he contracted eplasia rather than freezing himself on the slight chance that someone would effect a cure."

"You have eplasia?" she asked, backing away.

"Do I look like I have eplasia?" he asked.

"Your flesh says no, your emotions say yes."

"That's because my flesh doesn't know it yet," replied Nighthawk. "It's in the very early stages. You won't be able to notice it for another year or two—and by that time I'll be dead or cured."

"You should have told me before I agreed to come with you," said Melisande.

"It's like cancer used to be—deadly, but not contagious. You may contract it someday, but you won't catch it from me."

She stared at him for a moment, then relaxed. "Okay, you're telling the truth." She paused. "As you know it, anyway."

There was a high-pitched beeping sound.

"What was that?" she asked, as Nighthawk got to his feet and walked to the galley.

"Time for another shot of whiskey," he said, pulling out a bottle and taking a swallow.

She frowned. "You have to remind yourself to drink?"

"As a matter of fact, yes," answered Nighthawk.

"I don't understand."

"I woke up a month ago in a body that had never had a drink of alcohol. I work in a profession where a lot of information gets traded in taverns. The first few times I took a drink I was giddy and uncoordinated for an hour afterward. I'm trying to get my system used to it, so a few shots of whiskey won't affect my judgment or my reflexes."

"You're a very careful man."

"The graveyards are full of careless ones."

"Someone ought to collect your little homilies and put them in a book," she said with a smile.

"Are you volunteering?"

"Not me. My talents lie in other directions." Suddenly she looked around. "Where do I sleep?"

"We'll probably be two or three more days before we touch down," said Nighthawk. "How about a Deep-Sleep machine?"

She shook her head vigorously. "I don't trust them."

"I can vouch for at least one of them working for over a century."

"Not interested."

"All right," replied Nighthawk. "There are two cabins. You can have mine, and either Ito or I will sleep out here in the control room."

"Thank you," said Melisande. "Where is it?"

"You've already been to the head. Mine is the door just past it on the left."

"Just making sure. I wouldn't want to open it and find myself bumping into the nuclear pile."

She walked to the door, waited for it to melt before her, and walked into the cabin while the door quickly reconstituted itself behind her.

"You know," said Nighthawk, sitting down and ordering his chair to fold around him, "I could use some sleep myself."

He closed his eyes, and was soon breathing regularly.

I don't know, thought Kinoshita, looking at the Widowmaker with concerned eyes. *This guy is obsessed with the first clone. He seems stable enough, but I wonder . . .*

Suddenly he was aware of Melisande, standing in the doorway to her cabin.

"I read your concern," she said softly.

"It's a legitimate one," answered Kinoshita.

"Then let me address it: Jefferson Nighthawk is as normal and well adjusted as any man I've met."

She turned and went back into her room.

That's a pretty comforting statement, thought Kinoshita. *Until I remember just what kind of men you've been meeting . . .*

Chapter 6

The Blue Dragon wasn't a typical Frontier bar. For one thing, it was run by its namesake. For another, it catered to Men and aliens in almost equal percentages. For a third, it offered no sexual services. For a fourth, it didn't have any gaming tables.

It was also one of the few leads provided by Cassius Hill on the possible whereabouts of Ibn ben Khalid.

It was that first item, though, that made its reputation. The owner was a blue-skinned alien, covered with octagonal scales, with a face almost as elongated as a Shetland pony's. He stood erect and had opposable thumbs. He also possessed vestigial wings from an earlier point in his race's evolution when his progenitors either flew or, more likely, rode high upon the thermals.

His chest was angular and oddly shaped, as if once, a few thousand generations ago, his wings were much stronger and were manipulated by a coil of muscles that was clearly visible around his rib cage. He had a short, flat tail, one that in eons past had functioned as a rudder.

His eyes were the palest blue, and his teeth were a rich violet. He had two sets of nostrils, separated by a couple of inches, on each side of his long face. There were no ears, just pulsating slits on the side of his head.

He wasn't the only member of his race, but he was, so far as anyone knew, the only member that had migrated to a human-occupied planet in the Inner Frontier. Whenever anyone asked the name of his race, or the name or location of his home planet, he answered them promptly and truthfully—in his native language, which was an assortment of guttural clicks, grunts, and whistles.

He called himself Blue Eyes, and pretty soon so did everyone else.

"Good evening, good evening," he crooned as Nighthawk and Kinoshita entered his bar on Sylene IV, which circled a dull yellow sun, dragging two moons with it. "I don't think I've seen you here before."

"Probably we all look alike to you," answered Nighthawk wryly, looking around until he spotted Melisande nursing a drink at a table in the darkest corner of the place.

Blue Eyes threw back his head and hooted.

"Is that a laugh?" asked Nighthawk.

"You think only Men have a sense of humor?" shot back Blue Eyes. "Where are you two from and where are you heading, and how long can I entice you into staying on Sylene?"

"Don't tell me—you own the hotel, too."

"Okay, I won't tell you."

Nighthawk stared at Blue Eyes for a moment. "Never saw an alien like you before."

"Never will again, either," said Blue Eyes. "But let's keep in mind that on this world, you're as much an alien as I am."

"You speak the language very well," continued Nighthawk. "No accent, and no formality—your slang sounds very natural."

"Languages are easy for dragons," said Blue Eyes. "Giving up virgins—now *that* was hard." He threw back his head and hooted again.

"As long as you feel compelled to entertain us, the least I can do is buy you a drink."

"I never drink with the customers, but I'll be happy to sit with you for a while." He turned to the bar. "Nicholas, bring me my chair."

A young man, underweight and carelessly dressed, immediately stood up, walked over to a strangely configured chair, and carried it over to the empty table where Blue Eyes was waiting.

"Thank you," said the dragon. "Gentlemen, this is Nicholas Jory. He has spent the last three years recording everything I say in my native tongue and trying to create a dictionary of my language."

"How far along are you?" asked Kinoshita.

"About thirty words," said Nicholas. "Maybe thirty-two."

"In three years?"

"That's more progress than is made on a lot of alien tongues in the same period of time," replied Nicholas. He frowned thoughtfully, then continued. "The biggest problem is determining whether the alien is intelligent. A lot of nonsentient animals communicate by vocalizing."

"How long did it take you to learn Terran?" Kinoshita asked Blue Eyes.

"About a week." The dragon smiled—as much as he *could* smile, anyway. His jaws parted and his eyes narrowed. "It's a knack."

"The government could use you in the Alien Affairs section," remarked Nighthawk.

"The Oligarchy doesn't hire nonhumans, or hadn't you noticed?" said Blue Eyes.

"They used to," said Nighthawk.

"Not since the Domarian Rebellion," answered the dragon, as Kinoshita put his heel atop Nighthawk's toe and leaned on it.

All right, it happened in the past hundred years and I'm supposed to know about it. Now leave my toes alone.

"*I* used to work for them," volunteered Nicholas. He grimaced. "Until we had a slight disagreement about taxes."

"Oh?"

Suddenly Nicholas grinned. "They said taxes were mandatory, and I said they were voluntary. So I came out to the Frontier where there aren't any taxes at all."

"So let's all sit down and get to know one another," said Blue Eyes, finally lowering his bulk onto the chair Nicholas had brought. He signaled to the bartender, who brought over a bottle and three glasses.

"Sounds good to me," said Nighthawk, as he and Kinoshita sat down across from him.

"Try to get him mad," said Nicholas, picking up a chair from a nearby table and carrying it over.

"Why?" asked Nighthawk, curious.

"Because when he gets mad, he curses in his native language. The rest of the time he speaks Terran, just to annoy me."

"Be careful, my friend," said the dragon. "If you annoy me enough, I'll start speaking in dead tongues like English or Swahili and *really* drive you crazy."

"Can you really speak dead human languages?" asked Nighthawk.

"Of course," answered Blue Eyes. "Languages are easy. Giving up drugs is hard."

Nighthawk saw what he hoped was a small opening, and plunged in. "How about Arabic?"

"Arabic's a very broad word, Mr. . . . ah . . . you know, I never did catch your name."

"Nighthawk. Jefferson Nighthawk. And this is Ito Kinoshita."

"You know, I used to hear stories of a Jefferson Nighthawk," said the dragon. "He had quite a reputation."

"I've heard 'em too. But *that* Nighthawk lived more than a century ago."

"So they say," replied Blue Eyes. "Where were we?"

"We were talking about Arabic."

"And I was about to explain that what we know as Arabic probably covers a couple of hundred dialects. To say that two people are similar because they both speak Arabic is like saying that the Raphinites and the Yorbans are the same simply because they both breathe chlorine."

"Point noted."

"Still, I'm curious to know why you were interested in Arabic."

"Simple enough," said Nighthawk, finally pouring himself a glass of blue-tinted whiskey and taking a swallow. "Ibn ben Khalid is an Arabic name. If he has to issue orders and he's not sure that his communication system is secure, he can do it in an Arab dialect, and probably no one monitoring him would have any idea what he's saying."

"An intriguing thought," admitted Blue Eyes. "But I suspect Ibn ben Khalid is as ignorant of dead languages—including that one—as you yourself are."

"Still, it's an interesting idea," interjected Nicholas. "Maybe I'll suggest it to him the next time I see him."

Nighthawk wanted to ask, *Do you see him often?*, but fought back the urge.

"Lots of death tonight," remarked Blue Eyes. "Dead languages, dead gunfighters."

"Lot of death on the Frontier," responded Nighthawk.

"Maybe a little less than there used to be."

"Why should you think so?" asked Nighthawk.

"You brought up the reason—Ibn ben Khalid."

Speak up now, Ito, or you're going to find out what getting your toes ground under someone's heel really feels like.

"I hear he's nothing more than a kidnapper," said Kinoshita, as if he had somehow heard Nighthawk's thoughts.

"Actually, he's a *lot* more than a kidnapper," answered Blue Eyes. "I assume you're referring to Cassius Hill's daughter."

"They say he's holding her for ransom," continued Kinoshita. "That sure sounds like a common kidnapper to me."

"There's nothing common about him," said the dragon.

"I say he's a kidnapper and a murderer!" shouted Kinoshita, wondering just how far he could go before someone simply pulled a weapon and shot him.

"True," said Nighthawk. "But those aren't necessarily bad things to be when you're fighting for a just cause."

"When is murder ever good?" demanded Kinoshita.

"When your enemy is even worse," answered Nighthawk. "Maybe it's not pretty, but you do what you have to do."

"Let's not lose our tempers," said the dragon. "Ibn ben Khalid has never wronged anyone at this table."

"Damned right," chimed in Nighthawk. "And if he was here right now, I'd tell him so." *Damn! I wish I could look at some other faces in here. Are we loud enough, Melisande? Are they reacting?*

"In fact," added Blue Eyes, "I can tell you all a story about Ibn ben Khalid to prove my point."

"Spare us another of your meandering stories," said Nicholas.

"Yeah," added Kinoshita. "I don't need to hear you apologize for him."

"As you wish," said the dragon with a shrug that made every scale on his body shimmer.

Thanks a lot, pal. Don't overplay your goddamned role, okay? We need all the information we can get.

"So, Mr. Nighthawk, where do you come from and what do you do?"

"I come from out there," answered Nighthawk, waving his hand carelessly in a motion that encompassed roughly half the galaxy. "And I'm a troubleshooter."

"Trouble walks in and you shoot it?" asked Blue Eyes with another reptilian grin.

"That's perhaps a bit too literal," said Nighthawk. "I fix problems."

"What kind of problems?"

"What kind have you got?"

Blue Eyes sighed deeply. "It's been a long time since I've been with a lady dragon."

Nighthawk chuckled. "That kind isn't exactly in my line."

"I had a feeling it wasn't," replied Blue Eyes ruefully. He turned to Nicholas, who was pouring himself another drink. "Hey, go easy on that stuff. You've had half a bottle already."

Nicholas got up and staggered off without a word. Then, just in case his indignation had been missed or misinterpreted, he walked back, picked up his chair, tried to remember where he'd gotten it from, suddenly looked very confused, and sat down on it again.

"Did you have a nice trip?" asked Blue Eyes.

"Not bad, not bad," replied Nicholas. Suddenly he leaned forward until his head was on the table, and began snoring.

"I guess that's the end of today's language lesson," said Blue Eyes. Suddenly he uttered a totally incomprehensible sentence in his native tongue. "Just so you can tell him what he missed." He turned to Kinoshita. "I haven't yet asked you what *you* do, Mr. Kinoshita?"

Kinoshita jerked a thumb in Nighthawk's direction. "I'm with him," he said. "Until he decides to get us both killed by Ibn ben Khalid."

"I'm not going up against him," said Nighthawk. "Hell, I'm on his side."

"That's what I meant," said Kinoshita. "You can't trust a killer."

"I'd watch what I said about him if I were you," said Nighthawk ominously.

"Gentlemen, gentlemen," said Blue Eyes, rising to his feet. "I will not permit any altercations in this establishment."

Kinoshita made a vague gesture with his hand which could have meant anything from defiance to acquiescence, then also stood up.

"Okay, I know when I'm not wanted. I'm out of here." He turned and started walking to the door.

"Has he got a place to sleep?" asked Blue Eyes.

"That's not your problem," replied Nighthawk.

"You're absolutely right." He sat down again, staring at Nighthawk through his pale blue eyes. "I like you, Mr. Nighthawk. Tell me some more about yourself."

"There's not much to tell."

"Oh, I think there is. There's something about the way you carry yourself, something about the way you choose your words . . . something *dangerous*. Forgive an indelicate question, but how many men have you killed?"

"Forgive an indelicate answer, but go fuck yourself."

"I can, you know," answered Blue Eyes. "That's why I haven't spent my savings on a lady dragon."

"I don't want to destroy your self-confidence, but whether you can actually fuck yourself or not is a matter of complete indifference to me."

The dragon hooted his laughter again. He made a brief signal with his hand, and a moment later the bartender brought over a spherical bottle and a tall, thin glass. Blue Eyes opened the bottle, filled the glass halfway, then reached for the whiskey and filled it to the top. It began smoking and sizzling.

"I thought you didn't drink with the customers," noted Nighthawk.

"You were a customer when I said that. Now you're a friend."

"What *is* that stuff?"

"I suppose it really needs a name, doesn't it?" said Blue Eyes thoughtfully. "I first encountered it in the Deneb system. A mixture of Bilotei rum—it isn't really rum at all, but that's what they call it—and pure Sirian whiskey. Wonderful stuff." He took a sip. As he did so his eyes rolled back until only the whites showed, but Nighthawk couldn't tell if that was a reaction to the concoction or an inadvertent physical reaction caused by swallowing. "I think we'll name it after you, Mr. Nighthawk."

"A Nighthawk?"

"A Widowmaker."

"The Widowmaker died a century ago."

"All the more reason to find ways to keep his memory alive." He took another sip. "Though of course there are more meaningful ways."

"Oh?"

"That is, if your skills lie in the same direction."

"It's possible."

"How long will you be on Sylene, Mr. Nighthawk?"

Nighthawk shrugged. "How long do you want me to be here?"

"Another day, perhaps two, while I check you out."

"You won't be able to."

"Why not, pray tell?"

"I took this name less than a year ago. At the same time, I had laser surgery on my retinas and I had fingerprint grafts. I'm not on file anywhere, not with the Oligarchy, not with anyone else."

"A man who's not on file with the Oligarchy?" repeated the dragon. He threw back his head and hooted.

"What's so funny?"

He hooted once more, then finally managed to control himself. "What could possibly say more about your skills than that?"

Chapter 7

"Well?" demanded Nighthawk.

They were back on the ship, sipping coffee made from hybrid beans that had been imported from the green slopes of Peponi's mountains.

"Most of them didn't react at all," answered Melisande. "They couldn't care less about Ibn ben Khalid."

"Who *did* care?"

"The one you call Nicholas Jory," she replied. "Every time Ito would slander Khalid, it was all he could do to keep from showing his rage."

"Is there any way you can tell if he simply admires Khalid or if he knows something more, like where he is or how to reach him?"

She shook her head. "No, he was drinking too heavily. It was just rage."

"What else *could* it have been?" asked Kinoshita curiously.

"Fear. Worry. Concern. Either at the thought of you going after Khalid—"

"That's silly. He's got an army to protect him."

"—or the mention of Cassandra Hill, who could conceivably be stolen back from him."

"Ah," acknowledged Kinoshita, nodding. "What about Blue Eyes?"

"I can't read aliens well enough to tell you with any degree of certainty."

"He seemed just like us beneath the admittedly hideous surface."

"Absolutely not!" she responded. "Never make that assumption. What you saw was protective coloration. He has very little more in common with you than an insect does." She turned to Nighthawk. "So what is your next step?"

"I wait for Blue Eyes to check me out while I'm doing the same to him, and when he finds out that what I've told him is true—he can't find me in any computer in the Oligarchy—then I hope he'll try to recruit me."

"Oh, there's no question he wants to recruit you," agreed Kinoshita. "But for what? I think rum-running is at least as likely as serving in Ibn ben Khalid's army, such as it is."

"Probably you're right," said Nighthawk. "That's why we're not about to put all our eggs in one basket." He turned to Melisande. "I passed the local jail on the way back to the ship. There can't be ten cells there, and I'm sure they're not all occupied. Have the ship's computer print you up some credentials saying that you're with some charitable organization. Then buy some desserts at a local bakery, take 'em over to the jail, and explain that they're for the prisoners. The guards will want to harass you—until you give 'em a couple of cakes or pies, that is. Then they'll let you through."

"But my credentials are no good. Anyone can print them up."

"Right. And the guards will check anyone who wants something—but why should they check on someone who's giving things away?"

"And if I'm jailed?"

"Kinoshita will be right outside. If you're not out in an hour, he'll pay your bail or pay off any guards who need it in order to get you released."

"All right," said Melisande. "Once I'm in, what do I do?"

"Simple. Give a present to each prisoner, and mention Ibn ben Khalid and Cassandra Hill to each of them. Then remember if anyone reacts."

"Why?"

"Do *you* know where they are?"

"No, of course not."

"Well, neither do I. But if you get the kind of reaction from one of the prisoners that convinces you *he* knows, we'll spring him and take him with us."

"I thought *I* was what you needed."

"What I need is protection and insurance, and I plan to get all I can of both."

"What will you be doing in the meantime?"

"Sleeping," answered Nighthawk.

"Sleeping?" she repeated, half-amused and half-outraged.

"Who knows when I'll get another chance? In this business, you grab it when you can. The computer can put together Blue Eyes' profile for me while I'm asleep."

"If Melisande finds what you're looking for, do you want me to bail him out?" asked Kinoshita.

Nighthawk shook his head. "No, that'll be my decision."

"Why? Look at the time I could save you."

"Because if we guess wrong and he winds up trying to shoot us or warn Ibn ben Khalid, I'd hate to have to kill you for getting us into such a jam."

"Right," said Kinoshita promptly. "Your call."

"I'm glad we see eye to eye on things," said Nighthawk dryly.

Chapter 8

As Nighthawk walked back to The Blue Dragon, he got the distinct impression that he was being followed. He knew enough not to turn and look directly, but he could see swift, subtle reflections of motion in the store windows and on the metal doors of vehicles that he passed.

If someone wanted to kill him, they would have fired their weapons already, so he assumed that his shadow either wanted to talk with him or find out where he was going. And since there wasn't much doubt where he was going—it was the only place he'd gone the night before when he'd left the ship, and it was nighttime again—he decided that his tail wanted to talk.

The only question remaining was: make it easy, or make it hard? If they were recruiting a killer, he'd be well advised to duck into an alley—or whatever passed for alleys in this crazy-quilt checkerboard of human and alien streets—and lie in wait for his tracker, disarm him, possibly rough him up a little, and then find out who sent him. It would be an impressive display.

But he was pretty sure Ibn ben Khalid had more killers than he knew what to do with. This was juvenile thinking, the kind the younger Widowmaker clone was prey to.

No, the more he thought about it—and he thought very rapidly, given the circumstances—the more he was convinced that someone simply wanted to talk to him. Now, *why* someone should want to talk to Jefferson Nighthawk—for the Widowmaker had been dead a century, and no one here knew otherwise—was a mystery to him, but one he decided to solve.

He came to an alien restaurant that catered to Canphorites and Lodinites, looked in the window until he saw another flash of motion reflected in it, and then entered. The headwaiter, a furry orange marsupial of the Kragan race, looked terribly distressed when confronted by a Man, but managed to control itself long enough to lead Nighthawk to a table.

"We are pleased to serve you," it said into a T-pack that translated its voice into cold, unemotional Terran words and tones, "but I must advise you that you will be unable to metabolize most of the items on our menu."

"I'm game if you are," responded Nighthawk.

The Kragan listened to the translated words, then uttered a squawk loud enough to attract attention from the nearby tables—those few that weren't already staring at Nighthawk with hostility.

"I am not a game meat!" said the little marsupial. "You cannot eat me! We cannot eat each other!"

"Bad translation," said Nighthawk. "You really should learn to speak Terran."

"I suppose it never occurred to you to speak Kragan."

"No, it never did. I don't want your money; you want mine. That means you must make the accommodation."

The Kragan stared at him for a long moment. "You do not wish to eat me?"

"It will cheer you to no end to know that I find the thought totally repugnant."

"Good," said the Kragan. "What will you order?"

"Just water for the moment. I'll be joined very shortly, and then you can explain your menu to us."

"I see no other human," remarked the Kragan.

"I didn't say it was a human."

"Then what is it, so I can be alert for it when it enters?"

"That's not your concern," replied Nighthawk. "Whatever it is, it will find me."

"True," agreed the Kragan. "If you have an instinct for protective coloration, it is not functioning."

"Thank you for that observation. Now please get my water and then leave me alone."

"There is one more thing I must tell you," said the Kragan. "We do not accept Oligarchy credits."

Nighthawk pulled out a handful of gold Maria Theresa dollars and laid them on the table.

"Good enough?" he asked.

The Kragan looked, blinked, wrinkled its nostrils—which was as close as it could come to a satisfied smile—and left to get Nighthawk his glass of water. When it came back, it placed the water down on the table and reached for the dollars.

Nighthawk slapped its furry hand.

"Not until after I've ordered and eaten," he said.

"How do I know you won't pick up all the dollars and walk out with them?" asked the Kragan in what Nighthawk was sure were petulant tones prior to the T-pack's translating them into a dull monotone.

"How do I know you won't poison me?" he shot back.

The Kragan stared at him for a long moment, as if this was a fascinating new idea that bore serious consideration, and then waddled off.

Nighthawk sipped his water and looked around. There were seventeen Canphorites, eight Lodinites, a couple of Kragans, all trying very hard to pretend there wasn't a Man in their midst. One small Lodinite child, perhaps four years old and only two-thirds grown, stared at him openly, as if he'd never seen a Man before. He had, of course, but Nighthawk thought it was a fair bet that he'd never seen one inside an alien restaurant.

Finally he looked up at the walls. His first impression was that they were covered with works of non-representational art—but as he studied them more carefully, he saw certain themes and color schemes reappearing time and again, and decided they were probably *very* representational to the beings that frequented this restaurant.

Suddenly a tall alien—sleek, red, humanoid, almost gleaming in the dull light of the restaurant—entered and walked directly to Nighthawk's table.

"May I join you?" it asked in harsh, grating syllables.

Nighthawk nodded. "I assume you got tired of waiting for me to come out."

It was the alien's turn to nod. Its ears, though no larger than a man's, flopped wildly with the motion, reminding Nighthawk of nothing more than the recreations he had seen of African elephants.

"Why are you here?" asked the alien. "You cannot consume this food without becoming ill."

"I thought you'd rather speak to me here than at The Blue Dragon. But if I'm wrong, we can go there right now." He half rose from his chair.

"You are not wrong."

Nighthawk settled back down. "Have you got a name?"

"Everyone has a name, Jefferson Nighthawk."

"Would you care to tell me what it is?"

"In due time."

"All right, then—at least tell me what race you are?"

"It is I who shall ask the questions," said the alien.

"That's a matter of some debate," replied Nighthawk calmly. "It is I who has his gun trained on your belly beneath this lovely table."

The alien tensed, but chose not to verify the statement by looking.

"You cannot pronounce my name, but another Man I worked with many years ago called me Friday, and that is the name I use when dealing with Men. I am a member of the Projasti people of Czhimerich, which Men call Marius II."

"And I'm Jefferson Nighthawk, as you already seem to know. Now state your business, Friday."

"You are the Widowmaker," said Friday. "You are the most remarkable of all Men, for your appearance has not changed in more than one hundred Standard years."

"You saw me over a century ago?"

Friday nodded his head, setting his ears to flapping again. "My race is very long-lived. I saw you kill seven men without aid of any kind on—"

"—Dimitri IV," concluded Nighthawk.

"Then it *is* you."

"In a manner of speaking. But my question remains: why have you sought me out?"

"Where the Widowmaker goes, Men die. And now, after being gone for a century, you are back, and Men will die again." Friday paused. "For almost a century I have worked in the mines across the Inner Frontier, opening them when they were discovered, sealing them when they were played out. My specialty is explosives, and I tell you that there is none who knows them better. But one of the problems with a life span as long as the Projastis' is that eventually one becomes bored, even in a field where one has no equal." It paused and stared into Nighthawk's eyes. "I am tired of using my explosives on inanimate mines, Widowmaker. I wish to work with you."

"You don't even know who or what I'm up against."

"It makes no difference to me."

"What if I've been commissioned to blow up Marius II?" asked Nighthawk.

"*Have* you been?"

"No."

"All other worlds are equally unimportant to me."

"You just want to play with your explosives, right?" said Nighthawk.

"I want to kill *Men*."

"Why should I help you?"

"Why not? You will kill them for money and I will kill them for pleasure, and in the end, what difference will it make which of us does the killing?"

"How do I know you won't kill me, too?"

"*Can* you be killed?"

"Not by you."

"There you have it."

"How much do you propose to charge me for your services?"

"Nothing," responded Friday. "I will save you from failure and you will save me from boredom. It will be a fair trade."

Nighthawk stared at him for a long moment, waiting for a gut instinct, pro or con, to kick in. Finally it did.

"Okay," he said at last. "You're working for me now."

"When do we leave?"

"A day or two. You know which ship is mine?"

"I followed you from it."

"Right. Okay, then . . . vanish for a day and then come to the ship."

"I will go there right now."

"Do what I say. You might terrify one of the occupants, and the other might shoot you."

"All right, then: one day from this moment," agreed Friday.

"Aren't you curious to know who's on the other side?"

"I already know," said Friday.

"Oh?"

"You make war with Ibn ben Khalid."

"Why should you think so?"

"Against who else would the Widowmaker need my expertise?" answered Friday. "Have you been commissioned to kill him, or merely to rescue the human girl?"

"Both. You know where I can find them?"

"I have no idea. I did not expect to be at war with him until I recognized you." Friday paused. "How very exciting this is! Not only has the Widowmaker returned, but I am working for him, and together we shall kill millions of Men!"

"Try not to get *too* excited about wiping out my race."

"I will try," promised Friday with a dubious expression on his alien face.

Chapter 9

Blue Eyes looked up from his pocket computer as Nighthawk entered The Blue Dragon.

"Welcome back, my friend," he said. He deactivated the computer. "Numbers," he said. "I hate numbers."

"You don't look like you're losing money."

"I wasn't cut out to be a business owner."

"Then why don't you stop pretending to be one?"

Blue Eyes stared at Nighthawk for a long moment, then threw back his head, rolled his eyes, and hooted.

"You're *good,* Widowmaker! How long did it take you to find out?"

"Less than a day."

"That's all? And I've managed to keep it a secret for almost ten years."

"Maybe nobody else cared," suggested Nighthawk.

"While you were checking me out, I was doing the same to you."

"And?"

"You don't exist."

"I seem to remember explaining that to you."

"Let me finish," said Blue Eyes. "You don't exist—but you did once."

"I told you . . ."

"I know what you told me. But the Master Computer on Deluros VIII says you have the same fingerprints, voiceprint, and retinagram as the original Widowmaker. I'll wager that if you let me draw some blood or take a skin scraping, you've got the same DNA, too."

"Coincidence," said Nighthawk with a shrug.

"If you thought I'd believe that, you'd also think I was too stupid and gullible to work with."

"The Widowmaker was born more than a century and a half ago," said Nighthawk. "Do I look that old to you?"

"You look maybe two months old," said the dragon with as much of a grin as his facial structure allowed. "I pulled some strings and found out that the original Widowmaker has been frozen for more than a hundred years. He's still there." He stared at Nighthawk. "I've never seen a clone before. They did a fine job, Widowmaker."

"Better than the last one," agreed Nighthawk.

"They've cloned you more than once?" asked Blue Eyes, surprised.

"One other time."

"And that clone is . . . ?"

"Dead."

"Good. I don't think I'd feel comfortable in a galaxy with hundreds of Widowmakers on the loose."

"It's not going to happen. Cloning a human being is a felony on every world in the Oligarchy." Nighthawk walked over to the bar, reached down behind it, and brought up a bottle of Cygnian cognac. He opened it and took a swallow.

"Careful with that stuff!" cautioned Blue Eyes. "It costs me two hundred New Bombay rupees a bottle."

"It doesn't cost *you* a thing," replied Nighthawk. "Now that you know who I am, I think it's time you told me who pays the two hundred rupees, and why you're fronting for him."

"Haven't you guessed?"

"I never guess. *I* pulled some strings too, and my creators have a lot of strings to pull. It's Ibn ben Khalid."

"Right the first time," said Blue Eyes. "All the profits go into maintaining his organization."

"How many bars does he own across the Frontier?"

"Bars, restaurants, assay offices, hotels, boardinghouses—maybe three hundred, maybe a little more."

"Does he travel under his own name?"

"Depends on his mood."

"Does he ever show up here?"

"Once every few years."

Suddenly the dragon was staring into the cold muzzle of a sonic pistol.

"Have you told him I'm after him?"

Blue Eyes reached out and gently pushed the pistol aside. "If I had, you couldn't have made it from your ship to The Blue Dragon without being attacked."

"I was followed."

"Not by anyone connected to Ibn ben Khalid," said Blue Eyes. "And that's a fact."

"All right," said Nighthawk. "You work for him. *Why* haven't you warned him?"

"Look at me and tell me what you see."

"A dragon who's closer to getting blown away than he knows."

"The operative word, my friend, is 'dragon.' Not Man. What do *I* care if Ibn ben Khalid overthrows some human government and starts giving orders himself? What do I care if he doesn't? None of it affects me."

"I begin to appreciate your position," said Nighthawk. "The only thing that affects you is his death. Then The Blue Dragon gets a new owner, right?"

"Where does it say that greed must be confined to the race of Man?"

Nighthawk took another swallow of the cognac. "As long as it's not yours yet . . . " He closed the bottle and put it back behind the bar. "Are there likely to be any other claimants to The Blue Dragon and the hotel?"

"It depends on the circumstances of Ibn ben Khalid's death," replied Blue Eyes. "And how much of his organization remains."

"I couldn't care less about his organization. I just plan to do my job and get the hell out."

"Then yes, there will be claimants. Why?"

"I just want you to know that as long as you're willing to help me, I'll back up your claim." He paused. "I can be a pretty useful ally to have on your side."

"That's very thoughtful of you," said Blue Eyes. "And what if I decide at some point not to help you after all?"

"Then I'll mourn at your funeral."

"So much for a relationship based on mutual trust," said the dragon.

"Would you rather I lied to you?"

"I'd rather you didn't begin our partnership with a threat."

"First, I didn't *begin* with a threat; I ended with one. And second, I don't have any partners. You're working *for* me, not *with* me."

"I don't know if I'm all that pleased with this arrangement."

"You don't have to be. You'll be pleased when it's over and you can get obscenely rich from The Blue Dragon."

"First let's see if I live long enough, and if no one tries to take over the business while I'm gone," muttered the dragon. "You know, a million to two isn't a lot better odds than a million to one."

"Actually, it's a million to five."

"Well, that's a start. How many more are you going to recruit before you go after him?"

"None."

Blue Eyes possessed four separate and distinct stomachs. At that instant, he was sure all four were coming down with ulcers.

Chapter 10

"Did you find anyone?" asked Nighthawk, when he, Melisande, and Kinoshita were all together on the ship again.

"I found four men who believe in his cause, but no one who knows how to find him," answered Melisande. "Do you want to interview them further?"

"No. There are millions of men and women who came to the Frontier because they hate the Oligarchy. Most of them will believe in Ibn ben Khalid's cause. What I need is someone who knows where he is." He paused. "It's possible that I've got a couple. We'll have to find out."

"Who?" asked Kinoshita.

"The dragon and that linguist—what's his name?—Nicholas Jory. Blue Eyes admits that Khalid owns the bar and hotel, and Jory actually said that he'd seen him before."

"If that's the case, why did we waste our time at the jail?" demanded Kinoshita.

"Because I believe in being thorough. Since Melisande can't tell us for sure if the dragon's lying or not, we can never take his word for anything. And it's more than possible Jory was lying, building himself up. Why should a dead-broke drunken linguist have access to the most powerful revolutionary on the Frontier?"

"Now I'm confused again," said Kinoshita. "You just said you might have a couple of people who know how to find Ibn ben Khalid. Now you've all but eliminated them. So do they know how or not?"

"I plan to find out before we leave."

"Are you going to have Melisande check Jory out?"

"If it's convenient. Given that she seems to have trouble reading drunks, it probably won't be."

"Then how—?"

"There are ways," said Nighthawk so coldly that Kinoshita decided he didn't want to know what the ways were.

"So when do we plan to leave?"

"Tomorrow. I've recruited a couple of aliens to our team: Blue Eyes, and one you haven't met yet called Friday. They'll both show up about an hour before we take off."

"Do you trust them?" asked Kinoshita.

"I don't even trust *you*," responded Nighthawk.

Kinoshita looked offended, but chose not to argue, and a few minutes later Nighthawk got to his feet.

"Wait here," he said. "I've got to go out."

"We're not leaving for another day," protested Kinoshita. "Why should we have to stay in the ship until then?"

"So I'll know where to find you."

"You're getting awfully dictatorial."

"I'll let you know when this becomes a democracy," replied Nighthawk. "Either you take orders from me, or you walk. There's no third way." He put his hands on his hips. "Well?"

"You know the answer," said Kinoshita. "I'm staying. But you don't have to be such a goddamned dictator. You could ask instead of ordering."

"Waste of time."

"Why?"

"You might say no, and then I'd just have to order you."

Kinoshita smiled in spite of himself. "You've got a unique way of looking at things."

Nighthawk left the ship without returning his smile. It was dark, and there was a thick ground fog. He walked to within a block of The Blue Dragon, then sat down in the recessed entryway to a boardinghouse, his back propped against the wall, and waited.

Men and women came and went, aliens passed within feet of him without ever knowing he was there, and still he sat, absolutely motionless. If anyone *had* seen him, they would have thought he was asleep. They'd have been wrong. He was waiting for his quarry as patiently and silently as a jungle beast waits for *its* prey—and eventually his patience was rewarded.

He got to his feet and stepped out onto the pavement so quickly that the man he had been waiting for almost collided with him.

"I'm sorry!" said Nicholas, pivoting awkwardly and almost falling to the ground. "I didn't see you."

"That's all right," answered Nighthawk. "*I* saw *you*."

Suddenly the young man's eyes widened in recognition. "Nighthawk!" he exclaimed. "What are you doing here?"

"Waiting."

"For what? Or who?"

Nighthawk made no reply.

"For *me*?" said Nicholas at last. "Why?"

"We have to talk."

"About what?"

"Ibn ben Khalid."

"I don't know any more about him than you do," said Nicholas nervously.

"I've got a Balatai woman back on my ship," said Nighthawk. "She can tell me if you're lying."

"Bring her along. I've got nothing to hide."

"You said you would speak to Ibn ben Khalid next time you saw him," continued Nighthawk. "That implies you've seen him before."

"You misunderstood me!" protested Nicholas. "I meant that if I ever saw him, I'd speak to him."

Suddenly the cold muzzle of a sonic pistol was pressed against Nicholas' head.

"Let's try again," said Nighthawk.

"But I *told* you: I've never met him!"

"I know. But I don't believe you."

"You can't shoot me down in cold blood!" said Nicholas. "Blue Eyes told me all about you. You were a lot of things, but you were never a murderer!"

"I'm an officer of the law," said Nighthawk. "My credentials may be a century old, but they're still valid. And you're a tax evader."

"That's a goddamned misdemeanor!"

"But resisting arrest isn't."

"It'll be your word against—"

"Against what?"

Suddenly Nicholas froze. "All right. What do you want to know?"

"Where can I find him?"

"I don't know. He's stopped by The Blue Dragon twice in three years." Nicholas paused to regain his composure. "He and Blue Eyes go into the back room and come out a few minutes later. Then he has a drink and leaves. That's all I know!"

"Where does he come from?" asked Nighthawk. "Where does he go?"

"How the hell should I know?" shot back Nicholas. "He has to file a flight plan somewhere. Why don't you check the spaceport and leave me alone?"

"I already did. The spaceport doesn't have a record of Ibn ben Khalid landing here. He must have used another name. What was it?"

"I don't know!"

Nighthawk took the safety off the sonic pistol. "This will scramble your brains as if they were eggs over a campfire. It's not a death I'd wish on anyone." He paused. "I'm only going to ask once more: what name did he use?"

All the life seemed to go out of Nicholas. He slumped and seemed to sink within himself.

"I'm all out of answers," he said wearily. "I don't know what name he used. You might as well shoot and get it over with."

Nighthawk stared at him for a long moment, then put his pistol back in its holster.

"Go home."

"Soon," said Nicholas. "But first I'm going to The Blue Dragon for a drink."

"No. I mean, go *home*—back where you came from."

Nicholas frowned. "Are you ordering me off this planet?" he asked, puzzled.

Nighthawk shook his head. "No. But I'm taking the dragon with me tomorrow. You won't have anyone left to study."

"How long are you taking him for?"

"For as long as it takes to find Ibn ben Khalid."

"Finding him should be the easy part," observed Nicholas. "What comes next is harder." He paused, as if considering his options. "Still, you're the Widowmaker. You might actually pull it off. I think I'll wait until I hear you're dead before I leave the planet."

"I thought you wanted Blue Eyes, not me."

"If they can kill *you*, they'll have already killed *him*."

Nighthawk shrugged. "Do what you please."

"I'm free to go?"

"Yes. And tell Blue Eyes that I expect him to show up on time."

Nicholas scurried off into the fog.

Nighthawk walked around the area for another hour, not searching for anything in particular, but not without purpose. He looked at buildings, vehicles, Men, aliens, shadows, all with the uneasy feeling that something was wrong, that as careful as he'd been he had overlooked some tiny detail that could come back to haunt him. It was nothing he could put his finger on, but the feeling persisted, and he had learned in his previous incarnation never to ignore his instincts. So he walked, and searched, and walked and searched some more.

Finally he returned to the ship without having satisfied his doubts. He played every possible scenario over and over in his mind, but couldn't spot whatever it was that his subconscious felt he had missed.

Finally, after a couple of hours, he lay down on his bunk and drifted off to a troubled sleep.

Chapter 11

Friday ate insects. Preferably live ones.

Nighthawk, who in his prior life had spent a lot of time on the Inner Frontier with aliens, paid no attention. Kinoshita, who was sharing the control room with Nighthawk while the aliens shared his cabin, thought the habit was disgusting and said so. Blue Eyes found it amusing. Melisande took one quick peek at Friday's emotions, got a truer reading than she wanted or expected, and spent the rest of the voyage in her own cabin, trying not to read the emotions that were there for the perusing.

"Just how many of those things did you bring along?" asked Nighthawk as Friday withdrew a large, hairy, spiderlike insect from a pouch and started biting off the legs one by one.

"Enough," answered the alien.

"What do *they* eat while they're waiting to be eaten by you?" continued Nighthawk.

"Each other."

"Disgusting!" muttered Kinoshita for perhaps the tenth time.

Friday looked at him calmly. "You eat fish, which my race considers sacred."

"It's not the same thing at all," said Kinoshita. "At least everything I eat is dead before I eat it."

"Ah," said Friday. "I see now. It is moral to slaughter animals in a building constructed for that purpose, or to let a fish gasp for air for hours before it dies, as long as you yourself do not have to kill it."

"I've had about enough of you," muttered Kinoshita.

"Calm down," said Nighthawk.

"Damn it," complained Kinoshita. "Have you been watching and listening to him?"

"That's the way he's built. Try to treat him like an equal."

"Equals don't pull the legs off bugs and eat them!"

"This one does," said Friday, pulling another leg off the insect.

"What do we have him along for anyway?" persisted Kinoshita.

"He's our explosives expert."

"Do we need one?"

"I don't know," admitted Nighthawk. "But if we do, I don't want to have to go out searching for one."

Kinoshita stared at the impassive alien and fell silent. When Friday continued nibbling on the insect, he got up and left the galley.

"Touchy friend you've got there," said Blue Eyes, who had been an amused but silent observer of the little contretemps.

"He's not my friend."

"That's right—I forgot. You don't have any friends, do you?"

"None that I'm aware of," answered Nighthawk.

"Well, at least you've got a lady, which is more than the rest of us have."

"She's a part of the team, just like you."

Blue Eyes grinned. "You mean you don't rut in the muck and then stand guard while she lays her eggs?"

"Is that how blue dragons do it?"

"Probably not," answered Blue Eyes. "It's been so long, I can't remember exactly how we do it."

"Is he here for any reason other than to keep you amused?" asked Friday, biting through his insect's carapace with a sickening crunching noise.

"He's here to help me find Ibn ben Khalid."

"That's what *I'm* here for."

Nighthawk shook his head. "I'll need you after we find him." He turned back to Blue Eyes. "You'd better be right about Cellestra IV."

"I know he's been seen there a number of times," said Blue Eyes. "Maybe he's got a camp there, maybe he doesn't—but he sure passes through a lot."

"We'll be there in about five hours. Once we land, where do we go?"

Blue Eyes shrugged. "I've never been on Cellestra, remember? How would I know where someone like Ibn ben Khalid would be?"

"When he came to your world, what did he do?" asked Nighthawk.

"Took all the money out of my safe and left."

"He didn't get drunk, or stop by a drug den or a whorehouse or a bank?"

"Not to the best of my knowledge. He came in, ordered a drink, refused to pay for it, and after a couple of minutes he'd make me take him to my office and open the safe. Then he'd fill a bag with cash and walk out as bold as you please."

"Who saw him on Cellestra?" persisted Nighthawk.

"Beats the hell out of me," answered Blue Eyes. "Miners. Gamblers. Bounty hunters. Who knows? Not a lot of people announce their line of work when they come into my tavern for a drink." The dragon paused, then continued. "As for the governor, forget it—Cellestra doesn't *have* a governor. That's why there are so many bounty hunters there. *Some*one's got to enforce the law."

"What law?" asked Friday. "If there's no government, who made it?"

"A telling point," said Blue Eyes. "The minimal law as perceived by Men." He turned to Nighthawk. "I believe it comes from your holy book. Thou shalt not kill, thou shalt not steal. There's something about not coveting your friends' wives, too, but no one pays much attention to that."

"Sounds like just the kind of place I used to find work," commented Nighthawk.

"It's just the kind of place where Ibn ben Khalid can walk the streets with impunity," replied Blue Eyes. "No law."

"There's a million-credit price on his head. He starts walking down any street that's got a bounty hunter on it, he's a dead man."

"Perhaps they aren't all as opportunistic as you are."

"What's that supposed to mean?"

"Just that he's a hero on the Frontier. Maybe even the bounty killers believe in his cause."

"More likely, they know what will happen to them before they can leave the planet," put in Friday.

"You think he's that popular?" asked Nighthawk curiously.

"Empirical evidence would seem to confirm it."

"Empirical evidence?"

"He's still alive," said Blue Eyes.

"Maybe he's just lucky."

"Do you believe in luck?" asked Friday.

"No," admitted Nighthawk.

"Neither do I," said Friday.

"*I* do," put in Blue Eyes. "That's why I don't allow gambling in my establishment." He threw back his head and hooted in amusement, then sobered just as quickly. "Your friend Kinoshita's been lucky so far, too."

"Oh?"

"Yeah," said Blue Eyes. "He's lucky Friday hasn't killed him."

"Why is he here?" asked Friday. "I know why you and I have come, and the female is an empath, and this one"—he gestured disdainfully at the dragon—"may have information and at least knows what our prey looks like. But what does Kinoshita bring to the team?"

"He may be the most important cog," replied Nighthawk.

"Why?"

"When this is all over, assuming I live through it, I don't plan on going back. He'll know how my creators will react, who they'll contact, where they'll search for me."

"Your creators?"

Nighthawk made no reply, and the alien let the matter drop.

The ship altered course a few minutes later to avoid a meteor swarm, and Kinoshita emerged from his cabin to see what was happening. Friday promptly reached into his pouch and pulled out two more spiderlike insects, taking a bite of one and offering its squirming companion to Kinoshita.

"Get that away from me!" snapped the little man.

"I was just being friendly," said the alien calmly, putting the insect back.

"You mean you were just being Friday," said Blue Eyes with a hoot.

"Mind your own business, dragon," said Friday coldly.

"Who elected *you* leader?" demanded Blue Eyes. "I'll say what I want whenever I want."

"And I'll back him up!" snapped Kinoshita.

Suddenly Melisande emerged from her cabin and stood in the doorway to the galley, looking pale and nervous.

"You've got to stop!" she said weakly.

"Stop what?" asked Kinoshita.

"You know I'm an empath. I'm trying not to get involved, but there are too many savage emotions here. You could drive me insane before we ever encounter Ibn ben Khalid."

"I thought you couldn't read blue dragons," said Nighthawk.

"I can't," she said. "It's the other two."

"You can read my emotions?" asked Friday with open curiosity.

"Not all of them, and not clearly," replied Melisande. "But you have such hatred for Ito . . ."

"I *knew* it!" growled Kinoshita. He turned to Friday. "Do you want to have it out here or later? It makes no difference to me."

"That's enough," said Nighthawk. He looked at his motley crew. "Like it or not, you're a team. I chose you, I assembled you, and if anyone's going to do any killing around here, I'll be the one to do it. You don't have to like each other. You don't have to like *me*. You just have to remember that you're a team, and the first one who forgets it has to answer to me—and I promise you won't enjoy it. Is that clear?"

Kinoshita grudgingly nodded his agreement.

"What about you?" demanded Nighthawk of Friday.

"I will not strike the first blow in anger."

"Not good enough," said Nighthawk. "If you strike *any* blow, first, second, or three thousandth, in anger or in jest, you'll wish you hadn't. Do you understand?"

Friday nodded his head.

"That's not good enough. Say you understand."

"I understand," muttered the alien.

Nighthawk turned to Blue Eyes.

"Don't look at *me*. I'm the most peace-loving dragon you ever saw. I don't even carry a weapon."

"You could bite either of their heads off with that mouth," said Nighthawk.

"If I do, *then* you can threaten me."

Nighthawk stared into the dragon's clear blue eyes until the latter finally looked away.

"This is not a court of law, you have no legal rights, and I am not a compassionate man," said Nighthawk. "Try to keep that in mind."

"May I go back to my cabin now?" asked Melisande. "Or do you want to warn me too?"

"You know if I was telling the truth or not. That's enough. You can leave."

"Thank you," she said, turning and walking back the way she had come.

Nighthawk considered making Friday and Kinoshita shake hands, but he didn't know if that was a meaningful gesture for the alien, and he could tell that the thought of touching Friday made Kinoshita's flesh crawl.

This is some crew, he thought wryly. *I wonder if we can avoid killing each other long enough to find Ibn ben Khalid?*

Chapter 12

Cellestra was a dirty brown world without much in the way of natural resources. But it was an oxygen planet, and it possessed potable water, and it existed at a midpoint in the starlanes between the major Frontier worlds of Palinaros III and New Kenya. So, when it turned out that the soil wasn't rich enough for it to become a farming world, and that what lay beneath the soil wasn't really worth extracting, it became a trading world, a small but bustling center of commerce.

It was here that subspace messages were received from the Oligarchy and redirected farther into the Inner Frontier. A trio of import-export companies competed for the business of anyone shipping to or from the Frontier worlds. Thousands of preserved animal carcasses were shipped to the taxidermists who plied their trade on Cellestra. Banks traded in Oligarchy credits, New Kenya shillings, Maria Theresa dollars, Far London pounds, New Stalin rubles, Pukkah IV rupees, and a dozen other currencies, with the exchange rates changing and adjusting every ten seconds.

The population was close to twenty thousand Men, and perhaps three thousand aliens of various races, mostly Canphorites, Lodinites, and Mollutei. Almost all of them were involved in some form of interstellar commerce.

As Nighthawk's ship entered orbit around Cellestra, his radio came to life.

"Identify yourself, please," said a cold, almost mechanical voice.

"This is the *Olympus 6*, planet of registry Deluros VIII, commanded by Jefferson Nighthawk, two Standard days out of Sylene IV."

"Purpose of visit?"

"Commerce."

"Type of commerce?"

Kinoshita made a negative gesture.

"None of your damned business," answered Nighthawk.

"We are loading landing coordinates into your ship's computer," said the voice without missing a beat. "Enjoy your stay on Cellestra."

Blue Eyes hooted and Kinoshita grinned.

"You've never been here before," said Melisande. "How did you know we could get away without telling them our reason for landing?"

"Nighthawk *gave* him our reason for landing: commerce," answered Kinoshita. "This is the Frontier, not the Oligarchy. He had no authority to ask us what kind of business."

"That doesn't make sense. It's his world, after all. It must have laws."

"If you're a trading world, probably half of the goods that pass through are contraband. You don't attract a lot of business if word gets out that you're asking embarrassing questions."

"The voice also didn't ask if you had any nonhumans in your crew," added Friday. "That was another departure from Oligarchy procedure."

"They're still doing that?" asked Nighthawk.

"They've been doing it for four millennia," answered Friday. "Why should you think they have changed?"

Nighthawk shrugged. "Men are outnumbered thousands to one in the galaxy. You'd think we'd start making accommodations."

"The race that is in the ascendancy never makes accommodations," said Friday. "Fortunately, the galaxy has a long memory. Today Men possess the greatest technology and weaponry, and this has made an arrogant race even more arrogant. But you did not dominate the galaxy in times past, and the day will come when you do not do so in the future. I would not wish to be a Man on that day."

"I don't think you have to worry about it," said Kinoshita sardonically.

"I don't. As long as I can kill Men now, I am content."

"How about you?" asked Kinoshita, turning to Blue Eyes. "Do you feel that way too?"

"Absolutely not," answered the dragon with an amused hoot. "Man is the only race that believes in gratuities."

"So he wants us dead because we have the best weapons, and you want us alive because we're the biggest tippers?" said Kinoshita with a smile. "Well, that's probably as honest a pair of answers as I'm likely to hear."

"I could lie and say you're a physically lovely race," said Blue Eyes. "If it would make you happier, that is."

"Not at all," said Kinoshita. "But somehow, I get the distinct impression that lying would make *you* happier."

"Truth is a greatly overrated virtue, to quote your Jane Austen," agreed the dragon.

"If you say she said it, I'm sure she did—but somehow I don't think she was encouraging blue dragons to lie from morning till night for the sheer joy of it."

Blue Eyes shrugged. "It's all a matter of interpretation."

"Go strap yourselves in," interrupted Nighthawk. "We're about to land."

They touched down a few moments later, and emerged from the ship onto a slidewalk that took them to Customs. Given their appearance and the lack of any records of a current Jefferson Nighthawk, they passed through with a minimum of hassle.

"What now?" asked Melisande as they emerged from the spaceport into the warm Cellestra sunlight and took a broad, rapid-moving slidewalk toward the city center.

"Now we go into town and see what we can learn."

"I can already tell you that your presence is making most of the men we've passed very apprehensive."

"They don't know who I am," said Nighthawk.

"One look at you and they know generically," answered Melisande.

"That's encouraging," said Kinoshita.

"That I scare people?" said Nighthawk.

Kinoshita nodded. "They're not criminals. They're just spaceport employees and businessmen. They have no reason to be afraid of a man who might be a killer or a bounty hunter . . ."

". . . Unless they're afraid I've come for someone they don't want to see killed," concluded Nighthawk. He considered the notion. "It's a possibility."

"So, to repeat, what do we do now?" asked Melisande.

"We find a hotel. We've all been cooped up in that ship too long. We could use a little time away from each other, and a little room to stretch in. This isn't the Oligarchy, so there shouldn't be any trouble finding a place that will take all five of us." He paused. "Then, after dark, we'll go out looking for some sign that Ibn ben Khalid's here, or at least that someone can direct us to wherever he is."

"We'll look kind of strange, all five of us together," said Blue Eyes.

"That's why we'll split up." He faced Blue Eyes and Friday. "You two go to wherever the aliens hang out—even here on the Frontier, I can't believe they're rubbing shoulders with Men. Ito and I will hit the human gathering places. Melisande will come with me."

"Why not with Kinoshita?" she asked.

"Because if there's any trouble, I can protect you better—and until we learn where Ibn ben Khalid is, you're the most valuable member of the team. We'll arrange a meeting place later."

Nighthawk stepped onto a slower local slidewalk as they approached a small hotel, and his companions followed suit. The hostelry had seen better days, but it was clean enough, and it possessed a restaurant that catered to both humans and aliens. The five took a quintet of rooms at the far end of the fourth level, relaxed until dinnertime, and then descended to the main lobby.

"Friday, if they've got anything you can eat, I think it would be best for all parties concerned if you sat as far from us as possible," announced Nighthawk, and Kinoshita nodded approvingly.

"I have no more taste for dead flesh than you have for my form of nutrition," responded Friday. He stared directly at Kinoshita. "I just have better manners."

The alien walked off to the far end of the restaurant and seated himself.

Nighthawk and the rest of his party found an unoccupied table near the door, punched out their orders from the menu, and ate in relative silence.

Melisande kept shifting uncomfortably during the meal.

"Either you ate something that's making you sick, or you're getting a lot of bad vibrations," noted Nighthawk.

"It's very uncomfortable when so many people are so frightened," she admitted.

"Can't you turn it off?" he asked. "Like closing your eyes or plugging your ears?"

"How do you turn off your mind?" she shot back.

"There must be some way, or you'd have gone crazy years ago," he continued. "You can't be aware of every vicious, perverted emotion on the planet."

"Distance helps," she replied.

"How about walls?"

"Not really. Just distance."

"You must really have suffered on the ship."

"You find ways to cope," she said. "Friday hates all Men, but most of that hatred is beneath the surface. It comes out from time to time, but not often. And Kinoshita's emotions only flare up when he confronts Friday."

"What about me?" asked Blue Eyes.

"I can't read you at all," answered Melisande. "We're too different."

"And the boss?" asked Blue Eyes, gesturing toward Nighthawk.

She stared at Nighthawk for a long moment. "I've never met anyone quite like him. There's almost no emotional radiation at all. No apprehension, no fear, no hatred. This is all just a job to him. Nothing upsets him, and nothing seems to excite him."

"I suppose that's what makes him the Widowmaker," said Blue Eyes. "Probably the most you'll ever get from him is a sense of satisfaction at a job well done after he wipes out fifty or sixty bad guys."

"That's a terrible way to be" was her answer.

"It's the only way to survive when you put your life on the line so often," said Nighthawk.

"Life is more than surviving," she said.

"Not for everyone," he answered.

"What would you do if you weren't the Widowmaker?" asked Blue Eyes. "If you could do or be anything you want?"

"It's a silly question. I am what I am."

"But *if*," persisted the alien.

Nighthawk shrugged. "Grow things, I guess."

"Things?"

"Flowers, plants, animals," he answered vaguely. "I've killed enough things in my life. It might be interesting to try growing them for a change."

"What's stopping you?" asked Blue Eyes. "Your creators are half a galaxy away. You could vanish on the Frontier and they'd never find you."

"I have an obligation."

"To *them*?" said Blue Eyes contemptuously.

"To me."

"To yourself?"

"To a version of me that's lying in a frozen chamber on Deluros VIII," answered Nighthawk. "Once his future is secure, I'll worry about my own."

"I know how Men feel about their parents and siblings," continued Blue Eyes. "But how does a clone feel about his—what would you call it?—his original self?"

"He's not a separate person. He's a part of me, just as I'm a part of him."

"I don't understand."

"I don't either," admitted Nighthawk. "But I know what I feel."

"I wonder why cloning humans carries such heavy penalties?" mused Blue Eyes.

"All the legal problems," answered Kinoshita. "Is a man responsible for his clone's criminal actions? If DNA is found at the scene of a violent crime, whose is it? For the purposes of inheritance, who is more closely related—a man's son or his clone?"

"You would think they could solve them."

"They probably can—but they'd rather not," said Melisande. "Each of us likes to think he's unique. Clones would change all that."

"I don't know," said Kinoshita. "I never met the original Widowmaker, but I spent some time with the first clone, and he was nothing like this one."

"How was he different?" she asked.

"He was very immature, very impetuous—and he fell passionately in love with the first woman he saw."

"He was also two months old," said Nighthawk. "Not physically, but in every other way." He paused. "The poor bastard never had a chance."

"You speak as if you knew him," said Blue Eyes.

"I did more than know him," answered Nighthawk. "I *was* him."

"There!" said Melisande. "That's the first really powerful emotional reaction I've read since I met you."

"Emotions get in the way of things," said Nighthawk, his expression halfway between annoyed and embarrassed.

"I disagree," said Kinoshita. "Without lust and greed, the race would still be Earthbound."

"Lust and greed and curiosity," Melisande corrected him.

"Well, let's start satisfying our curiosity," said Nighthawk. He left his thumbprint on the bill, got to his feet, waited for the others to rise, and walked to the door.

Friday joined them, and a moment later Nighthawk's team had gone out into the cool Cellestra night in search of information about his quarry.

Chapter 13

"So where do we begin?" asked Melisande nervously as she and Nighthawk rode down the almost-empty slidewalk.

"Your choice," said Nighthawk. "Pick a tavern or a drug den or a coffee shop where the emotions aren't too painful. I want you to be able to read *new* emotions, passions I hope to raise; I assume its easier if you're not already overwhelmed."

"True," she said. "But why didn't you offer me the same choice back on Sylene IV?"

"Because my . . . ah . . . sponsors had tipped me that Ibn ben Khalid had been seen a couple of times in Blue Eyes' establishment. It wouldn't have made much sense to choose a barroom three blocks away, would it?"

"No," she admitted. Then: "How will you do it this time, without Kinoshita around to start an argument?"

Nighthawk shrugged. "I'm sure something will come to me." He paused. "I want you sitting in the light this time, where I can see your face without any difficulty. If anyone reacts to anything I say or do, just stare at him for a minute."

"I'll attract his attention," she said uneasily. "What if he tries to do something?"

"Then he'll find out what happens to people who bother the Widow-maker's friends."

"I'm comforted to hear that—but are you aware of how arrogant that sounds?"

"I've earned my arrogance," responded Nighthawk. "Would you rather I simpered and sucked my thumb and said 'Aw, shucks!' every time the subject of my abilities arose?"

"No," she said with a sigh. "I suppose not."

"How's this place?" asked Nighthawk, indicating an exotic-looking tavern.

She concentrated for a moment. "As good as any. They've got a very beautiful dancer."

"How can you tell?"

She smiled. "There's a lot of lust in the air. What would *you* credit it to?"

"Sounds logical. I think maybe we'd better go in as a couple."

"Why?"

"You're an attractive woman, and if you walk in alone, I imagine some of that lust is going to be directed toward you."

"That's thoughtful of you."

He shrugged. "Why make my job harder?"

She stared at him for a moment, then took his arm and entered the tavern with him.

It was a curious room, sixteen-sided, dark, with alien tapestries hanging on the walls. An almost-nude girl stood atop a huge transparent globe that rolled around a small stage in the middle of the room, and the girl's attempts to keep her balance bore such grace that Nighthawk decided she could have just as easily tapped or pirouetted on it had she so desired. The music seemed live, but he couldn't spot the band.

There were about thirty small tables circling the stage, about half of them occupied by Men, the rest empty. As far as Nighthawk could tell, the dancer and Melisande were the only two females in the place.

Nighthawk walked to a table very near the stage, pulled out a chair for Melisande, then sat down himself. He didn't see any sign of a waiter, either robotic or human, so he examined the table and found an almost invisible button which, when pressed, produced two drink menus. The selection was suitably exotic: Dust Whores, Blue Zebras, Green-and-Whites, Chiller Killers, even a wildly expensive bottle of seventy-five-year-old Alphard brandy. They each selected a drink, Nighthawk placed his thumb next to each on the menu, and a moment later two slots opened on the table and the drinks magically appeared.

"Anyone look likely?" asked Nighthawk, scanning the room.

"They *all* look dangerous," she replied.

"Looks can be deceiving."

"Don't you feel any fear or even apprehension?" she asked, staring at him.

He grinned. "If you don't know, we've got a serious problem."

"I can't detect any."

"This is my work. It doesn't pay to be nervous."

"There's a difference between controlling or ignoring your fear, and not feeling any at all."

"Maybe that's my edge, then."

"You're a very strange man, Jefferson Nighthawk."

"That's how you become a legend," he replied. The semi-nude girl finished her routine, and Nighthawk leaned over toward her. "We'd be happy to buy you a drink once you get your clothes back on," he said.

"I don't drink with the customers."

"Ah, but this is a drink in honor of Ibn ben Khalid," he said in a voice that was just loud enough to be overheard.

"You must not have heard me," replied the girl. "I don't drink with the customers."

"Next you'll be telling me you're a patriot," he said as she left the stage. Then he turned back to Melisande. "Well?"

"Nothing from her," she replied, "but when you mentioned Ibn ben Khalid I got a couple of rushes of emotion from somewhere in the room, and your comment about patriotism got one of them quite agitated."

"For us or against us?"

"I don't know," she said. "I read emotions, not thoughts—but given that we're two thousand light-years from the nearest Oligarchy world, I'd have to think it's *for* us."

"Let's find out," said Nighthawk.

He stood up, glass in hand.

"A toast to Ibn ben Khalid!" he said in a loud voice.

No one joined him.

"Bunch of goddamned cowards," he muttered, downing his drink and sitting down again. He looked at Melisande and asked softly, "Anything?"

"Everything," she answered. "Loyalty, outrage, love, hatred, even fear."

"Directed at me or at Ibn ben Khalid?"

"I don't know."

"It could mean they know him, or simply that they know *of* him. And that they love him and fear me, or the other way around." He grinned ruefully. "Empathy isn't an exact science, is it?"

"You knew what it was when you hired me."

"Don't get angry," he said, and suddenly looked around the room. "Or maybe that's the best thing for you to do?"

"I beg your pardon."

"If I slap you and pull my punch, can you fall and make it look real?"

"I don't know. I'm not an actress."

"Don't worry about it then," he said.

"What's this about?"

"I can't wait all night for someone to approach. Maybe we can precipitate some action."

"By hitting me?" she said. "I'll never be able to convince them I was really hurt."

"Yes you will," he assured her.

"But I—"

His hand shot out and slapped her, hard. She fell off her chair and rolled onto the floor.

"Get up!" he bellowed. "Get up and say that again!"

She sat erect, her eyes refusing to focus. He yanked her to her feet, dragged her to the door, and pushed her out into the street. "Wait for me at the hotel," he whispered, then reentered the tavern.

"Promises me a night's entertainment and then starts lecturing me about Cassius Hill's virtues," he announced, sitting down again at his table. "That bastard wouldn't know a virtue if it jumped up and spit in his face."

There was still no reaction, so he stood up.

"I've had my fill of this place," he said, walking back to the door and out into the street.

He had walked, swaying as if drunk, about forty feet when a voice called out from behind him.

"Hold on, friend!"

Nighthawk repressed a secret smile, then turned to see who was approaching him. It was one of the men from the tavern, a broad-shouldered beer-bellied man with a huge black beard and bold, glaring gray eyes.

"I couldn't help hearing what you had to say," said the man.

"And?"

"I happen to have fought under Cassius Hill's command in the war against the Borolites. He's a great man, and I take issue with what you said."

Wonderful. There are probably fifty Ibn ben Khalid supporters in the tavern, and I get the one who hates his guts.

"That's your privilege, brother," said Nighthawk at last. "I didn't mean any harm."

"Then you'd better apologize right here and now," said the man.

"Okay, I apologize."

The man seemed angrier than ever. "That's not good enough!"

Nighthawk noticed that a crowd had begun gathering.

Well, maybe it's not so bothersome after all. If I stand up for Ibn ben Khalid, maybe someone here will finally decide I'm on their side.

"It'll have to do," said Nighthawk. "It's all you're going to get."

"So you've found a little backbone after all," said the man with a dangerous smile.

"A little."

"Do you have anything to say before I rip you apart?"

"Yeah," said Nighthawk. "You and Cassius Hill can both go fuck yourselves."

The man bellowed a curse and charged, but Nighthawk was ready for him. He sidestepped, grabbed the man's arm, twisted it and put his weight into it, and the man somersaulted through the air, landing with a bone-jarring thud.

The man got to his feet slowly, brushed himself off, and stared at Nighthawk. He approached more slowly this time—and walked face-first into a spinning kick that sent him reeling.

"Who *are* you?" he demanded, wiping the blood from his face and approaching even more carefully this time.

"I'm the man you were going to rip apart," said Nighthawk.

The man approached him warily, feinting with his left. Nighthawk didn't wait for a second feint, but stepped inside and delivered six blows to the belly, so rapidly that most of the observers never saw the last four. His opponent collapsed, gasping for air.

Nighthawk looked around, hoping someone would approach to congratulate him or offer him a drink or show *some* form of solidity with a man who had just risked his life for Ibn ben Khalid. Instead, three men stepped forward, each with a drawn pistol—two sonic, one laser.

"I didn't know Cassius Hill was so popular," said Nighthawk wryly.

"We don't give a shit about politics," said one of the men. "But that was our friend you damned near killed."

"*He* attacked *me*."

"That doesn't make him any less our friend."

"Then take him home and tell him not to argue politics." *And don't make me kill you.*

"First we have to decide what to do about you."

"Just walk on," said Nighthawk. "I've got no argument with you."

"*We* have one with you," said the second man. "I saw the way you took him apart. You're no amateur. You should have warned him, or found some way to step aside."

"I apologized to him," said Nighthawk. "I'll apologize to you, too, if it'll make you feel any better." He paused. "But I'll only apologize once. Walk on."

"You're talking as if *you* have the drop on *us*," said the first man.

Nighthawk was about to reply when an ear-shattering explosion rang out. Bricks and debris rained down on him, and the ground shook beneath his feet. He threw himself to the ground, covering his head with his hands and wondering what the hell was happening. He could hear screams of agony nearby, and a moment later he felt a building collapse down the street.

Then an alien hand was on his shoulder, helping him to his feet.

"Are you all right?" asked Friday.

"Yes," said Nighthawk, looking around at a scene of total devastation. Wounded bodies littered the street, and a couple of men lay motionless, their bodies in such awkward positions that he knew instantly they were dead. "What the hell happened?"

"I saw three men with their weapons trained on you."

"You mean this was *your* doing?" demanded Nighthawk, wiping some blood from his left ear.

"It's my specialty."

"I didn't even know you had any explosives with you."

"I am never without them," said Friday.

Kinoshita came running up.

"What's going on?" he asked.

"This asshole wiped out half a city block," answered Nighthawk.

"I saved your life."

"My life was never in danger."

"You idiot!" snapped Kinoshita at Friday. "Look what you've done. How are we going to make contact with Ibn ben Khalid's people now?"

Men and women began regaining consciousness and staggered to their feet.

"That's the easy part," said Nighthawk. He turned to Friday. "All right, there's no undoing what happened. Get the hell back to the hotel— no, make that the ship—and stay there until you hear from me. Ito, find Blue Eyes and get him out of here. Take him to the ship and make him stay there. Melisande, too."

"Aren't you coming too?"

Nighthawk shook his head. "Not right away. I still have a job to do."

"Then at least let us help protect you."

"You too?" replied Nighthawk. "I don't need any protection. You can help me by getting the aliens to the ship and not letting them set foot outside it."

"All right," said Kinoshita. "But someone just killed and maimed a bunch of Ibn ben Khalid's supporters on your behalf. If I were you, I'd run like hell."

"You're not me."

"I don't see how you're going to get close to him now."

"By standing still," said Nighthawk. He looked up and down the street. "His people will find *me*."

Chapter 14

Nighthawk stood alone on the rubble, waiting patiently.

He didn't have long to wait. Within minutes he was surrounded by bruised and bloody men, all pointing weapons at him. Ambulances sped by, floating above the street, coming from and returning to the city's only hospital.

There were no police, but a pair of bounty hunters showed up, only to leave when they found out there was no price on his head. Finally the confusion and noise abated somewhat, and Nighthawk turned to face a middle-aged man, one he recognized from the tavern.

"Why am I being held?" he asked.

"Look around you."

"I'm not responsible for that. I was in plain view every second. I defended myself from one man, that's all."

"There's a red alien. We want him."

"What is that to me?" asked Nighthawk.

"We know he's your friend."

"I have no friends."

"He set off the explosives, and he was overheard saying he did it to save you. That's enough."

"What he did was *his* business. I didn't set off any bombs and I didn't kill any people. You have no right to keep me here."

"We want to know where the alien is. We think you can tell us." The man leaned forward. "I heard you in the tavern. I know you believe in Ibn ben Khalid's cause."

"So what?"

"So the alien killed six of Khalid's men."

"I'm sorry to hear that," said Nighthawk. "I may kill him myself."

"He works for you. Or with you. If we let you go, you'll just join him and leave Cellestra."

"How wise of you to know what I will or won't do," said Nighthawk. "If you're typical of the kind of men Ibn ben Khalid recruits, maybe I'd better reconsider who I support."

"Let's just kill him and be done with it!" snapped one of the men.

"I'm a supporter of Ibn ben Khalid, and you know that I didn't set off the bombs, and you want to kill me anyway? I wonder what Ibn ben Khalid would say if he were here."

"He'd probably say to kill you," said another man.

"If he would, then Cassius Hill's got nothing to worry about," said Nighthawk. "I've got more faith in his judgment than you do."

"Then turn the alien over to us."

"Not a chance."

"Why the hell not, if you had nothing to do with the bombing?"

Say it right, now, and put some fire in your eyes.

"Because I know what you're going to do to him. It's the same thing Men have been doing to aliens since the first day we found out we aren't alone in the galaxy, and I don't plan to be a part of it."

"But he's a killer!"

"Even a killer deserves a trial," said Nighthawk. "But he only gets it if he's a Man. If I tell you where the alien is hiding, you'll shoot him or string him up."

"You bet your ass we will!" said the first man. "He killed six of us!"

"Okay, he overreacted, and he deserves to go to jail for it. But I'm not going to turn him over to a bunch of human bigots who want to lynch him!"

"Who the hell are you calling a bigot?"

"Who's threatening to kill me if I don't turn over the alien?" shot back Nighthawk.

Are they actually buying this shit? I sure as hell can't tell by their faces—and I don't even know what Ibn ben Khalid feels about aliens. What if he's not a bleeding heart?

"Look, fella, whoever you are," said the first man, "if we don't find him, all we have is you, and you're going to have to answer for the bombing."

"Fine," said Nighthawk. "String *me* up—but I'm not turning an alien over to you until I know he's going to be safe in his jail cell and get a fair trial."

"We don't *have* a goddamned jail!" exploded the man. "And what's all this fair trial crap? You know he couldn't get a trial of any kind back in the Oligarchy."

"That's one of the reasons why we came out to the Frontier, isn't it?" shot back Nighthawk. "To get away from a government that wouldn't give an alien a fair chance."

The man stared at him for a long moment.

"All right," he said at last. "What was the alien doing here in the first place?"

"He was here on business."

"What kind?"

"You'd have to ask him."

"Damn it, I'm trying to be reasonable. Your companion just destroyed the better part of a city block and killed some of my friends."

"I'm sorry, and I'm sure if he's had time to reflect on it, *he's* sorry. He thought he was saving my life."

"Thought?" echoed another man. "You were two seconds away from getting blown to kingdom come."

"If you say so."

"You don't think so?" continued the man. "Hell, even the Widowmaker in his prime couldn't have gotten out of that spot alive."

Nighthawk shrugged and made no reply.

"Let's get back to what happened," said the first man. "You walked out of the tavern. Rigby followed you. Then what?"

"He asked me to apologize. I did."

"He attacked you for that?"

Nighthawk looked at his antagonist's still-unconscious body. "I don't know why the hell he attacked me. Ask him when he wakes up."

"Let's keep going. He attacked you. Why?"

"He didn't like my opinion of Cassius Hill," answered Nighthawk. "Or maybe he didn't like what I think about Ibn ben Khalid. It comes to the same thing."

"And you knocked him out?"

Nighthawk gestured to the unconscious Rigby. "There he is."

"Then what?"

"Then three of his friends came up with their guns drawn. I don't think they were going to shoot me, I think we were on the verge of talking things out—but my friend saw them and assumed they were about to kill me, and he did what he felt he had to do to save me."

"So you might say that the six men who were killed died because you were defending their leader?"

"It's a little simplistic, but if you want to say it, I won't disagree with you."

"You present us with a problem," continued the man. "You got into a fight defending a man we respect, that some of us all but worship. You refuse to turn the alien over to us for fear he won't get a fair trial."

"*Any* trial," Nighthawk corrected him.

"Any trial," amended the man. "Those are both virtues that we should respect. Yet it won't bring the six men back."

"Ibn ben Khalid's at war with Cassius Hill," said Nighthawk. "Casualties happen in wartime."

"I know. That's what we have to consider."

"Consider it until hell freezes over, but I'm not turning the alien over to you. If I have to be a seventh casualty, so be it. If I told you where he is, I'd be no better than Cassius Hill."

"We're going to have to talk this over," said the man. He turned to a couple of the younger men in the crowd. "Harry, Jason, keep him covered while we decide what to do."

The two men stepped forward, their guns trained on Nighthawk, while the rest of the men and women went into the tavern. Nighthawk stood motionless, seemingly oblivious of his two guards, for the better part of ten minutes. He still had three small concealed weapons, and felt confident that he could disable or kill the guards at any time, but it suited his purposes to wait for the judgment of the men and women who were currently deciding his fate.

Finally they emerged from the tavern, and the middle-aged man who seemed to be their leader walked up to Nighthawk.

"All right," he said. "You seem willing to die for your principles. We've decided that you deserve to live for them."

"I don't understand," said Nighthawk, who understood perfectly.

"We'd like you to join us, to fight for the cause."

"What about the alien?"

"He killed, he dies—but we'll find him ourselves."

"Fair enough," said Nighthawk. "How and where do I enlist?"

"You already have," said the man. "A statement of principle is as formal as it gets—and you've already made yours." He paused. "There are hundreds of thousands, maybe millions, of us all across the Frontier, waiting for the word."

"When will it come?"

"When Ibn ben Khalid decides we're ready."

"And when will that be?"

The man shrugged. "You'd have to ask him."

"I'd like to. Where is he?"

"Who knows?"

"Somebody must," said Nighthawk.

"If I knew, his enemies could torture it out of me, or drug me and make me reveal it. Much better that I don't know."

"I repeat: *some*body must know."

"There's a complex chain of command. You could follow it until you were a very old man and still never come to the end of it."

"Sounds inefficient to me," said Nighthawk. "If it takes that long to get to the top, it'll take as long for commands to come down."

"He's been one of us for less than three minutes and already he's criticizing the operation," said another man contemptuously.

"If I'm going to put my life on the line for Ibn ben Khalid, I'd like to meet him. If he's too busy to see me personally, and I can certainly understand that, I'd at least like to attend a speech or a rally. Everything I know about him is secondhand."

"Then why did you risk your life fighting Rigby?"

"First, I didn't risk my life, and second, everything I know about Cassius Hill is firsthand. I'll support anyone who's against him."

"Good answer," said the middle-aged man approvingly.

"Thanks," said Nighthawk. "*Now* will you tell me where I can find Ibn ben Khalid?"

"I don't know. None of us do."

"When's the last time he stopped off at Cellestra?"

"Never," said the man, surprised.

"Never?" repeated Nighthawk sharply.

The man shook his head. "Don't you think we'd know if he had? He's never been here."

Nighthawk stood motionless for a moment. He could almost hear a distinct *clink!* as another piece of the puzzle fell into place.

Chapter 15

Nighthawk entered the ship and ordered the hatch to close behind him.

"We were getting worried," said Blue Eyes, rising to greet him.

"*Some* of us were getting worried," Kinoshita corrected him. "I kept telling him that you were the Widowmaker, that if he was going to worry about anyone, he should be worrying about the townspeople who thought you were their prisoner."

"So what happened?" persisted Blue Eyes.

"I put on a performance," said Nighthawk. "They bought it, hook, line, and sinker."

"What does that mean?" asked Friday.

"It's an old expression, from the time Men were still Earthbound. In this instance, it means I've been welcomed into their organization, such as it is."

"Such as it is?" repeated Kinoshita, frowning.

"Ibn ben Khalid's not here."

"There *is* one other planet where I know he's been recently," said Blue Eyes.

"Oh?"

"Yes," continued the dragon. "A little world called Causeway. It's on the route from Jefferson II to Far London. The Oligarchy sent some agents in there, and from what I hear, he had them all tortured and killed."

"A resourceful man," remarked Nighthawk.

"Would an unresourceful man have survived this long?"

"Depends on the man and the situation," said Nighthawk.

"Do you want me to lay in a course for Causeway?" asked Blue Eyes. "I think its official name is Beta Dante IV."

"No, I'll do it," said Nighthawk. He turned to Kinoshita. "Take charge of getting our clearance to leave. Be polite and accommodating, but no one boards us or scans us. If you have to, take off without permission and get us up to light speed as fast as you can. I'd rather leave peacefully, but the main thing is to get the hell out of here. This world's a dead end." He paused. "Once we're a couple of dozen light-years out, let me know and I'll program the new destination."

"Why not now?"

"I want us to seem to be heading back to Sylene now, just in case anyone has any idea of following us. Once we're out of tracer range, we'll turn and head off for Causeway."

"I can do it."

"I know you can," said Nighthawk. "But if we make a mistake and allow someone to tail us, at least this way you won't bear the blame."

"Right," assented Kinoshita. "I can accept that."

Nighthawk allowed himself the luxury of a small smile. "I thought perhaps you could." He walked toward Melisande's cabin. "Is she in here?"

"Yes," said Kinoshita. "She didn't like what I was thinking about Friday."

"I can imagine," said Nighthawk. He stood beside the door. "I'll be out in a couple of minutes. Don't disturb us."

The door slid back, and he entered the cabin just before it closed again.

Melisande, who was sitting in the cabin's only chair, looked up from the book she was reading.

"What is it?" she asked.

"You tell me."

She stared at him. "There *is* something!" she said at last. "You're excited!"

"What else?"

She concentrated for a moment. "I don't know. Just that you're translating very powerful emotional radiation."

"But you don't know what it's about?"

"Not as an empath," she replied. "But I'd be awfully surprised if it doesn't concern Ibn ben Khalid."

"It does," said Nighthawk. "I don't want you leaving the cabin until we land."

"Why?"

"I don't want you to inadvertently reveal what you just discovered."

"Still why?"

"I have my reasons." Nighthawk paused. "Take your meals in here."

"How long will this trip last?"

"A couple of days."

"Who don't you trust?" asked Melisande. "Who am I not supposed to reveal this to?"

Nighthawk smiled. "Just stay in the cabin." He turned to the door, waited for it to open, and stepped back out into the corridor that led to the galley. A moment later he was in the control room.

"That was quick, even for a human," said Blue Eyes.

"That was vulgar, even for a dragon," Nighthawk shot back.

"Of course. Vulgarity is my charm."

Nighthawk walked over to Kinoshita, who was at the navigational computer.

"How's it going?"

"They're not happy about it, but they can't come up with a good reason to deny us permission to leave." He looked up at Nighthawk. "They've already requested permission to search the ship. I denied it."

"Have the sensors spotted any weaponry trained on us?"

Kinoshita shook his head. "No. They just haven't given us permission to take off."

"Scan deep space."

"Done."

"When's the next incoming ship due to hit the atmosphere?"

Kinoshita studied the holographic screen. "About forty Standard minutes."

"Okay, there's no likelihood of hitting it. Take off."

"You're sure?"

"They're not going to shoot until they *know* Friday's on the ship. The longer we stay on the ground, the more likely they are to find out."

Kinoshita gave the order to the computer, and a moment later the ship was streaking through the upper atmosphere of Cellestra. When it entered space, it jumped to light speed.

"Any pursuit?" asked Nighthawk.

"Not that I can find."

"We'll stay on this course for an hour or two, just in case they're tracking us. Then we'll head back to Causeway."

"Sounds good to me," said Kinoshita, finally looking up from the control panel.

Nighthawk turned to Friday. "I haven't had a chance to speak to you since you blew up those buildings."

"I saved your life."

"First of all, my life was in no danger. And second, even if it was, we both know that you did it because you enjoy *killing* Men, not *saving* them."

Nighthawk paused and stared at the red-skinned alien. "If you ever set off an explosive again without my permission, all bonds are broken, all agreements forgotten, and I will hunt you down and kill you like an animal. Do you understand?"

"Yes. The next time your life is threatened, you wish me to take no action at all."

"If that's the way you choose to interpret it."

"You should not alienate me, Widowmaker," said Friday. "I can be of enormous use to you."

"You can also be an enormous handicap," answered Nighthawk. "Actions have consequences. Yours came very close to getting me killed."

Friday stared at him, then turned his back and stared at a viewscreen.

"I would have liked to have heard your line of bullshit," said Blue Eyes. "You must have done some snappy talking to get those men to let you go."

"I told them what they wanted to hear."

"But you must have told them with sincerity," said the dragon. "No one can lie like a Man."

"You think not?" asked Nighthawk.

"Well, except maybe for blue dragons."

Blue Eyes threw back his head and hooted, and Nighthawk joined him. Kinoshita suddenly realized that it was the first time he'd heard the Widowmaker laugh in any of his incarnations. It wasn't a comforting sound.

After an hour Nighthawk sat down at the navigational computer, fed in the coordinates of the ship's destination, and walked to the galley, where he ordered a sandwich and a beer. Kinoshita and Blue Eyes joined him a few minutes later, while Friday continued staring at the viewscreen, back turned to the three of them.

"This is pretty awful stuff," offered Blue Eyes, indicating his drink.

"The galley wasn't programmed for your needs."

"An understatement," said Blue Eyes, tossing his cup in the atomizer and ordering a different concoction.

"Actually, the food's pretty good compared to some ships I've owned," said Kinoshita.

"I agree," said Nighthawk.

"I wonder how you managed to conquer the galaxy on such poor rations," said Blue Eyes.

"We only conquered a very small part of it," answered Kinoshita with a smile. "The rest we bought."

"You should have bought some good food synthesizers while you were at it."

"We did. It's hardly our fault that a human ship isn't equipped to feed a blue dragon with fangs that would give any child nightmares."

"If you two are going to argue about the food, wait until I've finished eating," said Nighthawk.

"I thought you liked it," said Blue Eyes.

"I do. But when you start talking about it, I think about what it really is instead of what it tastes like, and then I lose my appetite."

"Talk about self-delusion!" said the dragon with a hoot of amusement.

"It has its uses," said Nighthawk, finishing his sandwich and downing his beer.

"I thought you were the ultimate realist."

"I am," replied Nighthawk. "Who but a realist would admit the benefits of self-delusion?"

"That is either the stupidest or most intelligent remark I've heard in years," said Blue Eyes. "Now I'll have to spend the next day or two figuring out which."

Nighthawk got to his feet. "I think I'd better check on Melisande."

"Is she ill?" asked Kinoshita.

"Just a bit under the weather. She should be fine by the time we land."

He left the galley and returned to Melisande's cabin.

"I didn't expect to see you again for the duration of the trip," said Melisande, still sitting in the same chair.

"I need to know something."

"What?"

"Can you tell if someone's lying?"

"Someone on the ship? Probably not, if it's one of the aliens."

"No, a human, not Kinoshita or me."

"It all depends."

"On what?"

"On what kind of pressure he's under. Point a gun at him and he might be so scared that his fear of the gun will mask all other emotions. I might even read it as fear of telling the truth, and interpret that as a lie."

"Too bad."

"Why?"

"That's the very situation I had in mind," said Nighthawk.

"Who is it?"

"Who is *what*?"

"I'm not a fool, Nighthawk," said Melisande. "You were asking about a scenario you've already devised in your mind. You think that Ibn ben Khalid is masquerading as someone else. You think you know who. You want to confront him with your suspicions, probably at gunpoint. And you want me to tell you if he's lying or not. Isn't that what this is all about?"

"In essence."

"I'm sorry, but I can't give you a definite answer."

"I'll just have to proceed without one, then," said Nighthawk. He walked to the door. "I won't bother you again."

"I'm happy to have your company," she replied. "You're the most fascinating man I've met in a long time."

"I thought I didn't project any emotions."

"I misspoke. You don't *react* emotionally, but you do have emotions. Most of them are buried so deep that one of Friday's bombs probably couldn't get them out. I find that curious in so successful a man."

"Possibly because you mistake me for a successful man."

"You're a legend all over the Frontier," said Melisande. "You have more self-confidence than any man I know. You have never been defeated. That is my definition of a successful man."

"I would think a woman with your gifts wouldn't dabble on the surface of things," said Nighthawk.

"I don't understand."

"I was created with *all* of Jefferson Nighthawk's memories. Not just those that he possessed at age thirty-eight."

"Ah!" she said. "I see now!"

"Each time I see my face in a mirror, I expect to see the white of my cheekbones piercing through my diseased flesh," said Nighthawk. "I look at my hands, and I'm surprised not to see the skin peeled back from my knuckles and my fingernails missing." He paused uncomfortably. "You wondered that I didn't lust after you in the whorehouse. I learned not to. After all, what kind of woman could possibly be attracted to a man in an advanced state of eplasia? I watched myself dying of a disfiguring disease for the better part of two years, before they finally accepted my application to go into the deep freeze and await a cure. You learn to sublimate a lot of emotions when you go through something like that."

She nodded her head. "Yes, it makes much more sense now. You must forgive me, but like everyone else, I assumed you were what you appeared to be. I'll have to adjust."

"So will I," replied Nighthawk. "I'm on a mission now, and every move I've made since I was created has been directed toward accomplishing it. But when I've finally killed Ibn ben Khalid and returned Cassandra Hill to her father, I'm going to have to come to grips with the fact that every human I know except for you and Kinoshita has been dead for over a century, that most of the buildings are distant memories, that my knowledge of everything except weaponry and spaceships is a hundred years out of date."

"Frankly, I'm surprised that you're not even more repressed than you are," said Melisande.

"I haven't got time to be an emotional basket case," said Nighthawk. "I've got work to do."

"You don't take much pleasure in it."

"I did once. I will again."

He walked out of the room and let the door slide shut behind him, leaving Melisande to wonder how much longer he could remain simmering before the explosion came.

Chapter 16

"We're ready to land," announced Nighthawk as he instructed the autopilot to turn the controls over to the spaceport's computer.

"They didn't ask us to identify ourselves," noted Kinoshita. "That's very strange."

"They know who we are," said Nighthawk.

"You radioed ahead?"

"I didn't have to."

"I didn't know you've been to Causeway," said Blue Eyes.

"I haven't."

"I meant your ship."

"I know what you meant," said Nighthawk.

They fell silent then as the ship burst into the atmosphere and activated its heat shields. Another five minutes and it gently touched down on the reinforced concrete of the spaceport.

"That's it," said Nighthawk. "Let's go to work."

"Do you want to divide the place up, the way we did on Cellestra?" asked Kinoshita.

"No need to."

"I disagree," said Blue Eyes. "We can cover four times the ground if we go off on our own."

"But we don't have to," said Nighthawk, walking to the hatch and opening it. "I know where we're going."

Blue Eyes followed him to the hatch, then froze.

"What the hell's going on here?" he demanded.

"We're going after Ibn ben Khalid," answered Nighthawk.

"But this isn't Causeway!" snapped the dragon. "It's Sylene IV!"

"That's right," said Nighthawk. "This is where he is."

"Is this some kind of joke?" said Blue Eyes.

"No, it's not," said Nighthawk, drawing a pistol and aiming it at the dragon. "You slipped up."

"I don't know what you're talking about!"

"You told me that Ibn ben Khalid had been seen on Cellestra. His own followers, who had accepted me as one of them, told me that he'd never been there." Nighthawk paused. "Cellestra is two days closer to the Core than Sylene. Causeway is a couple of days closer than Cellestra. How far away from Sylene did you think you could lead me before I got tired of chasing ghosts?"

Blue Eyes glared at him. "If you're going to shoot, shoot. I don't have to listen to you too."

"I haven't decided if I'm going to shoot you," replied Nighthawk. "I admire loyalty, even if it's misdirected."

"Then what happens next?"

"You leave the ship and we go find Ibn ben Khalid. Melisande, you and Kinoshita come along. Friday, wait here; I don't need you blowing up anything else."

"If the adventure is to end here, I insist on coming along," said Friday.

Nighthawk stared at him for a long moment, then turned to Kinoshita. "Frisk him. Make sure he's not carrying anything that can go bang!"

Kinoshita slid his hands over the red alien with obvious distaste, then turned back to Nighthawk. "He's clean."

"Okay, you can come with us," said Nighthawk. "And don't forget what I told you on the ship about blowing things up without my approval."

"I will not forget," said Friday, joining them on the ground.

Nighthawk turned and began walking toward Customs, followed by his motley little crew. A few moments later they were cleared to leave the spaceport. He flagged down a vehicle and directed its computer to take them to The Blue Dragon.

"Why are we going there?" asked Blue Eyes.

"Nostalgia," replied Nighthawk, so ominously that the dragon fell silent, afraid to ask any more questions. Kinoshita never took his eyes off Friday, and every time the alien moved the little man's hand snaked down toward his weapon.

Melisande looked acutely uncomfortable, as indeed she was, with powerful and unpleasant emotions emanating from both Kinoshita and Friday. From Nighthawk all she could read was eagerness, an urge to confront whatever he thought was waiting at The Blue Dragon.

"You know, we don't have to do this," said Blue Eyes at last.

"Do what?" asked Nighthawk.

"Kill him."

"Yes, we do. That's why I was created."

"You don't even know him. He's a good man, Widowmaker."

"I'm not political. This is just business."

"It's *more* than business! You're killing an important man!"

"The fate of someone who's closer to me than a father or a brother depends on my killing him," said Nighthawk.

"You could *say* he was dead," urged Blue Eyes. "Your employers are half a galaxy away. They'd never know."

"I can't take the chance. The Widowmaker has got to survive."

"You *are* the Widowmaker."

Nighthawk shook his head. "I'm his shadow. He's depending on me. I can't let him down."

"Ibn ben Khalid might kill you instead."

"He might," admitted Nighthawk.

"What then?"

"Then Friday will blow up the whole damned city before he has a chance to get out of it," said Nighthawk.

The vehicle came to a stop in front of The Blue Dragon and hovered a few inches above the ground. Nighthawk paid the driver while his companions were getting out, then joined them in front of the entrance.

"I beg you," said Blue Eyes. "Let him live!"

Nighthawk stared at him emotionlessly, offered no reply, and finally entered the tavern, followed by the rest of his team.

As usual, The Blue Dragon was filled with a motley assortment of Men and aliens. There were two Canphorites, a Lodinite, four Gengi, a huge Bortai sitting alone in one corner, two other races that Nighthawk couldn't identify, and perhaps a dozen Men scattered at tables around the room.

Nighthawk and his companions sat down at a table near the entrance.

"Is he here?" asked Kinoshita, scanning the room.

"If he isn't, he will be soon," answered Nighthawk. "Order your drinks. I'm paying."

And then, just as the drinks were delivered to the table, a slender young man, carelessly dressed, his hair poorly combed, walked in and approached the bar.

"Stay here," said Nighthawk softly, as he got to his feet and walked across the tavern to confront the young man.

"You're back early," observed Nicholas Jory. "Did you find your man?"

"Eventually," said Nighthawk.

"Kill him?"

"Soon."

Blue Eyes got to his feet and approached the bar. "I'm sorry, Ibn ben Khalid. I tried to lead him away from you!"

Nicholas looked at Blue Eyes, then back to Nighthawk.

"So you've figured it out, have you?"

"It wasn't that difficult."

"And now you're going to kill me?"

"That's the general idea."

"What did I ever do to you?"

"It's what you did to Cassandra Hill," answered Nighthawk.

"You've never even met her," said Nicholas. "Why do you want to kill me over a woman you don't know?"

"I have my reasons."

"Why don't you use that brain of yours to come up with a reason to join my cause instead?"

"Not interested."

"I may kill *you,* you know."

"Anything's possible," replied Nighthawk.

"You don't believe it for a second, do you?" said Nicholas with a slight smile. "Maybe you should consider the fact that every man who wears a weapon out here is undefeated, just like you."

"That's why I never take anyone lightly," said Nighthawk.

"Well, I can see your mind's made up," said Nicholas, stepping away from the bar and positioning his hand over his sonic pistol. "Let's get on with it."

"Let's."

Nighthawk was a microsecond from going for his own weapon when suddenly the silence of the room was broken by the shout of a familiar voice.

"STOP!" yelled Melisande.

Chapter 17

Nighthawk froze, never taking his eyes off Nicholas Jory.

"You're making a terrible mistake!" said Melisande, getting to her feet and approaching the two men at the bar.

"Move and you're a dead man," said Nighthawk to Nicholas. Then, to Melisande: "What the hell's going on?"

"He's not Ibn ben Khalid!" she said.

"Just because he's seen to it that the Oligarchy has holographs of the wrong man?" demanded Nighthawk. "It's one of the oldest tricks in the book. You heard Blue Eyes. You heard Jory. They both admitted that he's Ibn ben Khalid!"

"You hired me for my ability," said Melisande urgently. "Make use of it, don't ignore it!"

Nighthawk drew his weapon before Nicholas quite realized what was happening, and pointed it at the young man.

"Put your hands on the bar," he ordered.

Nicholas complied.

Nighthawk frisked him briefly, disarmed him, and then stepped back.

"All right," he said to Melisande. "Talk to me. I thought you couldn't read Blue Eyes' emotions."

"I can't."

"And you're not a telepath."

"I'm not."

"Then how can you know for certain that this man's not Ibn ben Khalid?" persisted Nighthawk.

"I know from his emotions," answered Melisande. "When Blue Eyes addressed him as if he was Ibn ben Khalid, his reaction was shock and surprise. As he realized what Blue Eyes was doing, that was replaced by feelings of exultation and loyalty. He was willing to sacrifice his life to preserve Ibn ben Khalid's true identity. Finally, when you refused to be dissuaded, his only emotional reactions were sorrow and fear."

"Was there anything else?" asked Nighthawk. "Any other emotion at all?"

Melisande frowned for a moment, then looked up at Nighthawk. "Just one thing—a rush of conflicting emotions, too forceful and too contradictory for me to separate them, when you mentioned Cassandra Hill."

"Do you think he knows where she is?"

"I read feelings, not thoughts," replied Melisande. "I have no idea if he knows where she is."

"Thanks," said Nighthawk. "Go sit down. I'll take it from here."

She walked back to the table. As she passed Blue Eyes, who was still standing near the bar, he fell into step beside her.

"Not you," said Nighthawk.

Blue Eyes looked at him questioningly. "Are you talking to *me*?"

"Get your blue ass over here. You've got some explaining to do."

The dragon approached Nighthawk. "I was protecting my leader," he said with no show of fear. "I have no regrets. I did what I thought was best, and I'd do it again."

"You may not live long enough to do it again," said Nighthawk. "You've been lying to me ever since we met, and you almost got an innocent man killed by lying to me a couple of minutes ago."

"Nicholas Jory was willing to die for the cause. I commend him for his courage."

"I couldn't care less about your cause. I want to know where Ibn ben Khalid is."

"I'm sure you do," said Blue Eyes defiantly. "And after you kill me, you'll *still* want to know."

"Maybe I'll kill *him* instead," said Nighthawk, indicating Nicholas.

"He was willing to die two minutes ago to protect Ibn ben Khalid," responded the dragon. "I'm sure he still is. Do your worst."

"Or maybe I'll just find the girl and take her away until he's willing to talk."

Neither Nicholas nor Blue Eyes made any response, but Nighthawk was concentrating on Melisande, who had seated herself at the table some fifty feet away. She jumped like she'd been hit by a flying brick.

"She's here on Sylene, isn't she?" continued Nighthawk, staring intently at Nicholas.

"That's none of your damned business!"

"For the time being, it's my *only* business," Nighthawk replied. "Have you got Cassandra Hill stashed away at your place?"

"Go look. I'm not telling you anything."

You just did. If you're willing to have your rooms searched, she's not there. But she's got to be close. You're too nervous for her not to be.

He turned to face Blue Eyes. "You know where she is, don't you?"

"Why don't you just return to Deluros and leave us in peace?" answered the dragon. "You don't belong here. You don't belong anywhere. You should have died a century ago. Stop meddling in our business."

Nighthawk stared at the man and the dragon for a long moment, then turned to the tavern at large.

"All right," he said in a loud voice. "Everybody out. The bar's closed."

A few patrons looked at him curiously. He waved his gun in their direction.

"Now," he said.

Most of the Men and aliens got up and left. The Canphorites and a trio of Men remained.

"Ito, count to thirty and shoot any customers who are still in the tavern."

Kinoshita got to his feet, guns drawn, and faced the remaining patrons. The Canphorites made it out the door in ten seconds, the Men in twelve.

"All right," said Kinoshita to Nighthawk after the last of them had left. "What's going on?"

"I didn't want them to distract Melisande."

"Distract me from what?" she asked.

"You told me that proximity makes a difference in your ability to read emotions."

"Yes, but—"

"I want you to concentrate—hard," said Nighthawk. "Can you read anything that isn't coming from me, Kinoshita, Friday, or Jory?"

"You think that she's *here*?"

As Melisande uttered the words, she reeled as if she'd been hit.

"She's not at his place. And he just reacted at the suggestion, didn't he?"

"*Some*one did," she confirmed.

"All right. Tell me if you can read anyone else."

"I'll try."

"Don't bother," said a female voice from behind them, and they turned to see a slim, dark-haired woman in her late twenties stepping out through a sliding panel in the wall.

"Cassandra Hill, I presume?" said Nighthawk.

"Yes," she said.

"Are you all right?"

"Perfectly."

"I'm here to—"

"I know why you're here," said Cassandra Hill. "I'm sorry you've wasted your time, but I was not kidnapped by Ibn ben Khalid. I'm here of my own free will."

"What about the ransom demand?"

"Ibn ben Khalid saw a way to extort two million credits from my father. When you're in the revolution business, you do what you have to do."

"And you didn't object?"

"There is no love lost between my father and me. He's a vile, corrupt man, and I hope Ibn ben Khalid brings him to justice."

Nighthawk frowned. "That's too bad."

"Why?"

"I'm going to have to return you to him."

"But I've already told you—I wasn't kidnapped!" she said. "I'm here because I want to be here." She paused. "And if I know my father, I'll bet he's more interested in killing Ibn ben Khalid than in having me returned."

"True enough," admitted Nighthawk.

"Well, then?"

"I sympathize—but I don't have any choice."

"You can choose to walk away and forget you ever saw me," said Cassandra.

"It's not that simple," said Nighthawk. "The life of someone very important to me depends on my returning you to your father."

"I don't want to go back." She nodded her head toward Melisande. "Ask your Balatai woman."

Nighthawk turned to Melisande. "She's telling the truth, of course?"

"No."

"That's a lie!" snapped Cassandra.

"She doesn't want to go back," continued Melisande. "And she seems to genuinely hate her father. But there was a lot of insincerity in her answers—I would characterize it as misdirection."

"Once we find Ibn ben Khalid, we'll find out how much of what she said is the truth," said Kinoshita.

Melisande reeled again, like a boxer absorbing a blow to the head.

Well, I'll be damned, thought Nighthawk. *Suddenly the pieces fit together.*

"I think that would be a waste of time, don't you, Miss Hill?" said Nighthawk.

She stared coldly at him. "I don't think he could tell you anything I couldn't tell you myself."

"That remains to be seen," said Kinoshita.

"No it doesn't," said Nighthawk.

"What the hell are you talking about?"

Nighthawk looked at Cassandra Hill. "Do you want to tell him, or should I?"

"You do it," she replied.

"Tell me *what*?" demanded Kinoshita.

"Cassandra Hill is only one of her names," said Nighthawk. He paused for effect. "Say hello to Ibn ben Khalid."

Chapter 18

"You're crazy!" exclaimed Kinoshita.

"Am I?" responded Nighthawk. He gestured to Melisande. "Ask *her*."

"He's right," said the empath.

"But it doesn't make any sense!"

"It makes all the sense in the world," said Nighthawk. "We know she hates her father. We can assume he's as corrupt as most politicians, since he paid my law firm to oversee the performance of a highly illegal act—and, of course, he's also commissioned an illegal hit." Nighthawk paused. "I submit to you that that kind of corruption doesn't occur overnight. If Cassandra was appalled by it as an adolescent, she probably had access to enough information to start thwarting him. And since she didn't want to do it openly, for any number of reasons ranging from preserving her sources of information to preserving her life, she needed another identity."

"But Ibn ben Khalid is a *man's* name!"

"It just means she's better at misdirection than most of us," answered Nighthawk.

"Ibn ben Khalid has been operating out here for a decade," continued Kinoshita, not yet willing to admit he was wrong. "She'd have been a teenager then. Who would follow a teenaged girl into battle?"

"You still don't understand, do you?" said Nighthawk. "Think back, Ito. We've been all over the Frontier. How many of Ibn ben Khalid's followers have actually seen him? *That's* why there's such a complex chain of command. There are probably less than a dozen people out here who know Ibn ben Khalid is actually Cassandra Hill."

"Nineteen, to be exact," interjected Cassandra.

"Well, I'll be damned!" muttered Kinoshita.

"Probably you will be," she agreed. Suddenly she turned to Nighthawk. "Now that you know, what do you propose to do about it?"

"Nothing, for the moment."

"It is our mission to kill her," said Friday.

"Don't be a fool," shot back Nighthawk. "You don't think she'd have shown herself if we weren't covered, do you?" He looked at Cassandra. "How many guns are pointing at us right now?"

"Eight," she said. Then, "I know how good you are, Widowmaker. But they're well hidden; even *you* can't kill all of them before one of them gets in a fatal shot."

Nighthawk looked carefully around the tavern. "All right," he said. "You're calling the shots. What next?"

"Next? Next we talk."

"What about?"

"What are your intentions if you survive this meeting?" she said. "You're being paid to return Cassandra Hill and kill Ibn ben Khalid. You can't do both."

Nighthawk poured himself a drink. "I'll have to think about it."

"There's another alternative," said Cassandra.

"There usually is."

She looked at his team. "The rest of you go outside and wait for us. I want to talk to the Widowmaker alone."

They arose and began moving to the door.

"Just a minute!" she said firmly. "You—the red one!"

Friday turned back to her.

"Leave your weapons here on the table."

"Why just me?" demanded the alien.

"Because I don't trust you. Do what I say."

Friday shrugged, unstrapped his various pistols and knives, and placed them gently on the table, then walked out to join the others.

"You look approving," noted Cassandra, sitting down across from Nighthawk.

"You picked the right one. He'd just as soon kill the two of us as look at us."

"Then why is he working for you?"

"If he wasn't working for me, he'd be following me," answered Nighthawk. "At least this way I can keep an eye on him. And . . ." He paused.

"Yes?"

"We weren't going on a picnic," he continued. "He's good at his job."

"I heard about his 'job' on Cellestra."

"He thought he was coming to my rescue," said Nighthawk. "I can't fault him for that."

"You can fault his judgment."

Nighthawk shook his head. "It had nothing to do with judgment. He'll use any excuse he can find for killing Men. That excuse was better than most."

"What about the others?" asked Cassandra. "Do you trust them?"

"I don't trust anyone. But I'm willing to turn my back on them."

"They say that Kinoshita used to be a lawman out here on the Frontier."

"So I've been told," replied Nighthawk.

"Is he good at his work?"

"Relatively."

"But he's no Widowmaker?"

"No," answered Nighthawk. "He's no Widowmaker." He stared at her. "Are you going to make your offer pretty soon? I'm starting to get hungry."

"What offer?"

"It's pretty obvious," he said. "You want me to join you, and you're wondering whether to make the offer just to me, or to my whole team."

"Well, you're not stupid, I'll give you that."

"I never said I was."

"When you virtually accused poor Nicholas of being me, I had my doubts."

"I didn't have sufficient information," he replied. "He was dead drunk the first time Melisande encountered him. Once I realized Blue Eyes was leading me *away* from Ibn ben Khalid, I assumed the drunkenness was Jory's way of disguising his thoughts." Suddenly Nighthawk smiled. "How could I know he didn't have any?"

"He's a lot brighter than you think."

"He's willing to die for you, and you don't care a fig about him. I wouldn't call that bright."

"Not for *me*," she corrected him. "For the cause."

"Most tax dodgers are in favor of overthrowing the government," commented Nighthawk.

"He's more than that."

"If you say so."

She stared at him again. "I'll ask you once more: if I let you live, what do you plan to do?"

"I haven't decided."

"You will concede that I can have you killed before you reach the door?"

"I concede it," answered Nighthawk. "But I don't concede you can kill me before I can kill you."

"Why should either of us die? Especially for the benefit of someone as evil as my father?"

"I told you: I don't have a choice."

"Since when don't clones have free will?"

He stared at her.

"Oh, yes," Cassandra continued. "I know all about you, Jefferson Nighthawk. You're the second clone of the original Widowmaker. You were created for the sole purpose of returning me to my father."

"And killing Ibn ben Khalid."

"And killing Ibn ben Khalid," she agreed. "But you're out here, hundreds of thousands of light-years from Deluros VIII. What power do they hold over you? Why can't you just say no?"

"If I don't bring you back, I don't get paid," answered Nighthawk. "And if I don't get paid, the first Jefferson Nighthawk gets evicted from his cryonic chamber before they've completed the cure for his disease." He paused. "I kill *other* people. I'm not suicidal."

"And you feel it would be suicide?"

"He and I are one and the same."

"How much money does he need?"

Nighthawk shrugged. "Three million, four million, five million credits. Who knows? They're close to a cure, but they haven't got it yet."

She stared at him intently, then sipped the drink that Melisande had left behind. "What would you say to ten million credits?"

"Explain."

"Would you help me bring my father down if I paid you ten million credits?" she asked. "That could keep the original Nighthawk alive for a long time—and you'd be fighting on the right side."

"Which side I fight on makes no difference to me," said Nighthawk. "But I don't have any desire to kill you. If your offer is legitimate, I'd certainly have to consider it."

"Which side you fought on made a difference to you once," she continued. "I've studied your career. The Widowmaker killed an awful lot of Men and aliens, but he was always a lawman or a bounty hunter, never an outlaw."

"I was only feeding one of me then," he replied with an ironic smile.

"You can't convince me that you're not still an ethical man," she said adamantly.

"It's not my job to convince you of anything," said Nighthawk. "*You* have to convince *me* not to kill you or return you."

"I can offer you ten million reasons."

"Okay, where are they?"

"In my father's safe."

Nighthawk leaned back in his chair and considered it. "You're saying that there's no money unless we're successful, right?"

"In essence."

"And it could take months to assemble and prepare your forces for an attack on your father, and even then they'll probably be outnumbered."

"You can't take him by force, only by stealth and surprise," she said. "We'll have to go in with a carefully assembled team." She paused. "That's one of the reasons I need you. Like I said, I've studied your career. You've done this kind of thing more than once. I need your expertise."

"But you're not prepared to pay until we succeed?"

"That's right."

"I have to consider it," he said. "If we fail, you've killed two Widowmakers."

"If I kill you right now, I've done the same thing," she noted.

"True," he acknowledged.

"Consider something else," she continued. "If you succeed and return to Deluros, they're almost certain to terminate you. It would be very awkward to have a clone walking around, one who could identify the people who created him."

"I've known that from the moment I woke up on a lab table," he replied. "That's why I'm never going back to the Oligarchy."

"There's enough in my father's safe to keep the original Widowmaker alive *and* give you a stake for a new life."

He stared at her without replying.

"You're weakening, aren't you?" she said with a smile.

"I'm *considering.*"

He fell silent again.

"Well?" she demanded after another moment had passed. "Are you still considering?"

"No—I'm counting."

"Millions?"

"Men."

"I don't understand."

"If we're going to become partners, we have to trust each other," said Nighthawk. "Until you know I could have killed all eight of your gunmen and chose not to, you'll never be sure that I won't turn on you when the opportunity presents itself." He looked around the room. "Three behind the see-through mirror in back of the bar. Another one behind the door to the dressing room. One behind the picture that's hanging askew on the south wall. Two in the attic"—he pointed to the ceiling—"there and there. I haven't spotted the eighth yet."

"You're *good,*" she said, impressed. "I made the right choice."

"Not yet," he said, still scanning the room. Suddenly he smiled. "Oh, hell, I'm an asshole. The eighth one is *you.*"

She returned his smile, withdrew a tiny pistol that was attached to her wrist just inside her sleeve, and placed it on the table.

"So do we have a deal?"

"Yeah, I think we do."

"Good," she said. "I'll tell my people that your team can come and go freely."

"Tell them to keep an eye on the red alien," said Nighthawk. "He doesn't much care about sides, as long as he gets to kill Men."

She nodded and extended her hand. "Welcome to the cause, Widow-maker."

"Keep your cause," he said, taking her small hand in his own. "You'd just better be right about how much is in the safe."

Chapter 19

It was evening. Nighthawk's team had returned to the hotel, and he had remained behind at The Blue Dragon. There was an apartment above the bar, and Cassandra Hill had invited him upstairs to join her for dinner.

"This place is too tastefully decorated for it to belong to Blue Eyes," commented Nighthawk as he entered the place. "You've a good eye for art."

"You recognize some of the artists?" she asked.

"A few. The Morita sculpture is exquisite."

"I'm genuinely surprised," she said. "I never expected a man in your profession to have any knowledge of art."

"I've been sent out to retrieve it often enough."

"There's a difference between retrieving it and studying it."

"You think a man who kills for a living can't appreciate art?" he asked wryly.

"Well . . . I . . ."

"Let me tell you something," he said. "When you put your life on the line all the time, it heightens *all* your perceptions." He paused, staring at the sculpture. "Also, since you become aware of your mortality, you tend to appreciate those things that will outlive you. Morita died more than a millennia ago, and people still flock to see his work."

"I meant no offense," she said.

"None taken. I was just explaining."

"Well," she said, "you like artwork, so maybe my pride and joy won't be wasted on you. Follow me."

She led the way to a large room, paneled with imported hardwood. Three walls were covered with shelves, and the shelves themselves were covered with books. There were thousands of them, beautifully bound, many with gilt pages, a few with engraved covers, all with bent or broken spines that proved they were for reading rather than for decoration.

Nighthawk walked to the middle of the room, stood with his hands on his hips for a long moment, and then began examining the shelves.

"What do you think?" she asked.

"I've never seen so many books in one place," he replied.

"There used to be lots of libraries like this, I'm told, before you could fit an entire encyclopedia on a chip a tenth the size of my fingernail." She picked a volume up from the shelf. "I like the heft and smell of a book. The reading experience seems inadequate and lacking when you read from a holoscreen."

"I see you even have one by Tanblixt," noted Nighthawk.

"The greatest of the alien poets."

"I know. I've read him."

"Recently?"

He smiled. "About a century and a half ago."

She stared at him for a moment. "If there are any books you'd like to borrow . . ."

Nighthawk paused, then shook his head. "I'd be afraid something might happen to them," he said. "But if we're on Sylene for any length of time, I'd like to be able to read some right here in your library."

"You're welcome to." She paused. "You're a most unusual man, Widowmaker. It's very rare to find a cultured, educated man in your line of work."

"You find all kinds of men in my line of work," he replied. "There are as many reasons as there are practitioners."

"I would have thought most of you had an overdeveloped sense of justice, or perhaps a death wish," she said with a smile.

"Take a look at Friday," responded Nighthawk. "All he wants is the opportunity to kill Men. Justice means nothing to him, and I doubt that he ever considers his own mortality."

"He's an alien."

"Don't aliens count?"

"They have different motivations."

"Do they?" said Nighthawk. "An alien named Blue Eyes did his damnedest to lead me away from you, and when I came back he was willing to sacrifice both his life and Jory's to keep your identity a secret."

"That's Blue Eyes. He's one of us."

"I thought he was an alien."

She sighed. "You're right. Here I was, sounding like exactly what I'm fighting against."

"Suppose you tell me a little more about what you're fighting against?" suggested Nighthawk.

"I'll be happy to," she said. "Just let me serve our dinner first."

"You cook, too?"

"Not when I can help it," said Cassandra. "Actually, Nicholas cooked dinner tonight."

"You live with him?" asked Nighthawk.

"I live with *me*," she answered firmly. "Nicholas likes to cook."

"I always thought I'd take it up someday."

"Cooking?"

He nodded. "You visit a couple of hundred alien worlds and suddenly nice bland digestible food becomes very important to you." He smiled. "Especially when your life may depend upon not being sick."

"I never considered that."

"Stay in the revolution business long enough and you will," he assured her.

"Perhaps."

"Now suppose you tell me just how you got into the business," said Nighthawk.

"My father," she replied. "He's the most corrupt man alive."

"I think every girl believes that at one point or another. Most of them outgrow it. How come you didn't?"

"Because in my case it wasn't a fantasy. I've heard my father give orders to kill political rivals or ambitious subordinates. He's getting kick-backs from every contractor who ever worked for the planetary government, from every spaceship company that wants docking space at our orbiting hangars, from every interest group that wants a favor."

She paused for breath, and Nighthawk noticed that her cheeks were flushed. After a moment she brought their food to the table, and they both sat down.

"He's especially vicious toward our alien population. It's his policy to hold them without trial and without bail. Any alien who kills a Man is summarily executed without a trial. The penalty for a Man who kills any alien is two hundred credits." She grimaced at the memory. "So I decided that he had to be overthrown. I created the myth of Ibn ben Khalid to misdirect his attention, and began building an organization of Men and aliens who want to see Cassius Hill overthrown."

"They say you number over a million now," commented Nighthawk. "That's an impressive force."

"It's an inflated figure, just to scare him. Hell, if I had a million men, I'd have attacked already."

"You'd have lost."

"What are you talking about?" she demanded heatedly.

"He's got a standing army of close to four million men, and he's got—what?—something like thirty thousand ships. You're not going to overthrow him with a million men, or three million, or ten million."

"We will, if right is on our side."

"I'm no historian," said Nighthawk, "but it's my observation that God tends to favor the side with the best weapons and the most manpower."

"Are you saying he can't be overthrown?" she said. "Tyrants are overthrown every year."

"Not at all," he replied. "I said he can't be successfully attacked by a force ten times the size of the one that's at your disposal."

"Then what do you suggest?"

He stared at her for a long moment. "I don't know that I'm in a position to suggest anything. Remember: he's my employer."

"What if I showed you proof that he's every bit as evil and corrupt as I claim he is?" she asked.

"I believe you."

"But you insist that you owe him your loyalty?"

"I don't judge the men I hunt, and I don't judge the men I work for."

"Maybe it's time you started."

He shrugged. "Maybe it is," he agreed. "Let's discuss it while we eat."

"What's to discuss?" she said. "Either you're for me or you're against me. Or, in your case, either you're going to join me or you're going to try to take me back."

"Nothing's ever that simple."

"This is."

"*Nothing* is," he repeated. "I like you. I'm predisposed to like people who take moral stands, and I'm predisposed to like people who still read books. You're smart, and you're tough, and you've managed to convince a hell of a lot of people to join your cause. I believe everything you said about your father, and I have no admiration for those who take advantage of the weak."

"Well, then?"

"Half a galaxy away, on Deluros VIII, there's a cryonics chamber almost a mile beneath the surface of the planet. A few thousand men and women are frozen there. Most of them have diseases and are awaiting cures. A few committed crimes and are waiting for the statue of limitations to run out. A handful simply don't like the government or the economy, and are waiting for better times to live out the rest of their lives. There's even one, I'm told, a botanist who found a flower that only blooms once every three centuries, and wants to be alive to see it." Nighthawk took a bite of his meal, chewed it thoughtfully, and nodded approvingly.

"The one thing all these men and women have in common is that they're extremely wealthy," he went on. "Wealthy enough to be able to afford the enormous expense of remaining frozen. There's only one man there who *doesn't* have the financial wherewithal to remain frozen until his disease can be cured. His name is Jefferson Nighthawk. He's not my father, he's not my twin brother. He's *me*, and I can't let him down."

"I see."

"I told you: nothing is ever as simple as it seems," he said with a rueful smile. "If I don't deliver you to your father, I won't get paid—and if I don't get paid, the original version of me, the man who *is* the Widowmaker, who gave me his body and his memory so that I could protect his existence, is going to die. I won't allow that."

"So no matter what you feel about me or about my father, you're going to try to return me?"

" 'Try to' is a misstatement. If I decide to return you, I'll do it."

"Not without a fight," she promised.

"I'd expect one."

"Even the Widowmaker can die."

"I'm living proof of that," answered Nighthawk. "Or, rather, the original is dying proof of it."

"Then I guess the battle lines are drawn," said Cassandra. "Do you just plan to eat dinner, read a good book, and then carry me off?"

"There are always alternatives," said Nighthawk. "I thought we might explore some of them."

"I'm willing," she said. "What do you have in mind?"

"How liquid is your father?"

"I beg your pardon?"

"You said he has ten million credits in his safe. Are you guessing, or do you *know*?"

"Why?"

"Because ten million is enough to keep the original Nighthawk alive, and pay for my cure as well, once a cure is developed."

"He's got it, and more," she said decisively.

"If I helped overthrow him, I'd want that money as payment for my services."

"You've already said that Pericles V is impregnable. How will my agreeing to pay you make a difference?"

"What I said was an army of a million men couldn't overthrow your father," he said. "I didn't say there weren't other ways to accomplish it."

"Such as?"

"Well, most obviously, we try to lure him out here, where he's vulnerable, and kill him," said Nighthawk. He took a deep breath and let it out slowly. "And if that doesn't work, we'll do it the hard way."

"All right, Mr. Nighthawk," she said. "What's the hard way?"

"We take my team to Pericles V," he answered. "I assembled them for the purpose of killing one man, and that's still our purpose. Only now the man will be Cassius Hill instead of Ibn ben Khalid."

She stared at him. "I admire your confidence."

"I handpicked that team for a reason. They're not much to look at, and they don't get along very well—but they're goddamned good at what they do." He finished his food and shoved the plate aside. "Still, it'll be much easier if we can draw him out here, where he's not protected by so many men and devices."

"How will you do that?"

"It shouldn't be too hard," said Nighthawk. "After all, I've got something he wants."

"What is that?"

"You."

Chapter 20

Cassandra looked up from the book she was reading. "You're back again."

"Not much to do on this little dirtball," replied Nighthawk, as he entered her apartment. "At least you've got books I can read."

She put her book on a table and stared at him. "I've also got an army you can use."

He shook his head. "Too disorganized. And too outnumbered." He paused. "I keep telling you: you can't storm a well-armed fortress with a ragtag mob. Your father's probably got a ton of spies in your army, ready to tell him every order you give. And there's something else, too."

"Oh?"

"Only Blue Eyes and Jory and maybe a handful of others know you're Cassandra Hill. When the rest find out, your life won't be worth ten credits. At least half of them will think the creation of Ibn ben Khalid was a trick created by your father to pinpoint who was disloyal to him."

"Not after I explain it to them."

"This is the Frontier. There's going to be at least one man in each audience who doesn't feel like waiting for an explanation."

"You're wrong," she said adamantly. "These are *my* men. They're committed to my cause."

"Let's hope we don't have to find out. Much better to present them with a fait accompli."

"So when are you going to do it?" she asked.

"It's too soon," said Nighthawk.

She looked annoyed. "He's not getting any weaker, you know."

"I know. But I haven't been out here long enough. If I find Cassandra Hill and Ibn ben Khalid too easily, he'll think something's wrong."

"How can you be sure of that?" she demanded. "You don't even know him."

"I know that he's suspicious of just about everyone. It's not as if he hasn't got his share of enemies."

Cassandra nodded. "His share and more."

Nighthawk walked over to a bookcase and started scanning the titles. He pulled a couple out, thumbed through them, and put them back.

"Too much fiction," he announced at last.

"I beg your pardon?"

"You want to be a leader," he said. "You should be reading books about politics and leadership. Even Machiavelli. Ninety percent of your library is fiction." He grimaced in contempt. "Totally useless."

"It teaches you about people."

"It's filled with lies."

"Its plots are lies—but it's filled with truth. The good stuff, anyway."

"You want to be a leader," he noted. "How does a made-up story about people who never existed teach you anything about how real people think?"

"That's very strange," she said.

"What is?"

"It seems to me that you, the cold-blooded killer, should be the one who wants to escape into fiction."

"Me? Why?"

"As an alternative to the horrors and grimness of your occupation."

"I've been a lawman and a bounty hunter," answered Nighthawk. "I've never been a criminal."

"Meaning what?"

"There's nothing horrible about my work," he explained. "I bring felons to justice. There are times when it can be very satisfying."

"You take satisfaction in killing people?"

"Not as much, I suspect, as you'll take in the death of your father."

"That's different," she said. "It's personal."

"Are you saying you've assembled an army just to help you settle a personal grudge?" he asked.

"No, of course not. They're the dispossessed and disenfranchised."

"And you're their spokesman?"

"In a way."

"Then, in a way," he said, "I'm the ombudsman for all those people who have been swindled or killed by men with prices on their heads."

He half expected a furious outburst. Instead she threw back her head and laughed.

"You're a very intelligent man."

"Thank you."

"You're wasted in your current profession."

"I don't think so," he replied. "There are lots of bright men. There's only one Widowmaker."

"Perhaps."

"Perhaps?" he repeated.

"What about the original—the man you were cloned from?"

"As I told you, he's frozen until they come up with a cure for eplasia."

She made a face. "You hadn't said it was eplasia. Is there a chance you could catch it too?"

"There's considerably more than a chance," he said. "I've already got it."

She studied him, looking for some sign of it.

"It's in the very early stages," he continued. "You won't see any sign of it for another year or two."

"It's a horrible way to die!" she said with a shudder. "The skin just rots away until the body is exposed to so many infections that it finally can't fight them off any longer."

"I don't plan to die."

"No one ever plans to die. But we all do."

"Let me amend that, then. I don't plan to die from *eplasia*. They'll have a cure before much longer. That's why I'm here—to earn enough to keep the original Widowmaker alive and eventually cure him." He paused. "And I'll need some extra money for me."

"We'll get it," said Cassandra. She paused thoughtfully. "You should get quite a thrill when you meet him after you're both cured."

"I don't think I will."

"Get a thrill?"

"Meet him."

"Why not?"

"I don't know," he admitted. "I just have a feeling that the two of us should never meet, that it would somehow be like a time paradox where you meet yourself. I'm sure it won't destroy the universe or bring time to a stop, but I think it would be better if it never happens."

"Will he at least be able to thank you?"

"It's not necessary," said Nighthawk, and when she looked dubious, he added: "You don't thank yourself for brushing your teeth, or sterilizing a cut, do you? He's me, I'm him. This is just self-preservation."

"You must have some interesting nightmares," she said.

"A few," he admitted.

"Then why be something that disturbs you?"

"That's the kind of question men are supposed to ask of women who are in Melisande's line of work," he replied with a smile.

"I'm serious."

He shrugged. "I don't know," he replied. "It's one of those things you don't think about much. I guess I've just got a talent for it."

"How do you *know* you have a talent for it?" she persisted. "Did you kill the butler when you were three years old?"

"I suppose I might have, if we'd had one," he said with an amused smile.

"You're not very forthcoming."

"That's because it's *his* life, and I don't know if he'd want me to answer you or not."

"But you told me you had all of the original's memories," she said. "So it's your life as well."

"They're his memories, not mine," answered Nighthawk. "He's got a proprietary claim on them."

"I've never met anyone quite like you."

"I'll assume that's a compliment."

She fell silent, and he continued looking at the spines of her books, considering first one title, then another, and finally withdrawing one.

"What have you decided on?" she asked.

"Tanblixt," he replied.

"That's a collector's item," she noted. "It's in the original Canphorian."

"I can read it a bit."

"You continue to surprise me," said Cassandra.

"I've had to work with Canphorites in the past," he said. "They're easier to get along with if you try to learn their language."

"Even though the law demands that all aliens must learn Terran or equip themselves with T-packs?"

"Especially because of the law."

"Good," she said. "I approve."

"Of course you approve. You're Ibn ben Khalid."

"When I'm not being Cassandra Hill."

He smiled. "At least I'm always Jefferson Nighthawk, even if I don't always know *which* Jefferson Nighthawk I am."

She laughed again. "You're just not what I expected the Widowmaker to be like."

"You haven't seen the Widowmaker yet. Just Nighthawk."

"Aren't you one and the same?"

"No," he said. "I'm always Nighthawk. I'm only the Widowmaker when I have to be."

"With all our identities, I'm surprised the room doesn't feel more crowded," said Cassandra.

He smiled at her. "You're all right, Hill. I'm glad we're going after your father instead."

"I'm pleased you should think so."

He uttered a statement that was totally incomprehensible to her.

"Would you repeat that, please?" she asked.

He did so.

"What was that?"

"A compliment," said Nighthawk.

"In Canphorian?"

"Lodinese."

"You speak Lodinese too?"

"A little."

"You're a man of many accomplishments."

"I've tried to be," he said. "It's ironic that I'll only be remembered for one of them."

"It's the one that topples empires," she noted.

He shook his head emphatically. "Empires don't fall because the emperor dies. There's always another one eager to take his place. They fall, when they fall, because they're too corrupt *not* to fall."

"So you don't think my father's little empire will come tumbling down?"

"Maybe so, maybe not," answered Nighthawk. "It depends on the nature of the empire. Personally, I'll be satisfied if he has enough money to keep my progenitor alive."

"He has that, and more."

"We'll see."

"You don't believe me?"

"It's nothing personal. I don't believe anyone. Ever. That's how I lived to be sixty-one."

"You don't look sixty-one."

He smiled ruefully. "One of me does."

"That one's not getting any younger or any healthier," she said. "How soon do you think you can contact my father?"

"A few weeks, maybe a month."

"That's too long. I can have my army assembled here in less than two weeks."

"I told you before: I don't want your army."

"I know what you told me. But they're loyal and motivated. Surely you can find some way to use them."

"They'd just be cannon fodder," responded Nighthawk. "I'm a killer, not a general. I don't need them."

"But—"

"You really want to make them useful to us?" he interrupted her. "Have them assemble, publicly and noisily, on some world halfway across the Frontier. Maybe we can draw a few of your father's divisions out there to keep an eye on them. It might make our escape—assuming we live long enough to *attempt* an escape—easier." He paused. "But first, let's see if your father is dumb enough to come out here, before we do it the hard way."

"He'll come," she said firmly.

"Don't bet your last credit on it," said Nighthawk. "He didn't get where he is by being stupid."

"He paid whatever it cost to create you, just to rescue me," she said. "Of course he'll come. All this waiting is useless."

"You've waited this long to get to him," said Nighthawk. "Wait a few weeks more."

"No," she said. "It's time."

"You're sure?"

"I know him."

Personally, maybe. But I know him generically. And I've got a bad feeling about this.

"Okay," said Nighthawk aloud. "I'll contact him this afternoon."

"Good!" she said. "Now you can do me another favor."

"I'm not in the favor business."

"You won't mind this one," she said.

"Oh?"

"Pour us each a drink, and then translate some of Tanblixt's poems for me."

"You have a translation right there on the shelf," said Nighthawk, walking across the room to the bar, selecting a thirty-year-old Cygnian cognac, filling a pair of glasses, and handing one to her.

"I'd like to hear how *you* translate it."

"You're sure?"

She nodded. "And I like the way your voice sounds—possibly because I've yet to hear you threaten my life."

He stared at her and made no reply. Finally he took a sip of his drink, and a moment later he was reciting an intricate rhyming triplet about the incredible light refraction at sunset on Canphor VII.

Chapter 21

Nighthawk was sitting at a table in the bar, nursing a drink before making his transmission to Cassius Hill, when Ito Kinoshita entered and sat down next to him.

"What's up?" asked Nighthawk.

"I thought maybe *you* might tell *me*," replied Kinoshita. "We've been sitting around for days, waiting for action." He signaled for a beer, and took a long swallow when it arrived. "I think Friday may blow up the town this week, just to keep his hand in."

"I'll have work for him soon."

"And the rest of us?" asked Kinoshita.

"Are you that anxious to go out and shoot people?" asked Nighthawk.

"I'm anxious to stop feeling useless. We all are. We know why you originally assembled us . . . but we've *found* Ibn ben Khalid, so do we serve any further purpose?"

"A bigger one."

"Would you care to enlighten me?"

"Soon," said Nighthawk. "I have to speak to Cassandra's father first."

"Cassius Hill?" said Kinoshita sharply.

"That's right."

"Are you going to turn her over to him?"

Nighthawk shook his head. "If things were that simple, I wouldn't need you and the others."

"But he's your employer!"

"I'm sure it pleases him to think so," answered Nighthawk. "I don't plan to do anything to spoil the illusion."

Kinoshita stared at him for a long moment. "You've thrown in with her, haven't you?"

"In a way."

"In what way?" demanded Kinoshita, lighting a smokeless Altairian cigar. "Either you're with her or you're against her. It's as simple as that."

"Nothing's ever as simple as that," said Nighthawk.

"Just what have you got in mind?"

"I'm going to try to draw him out here to Sylene, hopefully with a huge cash box," said Nighthawk calmly. "If he comes, I'll kill him."

"You're kidding, right?"

"I never kid about business."

"You think he'll come alone, or with just one or two bodyguards?" scoffed Kinoshita. "Hell, he'll come with a whole division, and he won't get out of his ship until they've searched every inch of the landing field and secured his route to wherever you plan to meet him."

"I'd expect no less of a man who's been in power as long as Cassius Hill," agreed Nighthawk.

"Well, then?"

"I'll ask if he has the money with him, and Melisande will know if he's lying or not. If he's brought it along and left it in the ship, I'm sure Friday can rig something that will wipe out most of his landing party and maybe his ship's motive power while leaving the interior of the ship intact."

"And if he's got it with him?"

"Then you and I and Blue Eyes will figure out how to separate him from it."

Kinoshita snapped his fingers. "Just like that?"

"Just like that."

"You don't believe in long, intricate plans, do you?"

"The more intricate a plan is, the more likely it is to go wrong," answered Nighthawk. "Just like a machine. The more moving parts, the more likelihood of failure." Suddenly he sighed heavily. "Unfortunately, Hill himself is one more moving part than we need. That's why I'm uneasy."

"I don't follow you."

"If I'm attacking his headquarters, even with just my handpicked crew of five, *I'm* in control of things. I decide when we approach, how we get in, when we use force, when we retreat, whether we complete our mission or abort it. But if he comes here with his men, however many or few, *he* can disrupt the most carefully laid of plans."

"Seems to me we'll save a lot of lives if he comes here."

"Maybe."

"Did anyone ever tell you that you are not the most loquacious fellow in the world?"

"You did," answered Nighthawk. "Every time we were alone together on the ship."

"Well, I was right."

"Probably. Now I want you to do me a favor."

"What is it?"

"Tell Friday to get ready to travel."

"Just Friday?"

"Melisande, too."

"Now I'm confused," said Kinoshita. "I thought Hill was coming here, to Sylene."

"He's being invited. If he comes, fine. If not, I want them ready to go to Pericles V."

"Just them?" asked Kinoshita, trying to keep the resentment out of his voice.

"Just to talk," said Nighthawk. "I'm not going to war. Yet."

"Why not Blue Eyes or me?"

"She can tell me if he's lying, and Friday can blow up the whole god-damned planet if they kill me. I need you and Blue Eyes for other things."

"You're sure?"

"I'm sure." Nighthawk gestured toward the door. "You might as well start hunting them down."

Kinoshita downed his drink and walked to the door. Once there, he turned to face Nighthawk again.

"I hope to hell you know what you're doing," he said. "We've got the girl and Ibn ben Khalid in one package. That *is* what we came out here for, isn't it?"

"We came out here to secure the Widowmaker's future," said Night-hawk. "Since I'm his shadow, I'm best qualified to decide how to do it."

"I just keep wondering if you have your priorities straight. That's a very attractive woman, and you're just a couple of months old."

Nighthawk tapped his left temple with a forefinger. "I'm sixty-one up here," he said, and then slapped his chest. "And I'm thirty-eight everywhere else. If I was going to lose my head over the first woman I saw, like the previous clone did, I'd be sneaking into Melisande's bed every night."

Kinoshita stared at him for a long moment, then turned and left, mut-tering to himself. Nighthawk watched him walk away, then finished his drink, got to his feet, and headed off to Cassandra's subspace transmitter.

Chapter 22

"You'd better scram," said Nighthawk as he seated himself before the video transmission camera. "If he sees you, I'm going to have a hard time explaining why he's got to come out here with ransom money."

Cassandra nodded. "All right. And Jefferson?"

"Yes?"

"Be *very* careful. I don't think you can imagine how dangerous he is."

"I've faced dangerous men before," said Nighthawk.

"They were dangerous because they had guns. *He's* more dangerous because he's the man who pays for the bullets."

"Noted. Now leave."

She walked out the door, and a moment later he had contacted the governor's mansion on Pericles V.

"Name?" asked the bearded secretary at the other end.

"Jefferson Nighthawk."

"Where is your message originating from?"

"Sylene IV."

"And the purpose of this transmission?"

"I want to speak to Cassius Hill."

"That's quite impossible."

"You just tell him who's calling, sonny," said Nighthawk. "I guarantee he'll want to speak to me."

"I have instructions not to interrupt him, Mr. Nighthawk," said the secretary.

"That's up to you," said Nighthawk with a shrug. "But when he fires you for not putting my call through, remember that you were warned."

The secretary stared nervously at Nighthawk's hologram. "What, exactly, do you wish to speak to Governor Hill about?"

"That's none of your business," said Nighthawk. "Just get him."

"I have to tell him *something* besides your name!" said the secretary.

"It's your funeral," said Nighthawk, reaching out to deactivate the subspace tightbeam.

"Wait!" shouted the secretary suddenly.

Nighthawk froze.

"I'll see what I can do. Please stay where you are."

The screen went blank for a full minute, and then the secretary's image was replaced by that of a man in his mid-fifties, gray-haired and gray-eyed, with hard lines running down his face and jaw.

"Mr. Nighthawk," he said. "We meet at last." He puffed on a New Kentucky cigar, filling the air with clouds of white smoke. "Please forgive my fool of a secretary."

"It wasn't his fault," replied Nighthawk. "He has no idea who I am."

"I fired him anyway."

Nighthawk shrugged. "You do what you have to do. It's no skin off my ass."

"Good."

"What's good about it?"

"I don't tell you how to do your job," said Hill. "I don't want you telling me how to do mine."

"No problem," said Nighthawk. "Your job couldn't interest me less."

"Fine," said Hill. "Now let's talk about *your* job. I assume that's why you contacted me?"

"That's right."

"Well? Have you found him?"

Nighthawk nodded. "And her."

"Well, of course if you found *him* you'd find *her* too," said Hill. He puffed thoughtfully on his cigar for a long moment. "Is he dead?"

"No."

"Shit." Another puff. "I thought you were under orders to kill him. What went wrong?"

"I was under orders to bring your daughter back alive and well," answered Nighthawk. "I assumed that took precedence."

"Never assume a damned thing, Mr. Nighthawk," said Hill angrily. "All right. Where are they?"

"Not far."

"How far?"

"I don't think you really want me to say, just in case this is being monitored."

"What the fuck do *I* care if it's being monitored?" demanded Hill. "Where the hell are they?"

"Are you going to listen to me, or are you going to bluster?" asked Nighthawk.

Hill glared at him, then nodded his head. "Okay, Mr. Nighthawk, you have the floor. Make use of it."

"He wants to deal."

"Ibn ben Khalid?" asked Hill sharply.

"That's who we're talking about, isn't it?"

"Continue."

What do I need? Five million for the cryonics lab back on Deluros VIII, another million for my own medical treatment, more to live on . . .

"He'll turn her over to you for eight million credits, or its equivalent in Maria Theresa dollars."

"Eight million credits!" exploded Hill. "What does he think I'm made of—money?"

"He thinks you're a loving father who will pay to have his daughter returned unharmed."

"He wants small unmarked bills, no doubt," said Hill sardonically.

"He didn't say. But there's a condition."

"There always is. Out with it."

"He wants you to deliver the money in person."

"So he can blow me away the second I get off my ship," said Hill. "I know he's a bastard, but I never thought he was such a transparent bastard."

"That's where I come in," said Nighthawk.

"Explain."

"I'm the guarantor of the transaction. I guarantee your safety, I guarantee your daughter's safety, and I guarantee that you're not paying him off in bogus bills."

"Not good enough," said Hill. "He's got a million men."

"Not on Sylene IV, he doesn't," said Nighthawk.

"Is that where they are—him and my daughter?"

"No," said Nighthawk. "You come here. I make sure the money's real, and that you're not dragging an army or navy behind you, and then I take you to them."

"What's to stop him from killing both of us?" demanded Hill.

"Me."

"Still not good enough," said Hill, noting that his cigar had gone out and relighting it. "You may be the best, but when all is said and done, you're just one man. He's got a million of them."

Nighthawk caught himself just as he was about to say, in reassuring tones, "Spread all across the Frontier." *No sense letting him think there are so few men here he can march right in with his own forces.* Instead he said, "I've arranged for you to meet him with no one else present. If he reneges, we won't go in. Believe me, he wants his ransom money as much as you want your daughter."

"I don't doubt it," said Hill. "But I don't like the feel of this. Too many things can go wrong."

"Nothing will. That's what you created *me* for."

"I created you to kill Ibn ben Khalid and bring my daughter back to me!" snapped Hill. "And from where I'm sitting, you've failed."

"I can kill him tomorrow and bring you back a corpse, if that's what it takes to make you happy," said Nighthawk.

Hill glared at Nighthawk's image again, then lowered his head in thought. He looked up a moment later. "What does he need eight million credits for?"

"What does anyone need eight million credits for?"

"Is he buying guns for his army?"

"I've seen them," said Nighthawk. "And believe me, they've *got* guns."

"Payroll, then?"

"This is a revolution, Governor Hill. His army doesn't want money, just blood—yours."

Hill puffed away at his cigar without saying anything, and finally Nighthawk spoke again:

"It's up to you, Governor Hill. What do you want to do?"

There was still no answer.

"Do you want me to set up a meet with Ibn ben Khalid or not?" continued Nighthawk.

"There are too many intangibles," said Hill at last.

This time it was Nighthawk's turn to stare silently at the governor's image, waiting for him to clarify his meaning.

"Too many ways to walk into a trap. Too many ways to lose the money without getting what I want."

"You won't turn over the money until he turns over your daughter," Nighthawk explained patiently.

"That's *part* of what I want," said Hill. "I also want that wild-eyed radical scum dead, remember?"

"First one, then the other," said Nighthawk agreeably.

"It won't be that simple. We'll be walking onto *his* world, under *his* conditions. He'll have five hundred guns pointed at me the second I show up."

"What makes you think so?"

"Because that's what *I'd* do!" snapped Hill. "He's not stupid, you know."

"I know. In fact, he's remarkably well read."

"Most of these revolutionary fools are."

"I need to know your decision, Governor Hill. Are you coming out here?"

"Not yet. There's too much to be considered, too many preparations to make." He paused. "I want *you* to come to Pericles."

"I think you're making a mistake."

"I told you before: I don't like people telling me how to do my job."

"Your job is being a governor. Mine is getting your daughter back and killing Ibn ben Khalid."

"And since you haven't done it, I want you here to discuss strategy."

"All right. When?"

"Immediately."

"I can be there in about twenty Standard hours."

"Fine. And come alone."

"I have a friend who goes where I go," said Nighthawk.

"Human or alien?"

"Human."

"Male or female?"

"Female."

Hill considered it for a moment, then nodded. "All right. But no one else."

"Agreed."

"I'll see you tomorrow," said Nighthawk, deactivating the machine.

Cassandra returned a few minutes later.

"Well?" she said. "What do you think of him?"

"I'm very grateful to him."

"You're grateful?" she repeated with a frown.

"That's right."

"Why?"

"Because every now and then, I wonder about the moral and philosophical implications of my business. Then I meet someone like your father, and I realize that I was put here to kill men like that." He paused. "I find the thought of killing him very satisfying."

She stared at him. "You puzzle me. You love literature, and you have excellent manners, and you're considerate of my wishes, and you *seem* to have a well-developed sense of right and wrong—and every time I think I'm growing fond of you, you say something like that."

"And now you're not fond of me?" he asked.

"I wish I knew," she said in troubled tones.

Chapter 23

The ship settled down gently on the Pericles V landing strip.

"Are you certain that you don't want me to accompany you?" asked Friday, getting to his feet and stretching his legs, one at a time, as a dog might.

"You take one step outside the ship and they'll either blow you away or cancel the meeting," answered Nighthawk.

"Then I still don't see why you brought me."

"You like to blow things up, don't you?"

"Yes."

"If Melisande and I aren't back in twenty-four Standard hours, blow the whole fucking planet to kingdom come."

Friday smiled an alien smile. "I knew I would enjoy working with you, Widowmaker."

"Don't jump the gun," cautioned Nighthawk. "I have every expectation of being back here long before the deadline."

"Deadline," repeated Friday. "I like that word."

"Somehow I'm not surprised," muttered Nighthawk. He turned to Melisande. "Are you ready?"

She nodded her head.

"Okay," continued Nighthawk. "Remember, you don't have to say a word *during* the meeting. I just want to know afterward when he was lying and when he was telling the truth."

"I understand."

"I hope so."

"I'm not a fool, Nighthawk."

"Nobody's a fool," he replied. "But you'd be surprised how many people can pass for fools when things go wrong."

He ordered the hatch to open and escorted her out onto the tarmac. A vehicle with a built-in robotic chauffeur was waiting for them.

"Jefferson Nighthawk?" asked the mechanical driver.

"Yes."

"May I ask the name of your companion?"

"Her name's Melisande."

"That's a lovely name."

Melisande smiled, and Nighthawk suddenly winked at her.

"I was mistaken," he said. "Her name's Fungus."

"What an absolutely beautiful name!" said the driver enthusiastically.

Nighthawk grinned. "But everyone calls her Melisande."

"I see."

"You know," said Melisande, "I think that might be the first time I ever saw you smile."

"Stick around a decade and maybe I'll do it again," said Nighthawk. He looked ahead and leaned forward. "Driver, where are we going? The spaceport's off to your left."

"We are going to the governor's mansion, friend Nighthawk," replied the driver.

"Don't we have to clear Customs?"

"You already have."

"We have?"

"I have transmitted your retinagram, fingerprint, and bone structure to Security at the governor's mansion, and they have identified you as the clone of Jefferson Nighthawk, born 4933 G.E., still living." It paused. "I regret to inform you that we have not yet identified the woman Fungus, who prefers to be called Melisande."

"I was mistaken," said Nighthawk. "Her true name is . . ." He frowned and looked at Melisande. "What the hell *is* your real name?"

"Private."

"Whatever you wish."

"Am I to understand that the woman's name is Private?" asked the driver.

"No," said Nighthawk. "You are to understand that she does not choose to divulge her name, but that you may call her Melisande."

"It's a lovely name."

"We're delighted that you think so."

They took a sharp left turn and began speeding along a paved road that cut through some farm fields.

"To your left," announced the driver, "we are growing the mutated soybeans that form the staple of the Periclean diet. To your right, the hybrid cattle, imported from Earth itself, that yield 99.2 percent meat and only .8 percent fat. The tall plants just past the cattle pasture are native to this world, and closely resemble the nutritious Calaban fruit of Pollux IV. Have you any questions, friends Nighthawk and Melisande?"

"How long until we reach the governor's mansion?" asked Nighthawk.

"In terms of distance or time?"

"Whichever makes you happy."

"I am incapable of emotion," answered the driver. "I feel a certain mathematical satisfaction by answering a question completely and accurately. The answer to *your* question is 3.27 miles and/or four Standard minutes and nineteen seconds."

"Thanks," said Nighthawk. "Are you programmed to answer all questions?"

"Yes."

"Good. How many Security personnel are at the governor's mansion?"

"Please withdraw your question, friend Nighthawk."

"Why?"

"You have created a conflict within me. I am programmed to answer all questions, but I have been specifically forbidden to answer any question relating to Security."

Nighthawk was silent for a moment, and the vehicle started veering crazily.

"I withdraw the question."

"Thank you," said the driver as the vehicle once again began moving straight and true.

Nighthawk had been studying the countryside during the trip, filing bits and pieces away for future use. If he had to hide in this sector, that tree was hollow and this hill could shield him from the road. If he needed to get to the spaceport, an airsled could shave two minutes off the time it was taking this vehicle to get to the mansion while keeping to the roads. If he had to approach under cover of night, which means of approach offered the least number of obstacles? Could a ship land in one of these fields, and if so, in which one? Was the grass too tall and too dry to chance using a laser pistol? Were there enough trees and rock outcroppings to deflect the almost solid sound of a sonic gun?

A large estate soon came into view, and the vehicle made a beeline toward it.

"I have a question, driver," said Nighthawk.

"Yes?"

"The city looks to be about eight miles to the north. Isn't this very far out for a governor's mansion?"

"There have been attempts on Governor Hill's life," answered the driver. "His Security staff felt that he could be better protected in this location. When his physical presence is required, he is only a short trip from the various government buildings."

"And what are all those long low buildings to the left?" continued Nighthawk, staring at a series of concrete structures. "They look like barracks."

"They are. That's where his Security forces reside."

"He's got a lot of them, doesn't he?"

"I couldn't say," replied the driver. "I have no basis for comparison."

They pulled up to a shimmering gate and stopped.

"Force field?" asked Nighthawk.

"That is correct."

"What do we do now?"

"We wait. I have been identified. They are now checking you." The driver paused. "I am sorry, friend Nighthawk, but you will have to relinquish your sonic pistol, your projectile pistol, and the three knives you have secreted around your person. If you will place them here"—a hidden compartment opened up—"you may retrieve them when you leave."

Nighthawk did as he was requested, and the door to the compartment slid shut.

"What about my laser gun?" he asked out of curiosity. "Surely your Security system didn't miss it."

"Once inside the gate your laser pistol will be totally ineffective," answered the driver.

"How is that possible?"

"Our power plant projects a field that instantly drains the charge from your pistol, while simultaneously rendering your power pack impotent."

Good thing to remember. Someone ought to program you to be a little less forthcoming.

"The force field is still up," noted Nighthawk. "Maybe you should tell them to shut it off now that I'm disarmed."

"That will not be necessary," answered the driver as the vehicle slowly began moving forward. "Please do not stick your head or any limbs out beyond the limits of my body. I can neutralize the field, but only within the parameters of my physical structure."

Nighthawk watched as the vehicle went right through the force field. There was no bump, no jolt, no buzzing; one moment they were outside the property, the next they were inside, and the same force field that kept intruders out would now serve to keep Nighthawk in.

There was a long winding driveway leading to the front doorway of the mansion, where three men and a pair of robots stood guard. The vehicle slowed to a stop, and Nighthawk and Melisande got out.

"I will be waiting for you, friends Nighthawk and Melisande," said the driver. "I don't want to block traffic, so I will pull some forty meters ahead and then stop. Enjoy your visit."

"Friendliest damned car I ever met," said Nighthawk wryly to one of the guards, who ignored his comment.

"Please follow me," he said. "You are expected."

"I've been scanned, sonogrammed, and X-rayed," said Nighthawk. "I'd damned well better be expected."

He waited for Melisande to take his arm, then followed the guard into the mansion's enormous hexagonal foyer. The walls were a phosphorescent alien marble, with streaks of some shimmering metal running through them. Nighthawk noted them, but was more intent upon the number and placement of the doors.

They were led through the foyer to a grand circular stairway. The guard stopped at the foot of the stairs and signaled to a pair of robots.

"You will accompany Mr. Nighthawk and his companion up to the governor's office," he ordered.

"Yes, sir," answered the robot in a more grating monotone than the robotic driver had possessed. "Please follow me."

They ascended the stairs, then turned down a long corridor. At the end of it was a large outer office containing a number of comfortable chairs and sofas, as well as a selection of tasteful alien paintings, and another robot immediately approached and offered them their choice of drinks.

"Nothing for us," said Nighthawk. "We're here to see Cassius Hill."

"You are expected," said both robots almost in unison.

"Well?"

The robots exchanged mechanical glances.

"We do not understand the question, sir."

"If he's waiting for us, why don't you take us to him?" asked Nighthawk.

"There is a difference between the governor's expecting you and being ready to meet with you," explained the robots that had offered them the drinks. "He will signal me when he is ready to meet with you."

"You tell him he's got five minutes or I'm leaving," said Nighthawk. "Tell him that the Widowmaker doesn't like to be kept waiting."

"I will deliver your message immediately, sir," said the robot.

The robot stood at attention, and Nighthawk stared at it for a long moment, then said, "Well?"

"We do not understand the question, sir."

"I thought you were going to deliver my message to Cassius Hill."

"I already have, sir. He is aware that you will leave in"—slight pause—"two hundred and seven Standard seconds if he has not invited you into his office by that time." A longer pause. "Will there be anything else, sir?"

Nighthawk looked from one robot to the other. "Yes," he said at last.

"What can I do for you, sir?"

"Send this other robot away."

"I cannot do that, sir."

"Why not?"

"He is a Security robot, programmed to protect the governor. I am merely an office robot, unqualified to analyze the potential risk to the governor in any real or hypothetical situation. Therefore, I cannot order a Security robot to leave the governor's office."

"Who do you think might harm the governor?" asked Nighthawk.

"No one, sir."

"Then why can't you order him to leave?"

"Because I may be wrong, sir."

"You," said Nighthawk, turning to the Security robot. "Do you think he's wrong?"

"No, sir," answered the robot. "I think there is only a seventeen percent probability that he is wrong."

"That's rather a high probability, isn't it, given that we're unarmed?"

"If you were any human other than Jefferson Nighthawk, I would rate the probability at four percent."

"I'm flattered."

"I am pleased that you are flattered."

"Are you really?" asked Nighthawk.

"No, sir, but I have been programmed to respond with those or similar words."

"I thought robots couldn't lie."

The robot was silent for a moment, as if it were internally scanning some data. "You have been asleep for more than a century. During that time, the directive against lying has been eliminated from most robots."

Nighthawk considered the robot carefully. "What makes you think I've been asleep for a century?"

"You are Jefferson Nighthawk," said the robot, as if that was the only answer required.

Well, you're not infallible, thought Nighthawk. *That's a comfort of sorts.*

The other robot took a step forward. "The governor will see you now."

"I will accompany you," said the Security robot, walking toward a door that dilated to let the three of them pass through. They found themselves in a small office, manned by three more robots, all busy doing secretarial work. The Security robot led them to still another door, and this time when they passed through there was no doubt that they were in Cassius Hill's opulent office.

The governor, cigar in hand, sat behind a large desk made of an alien hardwood. The wall behind him was covered with holographs showing him in the company of the rich and the famous and, occasionally, the notorious. A Security robot was stationed in each of the four corners of the office. Nighthawk suddenly realized that Hill's desk and chair were on a small platform, so that seated visitors would have to look up to him.

"Mr. Nighthawk," acknowledged Hill, getting out of his chair and walking around the desk to shake Nighthawk's hand. "I'm glad to finally meet you in person."

"This is Melisande," said Nighthawk.

Hill glanced briefly at her. "She goes."

"I beg your pardon?"

"What kind of fool do you take me for?" demanded Hill. "Do you think I don't know a Balatai woman when I see one? We don't talk until she leaves."

"What have you got against Balatai women?" asked Nighthawk.

"Come on, Widowmaker," said Hill contemptuously. "If I was stupid enough to let her stay here, we wouldn't have anything to discuss." He turned to the Security robot that had escorted them to the office. "You! Take the woman back downstairs to wait for Nighthawk."

The robot took Melisande gently by the arm.

"Please come with me," it said.

She looked at Nighthawk, who nodded his acquiescence, then accompanied the robot out of the room.

"I'm disappointed in you," said Hill, sitting back down and puffing on his cigar. "Imagine thinking that I couldn't spot a Balatai woman!"

"They're very rare," said Nighthawk.

"Maybe they were a century ago, but not these days."

"Perhaps I was misinformed."

"You can't depend on your memories, you know," said Hill. "They're all a hundred years out of date. They'll betray you when you least expect it." Suddenly he leaned forward, his chin jutting out. "I'm the man who's responsible for your being alive, and I'm the man who's paying you. Why did you think you *needed* a Balatai woman in the first place?"

"I don't know you," said Nighthawk. "And therefore I don't trust you."

Hill considered Nighthawk's statement, and finally nodded his head. "I approve."

"I see you're not the most trusting man in the galaxy either," noted Nighthawk. "Four security robots in your office, and no Men."

"Robots are quicker to react and harder to kill," answered Hill promptly. "Also, their loyalty is programmed into them and can't be bought."

"They're a lot rarer where I come from."

"No," Hill corrected him. "Only *when* you come from." His cigar went out. He considered relighting it, finally tossed it into a tiny atomizer built into a corner of his desk, and lit another. "All right, Widowmaker. Talk to me. What's going on out there?"

"I found Ibn ben Khalid and your daughter."

"So you told me."

"He says that he wants eight million credits for her safe return."

"I know."

"Do you want the details?"

"No."

"No?" asked Nighthawk.

Hill snorted. "I wouldn't give him eight credits for that bitch! When I'm dead, she'll be first in line to dance on my grave." He stared across the desk at Nighthawk. "Sit down, Widowmaker. I don't like it when people stand. It makes me uneasy."

"I don't like looking up to people," replied Nighthawk. "I'll stand."

"I could have the robots make you sit."

"I wouldn't advise it," said Nighthawk so calmly that Hill decided not to force the issue.

"Sit, stand, do what you want," he muttered. "Just tell me about Ibn ben Khalid."

"He hasn't harmed her in any way."

"I don't give a shit about her!" snapped Hill. "She's hated me from the day she was born, and I hate her right back!"

"I thought you hired me to get her back," said Nighthawk.

"I hired you to find Ibn ben Khalid and kill him! I couldn't care less what happens to her!"

"That's not what I was told."

"Of course not," said Hill. "They wouldn't clone the Widowmaker just to eliminate a political upstart. I had to give them a reason that those weak-kneed bleeding-heart bastards back on Deluros could subscribe to." He paused. "You should be pleased. If I hadn't lied to them, you wouldn't exist."

"Why didn't you just send your navy out to kill him?" asked Nighthawk.

"You tell me where he is and I'll do just that," said Hill. "But in the meantime, there's no way I'm going to send them thousands of light-years away after some will-o'-the-wisp while he invades Pericles with his army."

"Or decimates your fleet."

Hill shrugged. "To be perfectly blunt, they're just cannon fodder. I'd happily see three million of them blown to hell in exchange for Ibn ben Khalid." He stared hard at Nighthawk. "In fact, if you will tell me where he's keeping my daughter, where he himself is . . ."

"Not a chance," said Nighthawk. "You're paying *me* to kill him, remember?"

"I'll pay you to tell me where he is."

"How much?"

"A million credits."

"Good-bye, Mr. Hill," said Nighthawk. "We have nothing further to discuss."

"Two million!"

"Go to hell, Mr. Hill. That won't keep the Widowmaker alive, and we both know it."

"*You're* the Widowmaker now!" retorted Hill. "We're alike, you and I. We both use force to get what we want, and we both know that life is the cheapest commodity on the Frontier. So don't pretend that you care any more about the first Widowmaker than I care about my soldiers or my daughter."

"I'm not here to argue motivations with you. I need money, and if you want my help, you're going to have to pay for it."

"All right," said Hill. "Sit down and we'll talk some business."

"I'll stand."

"I said sit."

"I heard what you said."

"You're going to have to learn who's in charge here," said Hill. "Number Three, help Mr. Nighthawk sit down."

One of the robots approached him, arms outstretched. Nighthawk ducked, grabbed a metallic arm, twisted it, and jerked suddenly—and the robot did an awkward somersault in the air and clanged heavily to the ground.

"Human or robot, leverage is leverage," said Nighthawk, never taking his eyes off the robot as it clambered awkwardly to its feet. "Now call it off before one of us gets hurt. You don't want the cost of replacing a robot, and like it or not you *can't* replace me."

Hill looked from Nighthawk to the robot. "At ease, Number Three," he said, and the robot walked back to its position in a corner of the room. "If I hadn't said that, he'd have killed you eventually."

"Perhaps."

"And if he couldn't, there are three more in this office who would have helped on my command."

"Proving what?"

"That when I give an order, I want it obeyed."

"I don't take orders," replied Nighthawk. "Not from you, not from anyone." He paused. "Why don't you *ask* me to sit down?"

"What?"

"You heard me: ask me to sit."

Hill frowned but complied. "Won't you please sit down, Mr. Nighthawk?"

"Thanks, I think I will," said Nighthawk, finally seating himself on a chair.

Some of the tension left Hill's face. "Now let's talk business."

"I'm listening."

"I want Ibn ben Khalid dead. If you can kill him this week, within seven Standard days, I'll pay you ten million credits."

"What about your daughter?"

"If she gets in the way of a laser beam or a bullet, well,"—Hill shrugged eloquently—"that's too bad, but she's very young and very foolish and unfortunately these things happen."

"And if she survives?"

Hill shook his head. "She doesn't."

Nighthawk stared at him. "I can see why you prefer surrounding yourself with robots."

"The life expectancy of men who were privy to my secrets was getting to be embarrassingly short," said Hill with a smile. "At least I know I can trust my robots. Each of them will burn out all its neural circuits before divulging anything that gets said in this room." Hill puffed on his cigar again, and the smoke almost obscured his face for a few seconds. "Well, Widowmaker, have we got a deal?"

"Can you pay in cash?"

"I thought you'd want it credited to your attorney's account."

"I don't trust lawyers."

Hill chuckled. "I agree. That's one thing that hasn't changed in a century." Suddenly the smile vanished. "Yes, I can pay you in cash."

"Then you've got a deal."

"Remember: I want him dead in one Standard week, or we're back to our original agreement and our original price." He paused. "Pull this off and you can walk away a rich man. Deluros never even has to know. Think about it."

"I've been thinking about it since yesterday," said Nighthawk.

"You're a man after my own heart, Widowmaker."

"Maybe I'll just cut it out right now."

"I don't find that very funny."

"Probably it isn't," said Nighthawk. "I don't have much of a sense of humor."

Suddenly Hill tensed. "Or was it a joke at all?" he demanded. "How much did Ibn ben Khalid offer you to kill *me*?"

"Not as much as you're offering me to kill him," answered Nighthawk. "He's only a poor corrupt man of the people; you're a rich one."

"A rich, well-protected one," said Hill pointedly. "You kill me, and you'll never make it out of the mansion alive. And even if you did, my Security forces would hunt you down long before you reached the spaceport. I assume you saw all the checkpoints as you drove up."

"I did."

"Good. Don't forget them."

"I don't plan to."

"That sounds like a threat," said Hill.

Nighthawk smiled. "Everything sounds like a threat to you. You're a very insecure man."

"I can live with my insecurities," said Hill. "Easier, I suspect, than you can live with being the ephemeral shadow of a real man."

"I may be a shadow," admitted Nighthawk. "I don't plan on being an ephemeral one."

"Then don't ever try to cross me," replied Hill. "And now, if we've no further business to discuss, get out. I may need you, but I find that I don't like you very much."

"No law says you have to," replied Nighthawk. "Just make sure the money's ready."

He turned and walked to the door, which remained closed until one of the robots stepped forward and escorted him out of the office. A few moments later he and Melisande were driving back to the spaceport, hoping that Friday wouldn't get overeager and blow the whole planet to smithereens before they reached the ship.

Chapter 24

"How did it go?" asked Cassandra when Nighthawk entered The Blue Dragon, accompanied by Melisande and Friday.

He looked around. The place still wasn't open for business, but Kinoshita and Blue Eyes were sitting at one table, and Jory was at another.

"That's some father you've got," he said at last.

"I know."

"I think he's as eager to see *you* dead as you are to see *him* dead."

"You told him I was Ibn ben Khalid?" she said angrily.

Nighthawk shook his head. "He hates you for yourself."

"Good," said Cassandra emphatically. "I'd hate to be something he admired."

"You're in no serious danger of that."

"So is he coming to Sylene?"

"Not a prayer," said Nighthawk. "Your father isn't a trusting man."

"Damn!"

"You didn't really think he'd come, did you?"

"No, but I'd hoped . . ."

"He *did* offer me ten million credits if I kill Ibn ben Khalid within the week."

Suddenly Cassandra tensed. "What did you tell him?"

"I told him I'd need it in cash."

"And he said?"

"No problem."

She stared at him. "And what are you going to do?"

"Kill him and take the money."

She relaxed visibly. "Good."

"Why didn't you kill him while you were there?" asked Blue Eyes.

"Because I'd like to live long enough to enjoy the money," answered Nighthawk.

"He's that well protected?" continued the dragon.

"He'd have been easy to kill. It would have been impossible to escape."

"So what do we do?" asked Kinoshita. "He won't come here, and you can't escape if you kill him there."

"We work out a way to kill him and escape."

"But you just said—"

"I was alone and expected. They knew when I was coming, with whom, who I was, what I could do." Nighthawk paused. "Next time I won't be alone, and they won't be expecting me."

"How many men are stationed on Pericles?" asked Blue Eyes.

"A few million."

"Against five of us?"

"Six," said Cassandra.

"Seven," chimed in Jory.

"That's still not the kind of odds to give one a sunny sense of confidence," said Blue Eyes wryly.

"You won't have to worry about more than a few hundred of them," said Nighthawk. "The rest will be stationed around Pericles V."

"Only a few hundred?" said the dragon unhappily. "I feel better already."

"Just a minute," said Kinoshita.

Everyone turned to him.

"He doesn't know that Cassandra is Ibn ben Khalid?"

"No," answered Nighthawk.

"That means he has no idea what Ibn ben Khalid looks like, right?"

"Right," said Nighthawk with a smile, as he saw where Kinoshita was leading him.

"So why not kill some outlaw out here, cut off his head, and present it to Hill as Ibn ben Khalid? Then take the money and run like hell before he figures out he's been had."

"By God, I *like* it!" bellowed Blue Eyes, slamming a fist down on the table.

"You know," said Jory, "it's not bad."

"It's out of the question!" said Cassandra furiously.

"Yes, it is," agreed Nighthawk. "Though two days ago I think I might have agreed to do it."

"What's happened in the past two days?" asked Blue Eyes.

"I've met Cassius Hill." Nighthawk paused and looked from one member of his band to the next. "He's got to die."

"You bet your ass he's got to!" snapped Cassandra.

"Hold on a minute," said Kinoshita. "If you think killing one corrupt politician will make the galaxy a better place for all Mankind or anything noble like that . . ."

"I know it won't," said Nighthawk.

"Then what makes you so suddenly noble?"

"It's not a matter of nobility, but of brainpower."

"I don't follow you."

"I met Cassius Hill. I spoke to him. He may be an evil man, but he's not a stupid one. He'll know in a matter of days, or weeks at most, that I didn't kill Ibn ben Khalid."

"So what?" said Kinoshita. "We'll be out on the Rim, or deep into the Spiral Arm, enjoying our money."

"You don't understand," said Nighthawk. "Once he figures out he's been duped, the first thing he's going to do is freeze the money in my attorneys' account, and see to it that the original Widowmaker is thrown out of the cryonics lab to die. I can't allow that."

"To hell with the original Widowmaker!" said Cassandra. "Cassius Hill has got to die as punishment for all the criminal acts he's performed. He's betrayed his people a hundred times over!"

"All right," said Kinoshita. "There's no sense shooting each other because we differ about *why* he has to die. The question now is how do we go about it?"

"We don't do anything for the next Standard week," said Nighthawk.

"Why not?" asked Friday, who was still unhappy about not being permitted to blow up the planet.

"Because he thinks I'm going to kill Ibn ben Khalid this week. That means he thinks Ibn ben Khalid is relatively close to Pericles V. As long as he believes that, his navy isn't going anywhere—and we don't want them around if we have to land there."

"So he's a coward in addition to everything else?" asked Blue Eyes.

"Not at all," answered Nighthawk. "It's just sound tactics not to disperse your forces when the enemy might be lurking nearby." He paused. "Still," he added, "maybe we can convince him to do just that."

"Oh?" said Cassandra. "How?"

"He's got to have followed me here—not Hill himself, but some of his men—or else he's managed to put some kind of trace on my ship."

"No one landed while I was in the spaceport," said Friday adamantly.

"It wouldn't have had to be a *person*," said Nighthawk. "This guy depends on machines more than most people do. It could have been anything that passed for a Service Mech. Anyway, I'm sure he's keeping tabs on the ship." He turned to Cassandra. "Based on your knowledge of him, is that a logical conclusion?"

"Absolutely."

"Good. Then all we have to do is have one of your men fly my ship halfway across the Inner Frontier. He'll think I'm after Ibn ben Khalid . . ."

". . . and once he thinks he knows where I am, he'll send half his navy there to be in on the kill and wipe out any of my forces that happen to be on the scene!" concluded Cassandra.

"Well, it *sounds* logical, anyway," said Nighthawk. "But will he do it? I mean, he didn't strike me as the most gullible man I've ever encountered."

"I really don't know," she said, frowning. Suddenly she looked up and smiled. "Unless he's convinced beyond any shadow of a doubt that Ibn ben Khalid is really there!"

"How do we convince him of that?" asked Kinoshita.

"We put *her* on the Widowmaker's ship," said Friday.

"Not a chance," said Cassandra. "I'm going to be in on the kill. But I can make a holographic recording, pleading for his help."

"Will he listen?" asked Kinoshita dubiously.

"Not sympathetically," said Cassandra. "But yes, he'll listen, because he'll have no reason to think it's phony."

All eyes turned to Nighthawk, who considered the suggestion for another minute, then nodded his head.

"Yeah, I think it'll work. And anything that might lower the odds is worth trying."

"Right," said Blue Eyes unhappily. "Send half his forces out after her, and it's only two million to seven."

"Oh, we'll have more than seven," said Nighthawk. "And half of his two million will be sound asleep."

"Well, that's wonderful," said the dragon. "You don't hang around casinos much, do you?"

"No. Why?"

"You've still got the shirt on your back. The way you compute fair odds, that's the only logical conclusion."

"Hey," said Nighthawk. "This is *your* cause. I'm just in it for the money."

"Thanks," said Blue Eyes. "I feel so much better now."

"Shut up!" said Cassandra.

"I was just teasing him," said Blue Eyes petulantly.

"Enough," she said. "This is serious business. You may be joking, but the odds *are* two million to seven."

"We'll start lowering them before we strike," said Nighthawk.

"Good," said Blue Eyes. "How?"

"As soon as I come up with an answer to that, you'll be among the first to know."

He got up and walked to the airlift behind the bar.

"Where are you going?" demanded Blue Eyes.

"I've had a long day," answered Nighthawk. "I'm going to go relax with a good book."

"That's *it*?" demanded the dragon. "That's all you're going to say about the overthrow of Cassius Hill?"

"For the moment."

Nighthawk floated gently upward to Cassandra's apartment. She joined him a few minutes later.

"He's a monster, isn't he?" she asked as the door slid shut behind her.

Nighthawk looked up from his book. "Blue Eyes?"

"My father!"

"I've seen better."

"I'll wager you've never seen worse."

"You're young yet," said Nighthawk. "I hope *you* never meet worse."

"He really wants me dead?"

"He insists on it."

She stood silent and motionless for a moment. "It's strange."

"What is?"

"He may be a monster, but he's still my father. The thought that he could want me dead . . ." She shook her head and shuddered.

"You want *him* dead," Nighthawk noted mildly.

"That's different. I've hated him my whole life."

"Maybe it's mutual."

"It couldn't be. How do you hate an infant? A little girl? He hardly knows me. How could he hate me so much?"

"I don't think he hates you," said Nighthawk. "I think you just annoy him."

"That's even worse!" she said. "To kill someone because she *annoys* you!"

"There are worse reasons," said Nighthawk. "Besides, it's just a guess."

"Probably an accurate one," replied Cassandra. "He doesn't know me well enough to hate me. In fact, when he finds out who Ibn ben Khalid really is, you may not have to kill him; the shock may do it for you."

"Try not to think about it."

"How can I stop thinking about it?" she demanded. "He's my *father*!"

"Just a toss of a coin. He could be anyone's father, you could be anyone's daughter."

"I don't believe that for a moment. Do you?"

"Not really. You've got some of his steel, a touch of his arrogance."

"I do?"

Nighthawk nodded. "I find them admirable qualities when they're not carried to excess."

"Thank you, I suppose."

"You've got his eyes, too."

"His are gray, mine are blue."

"Neither of you ever look away or blink. You're not afraid of what you see."

"Why should I be?"

"I'm the Widowmaker. I came here to kill you. And *he* has to know I've considered killing him."

"I'd rather you pointed out the differences between us," said Cassandra. "I hate the man."

"Well, you're a lot prettier."

She grimaced. "That's not what I meant."

"So much for romance," said Nighthawk wryly.

"I never expected a killer to be a romantic."

"Nonsense," answered Nighthawk. "Killers make the best romantics."

"Sure."

"We do," he insisted. "Sooner or later we have to convince ourselves that what we're doing is necessary, and ultimately good. What's more romantic than that?"

"Then why don't you stop this incessant talking and take me to bed?"

He stared at her, surprised. "Are you sure that's what you want? You don't know me."

"You're an attractive man. I'm an attractive woman. And we're both going to be dead in less than two weeks." She paused. "Blue Eyes isn't the only one who can compute the odds, you know. So we might as well make the most of it while we can."

Nighthawk got to his feet. "Sounds good to me."

He followed her to the bedroom.

"I plan to enjoy this," she said firmly.

"I'll do my best."

"How long has it been for you?"

He grinned at her as he began talking off his clothes. "Oh, a century, maybe a little longer."

"I hope you haven't forgotten how."

He hadn't.

Chapter 25

Nighthawk was sitting in The Blue Dragon three days later when Kinoshita entered and walked over to him.

"Mind if I sit down?" he asked.

"Be my guest."

"I saw your ship take off yesterday." Pause. "I guess you weren't on it."

"Not much gets past you, does it?" remarked Nighthawk dryly.

"I thought you might want to tell me about it."

"Not especially," said Nighthawk, sipping his drink.

"You refuse to?"

"I didn't say that."

"Well?"

"It's a decoy."

"Part of the plan you worked out with Cassandra Hill?" said Kinoshita.

"Do I detect a note of disapproval?" asked Nighthawk.

"Damn it, we're part of your team, me and Melisande and the aliens!" said Kinoshita angrily. "We all know you're sleeping with her, and nobody minds it, but we *do* mind being left out in the cold. If something's going on, if we're expected to risk our lives for her cause—*her* cause, not ours— then we think you should let us know just what's going on. We had no idea you'd even started!"

Nighthawk stared at him. Kinoshita looked at his expressionless face and cold eyes, and for just a moment he had an impulse to race for the door and consider himself lucky if he made it.

"All right," said Nighthawk at last. "Fair is fair. You've got a point."

He paused long enough to finish his drink and signal the bartender for another. "We're going to invade Pericles and take out Cassius Hill."

"We?" repeated Kinoshita. "You mean her army?"

Nighthawk shook his head. "Her army, such as it is, is ragtag, undisciplined, poorly armed, and spread all the hell over the Inner Frontier. More to the point, it's outnumbered four to one. If we approached the planet with it, we'd be blown out of the sky before our first ship could land."

"Then who's invading Pericles?"

"Us."

"Us?" repeated Kinoshita with a sick feeling in the pit of his stomach.

"You, me, her, Melisande, Friday, Blue Eyes, Jory, and maybe twenty of her most trusted men and women."

"Just a minute," said Kinoshita. "You're going to invade Cassius Hill's heavily guarded home world with an attack force of thirty men?"

"And women," said Nighthawk.

"You're good, Widowmaker," said Kinoshita. "Better than I thought, better than anyone I've ever seen. But you're nowhere near *that* good."

"I appreciate your confidence."

"It's not a matter of confidence," insisted Kinoshita. "It's a matter of numbers."

"Actually, it's a matter of planning."

"Cassius Hill has four million men on that planet. I don't care how widely dispersed they are. I don't care if half of them will be asleep. I don't care if he's isolated in his mansion with only ten thousand crack soldiers guarding him." Kinoshita paused and tried to regain his composure. "Look, even if you kill him, we've still got to get away from there. What'll we have—one ship? Three? Five? Against his entire fleet and his planetary defense system?"

"I've worked out some of the problems," said Nighthawk. "We won't move until I work out the rest."

"What about Cassandra?" continued Kinoshita.

"What about her?"

"I got the impression you cared about her."

"I do—not that it's any of your business."

"You can't," said Kinoshita, "or you wouldn't let her risk her life like this."

"You're a fool, Ito," said Nighthawk slowly. "It's not up to me to stop her. More to the point, I care about her precisely *because* she's willing to come along and risk her life for a cause she believes in."

"Can you trust her to do the right thing under pressure?"

"More than I trust anyone else. She's Ibn ben Khalid, isn't she?"

"You sound like you find that attractive," suggested Kinoshita.

"Out here on the Frontier the two things that count are courage and competence," said Nighthawk, "and she has them both. I'm glad that she's a good-looking woman, but I'd be just as attracted to her if she were three hundred pounds and pockmarked."

"Curious."

"What is?"

"I'd have thought that a man who lives for the moment would be more concerned with style than substance."

"What makes you think I live for the moment?" asked Nighthawk.

"Your profession."

"Never planning more than a moment at a time would be an admission of defeat," replied Nighthawk. "The first Widowmaker made it to his sixties, and if they come up with a cure for eplasia, he could make it to a hundred. He never once thought that he might die in the course of earning his living. I know: his memories are mine." He paused. "I want a woman with those same virtues—courage and competence. I found one." Another pause. "I'll tell you something else: it's more important to me that she reads books than that she's good in bed."

"Sure it is," said Kinoshita sardonically.

"Sooner or later you have to stop fucking and start talking," said Nighthawk. "I want someone who won't bore me to tears, someone to exchange ideas with."

"You are a constant source of amazement to me," admitted Kinoshita.

"That's because you bought into the myth. You think I live for killing—whereas what I really cherish are the hours and days *between* killings."

"Point taken."

"Is there anything else you want to ask?" said Nighthawk. "Let's get it over with now, because I don't plan to discuss my personal business with you again."

"Just that it seems a waste," said Kinoshita. "The rest of us have our reasons for following you, but if you care for Cassandra, why send her up against heavily armed soldiers?"

"You keep forgetting that this is *her* cause. I'm just in it for the money." He paused. "Besides, whether she weighs a hundred and ten pounds or three hundred and ten pounds, a gun is a hell of an equalizer."

"Okay, then I've got another question for you."

"I'm listening."

"What am *I* in it for?" asked Kinoshita. "*She's* in it to overthrow her father, and so are Jory and Blue Eyes. You're in it for the money. Melisande is here because you're paying her. Friday's here because he can't wait to blow up a few thousand Men. But what am *I* here for?"

"I thought you came along to watch me in action," remarked Nighthawk dryly.

"I know why I came this far," said Kinoshita irritably. "But why do *you* want me to come the rest of the way? I know you, Widowmaker—you never leave anything to chance. If you want me along, there's got to be a reason. I think I deserve to know what it is."

"Fair question," answered Nighthawk. "Your job is to stay alive."

Kinoshita frowned. "I don't understand."

"If only one person survives this operation, it has to be you."

"Me?" said Kinoshita, surprised. "Why?"

"Because you're the only one who's both trustworthy and knowledge-able enough to transfer the money I plan to appropriate into the Widow-maker's account at Hubbs, Wilkinson, Raith and Jiminez, and to make sure that Marcus Dinnisen and none of the others try to divert it for their own use."

"You don't trust them?"

"They're lawyers, aren't they?" replied Nighthawk, making no attempt to hide his contempt.

"How much money are we talking about?"

"At least five million, hopefully more. Your fee for seeing that it gets where it belongs will be ten percent."

Kinoshita grinned. "Suddenly I'm less opposed to attacking Pericles."

"Somehow I thought you might be."

"But I still don't understand someone who'd let the woman he loves go in there with guns blazing."

"No one's going anywhere with guns blazing," said Nighthawk. "This is not an enemy we can overpower."

"You know what I mean."

"I know exactly what you mean. Some men put women on a pedestal. I prefer to work side by side with them. My work just happens to be more dangerous than most."

Kinoshita shrugged. "Okay, I'm all through arguing. Do what you want with her. I can hardly object to your plans when I'm the designated survivor."

"I plan on all of us living through this," said Nighthawk. "You're just the one we're going to make absolutely sure survives."

"I appreciate it. When do we attack?"

"Not for a while. First, I want to make sure that a sizable number of Hill's ships are following mine."

"Where is it headed?"

"Socrates VII."

"That's clear across the Inner Frontier!"

"Right. And second, as I said, I have to work out the rest of the details."
Nighthawk paused. "We should be ready in six or seven Standard days."

"I hate to say this . . ."

"Yes?"

"Quite seriously," said Kinoshita with obvious reluctance, "if you're
going to protect someone's ass, make it Melisande's. You won't need an
empath in a pitched battle. You might need *me*."

"That's a generous offer," said Nighthawk. "But I'll definitely need an
empath."

"You're sure?"

"I'm sure."

"Then I guess I'll just have to live," said Kinoshita with a smile. "How
much of this can I tell the others?"

"I'll be speaking to each of them myself in the next day or two," said
Nighthawk. "We have a lot of details to sort out."

Kinoshita observed him thoughtfully. "You don't seem overly nervous."

"Should I be?"

"Well, you're about to take on four million soldiers with a handful of
untrained men, and to try to assassinate the best-protected politician on the
Inner Frontier," replied Kinoshita. "That would make most men a little
nervous."

"Most men," agreed Nighthawk.

"But not you?"

"Not the Widowmaker" was the calm reply.

Chapter 26

Melisande walked up to Nighthawk, who was standing in the street outside The Blue Dragon.

"You sent for me?" she said.

"Yes, I did," replied Nighthawk. "I need to know more about your power."

"Being a Balatai woman isn't so much a power as a curse," she replied. "You don't know what it's like to be bombarded by emotions every day of your life."

"Do you?"

She frowned. "What are you driving at?"

"Can you get away from them?"

"Sometimes."

"What's the closest someone can get before you can't avoid his emotions?"

"It depends on what he's feeling as well as his proximity," answered Melisande.

"That's not good enough."

"Why don't you tell me what you want, and I'll try to answer you."

"All right," said Nighthawk. "Pretend you're in the middle of a desert or a farm field, and there's a man a mile away, walking toward you. You can't see him. He's not mad at anyone. He's not frightened. He's not thinking lustful thoughts about his woman. He's not bursting with joy. He's just walking, his mind's kind of drifting, he's not noticing much of anything. How close would he have to be before you knew he was there?"

"I don't know," she said. "I might see him before I sensed him."

"It's midnight and this world doesn't have any moons."

"I assume there's a purpose to all this?" said Melisande.

"I wouldn't ask if there wasn't," replied Nighthawk. "Could you sense him at five hundred yards?"

"I don't know."

"Three hundred?"

"Damn it, *I don't know!*"

"Well, we're going to have to find out." He gestured toward The Blue Dragon. "How many men are in there right now?"

She closed her eyes, and the muscles in her face tightened as she concentrated.

"Seven."

"Six," said Nighthawk.

"I sense emotional radiations from seven."

"There's a bartender and five men."

"You're wrong."

"Oh—right. I forgot Cassandra. She's upstairs. Can you differentiate?"

"Can I tell that one of the seven is on the second floor? Not from out here, but when I'm inside I can."

Nighthawk took her by the arm and walked her one hundred yards down the street.

"Can you still read their radiations?" he asked.

"Of course."

"How many are there?"

She concentrated again, then looked at him, surprised. "Four."

"That's right. I told three of them to leave when they saw me walking you over here. Let's go a little farther."

He stopped two hundred yards from the tavern, and she stared at it.

"Six?"

"Are you asking me or telling me?"

She lowered her head for a moment, then looked up at him. "Six," she said firmly.

"Once more," he said, walking her another hundred yards away.

"Two," she said when they had stopped.

"You're sure?"

"Yes."

Nighthawk made a gesture, and Kinoshita walked out of the tavern and jabbed the air three times with a thumb.

"You missed one," said Nighthawk.

"Have I failed some kind of test?"

"Not at all," he replied. "We just had to know where your limit was.

It seems to be somewhere between two and three hundred yards, at least when no one's pitching any powerful emotions."

"All right," said Melisande. "Now that we know that, what are we supposed to do about it?"

"Ito will help you try to narrow it down even farther over the next few days," answered Nighthawk.

"And then?"

"And then, when we infiltrate Pericles V, you are going to be Friday's alarm system."

"I beg your pardon?"

"He's going to have to create a number of distractions. While he's planting his explosives, he's not going to be able to concentrate on anything else. *You're* going to let him know if anyone's coming."

"But why this experiment?" she asked. "If an armed guard thinks he hears something, or that he's spotted something, he'll radiate much stronger emotions, and . . ."

"We'll try to adjust for that," interrupted Nighthawk. "In the next couple of days, Ito will try to dope out your limits for men who are angry, or lustful, or frightened. But the most likely scenario, assuming we plan this properly, is that someone will be much more likely to stumble onto you by accident. So now we know if he's just patrolling an area that he patrols every night, and he has no reason to believe anyone's there, and you can spot his emotional radiation, he's probably within two hundred yards of you. That means you'll have to dope out some kind of signal with Friday that will either get him to freeze until the man passes, or kill him before he sees you."

"Now I see." She paused. "But if he's armed, how can you be sure Friday will be able to kill him? If there's any kind of commotion his friends might hear it."

"You'll have the advantage. You'll know he's there before he knows you are."

"*I'm* no killer. My question remains."

"When I hired you, you were in the business of making men think only about you. If need be, I'm sure you can do it long enough for Friday to sneak up and bludgeon him." Suddenly he smiled. "Trust me, if the first thing a man sees is *you,* he won't immediately start looking for an alien explosives expert."

"Just how many explosives is Friday going to plant?"

"As many as necessary."

"And how many Men will we be responsible for killing?" she continued.

"Less than you think."

"What if I say no?" asked Melisande.

Nighthawk sighed. "*Are* you saying no?"

"I'm considering it."

"Then you'll book passage back to Barrios II and that'll be the end of it."

"No repercussions, no threats at gunpoint from the Widowmaker?"

He shook his head. "This isn't what I hired you for. The rules of the game have changed, and so have the players. If you want to leave, I'll pay you what I owe you and see you safely to the spaceport."

She stared at him for a long moment. "You're telling the truth."

"Of course I'm telling the truth," said Nighthawk. "I know better than to lie to a Balatai woman."

"Everyone else knows you as a killer called the Widowmaker," said Melisande. "I know you as a man named Jefferson Nighthawk who has never lied to me. So I want to ask Jefferson Nighthawk one last question."

"Ask away."

"Is Cassius Hill really such a terrible man that you're willing to betray your creators, pervert your mission, and possibly sacrifice your life, just to bring him down?"

He looked into her eyes. "He is."

"And your feelings for Cassandra Hill haven't influenced you?"

"Possibly they have," he replied. "But not as much as meeting him did."

"All right, Jefferson Nighthawk," she said after a long pause, as she analyzed his emotions and found him to be telling the truth, at least as he knew it. "I'll do what you ask. And God have mercy on both our souls, as He'll be receiving them soon enough."

Chapter 27

Nighthawk stood at the bar of The Blue Dragon, waiting for Blue Eyes to bring him a drink.

"Are we *ever* leaving Sylene again?" asked the dragon as he approached Nighthawk, carrying a blue concoction in a uniquely shaped glass.

"You worked here for years. What's your hurry?"

"I know what's at the other end of the rainbow."

"It hasn't rained on Sylene for close to a century. All the water's underground. You wouldn't know a rainbow if it spit in your eye."

"It's an expression I picked up."

"Well, in answer to your question, what's at the other end of this particular rainbow is a lot of bloodshed, probably including yours. So I repeat: what's the rush?"

"For the first time I think we can take that bastard," answered Blue Eyes. "I'm anxious to do it."

"There's a handful of us and millions of them," noted Nighthawk.

"But you're the Widowmaker. You'll find a way. Besides . . ."

"Yes?"

"You wouldn't go there if you thought you wouldn't come out alive," said the dragon. "I've been watching you for weeks. You're the most cautious man I ever met." He paused. "Seems a strange characteristic in a man who was known all over the Frontier as a killer."

"I was a lawman, not an assassin," replied Nighthawk.

"Same thing. You killed people."

"I killed killers. It's not the same thing at all, though you'd never know it from a couple of biographies of the Widowmaker that I read in Cassandra's apartment."

"Six of one, half a dozen of the other," said Blue Eyes with a shrug. "The main thing is, I figure the closer to you I stay, the more likely I am to come out of this with my beautiful skin unblemished."

"You're not standing anywhere near me," said Nighthawk.

"Why not?"

"First, because you're mistaken about standing next to me being the safest place, and second, because I don't trust you."

"You've spent all this time with me and you don't trust me?" bellowed Blue Eyes. "Have I ever lied to you? Betrayed you? Tried to do you any harm?"

"Not to my knowledge."

"Well, then?"

"You're an alien, and—"

"So now you hate aliens, do you?" demanded the dragon.

"Let me finish," said Nighthawk calmly. "You're an alien, and Melisande can't read your emotions. That means until we're in a life-threatening situation, I can't be one hundred percent sure where you really stand, and that's too late."

"What about Friday? He's an alien too."

"She can read him."

"And what about Melisande herself?" continued Blue Eyes. "She's no more human than I am. She can read your emotions, but you can't read hers. How do you know *she* isn't manipulating you for her own ends? Why do you trust her, and not me—because she's got pink skin and I've got blue scales? She's a Balatai woman!"

"You say it like it's a separate species," replied Nighthawk. "Balatai is just a colony world. It was cut off from the Oligarchy, and before that the Democracy, for maybe fifteen or twenty generations, and when we finally made contact again, they had mutated and became empaths. But that doesn't mean they aren't human. They're human with an extra ability, that's all."

"And you trust any human over any alien, right?" persisted Blue Eyes.

"I'm a creature of my times," answered Nighthawk. "Humans don't betray their own. They did once, and I'm sure they will again, but not when we're outnumbered hundreds to one in the galaxy and trying to maintain our primacy."

"If they don't betray their own, why are we trying to overthrow Cassius Hill?"

"There's a difference between a crooked politician robbing his constituency, and that same man selling them out to some alien race. Cassius Hill's as poor an excuse for a man and a governor as you'll ever find, but even *he* wouldn't sell his people out to an alien power."

"I thought we were friends," said Blue Eyes.

"We are. I just define it differently."

"You're as bad as the rest of them," muttered the dragon. "Just the thought of touching one of us must make your skin crawl."

Nighthawk stared at him for a long moment. Finally he noticed the drink Blue Eyes had brought, took a swallow, and replaced it on the bar. "The closest friend I ever had was an alien."

"Sure."

"It's the truth. He was a Silverhorn."

"A Silverhorn? What's that?"

"A native of Bonara II. Mildly humanoid, covered with white fleece, and sporting a big silver horn on the top of his head. We were partners for three years."

"Let me guess," said Blue Eyes sardonically. "He took a laser blast or a bullet meant for you."

"No, it was meant for him; we had enough enemies to go around. But he *would* have taken one meant for me if he could have, and I'd have done the same."

"Then why can't you afford me the same trust?"

"He earned it; you haven't." Nighthawk paused. "You'll get your chance."

"So we come back to my initial question: when are we leaving Sylene?"

"Soon."

"How soon?"

"I'll let you know."

"You know already, don't you?" said Blue Eyes. "And you don't want to tell me."

"That's right."

"Have you told *anyone*?"

"No."

"Not even Cassandra?"

"No."

"Well, I suppose I can take some small comfort from the fact that you don't even trust the woman you're sleeping with."

"You take comfort from strange things," remarked Nighthawk.

"I don't suppose you're willing to tell me who else is coming with us—I mean, besides our original team and Cassandra?"

"I don't know yet."

"When *will* you know?"

"Soon."

"How will you choose them?"

"There are ways," answered Nighthawk.

Chapter 28

Nighthawk leaned up against a purple-boled tree in the small yard behind The Blue Dragon. He didn't have long to wait. A very young man, dressed in colorful silks and satins, and wearing shoes made from the sleek glistening skin of some alien reptile, approached him.

"I heard you were looking for men," announced the young man, throwing his coat open to reveal a truly stunning arsenal of weapons.

"That's right," said Nighthawk.

"You won't find anyone faster," said the young man confidently.

"If you say so," replied Nighthawk with a shrug. "Have you got a name?"

"Johnny Colt."

"That's a little old-fashioned, isn't it? Why not Johnny Laser?"

The young man's poise vanished momentarily. "There are already two Johnny Lasers on the Frontier, and there's a Johnny Blood out on the Rim," he replied unhappily. He pulled a pistol out of his belt and offered it, butt first, to Nighthawk. "But this is a genuine Colt, from the days when we were still Earthbound. Take a look at it. It's a museum piece. You wouldn't believe what it's worth on the market today."

Nighthawk didn't reach for the pistol. "I'm not a connoisseur."

"I thought you were the Widowmaker."

"I am," replied Nighthawk. "And take the Widowmaker's word for it: a hell of a lot more men are killed with weapons costing less than one hundred credits than with weapons costing over a thousand."

Johnny Colt returned the gun to its holster, looking somewhat perplexed.

"Well, am I in or out?" he asked.

"I plan to find out," said Nighthawk. He picked up three stones from the ground, walked to a fence some ten yards away, and lined them up at two-foot intervals. "Let's see what you can do with them."

"That's no challenge," said Johnny Colt contemptuously. "Let me stand a couple of hundred yards away."

"Forget it," said Nighthawk. "You hit anything with a pistol from two hundred yards and it's dumb luck. I don't want anyone shooting until they're as close to the enemy as you are to those rocks."

"Whatever you say." Johnny Colt faced the rocks, his fingers just above his pistol.

"Hold on," said Nighthawk.

"What now?"

"We're not having a fast-draw contest, and I'm not giving points for speed or form. I want your weapon to be in your hand before you confront the enemy." Nighthawk paused. "And one other thing."

"What?"

"Use your laser pistol."

"But my Colt is my trademark."

"It's a trademark that'll wake everyone for five miles in each direction," said Nighthawk. "This is supposed to be a covert operation."

Johnny Colt pulled out his laser pistol, held it steady with both hands, took aim at the three stones, and fired three short blasts. The first and third missed their targets; the second hit the middle stone.

"Kid, you're pissing away your advantage," commented Nighthawk.

"I don't know what you're talking about."

"One of the nice things about laser pistols, aside from the fact that they don't make a bang, is that you don't have to be all that accurate. You're shooting it just as if you were shooting bullets. Try keeping your finger on the trigger and spraying the target area."

Johnny Colt tried again, and this time he melted the other two stones.

"Not very sporting, is it?" said Nighthawk wryly.

"Not at all."

"Then it's lucky for you we're not going to a sporting contest, isn't it?"

Johnny Colt just grinned.

"Do you think you can remember to do that when people are shooting at you?" asked Nighthawk.

"Sure," said the young man. "Will I get a chance at Cassius Hill?"

"Probably not."

"You're saving him for yourself?"

"He's not a trophy; he's a target. I don't care who kills him, as long as he's dead."

"Then why not me?"

"Because if you're close enough to kill him, it means you've disobeyed my orders."

"I just want to leave my mark," explained Johnny Colt. "People will be talking about this for years. I want them to know I was there."

"We're not out for glory and we're not out for fame," said Nighthawk. "If we do our jobs right, no one will ever know we were responsible. If you can't live with that, then you're going to have to stay behind."

Johnny Colt frowned, then shrugged. "Whatever you say. Am I in or out?"

"I'll get back to you."

Johnny Colt wandered off, and Ito Kinoshita walked out into the yard.

"Very young and very eager."

"So were most of the men in most of the graveyards on the Frontier," replied Nighthawk dryly.

"Are you going to take him along?"

"I don't think so."

"Why not?"

"He's in love with that gun of his, and it'll alert every soldier in the area the first time he fires it."

"So tell him not to use it."

"It's his trademark," said Nighthawk sarcastically. "Imagine a seventeen-year-old kid having a trademark."

"Didn't you?"

"I still don't. It makes you too easy to identify."

"You don't think he's killed anyone, do you?" asked Kinoshita.

"Maybe a couple of old men who were looking the other way. But this kid never faced anyone who wasn't afraid to look into his eyes."

"How can you tell?"

"Instinct. Experience. Gut feeling."

"What if you're wrong?"

"Then he'll live to fight another day, and maybe write a folk song or two about how we died on Pericles V."

"You think we might die?"

"If everyone does their job, we might get in and out before they know what's happened," answered Nighthawk. "But there are an awful lot of them and just a handful of us. Getting killed is certainly a possibility."

"Then why risk it?"

"I've told you why: for the Nighthawk who's frozen beneath Deluros VIII."

"I know you can't turn Cassandra over to her father," said Kinoshita, "but can't you bring in some killers with prices on their heads? I mean, there must be *some* other way to raise the money."

"I don't know how quickly he'll need it," said Nighthawk. "I can't risk being late with it and having him thrown out onto the street." He paused. "So I'll plan as carefully as I can, and try to cover all the possibilities, and hope that someone in our little group was born lucky."

"You're about as lucky as anyone I know," offered Kinoshita. "Look how long you survived in such a dangerous profession."

"I'm good, not lucky."

"What's the difference?"

"Lucky people aren't walking around with eplasia," replied Nighthawk with an ironic smile.

"Point taken," admitted Kinoshita. He looked off and saw a slender woman approaching them. "I think you've got another volunteer."

The woman walked up to Nighthawk, totally ignoring Kinoshita. "They say you're looking for volunteers."

"That's right."

"Here I am."

"Name?"

"Pallas Athene."

"Strange name."

"It's for the Greek goddess," she replied. "People take any name they want out here. That's the one I wanted."

"Whatever makes you happy."

"Killing Cassius Hill will make me happy."

"Have you got a personal grudge, or are you just interested in making the Frontier a better place?"

"Do I ask you *your* motives?" she demanded. Before he could answer her, she whipped a knife out of her belt and hurled it at a low-flying avian. It caught the creature in the neck, killing it instantly. "*That's* all you have to know about me."

"That's enough to know," admitted Nighthawk. "You're in. I'll be in touch."

"Do you know where to find me?"

"You found me. I'll find you."

She walked away without another word.

"Give me two dozen like her and we just might pull this off," said Nighthawk.

"Take two thousand like her and you might conquer the whole god-damned Oligarchy," agreed Kinoshita.

"It's a thought."

"So, how soon are we ready?"

"I just told you: when I find two dozen more like her."

"That could take months."

"Or hours," said Nighthawk. "Or weeks. They'll show up when they show up. We're not offering any financial inducements, and besides, everyone I would offer it to has been dead for the better part of a century."

"Nicholas Jory was asking me why you haven't recruited *him*," said Kinoshita.

"I don't want him."

"He was willing to die to protect Cassandra's identity," noted Kinoshita.

"That's one of the reasons I don't want him," answered Nighthawk.

"I don't understand."

"It's undoubtedly noble that he was willing to die for her," said Nighthawk, "but I'd rather he'd tried to find some way to kill me instead. I don't want people who are willing to die. I want men and women who want to live, people like Pallas Athene who probably can't even conceive of their own deaths. Don't give me any noble sacrifices, just people who have every intention of returning to Sylene in one piece."

"It's an attitude that makes sense in you," said Kinoshita. "After all, you're the Widowmaker. But if *they* hold it, they're out of touch with reality."

"Haven't you figured it out yet?" said Nighthawk. "Nobody who is willing to face these odds without a reason is in touch with reality—and Cassandra and I are the only ones who've got a reason."

Well, at least it pleases you to think you have one, concluded Kinoshita.

Nighthawk looked up and saw a tall man approaching him. "Here comes another loser."

"That's a bit of a snap judgment, don't you think?"

"Look at his power pack," said Nighthawk. "It's flashing on empty."

"I never noticed."

"It's not your business to notice."

Kinoshita stared at Nighthawk for a long moment. *On the other hand, we're probably a hell of a lot better off taking three dozen madmen to Pericles than three dozen losers. I wish there were a third alternative . . . but the madmen and the losers constitute all the pieces. The sane ones own the game.*

Chapter 29

Kinoshita broke the silence aboard the ship.

"Pallas Athene reports that she and her team have landed," he announced.

"No problems?" asked Nighthawk.

"There don't seem to be any."

"What about the others?"

"No word from Friday and Melisande yet."

"How about Big Johann?"

Kinoshita shook his head. "Not a word. Do you want me to land?"

"No. Not until everyone else is down."

"I still don't see why we didn't all go in one ship," complained Blue Eyes.

"Why not just wave a flag and tell them we've come to assassinate the governor?" said Nighthawk wryly.

"We could have come as tourists on a spaceliner," said Blue Eyes defensively.

"Three dozen tourists from Sylene?"

"If we all had our passports and visas in order . . ." began the dragon without much conviction.

"I assume computers haven't gotten any stupider during the past century, and the ones I knew would have flashed every alarm they had if they'd been confronted by half as many tourists from a planet that is known to be sympathetic to Ibn ben Khalid," said Nighthawk. "Add to that that there probably haven't been ten tourists from Sylene in the past century, and—"

"Okay, okay," said Blue Eyes. "I get the picture."

Kinoshita looked up. "I just heard from Friday. He's on the ground. No problems."

"Good," said Nighthawk. "That leaves Big Johann's and Tuesday Eddie's groups." He checked his timepiece. "They should report any minute."

Nighthawk walked to the galley and poured himself a soft drink.

"Some ship!" muttered Blue Eyes, joining him. "Not a drop of booze on it."

"Liquor and action don't mix."

"Maybe they don't mix for *your* metabolism, but I find that a good Alphard brandy puts a fine edge on me."

"Then you'll have to make do without your edge," said Nighthawk.

"Your sympathy is appreciated" was the dragon's sardonic reply.

Nighthawk ignored him, finished his drink, tossed the container in an atomizer, and then returned to the control room.

"How are you holding up?" he asked of the girl sitting silently in a corner.

"I'm fine," said Cassandra. "Just anxious."

"You've waited this long," said Nighthawk. "You can wait another hour or two."

"I know."

"Well, *I* don't know," said Blue Eyes, joining them. "Why can't we land now?"

"Because I say so," replied Nighthawk.

"Look, you're the Widowmaker. You're the boss, and you're probably the only advantage we have—but so far you haven't told us what the hell is going on."

"Everyone knows what they have to do."

"But they don't know *why*," said the dragon. "If there's a master plan, and there'd damned well better be, no one knows it but you."

"Then no one can tell Cassius Hill what it is, can they?" said Nighthawk.

"You still think I'd tell him, just because I'm not human?" demanded Blue Eyes. "That I'd betray you because you *are?* Take a good look at Hill, Widowmaker—he's human too! Why would I betray one of you to the other?"

"I never said you would."

"You sure act like it," grumbled Blue Eyes.

"I haven't told anyone except Cassandra, and I only told her because someone has to coordinate things if I go down."

"But if you don't think there's a traitor . . . ?" began Blue Eyes.

"I don't think so," Nighthawk confirmed "But I could be wrong. If I don't tell any of you my plans, then it doesn't matter, does it?"

"Except that you could still be shot in the back."

"You tell me a surefire way to prevent that, and I'll listen."

Kinoshita stood up. "Big Johann has landed. But he's almost three miles off target."

Nighthawk sat down in the captain's chair. "All right. We'll give him an extra forty minutes. Get in touch with Pallas Athene and tell her to adjust her schedule."

"Will do," said Kinoshita. "There's no word from Tuesday Eddie yet."

"Let's assume he's being cautious rather than stupid."

"How will you know the difference?" asked Blue Eyes.

"If he's being cautious, he'll report in eventually. If he's been stupid, then he's dead already and we're not going to hear from him."

"How long are we willing to wait for Tuesday Eddie?" asked Kinoshita.

Nighthawk considered the question. "Ordinarily I'd say ten more minutes and then we move without him. But since we're giving Big Johann forty minutes, we might as well give the same to Tuesday Eddie." He paused. "Stupid name."

"He was born on a Tuesday, got married on a Tuesday, had his first son on a Tuesday, got divorced on a Tuesday, and killed his first man on a Tuesday," said Blue Eyes. "So he finally took it as his name."

"What's today?" asked Nighthawk.

"Monday."

"For another hour or so. Let's hope he doesn't hit for the cycle and die on a Tuesday."

"I thought you were supposed to be the optimist."

"I'm a realist. Sometimes it's the same thing; sometime's it's not. Tonight it's not."

"He's checking in . . ." said Kinoshita.

"He made it?"

Kinoshita shook his head. "He's been denied landing clearance."

"Why?"

"No reason."

"Can he get low enough to dump a shuttle before he cuts out?" asked Nighthawk.

Kinoshita put the question to Tuesday Eddie.

"He says he doesn't think so. Too many sensors covering him. Do you want him to open fire?"

"Hell no!" snapped Nighthawk. "They'd blow him out of the sky in five seconds."

"He wants to know what to do."

"Tell him to break out of orbit, then try about four hundred miles south. If he gets through, have him try to fly under the sensors and get back to his rendezvous point."

"It can't be done," said Kinoshita.

"Sure it can, if he's a good enough pilot. They can't spot anything flying less than eighty feet above the ground."

"Who the hell told you that?" asked Blue Eyes.

"Nobody had to tell me. I *know*—oh, shit!" Nighthawk grimaced. "Let me guess: they've perfected them during the past century, right?"

Kinoshita nodded.

"All right. Tell him to fake engine trouble and make an emergency landing. They'll never buy it, but if he thinks he can take them out, have him do it. Otherwise, fuck around with the engine for half an hour and take off for Sylene."

Kinoshita transmitted the message. "We probably won't hear from them again. Even if they pull it off, they're not going to break radio silence to announce that they've just taken out a squad of Hill's men."

"Right," said Nighthawk. "Okay, let me know when Big Johann's in place, and then we'll get this show on the road."

"Message incoming from Melisande."

"What does she want?"

"Friday's planted his bombs and wants to know when he can set them off."

"Not until I say so."

"She says he doesn't want to wait."

Nighthawk walked over to the console. "Put him on." He leaned over it. "Listen to me—this is Nighthawk." A moment later Friday's voice muttered an acknowledgment. "I didn't create this plan so you could go off and do what you want. If a single explosive is detonated before I give the word, I'll personally hunt you down and kill you before I leave this planet. Do you understand?"

Friday muttered a protest.

"They'll be just as dead if you wait another hour. The only difference is, you might live through this so you can kill more Men. Think about it."

He broke the connection and returned to his seat.

"Can you trust him?" asked Cassandra.

"Probably."

"He's afraid of you, right?" said Blue Eyes. "He knows you can kill him."

"He doesn't know any such thing," replied Nighthawk. "But if he kills me, there will be no one to lead him against more Men—and he favors quantity over quality."

"And he's out there with an empathic prostitute," said Cassandra. "And you're here with an alien bartender and a woman who's been masquerading as a man." She smiled wryly at him. "You put together some crew, Widowmaker."

He shrugged. "You work with what you've got."

And then, to the surprise of everyone, even those who knew him best, he settled back in his chair, closed his eyes, and fell asleep.

It was Kinoshita who gently touched his shoulder half an hour later.

"What is it?" asked Nighthawk, as alert as if he'd been awake the entire time.

"Big Johann's in position."

"Then it's time. Get landing coordinates from the spaceport."

"Got 'em," said Kinoshita a moment later. "But they're asking questions."

"I'll take it from here," said Nighthawk, walking over to the console.

"I require your name and the name and registration number of your ship," said a mechanical voice.

"This is Jefferson Nighthawk. My ship has no name. Its registration number is BD711507JH, and we're two days out from Sylene."

"Purpose of visit?"

"I was commissioned by Governor Cassius Hill to find and return his daughter, Cassandra. I've accomplished my mission. She's onboard with me."

"I must check this out."

"Let me land while you're checking it," said Nighthawk. "I'm very low on fuel."

Pause.

"You may land if you will first transmit a live image of Cassandra Hill."

"No problem. Cassandra, step over here near the holo transmitter." It was Nighthawk's turn to pause. "Got it?"

"Image received. You have permission to land. I have loaded the coordinates into your navigational computer."

"Thanks." Nighthawk cut the transmission. "Well, that's that."

"They'll be waiting for us with half the army!" protested Blue Eyes. "How long do you think it'll take them to find out that Hill wants her dead, not returned?"

"All night," said Nighthawk. "Why do you think we waited for Big

Johann to get into position? He's jamming all transmissions to and from the governor's mansion."

Suddenly Blue Eyes grinned. "You mean they can't contact him to tell him we're here?"

"That's the general idea."

"And I thought you were sending Big Johann out to wipe out some enemy squad."

"I know you did," said Nighthawk. "That's why I'm running this operation and you're not." He turned to Kinoshita. "How long before we touch down?"

"Maybe five minutes, maybe six."

"Are you packed?"

"Sonic pistol and laser pistol," said Kinoshita, touching the butt of each.

"Fully charged?"

"They'd better be."

"Double-check before we land." Nighthawk walked over to Blue Eyes. "Are your weapons in order?"

"Yes."

"I hope you know how to use them."

"Put me to the test," said the dragon.

"I don't have to. Cassius Hill will."

Nighthawk walked to a bulkhead, softly uttered its lock's combination, and waited while it slid back to reveal a very odd-looking weapon, half-pistol, half-rifle, with a large power pack and an unfamiliar configuration.

"What the hell is that?" asked Blue Eyes.

"A molecular imploder."

"I thought they were illegal everywhere in the galaxy!"

Nighthawk merely stared at him.

"Where did you get it?" continued the dragon.

"I had Pallas Athene pick it up for me." He paused. "She's a resourceful lady."

"Can these babies really do what I've heard?"

"Depends on what you've heard."

"That they turn everything they hit—people, buildings, vehicles—into jelly."

"You've heard right—deadly but localized."

"You'll *slaughter* them."

"This isn't a gentleman's contest, and it's not my intention to give the enemy an even chance," said Nighthawk. "Does that answer your next couple of questions?"

"You don't have to bite my head off," said Blue Eyes.

"Look," replied Nighthawk irritably, "I'm about to go into action against overwhelming odds. The likeliest outcome is that we'll all be killed. Even if we aren't, I'm going to blow away a lot of innocent men to get to one guilty one. So forgive me if I'm not in a friendly mood, okay?"

"All right, all right," said Blue Eyes, backing away. "Just remember who the enemy is."

Nighthawk turned to Cassandra. "You set?"

She patted each of her weapons.

"All right, Ito," he said. "Land the ship and let's get this show on the road."

Chapter 30

Nighthawk emerged from the ship and surveyed his surroundings, the molecular imploder held carefully in his hands. A moment later he was joined by Cassandra, Kinoshita, and Blue Eyes.

"Well?" asked the dragon.

"There probably aren't more than a dozen people here at this hour," replied Nighthawk. "See the west-facing section of the building?"

"Yes."

"It's yours."

"Mine?" asked Blue Eyes.

"Kill everyone in it."

"What about just taking them prisoner?"

"If you'd rather."

"*They're* not my enemies," said the dragon.

"Tell me that after one of them identifies you," said Nighthawk.

"I'll play it by ear."

"Do whatever you want," said Nighthawk. "But if any of them gets a message out, I won't wait for Hill's men to kill you. I'll do it myself."

"You could be a little more pleasant, you know," complained Blue Eyes.

"You could be a little more competent. We all have our shortcomings."

Blue Eyes glared at him, then pulled his laser pistol out of its holster and headed off in the direction Nighthawk had indicated.

"Well," said Nighthawk, "maybe he'll kill them and maybe he won't, but just to be on the safe side . . ."

He aimed the molecular imploder at the radio-transmitting tower. The metal turned to liquid and formed a large puddle on the roof of the spaceport. Inside the building a handful of men and women started moving rapidly, scurrying from desk to desk, trying to determine the cause of the problem, but as yet no one had looked out on the landing strip.

"Okay," said Nighthawk. "Ito, you've got the cargo area. Cassandra, go around to the exit and kill anyone who tries to get out."

They both acknowledged his orders with terse nods and went about their business, while Nighthawk approached the building. When he was some ten yards away he slung the imploder over a shoulder, withdrew a pair of pistols, and boldly entered the spaceport.

"Who the hell are—?" began a uniformed guard. He was dead before he could complete the sentence.

Nighthawk heard a slight noise behind him, spun around, and dropped two more guards with bursts of solid light. He heard agonized screams from the west end of the building, and assumed Blue Eyes was either a lousy marksman or a bit of a sadist, or perhaps both.

He carefully searched the Customs area. It seemed empty. He then began walking toward the cargo area to see how Kinoshita was doing when a laser beam whizzed by him, burning the lobe of his left ear. He threw himself to the floor, shattered the one dim light with his sonic pistol, and then tried to pinpoint the source of the laser fire.

For a long moment all was stillness and silence. He knew that all he had to do was entice his unseen opponent into firing once, and he'd know his position . . . but the opponent knew it too, and seemed content to outwait him. Nighthawk threw one of his knives noisily across the room, hoping to draw laser fire, but there was no response. Suddenly a brass cartridge rolled across the floor in his direction, and he resisted the urge to pull a weapon and blow it away.

Finally he began crawling across the room on his belly, hoping he could come across some sign—heavy breathing, the rubbing of a leather holster against a crisp military tunic, *something*—that would pinpoint his opponent's location. After a couple of minutes he half expected to wind up in his enemy's lap, and finally he stopped, convinced that that strategy could be suicidal.

He examined his weapons: laser pistols, sonic pistols, bullet pistol, knives, looking for a tactic, an edge. Finally he found one.

He placed a laser pistol on the floor, and silently removed its power pack. He pressed the "charge" button, but because the pistol was fully charged, the button immediately popped back out. He pressed the button again, withdrew a knife, and used it to hold the button in place, then carefully crawled about twenty feet away and waited.

It took exactly two minutes and twenty-six seconds for the pistol to overload. Then it exploded with a bright flash of light, and Nighthawk's opponent instantly fired at the light. Nighthawk pinpointed the source of the firepower and shot at it with his sonic pistol. There was a scream, then silence.

"Light," muttered Nighthawk, and instantly two dim bulbs came to life.

His antagonist was stretched out on the floor, pistol in hand. He walked over, rolled the body on its back with the toe of his boot, and thoughtfully studied the youthful face.

There was a sudden noise, and he noticed that Cassandra had entered the area.

"I saw all the lights go out, and I kept waiting for some signal that you were all right," she said. "I didn't want to walk into any gunfire."

"You did right."

She indicated the weapon that was still slung over his shoulder. "Why didn't you simply spray the room with the imploder?"

"Look around you."

"I don't understand," she said, surveying her surroundings.

"I'd have hit a weight-bearing wall." She looked puzzled. "These walls hold up the building," he explained. "It would probably have collapsed on me—and even if it hadn't, I don't need the Oligarchy coming after me."

"Why would they care?"

"I can get away with melting an antenna, but if I turn an entire spaceport into silly putty, I'm going to have the Navy on my tail for the rest of what figures to be a very brief life." He paused. "I assume the spaceport is secure?"

"No one tried to get out," she said.

"Yet."

"Ito and Blue Eyes are waiting out front. They didn't take any prisoners."

"Check the west wing; I don't trust that dragon."

"Has he ever lied to you?"

"No more than most men," answered Nighthawk.

She shrugged. "Where will you be?"

"Trying to locate the computer that talked to our ship—the one that has my name and the ship's registration number in it."

He found it before she returned, and used the imploder so that it was totally destroyed and there was no chance of experts later reconstructing the machine's memory.

"Two dead women, and nothing is stirring," announced Cassandra a moment later. "I suppose there could be some people hiding somewhere, but . . ."

"We can't spend all night looking for them, so we'll have to assume they don't exist," said Nighthawk. He looked around. "Okay, we're done with Phase One. We've landed, we've made it past Customs, and no one can identify us. Let's go."

They walked outside and joined Kinoshita and Blue Eyes.

"So far so good," said Nighthawk. "Now we pay a visit to the governor."

"There's a hell of a military vehicle sitting empty just across the road," noted Blue Eyes. "That baby could run through anything Hill's men throw at us."

"Forget it," replied Nighthawk. "We want a nice, simple, private vehicle."

"Why, when we could approach him safely in something like *that*?" persisted the dragon.

"Because something like that has probably got half a dozen communication devices, and since we don't know any of the codes or passwords, we'd be giving ourselves away before we went a mile." He paused. "Try to remember: if it comes to firepower, we're totally outgunned. We're trying to *sneak* in, not cut a swath through Hill's army."

Kinoshita stared at another vehicle. "By the same token, I assume we don't want a taxi?"

"I'd prefer not to use one," said Nighthawk. He looked around. "You see anything else?"

"No."

"Then we'll have to steal it. The second we get it moving, melt the radio."

Kinoshita frowned. "With the imploder?"

"One blast and you'd melt the whole car," said Nighthawk. "Use your laser."

"Uh . . . I think we're going to have a little problem here," said Kinoshita as they approached the vehicle.

"What is it?"

"This isn't like anything I've ever driven," said Kinoshita. "I mean, it *looks* like most of the vehicles I'm used to, but the panel is configured differently, and it sure doesn't seem to run on fusion." He peeked in through the window. "Hell, I don't even know how to start the damned thing." He turned to Blue Eyes. "You ever drive anything quite like this on any of the worlds you've been to?"

The dragon shook his head. "It shouldn't be too hard, though. How different can it be?"

"Different enough," said Kinoshita. "Unlike the other one, this *isn't* armored. You make any kind of mistake, however slight, and you've given us away. I mean, hell, the closer we get to Hill's mansion, the less leeway the guards will give us before they decide to shoot first and ask questions later."

"Enough talk," said Nighthawk, opening a door. "Get in. *I'm* driving."

"You?" repeated Kinoshita. "But you haven't driven a vehicle in a century! You have no idea how this works."

"I was in one just like it the last time I was on this world. I watched what the driver did."

He sat behind the panel, carefully touched the right screens in the right order, and the vehicle suddenly hummed with life.

"Well, I'll be damned!" said Kinoshita.

"I wouldn't be at all surprised," replied Nighthawk as the vehicle took off through the murky Periclean night.

Chapter 31

They'd gone a little more than nine miles when Nighthawk pulled the vehicle off the road and parked it behind a row of thick bushes.

"What now?" asked Blue Eyes.

"Now we walk."

"How far?"

"Maybe a mile, maybe a bit less."

"And you don't want to attract attention by driving the rest of the way, right?" continued the dragon.

"That's right."

"You don't think they're going to notice the four of us walking up to the front door?"

"First," answered Nighthawk, "we're not walking up to the front door, and second, I think they're going to have other things on their minds."

"Such as?"

Nighthawk activated his communicator and set it to Friday's channel.

"You still there, Friday?"

"Yes," replied the alien's voice.

"Any problems yet?"

"No."

"Okay. Count to twenty and give 'em hell—and then get your asses out of there."

Nighthawk didn't wait for a response. He deactivated the device and recommenced walking in the direction of the governor's mansion.

Twenty seconds later the horizon was lit up by a series of explosions. They circled to the east, each brighter and louder than the last.

"Where did he get his hands on so many explosives?" asked Blue Eyes.

"He's very creative," replied Nighthawk dryly. "Come on. Stop star-ing—it's not a fireworks display. We've got serious work to do."

"Shouldn't we wait until they empty out the mansion?"

"Everyone who's going has left already," answered Nighthawk. "Cas-sius Hill's not going to leave himself totally defenseless."

"Look!" said Kinoshita, pointing to the northeast. "That looks like laser fire! There are snipers out there!"

"That means Tuesday Eddie got through," said Nighthawk, increasing his pace.

"So that accounts for Tuesday Eddie and Friday," said Blue Eyes. "And I know Big Johann was jamming their transmissions. But where is Pallas Athene and her group?"

"Around," said Nighthawk.

"You *still* don't trust me?" demanded the dragon.

"It's not a matter of trust. If you're captured, you can't tell what you don't know."

"And what if *you're* captured?"

"I won't be," replied Nighthawk with such absolute calm and certainty that Blue Eyes was suddenly afraid of him.

"Is that it?" asked Kinoshita as the huge mansion came into view.

"That's it," said Cassandra coldly. "I've waited a long time for this day."

Blue Eyes started walking, prepared to use the extensive landscaping for cover, but Nighthawk laid a heavy hand on his shoulder. "Wait," he said.

"What for?" responded the dragon. "We're sitting ducks out here."

"This whole place is honeycombed with security devices," said Night-hawk.

"Then how—?"

"Shut up and listen."

Cassandra stared at the ground ahead of her, and finally looked up. "There's a web of sensors throughout the yard. They're about a foot off the ground so animals won't set them off. I'm wearing infrared lenses, so I can see them. Walk exactly where I walk, and you should be all right. When we get to where they're too closely aligned to walk between them, I'll crawl beneath them until I get to the power source and deactivate them."

She began walking in a complex route, turning every few steps, show-ing them how to avoid the unseen sensor beams, every now and then warning one of them that he was getting too near a beam. Finally, when they were perhaps two hundred yards from the house, she gestured them all to kneel down and wait for her signal.

She got onto her belly and slithered beneath the beams that only she could see. In a moment she was one with the darkness, and even Nighthawk, who possessed excellent night vision, couldn't spot her.

He made himself as comfortable as he could on the cool, damp lawn and contented himself with watching the now-sporadic explosions and increasing laser fire. After what seemed an hour, but was probably closer to ten minutes, Cassandra walked back and joined them.

"It's safe now," she whispered. "At least until we're inside the house."

"Then what?" asked Kinoshita.

"Guards, alarms, robots," she said. "You name it, he's got it."

"I assume you have a plan?" said Blue Eyes to Nighthawk. "Other than sending me up to the roof, I mean?"

"You know what you have to know," said Nighthawk.

"Damn it, I have a right to know what's going on!" persisted the dragon. *"Why* do I have to climb up to the roof? Cassandra says there are alarms in the house. The house is all lit up, so infrared lenses won't help. How are you going to get around them?"

"I'm not," responded Nighthawk.

"You're just going to blithely walk through the house setting them all off?"

"That's right."

"You're crazy!" snapped the dragon.

"You're welcome to think so," said Nighthawk, "but keep your voice down or you'll get us all shot before we even enter the mansion."

Blue Eyes glared at him, but didn't say anything more, and Nighthawk led his little party toward the house. When he was some eighty yards distant, he saw a number of troops on the driveway leading to the front entrance, and he changed directions, circling around to the back.

There were two uniformed men standing guard at the back of the mansion. Nighthawk put his finger to his lips, then gestured his group to stay put. He began sneaking up on the men, patient as Job, silent as death. When he was some twenty feet away, he pulled out a knife and hurled it into the throat of one man while leaping from the shadows onto the back of the other. A quick twist of the head, a loud *snap!,* and then all was still again.

Nighthawk signaled his party to join him, and a moment later they were all huddled in the shadows just outside the rear entrance.

"Blue Eyes, Ito, get these men out of sight."

They dragged the two guards off behind a row of thick, neatly trimmed shrubbery, then returned.

"You still plan to just walk right into the house?" demanded Blue Eyes.

"Yeah," said Nighthawk. "After Cassandra reconnects the outside alarm system."

"*Re*connects it?" exclaimed the dragon. "Why?"

"So I can set it off."

"What the hell are you talking about?"

"As you've pointed out, there's no way to get into the house without setting off dozens of alarms. So, since we can't avoid setting them off, the only thing to do is make the guards ignore them."

"How?"

"By setting off every outside alarm as well. Then these will just be one more set of alarms on the blink."

"You think he'll buy that while there are bombs going off and sniper fire, and his radio transmissions are being jammed?"

"Not initially," replied Nighthawk. "But eventually he'll have to, when his men check the grounds and can't find anyone setting off the alarms."

"And how are you going to accomplish that?"

"I'm not," said Nighthawk. "*You* are."

"Me?" demanded the dragon. "I want to be in on the kill!"

"You're going to make the kill possible," replied Nighthawk. He pointed to a staircase. "There's a set of stairs leading to one of the bedroom balconies. Once you're up there, you shouldn't have any trouble reaching the roof."

"You've been telling me since we left Sylene that I have to be able to get on the roof. I assumed there was some secret entrance up there."

"I wish there were."

"So I get onto the roof. What then?"

"Then you fire *this*"—Nighthawk handed him one of his sonic pistols—"randomly in every direction."

"A Screecher? I'll be spotted in three seconds!"

"No, you won't," said Nighthawk. "There's no light, and no explosion. The guards will be too far away to hear the hum . . . but the sensors are sensitive enough to react to it." He paused. "I want you to hit every area with that thing, to set off every system they've got. Don't hit any guards, just alarms. Especially toward the front of the mansion; that's where I want most of them congregated."

"And then you just walk in the back door and set off more alarms—and nobody pays attention?"

"That's the general idea."

"You know, it might work," admitted the dragon. Suddenly he tensed. "How do I get down after the place is teeming with guards?"

"Just be patient," said Nighthawk.

"For how long?"

"Ten minutes, twenty minutes, an hour," said Nighthawk with a shrug. "It depends on conditions inside. But either I'm going to kill Cassius Hill, in which case the whole planet will be after me and you can probably climb down and walk to the spaceport in broad daylight; or else he's going to kill me, and then you can testify that I forced you to do all this and swear everlasting fealty to him."

"He'll never believe me."

"Then you'd better hope I kill him, hadn't you?" responded Nighthawk with a smile. "Now get your ass up there, and don't start shooting until you see my signal."

Blue Eyes began cautiously climbing the stairs, muttering to himself. When he reached the balcony, he balanced precariously on the railing for a moment, then laboriously pulled himself onto the roof. He felt a surge of vertigo, lay as flat as he could, and waited until it passed. Finally he withdrew the sonic pistol, got carefully to his feet, and located Nighthawk, who was standing in the shadows just past the rear entrance.

Nighthawk waited for Cassandra to join him. He asked her something, she nodded her head, and he looked up at Blue Eyes, raised his hand above his head, and dropped it.

Wondering how he had gotten himself into such a situation, Blue Eyes trained the sonic pistol on a point some two hundred yards from the front door and pulled the trigger.

The response was deafening.

Chapter 32

As the guards streamed out of the house, looking for the intruders, Night-hawk motioned Cassandra and Kinoshita to keep to the shadows. Then, when Blue Eyes had set off at least a dozen different alarms, he walked in through a side door, spotted a security camera, and blew it away.

"Not you," he said, as Kinoshita followed him.

"Why not?"

"I told you before. You're the one who has to survive and get the money back to Deluros VIII. I can't take a chance on you getting killed inside the mansion."

"So where do you want me?"

"See that room on the second floor, the one with all the lights on?"

"Yes. Looks like he's got bars on the windows and the balcony door."

"Those bars are to keep people out, not in. It's Hill's office. Stay within sight of it. When I get the money, I'll toss it down to you."

"And if the yard is swarming with guards?"

"Then I'll find some way to distract them while Cassandra gets the money to you." He handed the molecular imploder to Kinoshita. "And if it gets really hairy, use this."

"I'm still not happy about this," said Kinoshita. "You could use me inside."

Nighthawk shook his head. "You'd be one more person I'd have to protect." Nighthawk briefly noted Kinoshita's hurt expression. "I'm sorry. I don't have time to be diplomatic."

He stepped aside as Cassandra entered, then closed the door behind him.

"Can he keep clear of the guards?" she asked as they walked through the small room.

"He's a good man. He'll stay clear."

Nighthawk paused before the door.

"What's on the other side of this?" he asked.

"A corridor. It leads to a staircase on the left, and a library and eventually the summer kitchen on the right."

"Summer kitchen?" he repeated.

"Where the staff cooks for outdoor functions. It used to be outside, but the insects on Pericles are not only large, they can be incredibly aggressive, so my father had it enclosed a few years ago."

"Are we likely to run into any guards in the corridor?" asked Nighthawk.

"Ordinarily, I'd say no. But with alarms going off all over, and the building's security board lit up like a Christmas tree, I can't be sure."

"All right," he said. "Stand back and let me go first."

"I'm armed too," she protested. "And don't forget—this is *my* battle."

"I'm going to be as blunt with you as I was with Kinoshita," said Nighthawk. "If there's more than one guard out there, you haven't got a chance. I'm the Widowmaker. This is what I do for a living. I guarantee it'll take more than two or three men to bring me down."

She seemed about to protest, realized that he was right, that his decision to go first was practical rather than noble or falsely heroic, and she stepped back.

"Open," muttered Nighthawk, and the door dilated. He stepped through, weapons in hand, and put a burst of laser fire through the security camera.

"Halt!" yelled a voice.

Nighthawk spun and fired, dropped a guard, then crouched down and shot two more as they raced down the stairs at the sound of the first one's voice.

He stood motionless, listening intently, for almost a full minute, then turned to Cassandra.

"All right, let's go," he said softly, heading toward the stairs.

"Not that way!" she whispered.

"They lead to your father's office, don't they?"

"And they're wired. The first step will read your weight and the structure of your foot, and since you're not in the computer, the second step will fry you to a crisp."

"Then how do we get up there?"

"There are three ways. Two will be guarded: the main staircase, and an airlift right next to it. The third way I discovered when I was a little girl—a secret stairway that I think he put in as an escape route—but I don't know if it's wired too."

"If it is, we won't have any warning before he activates it," said Nighthawk. "We'd better use one of the public routes and take our chances with the guards."

She nodded her agreement and set off down the corridor. When they reached the summer kitchen she stopped as Nighthawk destroyed yet another camera. He turned and saw her standing hesitantly, her face troubled.

"What is it?"

"Something's wrong," she said.

"What?"

She frowned. "There are always staff members here. This is where they cook their own food when it's not being used for some big ceremonial dinner."

"Nothing's wrong. There are dozens of alarms going off. They're all out looking for the bad guys—meaning us."

"Cooks don't carry weapons," she said. "*Someone* should be here."

As if on cue, the heavy metal door to the walk-in freezer opened and two middle-aged men walked out, each carrying slabs of meat.

"Freeze!" said Nighthawk softly.

One of the men was so startled he dropped his meat noisily to the floor and held his hands up. The other simply stared at Nighthawk as if he was the latest in a long line of minor irritations.

"Can you regulate the freezer's temperature from the inside?" asked Nighthawk.

"Yes," said one of the men.

"Okay. Go back inside."

"But—"

"No arguments. Just do it."

When both men were inside the freezer, Nighthawk began shutting the door.

"You're going to be here for a few hours, so raise the temperature and relax."

Before they could protest he had shut and locked the huge, gleaming door.

"So much for your missing men," he said, turning to Cassandra. "Now where do we go?"

"Follow me."

"*No!*" he said sharply. "I'll go first. You just tell me where."

"Out this door," she said, pointing, "then follow the corridor to the right, pass through the sitting room, and we're at the grand foyer."

"That's where the staircase is?"

"Yes."

"Okay, let's go."

He walked out into the corridor, a pistol in each hand, alert for the slightest noise or movement. Suddenly he heard the sound of footsteps coming through the country kitchen. He stepped back, passing Cassandra, waited with frightening calm until three men burst through the door, and fired. All three were dead before they hit the floor.

"Damn!" he muttered.

"What is it?" asked Cassandra.

"We should have set off more alarms inside the house. With only one sounding, they'll know security has been breached."

He walked back into the kitchen and blew out a window. The alarm went off, adding its whine to all the others.

Then he reentered the corridor and led the way to a large sitting room. He blew away the camera and gestured her to join him. As she did so, he shot out yet another window and activated the room's alarm.

"The main entrance is right past that door, you said?" he asked, indicating a massive door at the far end of the room.

She nodded. "The staircase and elevator will both be off to the left."

"How many men should be there?"

"Ordinarily there's a color guard of a dozen, plus a few minor functionaries," replied Cassandra. "But with all these alarms, who knows? They could all be outside, looking for enemies—or they could have smelled a ruse and tripled the guard."

A nearby explosion made the entire mansion shake.

"I hope he remembers he's not supposed to blow this place up until we're out of it," muttered Nighthawk.

"My father's got a couple of hundred men on call," she replied. "He couldn't get much closer."

"Never underestimate Friday," said Nighthawk. "He can blow them all to hell before you know it." He walked to the door. "Are you ready?"

She pulled her pistol out and nodded.

"Then let's go."

He ordered the door to open and burst into the grand foyer. There were eight uniformed men and a pair of robots standing guard. Five of the men were dead before they knew he was among them, and Cassandra downed two more. Nighthawk quickly turned his fire on the robots, melting the first with a laser blast and disrupting the circuits of the other with a solid burst of sound from his sonic pistol. The one remaining man turned and raced to the airlift.

"Get him!" snapped Nighthawk, still concentrating on the second robot, which was firing lethal pulse blasts from a finger that had been created for that purpose. He kept his sonic pistol trained on it, decided that the first robot was no longer a threat and added his laser fire to it, and heard a scream from the direction of the airlift just as the second robot finally collapsed, its limbs moving aimlessly, its weaponry no longer functional.

"Jesus, you're good!" said Cassandra admiringly. "You didn't need me at all, did you?"

"I needed you to stop that last one from warning your father or calling for reinforcements."

"He's stopped—but my father has to know *someone's* here by now." She paused. "I destroyed the airlift controls. We're going to have to climb the stairs."

"Doesn't make much difference," replied Nighthawk, staring at the dead bodies and deactivated robots. "We've protected our rear, and what's waiting for us will be waiting no matter which way we approach it."

"Yeah, we're okay unless someone enters the house," she agreed.

"No one will," he said, walking over to the entrance and fusing the lock with a blast from his laser pistol.

"Don't you think that will just alert them?" she asked.

"Probably."

"Then won't they immediately break the door down?"

"They can try," said Nighthawk. He checked his timepiece. "There's a six-foot lady who's going to have something to say about it in forty seconds or so," he added with a smile.

"Pallas Athene?"

"That's right," he said, starting to ascend the sweeping staircase.

"I was wondering what she was doing."

"Pretty much what we've been doing the last couple of minutes, but on the outside."

Nighthawk stopped at a landing, looking into every nook and cranny, peering into every shadow. When he decided it was safe, he climbed the rest of the stairs, then waited for Cassandra to catch up with him.

"So far so good," she said.

"That was the easy part," he replied. "Your father's no fool. You can bet the last hundred feet will be a hell of a lot harder than the first hundred."

He began walking cautiously along the corridor to Hill's outer office. Twice men emerged from rooms to stop him, and twice he shot them before they could take aim at him.

A robot emerged from the outer office and confronted them. Nighthawk turned his laser and sonic pistols on it, but with no discernible effect.

He looked around as the robot approached, spotted an overhead chandelier, and shot it loose from the ceiling. It fell heavily on the robot, which staggered and spent a moment getting free of it. During that time Nighthawk, no longer worried about keeping his presence secret, pulled out a projectile gun and fired a bullet into each of the robot's eyes. The sensors began smoking, and Nighthawk crouched down against a wall of the corridor, motioning to Cassandra to do the same. The robot continued walking in a straight line, crashed through a railing that overlooked the grand foyer, and fell some thirty feet to the marble floor below.

"Why the hell didn't my other weapons stop it, or even slow it down?" muttered Nighthawk, as much to himself as to Cassandra.

"It was made of a titanium alloy with a super-tight molecular bonding," she answered.

"I've seen titanium before," he replied. "But I never saw one that a laser couldn't even char."

"There have been a lot of advances in the last century," she said. "Don't count on your memories, because if it's a state-of-the-art security device, my father owns it."

"I'll keep it in mind," he said seriously, finally straightening up. He tucked the sonic pistol into his belt and kept the projectile gun out. "I think I may need this one."

"You'll need them all before you're through," she said. "My father's a dangerous man. I wish you'd kept the molecular imploder."

He shook his head. "Fire it at a man standing against a wall and you not only turn the man to liquid, you do the same to the wall. And, sometimes, the trees beyond the wall." He smiled. "You really don't want to use it on the second floor of a house with high ceilings. Besides, Ito has to get back to the ship. It's better that he has it."

He turned back to the outer office, approached it silently, and burst into the room, weapons at the ready, only to find that it was empty. He waited until she caught up with him, then went through the doorway to the inner office. A robot stood at attention, staring at him.

"Good evening, Mr. Nighthawk," it said. "How nice to see you once again."

Cassandra turned her gun on it, but Nighthawk held up a hand.

"He's just an office robot. He's not programmed for violence."

"But he'll warn my father we're here!"

"He already has."

"Governor Hill has no idea you are inside the building, Mr. Night-hawk," said the robot.

"You're lying, right?" said Nighthawk.

"That is correct, sir."

"Sit down behind a desk and keep your mouth shut."

"I think I should remain at my post, sir."

"If you don't sit down right now, I'll melt you with a laser," said Night-hawk. "Consider that carefully and then make your decision."

"I will be of greater use to my master if I sit down," announced the robot, walking over to a desk and seating itself behind it.

"How many men and robots has Cassius Hill got behind that next door?" asked Nighthawk, indicating Hill's office.

"None, sir."

"You're lying again."

"That is correct, sir."

"How many?"

"Three thousand and fourteen."

Nighthawk pointed his pistol at the robot. "If you lie once more, I'm going to blow your goddamned head off. Now, how many men and robots has he got protecting him?"

"Quite enough, sir," said the robot. "You may fire when ready."

"If you insist." Nighthawk squeezed the trigger and melted the robot from the neck up.

"What was that for?" asked Cassandra. "It was only a machine."

"No sense giving it a chance to tell every other robot on the grounds exactly where we are. Pallas Athene's good, but she's not *that* good."

"It probably told them already."

"Then that's what it gets for telling them," said Nighthawk irritably.

He cautiously approached the door to Hill's office. As he reached it, it dilated before him, allowing him and Cassandra to pass through.

Cassius Hill sat at his desk, flanked by four Security robots. He was elegantly dressed, and was smoking an Antarrean cigar.

"Good evening, Widowmaker," he said. He turned to Cassandra. "How very nice to see you too, my dear." Back to Nighthawk. "To what do I owe the pleasure of this visit?"

"You owe me five million credits," said Nighthawk. "I'd like it in cash."

"Nonsense," said Hill. "I told you I didn't want her back. I want Ibn ben Khalid."

"I know. You still owe me five million credits."

"I just told you, I—" Suddenly Hill's eyes widened and he stared at Cassandra. "Of *course!* What a fool I've been! No wonder I could never find out anything about Ibn ben Khalid's past! No wonder he always seemed to know my next move!" He stood up. "I commend you, Cassandra. I couldn't ask for a more exceptional daughter. You have everything it takes to succeed me in office." He paused, then added with mock sadness: "What a shame that I'm going to have to kill you."

"You're not killing anyone," said Nighthawk, leveling his pistol at Hill.

"Don't be a fool, Widowmaker. I'll admit you showed enormous resourcefulness to reach my office, but you'll never leave here alive if you kill me." He placed his hands on the desk and leaned forward. "You've fulfilled your commission. You've returned my daughter *and* presented me with Ibn ben Khalid. You're free to leave Pericles. The money will be transferred to your lawyers' account."

"What happens to *her*?"

"What happens to her is going to happen whether I kill you first or not."

"I don't think we have a deal," said Nighthawk. He pointed toward a solid-looking safe that stood in a corner. "Open your safe."

"No."

"I can open it whether I kill *you* first or not."

"You agreed to fulfill my commission," said Hill. "I was given to understand that the Widowmaker always honors his contracts."

"A lot can change in a century," said Nighthawk. "Open the safe."

"And then what?" said Hill. "You'll kill me anyway."

"I have no intention of killing you."

"You just admitted that you break your word—so why should I believe you?"

"Once I've got your money, what purpose would be served by my killing you?"

"If you let me live, I'll hunt you to the ends of the galaxy."

"I doubt it," said Nighthawk. "If I let you live, you'll be grateful for the gift of life and won't chance losing it by following me."

Hill stared at Nighthawk. "I could order my robots to kill you right now."

"I don't think so. They're programmed to protect you." He raised his voice. "The instant I see a robot move, I'll shoot Cassius Hill at point-blank range." He smiled at Hill. "All right, give them the order."

"This isn't over, Widowmaker. Every man has his weaknesses, including you. You've just signed your death warrant."

"I've been dead for a hundred years," replied Nighthawk. "There's no future in it." He pointed to the safe with one of his pistols. "Get busy."

Hill turned to Cassandra. "Have you nothing to say, daughter? No word of regret for turning against your father? No plea for forgiveness?"

"Just get the money," she said.

He shrugged, walked over to the safe, and rapidly touched a combination, then whispered a trio of code words so softly that Nighthawk couldn't hear them. The door swung open.

"There it is," said Hill, indicating the tall piles of crisp banknotes. "Little good may it do you."

"Step aside," said Nighthawk.

"This is your last chance, Widowmaker. You can still walk away."

"You're in no position to be giving orders."

"I'm Cassius Hill," he said, walking back to his desk. "I'm *always* in a position to give orders."

"Keep your gun trained on him," said Nighthawk. "If he or the robots make a move, shoot *him* first."

Nighthawk approached the safe, peered into it, then holstered his gun and reached in for the money with his left hand—

—and the door slammed shut—

—and the safe suddenly sprouted legs and grew to a height equal to Nighthawk's—

—and the safe developed arms that reached for Nighthawk's throat.

"Poor, stupid clone," said an amused Cassius Hill. "A lot can happen in a century. Meet the newest, finest security device on the market—a weapon that can assume any shape that I choose for it."

Nighthawk pulled out his laser pistol, but the safe—the Weapon—slapped it away.

"Call it off or she'll kill you!" he yelled as one of the metal arms clamped shut on his left shoulder.

"Call *her* off or I'll have *it* kill *you*," countered Hill.

Cassandra fired, and her father grabbed his right arm.

"The next one will take your head off," she said coldly.

Nighthawk uttered an involuntary groan as the metal hand crushed his shoulder. He continued bobbing and weaving to keep his head away from the second hand—but now the Weapon had sprouted three more arms, each longer than the first two.

"Now!" shouted Cassandra.

"All right," said Hill. He turned to the safe. "Kiss!"

Suddenly the metal arms flowed back into the walls of the Weapon, though the door still pressed against his left arm, holding it motionless.

"Kiss?" repeated Nighthawk, almost amused despite the agony of his crushed shoulder.

"I wanted a word an enemy wouldn't think to utter," said Hill almost conversationally, as if being confronted in his office by an armed assassin were an everyday occurrence. "What now? Do you kill me or do I kill you, or do we find some common ground?"

"Make it let go of my arm," said Nighthawk.

"I don't think so," replied Hill. "You're a very dangerous man, Widowmaker. Much better to keep you incapacitated until we've reached some understanding."

"Kiss," ordered Nighthawk.

"It only responds to *my* voice," explained Hill. "And 'kiss' is the command that makes its limbs vanish. It requires another word to make it let go of you—a word I have no intention of uttering."

Cassandra took a step nearer to him and aimed her pistol at a point between his eyes.

"No melodramatics, daughter," said Hill calmly. "His life isn't being threatened now, so you have no reason to threaten mine. And if you shoot me, my robots will kill you even faster than the Weapon will kill him."

"We can't stay like this forever," said Nighthawk.

"Then it's time to talk business," agreed Hill.

"Okay."

"But my business is only with you, Widowmaker. My daughter may inherit my paltry little estate someday, but what you and I have to say is of no concern to her."

"Fuck you!" snapped Cassandra, extending her arm so that her pistol was even closer to her father.

"Such language in a refined young revolutionary," said her father with mock distress.

"My arm's getting numb," said Nighthawk. "We've got to start talking soon."

"As soon as we're alone," said Hill.

Nighthawk turned to Cassandra. "I don't know how much longer I can stay conscious. You'd better do as he says."

"No goddamned way!" she protested.

"I'm in no position to argue!" he snapped. He looked back at Hill. "She can't go back to the outer office. She'll be a sitting duck if any of your men show up there."

"What do you propose?" asked Hill.

"I don't know," grated Nighthawk, grimacing in pain. "Is there some other way out of this room?"

Hill looked around. "Well, there's always the balcony."

"Fine. Lock her out there till we're done."

"What if she jumps down and runs away?"

"She'll break a leg, or your men will kill her."

"I'm not going anywhere!" snapped Cassandra.

Nighthawk stared at her. *Will you stop being tough and stop being noble and just remember who's waiting downstairs and what he's holding?*

"I suppose we'll have to wait until you pass out and she gets tired of pointing her gun at me," said Hill. He shrugged eloquently. "I never could do anything with her."

Jesus! You still *haven't figured it out!*

"Get the fuck out of here, you dumb bitch!" he yelled.

She glared at him, her face reflecting her fury, and stalked out onto the balcony without another word.

Good. Now just get over your mad long enough to look down before I pass out.

Hill closed the door behind her. "Well, here we are, Widowmaker," he said easily. "My offer still stands: you can walk away safely, and the money will be in your attorneys' account tomorrow."

"Fuck my attorneys," said Nighthawk. "I'm doing this for *me*, not *him*."

"Ah!" said Hill with a smile. "Enlightened sel-finterest. That certainly makes you more comprehensible to me." He paused. "Let me make sure we understand each other. I release you, I pay you off, and you leave my office. I don't know how many men you have out there"—he waved his hand in the general direction of Friday's bombs—"but you call them off and take them away with you." He paused and stared at Nighthawk. "Ibn ben Khalid you leave behind."

"Agreed."

Where the hell are you?

"Good. Now all that's left to discuss is your fee. I think three million credits sounds exceptionally generous."

"What happened to five million?"

"That was before you threatened my life. Besides, you've surely done a couple of million credits' damage to my property this evening, don't you think?"

"Probably."

"Well, then?"

"I'll give you two options," said Nighthawk. "You can pay me three million or eight million, it's up to you."

"What's the difference?" asked Hill, curious.

"For eight million, I don't come back and kill you."

"More threats? You are a very slow learner, Widowmaker." Hill sighed and stared at him for a long moment. "I'll tell you what I'm going to do," he said at last. "I'm going to accept your proposition and pay you the eight million. I truly don't relish spending the rest of my life looking over my shoulder for a man of your abilities."

"Good," said Nighthawk. "Then we have a deal."

"That's right." He lowered his gaze to the Weapon and uttered a single word: "*Bite!*"

Nighthawk bellowed in pain as he felt his hand severed at the wrist. He almost passed out as Hill ordered the door of the safe to open.

Nighthawk, finally free, rolled on the floor, then tore off his belt and wrapped it around his wrist to try to staunch the bleeding. As he did so, Hill reached into the safe and withdrew red-stained stacks of currency.

"To coin a phrase, here is your blood money, Widowmaker. And while I believe that you intended to keep your promise not to hunt me down, I think a little encouragement is always beneficial."

Nighthawk reached for his laser pistol, which was lying on the floor, but one of the robots pointed a deadly finger and shot it away.

"Breaking your word already?" asked Hill.

"The bleeding hasn't stopped," mumbled Nighthawk. "I've got to cauterize the wound!"

"Allow me," said Hill, reaching into his desk and withdrawing a laser pistol. He aimed it at the blood-drenched stump and fired. Nighthawk bellowed again and doubled over in pain. "Number Four," said Hill to one of his robots. "Go out onto the balcony and kill my daughter."

"Yes, Governor," replied the robot, walking to the door that led to the balcony.

There was a brief humming sound, and the robot became a small gray puddle on the floor.

"You remembered!" muttered Nighthawk as Cassandra strode into the room, fired the imploder at the other three robots, and then turned the Weapon into jelly.

"What the hell did he do to you?" she demanded, finally noting Nighthawk's arm.

"Don't worry about it!" grated Nighthawk. "Let's just get the hell out of here!"

She turned the imploder toward her father, who pointed his laser pistol at her.

"It's still a Mexican standoff," he said calmly.

"You think so, do you?"

She fired the imploder, and he was a puddle of liquid and juices before he could fire back.

"I forgot all about Kinoshita until you cursed at me," Cassandra said, helping Nighthawk to his feet. "That was so unlike you that it startled me and made me think."

"I must be weaker than I thought," he said unsteadily. "It feels like the whole room is shaking."

"Oh, shit!" she said. "It is! That bastard must have tied his life readings into the house system and rigged it! Now that he's dead the whole god-damned wing is falling apart!"

"Grab the money!"

She pulled a pair of bags out of her pocket, opened them, and quickly tossed one pile of money into one and a smaller pile into the other, as the room began shaking more violently. "Now what?" she asked.

Nighthawk staggered to the balcony door. "Throw the bigger bag down to Ito! And give him the imploder, too!"

She raced to the railing of the balcony, threw the money and imploder over it.

"What now?" she asked.

"That secret passage you mentioned. Where is it?"

She was about to lead him to it when the floor vanished beneath her and the office wing of the mansion collapsed.

Chapter 33

Nighthawk groaned and pushed a piece of timber off his chest. He reached down to remove another one from his leg, then realized that he was missing his left hand. As badly as that hurt, the pain in his crushed shoulder was worse.

Suddenly a tall, lean figure was standing over him, pulling timbers off his torso and legs.

"Cassandra . . ." he mumbled.

"She's all right. Don't waste your strength. Just lie still and I'll have you out in another minute."

He tried to focus his eyes, and finally realized that he was looking at Pallas Athene.

"What happened?" he asked, confused.

"The goddamned house collapsed," said Pallas Athene. "I assume you killed Hill?"

"Yes."

She nodded her head. "I've heard of this baby before. It's called the Vengeance System. You're lucky to be alive." She pulled the last piece of lumber off him and stared at him. "What the hell happened to you? You didn't lose your hand from *this*."

"It's a long story." Suddenly he sat up. "Where's Blue Eyes? We left him on the roof."

"Dead. He's about forty feet off to your left. Broke his neck in the fall."

"Damn!" He leaned back, exhausted from the effort. "Where's the rest of your team?"

"Scattered from here to my ship," replied Pallas Athene. "All dead."

"Too bad."

"They knew the odds." She paused. "So you got Cassius Hill!"

"*She* got him."

"I'm glad you left it to her," said Pallas Athene. "After all, she's Ibn ben Khalid. It was a damned generous thing for you to do."

"Generosity had nothing to do with it," replied Nighthawk. "She saved my life."

"Sure."

"She did!" he said heatedly.

"Okay, she did. Keep your voice down and don't waste your strength. You haven't got a lot to spare."

"Pull out my communicator," he said.

"Where is it?"

"One of my pockets, or inside my belt."

She frisked him gently and produced it.

"Activate it. Band 1193."

"Done."

"Johann, how's it going?"

No response.

"Johann, are you there?"

Silence.

"Are you sure it's on the right band?"

She checked again. "1193, just like you said."

"Shit. Try Band 2076."

"Okay."

"Eddie, come in. Tuesday Eddie, come in, damn it!"

No response.

"Is anyone else alive besides you, me, and her?" he asked weakly.

"Beats me. Where's Kinoshita?"

"He'd better be halfway to the spaceport by now," rasped Nighthawk. "Or the whole thing was for nothing."

"What do you mean, nothing?" she said. "We killed Cassius Hill, didn't we?"

"Right," he said. "We killed Cassius Hill. Get me onto my feet. If I stay on my back for another minute, I'm going to pass out."

She helped him up, and braced him for a moment until a wave of dizziness passed.

"Where's Cassandra?"

"Over here," said Pallas Athene, walking over to a crumpled body.

"I thought you said she was all right!"

"She is, considering. She has a major concussion and maybe a few fractured ribs. She was awake a couple of minutes ago; she could be a lot worse."

"Friday!" said Nighthawk suddenly. He adjusted the radio band. "Friday, are you there?"

"Of course I am here," said the alien's familiar voice. "This has been a wonderful night. A glorious night. I *knew* I was right to team up with you, Jefferson Nighthawk!"

"Is Melisande all right?"

"She is dead."

"How did it happen?"

"They swept the area with lasers. She never saw it coming, and I doubt that the man who killed her ever saw her. These things happen." There was a pause. "Have you any further orders, or should I return to my ship?"

Nighthawk swayed as he surveyed the carnage around him. "Stand by," he said at last. "I'll get back to you shortly."

He deactivated the communicator.

"The best killers survived," said Pallas Athene. "That's usually the way in war."

"At least it's over," he said. "The enemy's dead."

"You're not thinking clearly," she corrected him.

"What are you talking about?"

"The *general* is dead," she explained. "The army's still intact, minus a few thousand casualties, and tomorrow there'll be a new general."

"No," he said. "It wasn't a war. It's done."

"It won't be done as long as you're alive," she said. "Even those who hated Hill's guts will still try to hunt you down. You came onto their turf and you killed them where they lived. That requires vengeance."

"I don't plan to spend the rest of my life running," said Nighthawk.

"Then you'll make a stand and fight," replied Pallas Athene. "After all, you're the Widowmaker."

"I'm just his surrogate," answered Nighthawk. "What we did tonight was save the *real* Widowmaker."

"I don't understand."

"It doesn't matter; *I* understand." He looked around once more. "You killed everyone out front?"

"For the time being," she replied. "There'll be thousands of reinforcements bearing down on this place once they know what's been going on."

"They won't know until sunrise," said Nighthawk. "We jammed their signals and destroyed their transmitters."

"Okay, they won't know until sunrise," she said. "So what?"

"That's all the time we need."

"For what?"

"To end the war forever." He pulled out his communicator. "Friday, how far are you from the governor's mansion?"

"Perhaps a mile," answered the alien.

"Get here in the next half hour and blow the damned thing to smithereens. Then make it back to Sylene any way you can."

He tossed the communicator onto the rubble, then turned to Pallas Athene. "I left a vehicle about a mile up the road, behind some shrubs. Do you think you can find it?"

"If it's still there."

"Go get it and bring it back here."

She turned and started walking away without a word.

Nighthawk rummaged through his pockets and pouches with his remaining hand until he found what he was looking for: his metal ID card and passport cube. He placed them on the ground, reached for his laser pistol, suddenly realized that he didn't have it anymore, and walked over to Blue Eyes' corpse, where he appropriated the dragon's laser.

He returned to the card and the cube, put the weapon on a low-intensity setting, and fired it at them. The card turned black, and its edges curled from the heat, but when he took his finger off the trigger he could still make out part of his name and number. The cube melted, but he aimed the beam away from it before it was totally destroyed.

He waited a few minutes for the card and cube to cool, then picked them up and put them in a pocket. Finally he walked over to Cassandra, knelt down next to her, and gently stroked her hair.

She opened her eyes. "You're alive," she said.

"I'm a hard man to kill."

"When we couldn't find you, I thought you were buried under half the house," she said. "Then . . ." She frowned. "Then I can't remember anything."

"You passed out."

She was silent for a moment, and then looked up at him. "We did it, didn't we?"

"Yes, we did."

"I *knew* we could. And now it's finally over."

"Not quite. But soon."

Pallas Athene pulled up in the darkened vehicle. "There's no one on the roads yet," she said as she got out. "But that can't last long. We'd better get to the spaceport immediately."

"My ship won't be there," said Nighthawk. "Kinoshita's probably taken off by now. Where's yours?"

"A couple of miles south of here."

"Take Cassandra there and go back to Sylene." Suddenly he began looking around on the ground.

"You looking for this?" asked Pallas Athene, holding up the bag of money.

"Yeah. Take it with you."

"What about you?"

"I'll wait for Friday."

"Why not come with us?" she persisted. "My ship can handle a dozen men."

"I've got one last thing to do before I leave the planet."

"What?"

"I've got to kill the Widowmaker."

She frowned. "What the hell are you talking about?"

"After Friday blows the place," said Nighthawk, reaching into a pocket and removing the card and cube, "I'm going to bury these in the rubble." He forced a grim smile to his face. "And *that* ends the war."

Epilogue

In an orbiting hospital far out on the Rim, more than half a galaxy from the Inner Frontier, Nighthawk slowly opened his eyes and peered out through the bandages.

"How are you feeling?" asked Cassandra.

"Like a new man."

"Good," she said with a smile. "Because there's not very much of the old one left. New hand, new shoulder joint, and now a new face."

"The old one was a little too well known," replied Nighthawk.

"I can't wait for the bandages to come off, so I can start getting used to this one." She paused. "By the way, your surgeon took me aside and told me he thought he could detect the first signs of eplasia."

"I wouldn't be at all surprised if he was right," replied Nighthawk, wishing the bandages would allow him to smile.

"He says that they're within months of a cure."

"Good. Then the money will be enough to keep *him* alive."

"And to cure you."

"Medical science has managed to cure everything else," he said, flexing his artificial hand. "Why not eplasia?"

She sat down on the edge of the hospital bed. "Do you ever wish you could meet him?"

He considered the question for a long moment, then shook his head. "No. The younger one, the one who died on Solio II, *him* I'd have liked to have met, because I might have been able to help him. But the original? No, once they cure him, he won't need anyone's help."

"He'll be sixty-two years old in a world he won't be able to recognize," noted Cassandra. "Don't you think he'll need help adjusting?"

"He's the Widowmaker," said Nighthawk, as if that answered everything.

Which, in a way, it did.

THE WIDOWMAKER
UNLEASHED

To Carol,
as always

And to Ed Elbert:
friend,
producer,
keeper of promises

Chapter 1

The emaciated figure, its flesh hideously disfigured by the ravages of a virulent skin disease, lay perfectly still. Patches of shining white cheekbone protruded through the flesh of the face, knuckles pierced the skin of the hands, and even where the skin remained intact it looked like there was some malignancy crawling across it and discoloring it.

Suddenly a finger twitched. An eyelid flickered. The breathing, though weak, became more regular, and finally Jefferson Nighthawk opened his eyes.

"I'm starving!" he croaked.

"Of course you are," said the man in the white outfit. "You haven't eaten in more than a century."

"Am I cured, or did I just run out of money again?"

The man in white smiled. "You're not cured yet," he said. "I just brought you out of the deep freeze. But we finally *can* cure you, and we will in the coming weeks."

Nighthawk closed his eyes and sighed deeply. "Thank God!"

The man looked amused. "I thought the Widowmaker didn't believe in God."

"I believe in anyone or anything that keeps me alive," rasped Nighthawk.

The man in white leaned over him. "Do you remember my name?" he asked.

"Gilbert something."

"Gilbert Egan. I'm your physician. Or, to be more accurate, I've been your most recent attending physician while you were cryogenically frozen. In the coming days, you'll be in the hands of specialists."

"Help me up," said Nighthawk, reaching a hand weakly in Egan's direction.

"That wouldn't be a good idea, Mr. Nighthawk," said Egan. "Your body is riddled with eplasia, and you haven't used your muscles in . . . let me see . . . a hundred and twelve years."

"So it's 5106?"

"5106 Galactic Era," Egan confirmed.

"And my clone's been out there for five years?"

"Actually, your first clone died a few months after they created him."

"My *first* clone?"

Egan nodded. "They created a second clone two years later."

"I don't remember."

"I wouldn't allow them to wake you for that one. You were too weak. I felt we could only revive you one more time. This is it."

"This second clone—did he die, too?"

"Nobody knows. I have a feeling he's still alive somewhere out on the Rim, probably with a new name and a new face." Egan paused. "But he accomplished his purpose. He sent back enough money to keep you alive until the cure for your disease was discovered."

"I'll thank him when I see him."

Egan smiled and shook his head. "People have been looking for him for three years. You'll never find him."

"If I need to find him, I will," replied Nighthawk with certainty. Suddenly his body went limp. "What's the matter?" he asked, puzzled. "I've been awake for maybe two minutes and I'm exhausted."

"As I said, except for one five-minute interlude a few years ago, you've been in deep freeze for more than a century. All of your muscles have atrophied. Once we get you healthy again, you've got a lot of work to do with the physical therapist."

"Why am I so damned hungry?"

"All we did was slow your metabolism down to a crawl. We didn't stop it, or you'd have died. And no matter how slow it was, eventually you digested everything in your stomach. From time to time—actually, about every sixth year—we've fed you intravenously to keep you alive . . . but there's a difference between being alive and not being hungry."

"So can I get something to eat?"

"Not for a few days. We have to be sure your digestive system is functioning properly. A meal right now could kill you. As soon as you're moved to the hospital, we'll inject some proteins and carbohydrates directly into your bloodstream, enough to keep you going for a couple of days."

"Then what?"

"The doctors perform their magic and eradicate all traces of eplasia from your system—and then, since you still look like something from a child's worst nightmare, you'll undergo a month or more of reconstructive cosmetic surgery."

"How soon before I'm out of here and on my own?"

Egan shrugged. "That's up to you—two months, four months, a year, whatever it takes."

Nighthawk was silent for a moment. Then he spoke again: "There was another man last time you woke me."

"Yes," answered Egan. "Marcus Dinnisen. Your attorney."

"Where is he now?"

"Who knows?"

"*I* want to know. His firm is in charge of my money."

"Not anymore. Your second clone sent five million credits back with Ito Kinoshita and instructed him to pay it directly to us as we required it, rather than to allow the money to pass through Mr. Dinnisen's law firm."

"Were they robbing me?"

"I don't think so. It's just that your clone was not the most trusting soul I've ever encountered." Suddenly Egan smiled. "We were able to imprint your personality and memories on him."

"Who is this Kinoshita?" asked Nighthawk. "I never heard of him."

"He trained your first clone. The second one didn't really require any training, but Kinoshita accompanied him on his mission."

"Is he still around?"

"I believe so."

"And he's still got my money?"

"No. He deposited it in his own bank with instructions that they were to continue making payments to us, and were to release whatever remained only to you after you were cured."

"He sounds like a good man," said Nighthawk. "Pass the word that I want to see him after all this surgery is done."

"I'll contact him now. Your recovery will be a long, painful process. You could use a friend in the weeks to come."

"Just do what I said," replied Nighthawk, fighting back a surge of nausea and dizziness.

Egan nodded. "And now, if we have nothing further to discuss, I think it's time I transferred you to the hospital."

"Good," said Nighthawk. "The sooner we get this over with, the sooner I can do the two things I most want to do."

"What are they?" asked Egan curiously.

"Eat without getting sick, and look in a mirror without flinching."

Chapter 2

The small man entered the hospital room and walked to the foot of Nighthawk's bed. There were half a dozen tubes running into the old man's body, some dripping medication, some supplying nourishment, one delivering the recently synthesized enzyme that would finally trigger the cure to his eplasia.

"Who the hell are you?" demanded Nighthawk.

"My name is Ito Kinoshita."

Nighthawk instinctively extended a hand, saw the bones of his knuckles protruding through the rotted skin, and pulled it back, hiding it beneath the light blanket that covered him. "I'm told I owe you a debt of gratitude."

Kinoshita shook his head. "It was a pleasure to work with you." He paused. "Well, a version of you."

"You worked with both clones?"

"Not really. All I did with the first one was train him as best I could, and then they sent him out alone." Kinoshita frowned. "I warned them that he wasn't ready, but they wouldn't listen."

"Killed the first day out?" suggested Nighthawk.

"No, he was *you* at age twenty-three. He had your abilities, your instincts. Nobody could kill him."

"Then, what happened?"

"Innocence. Ignorance. Hormones." Kinoshita shrugged. "You name it."

"I don't understand," said Nighthawk.

"Physically he was twenty-three. But in actuality he was two months old. He had your skills, but not your experience. He didn't know whom to trust and whom not to, he couldn't spot a woman who was using him or a man who was conning him, and it cost him his life. He lasted a lot longer than I thought he would—long enough to fulfill his mission—but he was doomed from the day they created him."

"If he did what he was supposed to do, why was there a second clone?"

"Inflation," answered Kinoshita. "The money the first clone was paid bought you two extra years, but it took longer to come up with the cure for your disease, and the planet's inflation rate is running at twenty-two percent. There was nothing in the initial agreement that allowed your attorneys to dip into capital, and the medics wouldn't give them permission to awaken you. When the interest could no longer pay the bills, that would be the end of it—so they had to accept another commission on your behalf or you'd have been turned out."

"Tell me about the second clone," said Nighthawk. "You traveled with him?"

"By the time they created him, they'd found a way to give him all your memories." Kinoshita looked into the past and smiled. "There was never anything like him—except you, of course," he added hastily. "I remember once he was surrounded by a couple of hundred angry men on a planet called Cellestra. All I could think of was that those men were in a lot more trouble than they realized."

"Where is he now?"

"I've no idea. If he survived, he was going to go out to the Rim."

"*If* he survived?"

"We found a lot of evidence pointing to his death," said Kinoshita. "But he was so . . . so *indestructible* that I think he must have planted it to hide his tracks."

"And he gave you some money before that?"

"More than 'some,' " answered Kinoshita. "It's been keeping you alive for almost three years. Once you're out of the hospital, what remains of the principal is entirely yours."

"What do I owe you for your services?"

"I don't want anything. It was an honor to serve the Widowmaker." He looked meaningfully at Nighthawk. "It will be again, if you'll let me."

"The Widowmaker's history," said Nighthawk. "I'm a sixty-two-year-old man who's been on ice for more than a century. I don't know what this era is like."

"Neither did your clone, sir—but *he* adjusted."

"*He* had a mission," came the answer. "Me, I just want to enjoy being alive and healthy."

"What do you plan to do?"

Nighthawk shrugged. "Probably find some quiet backwater world and buy a few acres. Get myself a wife. Maybe grow some flowers. Catch up on my reading."

"A man like you?" said Kinoshita. "I don't believe it."

"What you believe is of no concern to me. I've been dying for a century and a quarter, and suddenly I've been given life and some semblance of health. I plan to spend the remainder of my years reveling in that gift."

"Well, I'm sure you mean it now . . ."

"You don't even know me," said Nighthawk. "What do you think gives you an insight into my plans?"

"I know you better than you think," responded Kinoshita. "I spent months with your second clone. Physically he was in his late thirties, but he had all the memories you have now—or, rather, that you had prior to waking up this last time. His foibles, his personality, his mind—they were all yours. He wasn't just *like* you. He *was* you." Kinoshita paused again. "And he had a partnership with Death the way most priests think they have with God. You may think you want flowers, but they're not for the Widowmaker."

"I told you . . ."

"I know what you told me. But you're the best there is, maybe the best there ever was. You were never an outlaw. You were a lawman and a bounty hunter. The men you killed deserved to die, and you never broke the law. I don't think you can turn your back on your God-given talent. It might even be sinful to contemplate it."

"Mr. Kinoshita . . ." began Nighthawk.

"Ito."

"Ito, then," he continued. "I can barely hold a fork in my hand, let alone a Burner or a Screecher. The bathroom's maybe twelve feet from my bed; I can't walk to it without help. I've been talking to you for about ten minutes; it's probably the longest I've been able to stay awake since they unfroze me. Whatever talent I once had is gone, and a sixty-two-year-old cripple with atrophied muscles isn't likely to get it back."

"You'll get it back," said Kinoshita with total confidence. "After all, you're the Widowmaker."

"I've made enough widows for one lifetime," said Nighthawk, leaning his head back on his pillow and closing his eyes. "I don't want to hear that word again."

"Whatever you say," replied Kinoshita. He watched the old man's chest rising and filling rhythmically, then added softly: "But you can't stop being what you are."

Chapter 3

Nighthawk wiped the sweat from his face without breaking stride.

"Faster," he said.

The doctor looked up from the treadmill controls. "I think you've done enough for one day, Mr. Nighthawk."

"You heard me."

"But—"

"Faster," he repeated.

The doctor shrugged and increased the speed. "The galaxy can wait an extra few weeks for the Widowmaker to make his reappearance," she said. "You're pushing yourself too hard."

"If I can keep pace, then I'm not pushing too hard. And if I can't, I'll fall off the damned thing soon enough and then you can say that you told me so."

"But what's the rush?"

"If you'd been lying flat on your back for a century, wouldn't *you* be in a hurry?" shot back Nighthawk.

"It's not as if you're in some kind of a race," she noted.

"All my life I had certain physical skills," said Nighthawk, forcing his legs to keep up with the treadmill. "During the past few years—make that the last few years before I submitted myself to the freezing process—I watched them desert me, one by one. I want them back."

"You're sixty-two years old. Surely you don't plan on being a bounty hunter again."

"I don't plan on ever firing another weapon again if I can help it."

"Then I don't see—"

"I want to know that I can if I have to."

"Then you should be practicing at a target range, not a treadmill."

"I also used to walk for miles. Maybe I'll never walk farther than from here to the front door of this place, but I'm not willing to give up that skill just because it's not vital to my existence. Why bother to read? You can live just as long without it. Why listen to music? It never increased anyone's life span." He paused, as more sweat poured down his face. "I want to be Jefferson Nighthawk again, not just some undernourished ghost who's pretending to be him. Does that make any sense to you?"

"Of course it does," she responded. "But I still don't see why you can't become the Jefferson Nighthawk you used to be in easy, reasonable stages, rather than risk hurting yourself. You're not fit."

"Because I admire excellence," said Nighthawk.

"What does *that* have to do with anything?" she asked, confused.

"When I was the Widowmaker, I wasn't just a competent bounty hunter. I wasn't just good with my weapons. I was the best! I worked at what I did and what I was until I couldn't get any better. That's the way I'm made, and I won't settle for being anything less than the best sixty-two-year-old Jefferson Nighthawk I can be."

"That's what I'm trying to help you be."

He shook his head, starting to pant from the exertion. "No. You're trying to help me be a reasonably fit and healthy old man. I'm trying to be Jefferson Nighthawk"—he gasped for breath—"and Jefferson Nighthawk doesn't *settle.*"

"He may not settle, but he gets red in the face, and his blood pressure gets too high, and he gets tired," said the doctor. "Let me turn off the treadmill."

"Don't touch it," said Nighthawk in a voice that had convinced more than one outlaw that surrender was the better part of valor.

"All right," she said, walking to the door. "If I don't hear you fall off, I'll be back in five minutes."

"Ten," he grated as she left.

"I thought you were going to raise flowers," remarked Kinoshita as he entered Nighthawk's room.

"I am."

"So why are you lifting weights?"

Nighthawk allowed himself the luxury of a smile. "You can never tell how deep the roots might be."

Kinoshita stared at the weights. "What are you up to now?"

"Forty pounds in each hand."

"Not bad."

"Not good."

"You've only been awake a month," said Kinoshita. "They spent three weeks curing your eplasia, and you've already undergone the first of your cosmetic surgeries. Given what you've undergone just since they brought you back, I'm surprised you can lift *five* pounds in each hand, let alone forty."

"The last surgery is scheduled for five weeks from today," said Nighthawk. "I plan to be in good enough shape to leave this place the day they finish."

"Are you talking about killing shape or walking-out shape?"

"They're one and the same."

Kinoshita sat down and grinned.

"What's so funny?" demanded Nighthawk.

"You know why I'm here?" responded Kinoshita.

"I haven't the slightest idea."

"The doctors are afraid you're going to work yourself to the point of physical collapse, and that your system has had so many shocks it might not be able to stand another."

"And you find that amusing, do you?" asked Nighthawk, continuing to raise and lower the weights. "Did my clones ever comment on your sense of humor?"

"What's amusing is that they asked me to speak to you. You have no family or close friends, and no one *really* knows you—but at least I knew your clones." He chuckled. "As if anyone who knew them would even *try* to talk you out of something you wanted to do."

"So you're not going to try?"

"Hey, I'm a fan," Kinoshita assured him. "Whatever you want to do is okay with me."

"Then why did you agree to come?"

"I figured if I didn't, they'd just get someone else who doesn't know that you don't argue with the Widowmaker." He grinned. "The hospital's got enough patients. They don't need another one."

"You're brighter than you look," said Nighthawk.

"Thanks."

"That wasn't necessarily a compliment."

Kinoshita stared approvingly at Nighthawk, who stood before a mirror, inspecting his face. The cheekbones still protruded where the flesh had been removed and not yet replaced, but the rest appeared to be reasonably healthy.

"Not bad," said Kinoshita. "A little older, a few more lines, but unquestionably Jefferson Nighthawk."

"A lot of it's second-generation Nighthawk. They took some skin scrapings, put them in a nutrient solution, did God knows what miracles to them, and then gave me new eyelids and a new nose. And my left ear's artificial, too."

"You can hardly call them artificial if they've got your DNA."

"They aren't the ones I was born with," said Nighthawk. "What would you call them?"

"Improvements," answered Kinoshita promptly.

"Not really," said Nighthawk. "A while back, there was a killer on the Inner Frontier called the One-Armed Bandit. Had a prosthetic arm that doubled as a laser rifle. Now, *he* had an improvement. All I've got are second-generation facial features. My eyes can't see into the infrared spectrum, my ears can't hear ultrasonic radio waves, my nose can't pick up the nurses' perfume. The only difference is that this week most of the staff doesn't wince when they look at my face."

"Don't belittle it," said Kinoshita. "That's a hell of a difference."

"Yeah, I suppose so."

"Besides, if you want 'improvements,' you can always get them. You're a rich man."

Nighthawk sighed. "I don't think my body can handle too many more operations. I'm not twenty-five anymore, or even fifty."

"And when you get right down to it, very few gardeners need a laser rifle instead of a green thumb."

"Point taken."

"So where do we plan to settle down and do our gardening?"

"We?"

Kinoshita nodded. "I used to think I was pretty good at my job until they hired me to train you—or, rather, your clones. I knew in less than a minute that I'd never seen anything like you, that I could work the rest of my life and never measure up. For a while it did pretty serious things to my ego, but then I saw what kind of work ethic was required to reach that level of accomplishment." He paused and sighed deeply. "I'm not made that way. I can admire what you do without aspiring to it—or without being willing to make the sacrifices you make to achieve it. So I'm willing to carry your bags, or hoe your garden, or answer your door, or do anything else to stay close enough to you to remind me why I'm *not* a lawman or a bounty hunter anymore. I figure I'll live a lot longer this way."

"I don't remember saying that I *wanted* company."

"You don't know it, but you *owe* me," said Kinoshita. "I sacrificed a lot for you—a whole career."

"I thought you wanted to live to a ripe old age. That's not in the cards for most lawmen."

"I could have made a substantial living as a trainer of lawmen, but your goddamned lawyers blacklisted me after I refused to turn your money over to them—which is probably the only reason you're alive today."

Nighthawk stared at him for a long moment. "All right," he said at last. "You're hired."

"As what?"

"Whatever I need: bodyguard, manservant, cook."

Kinoshita suddenly looked uncomfortable. "So what do I do now?" he said awkwardly.

Nighthawk considered for a moment. "Right now I need a barber. Give me a shave."

"A shave?" repeated Kinoshita, surprised.

"Right. If my face isn't attached properly, I want to know about it *before* I leave for the Frontier."

"You all packed?" asked Kinoshita, entering the hospital room for the last time.

"I don't have any possessions," replied Nighthawk. "I gave them all away a century ago."

Kinoshita laid a light blue outfit down on the bed. "I brought this for you."

Nighthawk made no attempt to hide his distaste. "Ugly," he muttered disapprovingly.

"It's the style—and besides, you'd look silly walking down the street in a hospital gown."

Nighthawk took off his gown and began getting dressed.

"Very impressive," said Kinoshita, looking at his lean, hard body. "You look like a heavyweight freehand fighter who's starved himself down to middleweight for a money fight. The muscles are there, but everything else is gone."

"I'll put the rest of my weight back on," Nighthawk assured him. "They didn't give me enough calories to compensate for all the exercising I did."

"Why didn't you ask for more?"

"I did. Once."

"And?"

"They didn't bring it."

"Why didn't you complain?"

"I don't beg," said Nighthawk, fastening his tunic. He straightened up. "How do I look?"

"Like an older version of the two clones," said Kinoshita. Suddenly he grinned. "I can't imagine why."

"Your sense of humor leaves a lot to be desired."

"By the way, I didn't bring you any weapons," said Kinoshita. "They're illegal on Deluros."

"What do I want a weapon for?"

"You're the Widowmaker."

"That was a long time ago."

"You are what you are."

"I think I prefer your humor to your philosophy." Nighthawk walked to the door and stepped out into the corridor. "Okay, let's go see what the galaxy looks like after all this time."

Chapter 4

It was a little house, small and neat, with white-painted walls, a green roof, a brick chimney, and an old-fashioned veranda with a swing and a rocking chair on it. Nighthawk knew the moment his vehicle pulled up in front of the house that he was going to buy it.

"But it's all trees and ravines," protested Kinoshita. "These are not the most productive two hundred acres I've ever seen. Even if you clear them, you can't farm them."

"Then we won't have to work very hard growing things, will we?" responded Nighthawk. He walked around to the side of the house. "We'll put a little pond right here, I think, and stick a few fish in it."

"We passed a river a mile back. It looked like there'd be good fishing there."

"Those fish are for eating. These will be for looking at." Nighthawk continued walking, then came to a stop near the corner of the house. "The garden'll be right here," he said, outlining a space with his hand.

"That's maybe ten feet by twenty," noted Kinoshita glumly. "Maybe less."

"It's big enough for me." He paused. "How deep did they say the well was?"

"Sixty feet."

"Okay," said Nighthawk. "Buy it."

"Don't you want to see the inside?" asked Kinoshita, surprised.

"One house is pretty much like another. If something needs fixing or changing, we'll fix or change it. Besides, I plan to spend most of my time sitting out here on the veranda."

"But—"

"Do it," said Nighthawk so softly that Kinoshita barely heard him and so firmly that all thoughts of protest vanished from the smaller man's mind. Nighthawk walked back to the vehicle. "Drop me at the bar back in town. I'll wait for you there while you take care of the details."

"Do you want a mortgage?"

Nighthawk shook his head. "Buy it outright. I don't like being beholden to anyone."

Kinoshita began driving the vehicle back down the winding, unpaved road. "I wish I knew what you find so charming about dirt roads and ancient houses. Hell, this planet doesn't even have fusion power yet! I thought we were buying a gentleman's farm on Pollux IV or some other major world, not a shack on some little dirtball nobody's ever heard of."

"I've seen my share of worlds. This one'll do."

"Tell me that when we run out of water, or the roof collapses from the snow."

"No one says you have to stay here," replied Nighthawk. "Take a third of the money and leave."

"And go where?" demanded Kinoshita.

"Someplace you like better."

"Not a chance," said Kinoshita adamantly. "I'm staying with you."

"Then shut up and drive. I'm an old man, and I haven't got the energy to argue."

They drove the next six miles in silence and finally reached the small town that had sprung up around Churchill II's primitive landing field. Then Kinoshita pulled to a stop in front of a nondescript tavern.

"It shouldn't take more than about ten minutes to transfer the funds, and maybe another five to transfer the title. I'll be back in fifteen or twenty minutes unless there's a hitch."

"I'll be here," said Nighthawk, getting out of the vehicle and walking into the tavern.

Force of habit made him pick out a table in the darkest corner of the room, and to sit with his back to the wall, so that he could see the doorway and the windows.

The table glowed and came to life. A holograph listing all the drinks available hovered in front of him, and a mechanical voice asked him to make a selection.

"Beer."

"We have two hundred and eighty-four brands from seventy-three worlds. You must be more specific."

"Have you got any local brews?"

"There are no breweries on Churchill II."

"Then select one for me."

"I am not programmed to perform that function."

"You can't randomize?"

"No I cannot, sir. If I were to select a brand you do not like, there is a fifty-seven-percent probability that you would refuse to pay for it. Our profit margin is forty-two percent. If I randomize for you, I must randomize for everyone—and if I select beer for everybody, the mathematical likelihood is that we will lose money on more than half our transactions."

"All right," said Nighthawk. "Give me whatever you've sold the most of today."

An instant later the top of the table irised right in front of him, and a tall glass of beer appeared just before the surface became solid again.

"That will be four credits, or one Maria Theresa dollar, or five Far London shillings, or . . ."

Nighthawk pressed his hand down on the table. "Read my thumbprint and bill my account on Deluros VIII."

"Reading . . . done." The mechanical voice was silent for a moment. Then: "Potential error."

"What's the problem?"

"You are Jefferson Nighthawk?"

"That's right."

"According to the Master Credit Computer on Deluros VIII, you are one hundred and seventy-four years old. My data banks tell me that no human, even of mutated stock, has ever lived past one hundred and forty-seven years."

"Well, now you'll have something to add to your data banks, won't you?"

"Have I your permission to read your retinagram?"

"Seems like a lot of trouble for four credits."

"Have I your permission to read your retinagram?" repeated the machine emotionlessly.

"Yeah, go ahead."

"Ready . . . checking . . . cross-checking . . . confirming. You *are* Jefferson Nighthawk."

"Fancy that," said Nighthawk, finally picking up his beer and taking a long swallow.

He sat in silence, observing his surroundings with an expert eye. Three middle-aged men sat at a table near the door, eating sandwiches they had brought with them and drinking beer. A young man whose clothes were too bright and whose weapon was too new and shiny stood at the bar, drinking some blue concoction. As he did so, the ice cubes, which were obviously not made of water, chimed musically. A woman sat as far from the men as possible, staring severely at the small glass in front of her.

Nighthawk nursed his beer, relishing the feel of the place, of not being on Deluros with its mile-high buildings and its thirty-three billion inhabitants. A small insect began crawling across the table. He considered killing it, then changed his mind, leaned back, and waited a few seconds for the table to sense, pinpoint, and atomize it.

The young man glanced over, momentarily attracted by the power surge in the table, and their eyes met. Nighthawk stared at him, calm and unblinking, and soon the young man frowned and turned away uncomfortably, as if he was not used to having people meet his gaze.

"Let's have something to watch!" snapped the young man.

"I possess a library of one thousand six hundred fifty-two sporting events, three thousand five hundred sixty-six dramatic entertainments, four hundred two documentaries . . ."

"There must have been a championship fight somewhere in the Oligarchy last week. Let's have it."

Instantly a life-sized holograph of two almost-naked men, their hands and feet heavily taped, appeared above the bar. They began circling each other, feinting and punching, throwing an occasional kick.

The fight was a dull one, with each party showing too much respect for the other's ability, and Nighthawk was glad when it ended some ten minutes later and the images vanished.

"Another," said the young man.

Nighthawk, who had no desire to watch another match, was about to get up and leave the tavern when Kinoshita walked through the doorway, looked around until he spotted him, and then walked over to his table.

"Any problems?" asked Nighthawk.

"None," answered Kinoshita. "Everything went smoothly. You now own an exceptional ugly house on two hundred useless acres. I hope you're thrilled."

"Satisfied, anyway."

"Since we're in a tavern, I suppose we might as well celebrate with a drink."

"Be my guest."

"What kind of beer did you have?"

Nighthawk shrugged. "Beats me."

"Any good?"

"It's decent enough."

"Two more beers," ordered Kinoshita.

"Cancel that," said Nighthawk as the table glowed with artificial life again.

"Canceled," said a mechanical voice.

"Make that one beer, same kind, and give me whatever that young man at the bar had. The blue drink that seemed to play a melody."

The young man suddenly looked up. "Cancel that," he said, swaggering over to the table.

"Have you got a problem, son?" asked Kinoshita.

"Who told you that you could order my drink, old man?" said the young man, never taking his eyes from Nighthawk.

"Do you know who you're talking to?" demanded Kinoshita.

"An old man who ordered something that's not his," came the answer. "Do *you* know who *you're* talking to? I'm Johnny Trouble." He continued staring at Nighthawk. "Ever hear of me?"

"I've heard of four or five Johnny Troubles."

"Yeah?" said Johnny Trouble, surprised.

Nighthawk nodded. "And a couple of Billy Troubles, too. They were all much deeper into the Frontier."

"How come I never heard of 'em?"

"It was before your time," said Nighthawk. He paused, then added: "And they all died young."

"Well, I'm Johnny Trouble now, and there's only one of me."

"Whatever you say."

"Take my word for it, one's enough," said Johnny Trouble. "Maybe you heard that the Widowmaker showed up a couple of years ago. I made him back down." Nighthawk found that thought amusing, and the young man glared at him suspiciously. "What are you smiling about?"

"I'm just happy that a man of your caliber is protecting my new world," replied Nighthawk easily. "Now can I order my drink?"

"I'm the guy who created it. It's mine. No one orders it without my permission."

"Whatever makes you happy," said Nighthawk. "May I have your permission?"

"What's it worth to you?"

Nighthawk sighed deeply. "Not as much as you think," he replied, getting slowly to his feet and holding his hands out from his body in plain view. "We don't want any trouble. We'll take our business elsewhere."

Kinoshita sat there, stunned.

"Come on, Ito," said Nighthawk. "We've upset this gentleman enough already."

Kinoshita stood up and followed Nighthawk to the door, while the young man, smiling smugly, stood in the center of the floor, hands on hips, watching them go.

"Are you all right?" asked Kinoshita when they were both outside and the door had shut behind them.

"Yeah, I'm fine."

"I wonder. The Nighthawks I knew would have taken that kid's gun away and pistol-whipped him with it."

"The Nighthawks you knew were twenty-three and thirty-eight years old. I've been dead for more than a century. It doesn't take that much of an effort to step aside when someone like that kid in there is feeling his testosterone."

"What if he'd pulled his gun?"

"He'd have killed me. I'm unarmed—and even if I was packed, I haven't held a weapon in my hands in a hundred and twelve years. It wouldn't have been much of a contest."

"So you're just going to withdraw from the world, and back down whenever someone challenges you?"

"I'm sixty-two years old. It's the best way I know to make it to seventy-two."

"I can't believe I'm speaking to the Widowmaker."

"You're not," said Nighthawk firmly. "Not anymore."

They reached the vehicle. "Where to now?" asked Kinoshita.

"Let's go home," said Nighthawk. Suddenly he smiled. "Let's go home," he said again.

"What's so funny?"

"I just realized that I've never had one before." He looked down the road. "It's about time. Let's go home." Then he nodded. "Yeah, I like the sound of it."

Chapter 5

Knowing what a perfectionist the second clone had been, Kinoshita expected Nighthawk to spend weeks, perhaps months, of intensive effort on the house until it exactly suited his tastes, but instead the older man bought some nondescript furniture and paid no further attention to the interior, except to spend one afternoon building a set of bookcases.

"No one reads books anymore," protested Kinoshita as he watched Nighthawk carefully creating the shelves.

"*I* do."

"That's silly. You can call up any book ever written on your computer."

"I don't have a computer."

"Then we'll buy one the next time we go into town."

"I don't *like* computers. I like the heft and feel and smell of a book."

"Do you know how much they cost?" demanded Kinoshita.

"I've got thousands of them stashed all over the Frontier," answered Nighthawk. "Damned near every place I've ever lived. I'll send for them one of these days."

"I think we'd better get you a computer anyway."

"Can it chop wood, or plant flowers, or light a fire?"

"Of course not."

"Then I don't want it and I don't need it," said Nighthawk decisively.

"Don't you want to know what's going on in the galaxy?" asked Kinoshita.

"Absolutely not. I'm retired, remember?"

"Are you retired from bounty hunting or from life?"

"A little of each, I think."

"You're getting into a rut."

"It's a rut I like."

And it *was* a pleasant enough rut. Every morning Nighthawk rose, forced himself to have breakfast—a meal he detested—and then spent the better part of an hour chopping wood. The house had both solar and nuclear heating systems, but Nighthawk enjoyed sitting by a fire, and he refused to sit in front of an artificial one.

At least, that was the reason he gave, and it was probably a valid one— but Kinoshita also noticed that he was adding muscle to his spare frame almost daily.

He also fetched a few gallons of water from the river each day, and Kinoshita *knew* that was to regain strength in his legs, since the house had three different water sources.

In the afternoons he went out hunting. The first five days he came back empty-handed, but after that he never failed to bring back something for the pot. There were some large herbivores in the nearby woods, five-hun-dred-pounders, but Nighthawk invariably brought home the amazingly quick, shifty little five-pound rabbitlike creatures that lived near the river. They made decent enough eating, but what it meant to Kinoshita was that the Widowmaker's aim and reflexes were back.

"Not bad," said Kinoshita, looking up from his most recent dinner. They took turns cooking, and this meal had been prepared by Nighthawk.

"I like the sauce," replied Nighthawk. "An Emran showed me how to make it, back on Silverdew."

"Still," continued Kinoshita, "don't you get a little tired of eating the same thing every day?"

"I ate the same thing every day for decades."

"What are you talking about?"

"Soya products," answered Nighthawk. "Oh, they all taste different, but they're essentially the same thing." He paused. "You set foot on a couple of hundred different worlds with different gravities and atmospheres, your body has enough adjusting to do. There's no sense overloading it with alien food, too."

"You were a careful man."

"Careless young men don't live to be careless old men, not in my profession."

"Do you miss it?"

"Soya food?"

"No. Your profession."

Nighthawk shook his head. "Not at all."

"It doesn't make sense," said Kinoshita. "You were the best there ever was."

"Oh, I doubt it."

"Who was better?"

Nighthawk lowered his head in thought for a moment, then looked up. "They say there was nobody as good as Peacemaker MacDougal and the Angel. And whoever killed Conrad Bland back on Walpurgis III had to be pretty good, too, considering the odds."

"That was thousands of years ago!" protested Kinoshita.

"I wasn't aware there was a time limit on being the best," responded Nighthawk with a wry smile. "You know, there was a carnival performer—I don't know if he really existed—who was supposed to be the best shot who ever lived. Can't recall his name—Singer, Jumper, something like that."

"Billybuck Dancer?"

"Yeah, that was it."

"I saw a statue of him back on Kargennian II," said Kinoshita. "It's covered with birdshit and graffiti, and part of it's crumbled away, but I could still make out the name at the base. Still, you can't help wondering how good he'd have been against something that could shoot back."

"Who knows?" answered Nighthawk. "Legend has it that he got killed in a gunfight." He paused. "Of course, sooner or later we all do."

"Not you," said Kinoshita adamantly.

"Even me."

"Not a chance. I've been watching you get yourself into shape," said Kinoshita. "You're almost ready."

Nighthawk shook his head. "You know the difference between a kid like Johnny Trouble and me? He's too young to know he can be killed. He never thinks about it. When he's in a fight, images of what could happen don't flash through his mind and make him pause. That's why all the killers out here are young. Once you realize that you can lose your life, you also start realizing just how precious it is. That makes you think, and thinking makes you hesitate, and you know what happens to he who hesitates."

"I spent months with your second clone," said Kinoshita, unimpressed. "He was physically thirty-eight, but he had your memories. Mentally and emotionally he was sixty-two. So why didn't he hesitate?"

"You'd have to ask him."

"I'm asking you. It's the same thing."

"Not quite. He was in perfect health, and he knew that they'd develop the cure for eplasia before he was riddled with it."

"Apples and oranges," protested Kinoshita. "He was sixty-two mentally, and he didn't hesitate."

"He had special knowledge."

"What special knowledge?"

"He knew that when he was in his fifties, he was still taking out twenty-two-year-old kids. Very few thirty-eight-year-olds have the absolute knowledge that they won't lose a nanosecond off their reflexes for another decade or more." Nighthawk sighed. "But I'm sixty-two, and I've been frozen for a century, and half my skin is artificial, and I know I'll never again be what I was."

"Okay, I concede," said Kinoshita. "But you still haven't really answered me: Do you miss the excitement?"

"Nothing very exciting about hunting down scum. You were a lawman. Did you find it exciting?"

"No, but . . ."

"But what?"

"But I wasn't the Widowmaker."

"Well, I'm not, either. I'm just Jefferson Nighthawk."

"I don't understand you at all. When you're the best at something . . ."

"You know what I was the best at?" said Nighthawk irritably. "I was the best at scaring women and children. I'd walk down the street, and they'd see my skin flaking off in front of their eyes, my bones jutting through it, and I'd give them nightmares for months to come." He paused. "After a while I started wearing gloves and a mask, so no one would have to see the effects of my disease. But word had gotten out. Young men didn't have to prove how tough they were by going up against me; now they proved it by trying to steal my mask so they could look at my face without getting sick—and not a hell of a lot of them were able to." Nighthawk's face twisted into a grimace as he paused for breath. "*That's* the Widowmaker's legacy— along with hundreds of terrified women and children, I could make strong men sick to their stomachs just by walking into a room."

"I'm sorry," said Kinoshita. "I hadn't realized . . ."

"It's all right," replied Nighthawk. "It's over now. And so is the Widowmaker."

"What made you finally choose to freeze yourself?"

"A doctor out on Binder X gave me six weeks to live, eight at the outside. I'd grown accustomed to scaring everyone who saw me, but I wasn't ready to die. He suggested that since I was sitting on a few million credits I check myself into the cryonics lab on Deluros VIII and wait for a cure. He thought it was maybe forty years off; he was seventy-two years short. Must be one hell of a disease."

"It was."

"I hope my clone got cured."

"He had enough money. I'm sure he did." Kinoshita paused. "Do you really plan to find him?"

Nighthawk shook his head. "What for? If he wanted to see me, he'd have left word. He did what he was created to do. If he wants to create a new identity and be left alone, I'll honor his wishes."

Nighthawk got up, cleaned off the table, and went outside to sit on a rocking chair.

"Lots of stars out tonight," he remarked when Kinoshita finally joined him.

Kinoshita looked up. "Lots of *worlds*." He paused. "I'll bet some of them are pretty interesting."

"I've seen a lot of worlds," said Nighthawk. "This one'll do as well as any."

"Are you just going to chop wood and hunt and fish all day, every day, forever?"

"Sounds good to me."

"Sounds boring as hell to me."

"Well, I'll be reading, too."

"How exciting."

"It's about all the excitement I can handle these days," said Nighthawk with a smile.

"And that's really all you plan to do?"

"Well, I've been thinking of joining a church."

Kinoshita laughed out loud. "You? The man who's sent a couple of hundred men and aliens straight to hell?"

"Yeah, me."

"Any particular religion?"

"Nope."

"Then why join?" persisted Kinoshita.

"Best place I can think of to meet a nice middle-aged widow woman."

"You want to get married?"

"I've lived alone all my life," answered Nighthawk. "I can't see much to recommend it."

"Aren't you a little old to change?"

Nighthawk shrugged. "Mankind adapts; that's what we do better than any other species." He leaned back on his chair. "I might be a little old to be sporting a young man's passion, but that doesn't mean I don't want to spend my final years with someone I care for." He paused and turned to his companion. "Nothing personal, but you aren't what I have in mind."

"I think I can live without being lusted after by the Widowmaker," answered Kinoshita with a laugh. "But if I can ask: Why a church?"

"I've spent a lot of time in bars and drug dens and whorehouses and gambling parlors, and I haven't seen an awful lot of women my age in them."

"Did you ever consider marrying a young one?"

Nighthawk shook his head. "Never once."

"Why not?"

"It's annoying enough having to put up with your less-than-subtle hints that I should go back to being the Widowmaker. I don't need some twenty-year-old wife looking for that same vicarious excitement."

"I'm not looking for vicarious excitement," said Kinoshita defensively.

"If you say so," answered Nighthawk, closing his eyes and rocking gently in his chair.

They sat in silence for almost half an hour. Then Kinoshita gently nudged him.

"Jefferson!" he whispered. "There's a Nightkiller about two hundred yards away, just beside that big tree."

"I know," answered Nighthawk softly. "I've been watching it for about ten minutes now. Looks more canine than feline, despite the fact that it can climb trees."

"Do you want to borrow my Burner or my Screecher?" asked Kinoshita.

"He's not bothering anyone," said Nighthawk. "And I'm tired of killing."

The Nightkiller, alerted by the sound of their voices, glared at them for a moment, then slunk off into the darkness.

"I hope he remembers you gave him a pass," said Kinoshita.

"He won't bother us."

"You think not?"

"We're not native to this world. He doesn't recognize us as prey."

"You go out hunting every day," Kinoshita pointed out. "He may recognize you as a competitor."

"There's food enough for all of us."

"He's only an animal. He may not be able to reason it out."

"Then I'll worry about it when the time comes."

Kinoshita looked at the old man, who had closed his eyes again and was rocking gently in his chair.

You were the greatest. I suppose if you want to spend the rest of your life stuck on this backwater world, that's not too much to ask, given all that you've accomplished. Who am I to insist that you keep bucking the odds until they finally catch up with you? I won't call you Widowmaker again.

Chapter 6

Kinoshita was awakened the next morning by the sound of the older man chopping wood.

"Good morning," said Nighthawk as Kinoshita stepped outside, shielding his eyes from the glare of the sun.

"You didn't wake me for breakfast."

"We'll eat in town. I've got some supplies to buy."

"Supplies?"

"Spices for the kitchen, seeds for the garden. Maybe a couple of new tunics; the ones I've got are getting a bit tight in the shoulders."

"Let me shave and shower and I'll be right with you."

"Tell you what," said Nighthawk. "I can use a little exercise." He buried his ax in a tree stump. "I'll start walking. You can pick me up along the way."

"Whatever you say," answered Kinoshita, idly wondering how many men Nighthawk's age could chop wood for an hour and then walk five miles into town.

Kinoshita took a long, leisurely, hot shower, atomized the hairs on his face, had a quick cup of coffee, and then set out for town in their vehicle. He caught up with Nighthawk after four miles.

"I thought maybe you'd gone back to sleep," said the older man as he climbed onto the passenger's seat.

"You said you wanted some exercise," replied Kinoshita defensively. He looked over. "Your shirt's drenched. I didn't think you could work up that kind of sweat from walking along a tree-shaded dirt road."

"Actually, I jogged for a couple of miles."

"You did?"

"Yeah." A guilty smile. "I didn't want anyone to see me in case I couldn't make it."

"You're getting into shape, no question about it," said Kinoshita. "Forgive me for asking, but just what are you getting into shape *for*?"

"I depended on my body for half a century, and it never betrayed me, never let me down," answered Nighthawk. "I never worried about stamina, or overweight, or blood pressure, or diabetes, or anything else. Then it proved as frail as everyone else's, and now that I've got a second chance, I plan to keep it in as good a condition as I can." He looked across at Kinoshita. "That's it. No hidden agenda, no secret goal. I've been deathly ill; now I just want to stay healthy."

"No argument," came the answer. "I just wonder, since you're becoming such a fanatic on the subject, why you haven't nagged me to get in better shape?"

"You're health is your own business, not mine."

"Now *that* sounds like the Nighthawk I used to know," said Kinoshita in satisfied tones.

"No reason why it shouldn't. We're the same."

They entered the town, and came to a stop in front of a farm supply store.

"You need me to help you carry anything?" asked Kinoshita as Nighthawk climbed out. The older man merely stared at him. "Sorry. Silly question."

Nighthawk entered the store and began looking at various displays.

"Morning, Mr. Nighthawk," said the clerk.

"Good morning, Jacob."

"Anything I can help you with?"

"Maybe. There's a brilliant yellow flower that grows on Greenwillow."

"Greenwillow?" repeated Jacob. "Give me a sec." He activated his computer. "Greenwillow."

"Greenwillow," repeated the machine. "Official name: Sunderman II. Location: the Inner Frontier."

"All right, Sunderman II. Yellow flower. Show me what you've got."

Holograms of fourteen flowers, all yellow, appeared in the air above the computer.

"Is it any of these, Mr. Nighthawk?" asked Jacob.

"Third from the left," answered Nighthawk. Jacob pointed to one. "No, *my* left."

"Okay, got it." Jacob uttered a brief command to the computer, read a screen, and looked up. "The local name for it is the Sunspot."

"Right," said Nighthawk. "That's it. How soon can you get me some?"

"How many?"

"Four or five dozen."

"First let me check and make sure it can survive in our soil." He spoke briefly to the machine. "Yes, it can take our gravity and soil. The atmosphere's no problem; neither is the water." He paused as more information appeared. "They're perennials, but a freeze, even a mild one, will wipe 'em out."

"Order them."

"Don't you want to know what the price is, Mr. Nighthawk?" asked Jacob.

"I'm sure you won't jack it up," said Nighthawk. "Just bill my account."

"All right. They'll be here in about a week. Can I help you with anything else?"

"Not today. I've still got to get over to the grocer's and then meet my friend."

"By the way, I saw Johnny Trouble walking around this morning," said the clerk. "I'd be careful. He seems to have taken a real dislike to you."

"Thanks for the warning," said Nighthawk.

He left the store, walked across the street, picked up the spices he wanted, and returned to the vehicle, which was empty. He looked into a couple of restaurant windows, spotted Kinoshita sitting down to an omelet made from imported eggs and mutated ham, and joined him.

"Thanks for waiting," said Nighthawk sardonically.

"I was starving."

"You must have been some lawman. What happened when you got hungry during a hot pursuit?"

"I ate. No sense going up against a killer in a weakened condition."

"A weakened condition is three bullets in your abdomen, or a hand sliced off by a Burner. What you're describing is a hungry condition."

"Make fun of me all you want," said Kinoshita defensively, "but I made it past forty without your skills. I must have done *something* right."

"Yeah," said Nighthawk, smiling. "You stopped for dinner while all the really dangerous outlaws got away."

"Have your fun," said Kinoshita, "but if you start talking about calories and diets, I'm going to get a room in town."

"Hell, eat all you want. Our days of chasing bad guys are over."

"Speaking of which, I saw that young gun going into the bar across the street."

"He starts his drinking early, doesn't he?" remarked Nighthawk.

"That's all you have to say?"

"There's no law against getting drunk before noon."

"If he sees you . . ."

"If he sees me, I'll step aside. It doesn't take all that much effort."

"I *still* don't understand you."

"I'm not wearing any weapons," said Nighthawk. "What would you have me do?"

Kinoshita sighed. "Nothing. It's none of my business."

"Right the first time."

Nighthawk called up a menu, made his selections, and ate in silence. Kinoshita kept looking nervously out the window for Johnny Trouble, but Nighthawk paid attention only to the meal in front of him.

When they were done they walked out to the vehicle.

"You want to jog back?" asked Kinoshita.

"I'm an old man," answered Nighthawk, climbing in. "In fact, right now I'm a stiff, tired old man. Two miles a day is plenty."

They had driven about half the distance when Nighthawk asked Kinoshita to stop.

"What is it?"

"That bird up there," said Nighthawk, pointing. "It's lovely. I wonder what it is?"

"What bird where?"

"Right over there. Eleven o'clock, about a quarter mile away. Top branch, to the left of the bole."

Kinoshita peered for a moment, then shook his head. "All I can see is a kind of reddish lump. You can actually make out details?"

"And colors."

"Well, there's sure as hell nothing wrong with your eyes."

"There never was. Eplasia doesn't affect the vision."

"So are you going to become a bird-watcher now?"

"No. It just caught my attention." Nighthawk paused thoughtfully. "You know, I *could* get into birding, now that I come to think of it."

Kinoshita shrugged. "Whatever makes you happy."

"I think a pastoral existence in my old age is what will make me happy. At least, it has so far." Suddenly he peered ahead and frowned.

"What is it?" asked Kinoshita, instantly alert. "What do you see?"

"I'm not sure. But get this thing moving and head for home—fast!"

Kinoshita peeled away on the dirt road.

"Shit!" muttered Nighthawk.

"What's the matter?" demanded Kinoshita, almost losing touch with the road as he raced around a turn.

"Smoke," said Nighthawk. "Plenty of it."

"Coming from near the house?"

"Very."

They sped on for another two miles, then halted fifty yards from the house, which was totally ablaze.

"What the hell could have happened?" demanded Kinoshita, emerging from the vehicle. "Maybe some embers from last night's fire?"

"This wasn't any accident," said Nighthawk grimly. He saw something fluttering from the stump where he had buried his ax, walked over, picked it up, and frowned.

"What is it?" asked Kinoshita, joining him.

"A message," he said, handing it over.

" *'This is for Colonel Hernandez!'* " Kinoshita read aloud.

"Who the hell *is* he?" said Nighthawk. "I never heard of any Colonel Hernandez."

"I have," said Kinoshita grimly.

"He's one of yours?"

Kinoshita shook his head. "No, Jefferson. You killed him."

"The hell I did."

"I know," said Kinoshita. "I was there."

Chapter 7

"Explain!"

"The first clone was created for Colonel James Hernandez of Solio II," answered Kinoshita. "He was the one who instigated the creation of the clone, and he paid the bill."

"Surely I didn't kill him for that?"

"The first clone didn't kill him at all. He—the clone—was as efficient a killer as you were at twenty-three, but mentally and emotionally he was only a few months old. He was naive and innocent, and it cost him his life."

"How?"

"He found out, somehow, that Hernandez was using him for his own ends, and he went to Solio and tried to kill him. I don't know all the details, but I'm told there was a woman involved. Anyway, it was a trap, and it was the clone who died."

"But he killed Hernandez in the process?"

Kinoshita shook his head. "No."

"Then who did?"

"The second clone."

"Did Hernandez pay for the second clone as well?" asked Nighthawk.

"No," said Kinoshita. "The second clone was commissioned by Cassius Hill, the governor of a world named Pericles. But the second clone found out what had happened to his predecessor, and he made it his business to settle accounts on the way to Pericles."

"And *he* killed Hernandez?"

"Right. I know; I was there."

"Then you know who else was there?"

"He shot him in the middle of a crowded restaurant on Solio II. In fact, he killed Hernandez and four or five bodyguards."

"So some survivor spotted one of us and burned the house down."

"What do you mean, 'one of us'?" demanded Kinoshita. "You're the one who killed him."

"I'll wager you've changed a hell of a lot less in the last three years than I have," answered Nighthawk. "I'm still twenty pounds lighter than I was in my prime, my hair is halfway between gray and white, my face is lined. It's much more likely that they recognized you and then doped out who I was."

Kinoshita was silent for a long moment. "You know," he admitted at last, "you've got a point."

"Well, at least you'll be able to identify them when we find them."

"I don't know that for a fact," answered Kinoshita. "I don't know if I could identify everyone who was in that restaurant. Besides, Hernandez was the most powerful man on the planet, and he was as corrupt as hell. If the new regime replaced all his cronies and loyalists, you could have thousands of embittered men and women out for revenge."

"Only half a dozen of which you might possibly recognize," suggested Nighthawk grimly. "Is that what you're trying to tell me?"

"Yeah, I think that's pretty much it."

Nighthawk stood, hands on hips, watching the last wall of the house collapse. "How much was it insured for?" he asked, surveying the damage.

"About twenty percent of cost."

"No more?"

"The land was worth eighty percent, and you still own it." Kinoshita paused. "Do you want to rebuild?"

"What's the point? They know where I live. They'll just come back."

"So what do we do?"

"We collect the insurance, put the land up for sale, and leave."

"Leave for where?"

"I don't know. We'll go deeper into the Frontier until we find another world."

"Should I get us a room at the hotel in town?" asked Kinoshita.

"Why?"

"I thought you might want to come back in a couple of days, when the ruins have cooled down, and see if there's anything left."

"It was a wood house. What the hell do you think will be left?"

"Well, actually, I was thinking we might find a clue as to who did this."

"I don't much give a damn," said Nighthawk. "If they're in town, you'll point them out to me. If they've already left the planet, I'm not about to spend the rest of my life tracking them down."

"Jefferson Nighthawk's just going to walk away?" demanded Kinoshita disbelievingly.

"Jefferson Nighthawk's going to vanish. I want a new identity before we settle on the next world. I don't plan to be a target for people I can't even recognize." He walked back to the vehicle. "There's nothing we can do here. Let's get going."

"The fire might spread."

"Let it. We're never coming back."

Kinoshita stared thoughtfully at him. *You're nowhere near as devastated as you should be. I thought you loved this place, that you wanted to spend the rest of your life here. But if you can just shrug and walk away, I was wrong. You're not quite the Widowmaker yet, or you'd be after whoever did this with blood in your eye; but you're not Jefferson Nighthawk, either, or you'd be more deeply affected. I don't know which one you're going to wind up being; in fact, I don't know which one I want you to be. Yet.*

"Are we just going to sit here all morning?" asked Nighthawk sardonically.

"Sorry," said Kinoshita, ordering the vehicle to accelerate.

"When we get to town, report the fire to the authorities, put in a claim for the insurance, and see if you can buy a new ship. If you can, trade ours in."

"Ours works fine."

"Ours is registered in my name. If there's an easier way to trace a man, I've never found it."

"So what name do you want me to register the new ship in?" asked Kinoshita.

"Shit!" muttered Nighthawk. "I'd forgotten. I won't get a new ID and passport until we're deeper into the Frontier." He sighed deeply. "All right, we'll keep the ship a little longer."

"What are you going to be doing while I'm talking to the insurance company and the police?"

"The fire department, not the police," Nighthawk corrected him.

"But it was arson!" protested Kinoshita.

Nighthawk pulled the message out of a pocket and ripped it to shreds, throwing the pieces out the window. "If they think it was arson, we'll be stuck here for a week, answering questions and filling out forms."

"You're the boss."

"Hold that thought." The vehicle slowed down as they approached the town. "Anyway, in answer to your question, I've got a bunch of things on order, everything from furniture to flowers. I've got to cancel them. And there's something I have to buy." They neared the feed store. "Drop me here. I'll meet you at the bar."

Nighthawk got out of the vehicle, walked into the store, and cancelled the morning's order. He walked up and down the street, doing the same thing at a hardware and a furniture store.

Finally he entered a small shop next to the restaurant.

An old, bald man squinted across the room at him. "I've seen you around, Mr. Nighthawk. Can I help you find something?"

"Probably. Do you handle just new equipment, or do you have some old stuff lying around?"

"Half and half. What are you looking for?"

"I'll know it when I see it," said Nighthawk, starting to examine the display cases. "Pull this one out, please."

"Nice choice. Belonged to a lawman. Kept him alive long enough to retire."

Nighthawk examined the laser pistol, hefted it, checked the sights with an expert eye.

"Power pack?"

"Right there."

"Where?"

"When's the last time you used a Burner?" asked the old man, curious.

"A long time ago," answered Nighthawk.

"It's right there in the handle."

"This?" asked Nighthawk, pointing to the tiny battery.

"Yeah, that's it."

"How long is it good for?"

"Depends how much you're using it. It'll hold up for a twenty-minute blast in a lab. In the field, when you stop and start, probably about half that."

"How much are the batteries?"

"Two hundred credits each. I can take Maria Theresa dollars or Far London pounds. Word is that there's been a revolution on New Stalin, so I'm not taking New Stalin rubles this week."

"I'll take the Burner, and a dozen batteries. Got a holster?"

"New or old?"

"Old. I want one that I know works."

"I can give you the one it came with. It's kind of ratty, but it'll hold the gun."

"Fine. Now show me your Screechers."

Nighthawk examined eight sonic pistols with an expert eye, chose the one he wanted, and picked up another dozen batteries fitted to that model.

"Anything else?"

"Something that makes a bang."

"Only got one, and it's brand-new."

"Let's have a look."

Nighthawk examined it, pulled the trigger several times, rolled the cylinder, and returned it to the old man.

"Won't do," he said.

"What's the matter with it?"

"Feels stiff."

"Of course it feels stiff. It's metal."

"I meant the mechanism."

"So oil it."

"I'd never trust it," said Nighthawk. "And if I don't trust it, I'll never use it—so why buy it in the first place?"

"You feel this way about every new weapon you buy?"

"I've never owned a new one."

"You owned many?" asked the old man dubiously.

"A few."

"Can I show you anything else?"

Nighthawk looked around, saw a knife with a serrated blade, slipped it comfortably inside his right boot. "Yeah, I'll take this, too. What's the total?"

The old man totaled up the amount, scanned Nighthawk's retinagram and thumbprint, waited for the bank's computer to validate them, transferred the money to his store's account, and began to wrap the weapons.

"Don't bother," said Nighthawk. He positioned the Burner's holster on his thigh, waited for it to bond with his trousers, then attached the Screecher's holster to the small of his back. He took the tiny batteries and shoved them into a pocket.

"You know," said the old man, "you look like a man who was used to carrying weapons once upon a time."

"Once upon a time I was."

"You develop a sudden grudge against someone?"

"Maybe someone's got a grudge against me."

"Who'd want to bother a dignified old guy like you?"

"Beats the hell out of me," said Nighthawk, walking toward the door. Suddenly he stopped.

"Hey, old man," he said.

"Yeah?"

"You have to register those weapons, don't you?"

"Yeah, but there's no problem. I know your name: Jefferson Night-hawk."

"Tell you what. Register them to Dr. Gilbert Egan of Deluros VIII, and I'll give you my vehicle. You can pick it up at the spaceport tonight."

"The papers are in it?"

"Right."

The old man grinned. "Dr. Egan, you got yourself a deal."

Nighthawk turned and walked out into the street. He looked around for Kinoshita, couldn't see him, and walked over to the bar. The doors irised, and as he walked in he found himself facing Johnny Trouble.

"Well, look who's here," said the young man in mocking tones.

"I'm just meeting a friend here," said Nighthawk. "I don't want any trouble."

"Looks to me like you came dressed for trouble, old man," said Johnny Trouble, gesturing toward the Burner at Nighthawk's side.

"Look, kid," said Nighthawk, "I've had a bad morning. I don't need any more hassles."

"Then take your Burner out real carefully, drop it on the floor, and buy me a beer, and you won't have any problems." Johnny Trouble flashed a grin at the handful of men who were seated at tables toward the back of the tavern.

"If I've done anything to offend you, I apologize," said Nighthawk. "I'm leaving the planet in another half hour, and you'll never have to see me again."

"Your money's good here. Your apologies aren't."

Nighthawk stared at him. "Back off, kid. I apologized once. I'm not going to do it again."

"Then you're going to wish you had," said Johnny Trouble, stepping closer.

Suddenly Nighthawk's right hand shot out, so fast that it was almost a blur, and slapped Johnny Trouble's face, hard. The young man spun around from the force of the blow. When he had completed the circle and was facing Nighthawk again, he found his nose two inches from the business end of the older man's Burner.

"Who *are* you?" demanded Johnny Trouble.

"You'll find out soon enough," answered Nighthawk. "Now take that pistol out—gently—and place it on the bar."

Johnny Trouble did as he was told.

Nighthawk placed his own pistol on the bar, an equal distance away.

"Okay, big shot," he said. "Are you ready to face down the Widow-maker a second time?"

Johnny Trouble stared into Nighthawk's cold, unblinking eyes, and didn't like what he saw there. He froze for a moment, then managed to shake his head vigorously.

"Then walk away and don't come back."

Johnny Trouble walked stiffly out the door.

There was a long silence. Then one of the men at the back of the tavern spoke up. "You really the Widowmaker?" he asked.

"Don't believe everything you hear," said Nighthawk, picking up his pistol and putting it back in his holster.

"Are you saying you're not?" asked a second man.

"I wouldn't believe *that*, either," said a third.

Nighthawk smiled at them, then walked out into the street. He saw his vehicle parked in front of the bank building that also housed the insurance agency, walked over, and sat in the passenger's seat. Kinoshita came out a moment later, spotted him, and joined him inside the vehicle.

"It'll be about two weeks before the adjusters send in their report," he announced. "They'll deposit the money in your account."

"That'll be fine," said Nighthawk.

"I looked into all the stores," continued Kinoshita. "I didn't see anyone I recognize."

"Then they're gone. No great surprise."

"So where to now?"

Nighthawk pointed at the sky. "Out there somewhere. We'll improvise as we go."

They drove to the spaceport.

"Damn!" exclaimed Kinoshita as they came to a stop. "You know what we forgot to do?"

"What?"

"Sell the vehicle."

"It's been taken care of," said Nighthawk, climbing out.

Kinoshita followed him as they walked through the spaceport and then out to where their ship was sitting.

"Something's wrong," said Nighthawk softly.

"What are you talking about?"

"Never mind. But when I give the word, hit the ground."

Kinoshita looked around, couldn't see any sign of life, and decided that the older man was being overly cautious. He was about to say so when Nighthawk yelled *"Duck!"*

Kinoshita hit the concrete and heard the hum of Nighthawk's Burner just above his head. There was a scream some thirty yards to his left.

"Okay, you can get up now," said Nighthawk.

"What happened?" asked Kinoshita, standing and brushing himself off. "Who was it?"

"A very foolish young man," said Nighthawk, walking over and turning the body face-up with his boot. There was a smoking hole between its dead, staring eyes.

"Johnny Trouble!" exclaimed Kinoshita.

"I *told* him it was an unlucky name," said Nighthawk, totally devoid of emotion.

You're peeking through again, thought Kinoshita. *You were buried so deep inside that old man, I thought you might never show up. But here you are, as cold and efficient as ever. You may rue the day they burned down your house and brought you back, but this much I know: Someone else is going to rue it even more.*

Chapter 8

Nighthawk looked at the image of the green world floating above the navigational computer.

"What do you think?" he asked.

"It's pretty enough, I suppose," replied Kinoshita noncommittally.

"Ninety-seven percent Earth gravity, breathable air, plenty of water."

"Has it got a name?"

"Alpha Spinoza IV."

"No," said Kinoshita. "I mean a *name*."

"Pondoro."

"What does it mean?"

"Who knows?" replied Nighthawk.

"What kind of population?"

"Two Tradertowns, nothing else that I can find. Population is about six hundred permanent residents, with a daily average of maybe fifteen hundred transients."

"It's not on the major trading routes," said Kinoshita. "Why so many transients?"

"It's a safari world. Half the transients are out hunting, and another quarter are getting ready to go out or preparing their trophies after coming back."

"Are you going to take up big-game hunting?" asked Kinoshita sardonically.

"Not me," answered Nighthawk with a smile. "I've hunted the biggest."

"Then what's the attraction?"

"It's small, it's underpopulated, it's off the main trade routes, and it looks pleasant enough. There'll be a constant stream of supply ships for the

Tradertowns and hunting lodges, so we shouldn't have too long to wait for anything we need. And with the very real possibility of a hunter getting ripped apart, I figure there's got to be decent medical care."

"Are you sick?"

"No."

"Well, then?"

"I'm an old man," replied Nighthawk, "and getting sick is what old men do."

"You're only sixty-two."

"I've been sick before, I'll be sick again. Not with the same thing, I hope, but it's inevitable."

"I don't think you're ready to move into a nursing home just yet," said Kinoshita.

"No, but when the time comes, I'll be ready to. I've seen otherwise rational men go a little crazy at the mention of nursing homes, as if they were synonymous with concentration camps."

"Still, it's hard to picture you needing or accepting help from anyone."

"Count on it." Nighthawk paused. "I came very close to dying once. I didn't like it."

"What about all those times you risked your life?" persisted Kinoshita.

"It went with the job . . . and I never risked my life if there was an alternative."

"How many times weren't there alternatives?"

"A few." Nighthawk looked at the pleasant green image again. "Yeah, I think we'll try our luck here."

They broke out of orbit and were soon on the ground. Nighthawk summoned a robot and had it take their luggage to Customs.

"Robots?" said Kinoshita, surprised. "On a world with only six hundred people?"

"They're not for the residents," answered Nighthawk. "They're for the tourists."

They rode the slidewalk to the spaceport's main building, and were soon being interviewed by Customs officials.

"May I have your passport, please?" asked the woman who was processing Nighthawk.

He handed it over. "I'm surprised."

"Oh? About what?"

"I've been on a lot of worlds. You're the first live Customs official I've encountered. Usually it's all computerized and dehumanized."

"We believe in the personal touch on Pondoro."

"It's appreciated."

"Which safari company will be meeting you, Mr. Nighthawk?" she asked.

"None."

"You haven't decided on one yet?"

"I'm not here for a safari."

Suddenly she smiled. "*That's* why we have live officials."

"I beg your pardon?"

"We're here to handle the unexpected," she explained. "You're the first visitor in more than a year who wasn't here to go hunting." She paused. "May I ask what business you have on Pondoro?"

"None."

"If you're just here for service or refueling, you needn't pass through Customs."

"I'm considering buying some property and settling down," said Nighthawk.

She ran his passport through her computer again. "You haven't been to Pondoro before," she said, staring at a screen that he couldn't see.

"I know."

She frowned. "There must be something wrong. It says that you're—"

"I know," interrupted Nighthawk. "A hundred and seventy-four years old."

"Yes."

"I've been in DeepSleep at the Cryonics Institute on Deluros VIII for a hundred and twelve years. You can check it out."

She uttered two short commands to her computer, then looked up.

"Welcome to Pondoro, Mr. Nighthawk. I'm delighted to see that you've made a complete recovery."

"Thank you," replied Nighthawk. "I wonder if I might make a request?"

"Certainly. What can I do for you?"

"You can keep my name to yourself. I'm sure your computer has told you who I am. I'd prefer to leave all that behind me and begin a new life here on Pondoro."

"I won't tell anyone," replied the woman. "But your name is registered in the computer, and it will remain there until you legally change it. At that time, if you'll contact me and show me proof of your new name, I can adjust the computer to reflect that."

"Thank you."

"I never thought I'd meet the Widowmaker," she said. "I saw holos of you when I was a little girl. Most people thought you'd been dead for almost a century even then."

"I wouldn't believe everything I saw if I were you," replied Nighthawk.

"Are you certain you wouldn't like to go on safari, a man like you?" she continued. "I can recommend some of our best companies."

"No, thanks."

"You're sure I can't change your mind?"

"I'm sure."

"Let me try anyway," she said, uttering more commands to her computer.

Suddenly, without moving, Nighthawk found himself in the middle of a forest. Standing some twenty feet away was a red-and-black catlike carnivore, some six hundred pounds, its orange unblinking eyes focused on him as it crept forward.

Nighthawk found to his surprise that he was holding a sonic rifle in his hands.

The carnivore roared once and leaped at him, and Nighthawk, with no time to raise the rifle to his shoulder, fired from the hip, spinning to his left to try to evade the creature—

—which froze in mid-leap. Instantly the forest and the weapon disappeared, and Nighthawk was once again in front of the Customs agent.

"What the hell was *that*?" he demanded.

"Just a sample," she replied. "The real thing is much more exciting."

"If you say so."

"So . . . can I interest you in a safari?"

He shook his head. "I told you what I'm here for."

"I know—but I get a commission for every safari I sell," she said apologetically. "We're a one-industry world."

"Does your industry include a hotel for people who haven't decided what company they want to use?"

"There's only one hotel in town. You'll find it easily enough."

"I thought there were two Tradertowns," said Nighthawk.

"There are. But the other is almost two thousand miles from here, in the southern hemisphere—or the eastern one, depending on which way you look at it."

"Has the hotel got a name?"

"The Pondoro Taylor." She paused. "The hotel, like our world, is named after John Taylor, one of the greatest big-game hunters in human history."

"Never heard of him," answered Nighthawk. "I thought our greatest hunter was Nicobar Lane."

"Taylor lived thousands of years earlier, back when we were still Earthbound."

"So why isn't the world named Taylor? What's Pondoro got to do with it?"

"Pondoro was his African name. I gather it was a native word for lion, and as an indication of his courage it was considered a mark of great respect."

"What's 'African'?"

"A city or country back on Earth, I'm not sure which." She paused. "The hotel supplies a computer in every room. I'm sure you can call the information up from your computer's data banks once you're there."

"Speaking of which, how do I get there?"

"Just pick up your luggage and glide out to the front of the spaceport," she answered. "You'll find some transport vehicles there. Enter whichever one you want and tell it where you want to go."

"Robot driver?"

"No driver at all," she replied. "Or, rather, the vehicle drives itself." She smiled. "Don't look so concerned, Mr. Nighthawk. I know they didn't exist when you entered DeepSleep, but we've only had one accident in the fifty-three years we've been using them."

She handed him back his passport card after her computer had added a Pondoro visa to its coding, and he joined Kinoshita at the front door of the spaceport.

"Very friendly people," said Kinoshita.

"They seem to be."

"Did you get the holo of the charging . . . I don't know what you'd call it—kind of dinosaur?"

"No, I got a cat."

"Amazing how quickly they can put you in the jungle, isn't it?"

"I don't think I was *put* in the jungle so much as surrounded by it," answered Nighthawk.

"Whichever."

They approached the first vehicle in line. The doors slid back to allow them to enter, and the robot accompanying them loaded their luggage.

"Where may I take you?" asked the vehicle.

"The Pondoro Taylor Hotel," answered Nighthawk.

The vehicle immediately sped off down the narrow road leading to the Tradertown.

"Is it any good?" asked Kinoshita.

"Is *what* any good?"

"This hotel."

"I hope so. It's the only one in this hemisphere."

Kinoshita looked out the window. "Pretty country. More savannah than forest, at least around here." A herd of herbivores caught his eye. "Some pretty grasseaters out there. Nice spiral horns on the males."

"There is no hunting allowed without a license," announced the vehicle.

"We weren't going to hunt," replied Nighthawk.

"Furthermore," continued the vehicle, ignoring his answer, "all areas within ten miles of the spaceport and the Tradertowns are protected reserves, where hunting and fishing are both illegal."

"Fine," said Nighthawk.

"I could supply you with a hard copy of all the safari companies based on Pondoro," offered the vehicle in its toneless voice, "as well as prices for their various services. Some of them will lead holographic as well as hunting safaris."

"That won't be necessary."

"Would you care for a list of all the game animals on Pondoro?" continued the vehicle. "I can produce holographs of each."

"No."

"Please inform me if you change your mind."

"You'll be the first to know," said Nighthawk. He turned to Kinoshita. "I've got a sinking feeling that this might not be as tranquil a world as I'd hoped."

"All the shooting?" suggested Kinoshita.

"All the selling."

They rode in silence and came to the Tradertown in another ten minutes.

"Not exactly typical," commented Nighthawk. "One bar, one casino, one weapon shop, one taxidermist, and twelve safari companies. Usually you've got half a dozen bars, drug dens, and whorehouses for every other building in town."

"We have reached the Pondoro Taylor Hotel," announced the vehicle as it pulled to a stop. "I have registered you for two single rooms. If you prefer to share a room—"

"Single rooms are fine," interrupted Nighthawk.

"My services will be billed to your personal account, Mr. Nighthawk."

"Fine," said Nighthawk. "Let us unload our bags and you can be on your way."

"I will take your luggage to the service entrance, and it will be delivered to your rooms." The vehicle waited for both of them to emerge, then quickly pulled around a corner of the building.

Nighthawk and Kinoshita approached the front desk, where a uniformed man awaited them.

"Welcome to the Taylor," he said. "Your rooms are on the second floor, keyed to your voiceprints. Just tell the doors to open and they'll respond."

"Which doors?" asked Kinoshita.

"The ones with your names on them in holographic displays," answered the man. "Is there anything I can do to make your stay more comfortable?"

"Yeah, there is," said Nighthawk.

"Excellent! I can recommend the very best safari guide, the finest weapon for—"

"All I want is the name of a realtor."

"A realtor?"

"Someone who sells real estate."

The man frowned. "I don't believe we have any, sir."

"What happens when you want to buy a piece of land?"

"I see!" responded the man. "You mean a private hunting preserve!" He paused. "Just ask the computer when you get to your room."

"Thanks," said Nighthawk. "One more thing. Where do we find a good meal?"

"I suppose you could get some sandwiches in the bar across the street," came the answer. "But the Taylor has the only restaurant in town."

"How late is it open?"

"It's open around the clock," answered the man. "You never know what time a ship might land, or when a safari might come in from the bush."

"Thanks," said Nighthawk. "We'll freshen up and unpack, and then come down for dinner."

He walked over to an airlift, followed by Kinoshita, and floated up to the second floor. They walked down the corridor until they came to doors with their names emblazoned, commanded them to open, and entered.

The luggage was already there, and after Nighthawk washed the dust from his hands and face he walked to the desk in the corner and activated the computer.

"How may I help you?" asked the machine.

"I want to relocate to Pondoro," said Nighthawk. "What properties are available?"

"With or without a domicile?"

"With, preferably."

"There are four private hunting lodges for sale, and one timeshare, all within forty miles of this Tradertown. Would you care to see them?"

"Please."

The five domiciles suddenly appeared above the computer. Beneath each was a price and a plat of the land.

"I'd like to see the four lodges tomorrow," said Nighthawk. "Who do I contact?"

"I have just arranged appointments at one-hour intervals beginning at noon," answered the computer. "Any empty vehicle near the hotel will take you there."

"Thank you. If I wish to make a bid, who do I make it *to*?"

"You will make your bid to me, and I will transmit it to the owners."

"Fair enough. Deactivate."

Nighthawk walked out into the hall, decided to wait for Kinoshita in the restaurant, and descended to the main floor.

Kinoshita joined him a few moments later.

"Did you learn anything?"

"There's a few places for sale. We'll visit them tomorrow afternoon."

"That means we get to sleep late?"

"*You* do. *I've* got to find someone who can give me a new ID and passport."

"In a typical Tradertown, I'd say you'd have your choice of forgers," said Kinoshita. "On this world, I'd be surprised if you can find even one."

"Lot of pretty pictures on the walls," commented Nighthawk, gesturing to the paintings and holographs of game animals.

"So what?"

"So any artist who can do that can do what I need. If I can't change my name legally, I'll hire one of them to make up some ID papers for me."

"Got a name chosen yet?"

"I'll think of one before morning."

They ate a meal of alien game meats and exotic produce, and then, because it was a lovely, cool night, they decided to sit outside before going off to bed.

The hotel had a veranda overlooking a small pond. Very few animals came by, but the building and its lights hadn't scared the birds off, and Nighthawk and Kinoshita sat on comfortable chairs, watching them.

"You know," remarked Kinoshita after a few minutes, "maybe there's something to this bird-watching after all."

"Maybe you've found a new hobby."

Three men walked out of the hotel's bar, headed for a table on the veranda. One of them stopped when he was a few feet from Nighthawk and stared at him.

Nighthawk stared back without saying a word.

"Mack! Blitz!" said the man, calling to his companions. "Come over and take a look."

Kinoshita tensed as the two other men joined their companion in front of Nighthawk.

"You got a problem, friend?" asked Nighthawk easily.

"Listen!" said the man. "It's *him*!"

"Boy, he sure as hell looks like him," agreed the one called Blitz. "And like Rimo says, he sounds like him, too."

"But it can't be," said Mack. "Take a *good* look. He's an old man. That was just a kid."

"Anyone can color his hair," said the first man, the one called Rimo. He took a step closer. "You ever been on a world called Tundra?"

"Tundra?" replied Nighthawk. "Never even heard of it."

"Damn it, that's *his* voice!" said Blitz.

"Maybe you remember the Marquis of Queensbury?"

Nighthawk shook his head. "I never heard of him, either. You're looking for someone else."

"Come on, guys," said Mack. "We're going out into the bush at daybreak. Let's get some sleep."

"Maybe we've found something to hunt right here," said Rimo doggedly.

"I've got no quarrel with anyone," said Nighthawk. "It's a lovely night out. Why not just enjoy it and go about your business?"

"Look at him!" said Mack. "He's got to be fifty-five, maybe sixty. It can't be the same guy."

"I don't care!" snapped Rimo. "I know who it is!"

Just be quiet and keep still, thought Kinoshita. *They've been drinking. Don't rile them. Any minute now they'll realize you can't be the twenty-three-year-old who killed the Marquis.*

"I've never seen you before in my life," offered Nighthawk.

"That's kind of funny, because *I've* sure as hell seen *you*!" said Rimo.

Don't egg him on. Just be quiet and polite and humble and they'll walk away.

"You must be mistaken," said Nighthawk.

"And *I* think you can't hide who you are behind a gray wig!" shot back Rimo.

Kinoshita sensed a change in his companion, took a quick look at Nighthawk's face, and had a sudden sick feeling in the pit of his stomach— because it wasn't Nighthawk's face anymore. It was the Widowmaker's.

"Son," said Nighthawk, "we've done enough talking, and you're standing in my way."

"You going somewhere?" demanded Rimo pugnaciously.

"No."

"Then what's your problem?"

"I'm watching birds."

"Are you?"

"And fools."

Shut up! You're an old man. They may be a little drunk, but there are three of them, damn it! And they're young.

"Who are you calling a fool?"

"If the shoe fits," replied Nighthawk. "You're looking for a kid. Do I look like one to you?"

"You look like an old man who hasn't got the brains to keep his mouth shut."

"And you look like three corpses."

"Corpses?" Rimo laughed. "We're not dead!"

"You will be soon enough if you don't walk on," said Nighthawk ominously.

"You don't have to do this!" whispered Kinoshita.

"*They* don't have to do this," answered Nighthawk, not lowering his voice. "I was just sitting here minding my own business."

Blitz's hand snaked down toward his laser pistol.

"Don't do it, son," warned Nighthawk.

Blitz's fingers grasped the handle of his gun. Nighthawk's hand flashed as he stood up, and suddenly a knife buried itself in Blitz's neck. Mack went for his gun, but Nighthawk's laser fried him before he could withdraw it.

"Who the hell *are* you?" demanded Rimo, who had been watching, too surprised to move.

"The name is Jefferson Nighthawk." Pause. "Now aren't you sorry you asked?"

"What happened to you?"

"I grew up," said Nighthawk grimly. "And now *I've* happened to *you*."

"Walk away!" said Kinoshita urgently. "Don't go for your gun and he'll let you live!"

"Fuck you!" snapped Rimo. "I'm going to be the man who killed the Widowmaker!"

He reached for his weapon, Nighthawk's Burner spewed out its deadly light again, and the younger man fell heavily to the ground.

Nighthawk stepped down from the veranda and nudged each body with his toe while his pistol was still trained on it, just in case there was a spark of life left. Finally he turned to Kinoshita. "Who the hell was the Marquis of Queensbury?"

"He was an outlaw, or maybe you'd call him a warlord," answered Kinoshita. "He controlled half a dozen worlds. Word has it that your first clone killed him."

"You never saw him?"

Kinoshita shook his head. "No."

"So along with Hernandez's men, I could run into the Marquis' men all the hell over the Frontier."

"It's possible."

"And of all these hundreds, maybe thousands, of men who have a grudge against the Widowmaker, you can identify five or six?"

"That's right."

"Shit!" muttered Nighthawk angrily. "All I want is to be left alone!"

You may think that's what you want, but you could have kept quiet and eventually they'd have gone away. Jefferson Nighthawk may want to be left alone, but the Widowmaker is growing stronger every day. I didn't think you were ready to take on three men at once, but he knew, didn't he?

"Well," said Nighthawk with a sigh, as the Widowmaker vanished to some secret place inside him, "let's find out who's in charge and report this. It'll look a lot better than if we just wait for them to find the bodies."

"Right," agreed Kinoshita.

We all have our agendas. You've got yours, which is out in the open. I've got mine, which I haven't confided to you. And I have a feeling the Widowmaker has his—and only he knows what it is.

Kinoshita sighed deeply.

I wonder what happens when they clash, as sooner or later they will?

Chapter 9

Nighthawk sat in the mayor's office, which happened to be a wood-paneled den at the Big Seven Safari Company.

"Damn it!" he said softly as he and Kinoshita waited for the mayor. "I'm an old man. My enemies have been dead for a century. I shouldn't have to watch my fucking back!"

"They weren't *your* enemies," said Kinoshita for perhaps the fifth time. "They were your clones'."

"Same goddamned thing!" snapped Nighthawk. "I've earned a little peace and quiet! I spent forty-five years on the Frontier, I went up against every human and alien outlaw I could find, I never ducked a fight, I never asked for favors." He took a deep breath, then released it slowly. "I've *done* my duty, damn it!"

"You could have let them walk away," suggested Kinoshita gently.

"They'd just have come back."

"You don't know that."

"I'm trying to be a man of peace," said Nighthawk irritably. "You know I am. But you can push *any* man just so hard and just so far—*even* a man of peace."

"Couldn't you have held off another ten seconds?" said Kinoshita. "Another fifteen? Maybe they'd have left."

"And if they had, maybe they'd have harassed some other old guy who *isn't* Jefferson Nighthawk."

"And maybe they wouldn't have."

"No more guessing games," said Nighthawk. "They went for their weapons. It was self-defense, and I don't think you're going to see a lot of mourners at their funerals."

A well-built middle-aged man, with shoulder-length silver hair and wearing an outfit made of native animal skins, entered the den, looking almost like a poster for his company. He spotted Nighthawk and walked up to him.

"Mr. Nighthawk?"

"Right," said Nighthawk, shaking his extended hand.

"My name is Hawkeye Silverbuck."

Nighthawk smiled. "It is?"

Silverbuck returned the smile. "It is now. And you must be Mr. Kinoshita."

"I am," replied Kinoshita.

"Pleased to meet you," said Silverbuck. "I am the mayor and chief law officer of Pondoro, as well as the owner of the Big Seven Safari Company." He paused. "Mr. Nighthawk, would you care to tell me exactly what happened in front of the Taylor just after nine o'clock tonight?"

"Three men thought I was someone else and threatened to kill me. When they went for their weapons I was forced to defend myself."

"Were there any witnesses?"

"I saw the whole thing," said Kinoshita. "He's telling the truth."

"Let me amend that," said Silverbuck with a smile. "Were there any witnesses who could reasonably be considered objective observers?"

"I don't know," said Nighthawk. "But that's the way it happened. And the moment it was over, I came here to report it to you."

"Did you do or say anything to encourage them?" asked Silverbuck.

"I tried to *dis*courage them. Why?"

"You say it was a case of mistaken identity. If you goaded them into a fight and they didn't know who they were facing, I would consider that tantamount to murder. After all, you *are* the Widowmaker."

"I *was* the Widowmaker," Nighthawk corrected him. "Now I'm just an old man looking for a place to live out his life."

"I think the presence of three dead bodies belies that statement," said Silverbuck. "I've checked, and there was paper on two of them." He smiled in amusement. "So now it's up to me to decide whether to pass the reward on to you or charge you for killing them."

"Bullshit," said Nighthawk. "If they were wanted men, how can you charge me with murder?"

"They were wanted for robbery. I know you've been away, but robbery is still not punishable by death."

"Then give me some sodium-P, or hook me up to a Neverlie Machine, and let's get this over with," said Nighthawk.

"I don't think that will be necessary," said Silverbuck. "I'm sure we can settle this quickly and amicably."

"Oh?" asked Nighthawk suspiciously.

"And I'll make sure you receive the reward."

"Not necessary."

"But I insist."

Nighthawk stared at him. "In exchange for what?"

"It's very simple. Leave Pondoro and promise never to come back."

"I didn't break the goddamned law!"

"It doesn't make any difference," replied Silverbuck. "Once word gets out that you're here, every young gun on the Inner Frontier will make a beeline for Pondoro to go up against you." He paused. "We do a lot of killing here, but we prefer to confine it to animals."

"They don't have to know I'm here. I plan to get new ID papers tomorrow."

"If you hadn't killed three men, I could probably keep your identity a secret, but now . . ." Silverbuck let his voice trail off. "It's a lot harder to change a police record than a Customs registration form—and yes, I'm aware that you plan to change it."

"Damn it!" snapped Nighthawk. "You have no legal right to make me leave!"

"I'm the only elected official and the only lawman on this planet, or at least on this half of it. My word carries the full force of the law, and I'm telling you we don't want you here." He paused. "Hell, *you* don't want to be here, either," he continued reasonably. "Go deeper into the Frontier, and establish a new identity *before* you land on the world where you want to live."

"I'm staying," said Nighthawk adamantly.

"I've already explained why it would be foolish to stay," said Silverbuck. "Why are you being so stubborn?"

"The Widow—" he began, and quickly caught himself. "*I* don't run from threats."

"No one's threatening you. I'm just telling you what will happen if you stay."

"You're the law. Your job is to protect me."

"I'm the law by default, Mr. Nighthawk," said Silverbuck. "No one else was willing to accept the position. But I spend most of my time on safari—and to be perfectly honest, I'd be a lot better protecting you from animals than men."

"Some lawman!" snorted Nighthawk contemptuously.

"You want the job?" shot back Silverbuck. "Just say the word and it's yours. Two thousand credits a month, and no one can deport you. Kill anyone you want; see if I give a damn."

"I'm retired."

"I saw what you did in your spare time."

"They went for their weapons."

"We're back where we started. I'm accepting your story, but I want you off the planet tomorrow—or I'll reopen the investigation."

"I'll let you know."

"Think about it very carefully," continued Silverbuck. "You don't want me as an enemy, Mr. Nighthawk. I know better than to go up against you; no one could pay me enough to do that. But I'll hide in a blind, and nail you from a quarter mile away. You'll never know what hit you—and I guarantee that with my rifles, I don't miss at four hundred yards."

Suddenly Silverbuck was looking down the barrel of Nighthawk's Burner.

"What makes you think I'll let you get four hundred yards away, Mr. Silverbuck?" asked Nighthawk in low tones.

Silverbuck raised his hands, too frightened to say anything.

"I've been threatened by experts," continued Nighthawk. "I don't rattle."

"You killed a lot of men," Silverbuck said with more confidence than he felt. "But you were always a lawman or a bounty hunter, never an outlaw. You won't kill me."

"I learned a long time ago never to bet more than I could afford to lose," replied Nighthawk. "Are you prepared to bet your life on that?"

Silverbuck shook his head.

Nighthawk lowered his Burner and put it back in its holster. "I'll leave when I'm ready to."

With that, he turned on his heel and walked out of the building. Kinoshita considered apologizing for his behavior, thought better of it, and followed him into the street.

"He's right, you know," said Nighthawk.

"Then why did you pull a gun on him?"

"There's a difference between being right and being arrogant. Telling me how he's going to kill me is arrogant."

"So what do we do now?"

Nighthawk was about to answer when there was a small commotion at the doorway to the tavern.

"That's him!" someone shouted.

"Did you hear what he did?"

"Is he really the Widowmaker?"

"He's an old man. How could he—?"
"—killed all three of them before they could get off a shot."
"Yeah? Well, wait till he goes up against Billy Tuesday!"
"I hear Backbreaker Kimani is already on his way here!"

"Yeah," said Nighthawk disgustedly as he turned and approached the doorway to the Taylor, "it's time to move again."

Chapter 10

Nighthawk sat at the controls of the ship, looking at the viewscreen. Kinoshita returned from the galley with some food and took his seat.

"Can I get you anything to eat?"

"No."

"Mind if I ask where we're going?"

"Go ahead."

"All right," said Kinoshita. "Where are we going?"

"I don't know."

Kinoshita stared at him for a long moment. "Are you mad at the whole galaxy, or just those members of it who remember the Widowmaker?"

Nighthawk made no reply, and Kinoshita ate his meal in silence.

"You mind if I say something?" he asked after a few more minutes had passed.

"Yes."

"Damn it, Jefferson, just how long are you going to be like this?"

"Until I feel differently."

"I could die of old age before that happens."

"*I'll* die of old age first."

"Not you," said Kinoshita. "You'll die taking on twenty men at once, all the while protesting that you just want to be left alone."

Nighthawk turned to him. "Just what the hell do you expect me to do?"

"The last clone had cosmetic surgery," Kinoshita pointed out. "He's got a new face and a new identity. No one will ever know who he is, or was. If you're so hot to live a peaceful life, why don't you do the same thing?"

"In case it's escaped your attention, I've *been* doing the same thing, and it hasn't helped a bit . . . so why bother? It was a lousy idea to begin with. I'm still Nighthawk; it's the Widowmaker I'm getting rid of. These are my face and my name. They're two of the things that define me. I don't see any reason to change them."

"I could give you four reasons," answered Kinoshita, "but they're all dead."

"I was in DeepSleep for a hundred and twelve years," said Nighthawk angrily. "I shouldn't have to hide who I am. My enemies should all be dead."

"But they're not. You yourself would be dead if we hadn't created two clones to earn enough money to keep you alive until a cure for your disease was found. But in the process, the clones made new enemies, enemies who haven't reverted to dust yet. Now, that's a fact, and all the arguments about what life *should* be like aren't going to change it." Kinoshita paused. "You know, so far we've only mentioned the Marquis and Colonel Hernandez. But the last thing your second clone did was kill Governor Cassius Hill and a few hundred of his best soldiers. He had a standing army of close to four million men and women who had a pretty soft touch until you came along. Probably most of them would like to see you dead, too."

"I assume you've got a point?" said Nighthawk dryly.

"Yes, I do. I think the odds are no worse than even that you're going to run into someone who has a grudge against the Widowmaker, or someone's who's out to make a reputation for himself, on just about every inhabited world on the Inner Frontier. If you think otherwise, you're blinding yourself to the facts. You need a new name *and* a new face."

"Forget it."

"But you yourself were going to get a new ID back on Pondoro!"

"I've given it a lot of thought the past few days." Nighthawk placed a finger to his cheek. "I spent five years looking for some trace of this face in the mirror. All I could find was some kid's nightmare. Now that it's back, it's staying."

"That's stupid!"

"That's me."

"The hell it is. Your clones were always willing to adapt to conditions. Why the hell aren't you?"

"My clones were young men with their whole lives ahead of them. I'm an old man, and most of my choices have been made, for better or worse. I'm through adapting to conditions; from now on, they can adapt to me."

"So you're going to keep killing men on each new world we come to?"

"I hope not. It's up to the men."

"It doesn't have to be."

"We're talking about my choices, not yours," said Nighthawk. "Why are you having such a problem with that?"

"You're good," said Kinoshita. "Even at sixty-two, you're far better than I was in my prime. You know, I seriously wondered if you had a chance against those three guys back on Pondoro, but you were never in any danger, were you?"

"Not really."

"I know," continued Kinoshita. "But you know something? As good as you are, I've seen better. And younger."

"Who?"

"Your clones. Either of them could take you out in a heartbeat."

"So what? One's dead, and the other's vanished with a new name and face."

"You're not following me," said Kinoshita. "If *they* could take you, probably there are others who could, too. You won't know and I won't know until you go up against one of them. I'd rather see you avoid it and live the life you keep saying you *want* to live."

"I *do* want to live it." Nighthawk's jaw muscles tightened noticeably as he grimaced. "I tried to walk away from that kid on Churchill, just as I tried to let those men on Pondoro walk away from me."

"So why didn't you?"

Nighthawk sighed deeply. "Because I've been the Widowmaker too long."

"You're not going to change, you know."

"I know."

"And someday, sooner or later, as you get slower and weaker, and the young men who want to challenge you get faster and stronger, one of them's going to kill you."

"At least it'll be quick," said Nighthawk with no sense of regret or resentment. "I've had my fill of the slow way."

"Wouldn't you rather never again be in a situation where you have to kill or be killed?" asked Kinoshita.

"If I've really got four or five million enemies out there, I'm just as likely to be backshot as called out."

"That's better somehow?" demanded Kinoshita sarcastically.

"Look," said Nighthawk. "I appreciate your concern. I hope you're wrong. I suspect that you're right. But this is the face I've lived with, and it's the one I'm going to die with."

"All right," said Kinoshita bitterly. "Get yourself killed. See if I care."

"You *do* care. What I can't figure out is why."

Kinoshita was about to reply when the ship's computer interrupted them.

"We are being followed by a Class J spacecraft," it announced.

"How long has it been on our tail?" asked Nighthawk.

"Twenty standard minutes. After fifteen minutes I attempted to elude it, as per your programming, but my evasive maneuvering was unsuccessful. I am a 341 Golden Streak; it is a 702 Bullet, which means that it is faster than I am."

"Find its port of origin and get its registration," ordered Nighthawk.

The computer was silent for a moment, and then spoke again: "Owned by the Starburst Corporation, seventeen hours out of Pondoro."

"How long since *we* left Pondoro?"

"Nineteen hours."

"Where are Starburst's corporate headquarters?"

"Tundra."

Nighthawk looked over at Kinoshita. "Not much question about it, is there?"

"None."

"Can you put it on the viewscreen?" asked Nighthawk.

"I can put a representation of a generic 702 Bullet on the screen. This particular ship is still out of range."

"If it's been chasing us since Pondoro, how come you only noticed it twenty minutes ago?"

"I do not know that it has been chasing us since it left Pondoro. It came within range of my sensors twenty-one minutes ago. I only know what it has done since then."

"Well," mused Nighthawk, "we can't outrun it, and there's no sense leading it to a planet we might want to settle on. I suppose the best thing to do is to talk to it."

"Make sure the damned thing isn't armed first," suggested Kinoshita.

"No Class J craft carries armaments," said the ship.

"Send it a greeting," ordered Nighthawk.

"Sending . . . done."

"Put any reply on visual and audio."

The holograph of a burly man suddenly appeared in front of Nighthawk and Kinoshita.

"Hello, Nighthawk," said the man with a toothy grin. "Tired of running?"

"No one's running."

"Are you going to tell me you didn't try to lose me about five minutes ago?"

"Automatic programming," answered Nighthawk. "I didn't even know you were there."

"Well, you know it now, and you'll know it when you land."

"Why are you following me?"

"You killed three of my friends."

"I never saw any of them before."

"Sure—and you don't know who I am, either." The man laughed in amusement.

"That's true."

"You disappoint me," said the man.

"Oh?"

"You were a lot of things back on Tundra, but you were never a liar. And now you've lied to me three times in less than a minute."

"I haven't lied at all."

"You said you didn't try to lose me, you said you didn't know the three men you murdered, and you said you didn't recognize me. Any way you count it, that comes to three."

"I killed those men in self-defense," said Nighthawk. "Don't make me do the same to you."

"Oh, I know better than to take you on alone," said the man. "After all, you're the Widowmaker—or at least that's what they say. But you're going to pay for killing my friends." He paused. "If it'll make you feel any better, I didn't mind your killing the Marquis. I never liked him much."

"I can't tell you how relieved that makes me feel," said Nighthawk dryly.

The man laughed again—a loud humorless laugh. "You want to tell me where your next port of call is, or are we going to have to do this the hard way?"

"The hard way, I think," said Nighthawk. "Computer, cut the transmission."

The holograph vanished instantly.

"What are we going to do?" asked Kinoshita. "We're not fast enough to lose him."

"I know."

"So what's next?" persisted Kinoshita. "I suppose we could try to lead him back to an Oligarchy world and—"

"I don't let the Oligarchy do my fighting for me," said Nighthawk.

"Then where *do* you plan to go?"

"Well, there's no sense blowing another habitable world by leading him to it."

"It sounds like he's got friends with him," offered Kinoshita.

"That's *their* problem," responded Nighthawk. "Mine is finding the best place to face him."

"You have something in mind?"

"Yeah, I think so. I've been in this section of the Frontier a couple of times before." He paused. "Computer, how far are we from Bolingbroke VI? In hours, not miles or parsecs."

"At this speed, encountering no ion storms, I can reach the Bolingbroke system in thirteen hours and twenty-seven minutes."

"Do it."

"Programming . . . done."

"Good, I'm going to grab something to eat."

Nighthawk walked off to the galley, and Kinoshita began questioning the computer about the Bolingbroke system.

"There are eleven planets, including four gas giants, and two asteroid belts. The seven inner planets possess atmospheres."

"How many oxygen worlds?"

"None."

"None?" exclaimed Kinoshita, surprised. "Then what is Bolingbroke VI?"

"It is a methane world, mean temperature minus seventy-three degrees Celsuis."

And that's where you want to face this guy and his henchmen? If they don't kill you, the planet will.

Chapter 11

Bolingbroke VI looked like it had been put together from a billion twinkling stars. Exquisite crystalline growths reached toward the distant sun, acting as prisms for its light. The ground was rough and uneven, as if covered by an infinite number of glass shards, each reflecting a different color.

"It looks like a big piece of rock candy," remarked Kinoshita.

"I suppose it does," said Nighthawk, testing all the joints of his protective suit.

"So what's the big attraction about facing them on Bolingbroke?"

"I like it here."

"That's *it*?" demanded Kinoshita. "You're standing out in the open on a frozen methane planet, ready to face God knows how many men, just because you like it here?"

Nighthawk smiled in amusement. "You never spoke like that to my clones, did you?"

"They wouldn't have permitted it," admitted Kinoshita.

"Lucky for you us old men are more tolerant, isn't it?" said Nighthawk, still smiling.

"Damn it!" said Kinoshita in frustration. "Can't you even tell me why we're here? I can help!"

"I don't need your help," replied Nighthawk. "I told you that when we landed. You'll be much safer if you just go back to the ship."

"Not a chance."

"Why?" asked Nighthawk. "Not only don't I need you, but you don't owe me a thing."

"I'm staying right here."

"You didn't answer me."

"*You* didn't answer *me*, either," shot back Kinoshita.

Nighthawk stared at him for a moment, then shrugged. "What the hell, you're a grown man. Suit yourself."

"I still don't know why you chose to face them on an airless planet."

"Bolingbroke's not airless," Nighthawk corrected him. "It has an atmosphere."

"Nothing anyone I know can breathe."

"That's not what I said."

"Okay, it's not airless. Big deal."

"It's important," said Nighthawk.

Kinoshita frowned. "If you say so . . . but I sure as hell can't see why."

"Hopefully, neither can *they*," said Nighthawk, pointing to the sleek silver ship that was plunging down toward the planet's surface.

Kinoshita looked up. "They'll be on the ground in another three minutes."

"Give or take," agreed Nighthawk.

"And you plan to just stand here in the open and wait for them?"

"That's right."

"If they land over there," continued Kinoshita, pointing to his left, "they can hide behind those outcroppings and shoot you down at their leisure."

"I imagine that's just what they'll try to do," agreed Nighthawk.

"Damn it! I'm supposed to be your partner! Why can't you tell me what the hell you have in mind?"

"I don't have any partners," replied Nighthawk firmly. "I appreciate your friendship and your loyalty, but I told you to stay in the ship. It's *your* decision to stand beside me, not mine."

"Will you please stop sounding like the goddamned Widowmaker and go back to being Jefferson Nighthawk?"

Nighthawk stared at him, but said nothing.

"Look, I'm sorry," said Kinoshita awkwardly. "I didn't mean that."

"Yes you did, and there's no need to apologize. I've never held it against a man for saying what he felt. Honesty is an underrated virtue these days."

Kinoshita shifted his weight awkwardly. "Just the same, I'm sorry."

"Fine."

"Let me know what you want me to do, and I'll do it. This is your show."

"You don't have to do anything. I thought I already told you that."

Kinoshita looked down at Nighthawk's hands. "Shit!" he exclaimed.

"What is it?"

"You wore the wrong gloves. Those are the metal-plated ones for working on the ship's engine. You'll have a hard time holding a pistol."

"I'll manage."

"I could go back right now and . . . No, of course you can't change them out here. Your hands would freeze. You'd better go to the ship and change while you can."

"There's no time," said Nighthawk, pointing to the pursuing ship, which had just touched down and was disgorging a handful of armed men.

"Six, seven, eight," counted Kinoshita. "*Eight!* Do you really think you can take eight men at once? I mean, maybe when you were thirty-eight, but now . . . ?"

"If I have to."

"If you have to? What does that mean?"

"It means I hope I don't have to," said Nighthawk calmly, as he turned to face his pursuers.

The largest of the eight men stopped by a glittering outcropping of purplish crystal. "You picked a hell of a planet to die on, Widowmaker," he said.

Nighthawk and Kinoshita picked up his radio signal with almost no static, and the former answered into his helmet's transmitter: "Then don't kill me."

The man threw back his head and laughed heartily. "You've got a wonderful sense of humor! I don't remember your having any back on Tundra. Five years bumming around the galaxy has done wonders for you."

"I don't suppose you'd like to tell me who you are, and why you're here?"

"Are you kidding?" demanded the man.

"I just want to know what name to put on your grave," came the answer. Kinoshita noted that even the tenor of the older man's voice had changed. Nighthawk had totally vanished; it was the Widowmaker speaking now.

The man gestured with his hand, and his seven cohorts instantly spread out, always keeping outcrops between themselves and Nighthawk.

"You got any short prayers, Widowmaker? I don't think you've got time for a long one."

"You're sure you want to go through with this?"

"Am *I* sure?" The man laughed again. "You got balls, Widowmaker; I'll give you that. But I've got eight guns, and we're well protected. You're two old men out in the open. What are you going to do now?"

"Applaud your superior generalship, I suppose," said Nighthawk.

He held his hands out so they could see he wasn't holding any weapons, then clapped them together once.

As metal plate struck metal plate, it was as if a bomb had exploded. At the sound of Nighthawk's hands striking each other, every outcrop within a quarter mile collapsed like so much broken glass, burying the men standing beside or behind them.

"Shoot this in the air," said Nighthawk, pulling a small bullet gun out of a hidden pouch on his thigh and handing it to Kinoshita. As Kinoshita began firing it every few seconds, creating ear-shattering explosion after explosion, Nighthawk withdrew his Burner and put a lethal burst of solid, silent light into each of the eight men as they struggled to dig themselves out from beneath the crystal shards.

"Jesus!" muttered Kinoshita, looking at the carnage. "Jesus!"

"You look upset," noted Nighthawk calmly as he walked back and rejoined him.

"I keep forgetting who you are," said Kinoshita. "It was like a walk in the park for you! Sixty-two years old, and you wiped out eight men without drawing a deep breath!"

"Would you be less impressed if I were thirty-two years old?" asked Nighthawk dryly.

"How the hell did you know it would work on an airless world?"

"I told you: it has an atmosphere. No air, no molecules. No molecules, no way for sound to travel."

"And that's why you wore the metal-plated gloves?"

"I knew they'd make a noise, and I couldn't be sure I could fire the pistol before they shot me down."

"You also had to know they'd stand next to the outcroppings," added Kinoshita.

"Well, I figured that between my reputation and a display of confidence, they'd make sure they had some cover before the shooting started. And by standing in the open, where they could see me if I made any sudden moves, it encouraged them to take cover before they pulled their weapons."

"It's just *business* to you, isn't it?"

Nighthawk shook his head. "It used to be my business. It isn't anymore."

"Sometimes you can't hide from who you are."

"I'm Jefferson Nighthawk."

"And the Widowmaker."

"That's not who I am. It's who I *was*."

Something in the tone of his voice convinced Kinoshita not to continue the discussion. Instead he walked over to the eight corpses, turning a few over with the toe of his boot, studying their faces.

"That's quite a haul," he said at last.

"There are no more men than there were five minutes ago," responded Nighthawk, unimpressed.

"That's not what I mean. I recognize three of these faces. I've seen them on Wanted posters. I'll bet there were prices on the others, too."

"Good," said Nighthawk. "It means I won't have to answer a charge of murder if they're ever found."

"Found?" asked Kinoshita, puzzled.

"Right. Let's get to work. We've got time to bury them before nightfall."

"Are you crazy? I'll bet the lot of them are worth more than half a million credits. Let's pack 'em in the cargo hold and take them to the nearest bounty station."

"Not interested."

"You're running through money pretty quickly," said Kinoshita. "Here's a chance to add to your bankroll. Legitimately."

"I said no."

"Why not?"

"Because I'm not the Widowmaker anymore. I'm retired. I don't kill men for bounties."

"You're crazy!" snapped Kinoshita. "They're already dead! What's wrong with hauling them to a bounty station?"

"Nothing's wrong with it," answered Nighthawk. "I'm just not going to do it."

"What *do* you plan to do for money?"

"If I need it, I'll work for it."

"And *this* wasn't work?" demanded Kinoshita.

"A century ago it was work. Today it was survival, nothing more."

"What *is* work?" persisted Kinoshita. "You're no farmer. You're no artist. You don't know shit about investing. You're too old to do heavy labor. If you're not going to claim these bounties, maybe you'd better consider becoming a marksman in a carnival like that Billybuck Dancer."

Nighthawk stared at him silently for a long moment, until Kinoshita shifted uncomfortably. Finally he spoke.

"These men were fools. I'd never chase someone onto a world of his own choosing. And having come here, they were even bigger fools for facing me. There's no price on my head, no reward for killing you. If they wanted to kill us, all they had to do was blow our ship away and then leave. We'd have no food, almost no oxygen, and no way of radioing for help."

"Son of a bitch!" exclaimed Kinoshita. "I never thought of that!"

"Neither did they," said Nighthawk, making no attempt to keep the contempt from his voice. "But just because *they* were fools, it doesn't mean all the men out here are fools. The Frontier is a hard place, and it breeds hard men and women. Most of the fools die young, and I don't plan to spend the rest of my life facing what's left. I told you: I spent enough time in death's company that I cherish the years that remain to me. The Widow-maker's retired. For good."

"But this is a different case," said Kinoshita. "No one's asking you to go out after the Oligarchy's Most Wanted list. These men are already dead, and there just happens to be paper on them. Why can't we just pack them in the hold and turn them in? You may never have had to worry about money before, but you do now. This ship cost a bundle, and you'll never recoup your loss on Churchill II, and . . ."

"I said no."

"But—"

"Why did they come after me?" asked Nighthawk.

"Because you killed three of their friends."

"And why did those three come after me?"

"Because your first clone killed the Marquis of Queensbury."

"So I killed one man, and three came after me. Then I killed those three, and eight more came after me. It's a fucking geometrical progression. I'm sure each them has half a dozen friends who will want my blood once they find out that I killed them . . . so it stops here. We bury them, we leave the planet, and no one ever knows what happened here." He paused. "And if no one knows, no one forces me to kill them. Otherwise, one of these days I'll have to go up against one I can't kill."

"All right," said Kinoshita. "I see your point."

"Then let's get to work."

Nighthawk burned eight graves in the ground with his laser. Then he and Kinoshita rolled the bodies into them and covered them with tons of crystal shards. Finally, because he was a thorough man, he blew away every outcropping within a mile of the graves, so no one could chance upon the one spot where the natural cover had been upset.

And, hopeful that he could finally live the life of tranquility he so coveted, Jefferson Nighthawk took off from Bolingbroke VI and sped deeper into the Inner Frontier.

Chapter 12

Nighthawk had been in a black mood since leaving the Bolingbroke system, and Kinoshita had given him as wide a berth as possible within the cramped confines of the ship.

They passed several inhabited worlds. Each time Nighthawk would find some reason not to set the ship down, and they sped farther and farther away from populated areas of the Inner Frontier.

Finally Kinoshita could take the silence no longer.

"Are you ever going to speak again?" he demanded, rotating his chair to face Nighthawk, who was sitting motionless in the captain's chair.

"I'm speaking right now."

"You know what I mean."

"I've got nothing to say," replied Nighthawk, staring without interest at one of the viewscreens at the front of the small cabin.

"Bolingbroke's nine days behind us and you haven't said ten words since we left," complained Kinoshita bitterly. "I'm going stir-crazy!"

"If you're unhappy, I'll drop you off anywhere you want," said Nighthawk.

"I don't want to be dropped off!" snapped Kinoshita. "I just need to hear a human voice."

"You're hearing it right now. Happy?"

"What the hell's the matter with you, Jefferson? We hid all the bodies on Bolingbroke. There's no chance that anyone's going to find them in this lifetime, probably not ever. No one's coming after you. You've got your health. So what's got you so pissed off?"

Nighthawk finally turned to face him. "I would think it'd be obvious," he said.

"Not to me."

"Look," said Nighthawk. "I went into the deep freeze for a hundred and twelve years. I'd become a monster, and I lived in pain every day for close to a decade before they put me under. I awoke to a universe where everything had changed, where every single person I knew had been dead for decades. But I told myself that I had one advantage: I wouldn't have the problems that usually accrue to retired men in my profession. There'd be no young guns out to build their reputations, no old guns with scores to settle. They were all dead, and I could spend my final years in some semblance of peace and tranquility."

He paused, and Kinoshita could see the bitterness on his face as well as hear it in his voice. "So what happens? I find out that not only don't I have that advantage, but I don't even know the men who want to kill me, or why they're after me."

"We *had* to create those clones to pay for your upkeep. You know that."

"Damn it, Ito—I didn't have to go into the fucking cryonics lab! I'm not afraid to die; a hundred and twelve years ago death would have come as a welcome relief. I submitted myself to the freezing process because I weighed all the possibilities, and I could see myself enjoying a comfortable, tranquil old age once they developed a cure. If I'd known that I was going to be hunted by men I never saw before . . ." He shrugged. "I think I might have endured the pain for one more month a century ago and gotten it over with."

"Don't even think that!" said Kinoshita firmly. "If you'd died, there would be a hell of a lot more evil abroad in the galaxy today."

Nighthawk stared curiously at him. "I don't know what you're talking about."

"Your clones did what they had to do, what they were created for," answered Kinoshita. "They went out and killed the bad guys—and for every enemy they made, they earned the gratitude of hundreds more."

"That's comforting in a detached, academic way," replied Nighthawk. "But no one's shooting at my clones."

"There are tens of thousands of oxygen worlds on the Frontier. I'm sure we can find one where nobody knows you, where no one's ever even heard of the Widowmaker."

"Didn't someone quote me some very discouraging odds about that not too long ago?" asked Nighthawk with an ironic smile.

"What do you want me to say?"

"Nothing," came the reply. "It was you who wanted *me* to talk, remember?"

"All right," said Kinoshita, leaning back in his chair and rotating it from one side to another. "We'll talk about something else."

"Fine."

"So how did you become, well, what you are, in the first place?"

"What I am is an old man, and I got here by outliving my friends and my enemies."

"You know what I mean," said Kinoshita doggedly. "I became a law-man because I saw my parents shot down in our own house by a thief who panicked when they stumbled upon him. How did you become the Widow-maker?"

Nighthawk shrugged. "I had a talent for killing people."

"What kind of answer is that?" demanded Kinoshita. "How did you know you had this talent? When did you develop it? According to the history books, you were already the Widowmaker when you were eighteen. How old were you when you killed your first man?"

"I was very young."

"How young?"

"Very." Kinoshita shot a quick look at Nighthawk, who seemed more disinterested in giving answers than uncomfortable about them.

"Whom did you kill?"

"Someone who deserved it." Nighthawk paused. "I don't think I've ever killed anyone who didn't deserve it. At least, once upon a time I thought that . . . but I suppose I could be wrong. Age tends to make you second-guess yourself."

"Who was the toughest killer you ever went up against?" continued Kinoshita.

"They were *all* tough."

"I mean—"

"I know what you mean," interrupted Nighthawk. "You want me to name one notorious outlaw, a Santiago or a Conrad Bland. Well, I can't."

"Why not?"

"Think of it this way: Just about everyone on the Frontier carries some kind of weapon, don't they?"

"Yes."

"Have you ever seen a dead man walking around with one?"

Kinoshita frowned. "Of course not. I don't know what you're getting at."

"What I'm trying to say is that every man you see walking around with a weapon in his holster is undefeated in mortal combat . . . and if there's paper on him, you know he's been a participant at least once. Reputations mean nothing. You have to treat each and every one of them as if they're the toughest opponent you'll ever face."

"You're a cautious man," remarked Kinoshita.

"That's how you stay alive out here."

"Your second clone was like that, too."

"Why shouldn't he have been?" replied Nighthawk. "After all, he was me."

"The first clone didn't possess that sense of caution."

"From everything I've been given to understand, the first clone was cannon fodder. They created him with no memories and sent him off on his mission."

"It was the best they could do at the time—and he did accomplish that mission."

"They should have waited until they found a way to give him my memories, the way you did with the second one."

"If they'd waited another two months, you'd have been awakened and evicted while you still had eplasia," answered Kinoshita.

"Still, it was murder, sending him out with no experience, no memory, nothing but some physical skills."

"They were *your* skills."

"There's a difference," said Nighthawk. "I developed them to survive in my environment. They became a part of me, and I used them intelligently. This poor clone may have had my gifts, but he couldn't possibly have had my instincts. *That's* why it was murder."

"The second clone thought so, too," said Kinoshita. "That's why he killed Colonel Hernandez."

"He saved me the trouble," said Nighthawk. "Or the pleasure."

"I thought you didn't take any pleasure from killing people," observed Kinoshita.

"Usually. But I think I'd take an enormous pleasure in avenging Jefferson Nighthawk."

"You make it sound like Colonel Hernandez killed you."

"He did. A version of me, anyway."

"Both of the clones seemed to feel an almost mystical bond with you," said Kinoshita. "Do you feel it, too?"

Nighthawk shook his head. "I'm the original. I don't owe either of them anything, except a vote of thanks for earning enough money to keep me alive. *They* owe *me* everything, including their existence."

"You know, you can be a cold son of a bitch sometimes."

"We can always go back to not talking."

"Not if you want me to stay sane, we can't."

"As you wish," said Nighthawk, getting to his feet. "But first I'm going to get a beer."

He walked to the galley, put in his order, waited a few seconds for the mechanism to respond, and made his way back to the pilot's chair.

"Next ship we buy knows how to chill its glasses," said Nighthawk, taking a long swallow of the beer.

"*Are* we buying another ship?"

"Depends on whether those guys back on Bolingbroke got off any messages to their friends," answered Nighthawk. "That's why I'm heading toward the Core on a straight line. It should make it easier to spot anyone who's chasing us."

"After nine days I think we're safe," offered Kinoshita. *What a damned silly thing to say. We're safe? Hell, whoever's not chasing the Widowmaker is the one who's safe.*

"Probably."

"And you've passed some interesting worlds the last couple of days."

"One world's pretty much like another."

"I disagree. There was a beautiful one on the outskirts of that last star cluster."

"I don't care if it's beautiful," interrupted Nighthawk. "I care if it's peaceful."

It may be peaceful now, but it won't be once you land on it. You attract trouble the way honey attracts flies.

"What exactly *are* you looking for?" asked Kinoshita. "Do you still want to grow flowers and watch birds?"

"I don't know," responded Nighthawk. "What I mostly want is to be left alone."

"I don't think it's your nature to be left alone." *And I have a feeling that it's not the galaxy's nature to leave you alone.*

"Well, like I told you once before, I'd like a wife, someone to grow old along with me." Kinoshita seemed about to say something and Nighthawk held up his hand. "Someone who doesn't look like you," he added with a smile.

"What happens to me when you find her?"

"What do you think should happen?"

"I'm not leaving you," said Kinoshita adamantly.

"Maybe not, but you're sure as hell sleeping at the other end of the house."

"I don't know if you're joking or not."

"About sleeping at the other end?" repeated Nighthawk. "Absolutely not."

"I mean about my staying."

"I don't know why you want to."

"I have my reasons."

"You plan to share them with me someday?" asked Nighthawk.

"Someday," promised Kinoshita.

Chapter 13

The world was called Tumbleweed. It was the only habitable planet within ten star systems, which gave it more traffic than such a nondescript world would ordinarily receive. There was a refueling station, a shipping depot, an assay office for mining claims in all the neighboring systems, a postal forwarding station for the worlds deeper into the Frontier, a single small city that had evolved from a Tradertown, a huge freshwater sea, and a few enormous totally-automated farms operated by robots laboring under the watchful eye of a tiny handful of human overseers.

"I've got a good feeling about this one," said Nighthawk as they stepped out of the ship.

"I hope you're right," said Kinoshita. "I'm tired of traveling."

"Nobody forced you to."

"I know."

"Well, let's get over to Customs."

Customs was nothing but a machine that registered their passports and added molecular long-term visas to them. Then they were transferred to a bullet-shaped transparent shuttle that glided inches above the ground and took them to the center of the small city.

"Lots of people here, compared to some of the worlds we've seen," remarked Nighthawk.

"Just the same, I'd hardly call it a megalopolis," answered Kinoshita.

"No, but it could mean property costs a little more." Nighthawk paused and turned to Kinoshita. "You've been keeping track of our finances. Where do we stand?"

Kinoshita pulled out a pocket computer and queried it, then looked up. "You've got a little less than two million credits," he announced. "As far as I can tell, the insurance money on Churchill hasn't come through yet, though it could just be slow registering in your account."

"Only two million?"

Kinoshita smiled in amusement. "What's so only about two million credits?"

"How much cash did you bring back with you from Pericles?"

"About five million. But the moment I entered the Oligarchy, it was subject to taxes . . . so it really came to just under three million."

"I'm a little confused," said Nighthawk. "The clones were created because the interest on my principal wasn't enough to pay the cryonics lab, right?"

"That's correct."

"But that was *interest*, and you made it up with the money you brought back. What happened to the principal? There must have been six or seven million credits' worth."

"The interest kept you frozen," answered Kinoshita. "The principal paid for the cure and the cosmetic surgery and your rehabilitation. In fact, it didn't quite pay for it; I had to add some of the Pericles money to it."

"Okay, that sounds reasonable enough," said Nighthawk with a shrug. "I was just wondering."

"It's your money. You have a right to ask."

"We have reached the city limits," announced the shuttle. "I require an address."

"I don't have an address," said Nighthawk. "Take us to the best hotel."

"I do not know which is the best hotel," answered the shuttle.

"Okay, take us to the most expensive hotel."

The shuttle immediately turned left, then right, and soon pulled up to a small hotel.

"Welcome to the Sand Castle," said the robot doorman, coming forward to take their luggage.

"I don't see any sand," remarked Nighthawk.

"This entire section of the city is built on a sand dune," explained the robot. "Hence the name of the hotel."

"I don't see any castle, either, but let it pass."

The robot, which had not been asked a question nor given an order, froze, trying to interpret what Nighthawk had said. Kinoshita stepped forward and directed it to take them to the hotel's registration desk.

Another robot greeted them and, after registering their voiceprints and retinas and matching their credit ratings to their thumbprints, assigned them a pair of rooms on the second floor.

"Have our baggage taken up to our rooms," said Nighthawk. "I want to grab some dinner. Where's your restaurant?"

"I regret to inform you that the Sand Castle's restaurant does not open until seven o'clock local time."

"Where's the closest open restaurant?"

"I am not programmed to send residents to our competition," replied the robot.

"Are you programmed to make value judgments?" asked Nighthawk.

"Yes, in certain instances."

Nighthawk pulled out a pistol. "All right, let's put that programming to the test."

"I must inform you that I have no sense of self-preservation and thus will not respond to threats to my person," said the robot.

"Shut up and listen," said Nighthawk. "If you don't tell me where I can find the closest restaurant, I'm going to blow out the two plate-glass windows in your lobby. I want you to compute their cost, compare it to the cost of losing my patronage for a single meal, and then make a decision."

"The closest restaurant is the Tumbleweed Roadhouse, one hundred thirty-seven feet to the south of this building, sir," said the robot instantly.

"I knew I could count on you," said Nighthawk, holstering his weapon. He turned to Kinoshita. "Let's go."

"What if he reports you to the law?" asked Kinoshita as they walked out the door and turned south.

"Do you know anyone who ever got arrested for threatening to shoot a window?"

"No," admitted Kinoshita with a smile. "No, I must admit I don't." He paused. "What would you have done if the robot hadn't answered?"

"Nothing. No sense shooting the place up if his programming wouldn't let him answer me."

They reached the Tumbleweed Roadhouse, an unprepossessing restaurant, and soon seated themselves at a table. A small, wiry blonde woman approached them.

"What'll it be, gentlemen?" she asked.

"A couple of beers and a menu," answered Nighthawk.

"Don't need a menu. We've got steak, and we've got stew. Take your choice."

"That's not much of a selection."

"My cook quit, my waiter's got the day off, and I don't believe in robots."

"So who did the cooking?" asked Kinoshita.

"I did. And it's a damned sight better than you'll get at the Sand Castle."

"What makes you think we're from the Sand Castle?"

"It's the only place in town that's too snobbish to serve dinner at dinnertime," she replied.

"You've got a point," said Nighthawk.

"So what'll you have?"

"You choose."

"You look like a steak-and-potato man to me."

"I've been a soya man for half a century. Time I started to get used to real meat again."

"Hey!" yelled a young man, dressed in colorful silks and satins and sporting an impressive array of weapons, from a nearby table where he sat with three of his friends. "Enough jabbering! We want some service."

"If you don't like it, complain to the owner," said the woman.

"Fine. Where is he?"

She turned to him and put her hands on her hips. "You're looking at her."

"You don't want to get me mad, lady," said the young man. "Just come over and take our orders."

"I'm taking this gentleman's order," she said. "And no one tells me what to do in my own place. If you don't like the service, there's the door."

"Go take care of them," said Nighthawk. "I don't want to cause any trouble."

"You're not causing any," she replied. "*They* are." She raised her voice. "And the more they cause, the longer they can wait. What's the point in owning your own place if you can't tell anyone to go to hell?"

"Goddammit, Sarah!" said another of the young men.

"You know what happened the last time you hassled me," she said ominously. "You want more of the same?"

"Come on, Sarah," he said defensively. "We just want some food."

"Then you can damned well wait your turn. You know I'm short-handed."

"What the hell did you do to him?" asked Kinoshita curiously. "The last time he hassled you, I mean?"

"I broke a chair over his head," she answered. "*Nobody* gives me orders in my own place. Two steaks, right?"

"Right," said Nighthawk.

"Don't you worry," she said to Kinoshita. "If he gets uppity, I'll protect you." She glanced at Nighthawk. "You don't look like you need any protecting."

She went off to wait on the other table, and returned with the steaks about ten minutes later.

"Hope you like 'em rare," she said.

"Rare'll do," answered Nighthawk.

"You here on business?"

"Nope."

"Just passing through?"

Nighthawk shrugged. "I don't know. We're looking for someplace to settle down."

She looked from Nighthawk to Kinoshita, then back again. "You two . . . ah . . . ?"

"Just friends."

"Well, if I can show you around, just ask."

"I thought you were all alone here."

"Look around," she said. "When those four would-be Widowmakers finish, you're all that's left."

"Widowmakers?" asked Nighthawk.

"Just an expression. There hasn't been a Widowmaker in more than a century."

"Well, as long as we're all the customers you've got, why not have a seat and a beer?" suggested Nighthawk. "My treat."

"I'll take the seat," she said, sitting down at the table. "But I'll take a rain check on the beer until the place is closed." She extended a hand. "I'm Sarah Jenner."

"Jefferson Nighthawk. And this is Ito Kinoshita."

"Nighthawk, Nighthawk," she repeated thoughtfully. "Seems I've heard that name before."

"I've never been here before."

"I've only been here five years myself. Hell, I don't think we've got two hundred natives on the whole world. If you grew up somewhere else, Tumbleweed looks idyllic; but if you grew up here, you can't wait to see the rest of the galaxy."

"Where are you from originally?"

"Pollux IV," she said. "Inner Frontier born and bred. I grew up on a farm out there."

"What brought you to Tumbleweed and what keeps you here?" asked Nighthawk. "As long as we're thinking of settling here, we ought to know what its virtues are."

"It's empty and it's clean," answered Sarah Jenner. "That's what got me here. And inertia keeps me here."

"Nothing else?"

"I've got a son," said Sarah. "It seemed like a nice place to raise him."

"If you're shorthanded, why not ask him to fill in here?"

"He's half the galaxy away, on Aristotle."

"The university planet?"

Sarah nodded. "It took every credit I had, but it's been worth it." She paused. "It's lonely without him. Still, I keep busy. I've got my business, and my reading, and my birds."

"You raise birds?" asked Kinoshita.

"I watch them."

"So does he."

She looked at Nighthawk with renewed interest. "You're a birder?"

"Not really. But I think I could become one."

"Hell, I'll take you out tomorrow morning," she said. "I know some wonderful places for watching." Suddenly she stopped. "That is, if you're interested."

"Why not?" said Nighthawk.

"I thought we were looking for property," said Kinoshita.

"Nothing wrong with property that's got birds on it," replied Nighthawk.

"I like you, Jefferson Nighthawk," she said. "You don't find many men out here who like birding."

"I like you, too," said Nighthawk. "You don't find many people anywhere who like to read."

"I *knew* it!" she said happily. "You're a reader, too!" She paused. "Tell me you're not a lawman before I get too fond of you."

"Why?"

"Because if you're here to apply for the job, it's only fair to tell you that you've got a life expectancy of less than two weeks."

"Oh?"

Sarah nodded. "That's another reason I sent my son away. Tumbleweed is a beautiful little world, but lately it's become a drug drop. They smuggle alphanella seeds from ten or twelve secret farms to the Oligarchy, and this is one of the drop points. The last couple of lawmen we had tried to stop the trade. They were damned good men." She pointed through a window. "They're buried about half a mile in that direction. So before I get too fond of you, I want to make sure you're not here for the job. I know they've been advertising it all across the Inner Frontier."

"I'm an old man. Why would I want to be a lawman?"

"You're not that old," she replied. "And you've got that look about you."

"What look?"

"I don't know. A look that says it wouldn't be a good idea to have you as an enemy."

"I just want to be left alone."

"Well, if you don't chew alphanella seeds or wear a badge, there's no reason why anyone should bother you," said Sarah. "Just don't stand too close to me if any strangers show up."

"Why not?"

"I'm on their hit list."

"The drug runners?"

She nodded. "Tumbleweed used to be a decent place to live. I want it to be again. So I reported them to the Oligarchy. They set up a sting operation on Raleigh II, and killed about ten of them . . . but one of the survivors found out that I was the informer, and since then there've been attempts on my life."

"And you're still here?"

"I'm harder to kill than you might think," she said, her expression a cross between pride and arrogance.

"Well, if you go around hitting young gunmen over the heads with chairs, I can believe it."

"It sounds like this world needs a protector," offered Kinoshita.

"At least one," agreed Sarah.

"I wonder where it can find one," continued Kinoshita.

"Beats the hell out of me," said Nighthawk, totally expressionless. "I just hope when he gets here, he protects me, too."

Sarah stared at him. "I said it before: You don't strike me as a man who needs protection."

"Sooner or later everyone needs it," said Nighthawk.

"Hey, Sarah, can we get some coffee?" asked the young man at the other table.

She stared at him impassively.

"Please," he added hastily.

"Happy to," she said, getting up and vanishing into the kitchen.

"Well?" asked Kinoshita.

"Well what?"

"Do you want me to spell it out?"

"I'm too old to go back to being a lawman. This place can find some other savior."

"And *her*?"

"I like her. She's bright and she's tough." He paused. "I think we'll stay in town a few days so I can keep an eye on her. Just in case."

"But you won't take the job?"

"I gave up the hero business a century ago."

"Sure you did."

"I did," repeated Nighthawk decisively.

You're fighting a losing battle, thought Kinoshita. *You can deny it all you want, but you can't help being the Widowmaker. That's why you're going to stay in town . . . and in a curious way, that's why I'm going to stay, too.*

Chapter 14

"Got one," said Nighthawk.

"Where?" asked Sarah, following him down the winding path between the tall trees and aiming her lens in the direction he was pointing.

"Top branch. Silver, almost phosphorescent. See how she shines when the sun hits her?"

"Yes, I see her now. She's gorgeous!" She lowered her lens and turned to him. "And you can see her with your naked eye? That's amazing!"

"I've always had pretty good eyesight."

"That's not just good—it's exceptional. Especially for a man in his fifties."

"Older than that."

"Oh?" she said. "How old are you, Jefferson?"

Nighthawk smiled ironically. "Well, there's some debate about that."

"It sounds like there's a story there."

"Someday I'll tell it to you." He looked back into the tree. "So what do you call that bird?"

"Officially, it's not a bird at all."

"It's not?"

"They only have birds on Earth. It's an avian—a flying animal. But it looks like a bird, and it acts like a bird, so I call it a bird."

"Makes sense to me. What kind of bird?"

"Almost none of them have been named yet," replied Sarah. "Avianology isn't one of Tumbleweed's more popular pastimes." She paused. "I guess that gives you the right to name her anything you want."

"I think I'll call her a Silver Sarah."

"I'm flattered." Suddenly, she smiled. "You know, if I were to let my hair grow out, it would almost be that color."

"Why don't you?"

"Being blonde makes me feel young."

"Is that important?"

"Don't *you* ever wish you were young again?"

He shook his head. "I'll settle for being old and alive. The graveyards are full of men who were young and foolish."

"I'll wager you put a lot of them there yourself," said Sarah.

"Why should you say that?"

"Just a guess." She shrugged and shifted the box lunch from one hand to the other. "Probably I'm wrong. I think I know most of the famous killers, good and bad, on the Frontier, but I've never seen you before. Your name rings a bell, but I can't quite place it."

"Don't blame yourself," replied Nighthawk. "You're a century too late."

"I don't understand."

"A hundred and twelve years ago I lay down to take a nap. I just woke up a few months back."

She stared at him curiously. "You were frozen?"

"Yes."

Her eyes widened. "On Deluros?"

He nodded.

"Oh, Jesus—you're *him*!"

"Probably."

"You're the Widowmaker! You're really him!" she continued excitedly. "I'd heard rumors, legends, that you'd contracted some horrible disease and had yourself frozen until it was cured, but no one ever knew any details. I knew you had that look about you! I knew it!" Suddenly she laughed and shook her head. "Here I am, babbling like a schoolgirl. I'm sorry."

"You're not afraid to be with the Widowmaker?"

"You always fought for the good guys," she replied.

"Sometimes I did bad things on their behalf," he pointed out.

"Necessary things. You were the best lawman and bounty hunter who ever lived."

"That was a long time ago. Before you were born. Hell, before your great-grandparents were born. Now I'm just an old man who wants to learn birding and catch up on my reading."

"You can tell me the truth, Jefferson," she said. "I'm on *your* side. You're here for the drug runners, aren't you?"

He shook his head. "I'm here for me."

"Really?"

"Really," replied Nighthawk. "Why did you inform on them in the first place? They'd surely have left you alone if you'd kept quiet."

"My son had a drug problem. He chewed alphanella. It almost killed him. When I found out where he was getting the seed, I blew the whistle." She stared at him. "I'd do it again."

"You must have known they'd come after you."

"I was hoping the Oligarchy's sting would nail them all," said Sarah. "But I'm prepared to live with the consequences of my actions."

"That's more than most people are prepared to do," noted Nighthawk.

"That's their problem."

"How many drug runners are there?"

"Who knows? Five, ten, twenty. They recruit killers of every shape and size from all over the Frontier." She smiled wryly. "A real equal-opportunity employer."

"Maybe the Widowmaker can lend a hand."

"It's not necessary," she replied. "You're not here for them, and I'm not afraid of them."

"I admire your courage," said Nighthawk. "But it does you no credit. Nobody in his right mind faces odds of twenty-to-one."

"*You* did."

Nighthawk smiled. "There are plenty of men who would swear that I was never in my right mind." The smile vanished. "Besides, it was my job. It's not yours."

"This is my home. I'm not running away."

"I'm not suggesting that you do," said Nighthawk. "I just think that you could use a little help."

"I appreciate your offer, but the answer is no," said Sarah adamantly. "I'm the one they want; I'm the one who has to cope with the situation."

"Whatever you say." Nighthawk walked along the path, searching for more birds. "There's a bright red one at ten o'clock."

"I know what you're thinking."

"I'm thinking that if you keep talking, you're going to frighten it away."

"You're thinking that you'll pretend to agree with me, but when the drug runners show up, you'll protect me."

"I'm too old to protect anyone." Nighthawk looked to his right. "Purple-and-gold one at three o'clock."

"I remember hearing legends about you when I was a girl," continued Sarah. "You were one of my heroes. You never walked away from a fight in your life."

"I ducked one for a hundred and twelve years."

"But when you were ready, you won."

Nighthawk looked uneasy. "*I* didn't win. The doctors did. And it took a pair of younger Widowmakers to pay them."

"I don't understand."

"I'm not totally sure I do, either," he replied. "Are you getting hungry? We could have lunch."

She stood in the trail in front of him, staring into his eyes. "Why *are* you here?"

"Just chance."

"I don't believe in chance."

"I didn't believe a healthy man could contract eplasia. Fat lot of good it did me."

"What was it like?"

"Pretty bad."

"I've heard of it, of course, but I've never seen anyone with it."

"Consider yourself lucky," said Nighthawk.

"I take it you don't want to talk about it?"

"I don't even want to think about it. Children dream of things that look half as bad and wake up screaming."

She set the basket down, pulled out a blanket, spread it on the ground, and sat down. Nighthawk joined her a moment later, and she passed him a sandwich and a container of beer, then served herself.

"What did you mean about two younger Widowmakers?"

"When I entered the cryonics lab, I left a fortune with my attorneys. They were to invest it conservatively and pay for my upkeep with the interest." He smiled wryly. "That's before Nadine Kirogi became Governor of Deluros VIII and started applying her theories to the economy. The result was twenty-three percent inflation for six years, and suddenly the interest wasn't enough to cover my expenses."

"What happened?" asked Sarah. "They obviously didn't throw you out in the street."

"What happened was that an offer came in for the Widowmaker's services. I was incapable of going out to the Frontier—hell, I was incapable of even standing up—but they decided to create a clone and send *him* out."

"I thought that was illegal."

"When did a little thing like legality bother doctors or lawyers?"

"So the clone went out and did what he was supposed to do?" she asked.

"I think so."

"You *think* so?"

"He was very young and very naive. He never made it back, and the man he was working for swore he didn't fulfill his contract." Nighthawk paused. "Of course, the man he was working for also killed him, so I tend to discount his statements. But the fact remains that the clone only earned half the money he was promised—the remainder was due upon completion of the job—and two years later I was in the same situation again. This time they managed to create a clone that possessed not only my skills but also my memories. I gather that caused him some difficulty—the memories were a century out of date—but he accomplished his mission, and that's why I'm here."

"Where is he now?"

Nighthawk shrugged. "Out on the Rim with a new name and a new face, according to Kinoshita."

"What has Kinoshita got to do with all this?"

"He trained the first clone."

"And the second?"

"The second didn't need any training, but Kinoshita traveled with him. He knew if he ever came back to Deluros they'd terminate him—after all, they'd broken half a dozen laws just by creating him—so he sent Kinoshita back with the money that kept me alive while he established a new identity."

"And you've never met him?"

"Never."

"Aren't you curious?"

"Not really. I know what I was like when I was forty-one, which is what he'd be now."

"But to see a perfect replica of yourself . . ."

"He's not a perfect replica anymore. And if he wanted to see me, he'd find me. I'm not hiding from anyone." He paused. "He did his job. He's under no further obligation to me or anyone else. I think if I were him—and in a way, I am—I'd have no desire to see the original, either. It's almost like coming face-to-face with your God, or your creator."

"That second clone—was he the one who caused all the ruckus on Pericles IV?"

"Yes."

"I should have known that nothing short of the Widowmaker could have pulled that off!"

"How could you know?" said Nighthawk. "The Widowmaker vanished a century ago."

"The Widowmaker is more than you, Jefferson," she explained. "It's you, and your clones, and your legend. You're more alive today than you ever were."

"Then maybe you should consider letting the Widowmaker help you."

Sarah shook her head. "For your own good, I can't let you do it."

"Don't worry about me," replied Nighthawk, totally without bravado. "Over the years a lot of men have tried to kill me. I'm still here."

"That's not it," she said.

"Then what's the problem? I like you, and I want to help you."

"You have no official standing here. And the Oligarchy's sting nailed all the known members of the gang. To the best of my knowledge, none of the men or aliens who are still at large have prices on their heads." She paused. "Don't you see? If you kill them, you're breaking the law. It seems ridiculous on the face of it, but you could conceivably be arrested for murder."

"We can sort it out later," answered Nighthawk. "If worse comes to worst, I'll just leave Tumbleweed and go further toward the Core."

"No," she said firmly. "I can't let you do it on my behalf."

"And that's the only reason?"

She stared at him silently for a long moment. "There could be as many as twenty of them."

"And you plan to face them alone?"

"Of course not," she responded. "But I plan to protect myself. This is my world; I know where to hide, how to set traps. What would *you* do?"

"I'd wait for them at the spaceport and explain they weren't wanted here."

"And when they laughed in your face?"

"Not many people laugh at me," said Nighthawk.

"You'd just stand there and face all twenty of them?" she said. "All by yourself?"

"Why don't you leave that to me?"

"Because I like you, too, and I don't want you getting killed on my behalf."

"I don't plan to get killed. I've spent too much time and energy and money staying alive."

"I appreciate your offer, Jefferson," she said, "but it's not your fight."

"We'll discuss it later," said Nighthawk, opening up his cannister of beer.

"Let's discuss it now," she insisted. "You have no legal right to kill any of them. If you face them and lose, you're dead; if you face them and somehow manage to win, you're a felon. I won't be responsible for that."

"All right," he said. "We'll do it your way."

"Thank you."

A long pause.

"Why are you looking at me like that?" he asked.

"You're a man who's gotten his way all his life," she replied. "You gave in too easily."

He smiled. "Try to be a more gracious winner."

"When I'm convinced I *have* won."

"No problem. I've never been an outlaw; I don't plan to start now."

They finished their meal in silence.

"You must have seen a lot of worlds," she said as they got to their feet and began following the trail again.

"A few."

"Tell me about them."

"There's not much to tell. I was always there on business. You start watching birds, you forget to watch for bullets and laser beams." He shrugged. "Besides, it's been over a century. Most of them will have changed beyond recognition by now."

"It seems sad to have been so many places and not to have any memories of them."

"Oh, I have memories. But not of the worlds; just what happened on them."

"Didn't you ever just want to relax?"

"I've been relaxing for the past hundred and twelve years," he replied. "It's an easy habit to get into. Now I'd like to relax for the rest of my life."

"So you really came here to settle down?"

"It seems remote. That's what I need."

"Why?"

"The less people, the less enemies."

"All your enemies should have been dead for fifty or sixty years," she said.

"You'd think so, wouldn't you?" he said with a trace of bitterness.

"What am I missing?"

"My clones managed to get a few thousand very dangerous people pissed at them." He paused. "At least I knew what *my* enemies looked like. These guys come out of nowhere, and I've never seen any of them before."

"The clones' enemies really come after you?"

"I'm the Widowmaker," said Nighthawk. "That's all they have to know."

"How long have you been out of the cryonics lab?"

"Maybe four or five months. Then I spent some time in the hospital, getting cosmetic surgery and regaining my strength, so I haven't been on my own too long—but it was long enough for them to burn down my house on Churchill, and I had to kill some of them on Pondoro, and more on Bolingbroke."

"And you didn't know any of them?"

"Not a one."

"Well, some deity with a sense of humor is getting even with you for giving children nightmares. You're living a nightmare yourself."

"At least I'm still living it," said Nighthawk. He ran a hand through his thick shock of gray hair. "Anyway, that's why I wanted a remote, sparsely populated little world like Tumbleweed. On a place like this I can see them coming."

"Perhaps," agreed Sarah. "But still, that's no way for anyone to live."

"Says the woman who's waiting for a gang of drug runners to come looking for her."

"I'll hide from them and set traps for them and whatever happens, that will be the end of it."

"If there's one thing I've learned, it's that that's *never* the end of it."

"Those bastards turned my son into a seed chewer. I informed on them, and I'd do it again." She set her jaw. "I did what I had to do. I'll take what comes."

"Well," said Nighthawk with a shrug, "If I can't talk you out of it, I can't talk you out of it." He started off down the dirt path. "Let's go find some birds."

They spent the next hour walking through the forest, spotting an occasional bird, exchanging an occasional reminiscence, just relaxing and enjoying each other's company. Nighthawk found himself attracted to her. It certainly wasn't her looks: he'd never been attracted to small, wiry women or to blondes. Probably it was her self-assurance and independence, two traits he admired wherever he found them.

Finally they came to the end of the path and found themselves back at her vehicle, which she had driven to the edge of the forest.

"Shall we go back to town?" she suggested.

"Might as well," replied Nighthawk. "I've got something to do there."

"Hunt for real estate?"

"Not just yet. I think I'll stay in town for a few days and get the feel of the place."

"I think that's a good idea. This isn't exactly a flourishing market. Any property that's for sale today will be for sale next week and next month . . . and probably even next year."

"Good."

"Then, if I'm not being too nosy," she continued, "what's your business?"

"Oh, mostly just paperwork. Where do I go to apply for citizenship?"

"We've only got one government building," she said. "It houses the mayor, the tax collector, the sheriff, the fire department, the building inspector, everything. Probably even the army, if we ever have one."

"Then that's where I want to go."

"It's on the next block," she said as they reached the outskirts of the city and turned onto the main street. "I'll drop you there."

"Fine."

"Would you care to join me for dinner when you're through?"

"Very much," said Nighthawk, as the vehicle came to a stop. "I'll come by as soon as I'm done here. It won't take long."

She left him at the door to the building, drove back to the restaurant, oversaw the changing of the shifts, and was just completing an order for the following week's supplies when Nighthawk walked in.

There was something different about his appearance. It took her about two seconds to spot what it was.

"What the hell is *that*?" she demanded, pointing to the glowing golden badge on his tunic.

He smiled wryly. "Well, I thought as long as I was going to stay here, I ought to be gainfully employed."

Chapter 15

Nighthawk spent an idyllic two weeks. He slept late, ate three hot meals a day, spent most of his time with Sarah Jenner, and his sole duties as a lawman consisted of arresting one unprotesting drunk.

"Maybe they won't come after all," said Kinoshita, sitting in a comfortable wooden chair opposite Nighthawk's desk one evening after dinner. "I mean, hell, there are millions of worlds. If they were smart, they'd open up two dozen new channels. No sense being predictable, not in their business."

"They'll come to Tumbleweed," said Nighthawk with absolute certainty.

"What makes you so sure? Like I said, there are hundreds of possible routes."

"Sarah's here, and they want her."

"You sure she's not just being hysterical?" asked Kinoshita.

"Does she strike you as the hysterical type?"

"No," admitted Kinoshita. "No, she doesn't." He paused. "You're getting fond of her, aren't you?"

"Is there some law against it?"

"No, of course not. But I hear talk that she's got a kid off at college somewhere who had some drug problems."

"I didn't say I was fond of the kid."

"I would think he comes with the mother."

"He's on Aristotle," replied Nighthawk. "It's not as if I have to help raise him. Besides, he may never come back. And if he does, he'll have a degree, which I suspect is more than you or I ever had."

"I'm not trying to interfere," said Kinoshita. "I just worry about you."

"I know. What I don't know is why." Nighthawk stared at him. "I keep thinking you're getting me confused with my clone. You've only known me since I woke up. You may think I'm him, but I'm not."

"I like you."

"That's a pretty lame answer," said Nighthawk. "One of these days I'm going to insist on the truth." He paused. "In the meantime, check with the spaceport and see what ships are due in tonight."

"It's two miles away!" protested Kinoshita.

"I didn't say to walk there. There's half a dozen communication devices in the office. Take your choice."

While Kinoshita was raising the spaceport, Nighthawk walked back to the cells to see if his prisoner needed some coffee, but the man was sleeping it off, and he chose not to wake him. He turned and walked quietly back to the office.

"I think they're on the way," announced Kinoshita.

"Explain."

"There's a ship of Darbeenan registry due to land in an hour. But according to its manifest, it's traveling practically empty, and it's only thirty-eight Standard hours out of Quixote."

"So?"

"They grow alphanella in the jungles of Quixote. And there are all kinds of servicing and refueling facilities there. Why should an empty ship that just took off land here less than two days later?"

"Okay, it makes sense."

"What are you going to do?"

"Whatever I do, I think I'd better do it at the spaceport. Except for you, no one else in this building looks capable of defending himself against the kind of men who figure to be on that ship."

"I'll come with you," said Kinoshita.

Nighthawk shook his head. "You'll stay with Sarah. If they get past me, I want you there."

"You're sure? If I stand with you, there's a lot less chance of them getting past us to Sarah."

"Just do what I say."

Kinoshita sighed. "All right."

"Thanks. I don't want her alerted, so just go on over, order a beer, and if she asks about me tell her I went to bed early. I'm an old man; she'll buy it."

Kinoshita got up and left, and Nighthawk went back to the cells, unlocked the door to the only occupied one, shook his inebriated prisoner awake, and told him to go home. He didn't think he'd be needing the space, but he knew there was a chance that he wouldn't survive the night and he saw no reason to let the drunk go without food and water until someone remembered he was there.

Then he went to check his armory. He searched through it until he found what he wanted, closed up his office, walked out to the official vehicle the planet had provided for him, and drove to the spaceport. He felt he had at least an hour to prepare for his visitors, and he made good use of it.

When the ship landed, he was the only living being on the grounds. He'd sent the skeleton staff home, and stood waiting as the entire crew of the ship—nine men and five aliens—approached the Customs building. They were a mean-looking bunch, all heavily armed.

When they were about thirty yards away, Nighthawk stepped out of the shadows.

"That's far enough," he said.

"Who the hell are you?" demanded one of the men.

"The law."

The man laughed. "You mean they went out and found themselves another sheriff?"

"Actually, my badge says I'm the Commissioner of Police," replied Nighthawk.

"What's the difference?"

"Not much. I'm still the law. And the law says that you have to state your business."

"You go to hell!" snapped the man.

"Then you'd better turn around and go back to your ship," said Nighthawk. "You're not welcome on Tumbleweed, now or any time in the future."

"Do you know who you're talking to, old man?"

"Yeah. I'm talking to a bunch of drug runners who are about to leave the planet."

"We're not here after you. Let us pass."

"Not a chance."

"You got a death wish?" demanded the man. "Look around you. There are fourteen of us."

"That's okay," said Nighthawk. "We've got a big graveyard."

The man looked at him unbelievingly. "Who the hell *are* you, old man?"

"I've had a lot of names," answered Nighthawk. "The one that stuck is the Widowmaker."

"You're *him*? I heard rumors that you were back!"

"For once, the rumors were right."

The man stared at him. "Even the Widowmaker can't take fourteen of us."

"There was a time when I could," answered Nighthawk. "These days I play it safe."

"What do you mean?" asked the man, looking into the shadows.

"Enough talk," said Nighthawk. "Go back to your ship." He paused. "Your weapons stay here."

The man never took his eyes from Nighthawk. "We're not here for you, Widowmaker. We have business with someone else. Let us by and we'll let you live."

"I don't make deals," answered Nighthawk. "Your weapons—now."

The man drew his laser pistol. Nighthawk was faster, and he fired at the man's feet, detonating a small explosive device that was all but invisible in the dim lighting. Four men and two aliens screamed in agony as the force of the explosion blew them twenty feet into the air. Nighthawk hit the other two devices he had planted, and suddenly there was only one remaining man, a teenager who had stood, motionless and transfixed, as the explosions decimated his companions.

Nighthawk stared at him, and put his burner away.

"All right, son," he said. "It's up to you. You can walk away, or you can go for your weapon. There are no more surprises, no more bombs. It's just you and me. Do you think you're up to facing the Widowmaker?"

The teenager stared nervously at him for a long moment, then shook his head.

"Then walk away, and don't let me ever see your face on Tumbleweed again."

"Where'll I go? What will I tell them?"

"I don't much care where you go, and you can tell your bosses that Tumbleweed is off-limits from now on."

"They'll come back for you."

"Like I said, we've got a big graveyard. There's room for everybody."

The teenager backed up a couple of steps, then hesitated and finally stopped.

"I can't go back and tell them that everyone else was killed," he said plaintively. "They'll never believe me. They'll think I sold them out!"

"That's not my problem," said Nighthawk.

"I can't do it!" yelled the teenager.

"Don't be a fool, son."

"No choice!" he wailed. "No choice!"

He reached for his weapon, and was dead before his fingers touched it.

"Stupid!" muttered Nighthawk, walking over and putting another blast into his body, just to be on the safe side. "Just stupid."

He walked to the drug runners' ship, pulled out yet another explosive, placed it into the exhaust vent, and detonated it. Then he walked to a hatch and opened it.

"If there's anyone inside, come out with your hands behind your head. I'm only going to ask you once."

There was no response.

A younger Nighthawk would have thought nothing of entering the strange, darkened ship and seeking out any enemies. The older Nighthawk simply closed the hatch and melted the lock with his laser pistol, leaving the ship sealed and disabled. If there was anyone aboard it, they'd be more than willing to listen to reason in three or four days.

He stopped at the security control room, canceled the red alert he had ordered and left word about the ship, then drove his vehicle into town, leaving it at his office and walking to the restaurant.

Kinoshita immediately got to his feet.

"It's over already?"

"Yeah, it's over," said Nighthawk, walking over to an empty table and sitting down.

Sarah came out of the kitchen.

"I thought you were asleep," she said.

"I will be soon. I had a little business to attend to first." He took his badge off and tossed it onto the table. "I won't be needing this anymore."

"What happened?" she demanded.

"They won't be bothering you anymore."

"Jesus!" she exclaimed, her eyes widening. "You killed them *all*?"

"They didn't give me much choice."

"Much choice? There must have been a whole gang of them! How did you do it?"

"In the safest way possible."

"Is that all you're going to say about it?" continued Sarah.

"Give me some coffee and a piece of pie, and I'll give you the sordid details."

"Why didn't you tell me they were coming?" she insisted. "It was *me* they were after! I could have helped!"

He stared at her without replying.

"All right, all right," she said with a sigh. "You're the Widowmaker. You didn't need any help." She paused. "But you knew you were going to face a whole gang of them. You should at least have taken Ito with you."

"He was where I wanted him."

"Protecting me?"

"There was no guarantee I could stop them."

"If *you* couldn't, how could *he*?"

"You'd be surprised what good men can do under pressure," answered Nighthawk. "And he's a good man."

"How many of them did you kill?"

"Fourteen."

"Fourteen?"

"It was legal. I had the badge, and it was self-defense. I even set up a holo camera to record it, just in case I'm ever challenged about it."

"Now, *that's* a holo I'd like to see!"

"It's digitized and locked under my seal in the spaceport's security computer. I'll pull it out if I need it in court. But I don't think I will."

"Damn it, Jefferson, you're just shrugging it off like it was all in a day's work. You could have been killed!"

"That *is* my work," answered Nighthawk. "Or at least it used to be."

"But you did it for me."

"I just figured I was better equipped to handle the situation than you were."

"I've had one man I care for die on me. I don't want it happening again."

"Your kid's father?"

"Yes."

"He was gunned down?"

"No," replied Sarah. "He was a decent, hardworking man, and I loved him. We never married, but we lived together for fourteen years." She paused. "He didn't die heroically. He contracted some disease that could have been cured in two weeks if we'd lived in the Oligarchy, but he hated the Oligarchy and wouldn't leave the Frontier even to save his own life. So I watched him die, bit by bit, and I'd swore I'd never watch someone I love die again."

"I spent a hundred and twelve years and tens of millions of credits *not* to die like that," said Nighthawk.

"There are other ways to die, even when you're the Widowmaker."

"One of them is hunger," he said, forcing a smile. "I'm still waiting for that coffee and pie."

She left without a word and returned from the kitchen a moment later.

"What do you do now?" she asked.

"Eat the pie, drink the coffee, and go to bed. It's been a long day and I'm an old man."

"Stop saying that!" she snapped. "Old men don't do what you did!"

"All right," he said. "I'm in a state of advanced middle age."

"Damn it, Jefferson! I'm trying to get a straight answer out of you. Are you staying or leaving?"

"On Tumbleweed? I'm staying."

"Alone?"

"I hope not. That depends on you."

"My house is a couple of miles out of town. Tell Ito to cancel your room at the hotel."

He stared at her for a long moment. She wasn't the idealized woman he had dreamed about; on the other hand, he had a feeling that a sixty-two-year-old eplasia victim who made a living by killing people wasn't her idealized man. He found her interesting, and comfortable to be with, and attractive enough to think of taking her to bed, and at this point, 174 years into his solitary life, that was enough.

"Sounds good to me," said Nighthawk.

Chapter 16

"What are you doing up?" asked Sarah, turning suddenly at the kitchen counter.

Nighthawk entered the room, wrapping a robe around himself. "I heard you tiptoeing around, so I thought I'd see if you were okay."

"Of course I am. I just wanted a cup of tea. I'm sorry; I didn't want to disturb you."

"It wasn't your fault," he assured her. "I've always been a light sleeper. It probably saved my life a dozen times. I don't imagine I'm about to change."

"Well, can I make you something to eat or drink, now that you're up?"

"Coffee will be fine," he said, sitting down at the kitchen table.

"Cream or sugar?"

"Black. And hot."

"I have some that's imported from Alphard," said Sarah. "Or do you prefer the local brand? I like it better."

Nighthawk shrugged. "Makes no difference," he said. "Coffee's coffee."

"Local, then. No sense wasting money."

"You don't have to worry about money anymore. I'm a rich man, relatively speaking."

"I'm willing to share. I'm not willing to be kept."

"I'm willing to share, too," said Nighthawk. "And one of the things I've got to share is money. I don't mind sharing your food and your house and your bed; I don't expect you to mind sharing my money."

"I'll share it when I need it. But I've always been frugal. I see no reason to change just because I'm living with the Widowmaker."

"You're living with Jefferson Nighthawk."

"Isn't it the same thing?"

"The Widowmaker's retired."

"I thought he showed up at the spaceport last night," said Sarah.

"That was his farewell appearance."

"Can I ask you a question?"

"Go ahead."

"Why?"

"Why what?"

"Why are you packing the Widowmaker away in mothballs?"

"Because I've been putting my life on the line since I was fifteen, and I'd like to stop."

"And do what?" asked Sarah. "Just how many birds can you watch?"

"More than you think," answered Nighthawk. "And I've got the better part of a lifetime's reading to catch up on. And I can do half a thousand other things I never had time to do when I was the Widowmaker."

Sarah shook her head. "Not you."

"Why not?"

"Look," she began, "I *wish* you could learn to relax, and grow old gracefully, but it's not you. You wake up the second you hear me tiptoeing two rooms away. You face fourteen gunmen at the spaceport and kill them all. You see things with your naked eye that I can barely see with my lens at full magnification." She paused and stared at him. "Like it or not, you're the Widowmaker. It's what you do, it's what you are, and I don't think you can hide from it."

"I wasn't the Widowmaker back on Churchill. I was enjoying my life until they burned my house down."

"How long were you there? A year?"

No answer.

"A month?"

Silence.

"Not even a month," said Sarah. "And you wound up killing Johnny Trouble—oh, I know all about it; Ito told me—and Johnny Trouble wasn't even responsible for the fire." She paused again. "Why don't you just admit that you're the best at what you do, maybe the best there ever was, and stop running away from who you are?"

"I'm an—"

"Don't give me that 'I'm an old man' crap again!" she said sharply. "You certainly didn't act like an old man in bed tonight."

"That's not the same thing."

She poured his coffee into a cup and handed it to him. "Could an old man have held off fourteen killers?"

"I planted explosives around the area before they showed up," answered Nighthawk. "I didn't have to shoot fourteen of them; I just had to hit a couple of bombs they didn't know were there. And when I killed those men back on Bolingbroke, I lured them into a situation where all I had to do was make a loud noise and they were buried under shattered crystal."

"Don't you realize what you're saying?" persisted Sarah. "You're even better now, because you use your brain as well as your physical gifts. You're like an athlete who may have lost a step, but makes up for it with added experience."

Nighthawk sipped his coffee thoughtfully. "I appreciate what you're saying," he replied at last. "But sooner or later every athlete knows it's time to hang it up. There's at least one man out there somewhere who could take me without working up a sweat—my second clone. And if there's one, why shouldn't there be more?"

"I'm not suggesting you go out looking for them," answered Sarah. "But I think you'll go stir-crazy if you do nothing but read and watch birds and sit around the house. Tumbleweed needs a police officer. Not much happens here, and I'm sure the drug runners won't come back, not after the way you decimated them—but there should be enough going on so you won't be bored to death. And there's one more thing."

"What?"

"Even if there are a few men out there who can take you, they're not likely to show up on Tumbleweed." She smiled. "You're not coming in to clean up some hellhole like you used to do all over the Inner Frontier a century ago; you'll just be keeping the peace on a tranquil little world where nothing too exciting ever happens."

"It happened tonight."

"That was an aberration."

"Most killings are."

"Are you going to consider what I said," said Sarah heatedly, "or are you going to spend what's left of the night arguing with me?"

"I'll give it some thought," said Nighthawk. "But there's one thing that you haven't taken into account."

"I don't want to hear any more age crap."

"No more age crap."

"Then what?"

"I'm tired of killing."

"*Can* someone like you be tired of killing?" she asked dubiously.

"Especially someone like me," he assured her. "I've run the race. I've faced more outlaws that most people can imagine, even given my reputation. I've faced them one at a time, and I've faced them in groups. I've faced men and women and aliens. I've put my life on the line more times than I can count. I've looked Death in the eye—and you know something? He's not a desperado holding a gun; he's me, Jefferson Nighthawk, with cheekbones sticking out through his flesh and skin the texture of sandpaper. I've done more than society has any right to ask me, and now I want to enjoy what time is left to me. Is that so goddamned much to ask?"

"No, it's not," she said seriously. "But I know you, maybe better than you know yourself. And I know what will and won't make you happy."

"If you think killing makes me happy . . ." he began.

"No, I believe you when you say it doesn't," she replied. "But keep the job anyway. You probably won't have to do anything more than lock up an occasional drunk, or arrest someone for illegal parking." Suddenly she laughed. "Or maybe close the Sand Castle for watering its drinks. But at least you won't wither away from boredom."

"After the life I've lived, withering away from boredom looks mighty appealing."

"You won't think so once you give it a try."

"There's nothing boring about a book," he said. "Or about being with a good woman."

"I'm flattered that you think so, and I hope you'll still think so a year from now, but—"

"I'm not looking just one year ahead," said Nighthawk. "I intend to spend the rest of my life here—and I'm planning on living a lot longer than a year."

"If a thousand outlaws couldn't kill you and eplasia couldn't kill you, I personally can't see any reason why you shouldn't live forever."

"Forever would be nice. I'll settle for seventy-five. Until I get there. Then I'll shoot for ninety."

"Twenty-eight years of lying on hammocks and looking at birds," she said. "Is that really what you want?"

"Maybe we'll do a little traveling," he said. "I was always so busy looking into shadows that I never saw what was out there in the sunlight."

"Speaking of sunlight," said Sarah, looking out the window, "I see that it's getting light out." She paused. "We might as well get dressed. I'm too wide awake to go back to sleep."

"Me, too," said Nighthawk, getting to his feet and following her into the bedroom.

They emerged, fully clothed, a few minutes later, just in time to hear footsteps shuffling up the stone path to the house.

"Good morning," said Kinoshita as Nighthawk walked across the living room and opened the door. "I saw your light on, so I figured you were awake."

"You're not going to make a daily habit of showing up at sunrise, are you?" asked Nighthawk.

"No," answered Kinoshita. "I just came by to give you something you left behind."

Nighthawk stared at him curiously.

"I thought this might come in handy," said Kinoshita, pulling Nighthawk's discarded badge out of his pocket and handing it to him.

"You, too?" said Nighthawk irritably.

"Tumbleweed needs a lawman, and you're the best." Kinoshita grinned. "After last night, the city fathers won't consider anyone else."

"I don't *want* to be a lawman!"

"You can't always have what you want. I'd take the job, but I'm not half as good as you, and we both know it." Kinoshita paused. "Besides, it'll keep you from getting bored."

"Did you two plot this out while I was at the spaceport?" demanded Nighthawk.

"No, but if she's urging you to take back the badge, I approve," said Kinoshita.

"Why?"

"On practical grounds. Word of what happened last night at the spaceport is going to get out. The bad guys will know someone wiped out one of their crews, and the good guys are already bragging about the lawman they hired. Whether you stay or go, someone's going to come after you. Maybe the drug runners' boss. Maybe his hired guns. Maybe some punk kids who want to test themselves against the lawman who killed fourteen bad guys at one time. But count on it: *someone's* going to come after you." He paused. "You might as well have the force of the law on your side."

Nighthawk looked slowly from Sarah to Kinoshita, then back again.

"You really think it's a good idea?" he asked her.

"I do."

He stared at the badge for a very long moment, then sighed deeply and bonded it to his tunic.

Chapter 17

It was almost two months before the first of them showed up.

Two idyllic months. It was the first time in his memory that Nighthawk was able to relax completely. He spent his days birding, reading, and working around the house. He built a deck off the kitchen, and a gazebo by the brook that ran behind the property. Then, because he was a realist, he also built a shooting range, where he practiced daily with his Burner, his Screecher, and his other weapons.

He also got his weight back up to where it had been more than a century ago, and none of it was fat. Sarah remarked that no one could eat as many calories as she was feeding him without turning soft as putty, but he worked them off almost as fast as he took them in.

True, he was the planet's official lawman, but it was such a peaceful little world that all he did was walk up and down the major streets once a day, check with the store owners to see if they had any complaints, and keep his office neat. About once a week he had to arrest a drunk, and a month into his tenure he broke up a fight, but that was the extent of it. He basically left Kinoshita to watch the office and call him if anything required his attention, and was grateful that almost nothing did.

"How long do you think it can last?" he said one day at breakfast.

"I thought you were happy here," answered Sarah, visibly upset. "Are you thinking of leaving?"

"I didn't ask how long we could last," he said reassuringly. "I was just wondering how long it'll be before they start showing up on Tumbleweed."

" 'They?' "

"The gunmen, the kids out to make a reputation, the men who want to be able to brag that they killed the Widowmaker."

"We're pretty far off the beaten track," she replied. "Why should anyone come here?"

"Well, I did take out a sizable portion of the drug cartel's muscle," responded Nighthawk. "Most kingpins can't let something like that go unchallenged. And I have a feeling your city fathers are bragging about the new cop on the beat, rather than going out of their way to keep his identity a secret."

"I told them not to."

"So did I." He smiled. "That probably held them in check for all of five minutes."

"So that's why you practice on those targets every day."

"It's going to happen sooner or later. I might as well be prepared for it." He looked over at her. "I'm enjoying every minute I spend with you. I plan to die only with the greatest reluctance."

"Well," said Sarah, "if Jefferson Nighthawk doesn't want to die, I don't suppose there's anyone in the galaxy who can kill him."

"That may have been true when I was twenty-five or thirty."

"I'm tired of you constantly referring to your age!" she said irritably. "You've accomplished things since you came out of the hospital that are beyond almost any man half your age."

"Half my age is eighty-seven," he said with a smile.

"Maybe I ought to treat you like an old man," she said. "Maybe I should leave you completely alone on the assumption that any excitement might bring on a stroke or a heart attack."

"You never know," he answered. "It might."

"Oh, shut up."

"Of course, it might not. Maybe we ought to go into the next room and find out which, just out of curiosity."

"In a long lifetime of being propositioned," said Sarah, "I think that may very well be the least romantic invitation I ever had." Suddenly she smiled. "Let's go and find out."

Nighthawk got to his feet. "Sounds good to me."

And then his communicator chimed.

"Ito, you can pick the damnedest times to bother me," he said in annoyed tones as Kinoshita's holograph appeared in the air in front of him.

"We've got a pair of young toughs who plan to bother you a lot more than I can," said Kinoshita's.

"Any paper on them?"

"Not that I can find."

"And they've said they're after me?"

"Not in so many words—but you take one look at them and they're adrenaline and testosterone and weapons . . . and why else could they be here?"

"Where are they now?"

"The Long Bar at the Sand Castle."

"Okay, they'll keep for an hour."

"You're not coming right away?"

"Soon. Let me know if they leave."

"Okay, you got it."

They broke the communication, and Nighthawk turned back to Sarah, who had paused by the bedroom door, listening to him.

"Now, where were we?" he said.

"You're kidding!" she replied incredulously.

"Do I look like I'm kidding?"

"But there are two men in town who've come to kill you!"

"Then this might be my last time," he said with a grin. "I hope you'll make it memorable."

"I can't believe it! How can you think about sex at a time like this?"

"What better time to think about it?"

"Most men would be worried about a pair of killers who were up to no good."

"Most men haven't been in this situation a couple of hundred times. I have."

She stared at him, frowning. "Every time I think I understand you, something like this happens and I realize I don't know you at all."

He sighed in resignation. "You really want me to go to town right this minute?"

"Hell, no! For all I know, it might be our last time." She paused. "I just don't know how you can concentrate on it."

"Well, you know us old guys—we can't think of more than one thing at a time."

"You say that once more and I will send you to town."

So he didn't, and she didn't, and later he got dressed again as she watched him from the bed.

"If you don't come back, I want you to know that I love you."

"I'll be back," he said. "There are men out there who can kill me, but they're all old enough to shave."

"Aren't you even a little bit concerned?"

"I didn't get this far by not respecting what any man with a weapon can do," he said. "But I know what I can do, too."

He bound his laser holster to his trousers after checking the Burner's battery, then tucked a Screecher into his belt under his tunic, and slid a knife into each boot.

"I'll be back in a little while," he said, walking to the doorway.

"I'll be here."

He got into the vehicle and drove to his office, where Kinoshita was waiting for him.

"Are they still in the Sand Castle?" he asked.

"Yes."

"Good," he said, sitting down and putting his feet up on his desk. "Let's give them another half hour."

"They're not going away," said Kinoshita. "Why not get it over with now?"

"They're in the Long Bar," replied Nighthawk. "My guess is that they're not drinking milk. As long as they want to fuck up their reaction times, I see no reason to stop them."

Kinoshita grinned. "I never thought of that."

"Did you check with Customs at the spaceport and find out who the hell they are?"

"You're not going to believe their names."

"Try me."

"Are you ready for this? They call themselves Billy Danger and the Lightning Kid."

Nighthawk laughed aloud. "You're kidding."

"I couldn't make up anything that ludicrous on the spur of the moment."

"I suppose not," agreed Nighthawk. "They were probably Billy Smith and Freddie Jones six months ago, skipping classes and chasing girls." He paused. "Too bad they had to come here. They're just begging for *someone* to kill them, walking around with those names." He shook his head. "Billy Danger."

"Watch out for the other one."

"The Lightning Kid?" asked Nighthawk. He chuckled. "My God, it's hard to say that name with a straight face."

"I think he's on something."

"Oh?"

"Twitches a lot. Wall-to-wall pupils. Billy Danger looks nervous as all hell, like he got talked into this. But the other one, there's something about him: he looks like torturing small animals is his favorite hobby."

"Okay, when they come out of there, let me know which is which."

"You'll know," said Kinoshita with absolute conviction.

And sure enough, when the two young men emerged from the Sand

Castle twenty minutes later, Nighthawk had no trouble spotting the Lightning Kid. He seemed almost brighter than the sun, dressed in metallic gold: tunic, pants, even belt, boots, and holsters. He wore a silver scarf around his neck, and skintight silver gloves. Nighthawk fought back the urge to laugh for a few seconds, then gave in to it.

"What do you think?" said Kinoshita.

"He looks like a fashion designer's worst nightmare."

"And the other one?"

Nighthawk looked at Billy Danger. He was flamboyantly dressed, though not compared to his companion. His shirt had oversized, puffy sleeves, his polished, shining boots came up almost to his knees, and his weapons would cost an average man a year's pay.

"Typical," said Nighthawk. "No surprises here."

"You sound like you've seen them before."

"A thousand times."

"You want me to stand with you?"

Nighthawk shook his head. "No paper on 'em, remember? You kill them, I have to arrest you."

"Just deputize me."

"Someday I will. But not for a couple of kids just out of diapers."

Nighthawk walked out the door and stood in the street, waiting for the two young men to approach him.

"Good morning," he said when they were about forty feet away. "I'm told that you have some business with me?"

"You can't be *him*!" said the Lightning Kid, obviously disappointed. "Look at you! You're an old man, and you're dressed just like everyone else."

"I know this is going to come as a shock to you," said Nighthawk, "but they don't give out a prize for the flashiest-dressed killer on the Frontier."

"It's him," said Billy Danger nervously. "I've seen holos of him. He's older, but it's him."

"You're sure?" asked the Lightning Kid, swaying slightly and trying to focus his eyes on Nighthawk.

"Believe me, it's the Widowmaker!" answered Billy Danger, and Nighthawk noticed a slight trembling in his hands.

"And now that you've seen me, why don't you go back home while you still can?"

"We're going to be the men who killed the Widowmaker," said the Lightning Kid.

"Go home now, and someday you may even grow up to become men."

"I want to see if you're as good as they say."

"Better," answered Nighthawk. He concentrated on Billy Danger. "Don't do anything foolish, kid. Have you ever killed anyone before?"

"Sure," blustered Billy Danger. "Lots of men."

"Bullshit. You're shaking like a leaf. I want you to consider something, kid: This is old hat to me. I've been facing young guns for more than a century, and I'm still here. I *know* what I can do. Until you know you can beat the Widowmaker, maybe you'd better go home and think seriously about what you mean to do."

Billy Danger was silent for a moment, as if he was actually considering Nighthawk's suggestion. Finally he spoke. "I can't. People will laugh."

"They won't laugh at your funeral. Is that what you want?"

"I've got to think about it."

"Don't take too long," said Nighthawk, walking a few steps closer.

"Hold it right there!" bellowed the Lightning Kid.

"Okay," said Nighthawk, stopping. "What now?"

"You're not going to talk *me* out of this!"

"I'm not even going to try," said Nighthawk. "It'll be a pleasure to kill you."

The young man frowned and blinked his eyes. "You can't kill me. I'm the Lightning Kid!"

"If *I* can't kill you, then the man in my office who's got his laser rifle trained on you certainly will."

"Where?" asked the Lightning Kid, turning awkwardly and trying to pinpoint Nighthawk's office window. As he did so, Nighthawk whipped out his Burner and melted both of the Kid's weapons in their holsters, then turned his gun on the other young man.

"Billy Danger, you've got to the count of five to pull your weapon or leave. It's your choice."

"Holster your weapon," said Billy Danger.

"My planet, my rules. The Burner stays out. One, two . . ."

"All right, all right—I'm leaving," said Billy Danger.

"And leave your weapons on the ground."

"But they cost my . . . me—"

"Consider it an object lesson."

Billy Danger seemed to be reconsidering, but before his hand could snake down toward his weapon, he took another look at the Burner that was trained on him and quickly unbound his holsters. They slid to the ground, and he began walking away.

"Spaceport's the other direction," said Nighthawk.

The young man turned and began walking again.

"I know it's painful, and a little humiliating," said Nighthawk. "You might remember that the next time you consider killing someone who never did you any harm."

Billy Danger didn't answer, but simply increased his pace, and Nighthawk turned his attention back to the Lightning Kid.

"What about you?" he said. "Are you willing to walk back to the spaceport?"

"Sure," said the Kid with a crazed laugh. "But I'll be back."

"I don't think so," said Nighthawk.

"You think melting a couple of guns will stop the Lightning Kid?"

"Probably not," admitted Nighthawk.

"Damned right, Widowmaker. Hell, I can always get more guns."

"Yeah, I suppose you can—but you'll need to learn how to fire them without a trigger finger." He burned away the Kid's two forefingers, as the young man screamed in pain. "I know it hurts—but remember, I could have killed you. After all, you came here to kill *me*."

"I'll get you for this!" yelled the Lightning Kid.

"Sure you will," said Nighthawk, unimpressed. "Now get the hell out of here before I get really mad at you."

The Lightning Kid, trying to clutch the stumps of his blackened, smoking forefingers, staggered past Nighthawk. As he did so, Nighthawk saw a movement out of the corner of his eye, and ducked just as Billy Danger, tears of fright and humiliation mingling on his cheeks, dove for him with a gleaming knife in his hand.

The blade opened a wound on Nighthawk's shoulder, and the shock made him drop his Burner.

"I'm sorry!" babbled Billy Danger. "I don't want to do this! But he's my partner—I've got to stand up for him!"

"He's an asshole," said Nighthawk, turning to face him. "You don't owe him a thing. You can still walk away."

"I wish I could, but I can't!"

Billy Danger charged again, and Nighthawk side-stepped and delivered a killing blow to the back of his neck. The young man fell to the street without a sound.

At exactly that instant, the Lightning Kid dove for the Burner Nighthawk had dropped. Nighthawk kicked him full in the face, and as the Kid sprawled on the ground the gun went flying. Nighthawk pulled his Screecher out of his belt and pointed it at the Kid.

"A very misguided boy is dead because of you," he grated. "I wouldn't mind blowing you away as well, so get up very slowly and don't make any sudden moves." The Kid looked at the Burner, which lay on the ground a few feet away. "Don't even think about it," continued Nighthawk. "Even if you reached it before I shot you, how are you going to fire the damned thing?"

And then, suddenly, with no warning, the Lightning Kid went berserk. He uttered an animal scream of rage and hurled himself at Nighthawk, who brought him up short with a stiff blow to the breastbone. The Kid shrieked, but never backed away, and began clawing manically at Nighthawk's face. The older man tried to sidestep, but found that he wasn't as quick as he'd thought he was, and an instant later the Kid's fingernails were raking the skin off his face. Nighthawk ducked, delivered two blows that would have stopped anyone who wasn't out of his mind on drugs and adrenaline, and the Kid dropped to his knees. But he was up a second later, this time with Billy Danger's wicked-looking knife in his hand, and he brought it down with all his strength, aiming at Nighthawk's chest.

What happened next was sheer instinct. Nighthawk's hand shot out, and the heel of it caught the Kid's nose, driving the bone and cartilage into the brain. The Kid screamed one last time, the knife dropped from his bloody hand, and he collapsed at Nighthawk's feet.

Kinoshita raced up to Nighthawk a moment later. "Nice job," he said.

"It was a fucking clumsy job," said Nighthawk disgustedly. "I shouldn't have had to kill the first one. I didn't even mean to kill *this* one, but I wasn't quick enough to take him out *without* killing him."

"It's over, and you're alive," said Kinoshita. "That's all that matters."

"It's just beginning," muttered Nighthawk. He looked at the two corpses and grimaced. "Shit!" he said unhappily. "This isn't the way it was supposed to be."

Chapter 18

He was a hero to all the planetary officials, who didn't hesitate to spread the word that Tumbleweed was now under the protection of the notorious Widowmaker. He tried to explain to them that this was hardly the way to keep reputation-seeking young guns away from the planet, but in their eyes he was everything legend had made him out to be: after all, he'd killed fourteen men single-handedly at the spaceport, and in case anyone doubted his abilities, he killed a pair of young toughs right out on Main Street in front of everyone.

Let them come with their best, was the officials' attitude; *we've* got the Widowmaker.

"They're fools," he muttered, for perhaps the thousandth time, while he was having breakfast with Sarah.

"Probably," she agreed. "But it's too late to do anything about it."

"We can leave."

"Tumbleweed is my home," she responded. "I don't want to leave."

"Neither do I. But they don't realize what's going to happen. I'm not sure even you do."

"A few guns will show up."

He shook his head. "Every ambitious killer on the Frontier will show up," he corrected her. "It used to happen every time I stayed in one place too long more than a century ago, and thanks to a bunch of hack writers and phony documentaries I'm more famous today than I was back then."

"It's been three weeks since you killed Billy Danger and the Lightning Kid," she said. "No one's showed up."

"It takes time for word to get around. They'll show up, all right. And they won't all be kids. Some of them will be men I can't take."

"You can take anyone."

"You, too?" he said irritably. "Trust me, I know my limitations."

"You're being too modest," she said. "But I'll make this concession: The day you feel someone has come to Tumbleweed to kill you, someone you think might succeed, I'll leave with you. Fair enough?"

"Fair enough."

"You know, you do have an advantage here that you never had before."

"You?"

"Me?" She chuckled and shook her head. "I was referring to Kinoshita. No one knows him, which means no one knows he's working for you."

"He puzzles me," said Nighthawk.

"Why?"

"Because I don't know who the hell he's working for, but it's not me. He was there at the hospital when I woke up, and he's been at my side ever since, but I'll be damned if I know why, and it bothers me."

"Maybe he just likes you."

Nighthawk smiled wryly. "I'm not that likable."

"I think you are."

He shook his head. "I give him orders. I don't listen to his advice. I get him into the damnedest scrapes. There's no reason why he should stick around."

"Why don't you ask him?"

"I have."

"And he hasn't answered?"

"Not exactly. He admits he's got a reason for being with me, but he hasn't told me what it is." Nighthawk paused. "When the time comes, I'll demand it."

"When will that be?"

He shrugged. "I can't tell you. But I'll know it when it's here."

They finished breakfast, then drove out to the countryside, where they took their daily walk through the woods. They spent a few hours looking at birds and identifying flowers—another new hobby—and then went back to town. After dropping her at the restaurant, Nighthawk parked the vehicle and began making his rounds.

All went routinely until he stopped at one of the smaller hotels.

"Good morning," he greeted the desk clerk.

"Good morning, Jefferson," came the reply. "Did those men find you?"

"What men?"

"Three men. They checked in, then asked where they could find you."

"Did they ask for Jefferson Nighthawk, or for the Widowmaker?"

"I can't really remember," admitted the clerk. "Is it important?"

"Probably not. Thanks."

Nighthawk walked back to his office, where he found Kinoshita doing some paperwork.

"Hi. What's up?"

"Three men are looking for me. Do you know who they are, or why they want to find me?"

"I can't know every enemy the two clones made," answered Kinoshita. "The first one went off on his own the second he hit the Frontier, and the second one got a few million people mad at him."

"Well, just the same, I want you to wander around town until you run into them and then tell me if you recognize them," said Nighthawk.

"What difference does it make?" asked Kinoshita. "If they're looking for you, there's just one reason."

"Because before I kill a man, or get killed by him, I'd like to know why."

"You know why—right now you're the biggest trophy on the Frontier."

"Maybe I can convince them that the bad guys are supposed to be the trophies."

"If they're here to kill you, they are the bad guys," answered Kinoshita.

"Just do what I say."

"You're the boss," said Kinoshita, getting up and walking to the door. "Have you got any idea where they're supposed to be right now?"

"Looking for me."

"They can't be too bright, or they'd have come right to the office." Kinoshita walked out the door and down the street while Nighthawk sat at his desk.

He had his computer pull the guest registrations from the hotel, after which he scanned their faces and names. There were five or six possibilities, but he couldn't recognize any of them, and he didn't have the budget or the patience to tie into the Master Computer on Deluros VIII and try to learn more about them.

Kinoshita returned about half an hour later.

"Well?"

"I found them. They're eating at your ladyfriend's place."

"Do they know she's my ladyfriend, as you so delicately put it?"

"I don't think so," answered Kinoshita. "I think they're just hungry."

"Do you know them?"

Kinoshita shook his head. "I never saw any of them before—which doesn't mean that they aren't from Tundra or Pericles. I mean, after all, there's no paper on you, and I can't imagine anyone's put out a hit on you."

"Paper's got nothing to do with it," answered Nighthawk. "If you want to get famous fast, you kill the Widowmaker."

"Well, what do you want to do about them?"

"They're not breaking any laws. Let's leave them alone for a while."

"These aren't like those kids you killed last month," said Kinoshita. "They're not going to get so drunk they're useless in a fight."

"Can you tell me anything about them?" asked Nighthawk. "Anything at all?"

"Just that they're tough-looking men, Jefferson. You may make their reputations, but I've got a feeling you're not the first man they've gone up against."

Nighthawk stood up. "Okay, then, I suppose I'd better go do something about them."

"I'll come with you."

"As you wish."

"You never let me join you before," noted Kinoshita.

"I always knew who my enemies were before. I don't want to confront the wrong men."

"Oh," said Kinoshita, visibly disappointed.

"You're a good man," said Nighthawk. "I don't want you getting killed on my account. I just want you to identify them."

"It would be an honor to die with the Widowmaker."

"First, I'm not the Widowmaker, and second, dying is never an honor. The object of the exercise is to kill the other guy."

They began walking toward the restaurant. Then, when they were half a block away, Nighthawk came to a dead stop.

"What is it?" asked Kinoshita.

"I just had a thought," he said.

"Oh?"

"Yeah. Let's go through the kitchen."

"Whatever you say."

They walked around to the back of the restaurant and entered through the service door.

"Hi," said Sarah, walking over to him. "I didn't expect to see you again till dinner."

Nighthawk signaled for silence, then walked to the doorway to the restaurant. There were three lean, dark-clad men sitting at a table by the front door.

"Are those the men?" he whispered.

Kinoshita nodded.

"Wait here," he said, and walked out the service door. He was back in less than a minute.

"What are they drinking?"

"Coffee," answered Sarah.

"Bring me a fresh pot."

She did as he asked. He lifted the top and dropped five small pills into it.

"What was that?" she asked.

"That was a gunfight-avoider I borrowed from the pharmacy," said Nighthawk. "There's enough in those pills to put a platoon to sleep, let alone three men. Take it out and leave it on the table. Don't offer to pour. I don't want them thinking anyone's anxious for them to drink."

Sarah took the container, walked out into the restaurant and over to the three men before anyone could ask for a refill, and left the pot in the middle of their table.

"Now what?" whispered Kinoshita.

"Now you go to the doctor's office. Get three airsleds and bring them back here. We'll need them to cart these guys off to jail."

"They haven't broken any laws, you know."

"Then I probably can't hold them more than a year or two, can I?" replied Nighthawk.

Kinoshita shrugged, walked out the back, and began hunting up the airsleds. Nighthawk poured himself a cup of coffee, sat down on a stool, and sipped it, as Sarah kept watch on the three men. For the longest time it seemed to her that they were never going to refill their cups, but finally they did, and within a minute all three seemed to be talking and gesticulating in slow motion.

She reported their behavior to Nighthawk, who walked into the restaurant just as they were losing consciousness, assured the other patrons that there was nothing to worry about, and laid the three men gently on the floor.

Kinoshita showed up a few minutes later with the airsleds. He and Nighthawk lifted each man onto a sled, then ushered them out the front door and over to the jail, where Nighthawk disarmed them and locked all three of them in a single cell.

"How long are they out for?" asked Kinoshita, staring at the three motionless men.

"Maybe three hours, maybe four. I'll be back in late afternoon to have a little chat with them. Give them water if they ask for it; nothing else."

"No food?"

"I wouldn't want them to be too comfortable when I speak to them," said Nighthawk.

"Where will you be if I need you?"

"You won't."

"But *if* I do."

"I'll be taking a nap at Sarah's place."

"You can sleep at a time like this?" asked Kinoshita incredulously.

"I've just had a strenuous morning of bird-watching and not killing three men," said Nighthawk with just the trace of a smile. "That's about all a man of my advanced years can handle before lunch."

Chapter 19

"Good afternoon," said Nighthawk, sitting comfortably on a chair just outside the cell. "How are we feeling?"

"Like shit warmed over," groaned one of the three men, holding his head. "What the hell was in that coffee?"

"A little something that any doctor could lose his license for prescribing," answered Nighthawk with a smile.

"Why are we here?" asked another of the men.

"I thought we should have a little chat."

"What about?"

"Life. Death. Things like that."

"If you're going to kill us, get it over with," said the man. "But don't talk us to death."

"If I wanted to kill you," said Nighthawk, "I could have done it this morning."

"Why didn't you?"

"It would just attract more scum to Tumbleweed. We want to be left alone here." He paused. "More to the point, I want to be left alone." He stared at the three men. "You came here to kill me. Was it your own idea, or did someone hire you?"

The three men looked at each other. Finally the first of them shrugged and turned back to Nighthawk.

"It was our idea."

"Why?"

Silence.

Nighthawk pointed a pistol at them. "You're in a lousy bargaining position. I want an answer."

"All right," said the nearest man. "We're for hire, and the men who killed the Widowmaker can charge top prices."

"Do you know why?"

The man stared at him, but offered no reply.

"You'd command a higher price because men have been trying to kill me for a century and a half, and I'm still here." Nighthawk's contempt for their abilities was reflected in his expression. "Did you ever stop to ask yourself why that should be, why so many men have tried to kill me and none have succeeded?"

"We know you're good. That's why there are three of us."

"Maybe you'd better take up a different profession," suggested Nighthawk. "You're not the brightest gunfighters I ever met. In fact, the only reason you're still alive is because you were dumb enough to come to my world and eat and drink everything that was put in front of you without testing it—not exactly a survival trait out here."

"The only reason *you're* alive is because you drugged us instead of facing us," said the largest of the men, speaking for the first time.

Nighthawk tossed a small, octagonal coin from the Hesperite system to the man. "Throw it at the wall over there."

The man caught the coin, stared curiously at Nighthawk for a moment, then shrugged and hurled the coin at the far wall of the cell. Nighthawk, without ever getting out of his chair, drew his Burner and melted the coin in midair.

"I'm just as good with my other hand," he said. "Maybe even better. Now, do you *really* want to face me?"

There were no answers, but they were unable to hide their sudden reluctance.

"I'll interpret that as a negative answer," continued Nighthawk. "Now, if I let you out of your cell and point you toward the spaceport, can I reasonably expect you to get the hell off the planet and never return?"

More silence. Finally the largest man nodded his head.

"What about our weapons?"

"They're on your ship. The power packs stay here."

"Power packs cost money."

"So do triple funerals," replied Nighthawk. "Do you want to pay for new packs, or have Tumbleweed pay for the funerals?"

The men glared at him, but offered no response.

Nighthawk uttered the code that opened the cell.

The three men walked to the door. Two of them walked out in the street. The third, who hadn't spoken at all, turned to Nighthawk, his body tense.

"Don't even think of it," said Nighthawk.

"You're an old man. Get rid of those weapons and I can take you."

"I doubt it—but I didn't get to be an old man by accepting stupid challenges."

"The Widowmaker's backing down?" said the man contemptuously.

"The Widowmaker's offering you your life," replied Nighthawk. "A smart man would take it and leave."

The man didn't move. "I could have taken you with a gun, too."

"Sure you could."

"Anyone can melt a coin with a Burner. You just spray the whole area."

"If you say so. Now get the hell out of here before I lock you up again."

"I'll be back, you know."

"That's fine by me. The cemetery won't be full for years yet."

The man glared at him for a long moment, then finally turned and walked out after his companions.

Nighthawk stood by his window, watching them until they caught the shuttle to the spaceport.

The man probably *would* be back. Nighthawk wondered if he'd have let him walk away a century ago, and concluded, to his surprise, that he probably wouldn't have.

The Widowmaker didn't believe in letting enemies live. He killed calmly and efficiently, without emotion, without regret. If a man came to a world to kill him, that man was, by definition, a mortal enemy, and the Widowmaker didn't allow mortal enemies to live.

The Widowmaker also didn't second-guess himself—which he viewed as further proof that he was no longer the Widowmaker.

Chapter 20

Finally the men that Nighthawk had been expecting, generically at least, arrived on Tumbleweed.

He was sitting on Sarah's porch, reading a book, when she came out from town to speak to him.

"What's the problem?" he asked. "You look troubled."

"It's time to leave."

"You're throwing me out?"

"I'm coming with you," she replied. "We're both leaving this world."

"What the hell's going on?"

"We always knew the time would come," said Sarah. "Well, it's here. Let's pack up and go."

Nighthawk put the book down on a small table and got to his feet. "I'll go when I'm ready," he said. "And I don't feel ready yet. I want to know what put this scare into you."

"All right," she said, looking into his eyes. "Two men came to Tumbleweed. They haven't said that they're here for you, but that has to be the reason."

"Men have come here for me before."

"Not like these two," she said.

"Tell me about them."

"There's nothing to tell," answered Sarah. "There's just something about them. You take one look and you know they're born killers."

"They're probably a couple of businessmen who dressed up to impress the locals," said Nighthawk.

"Don't humor me, Jefferson," said Sarah. "I've seen them come and go, and I've never seen anyone like these two. Maybe you could have taken one of them in your prime, but . . ."

"This isn't like you," said Nighthawk. "Usually you're the one who wants me to go slay dragons for you, and I'm the reluctant knight."

"These dragons are different."

"You don't mind if I go see for myself?"

"The hell I don't!" she snapped. "If you go into town, you'll never come back!"

"I appreciate your confidence," he replied ironically.

"I spent a long time waiting for someone like you," she said. "I don't want to lose you this soon."

"I've got to at least see them, you know."

"I'm begging you not to."

"Tell you what," he said, removing his holster and laying his various pistols down next to the book. "I'll leave all my weapons here. They won't enhance their reputations by shooting down an unarmed man."

"I have a feeling their reputations don't *need* enhancing," she replied.

He walked over to the vehicle. "I'll be back soon."

"I hope so."

"But you doubt it?"

"You're the best I've ever seen . . . but they're what you were thirty years ago."

"Thirty years ago I was a skeleton in a cryonics chamber," he responded. "I didn't go through all that so I could be shot down on the streets of Tumbleweed."

He got into the vehicle and took off for town. He decided not to park at his office—there was no sense announcing his identity to whoever might be looking for him—so he parked well past the Sand Castle and began walking slowly down the street. He looked into the restaurant to see if the men who had so frightened Sarah were there, but there was just a pair of elderly women having tea.

Finally he walked to Tavern Row, a stretch of the street that held three taverns in a row, and looked into the first. Things seemed pretty dull—a few drinkers, a couple of men and a Canphorite playing *jabob*. The second tavern hadn't even opened for business yet.

He walked into the third, which was relatively crowded for this early in the day, and saw two elegantly tailored gray-clad men standing at the bar, each wearing tight-fitting custom-made gloves. Even though they were motionless, there was a certain grace about them, a potential that was immediately evident.

Nighthawk walked to a table, sat down, ordered a beer off the holographic menu, and studied the two men.

"Your name Nighthawk?" asked one of the men, staring at him in the mirror behind the bar.

"That's right."

"Then I insist that you let us pick up the tab for that beer."

"Whatever makes you happy," answered Nighthawk.

"I think it'd make us happy to join you at your table."

"Be my guest."

"Thanks. We will."

The two men walked over and sat down on each side of him.

"I'm Mr. Dark," said the one who had been speaking. "This is my friend, Mr. Night."

"Night and Nighthawk," offered Mr. Night. "Maybe we're related."

"Anything's possible."

"No, there are certain things that aren't possible," said Mr. Night. "Would you like an example?"

"If you insist."

"It's not possible that you can survive a fight with us."

"If you say so."

"You're allowed to disagree," said Mr. Dark, dabbing at this mouth with a silk handkerchief. "In fact, you could come out into the street and disagree with us right now, if you're so inclined."

Nighthawk held his arms out from his body. "I certainly can't survive a fight while I'm unarmed."

"I've heard stories that you're just as good without a weapon."

"I might have been once, but that was a long time ago. You wouldn't get much pleasure giving a beating to a feeble old man like me."

"No one else in this town seems to think you're all that feeble."

"That's because they hope you'll come after me instead of them," said Nighthawk with a smile.

"And that's just what we've done."

"I can't imagine why."

"Surely you're kidding!" said Mr. Dark.

"Not at all," said Nighthawk. "If you win, they'll say you can kill a tired old man, and if you lose, they'll say you can't. Either way, what good will it do you?"

"I have a feeling that Mr. Nighthawk doesn't take us seriously, Mr. Dark," said Mr. Night.

"Perhaps he needs a demonstration, Mr. Night," suggested Mr. Dark.

Before Nighthawk could respond, they had each whipped out their

Burners and melted off the tops of some fifty bottles of bar stock without their beams of deadly light hitting anything else or doing any damage to the rest of the place. The entire demonstration took less than two seconds from start to finish.

"What do you think, Mr. Nighthawk?" asked Mr. Dark as customers who had thrown themselves to the floor began getting up and looking around, trying to figure out exactly what had happened.

"I think we'll probably have to add all that to your bar bill."

"He's still not taking us seriously, Mr. Night," said Mr. Dark.

"I suppose the only way to get his attention is to break some laws, Mr. Dark," replied his companion.

"Or possibly kill a friend or two of his," agreed Mr. Dark. He turned to Nighthawk. "I wonder: Does a man like you have any friends?"

"Not many," admitted Nighthawk. "But you know that. It goes with the territory."

"True," answered Mr. Dark.

"Just out of curiosity, who sent you?" asked Nighthawk.

"No one," said Mr. Night.

"Then why are you here?" continued Nighthawk. "What did I ever do to you?"

"You got here first."

Nighthawk nodded thoughtfully. "Good answer."

"I'm glad you approve," said Mr. Night. "Perhaps you'll show your appreciation by taking us up on our offer."

"Not right now."

"Sooner or later you'll have to, you know," said Mr. Dark.

"Later, I think."

"If you're frightened, you might consider calling just one of us out," said Mr. Night. "Either one of us. It makes no difference."

"Will the other want to give up all credit for killing the Widowmaker?" asked Nighthawk.

"We're a team, Mr. Nighthawk," said Mr. Dark. "We share in all things."

"That must startle your ladyfriends from time to time," suggested Nighthawk.

"We don't have any ladyfriends."

"Oh?"

"Like I said, we're a team. Each of us is all the other needs."

Mr. Night stared at Nighthawk. "I think he disapproves of us, Mr. Dark."

"Probably, Mr. Night," agreed Mr. Dark. He turned to Nighthawk. "The cemeteries are filled with men who disapproved of us."

"I don't doubt it," said Nighthawk. His hand, which had been resting on his knee, slipped gently down to the top of his boot, where his knife was concealed. He considered pulling it out, but knew he wasn't fast enough to kill them both, or probably even one, before they shot him, not even with the element of surprise in his favor. When he was twenty, or thirty, he'd have tried; at forty, probably . . . but not now.

They didn't frighten him the way they terrified Sarah. He'd been dealing with men like this all his life. He wasn't afraid to face them, and he wasn't afraid to die—but he couldn't see any reason to throw his life away, and he knew that's what he'd be doing if he took them on. He would never admit it to them, but their demonstration of their skills had been that impressive. In his youth he might have been the tiniest fraction of a second faster, the slightest degree more accurate . . . but his youth was farther in the past than most men's, and he was realist enough to know that he couldn't take Mr. Dark or Mr. Night today, not even if he were armed and facing them on his own terms.

"I suppose we could try to humiliate him in front of all the people here who seem to worship him," said Mr. Dark.

"I don't know," replied Mr. Night. "Mr. Nighthawk strikes me as a man who has no quality of shame. I don't think he *can* be humiliated."

"Perhaps you're right," agreed Mr. Dark. "Of course, we'll never know until we try."

"He *is* the only lawman on Tumbleweed," noted Mr. Night. "Maybe we should break some laws and see what happens."

"He'd probably have to arrest us," said Mr. Dark.

"Really?" said Mr. Night, pulling out his Screecher and aiming it at the huge mirror behind the bar. He pulled the trigger and the mirror shattered into a thousand pieces. "You mean he might want to arrest me for something as innocent and fun-loving as that?"

"You never can tell," said Mr. Dark as pandemonium ensued and the bartender and all the customers fled into the street.

"He hasn't arrested me yet," said Mr. Night. "Maybe if I shot some innocent bystanders . . ."

"Oh, I don't think that will be necessary, will it, Mr. Nighthawk?" said Mr. Dark. "I think you'll go home, confront your demons, and face us later today, won't you?"

"I'd say it's a pretty strong possibility," said Nighthawk.

"I think it would be a good idea," continued Mr. Dark. "Because as you may well have guessed, we do have ways of getting the locals to tell us where you live. If we have to go to the trouble of seeking you out at your home, we'll probably be in such a foul mood that we'll burn it down and kill anyone who runs out of it."

"We mean anyone besides yourself, of course," added Mr. Night.

"Just out of curiosity, did you two burn down a house I had back on Churchill II?" asked Nighthawk.

"Someone has appropriated our methods?" said Mr. Dark, feigning shock. "I'm appalled."

"Of course it wasn't us," said Mr. Night. "The proof of it is that you're still alive."

Nighthawk got to his feet. "I assume you're not going anywhere?"

"Not until we do what we came here to do," answered Mr. Dark.

"I'll see you later, then."

"May I ask a question?"

"Be my guest."

"Why did you come here unarmed?"

"I like to scout out the opposition," said Nighthawk.

"And?"

"And now that I know I can beat you," he lied, "I'm going home to get my weapons."

For just a moment Mr. Dark looked unsure of himself. "Maybe we should kill you now."

"Maybe," agreed Nighthawk. "But you won't. How would it sound— two amateurs shoot down the king when he's not armed?"

"Leave," said Mr. Night. "We'll be waiting for you."

Nighthawk walked to the door, then out into the street and toward his vehicle. When he reached it, he entered it and drove it to Sarah's house, where Sarah and Kinoshita were waiting for him.

"I half-expected never to see you again," she said.

"I told you I'd be back."

"I contacted Ito and asked him to come out here. I hope that if I can't talk you into leaving, maybe he can."

"I've checked them out," said Kinoshita. "They hire out as a team. They've killed thirty-eight men between them."

"I can believe that," said Nighthawk. "They're pretty good. Almost as good as I used to be." He smiled wryly. "They gave me a demonstration."

"Can you take them?"

"Not a chance."

"Can *we* take them?" persisted Kinoshita.

Nighthawk shook his head. "Don't come back with me. You'd just be a cannon fodder."

"Well, if you know you can't beat them, let's get the hell off the planet," said Sarah.

Nighthawk looked at her for a long moment. "I'm tired of running. It's not my nature."

"But you admit they'll kill you."

"If I run, they'll just shoot up Tumbleweed. A lot of innocent people will die."

"The hell they will," said Sarah. "They want you, not Tumbleweed."

"Look," he said. "I'm not anxious to die. I've avoided fights before for what I thought were good reasons, and I wish I could avoid this one—but if I run, they'll follow me to the next world. And if they don't, then just about the time we build a house and decide to stay, someone just as deadly will show up. I want to live in peace, but I've already deserted Churchill and Pondoro; I'm not going to keep running the rest of my life. I had hoped I could live another twenty or thirty years, but if I can't, I can't. I've lived with Death for a long time; I'm not afraid of it. And who knows? Maybe they're not as good as they think, and maybe I'm better than you think."

He stared defiantly at Sarah. From somewhere behind him he heard Kinoshita's voice mutter "Jefferson, I'm sorry!" but before he could turn around, a gun barrel came down hard on his head, and he fell, unconscious, to the floor.

Chapter 21

Nighthawk opened his eyes, saw three Sarahs standing in front of him, and closed them again.

"He's awake," he heard her say.

"Good," said Kinoshita. "For a minute there, I was afraid I'd done him some real harm."

Nighthawk reopened his left eye and was able to focus it just enough to see that he was inside his spaceship.

"What the hell happened?" he mumbled, trying to get to his feet, only to find that he was bound to a chair.

"I saved your life," said Kinoshita. "Of course, you may not view it that way, so I thought it might be best to restrain you until I could explain."

"What did you hit me with?" asked Nighthawk. "It felt like a piano."

"The barrel of a laser rifle," said Kinoshita. "Good thing you're a rich man. That was a damned valuable weapon that will never work again."

"Here," said Sarah, placing a small pill in his mouth and holding a cup of water to his lips. "Swallow."

Nighthawk did as she said, and found, to his amazement, that his pain subsided and his vision cleared within half a minute.

"Better?" she asked.

He nodded, half expecting the motion to set off new agonies within his skull, but there was no discomfort.

"Okay," said Kinoshita, uttering a code that released the bonds. "You're free now."

"Why did you do it?" asked Nighthawk, tenderly touching the lump on the back of his head.

"You were about to commit suicide, remember?"

"I might have won."

"We both know you wouldn't have."

"It makes no difference," snapped Nighthawk. "You had no right—" He stood up, was overcome by alternating waves of nausea and dizziness, and collapsed back onto his chair.

"Careful," said Kinoshita. "That was a hell of a concussion. It'd be a good idea not to make any sudden movements for the next couple of days."

Nighthawk was silent for a moment, until the dizziness passed.

"Where are we heading?" he asked.

"I don't know," answered Kinoshita. "As soon as I make sure that your two friends aren't on our tail, we can discuss a location."

"You just tell us where to drop you," said Nighthawk. "We'll take it from there."

"No chance," said Kinoshita firmly. "We're partners, remember?"

"The hell we are. Partners don't whack partners with rifle barrels."

"That's some fucking gratitude after I stop you from getting your damned head blown off," said Kinoshita.

"Gratitude be damned," said Nighthawk. "You've been skirting the subject ever since I got out of the hospital, and now I want a straight answer or we part ways. Why have you attached yourself to me?"

Kinoshita stared at him for a long moment, trying to make up his mind.

"All right," he said at last. "I made a promise."

"To who?"

"To the Widowmaker."

"What are you talking about?" demanded Nighthawk. "*I'm* the Widowmaker."

"You weren't when I made it."

"Explain."

"It was on Pericles, just after your second clone killed Cassius Hill," said Kinoshita. "He gave me the money that would keep you alive."

"I know that."

"There was more, though. He knew you'd be an old man, and possibly a sick one—certainly one who was a century out of date. He asked me to watch over you, and I promised him that I would."

"Bullshit."

"I swear it's the truth."

"He had to know that even at sixty-two I could take you without drawing a deep breath. There's no way he would have asked you to protect me."

"I didn't say *protect*," shot back Kinoshita. "I trained the first clone, and I fought for the second. I've done whatever *you've* asked me to do. I serve the Widowmaker; this little incident on Tumbleweed is one of the very few times any of you have needed protection." He paused. "Now that the clone has changed his face and his name, and you're back on the Frontier, you're the Widowmaker again, and you're the man to whom I owe my allegiance."

"Are you in touch with this clone?"

"Not directly. I leave messages at a blind electronic address. I assume he picks them up."

Nighthawk sat in silence, considering what he'd heard. Finally he looked at Kinoshita and spoke: "You serve the Widowmaker?"

"That's right."

"And that's me?"

"Yes."

"Then I want you to contact my clone and tell him that if he's not willing to be the Widowmaker anymore, you're through leaving messages for him."

"But—"

"If he's not the Widowmaker and I am, then your loyalty is to me, right?"

"Yes, but—"

"Then tell him you're all through sending messages. Wherever we wind up, I don't want *anyone* to know, not even him."

"You insist?"

"I do." He turned to Sarah. "Did you know about this?"

"No," she replied. "I'm as surprised as you are."

He looked at Kinoshita. "Okay, make up your mind: Are you serving *me* or *him*?"

"Despite your frequent protestations to the contrary, you're the Widowmaker again. I'm your man."

"Tell him I ordered you to cut off communications. No sense having him blame you for it."

Kinoshita nodded in assent.

"Maybe he'll seek you out himself, now that he can't keep tabs on you through Ito," suggested Sarah.

"He won't."

"How do you know?"

"It's difficult to explain," said Nighthawk. "Without me, there'd be no him. The reverse isn't true. I don't mind the thought of meeting him; he's very much like a son, from my viewpoint. But from his, I'm almost a god; he was created in my image, with my memories, for the sole purpose of keeping me alive. That was his mission, his only reason for existence." He sighed and shook his head. "No, he won't want to meet me in person." He glanced at Kinoshita. "Will he?"

"No, he absolutely refuses." Suddenly he smiled. "You should be grateful that he's the one I'm in contact with."

"Why?"

"I'm told the first clone was less religious, so to speak. He wanted to kill you."

"Still why?"

Kinoshita shrugged. "I don't know. My guess is that he felt like a shadow, or a surrogate, and the only way he could feel like a true human being was to be the *only* Nighthawk."

"That doesn't make sense. I can see why the second clone feels the way he does, but even when I was a young man, I don't think I was as stupid as you make the first clone sound."

"That's why he died," answered Kinoshita promptly. "He *wasn't* you, not where it counted. He had your physical attributes, but not your memories or your experience. Truth to tell, I don't think he *wanted* to be the Widowmaker." He frowned. "I wish he had taken me with him on his assignment. I might have been able to help him."

"Well, you helped the second one."

Kinoshita snorted his disagreement. "He never needed my help. Or anyone else's, for that matter."

"He seems to have made quite an impression on you," noted Nighthawk.

"He was *you*," answered Kinoshita. "At the height of your powers. Before you decided you didn't especially want to be you any longer."

"I like being *me*. I'm Jefferson Nighthawk. I don't want to be the Widowmaker anymore."

"This is getting a little too schizophrenic for me," interjected Sarah. "I think it's time to start considering our options."

"It's too soon," replied Kinoshita. "It'll be another ten or twelve Standard hours before we can be sure no one's following us."

"That doesn't mean we can't *consider* what to do," insisted Sarah. "We should have some plan of action. Two plans, really—one if we're being followed, one if we're not."

"If we're being followed, the only course of action is to lose them," said Kinoshita. "We're not going to fight them, ship to ship or man to man."

"All right," said Sarah. "Then let's see what worlds are within reach, on the assumption that no one's coming after us."

Kinoshita brought up a holograph showing their sector of the Inner Frontier, and had the navigational computer highlight every oxygen world that had been colonized.

"Fare-Thee-Well, Giancola II, Chrysler IV, New Angola, Lower Volta, Rashomon, Purpleveldt, Tigerstripe III, Nelson 23, Tallgrass . . ." Kinoshita's voice droned on and on, identifying each world.

"How about this one?" asked Sarah, pointing to a blue-and-green world about the size of Tumbleweed.

"Thaddeus," said Kinoshita.

"Thaddeus? That's a human name. Who was he?"

"I don't know. It could be the name of the navigator who first discovered the world, or the Pioneer who opened it up, or one of the planet's more famous citizens."

"It looks interesting."

"It looks like every other world," commented Nighthawk dryly.

"That's not so, Jefferson," she said. "Look at how much water it has. And cloud cover. Except for its size and location, it could be Earth itself."

"And except for my name, my looks, and my profession, I could be a chorus girl."

"All right, all right," she said. "Which world do *you* want to land on?"

"Makes no difference to me," answered Nighthawk. "Thaddeus is as good as any."

"Good." She turned to Kinoshita. "When you know for sure we're not being followed, divert to Thaddeus."

"All right," he said. "Let's get a readout and see what we can learn about it." He uttered a terse command to the computer, and instantly a series of notations appeared and hovered before their eyes:

Planet: Alpha Flint IV
Local Name: Thaddeus
Atmosphere: 19% oxygen, 78% nitrogen, 3% inert gases
Gravity: 98% Deluros VIII normal
Population: 18,203 humans, no indigenous sentient species

Currency: Maria Theresa dollars. Most locals will accept Far London pounds or New Tanganyika shillings. The Oligarchy credit is not honored.

"Is that okay with you?" asked Sarah.

"Yeah," said Nighthawk. "I've got enough Far London pounds to see us through until I convert my credits."

"I wonder why they don't accept them?" mused Kinoshita.

"The farther you get from the Oligarchy, the more certain the people are that it won't last any longer than the Republic or the Democracy did, and they don't want to be stuck with useless money."

"But that's silly!" protested Kinoshita. "The Republic and the Democracy each lasted for over two millennia, and their currency was always honored by their successors."

"Well, then," said Nighthawk, "just accept the fact that Frontier folk haven't got much use or faith in whoever's ruling the galaxy this month." He paused, blinking furiously, and turned to Sarah. "Give me another pill. Everyone's getting blurry again."

She did as he asked, and a moment later he was sleeping peacefully, while she sat down next to him, clasping his limp right hand in her own smaller ones.

It was ten hours later when he woke again, this time feeling physically healthy but starving. He and Sarah vanished into the galley for half an hour, and when he reemerged, sated, Kinoshita announced that they had not been followed and were now approaching Thaddeus.

They landed within an hour, summoned a robotic cart, and had it unload their luggage.

"Where to?" asked Nighthawk.

"I must take your luggage through Customs," replied the robot. "If you'll head seventeen degrees to the northeast, you will come to the Immigration Station, where you will be processed. You can pick up your things once you have passed through."

"Thanks," said Nighthawk. They headed off in the direction the robot had indicated until they came to Immigration, a small, computerized station that was able to handle only one person at a time.

Nighthawk stepped forward.

"Name?" asked the computer.

"Jefferson Nighthawk."

"Occupation?"

"Retired."

"Purpose of visit?"

"Tourism."

"Thaddeus is an agricultural and mining world with no tourist industry."

"It's also possible that I might choose to become a permanent resident of Thaddeus."

"Alone, or with the other members of your party?"

"With my party."

"I must access your primary bank account to ascertain that you have sufficient funds so you will not become a burden to the Thaddeus economy."

"My primary account is on Deluros VIII, but it's in credits," answered Nighthawk. "I do have some accounts in Far London pounds, if you'd prefer."

"With your permission, I will access all of them."

"Fine."

The computer read the microscopic account numbers on Nighthawk's passport, paused for some ten or twelve seconds, and then returned the passport.

"I am pleased to welcome you to Thaddeus."

"I'll need a map and a list of hotels, restaurants, and realtors."

"Processing your request . . . done." The map and lists suddenly appeared. "Here you are."

"Thanks."

Nighthawk walked through the station and waited for Sarah and Kinoshita to join him. They rented an airbus and drove it to the nearby town, then registered in the hotel—a room for Kinoshita, a suite for Nighthawk and Sarah.

"I should contact my son and tell him where I am," she remarked as they finished unpacking.

"Wait."

"Why?"

"Let's make sure we like it here first."

"All right—but we left Tumbleweed in such a hurry that I never told him we were going."

"He's half a galaxy away, and he contacts you about once every ten days—and only to ask for money. He can wait for a week or so."

She sighed. "I suppose so."

Nighthawk got to his feet. "I'd like a beer. You want to join me? I'll order from room service."

"I think I'd rather take a bath," she replied. "We were cooped up in that stuffy little ship for a long time."

He shrugged. "As you wish. I think I'll go down to the bar. I'll be back in time for dinner."

He left, took the airlift down to the main floor, and entered the hotel's bar, where he ordered a beer and took it over to an empty table. While he was wondering whether to call Kinoshita and treat him to a drink, a young man, dressed in brilliant colors, walked up.

"You're *him*, ain't you?" said the young man.

"I'm me," said Nighthawk.

"You can't fool me," said the young man. "I've seen your holo a hundred times. You're older, but you're him. You're the Widowmaker."

"You want an autograph, right?" said Nighthawk sardonically.

"I want to be the man who killed the Widowmaker."

"You and ten thousand others," said Nighthawk. "Go home, son, while you still can."

"You're afraid to face me, right?"

"Okay, I'm afraid to face you. You made the Widowmaker back down. Now go away."

"Goddamn!" said the young man. "You really *are* afraid to face me, aren't you?"

"Right as rain, kid. Now leave me alone."

The young man was silent for a moment, lost in thought. Finally he spoke again: "No, I got to fight you. If I tell people you backed down, they'll never believe me. But if I kill you, they'll *have* to believe me."

"I'm not fighting anyone," said Nighthawk. "Beat it. Or sit down and I'll buy you a beer."

"Oh, you'll fight me, Widowmaker," said the young man confidently.

"You think so, do you?"

"I saw the woman you came in with. You'll fight me now, or you'll fight me after I kill her, but one way or the other you'll—"

He was dead, his forehead a bubbling, smoking goo, before he could get out the final words.

Nighthawk was on his feet instantly, looking around for other challengers. There were eight men and a woman in the bar. None seemed disposed to go for their weapons.

"He called me out," said Nighthawk. "I tried to send him on his way."

"We all heard, Widowmaker," replied the nearest man.

"You know who I am?"

"He wasn't exactly trying to keep it a secret." The man looked down at the corpse. "Still, that wasn't what I'd call self-defense. He never knew what hit him."

"That's what will happen to anyone who threatens the woman I travel with," said Nighthawk. "You might pass the word."

As he walked out the door and took the airlift back to his suite, he knew that word of the incident would spread, and from now on every young punk out to make a reputation would goad him into a fight by threatening Sarah.

Something had to be done—and by the time he got off the airlift, he knew what that something was.

Chapter 22

"I want you to stay in the suite until word gets out that I've left the planet," said Nighthawk. "Order your meals here. Don't go outside for any reason. Then, after a couple of days, pack up and book passage to Serengeti."

"The zoo world?"

"Right. Go to the western continent. There's only one lodge there, so you'll be easy for me to find." He frowned. "At least, there used to only be one lodge. It's been a long time since I was there." He paused. "Don't worry if I don't show up right away. It could be a couple of months."

"Where will you be in the meantime?"

"I have work to do."

"Why can't I come with you?"

"Don't make me answer that," said Nighthawk. "It'll just hurt your feelings."

"I want to know."

He looked into her eyes. "You'd be in the way."

"Oh, Jesus—who are you going to kill?"

"Just do what I ask, all right?"

She wasn't happy, but finally she stopped arguing and agreed.

Three men sat in a lobby at the Newton II spaceport. They all wore weapons, as almost everyone did on the Inner Frontier, but they were relaxed, drinks in hand, joking with one another.

Jefferson Nighthawk approached them from behind. None of the three paid him any attention. He pulled out his projectile pistol and swiftly and efficiently put a bullet into each of their heads.

A woman screamed. A number of people ducked or threw themselves to the floor. Two spaceport security men raced over, weapons in hand.

Nighthawk held up his passport and his ancient but still-valid license. "My name is Jefferson Nighthawk, and I'm a licensed bounty hunter. There was paper on these three men." He produced hard copies of the Wanted posters.

"Sonofabitch!" exclaimed one of the security men. "The Widow-maker—in *my* spaceport!"

The second security man checked the holographs against the dead men's faces and IDs.

"It's them, all right."

Nighthawk turned to the small man who was standing some fifty feet away.

"Get the body bags and put 'em on ice."

Kinoshita nodded and went about his work.

Her name was Jenny the Dart, and she was a freelance assassin whose weapon of choice was a tailor-made pistol that shot poison darts with deadly accuracy.

She was just emerging from a chic restaurant on Roosevelt III when she found herself facing Jefferson Nighthawk.

"Hello, Jenny," he said.

"Do I know you?" she asked.

"No reason why you should."

"What do you want with me?" she demanded.

"You've killed seventeen innocent men and women, Jenny," said Nighthawk.

"Innocent of *what*?" she said contemptuously.

"That's not for me to answer. You're worth two million credits dead or alive. The choice is yours."

She made the wrong choice, and fell lifeless to the pavement less than a second later.

"Ito! Take care of her."

He called himself Will Shakespeare, which was a pretty impressive name for a man who had never learned to read or write. But he knew that everyone respected Shakespeare, even though he'd been dead for more than six millennia, and he decided that they'd respect anyone who wore Shakespeare's name.

Of course, the fact that he'd killed more than fifty men and aliens didn't hurt, either.

He was after Number 51 when a tall, slender, gray-haired man blocked his way.

"Who the hell are you?" demanded Will.

"Francis Bacon," said Nighthawk.

"Step aside, old man."

"I'm afraid I can't do that. I'm pissed at you for stealing all my plays."

Will Shakespeare was still trying to figure out what Francis Bacon was talking about when the laser burned a smoking hole in his chest.

The last of them bore the simplest name and the biggest reward. It was an alien known simply as Bug, and it wore no weapons at all. Instead, it killed with the natural fluids of its body, spitting them as far as thirty feet with enormous force and accuracy, then watching as they instantly ate into flesh and bone until all was swiftly dissolved.

Nighthawk found Bug in the squalid Alien Quarter on Pretorius V, making its rounds of the quarter, exacting tribute from the other aliens for not killing them this month.

He approached Bug directly and silently, which had always worked up to this point, for the killers he approached had no reason to be apprehensive about his presence, and were totally secure in their gifts.

But Bug knew that Men didn't enter the Alien Quarter without a reason—and the only reason a Man would approach it was the four-million-credit reward. Bug waited until Nighthawk was twenty feet away, then ejected a stream of deadly spittle from its mouth. Nighthawk had been quicker in his youth, but he was still fast enough to throw himself to the ground beneath the alien's saliva, pulling out his Burner and firing it as he fell.

It was a fatal shot—but Bug's race possessed exceptional vitality, and even though it knew he would soon be dead, it still had enough strength to raise itself on what passed for its knees, face Nighthawk, and eject another lethal stream.

Nighthawk was ready, and turned it to steam even as it flew toward him, then burned out Bug's eyes, just in case it had the strength to spit once more before it died.

It was an intelligent maneuver, for Bug didn't collapse for another thirty seconds.

Nighthawk got to his feet and surveyed his surroundings. Dozens of aliens of all races were staring at him, but none was approaching.

"Ito! Get this garbage off the street."

* * *

They were eleven days out of Thaddeus, and were on their way to the
Binder X bounty station to turn in the bodies and collect the rewards.

"Six bodies, fifteen million credits," intoned Kinoshita. "That's a lot
of money."

"I *need* a lot of money."

"Now that you're the Widowmaker again, it seems to me that you can
get money whenever you want it."

"How many times do I have to tell you that I'm not the Widowmaker?"

"After these last two weeks?" said Kinoshita. "One hell of a lot more
times than you have, and then I still won't believe you."

"You're a fool."

*If I'm a fool for thinking that the Widowmaker is back in business and
has just killed six outlaws for the bounties,* thought Kinoshita, *just what
does that make* you?

Chapter 23

"Okay, you've got your money," said Kinoshita as their ship reached light speed and left the Binder system far behind them. "What now?"

"Now I spend it."

Kinoshita blinked rapidly. "All of it?"

"That's right."

"You must be buying Sarah one hell of a present."

"A very ephemeral one," answered Nighthawk.

"So where are we going?"

"I know where *I'm* going. I don't know if you'll want to come along."

"I told you before," replied Kinoshita. "I go where the Widowmaker goes."

"And I told you: I'm not the Widowmaker."

"All right," said Kinoshita. "I go where *you* go. Do you like that better?"

"You may change your mind."

"Try me."

"I'm going to Deluros."

"Deluros?" repeated Kinoshita, surprised. "What the hell is there to do on Deluros?" He looked sharply at Nighthawk. "Are you going back to kill your lawyer?"

Nighthawk smiled. "You know, that's a tempting thought—but no."

"What then?"

"I can't tell you."

"Why the hell not?"

"Because you and I have always been lawmen, and I'm going to commit a felony—probably several of them. If I'm captured, I know I can't be

broken. You're a good man, Ito, but I don't know that with the right combination of torture and drugs you won't talk." He paused. "And since I can't
tell you my reasons for going to Deluros, I officially release you from
whatever duty or fealty you feel you owe me."

"Do you want me to come or not?" asked Kinoshita bluntly.

"You can make my mission a little easier if you come with me, but I'll
accomplish it regardless."

"Okay, I'm coming."

"You're sure you don't want to consider it?"

"I *did* consider it. I'm coming."

"Then, thank you."

"Everything we've done since we left Thaddeus was part of a plan,
right?"

"That's right."

"You really plan to commit a felony?"

"At least one."

"I hope to hell you know what you're doing," said Kinoshita.

"That makes two of us," answered Nighthawk.

Chapter 24

Deluros VIII was a freak.

It possessed ten times Earth's surface area, with an almost identical atmosphere and gravity, two large freshwater oceans, and enough landmass to house thirty-three billion bureaucrats in some semblance of comfort. It was right in the middle of the most populous, star-studded section of the galaxy, while Earth was isolated not even in the galactic suburbs, but out in the rural extremities of the Spiral Arm.

Man began moving his seat of government to Deluros VIII during the middle years of the Republic, and by the time of the Oligarchy, almost four millennia later, even huge, awesome Deluros VIII was inadequate to the task of ruling Man's empire.

There were fourteen other planets in the Deluros system. The outer six were all gas giants, totally useless for Man's purposes, but Deluros VIII provided the answer to the Oligarchy's problem. After consultation with hundreds of leading scientists, it was decided to break it apart with a number of carefully placed and extremely powerful explosive charges. The small fragments, as well as the larger irregular ones, were then totally obliterated. The remaining forty-eight planetoids were turned over to the largest governmental departments of the Oligarchy: one was reserved for Agriculture, one for Alien Affairs, one for Exobiology, and so on. (The military promptly claimed the four largest, and was soon feeling cramped for space.) Domes were erected on each planetoid, worldwide bureaucratic complexes were constructed, and life-support systems were implemented. The orbits of the planetoids were adjusted so that they danced their slow minuet around huge Deluros millions of miles from each other, and tens of thousands of ships sped daily between the enormous ruling world of the Oligarchy and its forty-eight extensions.

"You know," remarked Kinoshita, staring at the viewscreen as they approached their destination, "every time I see Deluros VIII I feel like some kind of country bumpkin. The last time I was stationed here they announced that you could finally reach any location on the planet without taking a step outside. Can you imagine that—a single building that covers the whole goddamned planet?"

"I seem to remember some parks, and some outdoor pavilions," said Nighthawk.

"Oh, I didn't mean to imply that every inch of the planet is a building. It's got courtyards and atriums—some of them extending for hundreds of acres. I'm just saying that you don't *have* to step outside to get from any point to any other point unless you want to—and sometimes not even if you want to."

"I suppose they think that's something to be proud of."

"They think it's an achievement unmatched in the history of architecture."

"Then they belong here," said Nighthawk, making no effort to hide his distaste.

"There are worse places to be," said Kinoshita. "It's got the best restaurants and theaters and art galleries and sports stadiums and hotels in the galaxy."

"No argument," replied Nighthawk. He studied the screen, which was showing a transmitted view of the world, as seen from a height of some forty miles. "It's got everything you could ever want—except character."

"You think those dry, dusty, underpopulated worlds we work on have character?"

"When you're standing on one of them, you know it's that world and not any other."

"You know it on Deluros, too," responded Kinoshita. "It's the only world where the buildings are so tall that there are only a few places where you can stand on the ground and still see the sky."

"And you think that's a good thing, do you?"

"I didn't say that. I said it makes Deluros as unique as any Frontier world."

"You can meet every man who lives on a Frontier world before you can find a given location on Deluros."

"That's because you're a stranger here. I've lived on Deluros VIII. It's the most logically laid-out city I've ever seen. What it lacks in character it makes up for in order."

"If you say so."

Nighthawk went to the galley for a beer. When he came back, they had entered an orbit some six hundred miles above the huge planet's surface. Once, centuries ago, there had been many spaceports on Deluros VIII, but after the increasing congestion caused numerous fatal crashes, the planetary planners gave in to the inevitable and created dozens (then hundreds, and still later thousands) of orbiting hangars. Ships docked at the hangars, Customs and Immigration were to be cleared hundreds of miles above the surface, and only authorized government-run shuttles were allowed to transfer the tens of millions of daily (and sometimes hourly) travelers to and from the planet.

The ship's radio suddenly came to life.

"Please identify yourself and your ship," said a cold, emotionless voice that might or might not have been human.

"My name is Jefferson Nighthawk, passport number M3625413C, fifteen days out of Alpha Flint IV on the Inner Frontier. My ship is a Class H 341 Golden Streak, registration number 677LR2439. Crew of two: myself and Ito Kinoshita."

"I have just uploaded a list of 174 contraband substances into your ship's computer. Are you carrying any of them?"

"I doubt it, but I won't know until I study the list."

"You have a Class H ship. *It* can answer." Pause. "In fact, it just has. You are cleared to dock at Hangar 113H. I will feed the coordinates and bay number to your navigational computer."

"Fine. Is that all?"

"Have you a place to stay? I can make reservations at more than six thousand hotels."

"I'd like a two-bedroom suite in the vicinity of the John Ramsey Memorial Medical Center. Price is no object."

"Done. You have a guaranteed suite at the Wellington Arms Hotel, a six-mile underground monorail ride from the John Ramsey Memorial Medical Center. Your confirmation number is 10733422. If you choose to cancel your reservation, you must inform the hotel by 1800 hours, Deluros North Central Time."

"Thank you."

"When you clear Customs and Immigration, take either a blue-coded or orange-coded shuttle, then transfer to a Sector 179 shuttle at the Ten-Mile Platform."

"Blue or orange?" repeated Nighthawk.

"That is correct. Any other shuttle will land you on the wrong platform, and you will be thousands of miles from your destination."

"Thank you."

"My deep scanner informs me that you are wearing the following weapons: a laser pistol, a sonic pistol, a projectile pistol, and two knives; and that Ito Kinoshita is wearing a laser pistol and a sonic pistol." The voice paused. "You will have to leave these aboard your ship, as weapons are not permitted on Deluros VIII."

"I'm a licensed bounty hunter," said Nighthawk. "Most planets have a provision that allows bounty hunters to carry registered weapons."

"Deluros VIII did indeed have such a provision," said the voice, "but it was repealed in 5073 G.E. You are not permitted to bring any weapons with you."

"All right. Is there anything else?"

"I have no further questions, though of course Immigration and Customs will have their own questions to ask you. Your ship will finish docking in approximately ninety seconds. I can answer any questions you may have during that time."

"None," said Nighthawk, breaking the connection. He looked at Kinoshita. "Can you say 'overregulated'?" he asked wryly.

"It may be overregulated, but there hasn't been an assassination on Deluros in almost two decades."

"What about simple everyday murders?"

"Most husbands and wives don't need guns to kill each other," replied Kinoshita with a smile.

"A point well taken," said Nighthawk.

There was a momentary silence. Then: "Why did you want your weapons?" asked Kinoshita.

"I feel comfortable with them."

"I wish you'd stop lying to me," said Kinoshita. "I'm here in your service. I'm prepared to lay down my life for you. I'll continue to do it whether you lie or not, but I'd feel less like a fool if you'd start telling me the truth."

"You'll know soon enough," said Nighthawk. "And I don't plan on firing any weapons."

"Then why do you think you need them?"

Nighthawk shrugged. "Things don't always go according to plan."

The ship shuddered as it docked in its bay, and a moment later Nighthawk and Kinoshita were in one of many long lines at the Immigration center. The questions were more numerous and more thorough than on the Frontier worlds, but eventually they got through them, had temporary visas added to their passport cards, and accompanied their luggage through the Customs scanners.

Finally they went to the Deluros Departure Terminal, walked past some two dozen shuttles carrying the wrong color coding, finally found a blue-coded one, and boarded it along with almost a thousand other passengers. It took less than two minutes to fill to capacity, and then they were floating down to the enormous Ten-Mile Platform, which encircled the planet like a wedding ring. Here they took a seemingly endless tram ride until they came to a Sector 179 shuttle and boarded it.

It took this somewhat larger shuttle almost ten minutes to fill to capacity, and then it took off for the surface. They landed gently on a rooftop some two miles above the ground, took an airlift to the subbasement level, and found themselves in an enormous monorail station. Hundreds of tracks crossed the area, heading out in all directions, and as quickly as one train departed another instantly appeared to take its place.

"So how do we find the Wellington Arms?" muttered Nighthawk.

"We ask," said Kinoshita, walking to one of a hundred Tourist Aid computers along the wall.

"Good afternoon," said the computer as its lens registered his proximity. "How may I help you?"

"How do I get to the Wellington Arms from here?" asked Kinoshita.

"Take Monorail Number 206 South to Station RL—that will be four stops from here. Transfer to Monorail Number 1701 East, and exit at Station SC."

"And we're there?"

"You will be within walking distance," answered the computer. "Once you are at Station SC, ask another Tourist Aid computer for exact directions."

"Thanks," said Kinoshita. He turned to Nighthawk. "That's the way you do it around here. There are natives who still need these damned things to get around." He walked toward the platform for Monorail Number 206 South, and Nighthawk fell into step beside him. "I don't imagine things have changed all that much in a century. Don't you remember using the computers when you came here before?"

"I was ninety percent dead," answered Nighthawk. "I don't remember much of anything." He glanced around at the mass of humanity, each hurrying toward one of the six hundred monorails. "Just as well," he added. "If this is living, I think I'd prefer death." He looked around contemptuously. "Hell, I'd welcome it."

"You've been on the Frontier too long."

"And you haven't been there long enough," countered Nighthawk.

They soon reached the platform, caught a tram, and within a few minutes had transferred at Station RL, ridden another mile, and exited at Station SC.

This time it was Nighthawk who approached the computer to get directions to the hotel—"One block east of Exit 14, turn north 172 feet to the front door, enter, turn left 80 feet to the registration desk"—and in a few minutes they were finally in their suite.

A robot brought their luggage up to the room, explained how to use the plethora of gimmicks and gadgets that had been built into the suite, and then made a graceful retreat.

"Nice place," said Kinoshita, walking around the sitting room that connected the two large bedrooms. "I wonder how much it's costing you?"

"I'm sure they'll tell me before I leave."

"You ready to talk yet?"

"We've been talking all day."

"You know what I mean," said Kinoshita. "Why are we here? What is there on Deluros that managed to pull you halfway across the galaxy?"

"Nothing," said Nighthawk. "Yet."

"I don't understand."

"That's just as well."

"Damn it, Jefferson!"

Nighthawk walked to the door. "I'm going out for a while. Wait here for me. If I'm not back by morning, check to see if I'm being held in one of the local police stations, and if I am, bail me out."

"That's all?" said Kinoshita. "Can't I do anything more?"

"Yes, you can," replied Nighthawk. "I need a piece of information from you. Once you give it to me, you'll figure it all out or you're a lot dumber than I think you are."

Kinoshita stared curiously at him. "I know something of value to you?"

"It's nothing I can't find out for myself, but you can save me some time and give me some details I can't get anywhere else."

"If it's mine to give, you're welcome to it," said Kinoshita. "What is it?"

"An address."

Chapter 25

Gilbert Egan rode the walkway down the long underground corridor to his office, passing a pair of security checkpoints. He stood before his door, waited for the scanners to register his retina, weight, and bone structure, and entered.

The door slid shut behind him, and Egan walked over to his cluttered desk. He stopped, startled, when he saw the man sitting behind it.

"Good morning, Dr. Egan," said Nighthawk. "Pull up a chair. We've got some business to discuss."

"Who the hell are you?" demanded Egan.

"You really don't recognize me?"

"Should I?" asked Egan, staring at him. Then: "Shit! You're Nighthawk!"

"That's right."

"What are you doing here?" demanded Egan. "How did you get in?"

"I never saw a security system I couldn't crack," said Nighthawk.

"But you missed a century of technological improvement!" Egan pointed out.

"Yeah . . . but I'm the Widowmaker."

"You realize you've broken at least one law, sneaking in here, possibly several."

"Suppose you let me worry about that," said Nighthawk.

"Fine," said Egan, getting to his feet. "You can discuss it with the authorities." He walked to the door.

"Take one step outside or call for help and I'll break another law," said Nighthawk, and Egan turned to find himself covered by a Burner.

"How the hell did you get a gun on Deluros?" demanded Egan, half frightened, half outraged.

"I have my methods."

"What do you want?" asked Egan. "If it's money . . ."

"Shut up and listen," said Nighthawk. "All I want from you is a favor. As for money, I'm prepared to pay you ten million credits for it."

"Ten million credits?" repeated Egan unbelievingly. "Who do you want me to kill?"

"No one. In fact, quite the opposite."

"I don't know what you're talking about."

"There have been two clones of me already," said Nighthawk. "I want a third one."

"Your eplasia has been cured, and you seem to be in good health," said Egan. "Why do you want another clone?"

"My reasons are no concern of yours. I want it, and I'm prepared to pay handsomely for it."

"Creating a clone is a felony, punishable by—"

"Five million is for your skill," interrupted Nighthawk. "The other five million is for the risk."

"Look," said Egan, "even if I wanted to, you've got the wrong man. I'm just a doctor who specializes in cryonics."

"I'm offering to make you a filthy-rich doctor."

"Mr. Nighthawk, my job was keeping you alive. That's what I do. Others cloned you; I didn't."

"You know who they were." Nighthawk tossed a thick envelope on the desk. "There's ten million credits in there in unmarked bills. Talk one of them into it for two million and you've earned eight million credits for ten minutes' work."

"How long have I got to make up my mind?"

"About a minute," said Nighthawk. "If your answer is no, that's the end of it—with this stipulation: If you tell anyone I was here, I'll kill you. And believe me, I can do it before they can stop me."

"I believe you."

"Thirty seconds left."

"All right," said Egan. "I'll do it."

He reached for the envelope, but Nighthawk was faster, pulling it back. He opened it up, pulled out five million credits, and placed them on the desk.

"A down payment," he said. "You get the other half when I get the clone."

Chapter 26

It was an hour after midnight as Nighthawk approached Egan's exclusive apartment, more than a mile above the planet's surface.

Security was tight in the luxury titanium-and-glass structure. He had to get a robotic doorman to announce his presence while still on the main floor. After he was cleared, his ID and retina were read by the airlift before it ascended, and when he got off at the 353rd floor he went through the entire process again before he was permitted to leave the vicinity of the lift.

There was a final scanning at Egan's front door, and at last he was allowed to enter the apartment. A sleek, shining robot butler greeted him and ushered him into a huge, sprawling room with constantly changing murals on the walls. State-of-the-art furniture floated gently a few inches above a plush carpet with an almost hypnotically swirling pattern, and a huge window looked down on a cloud layer.

Two men were waiting for him. Egan stepped forward to greet him.

"Jefferson Nighthawk, I'd like you to meet . . . ah . . . Doctor X." Egan gestured toward his companion. "Doctor X, Jefferson Nighthawk."

"I've worshiped you ever since I was a boy," said Doctor X, and as he extended his hand, Nighthawk saw that he was a rather pudgy man in his mid-forties. "I'm thrilled to meet you in the flesh. I was responsible for one of your clones—the one who met such an unfortunate end in the Solio system."

"Egan's explained the situation to you?"

"Yes."

"And you're willing?"

"That's why I'm here. I have only one stipulation: I would like your assurance that both you and the clone will be returning to the Inner Frontier, and will not attempt to reside in the Oligarchy. It could be most awkward if the authorities learned of this."

"You have my word."

There was an uneasy pause.

"Aren't you going to insist on knowing my real name?" asked Doctor X.

"Will knowing it make the operation go any smoother?" asked Nighthawk.

"No, of course not."

"Then why should I care?"

"Well, I thought—"

"The police can't extract what I don't know," explained Nighthawk. *And besides, Ito will be following you home later tonight, so if you do betray me, he'll know who to kill.*

"A very reasonable attitude," said Doctor X, looking much relieved. "When do you wish the process to begin?"

"What's wrong with tomorrow?"

Doctor X shook his head. "I can't be ready by then."

"Why not?" asked Nighthawk. "You're the cloning expert. I assume you have access to everything you need."

"It's not that simple, Mr. Nighthawk," explained the medic. "When your first two clones were created, we had the protection of the most powerful law firm on Deluros VIII, so we didn't have to be quite so secretive. But for *this* procedure, security must be absolute, as we all face many years of imprisonment if we should be apprehended. I'll need at least three days to set up a lab, perhaps four. Then I'll be ready to take some skin scrapings from you."

"All right," said Nighthawk. "How many people will be involved in the project?"

"Four at most, all of them trusted aides of many years' standing—and all of them men and women who worked on your first clone."

"And how long will the whole process take?"

"The science of cloning has made phenomenal strides, despite government opposition," said Doctor X. "We can have a fully grown clone operational in six to eight weeks. The progress in nutrient solutions alone has been—"

"I don't care *how* it gets done," Nighthawk interrupted him. "Only *when*."

"I assume you care about more than that," responded Doctor X.

"For example?"

"For example, what physical age should the clone be?"

Nighthawk considered for a moment. "Twenty-five."

"If you wish, we can supply him with your memories, right up to the instant of his creation."

"What will that require?"

"Just you."

"Explain."

"The transfer of memories is rather like uploading data from one computer to another, but because the brain is so much more complex and subtle, it's a much longer process. I'd have to put you under for almost three days. There's some minimal danger involved in being anesthetized for so long, but you seem to be in fine physical condition. I think you can handle it."

"Out of the question."

"There's no other way. That's how your second clone received your memories. Of course, you were already unconscious; frozen, in fact."

"The answer is no."

"It won't hurt at all," Doctor X assured him.

"I'm not worried about a little pain," said Nighthawk. "But I'm commissioning a felony, and I've already made both of you wealthy men. There's no guarantee that you won't simply forget to wake me up."

"I assure you—"

"I'm sure you do," said Nighthawk, "but what are your assurances worth to a dead man?"

The doctor shrugged. "I don't know what I can say to convince you . . ."

"The only way I can be convinced is to have a confederate standing next to you with a gun—but that might make you nervous, and I don't want you doing the wrong thing at the wrong time." *Hell, in a way, it's just as well he won't have my memories. I don't want to be the Widowmaker anymore; he's got to revel in it.*

"All right," agreed the doctor with obvious reluctance. "We'll attach him to educator tapes day and night for the final month of his development. He'll enter the world with a basic education, fully able to speak, read, and write."

"That'll be good enough," said Nighthawk. "I'll handle it from there."

"We'll also have to give him a childhood," added Doctor X. "They'll be false memories, of course, but pleasant ones."

"No," said Nighthawk.

"I beg your pardon?"

"No memories are better than false ones."

"You're speaking from ignorance, Mr. Nighthawk," replied Doctor X. "If he enters the world as an adult with no memories at all, he'll soon be a basket case. As he develops his own very real memories and you educate him, the ones we give him will soon fade."

"You're sure?"

"We kept tabs on the first clone until he left on his mission—and by that time, only a month or two into his existence, he had already jettisoned most of his false memories."

"You mean, forgotten them?"

"In a way. Once your new clone knows his memories are false, he will—how can I explain it?—push them into the attics and basements of his mind, replacing them with experiences he has undergone, experiences he knows to be true."

"How can he do that?"

"When you see an exceptionally realistic holographic entertainment, or experience a vivid dream, you accept it as real while it's happening—but once it's over and you realize that it was merely an illusion of reality, you have no difficulty separating it from real experiences, have you? Your clone will do much the same thing."

"You'd better be right," said Nighthawk. "This clone is going to be under enough pressure from the real world. I don't want him hallucinating or going schizoid because he can't tell his real experiences from his false ones."

"It won't happen," said Doctor X firmly.

"It better not."

Doctor X stared at Nighthawk for a long moment. "May I ask exactly why you want me to create him?"

"You can ask."

"You can trust to my discretion, Mr. Nighthawk."

"I'm sure I can," replied Nighthawk. He smiled humorlessly. "And my clone can trust to mine."

Another awkward silence.

"If we have nothing further to say to each other, I think I shall take my leave of you," said Doctor X.

"We have one thing further to say, or rather, *you* have," said Nighthawk. "I want an address."

"Where we're creating the clone, you mean?"

"That's the only address that interests me," said Nighthawk.

"As soon as I know, I'll tell Gilbert, and he can tell you. But I warn you, Mr. Nighthawk—we must have complete secrecy. Knowing where the clone is being created does not mean you will be allowed access after the day we take the scrapings."

"Suppose you let *me* worry about that."

Egan was unable to suppress an amused chuckle.

Chapter 27

The handsome young man opened his eyes and tried to focus them.

"Where am I?" he rasped.

"Take it easy, son," said Doctor X. "You're just fine."

"Who are you?" Suddenly the young man looked very confused. "Who am *I*?"

"You're in a very private hospital," said Doctor X. "This gentleman standing next to me is Jefferson Nighthawk. He'll answer all your questions."

He nodded to Nighthawk, then left the room.

Nighthawk walked over to the bed. "How do you feel?"

"I don't know. Nothing hurts—but I can't remember how I got here."

"I'll be happy to tell you. But let's wait a few moments until you've got all your wits about you. You've been asleep a long time."

The young man stared at Nighthawk, puzzled. "Do I know you?"

"Not yet, but you will."

"What was your name again?"

"Jefferson Nighthawk."

The young man blinked furiously. "I seem to remember something about a Jefferson Nighthawk, something I heard or read when I was a kid. Were you an athlete or something?"

Nighthawk smiled. "Something."

"Wait a minute," said the young man, his face taut with concentration. "Now I remember! You're the Widowmaker!"

"That's right."

"But you've been dead for a century!"

"Not quite," replied Nighthawk. "I contracted an incurable disease, and I voluntarily submitted myself to cryonic freezing for a century—until it wasn't incurable any longer."

"Well, I'm thrilled to meet you," said the young man. "But what interest does a famous lawman like you have in someone like me?"

"More than you can imagine."

The young man looked expectantly at him.

"I don't like beating about the bush," continued Nighthawk, "and I don't think you do, either. So I'm going to tell you some things that are going to be difficult for you to accept. You won't believe them at first, but they're true nonetheless. Are you ready for them?"

The young man sat up, and just as quickly collapsed back onto the bed.

"Damn!" he muttered. "What's the matter with me?"

"Nothing."

"There's *something* wrong, maybe the same disease you had," he continued. "I can't even sit up by myself."

"You'll contract the disease eventually," said Nighthawk, not without sympathy, "but you don't have it now. You can sit up, and if you try a few more times, you'll do it without any problems." He paused. "You're not sick. You're just using muscles that you've never used before."

"What are you talking about?" said the young man. "All I'm doing is sitting up."

"Listen to me, son," said Nighthawk. "You haven't used *any* of your muscles. Ever."

The young man stared at him. "All right, who the hell are you really?"

"I told you: Jefferson Nighthawk."

"You also told me you're more than a century old, and that I've never used any of my muscles before. Why should I believe anything you say?"

"Only one reason," said Nighthawk. "I'm telling you the truth. I *am* Jefferson Nighthawk." He paused, staring at the young man. "And so are you."

"What asylum did you escape from?"

"Here," said Nighthawk, handing a small mirror to him. "Take a good, hard look."

The young man studied himself very carefully, occasionally glancing up at Nighthawk with a curious expression on his face. Finally he handed the mirror back.

"What am I—your son?"

"Not quite."

"I'm not in the mood for guessing games."

"You're my clone," said Nighthawk.

The young man grabbed the mirror back and studied it even more intently. Finally he shook his head vigorously. "You're crazy! I remember things, things from when I was a boy!"

"I know. Those are memories you've been allowed to borrow until you get some of your own."

"Bullshit! Nobody borrows memories!"

"You think not?" said Nighthawk. "You remember growing up on a farm on Pollux IV. You always wanted a dog, and finally your father imported one from Earth itself. You called him Snapper. He drowned when the two of you were swimming in the river together, and you blamed yourself for years. Your first love was Becky Raymond from the neighboring farm, but you never told her. When you were fourteen, you—"

"Enough!" shouted the young man. He stared at Nighthawk. "I never mentioned Becky to *anyone*, not even my brother!"

"I know."

The young man looked distressed. "*Was* there a Becky?"

"Yes," said Nighthawk, not without sympathy. "But not in your past. In someone else's."

The young man was silent for a very long moment. Finally he spoke: "I thought clones were illegal."

"They are."

"Then how—?"

"I paid a lot of people off."

"Why?"

"That's something we have to talk about. I think we'd better wait until you've assimilated what I've already told you. Tomorrow, perhaps."

"Now," said the young man firmly. "You've just told me that yesterday I was a blob of protoplasm, and today I'm a younger version of you. I want to know why."

"Good," said Nighthawk approvingly. "I don't like procrastination in my Jefferson Nighthawks."

"You make it sound like I'm not the only clone."

"You're the third—though you're the first I've laid eyes on."

"I take it the first two didn't make it out of the lab?" said the young man.

"They made it out," said Nighthawk. "The first one was killed. The second one's still out there somewhere, with a new name and a new face."

"Why do you need so many clones? In fact, why do you need any at all?"

"While I was frozen here on Deluros, inflation was so rampant that I was in danger of running out of money before they found a cure for my disease. Someone on the Frontier offered a lot of money for a clone that

could wipe out some enemies. That was the first one. He did his job, but
didn't outlive it. That bought me a few years. The second clone bought me
the rest of the time I needed."

"And you're cured now?"

"That's right."

"So why am I here?"

"I need you for a totally different reason." Nighthawk smiled ruefully.
"It seems that the galaxy needs a Widowmaker more than this particular
Widowmaker needs the galaxy."

"I don't know what you're talking about."

"I'm an old man," said Nighthawk. "I've got a woman I care for, I'm
tired of killing, and I want to live out the rest of my life in peace."

"So?"

"There are a couple of million men and women out there who want
the Widowmaker dead, enemies the first two clones made, enemies I don't
even recognize. I killed some of them in self-defense, but now word is out
that the Widowmaker is back on the Frontier, and every punk kid who's out
to make a name for himself is seeking me out." He paused. "Do you see
where this is leading?"

"Yeah," said the young man, staring at him curiously. "I think so."

"Well, let me eliminate any doubts right here and now," said Nighthawk. "Son, I created you to take over the family business."

Chapter 28

They had no trouble leaving the Deluros system. Nighthawk, with five million credits still in his possession, spent a million on the best fake fingerprints, retinagrams, and passport money could buy, and the scanners never once blinked as they passed the clone through.

It took them three days to reach Serengeti and pick up Sarah, who was less surprised than Nighthawk had expected, and then they went deep into the Inner Frontier, finally landing on Dustdevil, an arid little world circling an unimpressive binary.

Then Nighthawk began the task of training the new Widowmaker.

"Kinoshita will teach you everything you need to know about shooting and freehand fighting," said Nighthawk. "He did a fine job with the first clone, who was just about your age."

"Then why did the clone die?" asked the young man.

"Not for lack of physical abilities. You've got every one I ever possessed, and you're not even in your prime yet." Nighthawk paused. "The problem with the clone was that his head wasn't on right. Ito will train your body; I'll train your mind."

The young man flew through the air and landed heavily on his back.

"You cheated!" he said accusingly.

"Of course I cheated," said Kinoshita. "You think murderers and assassins don't cheat? Let's try it again."

"Give me a minute to catch my breath."

Kinoshita walked over. "Sure, kid. Take your time." Suddenly he kicked the young man full in the face.

"You son of a bitch!"

"First rule of the game, kid," said Kinoshita. "Never trust a killer."

"I'm surprised the first clone didn't kill you," muttered the young man, getting to his feet and facing his antagonist.

"He tried," said Kinoshita, dodging a heavy blow, grabbing an arm, and twisting suddenly. "But just like you, he telegraphed."

The young man went sprawling again.

"I thought you were going to—"

"Never picture what you think I might do, kid," said Kinoshita. "If you do, that's what you're subconsciously prepared for. And if I do anything else, it takes you a fraction of a second to adjust."

"I wonder if the pair of you aren't wasting your time," said the young man. "I don't think I'll ever be good enough to take you."

"Of course you will—and sooner than you think. After all, you're Jefferson Nighthawk."

"Okay," said the young man, getting back to his feet. "Let's try again."

A moment later he went flying again—but this time he was a fraction of an inch and a fraction of a second closer to landing a near-deadly blow on Kinoshita.

Every afternoon and every evening they would sit in the living room, man and clone, and the master would lecture the pupil.

"The thing to remember," said Nighthawk, "is that by the time there's paper on a man, he's no longer wanted on suspicion of anything. He's a killer, and while some of them are the nicest men and women you'd ever want to meet, the Widowmaker lives by a simple code: To feel compassion toward a killer is an insult to his victims."

"What if he begs for mercy?"

"You don't give him a chance to," responded Nighthawk. "This isn't some holo drama where two gunmen face each other on the street. You're the good guy; always remember that. The law's on your side. And being the good guy gives you certain advantages. You know what your enemy looks like; he doesn't know who you are. You know his history; he doesn't know yours. You can study him at your leisure; he can't study you. And when you're ready to take him, you don't have to call him out and give him a chance to blow you away. If he's sitting at a bar or a card table or a restaurant, you walk up behind him and put a bullet or a beam in his ear."

"Women, too?"

"You think a woman with a Burner or a Screecher can't kill you just as dead as a man can?"

"I was raised not to—"

"When a woman takes a shot at you, you'd better overcome your feelings—or you're dead."

"Okay, there are four targets at three hundred yards," said Kinoshita. "Blow 'em away."

The young man drew his Burner and fired it, hitting three and missing one.

"Not bad. Not good, but not bad."

"Why is this important? Who am I going to shoot from this far away?"

"Hopefully no one."

"Then why—"

"You can't always get in close to the man you're after. Sometimes it's a matter of taking him out from a quarter mile away or letting him escape."

"All right. Let me try again."

This time he hit all four.

"Not bad."

"Damned good, if you ask me," said the young man.

"I didn't ask you." Kinoshita held up a stopwatch. "You hit four targets in three seconds. If those were men, the last two had time to blow you away. Let's cut that time in half."

"Then what?"

"Then you do it with the other hand. And with every other weapon we've got around here. And then you do it at four hundred yards, and at five hundred."

"Five hundred? It can't be done.

"Sure it can. That old man in the house can still do it, and you're going to be better than he ever was."

"Do you really think so?"

Kinoshita smiled. "Kid, training Widowmakers is one of the very best things I do."

After a month, Nighthawk said good-bye to Sarah and Kinoshita and took the clone to Barrios II, home of the Gomorrah Palace, the biggest whorehouse on the Inner Frontier.

Nighthawk picked up the tab as the young man went to bed with a different woman every morning and evening for five days.

"Aren't you interested in sampling their wares at all?" asked the young man as he emerged from yet another bedroom.

"I've got what I want waiting for me back on Dustdevil." He paused. "I think it's about time we were getting back there."

"Well, I want to thank you for bringing me here."

"No need to thank me. It's part of your education."

"It is?"

Nighthawk nodded. "The first clone died because he let his hormones rule his mind, and it impaired his judgment. He fell for the first woman he saw, and eventually she proved his undoing. I don't want that happening to you."

The young man frowned. "And what I've been doing this past week will prevent it?"

"It's probably not in the textbooks, but yeah, it will."

"How?"

"By showing you that sex is enjoyable no matter who you have it with, and that all women are pretty much the same between their legs—just like all men. It's what's between their ears that makes you decide whether or not to slay a dragon for them."

"You've got an interesting way of making your point."

"I know what would impress me," said Nighthawk, "so I know what will leave a lasting impression on you."

And, of course, it did.

While Kinoshita spent the next sixty days honing the young man's marksmanship and fighting abilities, Nighthawk took over at nights, lecturing on strategy, preparing him for the thousand situations he might confront. Then one day he pulled out a nondescript bottle of whiskey and poured each of them a glass.

"I don't like it," said the young man, making a face. "It burns my throat as it goes down."

"You don't have to like it," said Nighthawk. "You just have to learn to hold it, to drink and not let it affect your judgment or your abilities."

"Why?"

"Because a lot of information you need will be obtained in taverns, and if you're not used to drinking, it could have a very adverse effect on your reactions."

"You're sure I have to do this?"

"Trust me, you'll learn to enjoy this before long." Nighthawk paused. "Once I know you can handle your liquor, we'll start on a couple of very mild drugs that you'll use in situations where you've got to visit drug dens. You'll enjoy them, too, but don't forget that the object of the exercise is to build up a resistance to them."

"How will you know when I've built up enough resistance?"

"When you can drink a pint of booze, outscore me at the shooting range, and then beat the crap out of Kinoshita."

"You really think I'll be able to do all that?" asked the young man dubiously.

"Sooner than you think," promised Nighthawk.

And finally the young man was as ready as Nighthawk and Kinoshita could make him.

"That's it," said Nighthawk. "I've taught you everything I can. Today you are the Widowmaker."

"It's awkward to be called nothing but Kid or Son or even Widowmaker. I need a name."

"That seems fair enough. What name do you like?"

"Considering my pedigree, yours—now that I'll be leaving soon and it won't cause any confusion."

"Then you can have it," said Nighthawk.

"What name will you take?"

"I've got a name. I've had it for a century and a half, and I'm not about to change it." Nighthawk paused. "Tell you what: For the very brief amount of time we're still together, you can be Jeff and I'll be Jefferson, just so we'll know who Ito and Sarah are speaking to."

"Sounds good to me."

"Fine. Now let's grab some dinner, and get a good night's sleep. You've got a big day ahead of you tomorrow."

"I do?"

"Yeah," said Nighthawk. "We're going to find out just how good a teacher I am."

"Great!" said Jeff, unable to hide his enthusiasm. "What are we doing?"

"We're going to a little world called Tumbleweed."

Chapter 29

Nighthawk walked into the tavern, looked around at the empty tables, then walked over to the bar and ordered a beer.

"A word of advice," said the bartender. "Take your beer and leave."

"Oh?"

"Those two guys who ran you out of here are still on the planet. Somebody's got to have spotted you, and they'll know about it soon, if they don't already."

"Thanks for the tip."

"A lot of people blame you for cutting and running back when they showed up," said the bartender. "Not me. They didn't see what those two guys could do; *I* did." He paused. "I don't think you could have taken them both even when you were a young man, no matter what everyone says about you. Besides, Tumbleweed never did anything for you; I don't figure you owe us anything. I mean, hell, you already killed that whole gang of drug runners out at the spaceport. Everyone knew they'd be there, but only you went out to face them. I figure *we* owe *you*."

"I appreciate that," said Nighthawk. He picked up the beer and walked to a table.

"Then appreciate a little friendly advice and get the hell out of here while you still can."

"Not today."

"They'll be here any minute," said the bartender. "Take my word for it."

"I'm sure they'll be here," replied Nighthawk. "But they don't want me."

The bartender shrugged. "Well, I did my best." He went back to polishing glasses and sorting oddly shaped bottles of alien liquor.

Nighthawk slowly sipped at the beer. When he'd finished half the glass, Mr. Dark, dressed in an elegantly tailored dark gray outfit and shining boots, entered the tavern. He was followed a moment later by Mr. Night, clad in a severely cut black outfit with matching boots and holster.

"Well, look who's come back to visit us, Mr. Night," said Mr. Dark, staring at Nighthawk.

"I think he was very rude to leave so suddenly the last time we met," said Mr. Night. "You hurt my feelings, Mr. Nighthawk."

"You have feelings?" asked Nighthawk.

"There!" said Mr. Night in mock distress. "See? You did it again!"

"Still," said Mr. Dark, "we're very glad you came back, whatever your reasons."

"Are you really?"

"Certainly," said Mr. Dark, withdrawing a colorful silk handkerchief and dusting an invisible speck from his tunic. "We have some unfinished business, if you'll recall."

"And this time," added Mr. Night, "I don't think we'll let you leave the tavern until we conclude it."

"I have no business with you," said Nighthawk.

"Ah, dear me," said Mr. Dark, "the poor man's memory has left him. I suppose that happens when you reach a certain age."

"True," agreed Mr. Night. "We'd almost be doing him a service, putting him out of his misery now that his mind has ceased to function properly. He'd probably thank us if he understood the true nature of our actions."

"You talk too much," said Nighthawk, taking another swallow of his beer.

"Bold words for an old man who's about to die, Widowmaker," said Mr. Dark.

"Wrong on both counts," said Nighthawk.

The two men stared at him curiously.

"Would you care to explain yourself?" said Mr. Night.

"First, I'm not about to die, and second, I'm not the Widowmaker."

"What new foolishness is this?" demanded Mr. Dark. "You're Jefferson Nighthawk, aren't you?"

"Yeah, that's right."

"Then you're the Widowmaker."

Nighthawk smiled and shook his head. "Not anymore. In fact, he's standing right behind you."

They turned to find themselves facing the clone, who stood in the doorway.

"Gentlemen," continued Nighthawk, "say hello to the new Widowmaker."

"What are you talking about?" said Mr. Night suspiciously.

"We had a drawing, and he won."

"He looks a lot like you," said Mr. Dark.

"Good genes."

"Son? Grandson? Nephew?"

"Yes," answered Nighthawk. "And that's all I've got to say to you." He gestured to the young man. "From this point on, talk to *him*."

"But talk quickly," added Jeff. "My lunch is getting cold, and all I really want to do is kill you and get back to it."

"He *talks* like a Widowmaker, Mr. Dark," said Mr. Night. "What do you think?"

"I think he's trying to frighten us, Mr. Night," said Mr. Dark.

"Is it working?" asked Mr. Night.

"Not that I notice," said Mr. Dark, turning to face the young man. "What's your name, substitute Widowmaker?"

"Destiny," said the young man.

"I beg your pardon?"

"Fate. Death. Take your choice."

"Pretty damned silly names, if you ask me."

"I didn't. But if you don't like them, I'm also Jefferson Nighthawk."

"You borrowed the name as well as the title?"

"I inherited it."

"Poor boy," said Mr. Night. "You're about to inherit what we had planned for *him*."

"And you're about to inherit two plots in the local cemetery," answered Jeff. "I reserved them this morning, once I knew you were still on the planet."

"You sound pretty confident when we're standing side by side," said Mr. Dark. He began edging away from his partner. "Are you just as confident when we stand apart?"

"It just means you won't hit each other when you fall."

You're talking too much, enjoying it too much. Don't wait for them. Just pull your guns and blow them away. They're talking for a reason; start paying attention to what they're saying and you're a dead man.

"Well, that's very considerate of you, isn't it, Mr. Night?" said Mr. Dark.

"Absolutely," agreed Mr. Night. "In fact, I don't know when I've met a more considerate doomed man."

As Mr. Night spoke, Mr. Dark went for his weapon. Jeff drew his guns faster than Nighthawk's eye could follow. Before Mr. Dark's gun could even clear its holster, he and his partner were both dead, each with a smoking black hole placed directly between their eyes. Mr. Night got off a single wild shot as he fell across a table; it hit a century-old bottle of Cygnian cognac, spraying the kneeling bartender with broken glass and wildly expensive liquor.

Nighthawk got up, walked over, and stared at the corpses, then looked at Jeff.

"How did I do?" asked the clone.

"Goddamn!" exclaimed Nighthawk. "I was as good as the legends say!"

"Better, even," offered Jeff.

"I thought you were going to get yourself killed with all that talking."

"Oh, that," said Jeff with a shrug. "I was just waiting for one of them to go for his weapon."

"Why?" asked Nighthawk. "I've told you over and over that it's not a sporting contest. You don't have to be a gentleman about it."

"I knew I could take them," answered Jeff calmly. "I just wanted to see how good they were."

"You'd never seen them in action before. How could you know you'd take them?"

"I'm the Widowmaker."

There was a long, thoughtful pause.

"Yeah," agreed Nighthawk. "I guess now you are."

Chapter 30

The new Widowmaker loved his work. He loved the competition, the fame, the adulation, even the notoriety. As word spread across the Frontier worlds that he was back in business, he liked the fact that people whispered and pointed as he walked past. He liked the service he got in hotels and restaurants and taverns, he liked the willingness of the women he met and the subservience of the men.

His career had begun on Tumbleweed, but he remained there only a few hours.

He tracked down three murderers on Giancola II and killed them all.

He killed four more on Greenveldt, even though they were lying in wait for him.

Backbreaker Kimani called him out on New Angola, and though Kimani was seven feet tall, four hundred pounds of rock-hard muscle, and a former freehand heavyweight champion, the young Widowmaker killed him in hand-to-hand combat.

By the time he reached Chrysler IV, his reputation had preceded him. The entire Wilconi Gang was waiting for him, all twelve of them. Nighthawk offered to lend a hand, but Jeff rejected the offer, walked into an obvious death trap, and killed them all, suffering only a single flesh wound in his left leg.

He followed Lady Platinum to her hideout on Fare-Thee-Well, took her prisoner as she tried to seduce him, and broke both her arm and her jaw when she pulled a hidden knife on him.

His final test came on Lower Volta. Nighthawk didn't even know he was going there, and would have advised him to at least take Kinoshita along. But he went in alone, against the rest of the drug runners that Nighthawk had killed months earlier on Tumbleweed, and picked them off one by one until all forty were dead.

"I couldn't have done better myself," admitted Nighthawk when Jeff returned to their home base on Dustdevil and told him of his exploits on Lower Volta.

"I *am* yourself," replied Jeff with a smile.

"Yes, you are," said Nighthawk. "Sometimes I forget."

"You must have loved your life before you came down with eplasia," said Jeff enthusiastically.

"I don't know that I ever thought about it. I had a job, and I did the best I could at it."

"Now there are three of us abroad in the galaxy—you, me, and the second clone. Do you know what we could accomplish if we joined forces?"

"I don't know the other clone's name or how to contact him," said Nighthawk. "Besides, he doesn't want anything to do with me—or, by extension, you." He paused. "And I created you so that I could finally retire and be left alone."

"I know," he said wistfully. "Still, it would have been fun."

Nighthawk smiled. "I trained you just right, and I made you the right age."

"What do you mean?"

"I mean I haven't thought of my work as fun since I was twenty-five."

"How could you not enjoy it?" replied Jeff. "People know me everywhere I go." He grinned. "And you can't beat the pay."

"The pay is commensurate with the risk."

"Hell, even the risk is exciting."

"Well, you didn't inherit my outlook, that's for goddamned sure," said Nighthawk. "I was right not to give you my mind. You might as well enjoy yourself for as long as you can."

"With your skills, I just might live forever," said the young man.

"I approve," said Nighthawk. "That's the only way for a man in your profession to feel. If you ever start thinking that Death happens to you instead of to other people, it's time to hang it up." He paused. "We haven't discussed it, but someday, in a year or a decade, you're going to wake up and think you're developing a rash over your whole body. You'll wonder what you ate, or rubbed against, and when you can't come up with an answer, you'll wonder exactly what was in the atmosphere of the last world you visited. And the whole time you're wondering, the rash will get worse, and soon you'll understand that it's not a rash after all. Your skin will literally start rotting away, and you'll realize that the problem isn't external, but internal, that you have eplasia."

"Maybe I won't get it."

"You're a genetic duplicate of me, which means you've got my weakness for it programmed into you. You'll get it, all right. The good news is that it's finally curable. All I want to tell you is to not wait until you're sure that's what it is. The moment you see a rash, get to a doctor—quick. If it's actually a rash and nothing worse, you haven't lost anything. But if he says it's eplasia, go to the best clinic you can find, and have them treat you immediately."

"I'll go to the one that cured you."

Nighthawk shook his head. "That's on Deluros, and we can't know that Egan and his friend have kept their silence. You're illegal, remember?" Nighthawk paused in thought. "No, go to a world named Safe Harbor. I've never been there, but I'm told that they've got a hell of a medical facility—and that they have no use for the Oligarchy. If they find out you're a clone, they'll probably work all the harder to keep you alive."

"How come you didn't use it?" asked Jeff.

"There was no cure back then. I had to go to Deluros VIII to get frozen and wait for a cure."

"Okay, I'll watch for it. Just a simple rash, right?"

"Right."

Nighthawk leaned back comfortably on his chair. "Okay, it's finally done."

"What is?"

"Your education. That was the last thing I had to tell you."

"I'll be leaving in the morning," said Jeff. "Will you and Sarah and Ito be staying here after I leave?"

"I don't think so," said Nighthawk. "It's really not much of a world. I think we'll try settling on Tallgrass. They say it's a lot prettier."

"I'll check in with you from time to time."

"Please do. I'd like to keep up with who I've killed recently."

Chapter 31

Tallgrass was pretty and green and temperate, with a pair of Tradertowns, a handful of farms, one large gold mine, and not much else. They bought a small home a few miles out from the larger Tradertown.

Nighthawk and Sarah spent a month remodeling it and putting it in order, while Kinoshita traveled to Nelson 23 with the clone, who captured three of the four Jimana Sisters, while killing the fourth.

"You know," said Sarah when they had finished working on the house, "I think I'm going to like this world even better than Tumbleweed."

"You're supposed to," replied Nighthawk. "That's why we moved here."

"You know what it doesn't have?" she continued. "A restaurant."

"You don't have to work," said Nighthawk. "I've still got a couple of million credits left, and nothing to spend it on."

"Look," she said, "you spent your whole life hunting down killers and rapists and the like, and now you want to rest. That's fine. But I *enjoy* working, and I'm good at what I do."

"I didn't say you couldn't work," replied Nighthawk quickly. "I said you didn't have to. I don't own you; you're free to do whatever you want to do. If you want to start a restaurant, start one. I'll be your best customer."

"Good. There's an empty storefront in town. I want to take a look at it. If there's room in the back for a kitchen, it's just about the right size."

"All right," said Nighthawk. "Let's go take a look at it."

They drove down the winding dirt road to the Tradertown and parked in front of the empty building.

"The realtor gave me the entry code," said Sarah, walking up to the door and uttering a seven-digit number. The door irised, and the two of them walked into the storefront.

"It looks smaller than the one you had on Tumbleweed," remarked Nighthawk.

"It is," she replied. "But I had an oversized kitchen there. I can accomplish the same here with half the space. Then, if we break through this wall"—she indicated the wall in question—"we could have, let me see, oh, probably six tables for two, four or five for four, and one for six. And of course we could push them together for larger parties." She began walking around the empty room. "Let's see. We'll need public rest rooms, and they'll take up some space, and—"

A single shot rang out, and the plate-glass front window shattered.

Nighthawk raced across the room and unceremoniously threw Sarah to the floor as a laser beam burned a hole in the wall directly behind where she had been standing.

"What's happening?" she asked, confused.

"Quiet!" he whispered. "And don't move."

Ten more bullets ripped into the walls, and a pair of laser beams began sweeping the room at waist height.

"Who is it?" demanded Sarah. "Nobody here knows us. There must be some mistake!"

"People don't shoot at me by mistake," muttered Nighthawk, slithering across the glass-covered floor on his stomach.

He raised his head a few inches, then ducked as one of the lasers sought him out.

"Come on out, Widowmaker!" yelled a voice. "We know you're in there!"

"Sarah, can you get to the back door?"

She nodded.

"Do it," instructed Nighthawk. "But don't go out, just in case there are more of them waiting back there for us. Let me know when you've made it and I'll join you."

Sarah crawled to the rear entrance, and Nighthawk got there a moment later.

"What now?"

"We're dead meat if we stay here," he said. "Those lasers will have the place in flames in another minute." He pulled out his own Burner. "I'm going out first. If you don't hear my gun hum, count to five and come out after me."

"And if I *do* hear shooting?"

He withdrew his Screecher and handed it to her. "Then do the best you can." He paused. "I don't think they're back there, though, or there'd have been gunfire from that direction, too. If no one's waiting for us out back, hide in the first building you come to."

"What are *you* going to do?"

"What I thought I was all through doing," he said bitterly.

He edged out the back door, Burner in hand. She waited, didn't hear the hum of Burners firing, and followed him. No one shot at her, and she headed off to her right, while he began moving left in a crouching trot, keeping to the shadows of buildings wherever he could.

When he'd gone to the end of the block, he sneaked a look back and saw that the building was indeed in flames. Three men were standing in the street in front of it, two armed with Burners, one with a bullet gun, obviously waiting for him to come running out of the smoking storefront.

Nighthawk edged around the corner. He was perhaps forty yards from them now, and they still hadn't seen him. He saw frenzied activity at the far end of the Tradertown, some three blocks away, and knew he'd have to move quickly before the firefighters ran headfirst into the three would-be killers.

Nighthawk fired his Burner, and one of the three men dropped to the ground. The other two turned to face him, and he fired again. The man with the bullet gun spun around, his gun flying into the burning building, then fell to his knees, blood gushing out of his midsection.

The third man hastily fired at Nighthawk and missed. Nighthawk burned his gun hand away, then melted his burner where it lay on the street before he could reach it with his remaining hand.

"Who are you?" demanded Nighthawk coldly. "What do you want from me?"

"We came to kill you, you bastard!" grated the man with one hand.

"You made a mistake," said Nighthawk coldly. "I'm not the Widowmaker. He's off hunting scum like you."

"Fuck him!" spat the man. "You're the one who killed our brother on Bolingbroke!"

"Bolingbroke?" repeated Nighthawk. "That's what this is about?"

"We know you've come back from wherever you were hiding all those years. You've killed people all over the Frontier, and now you think you can hide from us by letting some other guy call himself the Widowmaker! Well, it's not going to work! You're a dead man!" The man reached into a pocket for a tiny pistol, and Nighthawk fired and killed him before he could bring it into play.

The man who had been kneeling suddenly fell over on his side, also dead.

"Shit!" muttered Nighthawk. "I created a Widowmaker, gave him my genes and my skill and my name, and sent him out to take my place." He stared disgustedly at the three corpses. "This wasn't supposed to happen!"

Chapter 32

Nighthawk sat in a bar on Keepsake, a grubby little Frontier world. He'd been there for two hours, silent, sullen, unwilling to speak to any of the men and women around him.

As he was downing yet another drink, there was a commotion at the doorway.

"He killed Red Devil Korbite!" exclaimed one of the men.

"I'm buying for the house," said a familiar voice. "To law and order—may it always be shorthanded and in need of bounty hunters!"

Nighthawk looked up. "*I* was in need of a bounty hunter last week," he said, slurring his words slightly. "Where the hell were you?"

Jeff entered the tavern and approached Nighthawk. "What are you do-ing here?"

"Waiting for you. I heard Korbite was on Keepsake."

"He was. I'll buy you a drink to celebrate his timely demise."

"I don't give a shit what you're celebrating," said Nighthawk. "Sarah was almost killed last week."

Jeff's demeanor was instantly serious. "She was? Is she all right?"

"She's all right."

"Who did it? I'll take care of—"

"I already took care of them," said Nighthawk.

"Good. Then it's over."

"It's not over," said Nighthawk bitterly. "It's never over. I created you, and they're still coming after me."

"I thought you said they were after her."

"She was with me," said Nighthawk. "Not the safest place to be these days."

"I'm sorry to hear about it," said Jeff, "but what do you expect me to do?"

"I want you back on—" Nighthawk stopped, suddenly aware of the crowd. "I want you back on my new world, and I want you to stay there until I know no one else is looking for me."

"Don't be ridiculous. That could take years!"

"You're a young man. You've got years to spare."

"I've got more important things to do."

"I *created* you!" snapped Nighthawk. "I'm your goddamned god! What's more important than protecting me?"

"How many men have you killed since they woke you up?" shot back Jeff. "You can protect yourself."

"I don't have to protect myself. That's what you're for!"

"I'm not a fucking puppet!" yelled Jeff. "I'm my own man. You don't pull my strings!"

"Listen, kid," said Nighthawk, "I created you, and I can uncreate you."

Jeff laughed contemptuously. "Are you threatening me, old man?"

"You bet your ass I'm threatening you. I'm not going to have Sarah killed, or be assassinated myself, because you're too busy chasing glory and big rewards. Everything you are you owe to me. That ought to be worth a little loyalty."

Suddenly the young man stared sharply at Nighthawk. "How long have you been drinking?"

"None of your business."

"I thought you could hold your liquor," said Jeff. "I guess I was wrong. You're not making any sense."

"You think it makes sense to turn your back on Sarah and me when I tell you we need you?"

"Look," said Jeff soothingly. "We can work this out. You're drunk now, and not thinking clearly. You can sleep it off in my ship, and we'll talk in the morning."

"I don't want your ship or your sympathy!" said Nighthawk. "I just want you to remember who put you here and who you owe for it!"

"I'm sorry you got old, and I'm sorry you've made enemies—but they go with the territory. There'll be people wanting to kill Jefferson Nighthawk as long as Jefferson Nighthawk's alive. Why don't you take a new name and maybe get a new face? It wouldn't be the first time someone's done that," he added meaningfully.

"I've spent enough of my time in hospitals. I just want to spend the rest of it in peace."

"Then go where they can't find you," Jeff shot back. "But don't drag *me* into it. You created me for a purpose, and I'm fulfilling it."

"The hell you are."

"I'm here to bring in the worst of the bad guys, the ones no one else can take—not to protect a broken-down old man whose past is starting to catch up with him."

"So that's what you think I am—a broken-down old man?"

"Look, I'm sorry I said it, okay?" said Jeff. "Just back off and calm down."

"This is a broken-down old man who taught you everything you know, and can still take you in a fair fight."

"Fine," said Jeff. "You can take me. Now try to calm down."

"Don't you give me orders!" bellowed Nighthawk. Before Jeff could react, he reached out and landed a heavy right to the young man's jaw.

Jeff fell to the floor, rolled once, and came up with guns in both hands. He found himself looking down the barrel of Nighthawk's Burner.

"Put 'em back where you got 'em," said Nighthawk. *"Very* slowly."

Jeff did as he was ordered.

"If you want to pull 'em out again, just say the word and we'll step out into the street."

"I don't want to kill you," said the young man. "You're like a father to me. *More* than a father."

"Funny," said Nighthawk. "You don't feel like a son to me."

"I'm sorry about that."

"You come back with me or you're going to be a lot sorrier."

"What the hell," said Jeff. "If it means that much to you . . ."

"It does."

"Then I'll come." He extended his hand. "Friends again?"

"Why not?" agreed Nighthawk, taking the young man's hand.

Jeff instantly pulled, twisted, and threw all his weight behind it. Nighthawk flew through the air and landed heavily on his back. He tried to reach for his Burner, but Jeff was too quick for him, and planted his foot on the older man's right hand.

"You're drunk," said Jeff, pointing a Screecher at him. "That's the only reason I'm letting you live." He squatted down and removed Nighthawk's Burner. "I know you always keep a knife in each boot. Reach for either of them and I'll blow both of your legs away."

Nighthawk glared at him, but said nothing.

"All right," continued Jeff. "Now I want you to listen very carefully to me, old man, because I'm only going to say this once. I'm the Widow-maker. If you ever try to give me orders again, I'll kill you. If you try to publicly humiliate me again the way you did today, I'll kill you. If you follow me, I'll kill you. Do you understand?"

Nighthawk still made no reply.

"I'm leaving now," said Jeff. "I'm going out after Consuela Blood, and if you're here when I get back, I'll kill you."

He stepped away, tucked Nighthawk's Burner into his belt, and backed toward the door as Nighthawk slowly got to his feet.

"You're going to regret that," said the older man.

"Just remember what I said," replied Jeff. "If you're still here, I'll kill you."

"I'll be waiting," promised Nighthawk.

Chapter 33

The clone returned to Keepsake nine days later, with Consuela Blood's preserved body in his cargo hold. Even before he left the landing field—no one would dignify the little strip of barren ground by calling it a spaceport—he noticed the crowd.

"What's going on?" he asked one of the bystanders who lined his way to the tavern.

"Everyone's here to see the shoot-out."

"What shoot-out?"

"You and the old man," replied another member of the crowd.

"Nighthawk?" replied Jeff. "He's sobered up and gone home by now."

"The hell he has. He's waiting for you, just like he said he would."

"That's suicidal," said Jeff, never slowing his pace as he approached the tavern. "I'm everything he used to be. He hasn't got a chance."

"He thinks he has."

"He was drunk. Once his brain starts working, he'll realize that there's only one way it could end."

"I'm telling you, he's waiting for you."

"How could he be that—?"

The young man broke off in midsentence as Nighthawk stepped out into the street.

"Why aren't you home with Sarah?"

"I've got business here," said Nighthawk.

"Have you been drinking again?"

"Not a drop."

Jeff frowned. "You remember what I said I'd do if you were still here?"

"I remember," said Nighthawk.

"It doesn't have to be like this. I still owe you something. You can leave right now, and I won't stop you."

"The Widowmaker doesn't cut and run from anyone."

"You're not the Widowmaker anymore," said Jeff. "*I* am."

"I say the survivor is," said Nighthawk, crouching as he pulled out his Burner.

He was fast, almost as fast as he'd been a century ago—but the clone was faster. Jeff fired his Screecher once, and Nighthawk literally flew back through the air, landed with a thud, and lay still.

Jeff walked over and looked down at the old man. Blood gushed out of his nostrils and ears, and his face was already discolored where dozens of tiny veins had burst under the onslaught of solid sound.

Finally Jeff looked up at the crowd.

"You all saw it," he said. "He went for his weapon first. It was self-defense."

"More than that," mused an elderly bystander. "It was inevitable."

Chapter 34

Sarah and Kinoshita picked up the body and took it back to Tallgrass for burial. And when they brought it home, instead of taking it to the cemetery where the headstone was already planted, they laid it on its bed and kept watch over it.

Finally, after two days, an eyelid flickered.

"Where am I?" whispered Nighthawk.

"You're home," said Sarah.

"I can't hear you."

"You're home!" Sarah half-shouted.

"God, I feel awful."

"You *should* feel awful," said Kinoshita, raising his voice. "You were nailed by a Screecher at near-fatal force."

"Anything less and someone might have seen through it." Nighthawk winced. "My head's killing me. Give me something for the pain."

"I already have," said Sarah. "It should subside in a few minutes. But you'll be in pain on and off for the next few weeks. Nobody's ever had a concussion quite like yours." She paused. "I think your hearing's pretty much gone. We'll have to see a doctor to enhance it."

"Old guys are allowed to be hard of hearing," said Nighthawk. He tried to smile, but the effort brought on another paroxysm of pain, and he lost consciousness.

When he awoke two hours later, Sarah and Kinoshita were still by his bedside, and the pain had subsided somewhat.

"Did it work?"

"Looks like it," replied Kinoshita. "Giving it a nine-day buildup was a good idea; an awful lot of people showed up to see you get killed. There are reports of your death all over the subspace radio bands."

"Good," said Nighthawk. "Then I can finally live the life I want to live, and he can live the life he wants." He reached out and clasped Sarah's hand in his own. "I just wish there'd been a better way to arrange it."

"It's over now," she said.

"Yeah, I think it probably is," agreed Nighthawk.

"Are you going to stay on Tallgrass?" asked Kinoshita.

"No. They found me here once already. I think we'll leave the Inner Frontier altogether, maybe go settle in the Spiral Arm where no one has ever seen me before."

"I wish you well," said Kinoshita. He stood up and walked to the door.

"You're coming with us, aren't you?" asked Sarah.

"I can't," said Kinoshita.

"Why not?"

"I'm a Samurai, like my ancestors."

"What's a Samurai?" asked Sarah.

"A warrior who serves his feudal lord," replied Kinoshita. "One whose life and death is at the disposal of his master."

"This is your master right here!" insisted Sarah, indicating Nighthawk.

"Not anymore," interjected Nighthawk weakly. He looked at Kinoshita. "It's time to leave. We both know that your duty lies elsewhere."

"Where?" demanded Sarah.

"He's waiting for me, somewhere out there beyond Keepsake," said Kinoshita.

"Serve him well," said Nighthawk. "He doesn't know it, but he needs you. He's got a lot more to learn."

Kinoshita turned to the man on the bed. "It's been an honor to know you." He shifted his feet awkwardly. "I wish I could stay . . ."

"I know," said Nighthawk.

"But you are merely Jefferson Nighthawk," he said as he opened the door. "And I serve the Widowmaker."

About the Author

Mike Resnick is one of the major names in science fiction, both as a writer and as an editor. He is the author of almost forty novels, eight collections, and more than one hundred stories and has edited twenty-five anthologies. He has been nominated for seventeen Hugos and eight Nebulas since 1989 and has won three Hugos and a Nebula, as well as scores of lesser awards. Among his best-known works are *Santiago, Ivory, Soothsayer, Paradise,* and the Kirinyaga stories, which have become the most honored story cycle in science fiction history. He lives with his wife, Carol, in Cincinnati, Ohio.